FRONTIER LEGENDS: THE ZANE CHRONICLES

Betty Zane, The Spirit of the Border & The Last Trail

ZANE GREY

Cover by: Filibook Covers

Oregon Trail (1869) by Albert Bierstadt (1830–1902)

Published by: Fili Public

Filibooks ApS

info@filibooks.com

CVR: 37100161

∼

Paperback ISBN: 978-87-93494-46-6
Ebook ISBN: 978-87-93494-47-3

CONTENTS

BETTY ZANE

THE SPIRIT OF THE BORDER

THE LAST TRAIL

BETTY ZANE

CONTENTS

DEDICATION

To the Betty Zane Chapter of the Daughters of the Revolution this book is respectfully dedicated by the author.

NOTE

In a quiet corner of the stately little city of Wheeling, West Va., stands a monument on which is inscribed:

"By authority of the State of West Virginia to commemorate the siege of Fort Henry, Sept 11, 1782, the last battle of the American Revolution, this tablet is here placed."

Had it not been for the heroism of a girl the foregoing inscription would never have been written, and the city of Wheeling would never have existed. From time to time I have read short stories and magazine articles which have been published about Elizabeth Zane and her famous exploit; but they are unreliable in some particulars, which is owing, no doubt, to the singularly meagre details available in histories of our western border.

For a hundred years the stories of Betty and Isaac Zane have been familiar, oft-repeated tales in my family—tales told with that pardonable ancestral pride which seems inherent in every one. My grandmother loved to cluster the children round her and tell them that when she was a little girl she had knelt at the feet of Betty Zane, and listened to the old lady as she told of her brother's capture by the Indian Princess, of the burning of the Fort, and of her own race for life. I knew these stories by heart when a child.

Two years ago my mother came to me with an old note book which had been discovered in some rubbish that had been placed in the yard to burn. The book had probably been hidden in an old picture frame for many years. It belonged to my great-grandfather, Col. Ebenezer Zane. From its faded and time-worn pages I have taken the main facts of my story. My regret is that a worthier pen than mine has not had this wealth of material.

In this busy progressive age there are no heroes of the kind so dear to all lovers of chivalry and romance. There are heroes, perhaps, but they are the patient sad-faced kind, of whom few take cognizance as they hurry onward. But cannot we all remember some one who suffered greatly, who accomplished great deeds, who died on the battlefield—some one around whose name lingers a halo of glory? Few of us are so unfortunate that we cannot look backward on kith or kin and thrill with love and reverence as we dream of an act of heroism or martyrdom which rings down the annals of time like the melody of the huntsman's horn, as it peals out on a frosty October morn purer and sweeter with each succeeding note.

If to any of those who have such remembrances, as well as those who have not, my story gives an hour of pleasure I shall be rewarded.

PROLOGUE

On June 16, 1716, Alexander Spotswood, Governor of the Colony of Virginia, and a gallant soldier who had served under Marlborough in the English wars, rode, at the head of a dauntless band of cavaliers, down the quiet street of quaint old Williamsburg.

The adventurous spirits of this party of men urged them toward the land of the setting sun, that unknown west far beyond the blue crested mountains rising so grandly before them.

Months afterward they stood on the western range of the Great North mountains towering above the picturesque Shenandoah Valley, and from the summit of one of the loftiest peaks, where, until then, the foot of a white man had never trod, they viewed the vast expanse of plain and forest with glistening eyes. Returning to Williamsburg they told of the wonderful richness of the newly discovered country and thus opened the way for the venturesome pioneer who was destined to overcome all difficulties and make a home in the western world.

But fifty years and more passed before a white man penetrated far beyond the purple spires of those majestic mountains.

One bright morning in June, 1769, the figure of a stalwart, broad shouldered man could have been seen standing on the wild and rugged promontory which rears its rocky bluff high above the Ohio river, at a point near the mouth of Wheeling Creek. He was alone save for the companionship of a deerhound that crouched at his feet. As he leaned on a long rifle, contemplating the glorious scene that stretched before him, a smile flashed across his bronzed cheek, and his heart bounded as he forecast the future of that spot. In the river below him lay an island so round and green that it resembled a huge lily pad floating placidly on the water. The fresh green foliage of the trees sparkled with glittering dewdrops. Back of him rose the high ridges, and, in front, as far as eye could reach, extended an unbroken forest.

Beneath him to the left and across a deep ravine he saw a wide level clearing. The few scattered and blackened tree stumps showed the ravages made by a forest fire in the years gone by. The field was now overgrown with hazel and laurel bushes, and intermingling with them were the trailing arbutus, the honeysuckle, and the wild rose. A fragrant perfume was wafted upward to him. A rushing creek bordered one edge of the clearing. After a long quiet reach of water, which could be seen winding back in the hills, the stream tumbled madly over a rocky ledge, and white with foam, it hurried onward as if impatient of long restraint, and lost its individuality in the broad Ohio.

This solitary hunter was Colonel Ebenezer Zane. He was one of those daring men, who, as the tide of emigration started westward, had left his friends and family and had struck out alone into the wilderness. Departing from his home in Eastern Virginia he had plunged into the woods, and after many days of hunting and exploring, he reached the then far Western Ohio valley.

The scene so impressed Colonel Zane that he concluded to found a settlement there. Taking "tomahawk possession" of the locality (which consisted of blazing a few trees with his tomahawk), he built himself a rude shack and remained that summer on the Ohio.

In the autumn he set out for Berkeley County, Virginia, to tell his people of the magnificent country he had discovered. The following spring he persuaded a number of settlers, of a like spirit with himself, to accompany him to the wilderness. Believing it unsafe to take their families with them at once, they left them at Red Stone on the Monongahela river, while the men, including Colonel Zane, his brothers Silas, Andrew, Jonathan and Isaac, the Wetzels, McCollochs, Bennets, Metzars and others, pushed on ahead.

The country through which they passed was one tangled, most impenetrable forest; the axe of the pioneer had never sounded in this region, where every rod of the way might harbor some unknown danger.

These reckless bordermen knew not the meaning of fear; to all, daring adventure was welcome, and the screech of a redskin and the ping of a bullet were familiar sounds; to the Wetzels, McCollochs and Jonathan Zane the hunting of Indians was the most thrilling passion of their lives; indeed, the Wetzels, particularly, knew no other occupation. They had attained a wonderful skill with the rifle; long practice had rendered their senses as acute as those of the fox. Skilled in every variety of woodcraft, with lynx eyes ever on the alert for detecting a trail, or the curling smoke of some camp fire, or the minutest sign of an enemy, these men stole onward through the forest with the cautious but dogged and persistent determination that was characteristic of the settler.

They at length climbed the commanding bluff overlooking the majestic river, and as they gazed out on the undulating and uninterrupted area of green, their hearts beat high with hope.

The keen axe, wielded by strong arms, soon opened the clearing and reared stout log cabins on the river bluff. Then Ebenezer Zane and his followers moved their families and soon the settlement began to grow and flourish. As the little village commenced to prosper the redmen became troublesome. Settlers were shot while plowing the fields or gathering the harvests. Bands of hostile Indians prowled around and made it dangerous for anyone to leave the clearing. Frequently the first person to appear in the early morning would be shot at by an Indian concealed in the woods.

General George Rodgers Clark, commandant of the Western Military Department, arrived at the village in 1774. As an attack from the savages was apprehended during the year the settlers determined to erect a fort as a defense for the infant settlement. It was planned by General Clark and built by the people themselves. At first they called it Fort Fincastle, in honor of Lord Dunmore, who, at the time of its erection, was Governor of the Colony of Virginia. In 1776 its name was changed to Fort Henry, in honor of Patrick Henry.

For many years it remained the most famous fort on the frontier, having withstood numberless Indian attacks and two memorable sieges, one in 1777, which year is called the year of the "Bloody Sevens," and again in 1782. In this last siege the British Rangers under Hamilton took part with the Indians, making the attack practically the last battle of the Revolution.

CHAPTER 1

THE ZANE FAMILY WAS A REMARKABLE ONE IN EARLY DAYS, AND MOST OF its members are historical characters.

The first Zane of whom any trace can be found was a Dane of aristocratic lineage, who was exiled from his country and came to America with William Penn. He was prominent for several years in the new settlement founded by Penn, and Zane street, Philadelphia, bears his name. Being a proud and arrogant man, he soon became obnoxious to his Quaker brethren. He therefore cut loose from them and emigrated to Virginia, settling on the Potomac river, in what was then known as Berkeley county. There his five sons, and one daughter, the heroine of this story, were born.

Ebenezer Zane, the eldest, was born October 7, 1747, and grew to manhood in the Potomac valley. There he married Elizabeth McColloch, a sister of the famous McColloch brothers so well known in frontier history.

Ebenezer was fortunate in having such a wife and no pioneer could have been better blessed. She was not only a handsome woman, but one of remarkable force of character as well as kindness of heart. She was particularly noted for a rare skill in the treatment of illness, and her deftness in handling the surgeon's knife and extracting a poisoned bullet or arrow from a wound had restored to health many a settler when all had despaired.

The Zane brothers were best known on the border for their athletic prowess, and for their knowledge of Indian warfare and cunning. They were all powerful men, exceedingly active and as fleet as deer. In appearance they were singularly pleasing and bore a marked resemblance to one another, all having smooth faces, clear cut, regular features, dark eyes and long black hair.

When they were as yet boys they had been captured by Indians, soon after their arrival on the Virginia border, and had been taken far into the interior, and held as captives for two years. Ebenezer, Silas, and Jonathan Zane were then taken to Detroit and ransomed. While attempting to swim the Scioto river in an effort to escape, Andrew Zane had been shot and killed by his pursuers.

But the bonds that held Isaac Zane, the remaining and youngest brother, were stronger than those of interest or revenge such as had caused the captivity of his brothers. He was loved by an Indian princess, the daughter of Tarhe, the chief of the puissant Huron race. Isaac had escaped on various occasions, but had always been retaken, and at the time of the opening of our story nothing had been heard of him for several years, and it was believed he had been killed.

At the period of the settling of the little colony in the wilderness, Elizabeth Zane, the only sister, was living with an aunt in Philadelphia, where she was being educated.

Colonel Zane's house, a two story structure built of rough hewn logs, was the most comfortable one in the settlement, and occupied a prominent site on the hillside about one hundred yards from the fort. It was constructed of heavy timber and presented rather a forbidding appearance with its square corners, its ominous looking portholes, and strongly barred doors and windows. There were three rooms on the ground floor, a kitchen, a magazine room for military supplies, and a large room for general use. The several sleeping rooms were on the second floor, which was reached by a steep stairway.

The interior of a pioneer's rude dwelling did not reveal, as a rule, more than bare walls, a bed or two, a table and a few chairs—in fact, no more than the necessities of life. But Colonel Zane's house proved an exception to this. Most interesting was the large room. The chinks between the logs had been plastered up with clay and then the walls covered with white birch bark; trophies of the chase, Indian bows and arrows, pipes and tomahawks hung upon them; the wide spreading antlers of a noble buck adorned the space above the mantel piece; buffalo robes covered the couches; bearskin rugs lay scattered about on the hardwood floor. The wall on the western side had been built over a huge stone, into which had been cut an open fireplace.

This blackened recess, which had seen two houses burned over it, when full of blazing logs had cheered many noted men with its warmth. Lord Dunmore, General Clark, Simon Kenton, and Daniel Boone had sat beside that fire. There Cornplanter, the Seneca chief, had made his famous deal with Colonel Zane, trading the island in the river opposite the settlement for a barrel of whiskey. Logan, the Mingo chief and friend of the whites, had smoked many pipes of peace there with Colonel Zane. At a later period, when King Louis Phillippe, who had been exiled from France by Napoleon, had come to America, during the course of his melancholy wanderings he had stopped at Fort Henry a few days. His stay there was marked by a fierce blizzard and the royal guest passed most of his time at Colonel Zane's fireside. Musing by those roaring logs perhaps he saw the radiant star of the Man of Destiny rise to its magnificent zenith.

One cold, raw night in early spring the Colonel had just returned from one of his hunting trips and the tramping of horses mingled with the rough voices of the negro slaves sounded without. When Colonel Zane entered the house he was greeted affectionately by his wife and sister. The latter, at the death of her aunt in Philadelphia, had come west to live with her brother, and had been there since late in the preceding autumn. It was a welcome sight for the eyes of a tired and weary hunter. The tender kiss of his comely wife, the cries of the delighted children, and the crackling of the fire warmed his heart and made him feel how good it was to be home again after a three days' march in the woods. Placing his rifle in a corner and throwing aside his wet hunting coat, he turned and stood with his back to the bright blaze. Still young and vigorous, Colonel Zane was a handsome man. Tall, though not heavy, his frame denoted great strength and endurance. His face was smooth, his heavy eyebrows met in a straight line; his eyes were dark and now beamed with a kindly light; his jaw was square and massive; his mouth resolute; in fact, his whole face was strikingly expressive of courage and geniality. A great wolf dog had followed him in and, tired from travel, had stretched himself out before the fireplace, laying his noble head on the paws he had extended toward the warm blaze.

"Well! Well! I am nearly starved and mighty glad to get back," said the Colonel, with a smile of satisfaction at the steaming dishes a negro servant was bringing from the kitchen.

"We are glad you have returned," answered his wife, whose glowing face testified to the pleasure she felt. "Supper is ready—Annie, bring in some cream—yes, indeed, I am happy that you are home. I never have a moment's peace when you are away, especially when you are accompanied by Lewis Wetzel."

"Our hunt was a failure," said the Colonel, after he had helped himself to a plate full of roast wild turkey. "The bears have just come out of their winter's sleep and are unusually wary at this time. We saw many signs of their work, tearing rotten logs to pieces in search of grubs and bees' nests. Wetzel killed a deer and we baited a likely place where we had discovered many bear tracks. We stayed up all night in a drizzling rain, hoping to get a shot. I am tired out. So is Tige. Wetzel did not mind the weather or the ill luck, and when we ran across some Indian sign he went off on one of his lonely tramps, leaving me to come home alone."

"He is such a reckless man," remarked Mrs. Zane.

"Wetzel is reckless, or rather, daring. His incomparable nerve carries him safely through many dangers, where an ordinary man would have no show whatever. Well, Betty, how are you?"

"Quite well," said the slender, dark-eyed girl who had just taken the seat opposite the Colonel.

"Bessie, has my sister indulged in any shocking escapade in my absence? I think that last trick of hers, when she gave a bucket of hard cider to that poor tame bear, should last her a spell."

"No, for a wonder Elizabeth has been very good. However, I do not attribute it to any unusual change of temperament; simply the cold, wet weather. I anticipate a catastrophe very shortly if she is kept indoors much longer."

"I have not had much opportunity to be anything but well behaved. If it rains a few days more I shall become desperate. I want to ride my pony, roam the woods, paddle my canoe, and enjoy myself," said Elizabeth.

"Well! Well! Betts, I knew it would be dull here for you, but you must not get discouraged. You know you got here late last fall, and have not had any pleasant weather yet. It is perfectly delightful in May and June. I can take you to fields of wild white honeysuckle and May flowers and wild roses. I know you love the woods, so be patient a little longer."

Elizabeth had been spoiled by her brothers—what girl would not have been by five great big worshippers?—and any trivial thing gone wrong with her was a serious matter to them. They were proud of her, and of her beauty and accomplishments were never tired of talking. She had the dark hair and eyes so characteristic of the Zanes; the same oval face and fine features: and added to this was a certain softness of contour and a sweetness of expression which made her face bewitching. But, in spite of that demure and innocent face, she possessed a decided will of her own, and one very apt to be asserted; she was mischievous; inclined to coquettishness, and more terrible than all she had a fiery temper which could be aroused with the most surprising ease.

Colonel Zane was wont to say that his sister's accomplishments were innumerable. After only a few months on the border she could prepare the flax and weave a linsey dresscloth with admirable skill. Sometimes to humor Betty the Colonel's wife would allow her to get the dinner, and she would do it in a manner that pleased her brothers, and called forth golden praises from the cook, old Sam's wife who had been with the family twenty years. Betty sang in the little church on Sundays; she organized and taught a Sunday school class; she often beat Colonel Zane and Major McColloch at their favorite game of checkers, which they had played together since they were knee high; in fact, Betty did nearly everything well, from baking pies to painting the birch bark walls of her room. But these things were insignificant in Colonel Zane's eyes. If the Colonel were ever guilty of bragging it was about his sister's ability in those acquirements demanding a true eye, a fleet foot, a strong arm and a daring spirit. He had told all the people in the settlement, to many of whom Betty was unknown, that she could ride like an Indian and shoot with undoubted skill; that she had a generous share of the Zanes' fleetness of foot, and that she would send a canoe over as bad a place as she could find. The boasts of the Colonel remained as yet unproven, but, be that as it may, Betty had, notwithstanding her many faults, endeared herself to all. She made sunshine and happiness everywhere; the old people loved her; the children adored her, and the broad shouldered, heavy footed young settlers were shy and silent, yet blissfully happy in her presence.

"Betty, will you fill my pipe?" asked the Colonel, when he had finished his supper and had pulled his big chair nearer the fire. His oldest child, Noah, a sturdy lad of six, climbed upon his knee and plied him with questions.

"Did you see any bars and bufflers?" he asked, his eyes large and round.

"No, my lad, not one."

"How long will it be until I am big enough to go?"

"Not for a very long time, Noah."

"But I am not afraid of Betty's bar. He growls at me when I throw sticks at him, and snaps his teeth. Can I go with you next time?"

"My brother came over from Short Creek to-day. He has been to Fort Pitt," interposed Mrs. Zane. As she was speaking a tap sounded on the door, which, being opened by Betty, disclosed Captain Boggs his daughter Lydia, and Major Samuel McColloch, the brother of Mrs. Zane.

"Ah, Colonel! I expected to find you at home to-night. The weather has been miserable for hunting and it is not getting any better. The wind is blowing from the northwest and a storm is coming," said Captain Boggs, a fine, soldierly looking man.

"Hello, Captain! How are you? Sam, I have not had the pleasure of seeing you for a long time," replied Colonel Zane, as he shook hands with his guests.

Major McColloch was the eldest of the brothers of that name. As an Indian killer he ranked next to the intrepid Wetzel; but while Wetzel preferred to take his chances alone and track the Indians through the untrodden wilds, McColloch was a leader of expeditions against the savages. A giant in stature, massive in build, bronzed and bearded, he looked the typical frontiersman. His blue eyes were like those of his sister and his voice had the same pleasant ring.

"Major McColloch, do you remember me?" asked Betty.

"Indeed I do," he answered, with a smile. "You were a little girl, running wild, on the Potomac when I last saw you!"

"Do you remember when you used to lift me on your horse and give me lessons in riding?"

"I remember better than you. How you used to stick on the back of that horse was a mystery to me."

"Well, I shall be ready soon to go on with those lessons in riding. I have heard of your wonderful leap over the hill and I should like to have you tell me all about it. Of all the stories I have heard since I arrived at Fort Henry, the one of your ride and leap for life is the most wonderful."

"Yes, Sam, she will bother you to death about that ride, and will try to give you lessons in leaping down precipices. I should not be at all surprised to find her trying to duplicate your feat. You know the Indian pony I got from that fur trader last summer. Well, he is as wild as a deer and she has been riding him without his being broken," said Colonel Zane.

"Some other time I shall tell you about my jump over the hill. Just now I have important matters to discuss," answered the Major to Betty.

It was evident that something unusual had occurred, for after chatting a few moments the three men withdrew into the magazine room and conversed in low, earnest tones.

Lydia Boggs was eighteen, fair haired and blue eyed. Like Betty she had received a good education, and, in that respect, was superior to the border girls, who seldom knew more than to keep house and to make linen. At the outbreak of the Indian wars General Clark had stationed Captain Boggs at Fort Henry and Lydia had lived there with him two years. After Betty's arrival, which she hailed with delight, the girls had become fast friends.

Lydia slipped her arm affectionately around Betty's neck and said, "Why did you not come over to the Fort to-day?"

"It has been such an ugly day, so disagreeable altogether, that I have remained indoors."

"You missed something," said Lydia, knowingly.

"What do you mean? What did I miss?"

"Oh, perhaps, after all, it will not interest you."

"How provoking! Of course it will. Anything or anybody would interest me to-night. Do tell me, please."

"It isn't much. Only a young soldier came over with Major McColloch."

"A soldier? From Fort Pitt? Do I know him? I have met most of the officers."

"No, you have never seen him. He is a stranger to all of us."

"There does not seem to be so much in your news," said Betty, in a disappointed tone. "To be sure, strangers are a rarity in our little village, but, judging from the strangers who have visited us in the past, I imagine this one cannot be much different."

"Wait until you see him," said Lydia, with a serious little nod of her head.

"Come, tell me all about him," said Betty, now much interested.

"Major McColloch brought him in to see papa, and he was introduced to me. He is a southerner and from one of those old families. I could tell by his cool, easy, almost reckless air. He is handsome, tall and fair, and his face is frank and open. He has such beautiful manners. He bowed low to me and really I felt so embarrassed that I hardly spoke. You know I am used to these big hunters seizing your hand and giving it a squeeze which makes you want to scream. Well, this young man is different. He is a cavalier. All the girls are in love with him already. So will you be."

"I? Indeed not. But how refreshing. You must have been strongly impressed to see and remember all you have told me."

"Betty Zane, I remember so well because he is just the man you described one day when we were building castles and telling each other what kind of a hero we wanted."

"Girls, do not talk such nonsense," interrupted the Colonel's wife who was perturbed by the colloquy in the other room. She had seen those ominous signs before. "Can you find nothing better to talk about?"

Meanwhile Colonel Zane and his companions were earnestly discussing certain information which had arrived that day. A friendly Indian runner had brought news to Short Creek, a settlement on the river between Fort Henry and Fort Pitt of an intended raid by the Indians all along the Ohio valley. Major McColloch, who had been warned by Wetzel of the fever of unrest among the Indians—a fever which broke out every spring—had gone to Fort Pitt with the hope of bringing back reinforcements, but, excepting the young soldier, who had volunteered to return with him, no help could he enlist, so he journeyed back post-haste to Fort Henry.

The information he brought disturbed Captain Boggs, who commanded the garrison, as a number of men were away on a logging expedition up the river, and were not expected to raft down to the Fort for two weeks.

Jonathan Zane, who had been sent for, joined the trio at this moment, and was acquainted with the particulars. The Zane brothers were always consulted where any question concerning Indian craft and cunning was to be decided. Colonel Zane had a strong friendly influence with certain tribes, and his advice was invaluable. Jonathan Zane hated the sight of an Indian and except for his knowledge as a scout, or Indian tracker or fighter, he was of little use in a council. Colonel Zane informed the men of the fact that Wetzel and he had discovered Indian tracks within ten miles of the Fort, and he dwelt particularly on the disappearance of Wetzel.

"Now, you can depend on what I say. There are Wyandots in force on the war path. Wetzel told me to dig for the Fort and he left me in a hurry. We were near that cranberry bog over at the foot of Bald mountain. I do not believe we shall be attacked. In my opinion the Indians would come up from the west and keep to the high ridges along Yellow creek. They always come that way. But of course, it is best to know surely, and I daresay Lew will come in to-night or to-morrow with the facts. In the meantime put out some scouts back in the woods and let Jonathan and the Major watch the river."

"I hope Wetzel will come in," said the Major. "We can trust him to know more about the Indians than any one. It was a week before you and he went hunting that I saw him. I went to Fort Pitt and tried to bring over some men, but the garrison is short and they need men as much as we do. A young soldier named Clarke volunteered to come and I brought him along with me. He has not seen any Indian fighting, but he is a likely looking chap, and I guess will do. Captain Boggs will give him a place in the block house if you say so."

"By all means. We shall be glad to have him," said Colonel Zane.

"It would not be so serious if I had not sent the men up the river," said Captain Boggs, in anxious tones. "Do you think it possible they might have fallen in with the Indians?"

"It is possible, of course, but not probable," answered Colonel Zane. "The Indians are all across the Ohio. Wetzel is over there and he will get here long before they do."

"I hope it may be as you say. I have much confidence in your judgment," returned Captain Boggs. "I shall put out scouts and take all the precaution possible. We must return now. Come, Lydia."

"Whew! What an awful night this is going to be," said Colonel Zane, when he had closed the door after his guests' departure. "I should not care to sleep out to-night."

"Eb, what will Lew Wetzel do on a night like this?" asked Betty, curiously.

"Oh, Lew will be as snug as a rabbit in his burrow," said Colonel Zane, laughing. "In a few moments he can build a birch bark shack, start a fire inside and go to sleep comfortably."

"Ebenezer, what is all this confab about? What did my brother tell you?" asked Mrs. Zane, anxiously.

"We are in for more trouble from the Wyandots and Shawnees. But, Bessie, I don't believe it will come soon. We are too well protected here for anything but a protracted siege."

Colonel Zane's light and rather evasive answer did not deceive his wife. She knew her brother and her husband would not wear anxious faces for nothing. Her usually bright face clouded with a look of distress. She had seen enough of Indian warfare to make her shudder with horror at the mere thought. Betty seemed unconcerned. She sat down beside the dog and patted him on the head.

"Tige, Indians! Indians!" she said.

The dog growled and showed his teeth. It was only necessary to mention Indians to arouse his ire.

"The dog has been uneasy of late," continued Colonel Zane "He found the Indian tracks before Wetzel did. You know how Tige hates Indians. Ever since he came home with Isaac four years ago he has been of great service to the scouts, as he possesses so much intelligence and sagacity. Tige followed Isaac home the last time he escaped from the Wyandots. When Isaac was in captivity he nursed and cared for the dog after he had been brutally beaten by the redskins. Have you ever heard that long mournful howl Tige gives out sometimes in the dead of night?"

"Yes I have, and it makes me cover up my head," said Betty.

"Well, it is Tige mourning for Isaac," said Colonel Zane

"Poor Isaac," murmured Betty.

"Do you remember him? It has been nine years since you saw him," said Mrs. Zane.

"Remember Isaac? Indeed I do. I shall never forget him. I wonder if he is still living?"

"Probably not. It is now four years since he was recaptured. I think it would have been impossible to keep him that length of time, unless, of course, he has married that Indian girl. The simplicity of the Indian nature is remarkable. He could easily have deceived them and made them believe he was content in captivity. Probably, in attempting to escape again, he has been killed as was poor Andrew."

Brother and sister gazed with dark, sad eyes into the fire, now burned down to a glowing bed of coals. The silence remained unbroken save for the moan of the rising wind outside, the rattle of hail, and the patter of rain drops on the roof.

CHAPTER 2

FORT HENRY STOOD ON A BLUFF OVERLOOKING THE RIVER AND commanded a fine view of the surrounding country. In shape it was a parallelogram, being about three hundred and fifty-six feet in length, and one hundred and fifty in width. Surrounded by a stockade fence twelve feet high, with a yard wide walk running around the inside, and with bastions at each corner large enough to contain six defenders, the fort presented an almost impregnable defense. The blockhouse was two stories in height, the second story projecting out several feet over the first. The thick white oak walls bristled with portholes. Besides the blockhouse, there were a number of cabins located within the stockade. Wells had been sunk inside the inclosure, so that if the spring happened to go dry, an abundance of good water could be had at all times.

In all the histories of frontier life mention is made of the forts and the protection they offered in time of savage warfare. These forts were used as homes for the settlers, who often lived for weeks inside the walls.

Forts constructed entirely of wood without the aid of a nail or spike (for the good reason that these things could not be had) may seem insignificant in these days of great nasal and military garrisons. However, they answered the purpose at that time and served to protect many an infant settlement from the savage attacks of Indian tribes. During a siege of Fort Henry, which had occurred about a year previous, the settlers would have lost scarcely a man had they kept to the fort. But Captain

Ogle, at that time in charge of the garrison, had led a company out in search of the Indians. Nearly all of his men were killed, several only making their way to the fort.

On the day following Major McColloch's arrival at Fort Henry, the settlers had been called in from their spring plowing and other labors, and were now busily engaged in moving their stock and the things they wished to save from the destructive torch of the redskin. The women had their hands full with the children, the cleaning of rifles and moulding of bullets, and the thousand and one things the sterner tasks of their husbands had left them. Major McColloch, Jonathan and Silas Zane, early in the day, had taken different directions along the river to keep a sharp lookout for signs of the enemy. Colonel Zane intended to stay in his oven house and defend it, so he had not moved anything to the fort excepting his horses and cattle. Old Sam, the negro, was hauling loads of hay inside the stockade. Captain Boggs had detailed several scouts to watch the roads and one of these was the young man, Clarke, who had accompanied the Major from Fort Pitt.

The appearance of Alfred Clarke, despite the fact that he wore the regulation hunting garb, indicated a young man to whom the hard work and privation of the settler were unaccustomed things. So thought the pioneers who noticed his graceful walk, his fair skin and smooth hands. Yet those who carefully studied his clearcut features were favorably impressed; the women, by the direct, honest gaze of his blue eyes and the absence of ungentle lines in his face; the men, by the good nature, and that indefinable something by which a man marks another as true steel.

He brought nothing with him from Fort Pitt except his horse, a black-coated, fine limbed thoroughbred, which he frankly confessed was all he could call his own. When asking Colonel Zane to give him a position in the garrison he said he was a Virginian and had been educated in Philadelphia; that after his father died his mother married again, and this, together with a natural love of adventure, had induced him to run away and seek his fortune with the hardy pioneer and the cunning savage of the border. Beyond a few months' service under General Clark he knew nothing of frontier life; but he was tired of idleness; he was strong and not afraid of work, and he could learn. Colonel Zane, who prided himself on his judgment of character, took a liking to the young man at once, and giving him a rifle and accoutrements, told him the border needed young men of pluck and fire, and that if he brought a strong hand and a willing heart he could surely find fortune. Possibly if Alfred Clarke could have been told of the fate in store for him he might have mounted his black steed and have placed miles between him and the frontier village; but, as there were none to tell, he went cheerfully out to meet that fate.

On this is bright spring morning he patrolled the road leading along the edge of the clearing, which was distant a quarter of a mile from the fort. He kept a keen eye on the opposite side of the river, as he had been directed. From the upper end of the island, almost straight across from where he stood, the river took a broad turn, which could not be observed from the fort windows. The river was high from the recent rains and brush heaps and logs and debris of all descriptions were floating down with the swift current. Rabbits and other small animals, which had probably been surrounded on some island and compelled to take to the brush or drown, crouched on floating logs and piles of driftwood. Happening to glance down the road, Clarke saw a horse galloping in his direction. At first he thought it was a messenger for himself, but as it neared him he saw that the horse was an Indian pony and the rider a young girl, whose long, black hair was flying in the wind.

"Hello! I wonder what the deuce this is? Looks like an Indian girl," said Clarke to himself. "She rides well, whoever she may be."

He stepped behind a clump of laurel bushes near the roadside and waited. Rapidly the horse and rider approached him. When they were but a few paces distant he sprang out and, as the pony shied and reared at sight of him, he clutched the bridle and pulled the pony's head down. Looking up he encountered the astonished and bewildered gaze from a pair of the prettiest dark eyes it had ever been his fortune, or misfortune, to look into.

Betty, for it was she, looked at the young man in amazement, while Alfred was even more surprised and disconcerted. For a moment they looked at each other in silence. But Betty, who was scarcely ever at a loss for words, presently found her voice.

"Well, sir! What does this mean?" she asked indignantly.

"It means that you must turn around and go back to the fort," answered Alfred, also recovering himself.

Now Betty's favorite ride happened to be along this road. It lay along the top of the bluff a mile or more and afforded a fine unobstructed view of the river. Betty had either not heard of the Captain's order, that no one was to leave the fort, or she had disregarded it altogether; probably the latter, as she generally did what suited her fancy.

"Release my pony's head!" she cried, her face flushing, as she gave a jerk to the reins. "How dare you? What right have you to detain me?"

The expression Betty saw on Clarke's face was not new to her, for she remembered having seen it on the faces of young gentlemen whom she had met at her aunt's house in Philadelphia. It was the slight, provoking smile of the man familiar with the various moods of young women, the expression of an amused contempt for their imperiousness. But it was not that which angered Betty. It was the coolness with which he still held her pony regardless of her commands.

"Pray do not get excited," he said. "I am sorry I cannot allow such a pretty little girl to have her own way. I shall hold your pony until you say you will go back to the fort."

"Sir!" exclaimed Betty, blushing a bright-red. "You—you are impertinent!"

"Not at all," answered Alfred, with a pleasant laugh. "I am sure I do not intend to be. Captain Boggs did not acquaint me with full particulars or I might have declined my present occupation: not, however, that it is not agreeable just at this moment. He should have mentioned the danger of my being run down by Indian ponies and imperious young ladies."

"Will you let go of that bridle, or shall I get off and walk back for assistance?" said Betty, getting angrier every moment.

"Go back to the fort at once," ordered Alfred, authoritatively. "Captain Boggs' orders are that no one shall be allowed to leave the clearing."

"Oh! Why did you not say so? I thought you were Simon Girty, or a highwayman. Was it necessary to keep me here all this time to explain that you were on duty?"

"You know sometimes it is difficult to explain," said Alfred, "besides, the situation had its charm. No, I am not a robber, and I don't believe you thought so. I have only thwarted a young lady's whim, which I am aware is a great crime. I am very sorry. Goodbye."

Betty gave him a withering glance from her black eyes, wheeled her pony and galloped away. A mellow laugh was borne to her ears before she got out of hearing, and again the red blood mantled her cheeks.

"Heavens! What a little beauty," said Alfred to himself, as he watched the graceful rider disappear. "What spirit! Now, I wonder who she can be. She had on moccasins and buckskin gloves and her hair tumbled like a tomboy's, but she is no backwoods girl, I'll bet on that. I'm afraid I was a little rude, but after taking such a stand I could not weaken, especially before such a haughty and disdainful little vixen. It was too great a temptation. What eyes she had! Contrary to what I expected, this little frontier settlement bids fair to become interesting."

The afternoon wore slowly away, and until late in the day nothing further happened to disturb Alfred's meditations, which consisted chiefly of different mental views and pictures of red lips and black eyes. Just as he decided to return to the fort for his supper he heard the barking of a dog that he had seen running along the road some moments before. The sound came from some distance down the river bank and nearer the fort. Walking a few paces up the bluff Alfred caught sight of a large black dog running along the edge of the water. He would run into the water a few paces and then come out and dash along the shore. He barked furiously all the while. Alfred concluded that he must have been excited by a fox or perhaps a wolf; so he climbed down the steep bank and spoke to the dog. Thereupon the dog barked louder and more fiercely than ever, ran to the water, looked out into the river and then up at the man with almost human intelligence.

Alfred understood. He glanced out over the muddy water, at first making out nothing but driftwood. Then suddenly he saw a log with an object clinging to it which he took to be a man, and an Indian at that. Alfred raised his rifle to his shoulder and was in the act of pressing the trigger when he thought he heard a faint halloo. Looking closer, he found he was not covering the smooth polished head adorned with the small tuft of hair, peculiar to a redskin on the warpath, but a head from which streamed long black hair.

Alfred lowered his rifle and studied intently the log with its human burden. Drifting with the current it gradually approached the bank, and as it came nearer he saw that it bore a white man, who was holding to the log with one hand and with the other was making feeble strokes. He concluded the man was either wounded or nearly drowned, for his movements were becoming slower and weaker every moment. His white face lay against the log and barely above water. Alfred shouted encouraging words to him.

At the bend of the river a little rocky point jutted out a few yards into the water. As the current carried the log toward this point, Alfred, after divesting himself of some of his clothing, plunged in and pulled it to the shore. The pallid face of the man clinging to the log showed that he was nearly exhausted, and that he had been rescued in the nick of time. When Alfred reached shoal water he slipped his arm around the man, who was unable to stand, and carried him ashore.

The rescued man wore a buckskin hunting shirt and leggins and moccasins of the same material, all very much the worse for wear. The leggins were torn into tatters and the moccasins worn through. His face was pinched with suffering and one arm was bleeding from a gunshot wound near the shoulder.

"Can you not speak? Who are you?" asked Clarke, supporting the limp figure.

The man made several efforts to answer, and finally said something that to Alfred sounded like "Zane," then he fell to the ground unconscious.

All this time the dog had acted in a most peculiar manner, and if Alfred had not been so intent on the man he would have noticed the animal's odd maneuvers. He ran to and fro on the sandy beach; he scratched up the sand and pebbles, sending them flying in the air; he made short, furious dashes; he jumped, whirled, and, at last, crawled close to the motionless figure and licked its hand.

Clarke realized that he would not be able to carry the inanimate figure, so he hurriedly put on his clothes and set out on a run for Colonel Zane's house. The first person whom he saw was the old negro slave, who was brushing one of the Colonel's horses.

Sam was deliberate and took his time about everything. He slowly looked up and surveyed Clarke with his rolling eyes. He did not recognize in him any one he had ever seen before, and being of a sullen and taciturn nature, especially with strangers, he seemed in no hurry to give the desired information as to Colonel Zane's whereabouts.

"Don't stare at me that way, you damn nigger," said Clarke, who was used to being obeyed by negroes. "Quick, you idiot. Where is the Colonel?"

At that moment Colonel Zane came out of the barn and started to speak, when Clarke interrupted him.

"Colonel, I have just pulled a man out of the river who says his name is Zane, or if he did not mean that, he knows you, for he surely said 'Zane.'"

"What!" ejaculated the Colonel, letting his pipe fall from his mouth.

Clarke related the circumstances in a few hurried words. Calling Sam they ran quickly down to the river, where they found the prostrate figure as Clarke had left it, the dog still crouched close by.

"My God! It is Isaac!" exclaimed Colonel Zane, when he saw the white face. "Poor boy, he looks as if he were dead. Are you sure he spoke? Of course he must have spoken for you could not have known. Yes, his heart is still beating."

Colonel Zane raised his head from the unconscious man's breast, where he had laid it to listen for the beating heart.

"Clarke, God bless you for saving him," said he fervently. "It shall never be forgotten. He is alive, and, I believe, only exhausted, for that wound amounts to little. Let us hurry."

"I did not save him. It was the dog," Alfred made haste to answer.

They carried the dripping form to the house, where the door was opened by Mrs. Zane.

"Oh, dear, another poor man," she said, pityingly. Then, as she saw his face, "Great Heavens, it is Isaac! Oh! don't say he is dead!"

"Yes, it is Isaac, and he is worth any number of dead men yet," said Colonel Zane, as they laid the insensible man on the couch. "Bessie, there is work here for you. He has been shot."

"Is there any other wound beside this one in his arm?" asked Mrs. Zane, examining it.

"I do not think so, and that injury is not serious. It is lose of blood, exposure and starvation. Clarke, will you please run over to Captain Boggs and tell Betty to hurry home! Sam, you get a blanket and warm it by the fire. That's right, Bessie, bring the whiskey," and Colonel Zane went on giving orders.

Alfred did not know in the least who Betty was, but, as he thought that unimportant, he started off on a run for the fort. He had a vague idea that Betty was the servant, possibly Sam's wife, or some one of the Colonel's several slaves.

Let us return to Betty. As she wheeled her pony and rode away from the scene of her adventure on the river bluff, her state of mind can be more readily imagined than described. Betty hated opposition of any kind, whether justifiable or not; she wanted her own way, and when prevented from doing as she pleased she invariably got angry. To be ordered and compelled to give up her ride, and that by a stranger, was intolerable. To make it all the worse this stranger had been decidedly flippant. He had familiarly spoken to her as "a pretty little girl." Not only that, which was a great offense, but he had stared at her, and she had a confused recollection of a gaze in which admiration had been ill disguised. Of course, it was that soldier Lydia had been telling her about. Strangers were of so rare an occurrence in the little village that it was not probable there could be more than one.

Approaching the house she met her brother who told her she had better go indoors and let Sam put up the pony. Accordingly, Betty called the negro, and then went into the house. Bessie had gone to the fort with the children. Betty found no one to talk to, so she tried to read. Finding she could not become interested she threw the book aside and took up her embroidery. This also turned out a useless effort; she got the linen hopelessly twisted and tangled, and presently she tossed this upon the table. Throwing her shawl over her shoulders, for it was now late in the afternoon and growing chilly, she walked downstairs and out into the Yard. She strolled aimlessly to and fro awhile, and then went over to the fort and into Captain Bogg's house, which adjoined the blockhouse. Here she found Lydia preparing flax.

"I saw you racing by on your pony. Goodness, how you can ride! I should be afraid of breaking my neck," exclaimed Lydia, as Betty entered.

"My ride was spoiled," said Betty, petulantly.

"Spoiled? By what—whom?"

"By a man, of course," retorted Betty, whose temper still was high. "It is always a man that spoils everything."

"Why, Betty, what in the world do you mean? I never heard you talk that way," said Lydia, opening her blue eyes in astonishment.

"Well, Lyde, I'll tell you. I was riding down the river road and just as I came to the end of the clearing a man jumped out from behind some bushes and grasped Madcap's bridle. Imagine! For a moment I was frightened out of my wits. I instantly thought of the Girtys, who, I have heard, have evinced a fondness for kidnapping little girls. Then the fellow said he was on guard and ordered me, actually commanded me to go home."

"Oh, is that all?" said Lydia, laughing.

"No, that is not all. He—he said I was a pretty little girl and that he was sorry I could not have my own way; that his present occupation was pleasant, and that the situation had its charm. The very idea. He was most impertinent," and Betty's telltale cheeks reddened again at the recollection.

"Betty, I do not think your experience was so dreadful, certainly nothing to put you out as it has," said Lydia, laughing merrily. "Be serious. You know we are not in the backwoods now and must not expect so much of the men. These rough border men know little of refinement like that with which you have been familiar. Some of them are quiet and never speak unless addressed; their simplicity is remarkable; Lew Wetzel and your brother Jonathan, when they are not fighting Indians, are examples.

On the other hand, some of them are boisterous and if they get anything to drink they will make trouble for you. Why, I went to a party one night after I had been here only a few weeks and they played a game in which every man in the place kissed me."

"Gracious! Please tell me when any such games are likely to be proposed and I'll stay home," said Betty.

"I have learned to get along very well by simply making the best of it," continued Lydia. "And to tell the truth, I have learned to respect these rugged fellows. They are uncouth; they have no manners, but their hearts are honest and true, and that is of much greater importance in frontiersmen than the little attentions and courtesies upon which women are apt to lay too much stress."

"I think you speak sensibly and I shall try and be more reasonable hereafter. But, to return to the man who spoiled my ride. He, at least, is no frontiersman, notwithstanding his gun and his buckskin suit. He is an educated man. His manner and accent showed that. Then he looked at me so differently. I know it was that soldier from Fort Pitt."

"Mr. Clarke? Why, of course!" exclaimed Lydia, clapping her hands in glee. "How stupid of me!"

"You seem to be amused," said Betty, frowning.

"Oh, Betty, it is such a good joke."

"Is it? I fail to see it."

"But I can. I am very much amused. You see, I heard Mr. Clarke say, after papa told him there were lots of pretty girls here, that he usually succeeded in finding those things out and without any assistance. And the very first day he has met you and made you angry. It is delightful."

"Lyde, I never knew you could be so horrid."

"It is evident that Mr. Clarke is not only discerning, but not backward in expressing his thoughts. Betty, I see a romance."

"Don't be ridiculous," retorted Betty, with an angry blush. "Of course, he had a right to stop me, and perhaps he did me a good turn by keeping me inside the clearing, though I cannot imagine why he hid behind the bushes. But he might have been polite. He made me angry. He was so cool and—and—"

"I see," interrupted Lydia, teasingly. "He failed to recognize your importance."

"Nonsense, Lydia. I hope you do not think I am a silly little fool. It is only that I have not been accustomed to that kind of treatment, and I will not have it."

Lydia was rather pleased that some one had appeared on the scene who did not at once bow down before Betty, and therefore she took the young man's side of the argument.

"Do not be hard on poor Mr. Clarke. Maybe he mistook you for an Indian girl. He is handsome. I am sure you saw that."

"Oh, I don't remember how he looked," said Betty. She did remember, but would not admit it.

The conversation drifted into other channels after this, and soon twilight came stealing down on them. As Betty rose to go there came a hurried tap on the door.

"I wonder who would knock like that," said Lydia, rising "Betty, wait a moment while I open the door."

On doing this she discovered Clarke standing on the step with his cap in his hand.

"Why, Mr. Clarke! Will you come in?" exclaimed Lydia. "Thank you, only for a moment," said Alfred. "I cannot stay. I came to find Betty. Is she here?"

He had not observed Betty, who had stepped back into the shadow of the darkening room. At his question Lydia became so embarrassed she did not know what to say or do, and stood looking helplessly at him.

But Betty was equal to the occasion. At the mention of her first name in such a familiar manner by this stranger, who had already grievously offended her once before that day, Betty stood perfectly still a moment, speechless with surprise, then she stepped quickly out of the shadow.

Clarke turned as he heard her step and looked straight into a pair of dark, scornful eyes and a face pale with anger.

"If it be necessary that you use my name, and I do not see how that can be possible, will you please have courtesy enough to say Miss Zane?" she cried haughtily.

Lydia recovered her composure sufficiently to falter out:

"Betty, allow me to introduce—"

"Do not trouble yourself, Lydia. I have met this person once before to-day, and I do not care for an introduction."

When Alfred found himself gazing into the face that had haunted him all the afternoon, he forgot for the moment all about his errand. He was finally brought to a realization of the true state of affairs by Lydia's words.

"Mr. Clarke, you are all wet. What has happened?" she exclaimed, noticing the water dripping from his garments.

Suddenly a light broke in on Alfred. So the girl he had accosted on the road and "Betty" were one and the same person. His face flushed. He felt that his rudeness on that occasion may have merited censure, but that it had not justified the humiliation she had put upon him.

These two persons, so strangely brought together, and on whom Fate had made her inscrutable designs, looked steadily into each other's eyes. What mysterious force thrilled through Alfred Clarke and made Betty Zane tremble?

"Miss Boggs, I am twice unfortunate," said Alfred, tuning to Lydia, and there was an earnest ring in his deep voice "This time I am indeed blameless. I have just left Colonel Zane's house, where there has been an accident, and I was dispatched to find 'Betty,' being entirely ignorant as to who she might be. Colonel Zane did not stop to explain. Miss Zane is needed at the house, that is all."

And without so much as a glance at Betty he bowed low to Lydia and then strode out of the open door.

"What did he say?" asked Betty, in a small trembling voice, all her anger and resentment vanished.

"There has been an accident. He did not say what or to whom. You must hurry home. Oh, Betty, I hope no one has been hurt! And you were very unkind to Mr. Clarke. I am sure he is a gentleman, and you might have waited a moment to learn what he meant."

Betty did not answer, but flew out of the door and down the path to the gate of the fort. She was almost breathless when she reached Colonel Zane's house, and hesitated on the step before entering. Summoning her courage she pushed open the door. The first thing that struck her after the bright light was the pungent odor of strong liniment. She saw several women neighbors whispering together. Major McColloch and Jonathan Zane were standing by a couch over which Mrs. Zane was bending. Colonel Zane sat at the foot of the couch. Betty saw this in the first rapid glance, and then, as the Colonel's wife moved aside, she saw a prostrate figure, a white face and dark eyes that smiled at her.

"Betty," came in a low voice from those pale lips.

Her heart leaped and then seemed to cease beating. Many long years had passed since she had heard that voice, but it had never been forgotten. It was the best beloved voice of her childhood, and with it came the sweet memories of her brother and playmate. With a cry of joy she fell on her knees beside him and threw her arms around his neck.

"Oh, Isaac, brother, brother!" she cried, as she kissed him again and again. "Can it really be you? Oh, it is too good to be true! Thank God! I have prayed and prayed that you would be restored to us."

Then she began to cry and laugh at the same time in that strange way in which a woman relieves a heart too full of joy. "Yes, Betty. It is all that is left of me," he said, running his hand caressingly over the dark head that lay on his breast.

"Betty, you must not excite him," said Colonel Zane.

"So you have not forgotten me?" whispered Isaac.

"No, indeed, Isaac. I have never forgotten," answered Betty, softly. "Only last night I spoke of you and wondered if you were living. And now you are here. Oh, I am so happy!" The quivering lips and the dark eyes bright with tears spoke eloquently of her joy.

"Major will you tell Captain Boggs to come over after supper? Isaac will be able to talk a little by then, and he has some news of the Indians," said Colonel Zane.

"And ask the young man who saved my life to come that I may thank him," said Isaac.

"Saved your life?" exclaimed Betty, turning to her brother, in surprise, while a dark red flush spread over her face. A humiliating thought had flashed into her mind.

"Saved his life, of course," said Colonel Zane, answering for Isaac. "Young Clarke pulled him out of the river. Didn't he tell you?"

"No," said Betty, rather faintly.

"Well, he is a modest young fellow. He saved Isaac's life, there is no doubt of that. You will hear all about it after supper. Don't make Isaac talk any more at present."

Betty hid her face on Isaac's shoulder and remained quiet a few moments; then, rising, she kissed his cheek and went quietly to her room. Once there she threw herself on the bed and tried to think. The events of the day, coming after a long string of monotonous, wearying days, had been confusing; they had succeeded one another in such rapid order as to leave no time for reflection. The meeting by the river with the rude but interesting stranger; the shock to her dignity; Lydia's kindly advice; the stranger again, this time emerging from the dark depths of disgrace into the luminous light as the hero of her brother's rescue—all these thoughts jumbled in her mind making it difficult for her to think clearly. But after a time one thing forced itself upon her. She could not help being conscious that she had wronged some one to whom she would be forever indebted. Nothing could alter that. She was under an eternal obligation to the man who had saved the life she loved best on earth. She had unjustly scorned and insulted the man to whom she owed the life of her brother.

Betty was passionate and quick-tempered, but she was generous and tender-hearted as well, and when she realized how unkind and cruel she kind been she felt very miserable. Her position admitted of no retreat. No matter how much pride rebelled; no matter how much she disliked to retract anything she had said, she knew no other course lay open to her. She would have to apologize to Mr. Clarke. How could she? What would she say? She remembered how cold and stern his face had been as he turned from her to Lydia. Perplexed and unhappy, Betty did what any girl in her position would have done: she resorted to the consoling and unfailing privilege of her sex—a good cry.

When she became composed again she got up and bathed her hot cheeks, brushed her hair, and changed her gown for a becoming one of white. She tied a red ribbon about her throat and put a rosette in her hair. She had forgotten all about the Indians. By the time Mrs. Zane called her for supper she had her mind made up to ask Mr. Clarke's pardon, tell him she was sorry, and that she hoped they might be friends.

Isaac Zane's fame had spread from the Potomac to Detroit and Louisville. Many an anxious mother on the border used the story of his captivity as a means to frighten truant youngsters who had evinced a love for running wild in the woods. The evening of Isaac's return every one in the settlement called to welcome home the wanderer. In spite of the troubled times and the dark cloud hanging over them they made the occasion one of rejoicing.

Old John Bennet, the biggest and merriest man in the colony, came in and roared his appreciation of Isaac's return. He was a huge man, and when he stalked into the room he made the floor shake with his heavy tread. His honest face expressed his pleasure as he stood over Isaac and nearly crushed his hand.

"Glad to see you, Isaac. Always knew you would come back. Always said so. There are not enough damn redskins on the river to keep you prisoner."

"I think they managed to keep him long enough," remarked Silas Zane.

"Well, here comes the hero," said Colonel Zane, as Clarke entered, accompanied by Captain Boggs, Major McColloch and Jonathan. "Any sign of Wetzel or the Indians?"

Jonathan had not yet seen his brother, and he went over and seized Isaac's hand and wrung it without speaking.

"There are no Indians on this side of the river," said Major McColloch, in answer to the Colonel's question.

"Mr. Clarke, you do not seem impressed with your importance," said Colonel Zane. "My sister said you did not tell her what part you took in Isaac's rescue."

"I hardly deserve all the credit," answered Alfred. "Your big black dog merits a great deal of it."

"Well, I consider your first day at the fort a very satisfactory one, and an augury of that fortune you came west to find."

"How are you?" said Alfred, going up to the couch where Isaac lay.

"I am doing well, thanks to you," said Isaac, warmly shaking Alfred's hand.

"It is good to see you pulling out all right," answered Alfred. "I tell you, I feared you were in a bad way when I got you out of the water."

Isaac reclined on the couch with his head and shoulder propped up by pillows. He was the handsomest of the brothers. His face would have been but for the marks of privation, singularly like Betty's; the same low, level brows and dark eyes; the same mouth, though the lips were stronger and without the soft curves which made his sister's mouth so sweet.

Betty appeared at the door, and seeing the room filled with men she hesitated a moment before coming forward. In her white dress she made such a dainty picture that she seemed out of place among those surroundings. Alfred Clarke, for one, thought such a charming vision was wasted on the rough settlers, every one of whom wore a faded and dirty buckskin suit and a belt containing a knife and a tomahawk. Colonel Zane stepped up to Betty and placing his arm around her turned toward Clarke with pride in his eyes.

"Betty, I want to make you acquainted with the hero of the hour, Mr. Alfred Clarke. This is my sister."

Betty bowed to Alfred, but lowered her eyes instantly on encountering the young man's gaze.

"I have had the pleasure of meeting Miss Zane twice today," said Alfred.

"Twice?" asked Colonel Zane, turning to Betty. She did not answer, but disengaged herself from his arm and sat down by Isaac.

"It was on the river road that I first met Miss Zane, although I did not know her then," answered Alfred. "I had some difficulty in stopping her pony from going to Fort Pitt, or some other place down the river."

"Ha! Ha! Well, I know she rides that pony pretty hard," said Colonel

Zane, with his hearty laugh. "I'll tell you, Clarke, we have some riders here in the settlement. Have you heard of Major McColloch's leap over the hill?"

"I have heard it mentioned, and I would like to hear the story," responded Alfred. "I am fond of horses, and think I can ride a little myself. I am afraid I shall be compelled to change my mind."

"That is a fine animal you rode from Fort Pitt," remarked the Major. "I would like to own him."

"Come, draw your chairs up and he'll listen to Isaac's story," said Colonel Zane.

"I have not much of a story to tell," said Isaac, in a voice still weak and low. "I have some bad news, I am sorry to say, but I shall leave that for the last. This year, if it had been completed, would have made my tenth year as a captive of the Wyandots. This last period of captivity, which has been nearly four years, I have not been ill-treated and have enjoyed more comfort than any of you can imagine. Probably you are all familiar with the reason for my long captivity. Because of the interest of Myeerah, the Indian Princess, they have importuned me for years to be adopted into the tribe, marry the White Crane, as they call Myeerah, and become a Wyandot chief. To this I would never consent, though I have been careful not to provoke the Indians. I was allowed the freedom of the camp, but have always been closely watched. I should still be with the Indians had I not suspected that Hamilton, the British Governor, had formed a plan with the Hurons, Shawnees, Delawares, and other tribes, to strike a terrible blow at the whites along, the river. For months I have watched the Indians preparing for an expedition, the extent of which they had never before undertaken. I finally learned from Myeerah that my suspicions were well founded. A favorable chance to escape presented and I took it and got away. I outran all the braves, even Arrowswift, the Wyandot runner, who shot me through the arm. I have had a hard time of it these last three or four days, living on herbs and roots, and when I reached the river I was ready to drop. I pushed a log into the water and started to drift over. When the old dog saw me I knew I was safe if I could hold on. Once, when the young man pointed his gun at me, I thought it was all over. I could not shout very loud."

"Were you going to shoot?" asked Colonel Zane of Clarke.

"I took him for an Indian, but fortunately I discovered my mistake in time," answered Alfred.

"Are the Indians on the way here?" asked Jonathan.

"That I cannot say. At present the Wyandots are at home. But I know that the British and the Indians will make a combined attack on the settlements. It may be a month, or a year, but it is coming."

"And Hamilton, the hair buyer, the scalp buyer, is behind the plan," said Colonel Zane, in disgust.

"The Indians have their wrongs. I sympathize with them in many ways. We have robbed them, broken faith with them, and have not lived up to the treaties. Pipe and Wingenund are particularly bitter toward the whites. I understand Cornplanter is also. He would give anything for Jonathan's scalp, and I believe any of the tribes would give a hundred of their best warriors for 'Black Wind,' as they call Lew Wetzel."

"Have you ever seen Red Fox?" asked Jonathan, who was sitting near the fire and as usual saying but little. He was the wildest and most untamable of all the Zanes. Most of the time he spent in the woods, not so much to fight Indians, as Wetzel did, but for pure love of outdoor life. At home he was thoughtful and silent.

"Yes, I have seen him," answered Isaac. "He is a Shawnee chief and one of the fiercest warriors in that tribe of fighters. He was at Indian-head, which is the name of one of the Wyandot villages, when I visited there last, and he had two hundred of his best braves with him."

"He is a bad Indian. Wetzel and I know him. He swore he would hang our scalps up in his wigwam," said Jonathan.

"What has he in particular against you?" asked Colonel Zane. "Of course, Wetzel is the enemy of all Indians."

"Several years ago Wetzel and I were on a hunt down the river at the place called Girty's Point, where we fell in with the tracks of five Shawnees. I was for coming home, but Wetzel would not hear of it. We trailed the Indians and, coming up on them after dark, we tomahawked them. One of them got away crippled, but we could not follow him because we discovered that they had a white girl as captive, and one of the red devils, thinking we were a rescuing party, had tomahawked her. She was not quite dead. We did all we could to save her life. She died and we buried her on the spot. They were Red Fox's braves and were on their way to his camp with the prisoner. A year or so afterwards I learned from a friendly Indian that the Shawnee chief had sworn to kill us. No doubt he will be a leader in the coming attack."

"We are living in the midst of terrible times," remarked Colonel Zane. "Indeed, these are the times that try men's souls, but I firmly believe the day is not far distant when the redmen will be driven far over the border."

"Is the Indian Princess pretty?" asked Betty of Isaac.

"Indeed she is, Betty, almost as beautiful as you are," said Isaac. "She is tall and very fair for an Indian. But I have something to tell about her more interesting than that. Since I have been with the Wyandots this last time I have discovered a little of the jealously guarded secret of Myeerah's mother. When Tarhe and his band of Hurons lived in Canada their home was in the Muskoka Lakes region on the Moon river. The old warriors tell wonderful stories of the beauty of that country. Tarhe took captive some French travellers, among them a woman named La Durante. She had a beautiful little girl. The prisoners, except this little girl, were released. When she grew up Tarhe married her. Myeerah is her child. Once Tarhe took his wife to Detroit and she was seen there by an old Frenchman who went crazy over her and said she was his child. Tarhe never went to the white settlements again. So you see, Myeerah is from a great French family on her mother's side, as this is old Frenchman was probably Chevalier La Durante, and Myeerah's grandfather."

"I would love to see her, and yet I hate her. What an odd name she has," said Betty.

"It is the Indian name for the white crane, a rare and beautiful bird. I never saw one. The name has been celebrated among the Hurons as long as any one of them can remember. The Indians call her the White Crane, or Walk-in-the-Water, because of her love for wading in the stream."

"I think we have made Isaac talk enough for one night," said Colonel Zane. "He is tired out. Major, tell Isaac and Betty, and Mr. Clarke, too, of your jump over the cliff."

"I have heard of that leap from the Indians," said Isaac.

"Major, from what hill did you jump your horse?" asked Alfred.

"You know the bare rocky bluff that stands out prominently on the hill across the creek. From that spot Colonel Zane first saw the valley, and from there I leaped my horse. I can never convince myself that it really happened. Often I look up at that cliff in doubt. But the Indians and Colonel Zane, Jonathan, Wetzel and others say they actually saw the deed done, so I must accept it," said Major McColloch.

"It seems incredible!" said Alfred. "I cannot understand how a man or horse could go over that precipice and live."

"That is what we all say," responded the Colonel. "I suppose I shall have to tell the story. We have fighters and makers of history here, but few talkers."

"I am anxious to hear it," answered Clarke, "and I am curious to see this man Wetzel, whose fame has reached as far as my home, way down in Virginia."

"You will have your wish gratified soon, I have no doubt," resumed the Colonel. "Well, now for the story of McColloch's mad ride for life and his wonderful leap down Wheeling hill. A year ago, when the fort was besieged by the Indians, the Major got through the lines and made off for Short Creek. He returned next morning with forty mounted men. They marched boldly up to the gate, and all succeeded in getting inside save the gallant Major, who had waited to be the last man to go in. Finding it impossible to make the short distance without going under the fire of the Indians, who had rushed up to prevent the relief party from entering the fort, he wheeled his big stallion, and, followed by the yelling band of savages, he took the road leading around back of the fort to the top of the bluff. The road lay along the edge of the cliff and I saw the Major turn and wave his rifle at us, evidently with the desire of assuring us that he was safe. Suddenly, on the very summit of the hill, he reined in his horse as if undecided. I knew in an instant what had happened. The Major had run right into the returning party of Indians, which had been sent out to intercept our reinforcements. In a moment more we heard the exultant yells of the savages, and saw them gliding from tree to tree, slowly lengthening out their line and surrounding the unfortunate Major. They did not fire a shot. We in the fort were stupefied with horror, and stood helplessly with our useless guns, watching and waiting for the seemingly inevitable doom of our comrade. Not so with the Major! Knowing that he was a marked man by the Indians and feeling that any death was preferable to the gauntlet, the knife, the stake and torch of the merciless savage, he had grasped at a desperate chance. He saw his enemies stealthily darting from rock to tree, and tree to bush, creeping through the brush, and slipping closer and closer every moment. On three sides were his hated foes and on the remaining side—the abyss. Without a moment's hesitation the intrepid Major spurred his horse at the precipice. Never shall I forget that thrilling moment. The three hundred savages were silent as they realized the Major's intention. Those in the fort watched with staring eyes. A few bounds and the noble steed reared high on his hind legs. Outlined by the clear blue sky the magnificent animal stood for one brief instant, his black mane flying in the wind, his head thrown up and his front hoofs pawing the air like Marcus Curtius' mailed steed of old, and then down with a crash, a cloud of dust, and the crackling of pine limbs. A long yell went up from the Indians below, while those above ran to the edge of the cliff.

With cries of wonder and baffled vengeance they gesticulated toward the dark ravine into which horse and rider had plunged rather than wait to meet a more cruel death. The precipice at this point is over three hundred feet in height, and in places is almost perpendicular. We believed the Major to be lying crushed and mangled on the rocks. Imagine our frenzy of joy when we saw the daring soldier and his horse dash out of the bushes that skirt the base of the cliff, cross the creek, and come galloping to the fort in safety."

"It was wonderful! Wonderful!" exclaimed Isaac, his eyes glistening. "No wonder the Indians call you the 'Flying Chief.'"

"Had the Major not jumped into the clump of pine trees which grow thickly some thirty feet below the summit he would not now be alive," said Colonel Zane. "I am certain of that. Nevertheless that does not detract from the courage of his deed. He had no time to pick out the best place to jump. He simply took his one chance, and came out all right. That leap will live in the minds of men as long as yonder bluff stands a monument to McColloch's ride for life."

Alfred had listened with intense interest to the Colonel's recital. When it ended, although his pulses quickened and his soul expanded with awe and reverence for the hero of that ride, he sat silent. Alfred honored courage in a man more than any other quality. He marvelled at the simplicity of these bordermen who, he thought, took the most wonderful adventures and daring escapes as a matter of course, a compulsory part of their daily lives. He had already, in one day, had more excitement than had ever befallen him, and was beginning to believe his thirst for a free life of stirring action would be quenched long before he had learned to become useful in his new sphere. During the remaining half hour of his call on his lately acquired friends, he took little part in the conversation, but sat quietly watching the changeful expressions on Betty's face, and listening to Colonel Zane's jokes. When he rose to go he bade his host good-night, and expressed a wish that Isaac, who had fallen asleep, might have a speedy recovery. He turned toward the door to find that Betty had intercepted him.

"Mr. Clarke," she said, extending a little hand that trembled slightly. "I wish to say—that—I want to say that my feelings have changed. I am sorry for what I said over at Lydia's. I spoke hastily and rudely. You have saved my brother's life. I will be forever grateful to you. It is useless to try to thank you. I—I hope we may be friends."

Alfred found it desperately hard to resist that low voice, and those dark eyes which were raised shyly, yet bravely, to his. But he had been deeply hurt. He pretended not to see the friendly hand held out to him, and his voice was cold when he answered her.

"I am glad to have been of some service," he said, "but I think you overrate my action. Your brother would not have drowned, I am sure. You owe me nothing. Good-night."

Betty stood still one moment staring at the door through which he had gone before she realized that her overtures of friendship had been politely, but coldly, ignored. She had actually been snubbed. The impossible had happened to Elizabeth Zane. Her first sensation after she recovered from her momentary bewilderment was one of amusement, and she laughed in a constrained manner; but, presently, two bright red spots appeared in her cheeks, and she looked quickly around to see if any of the others had noticed the incident. None of them had been paying any attention to her and she breathed a sigh of relief. It was bad enough to be snubbed without having others see it. That would have been too humiliating. Her eyes flashed fire as she remembered the disdain in Clarke's face, and that she had not been clever enough to see it in time.

"Tige, come here!" called Colonel Zane. "What ails the dog?"

The dog had jumped to his feet and ran to the door, where he sniffed at the crack over the threshold. His aspect was fierce and threatening. He uttered low growls and then two short barks. Those in the room heard a soft moccasined footfall outside. The next instant the door opened wide and a tall figure stood disclosed.

"Wetzel!" exclaimed Colonel Zane. A hush fell on the little company after that exclamation, and all eyes were fastened on the new comer.

Well did the stranger merit close attention. He stalked into the room, leaned his long rifle against the mantelpiece and spread out his hands to the fire. He was clad from head to foot in fringed and beaded buckskin, which showed evidence of a long and arduous tramp. It was torn and wet and covered with mud. He was a magnificently made man, six feet in height, and stood straight as an arrow. His wide shoulders, and his muscular, though not heavy, limbs denoted wonderful strength and activity. His long hair, black as a raven's wing, hung far down his shoulders. Presently he turned and the light shone on a remarkable face. So calm and cold and stern it was that it seemed chiselled out of marble. The most striking features were its unusual pallor, and the eyes, which were coal black, and piercing as the dagger's point.

"If you have any bad news out with it," cried Colonel Zane, impatiently.

"No need fer alarm," said Wetzel. He smiled slightly as he saw Betty's apprehensive face. "Don't look scared, Betty. The redskins are miles away and goin' fer the Kanawha settlement."

CHAPTER 3

MANY WEEKS OF QUIET FOLLOWED THE EVENTS OF THE LAST CHAPTER. The settlers planted their corn, harvested their wheat and labored in the fields during the whole of one spring and summer without hearing the dreaded war cry of the Indians. Colonel Zane, who had been a disbursing officer in the army of Lord Dunmore, where he had attained the rank of Colonel, visited Fort Pitt during the summer in the hope of increasing the number of soldiers in his garrison. His efforts proved fruitless. He returned to Fort Henry by way of the river with several pioneers, who with their families were bound for Fort Henry. One of these pioneers was a minister who worked in the fields every week day and on Sundays preached the Gospel to those who gathered in the meeting house.

Alfred Clarke had taken up his permanent abode at the fort, where he had been installed as one of the regular garrison. His duties, as well as those of the nine other members of the garrison, were light. For two hours out of the twenty-four he was on guard. Thus he had ample time to acquaint himself with the settlers and their families.

Alfred and Isaac had now become firm friends. They spent many hours fishing in the river, and roaming the woods in the vicinity, as Colonel Zane would not allow Isaac to stray far from the fort. Alfred became a regular visitor at Colonel Zane's house. He saw Betty every day, but as yet, nothing had mended the breach between them. They were civil to each other when chance threw them together, but Betty usually left the room

44

on some pretext soon after he entered. Alfred regretted his hasty exhibition of resentment and would have been glad to establish friendly relations with her. But she would not give him an opportunity. She avoided him on all possible occasions. Though Alfred was fast succumbing to the charm of Betty's beautiful face, though his desire to be near her had grown well nigh resistless, his pride had not yet broken down. Many of the summer evenings found him on the Colonel's doorstep, smoking a pipe, or playing with the children. He was that rare and best company—a good listener. Although he laughed at Colonel Zane's stories, and never tired of hearing of Isaac's experiences among the Indians, it is probable he would not have partaken of the Colonel's hospitality nearly so often had it not been that he usually saw Betty, and if he got only a glimpse of her he went away satisfied. On Sundays he attended the services at the little church and listened to Betty's sweet voice as she led the singing.

There were a number of girls at the fort near Betty's age. With all of these Alfred was popular. He appeared so entirely different from the usual young man on the frontier that he was more than welcome everywhere. Girls in the backwoods are much the same as girls in thickly populated and civilized districts. They liked his manly ways; his frank and pleasant manners; and when to these virtues he added a certain deferential regard, a courtliness to which they were unaccustomed, they were all the better pleased. He paid the young women little attentions, such as calling on them, taking them to parties and out driving, but there was not one of them who could think that she, in particular, interested him.

The girls noticed, however, that he never approached Betty after service, or on any occasion, and while it caused some wonder and gossip among them, for Betty enjoyed the distinction of being the belle of the border, they were secretly pleased. Little hints and knowing smiles, with which girls are so skillful, made known to Betty all of this, and, although she was apparently indifferent, it hurt her sensitive feelings. It had the effect of making her believe she hated the cause of it more than ever.

What would have happened had things gone on in this way, I am not prepared to say; probably had not a meddling Fate decided to take a hand in the game, Betty would have continued to think she hated Alfred, and I would never have had occasion to write his story; but Fate did interfere, and, one day in the early fall, brought about an incident which changed the whole world for the two young people.

It was the afternoon of an Indian summer day—in that most beautiful time of all the year—and Betty, accompanied by her dog, had wandered up the hillside into the woods. From the hilltop the broad river could be seen winding away in the distance, and a soft, bluish, smoky haze hung over the water. The forest seemed to be on fire. The yellow leaves of the poplars, the brown of the white and black oaks, the red and purple of the maples, and the green of the pines and hemlocks flamed in a glorious blaze of color. A stillness, which was only broken now and then by the twittering of birds uttering the plaintive notes peculiar to them in the autumn as they band together before their pilgrimage to the far south, pervaded the forest.

Betty loved the woods, and she knew all the trees. She could tell their names by the bark or the shape of the leaves. The giant black oak, with its smooth shiny bark and sturdy limbs, the chestnut with its rugged, seamed sides and bristling burrs, the hickory with its lofty height and curled shelling bark, were all well known and well loved by Betty. Many times had she wondered at the trembling, quivering leaves of the aspen, and the foliage of the silver-leaf as it glinted in the sun. To-day, especially, as she walked through the woods, did their beauty appeal to her. In the little sunny patches of clearing which were scattered here and there in the grove, great clusters of goldenrod grew profusely. The golden heads swayed gracefully on the long stems Betty gathered a few sprigs and added to them a bunch of warmly tinted maple leaves.

The chestnuts burrs were opening. As Betty mounted a little rocky eminence and reached out for a limb of a chestnut tree, she lost her footing and fell. Her right foot had twisted under her as she went down, and when a sharp pain shot through it she was unable to repress a cry. She got up, tenderly placed the foot on the ground and tried her weight on it, which caused acute pain. She unlaced and removed her moccasin to find that her ankle had commenced to swell. Assured that she had sprained it, and aware of the serious consequences of an injury of that nature, she felt greatly distressed. Another effort to place her foot on the ground and bear her weight on it caused such severe pain that she was compelled to give up the attempt. Sinking down by the trunk of the tree and leaning her head against it she tried to think of a way out of her difficulty.

The fort, which she could plainly see, seemed a long distance off, although it was only a little way down the grassy slope. She looked and looked, but not a person was to be seen. She called to Tige. She remembered that he had been chasing a squirrel a short while ago, but now there was no sign of him. He did not come at her call. How annoying! If Tige were only there she could have sent him for help. She shouted several times, but the distance was too great for her voice to carry to the fort. The mocking echo of her call came back from the bluff that rose to her left. Betty now began to be alarmed in earnest, and the tears started to roll down her cheeks. The throbbing pain in her ankle, the dread of having to remain out in that lonesome forest after dark, and the fear that she might not be found for hours, caused Betty's usually brave spirit to falter; she was weeping unreservedly.

In reality she had been there only a few minutes—although they seemed hours to her—when she heard the light tread of moccasined feet on the moss behind her. Starting up with a cry of joy she turned and looked up into the astonished face of Alfred Clarke.

Returning from a hunt back in the woods he had walked up to her before being aware of her presence. In a single glance he saw the wildflowers scattered beside her, the little moccasin turned inside out, the woebegone, tearstained face, and he knew Betty had come to grief.

Confused and vexed, Betty sank back at the foot of the tree. It is probable she would have encountered Girty or a member of his band of redmen, rather than have this young man find her in this predicament. It provoked her to think that of all the people at the fort it should be the only one she could not welcome who should find her in such a sad plight.

"Why, Miss Zane!" he exclaimed, after a moment of hesitation. "What in the world has happened? Have you been hurt? May I help you?"

"It is nothing," said Betty, bravely, as she gathered up her flowers and the moccasin and rose slowly to her feet. "Thank you, but you need not wait."

The cold words nettled Alfred and he was in the act of turning away from her when he caught, for the fleetest part of a second, the full gaze of her eyes. He stopped short. A closer scrutiny of her face convinced him that she was suffering and endeavoring with all her strength to conceal it.

"But I will wait. I think you have hurt yourself. Lean upon my arm," he said, quietly.

"Please let me help you," he continued, going nearer to her.

But Betty refused his assistance. She would not even allow him to take the goldenrod from her arms. After a few hesitating steps she paused and lifted her foot from the ground.

"Here, you must not try to walk a step farther," he said, resolutely, noting how white she had suddenly become. "You have sprained your ankle and are needlessly torturing yourself. Please let me carry you?"

"Oh, no, no, no!" cried Betty, in evident distress. "I will manage. It is not so—very—far."

She resumed the slow and painful walking, but she had taken only a few steps when she stopped again and this time a low moan issued from her lips. She swayed slightly backward and if Alfred had not dropped his rifle and caught her she would have fallen.

"Will you—please—for some one?" she whispered faintly, at the same time pushing him away.

"How absurd!" burst out Alfred, indignantly. "Am I then, so distasteful to you that you would rather wait here and suffer a half hour longer while I go for assistance? It is only common courtesy on my part. I do not want to carry you. I think you would be quite heavy."

He said this in a hard, bitter tone, deeply hurt that she would not accept even a little kindness from him. He looked away from her and waited. Presently a soft, half-smothered sob came from Betty and it expressed such utter wretchedness that his heart melted. After all she was only a child. He turned to see the tears running down her cheeks, and with a suppressed imprecation upon the wilfulness of young women in general, and this one in particular, he stepped forward and before she could offer any resistance, he had taken her up in his arms, goldenrod and all, and had started off at a rapid walk toward the fort.

Betty cried out in angry surprise, struggled violently for a moment, and then, as suddenly, lay quietly in his arms. His anger changed to self-reproach as he realized what a light burden she made. He looked down at the dark head lying on his shoulder. Her face was hidden by the dusky rippling hair, which tumbled over his breast, brushed against his cheek, and blew across his lips. The touch of those fragrant tresses was a soft caress. Almost unconsciously he pressed her closer to his heart. And as a sweet mad longing grew upon him he was blind to all save that he held her in his arms, that uncertainty was gone forever, and that he loved her. With these thoughts running riot in his brain he carried her down the hill to Colonel Zane's house.

The negro, Sam, who came out of the kitchen, dropped the bucket he had in his hand and ran into the house when he saw them. When Alfred reached the gate Colonel Zane and Isaac were hurrying out to meet him.

"For Heaven's sake! What has happened? Is she badly hurt? I have always looked for this," said the Colonel, excitedly.

"You need not look so alarmed," answered Alfred. "She has only sprained her ankle, and trying to walk afterward hurt her so badly that she became faint and I had to carry her."

"Dear me, is that all?" said Mrs. Zane, who had also come out. "We were terribly frightened. Sam came running into the house with some kind of a wild story. Said he knew you would be the death of Betty."

"How ridiculous! Colonel Zane, that servant of yours never fails to say something against me," said Alfred, as he carried Betty into the house.

"He doesn't like you. But you need not mind Sam. He is getting old and we humor him, perhaps too much. We are certainly indebted to you," returned the Colonel.

Betty was laid on the couch and consigned to the skillful hands of Mrs. Zane, who pronounced the injury a bad sprain.

"Well, Betty, this will keep you quiet for a few days," said she, with a touch of humor, as she gently felt the swollen ankle.

"Alfred, you have been our good angel so often that I don't see how we shall ever reward you," said Isaac to Alfred.

"Oh, that time will come. Don't worry about that," said Alfred, jestingly, and then, turning to the others he continued, earnestly. "I will apologize for the manner in which I disregarded Miss Zane's wish not to help her. I am sure I could do no less. I believe my rudeness has spared her considerable suffering."

"What did he mean, Betts?" asked Isaac, going back to his sister after he had closed the door. "Didn't you want him to help you?"

Betty did not answer. She sat on the couch while Mrs. Zane held the little bare foot and slowly poured the hot water over the swollen and discolored ankle. Betty's lips were pale. She winced every time Mrs. Zane touched her foot, but as yet she had not uttered even a sigh.

"Betty, does it hurt much?" asked Isaac.

"Hurt? Do you think I am made of wood? Of course it hurts," retorted Betty. "That water is so hot. Bessie, will not cold water do as well?"

"I am sorry. I won't tease any more," said Isaac, taking his sister's hand. "I'll tell you what, Betty, we owe Alfred Clarke a great deal, you and I. I am going to tell you something so you will know how much more you owe him. Do you remember last month when that red heifer of yours got away. Well, Clarke chased her away and finally caught her in the woods. He asked me to say I had caught her. Somehow or other he seems to be afraid of you. I wish you and he would be good friends. He is a mighty fine fellow."

In spite of the pain Betty was suffering a bright blush suffused her face

49

at the words of her brother, who, blind as brothers are in regard to their own sisters, went on praising his friend.

Betty was confined to the house a week or more and during this enforced idleness she had ample time for reflection and opportunity to inquire into the perplexed state of her mind.

The small room, which Betty called her own, faced the river and fort. Most of the day she lay by the window trying to read her favorite books, but often she gazed out on the quiet scene, the rolling river, the ever-changing trees and the pastures in which the red and white cows grazed peacefully; or she would watch with idle, dreamy eyes the flight of the crows over the hills, and the graceful motion of the hawk as he sailed around and around in the azure sky, looking like a white sail far out on a summer sea.

But Betty's mind was at variance with this peaceful scene. The consciousness of a change, which she could not readily define, in her feelings toward Alfred Clarke, vexed and irritated her. Why did she think of him so often? True, he had saved her brother's life. Still she was compelled to admit to herself that this was not the reason. Try as she would, she could not banish the thought of him. Over and over again, a thousand times, came the recollection of that moment when he had taken her up in his arms as though she were a child. Some vague feeling stirred in her heart as she remembered the strong yet gentle clasp of his arms.

Several times from her window she had seen him coming across the square between the fort and her brother's house, and womanlike, unseen herself, she had watched him. How erect was his carriage. How pleasant his deep voice sounded as she heard him talking to her brother. Day by day, as her ankle grew stronger and she knew she could not remain much longer in her room, she dreaded more and more the thought of meeting him. She could not understand herself; she had strange dreams; she cried seemingly without the slightest cause and she was restless and unhappy. Finally she grew angry and scolded herself. She said she was silly and senti-mental. This had the effect of making her bolder, but it did not quiet her unrest. Betty did not know that the little blind God, who steals unawares on his victim, had marked her for his own, and that all this sweet perplexity was the unconscious awakening of the heart.

One afternoon, near the end of Betty's siege indoors, two of her friends, Lydia Boggs and Alice Reynolds, called to see her.

Alice had bright blue eyes, and her nut brown hair hung in rebellious curls around her demure and pretty face. An adorable dimple lay hidden in her rosy cheek and flashed into light with her smiles.

"Betty, you are a lazy thing!" exclaimed Lydia. "Lying here all day long doing nothing but gaze out of the window."

"Girls, I am glad you came over," said Betty. "I am blue. Perhaps you will cheer me up."

"Betty needs some one of the sterner sex to cheer her," said Alice, mischievously, her eyes twinkling. "Don't you think so, Lydia?"

"Of course," answered Lydia. "When I get blue—"

"Please spare me," interrupted Betty, holding up her hands in protest. "I have not a single doubt that your masculine remedies are sufficient for all your ills. Girls who have lost their interest in the old pleasures, who spend their spare time in making linen and quilts, and who have sunk their very personalities in a great big tyrant of a man, are not liable to get blue. They are afraid he may see a tear or a frown. But thank goodness, I have not yet reached that stage."

"Oh, Betty Zane! Just you wait! Wait!" exclaimed Lydia, shaking her finger at Betty. "Your turn is coming. When it does do not expect any mercy from us, for you shalt never get it."

"Unfortunately, you and Alice have monopolized the attentions of the only two eligible young men at the fort," said Betty, with a laugh.

"Nonsense there plenty of young men all eager for our favor, you little coquette," answered Lydia. "Harry Martin, Will Metzer, Captain Swearengen, of Short Creek, and others too numerous to count. Look at Lew Wetzel and Billy Bennet."

"Lew cares for nothing except hunting Indians and Billy's only a boy," said Betty.

"Well, have it your own way," said Lydia. "Only this, I know Billy adores you, for he told me so, and a better lad never lived."

"Lyde, you forget to include one other among those prostrate before Betty's charms," said Alice.

"Oh, yes, you mean Mr. Clarke. To be sure, I had forgotten him," answered Lydia. "How odd that he should be the one to find you the day you hurt your foot. Was it an accident?"

"Of course. I slipped off the bank," said Betty.

"No, no. I don't mean that. Was his finding you an accident?"

"Do you imagine I waylaid Mr. Clarke, and then sprained my ankle on purpose?" said Betty, who began to look dangerous.

"Certainly not that; only it seems so odd that he should be the one to rescue all the damsels in distress. Day before yesterday he stopped a runaway horse, and saved Nell Metzer who was in the wagon, a severe shaking up, if not something more serious. She is desperately in love with him. She told me Mr. Clarke—"

"I really do not care to hear about it," interrupted Betty.

"But, Betty, tell us. Wasn't it dreadful, his carrying you?" asked Alice, with a sly glance at Betty. "You know you are so—so prudish, one may say. Did he take you in his arms? It must have been very embarrassing for you, considering your dislike of Mr. Clarke, and he so much in love with—"

"You hateful girls," cried Betty, throwing a pillow at Alice, who just managed to dodge it. "I wish you would go home."

"Never mind, Betty. We will not tease anymore," said Lydia, putting her arm around Betty. "Come, Alice, we will tell Betty you have named the day for your wedding. See! She is all eyes now."

The young people of the frontier settlements were usually married before they were twenty. This was owing to the fact that there was little distinction of rank and family pride. The object of the pioneers in moving West was, of course, to better their condition; but, the realization of their dependence on one another, the common cause of their labors, and the terrible dangers to which they were continually exposed, brought them together as one large family.

Therefore, early love affairs were encouraged—not frowned upon as they are to-day—and they usually resulted in early marriages.

However, do not let it be imagined that the path of the youthful swain was strewn with flowers. Courting or "sparking" his sweetheart had a painful as well as a joyous side. Many and varied were the tricks played on the fortunate lover by the gallants who had vied with him for the favor of the maid. Brave, indeed, he who won her. If he marched up to her home in the early evening he was made the object of innumerable jests, even the young lady's family indulging in and enjoying the banter. Later, when he come out of the door, it was more than likely that, if it were winter, he would be met by a volley of water soaked snowballs, or big buckets of icewater, or a mountain of snow shoved off the roof by some trickster, who had waited patiently for such an opportunity. On summer nights his horse would be stolen, led far into the woods and tied, or the wheels of his wagon would be taken off and hidden, leaving him to walk home. Usually the successful lover, and especially if he lived at a distance, would make his way only once a week and then late at night to the home of his betrothed. Silently, like a thief in the dark, he would crawl through the grass and shrubs until beneath her window. At a low signal, prearranged between them, she would slip to the door and let him in without disturbing the parents. Fearing to make a light, and perhaps welcoming that excuse to enjoy the darkness beloved by sweethearts, they would sit quietly, whispering low, until the brightening in the east betokened the break of day, and then he was off, happy and lighthearted, to his labors.

A wedding was looked forward to with much pleasure by old and young. Practically, it meant the only gathering of the settlers which was not accompanied by the work of reaping the harvest, building a cabin, planning an expedition to relieve some distant settlement, or a defense for themselves. For all, it meant a rollicking good time; to the old people a feast, and the looking on at the merriment of their children—to the young folk, a pleasing break in the monotony of their busy lives, a day given up to fun and gossip, a day of romance, a wedding, and best of all, a dance. Therefore Alice Reynold's wedding proved a great event to the inhabitants of Fort Henry.

The day dawned bright and clear. The sun, rising like a ball of red gold, cast its yellow beams over the bare, brown hills, shining on the cabin roofs white with frost, and making the delicate weblike coat of ice on the river sparkle as if it had been sprinkled with powdered diamonds. William Martin, the groom, and his attendants, met at an appointed time to celebrate an old time-honored custom which always took place before the party started for the house of the bride. This performance was called "the race for the bottle."

A number of young men, selected by the groom, were asked to take part in this race, which was to be run over as rough and dangerous a track as could be found. The worse the road, the more ditches, bogs, trees, stumps, brush, in fact, the more obstacles of every kind, the better, as all these afforded opportunity for daring and expert horsemanship. The English fox race, now famous on three continents, while it involves risk and is sometimes dangerous, cannot, in the sense of hazard to life and limb, be compared to this race for the bottle.

On this day the run was not less exciting than usual. The horses were placed as nearly abreast as possible and the starter gave an Indian yell. Then followed the cracking of whips, the furious pounding of heavy hoofs, the commands of the contestants, and the yells of the onlookers. Away they went at a mad pace down the road. The course extended a mile straight away down the creek bottom. The first hundred yards the horses were bunched. At the ditch beyond the creek bridge a beautiful, clean limbed animal darted from among the furiously galloping horses and sailed over the deep furrow like a bird. All recognized the rider as Alfred Clarke on his black thoroughbred. Close behind was George Martin mounted on a large roan of powerful frame and long stride. Through the willows they dashed, over logs and brush heaps, up the little ridges of rising ground, and down the shallow gullies, unheeding the stinging branches and the splashing water. Half the distance covered and Alfred turned, to find the roan close behind. On a level road he would have laughed at the attempt of that horse to keep up with his racer, but he was beginning to fear that the strong limbed stallion deserved his reputation. Directly before them rose a pile of logs and matted brush, placed there by the daredevil settlers who had mapped out the route. It was too high for any horse to be put at. With pale cheek and clinched teeth Alfred touched the spurs to Roger and then threw himself forward. The gallant beast responded nobly. Up, up, up he rose, clearing all but the topmost branches. Alfred turned again and saw the giant roan make the leap without touching a twig. The next instant Roger went splash into a swamp. He sank to his knees in the soft black soil. He could move but one foot at a time, and Alfred saw at a glance he had won the race. The great weight of the roan handicapped him here. When Alfred reached the other side of the bog, where the bottle was swinging from a branch of a tree, his rival's horse was floundering hopelessly in the middle of the treacherous mire. The remaining three horsemen, who had come up by this time, seeing that it would be useless to attempt further efforts, had drawn up on the bank. With friendly shouts to Clarke, they acknowledged themselves beaten. There were no judges required for this race, because the man who reached the bottle first won it.

The five men returned to the starting point, where the victor was greeted by loud whoops. The groom got the first drink from the bottle, then came the attendants, and others in order, after which the bottle was put away to be kept as a memento of the occasion.

The party now repaired to the village and marched to the home of the bride. The hour for the observance of the marriage rites was just before the midday meal. When the groom reached the bride's home he found her in readiness. Sweet and pretty Alice looked in her gray linsey gown, perfectly plain and simple though it was, without an ornament or a ribbon.

Proud indeed looked her lover as he took her hand and led her up to the waiting minister. When the whisperings had ceased the minister asked who gave this woman to be married. Alice's father answered.

"Will you take this woman to be your wedded wife, to love, cherish and protect her all the days of her life?" asked the minister.

"I will," answered a deep bass voice.

"Will you take this man to be your wedded husband, to love, honor and obey him all the days of your life?"

"I will," said Alice, in a low tone.

"I pronounce you man and wife. Those whom God has joined together let no man put asunder."

There was a brief prayer and the ceremony ended. Then followed the congratulations of relatives and friends. The felicitations were apt to be trying to the nerves of even the best tempered groom. The hand shakes, the heavy slaps on the back, and the pommeling he received at the hands of his intimate friends were as nothing compared to the anguish of mind he endured while they were kissing his wife. The young bucks would not have considered it a real wedding had they been prevented from kissing the bride, and for that matter, every girl within reach. So fast as the burly young settlers could push themselves through the densely packed rooms they kissed the bride, and then the first girl they came to.

Betty and Lydia had been Alice's maids of honor. This being Betty's first experience at a frontier wedding, it developed that she was much in need of Lydia's advice, which she had previously disdained. She had rested secure in her dignity. Poor Betty! The first man to kiss Alice was George Martin, a big, strong fellow, who gathered his brother's bride into his arms and gave her a bearish hug and a resounding kiss. Releasing her he turned toward Lydia and Betty. Lydia eluded him, but one of his great hands clasped around Betty's wrist. She tried to look haughty, but with everyone laughing, and the young man's face expressive of honest fun and happiness she found it impossible. She stood still and only turned her face a little to one side while George kissed her. The young men now made a rush for her. With blushing cheeks Betty, unable to stand her ground any longer, ran to her brother, the Colonel. He pushed her away with a laugh. She turned to Major McColloch, who held out his arms to her. With an exclamation she wrenched herself free from a young man, who had caught her hand, and flew to the Major. But alas for Betty! The Major was not proof against the temptation and he kissed her himself.

"Traitor!" cried Betty, breaking away from him.

Poor Betty was in despair. She had just made up her mind to submit when she caught sight of Wetzel's familiar figure. She ran to him and the hunter put one of his long arms around her.

"I reckon I kin take care of you, Betty," he said, a smile playing over his usually stern face. "See here, you young bucks. Betty don't want to be kissed, and if you keep on pesterin' her I'll have to scalp a few of you."

The merriment grew as the day progressed. During the wedding feast great hilarity prevailed. It culminated in the dance which followed the dinner. The long room of the block-house had been decorated with evergreens, autumn leaves and goldenrod, which were scattered profusely about, hiding the blackened walls and bare rafters. Numerous blazing pine knots, fastened on sticks which were stuck into the walls, lighted up a scene, which for color and animation could not have been surpassed.

Colonel Zane's old slave, Sam, who furnished the music, sat on a raised platform at the upper end of the hall, and the way he sawed away on his fiddle, accompanying the movements of his arm with a swaying of his body and a stamping of his heavy foot, showed he had a hearty appreciation of his own value.

Prominent among the men and women standing and sitting near the platform could be distinguished the tall forms of Jonathan Zane, Major McColloch and Wetzel, all, as usual, dressed in their hunting costumes and carrying long rifles. The other men had made more or less effort to improve their appearance. Bright homespun shirts and scarfs had replaced the everyday buckskin garments. Major McColloch was talking to Colonel Zane. The genial faces of both reflected the pleasure they felt in the enjoyment of the younger people. Jonathan Zane stood near the door. Moody and silent he watched the dance. Wetzel leaned against the wall. The black barrel of his rifle lay in the hollow of his arm. The hunter was gravely contemplating the members of the bridal party who were dancing in front of him. When the dance ended Lydia and Betty stopped before Wetzel and Betty said: "Lew, aren't you going to ask us to dance?"

The hunter looked down into the happy, gleaming faces, and smiling in his half sad way, answered: "Every man to his gifts."

"But you can dance. I want you to put aside your gun long enough to dance with me. If I waited for you to ask me, I fear I should have to wait a long time. Come, Lew, here I am asking you, and I know the other men are dying to dance with me," said Betty, coaxingly, in a roguish voice.

Wetzel never refused a request of Betty's, and so, laying aside his weapons, he danced with her, to the wonder and admiration of all. Colonel

Zane clapped his hands, and everyone stared in amazement at the unprecedented sight Wetzel danced not ungracefully. He was wonderfully light on his feet. His striking figure, the long black hair, and the fancifully embroidered costume he wore contrasted strangely with Betty's slender, graceful form and pretty gray dress.

"Well, well, Lewis, I would not have believed anything but the evidence of my own eyes," said Colonel Zane, with a laugh, as Betty and Wetzel approached him.

"If all the men could dance as well as Lew, the girls would be thankful, I can assure you," said Betty.

"Betty, I declare you grow prettier every day," said old John Bennet, who was standing with the Colonel and the Major. "If I were only a young man once more I should try my chances with you, and I wouldn't give up very easily."

"I do not know, Uncle John, but I am inclined to think that if you were a young man and should come a-wooing you would not get a rebuff from me," answered Betty, smiling on the old man, of whom she was very fond.

"Miss Zane, will you dance with me?"

The voice sounded close by Betty's side. She recognized it, and an unaccountable sensation of shyness suddenly came over her. She had firmly made up her mind, should Mr. Clarke ask her to dance, that she would tell him she was tired, or engaged for that number—anything so that she could avoid dancing with him. But, now that the moment had come she either forgot her resolution or lacked the courage to keep it, for as the music commenced, she turned and without saying a word or looking at him, she placed her hand on his arm. He whirled her away. She gave a start of surprise and delight at the familiar step and then gave herself up to the charm of the dance. Supported by his strong arm she floated around the room in a sort of dream. Dancing as they did was new to the young people at the Fort—it was a style then in vogue in the east—and everyone looked on with great interest and curiosity. But all too soon the dance ended and before Betty had recovered her composure she found that her partner had led her to a secluded seat in the lower end of the hall. The bench was partly obscured from the dancers by masses of autumn leaves.

"That was a very pleasant dance," said Alfred. "Miss Boggs told me you danced the round dance."

"I was much surprised and pleased," said Betty, who had indeed enjoyed it.

"It has been a delightful day," went on Alfred, seeing that Betty was still confused. "I almost killed myself in that race for the bottle this morning. I never saw such logs and brush heaps and ditches in my life. I am sure that if the fever of recklessness which seemed in the air had not suddenly seized me I would never have put my horse at such leaps."

"I heard my brother say your horse was one of the best he had ever seen, and that you rode superbly," murmured Betty.

"Well, to be honest, I would not care to take that ride again. It certainly was not fair to the horse."

"How do you like the fort by this time?"

"Miss Zane, I am learning to love this free, wild life. I really think I was made for the frontier. The odd customs and manners which seemed strange at first have become very acceptable to me now. I find everyone so honest and simple and brave. Here one must work to live, which is right. Do you know, I never worked in my life until I came to Fort Henry. My life was all uselessness, idleness."

"I can hardly believe that," answered Betty. "You have learned to dance and ride and—"

"What?" asked Alfred, as Betty hesitated.

"Never mind. It was an accomplishment with which the girls credited you," said Betty, with a little laugh.

"I suppose I did not deserve it. I heard I had a singular aptitude for discovering young ladies in distress."

"Have you become well acquainted with the boys?" asked Betty, hastening to change the subject.

"Oh, yes, particularly with your Indianized brother, Isaac. He is the finest fellow, as well as the most interesting, I ever knew. I like Colonel Zane immensely too. The dark, quiet fellow, Jack, or John, they call him, is not like your other brothers. The hunter, Wetzel, inspires me with awe. Everyone has been most kind to me and I have almost forgotten that I was a wanderer."

"I am glad to hear that," said Betty.

"Miss Zane," continued Alfred, "doubtless you have heard that I came West because I was compelled to leave my home. Please do not believe everything you hear of me. Some day I may tell you my story if you care to hear it. Suffice it to say now that I left my home of my own free will and I could go back to-morrow."

"I did not mean to imply—" began Betty, coloring.

"Of course not. But tell me about yourself. Is it not rather dull and lonesome here for you?"

"It was last winter. But I have been contented and happy this summer. Of course, it is not Philadelphia life, and I miss the excitement and gayety of my uncle's house. I knew my place was with my brothers. My aunt pleaded with me to live with her and not go to the wilderness. I had everything I wanted there—luxury, society, parties, balls, dances, friends—all that the heart of a girl could desire, but I preferred to come to this little frontier settlement. Strange choice for a girl, was it not?"

"Unusual, yes," answered Alfred, gravely. "And I cannot but wonder what motives actuated our coming to Fort Henry. I came to seek my fortune. You came to bring sunshine into the home of your brother, and left your fortune behind you. Well, your motive has the element of nobility. Mine has nothing but that of recklessness. I would like to read the future."

"I do not think it is right to have such a wish. With the veil rolled away could you work as hard, accomplish as much? I do not want to know the future. Perhaps some of it will be unhappy. I have made my choice and will cheerfully abide by it. I rather envy your being a man. You have the world to conquer. A woman—what can she do? She can knead the dough, ply the distaff, and sit by the lattice and watch and wait."

"Let us postpone such melancholy thoughts until some future day. I have not as yet said anything that I intended. I wish to tell you how sorry I am that I acted in such a rude way the night your brother came home. I do not know what made me do so, but I know I have regretted it ever since. Will you forgive me and may we not be friends?"

"I—I do not know," said Betty, surprised and vaguely troubled by the earnest light in his eyes.

"But why? Surely you will make some little allowance for a naturally quick temper, and you know you did not—that you were—"

"Yes, I remember I was hasty and unkind. But I made amends, or at least, I tried to do so."

"Try to overlook my stupidity. I will not give up until you forgive me. Consider how much you can avoid by being generous."

"Very well, then, I will forgive you," said Betty, who had arrived at the conclusion that this young man was one of determination.

"Thank you. I promise you shall never regret it. And the sprained ankle? It must be well, as I noticed you danced beautifully."

"I am compelled to believe what the girls say—that you are inclined to the language of compliment. My ankle is nearly well, thank you. It hurts a little now and then."

"Speaking of your accident reminds me of the day it happened," said Alfred, watching her closely. He desired to tease her a little, but he was not sure of his ground. "I had been all day in the woods with nothing but my thoughts—mostly unhappy ones—for company. When I met you I pretended to be surprised. As a matter of fact I was not, for I had followed your dog. He took a liking to me and I was extremely pleased, I assure you. Well, I saw your face a moment before you knew I was as near you. When you heard my footsteps you turned with a relieved and joyous cry. When you saw whom it was your glad expression changed, and if I had been a hostile Wyandot you could not have looked more unfriendly. Such a woeful, tear-stained face I never saw."

"Mr. Clarke, please do not speak any more of that," said Betty with dignity. "I desire that you forget it."

"I will forget all except that it was I who had the happiness of finding you and of helping you. I cannot forget that. I am sure we should never have been friends but for that accident."

"There is Isaac. He is looking for me," answered Betty, rising.

"Wait a moment longer—please. He will find you," said Alfred, detaining her. "Since you have been so kind I have grown bolder. May I come over to see you to-morrow?"

He looked straight down into the dark eyes which wavered and fell before he had completed his question.

"There is Isaac. He cannot see me here. I must go."

"But not before telling me. What is the good of your forgiving me if I may not see you. Please say yes."

"You may come," answered Betty, half amused and half provoked at his persistence. "I should think you would know that such permission invariably goes with a young woman's forgiveness."

"Hello, here you are. What a time I have had in finding you," said Isaac, coming up with flushed face and eyes bright with excitement. "Alfred, what do you mean by hiding the belle of the dance away like this? I want to dance with you, Betts. I am having a fine time. I have not danced anything but Indian dances for ages. Sorry to take her away, Alfred. I can see she doesn't want to go. Ha! Ha!" and with a mischievous look at both of them he led Betty away.

Alfred kept his seat awhile lost in thought. Suddenly he remembered that it would look strange if he did not make himself agreeable, so he got up and found a partner. He danced with Alice, Lydia, and the other young ladies. After an hour he slipped away to his room. He wished to be alone.

He wanted to think; to decide whether it would be best for him to stay at the fort, or ride away in the darkness and never return. With the friendly touch of Betty's hand the madness with which he had been battling for weeks rushed over him stronger than ever. The thrill of that soft little palm remained with him, and he pressed the hand it had touched to his lips.

For a long hour he sat by his window. He could dimly see the broad winding river, with its curtain of pale gray mist, and beyond, the dark outline of the forest. A cool breeze from the water fanned his heated brow, and the quiet and solitude soothed him.

CHAPTER 4

"GOOD MORNING, HARRY. WHERE ARE YOU GOING SO EARLY?" CALLED Betty from the doorway.

A lad was passing down the path in front of Colonel Zane's house as Betty hailed him. He carried a rifle almost as long as himself.

"Mornin', Betty. I am goin' 'cross the crick fer that turkey I hear gobblin'," he answered, stopping at the gate and smiling brightly at Betty.

"Hello, Harry Bennet. Going after that turkey? I have heard him several mornings and he must be a big, healthy gobbler," said Colonel Zane, stepping to the door. "You are going to have company. Here comes Wetzel."

"Good morning, Lew. Are you too off on a turkey hunt?" said Betty.

"Listen," said the hunter, as he stopped and leaned against the gate. They listened. All was quiet save for the tinkle of a cow-bell in the pasture adjoining the Colonel's barn. Presently the silence was broken by a long, shrill, peculiar cry.

"Chug-a-lug, chug-a-lug, chug-a-lug, chug-a-lug-chug."

"Well, it's a turkey, all right, and I'll bet a big gobbler," remarked Colonel Zane, as the cry ceased.

"Has Jonathan heard it?" asked Wetzel.

"Not that I know of. Why do you ask?" said the Colonel, in a low tone. "Look here, Lew, is that not a genuine call?"

"Goodbye, Harry, be sure and bring me a turkey," called Betty, as she disappeared.

"I calkilate it's a real turkey," answered the hunter, and motioning the lad to stay behind, he shouldered his rifle and passed swiftly down the path.

Of all the Wetzel family—a family noted from one end of the frontier to the other—Lewis was as the most famous.

The early history of West Virginia and Ohio is replete with the daring deeds of this wilderness roamer, this lone hunter and insatiable Nemesis, justly called the greatest Indian slayer known to men.

When Lewis was about twenty years old, and his brothers John and Martin little older, they left their Virginia home for a protracted hunt. On their return they found the smoking ruins of the home, the mangled remains of father and mother, the naked and violated bodies of their sisters, and the scalped and bleeding corpse of a baby brother.

Lewis Wetzel swore sleepless and eternal vengeance on the whole Indian race. Terribly did he carry out that resolution. From that time forward he lived most of the time in the woods, and an Indian who crossed his trail was a doomed man. The various Indian tribes gave him different names. The Shawnees called him "Long Knife;" the Hurons, "Destroyer;" the Delawares, "Death Wind," and any one of these names would chill the heart of the stoutest warrior.

To most of the famed pioneer hunters of the border, Indian fighting was only a side issue—generally a necessary one—but with Wetzel it was the business of his life. He lived solely to kill Indians. He plunged recklessly into the strife, and was never content unless roaming the wilderness solitudes, trailing the savages to their very homes and ambushing the village bridlepath like a panther waiting for his prey. Often in the gray of the morning the Indians, sleeping around their camp fire, were awakened by a horrible, screeching yell. They started up in terror only to fall victims to the tomahawk of their merciless foe, or to hear a rifle shot and get a glimpse of a form with flying black hair disappearing with wonderful quickness in the forest. Wetzel always left death behind him, and he was gone before his demoniac yell ceased to echo throughout the woods. Although often pursued, he invariably eluded the Indians, for he was the fleetest runner on the border.

For many years he was considered the right hand of the defense of the fort. The Indians held him in superstitious dread, and the fact that he was known to be in the settlement had averted more than one attack by the Indians.

Many regarded Wetzel as a savage, a man who was mad for the blood of the red men, and without one redeeming quality. But this was an unjust opinion. When that restless fever for revenge left him—it was not always with him—he was quiet and peaceable. To those few who knew him well he was even amiable. But Wetzel, although known to everyone, cared for few. He spent little time in the settlements and rarely spoke except when addressed.

Nature had singularly fitted him for his pre-eminent position among scouts and hunters. He was tall and broad across the shoulders; his strength, agility and endurance were marvelous; he had an eagle eye, the sagacity of the bloodhound, and that intuitive knowledge which plays such an important part in a hunter's life. He knew not fear. He was daring where daring was the wiser part. Crafty, tireless and implacable, Wetzel was incomparable in his vocation.

His long raven-black hair, of which he was vain, when combed out reached to within a foot of the ground. He had a rare scalp, one for which the Indians would have bartered anything.

A favorite Indian decoy, and the most fatal one, was the imitation of the call of the wild turkey. It had often happened that men from the settlements who had gone out for a turkey which had been gobbling, had not returned.

For several mornings Wetzel had heard a turkey call, and becoming suspicious of it, had determined to satisfy himself. On the east side of the creek hill there was a cavern some fifty or sixty yards above the water. The entrance to this cavern was concealed by vines and foliage. Wetzel knew of it, and, crossing the stream some distance above, he made a wide circuit and came up back of the cave. Here he concealed himself in a clump of bushes and waited. He had not been there long when directly below him sounded the cry, "Chug-a-lug, Chug-a-lug, Chug-a-lug." At the same time the polished head and brawny shoulders of an Indian warrior rose out of the cavern. Peering cautiously around, the savage again gave the peculiar cry, and then sank back out of sight. Wetzel screened himself safely in his position and watched the savage repeat the action at least ten times before he made up his mind that the Indian was alone in the cave. When he had satisfied himself of this he took a quick aim at the twisted tuft of hair and fired. Without waiting to see the result of his shot—so well did he trust his unerring aim—he climbed down the steep bank and brushing aside the vines entered the cave. A stalwart Indian lay in the entrance with his face pressed down on the vines. He still clutched in his sinewy fingers the buckhorn mouthpiece with which he had made the calls that had resulted in his death.

"Huron," muttered the hunter to himself as he ran the keen edge of his knife around the twisted tuft of hair and tore off the scalp-lock.

The cave showed evidence of having been inhabited for some time. There was a cunningly contrived fireplace made of stones, against which pieces of birch bark were placed in such a position that not a ray of light could get out of the cavern. The bed of black coals between the stones still smoked; a quantity of parched corn lay on a little rocky shelf which jutted out from the wall; a piece of jerked meat and a buckskin pouch hung from a peg.

Suddenly Wetzel dropped on his knees and began examining the footprints in the sandy floor of the cavern. He measured the length and width of the dead warrior's foot. He closely scrutinized every moccasin print. He crawled to the opening of the cavern and carefully surveyed the moss.

Then he rose to his feet. A remarkable transformation had come over him during the last few moments. His face had changed; the calm expression was replaced by one sullen and fierce: his lips were set in a thin, cruel line, and a strange light glittered in his eyes.

He slowly pursued a course lending gradually down to the creek. At intervals he would stop and listen. The strange voices of the woods were not mysteries to him. They were more familiar to him than the voices of men.

He recalled that, while on his circuit over the ridge to get behind the cavern, he had heard the report of a rifle far off in the direction of the chestnut grove, but, as that was a favorite place of the settlers for shooting squirrels, he had not thought anything of it at the time. Now it had a peculiar significance. He turned abruptly from the trail he had been following and plunged down the steep hill. Crossing the creek he took to the cover of the willows, which grew profusely along the banks, and striking a sort of bridle path he started on a run. He ran easily, as though accustomed to that mode of travel, and his long strides covered a couple of miles in short order. Coming to the rugged bluff, which marked the end of the ridge, he stopped and walked slowly along the edge of the water. He struck the trail of the Indians where it crossed the creek, just where he expected. There were several moccasin tracks in the wet sand and, in some of the depressions made by the heels the rounded edges of the imprints were still smooth and intact. The little pools of muddy water, which still lay in these hollows, were other indications to his keen eyes that the Indians had passed this point early that morning.

The trail led up the hill and far into the woods. Never in doubt the hunter kept on his course; like a shadow he passed from tree to tree and from bush to bush; silently, cautiously, but rapidly he followed the tracks of the Indians. When he had penetrated the dark backwoods of the Black Forest tangled underbrush, windfalls and gullies crossed his path and rendered fast trailing impossible. Before these almost impassible barriers he stopped and peered on all sides, studying the lay of the land, the deadfalls, the gorges, and all the time keeping in mind the probable route of the redskins. Then he turned aside to avoid the roughest travelling. Sometimes these detours were only a few hundred feet long; often they were miles; but nearly always he struck the trail again. This almost superhuman knowledge of the Indian's ways of traversing the forest, which probably no man could have possessed without giving his life to the hunting of Indians, was the one feature of Wetzel's woodcraft which placed him so far above other hunters, and made him so dreaded by the savages.

Descending a knoll he entered a glade where the trees grew farther apart and the underbrush was only knee high. The black soil showed that the tract of land had been burned over. On the banks of a babbling brook which wound its way through this open space, the hunter found tracks which brought an exclamation from him. Clearly defined in the soft earth was the impress of a white man's moccasin. The footprints of an Indian toe inward. Those of a white man are just the opposite. A little farther on Wetzel came to a slight crushing of the moss, where he concluded some heavy body had fallen. As he had seen the tracks of a buck and doe all the way down the brook he thought it probable one of them had been shot by the white hunter. He found a pool of blood surrounded by moccasin prints; and from that spot the trail led straight toward the west, showing that for some reason the Indians had changed their direction.

This new move puzzled the hunter, and he leaned against the trunk of a tree, while he revolved in his mind the reasons for this abrupt departure —for such he believed it. The trail he had followed for miles was the devious trail of hunting Indians, stealing slowly and stealthily along watching for their prey, whether it be man or beast. The trail toward the west was straight as the crow flies; the moccasin prints that indented the soil were wide apart, and to an inexperienced eye looked like the track of one Indian. To Wetzel this indicated that the Indians had all stepped in the tracks of a leader.

As was usually his way, Wetzel decided quickly. He had calculated that there were eight Indians in all, not counting the chief whom he had shot. This party of Indians had either killed or captured the white man who had been hunting. Wetzel believed that a part of the Indians would push on with all possible speed, leaving some of their number to ambush the trail or double back on it to see if they were pursued.

An hour of patient waiting, in which he never moved from his position, proved the wisdom of his judgment. Suddenly, away at the other end of the grove, he caught a flash of brown, of a living, moving something, like the flitting of a bird behind a tree. Was it a bird or a squirrel? Then again he saw it, almost lost in the shade of the forest. Several minutes passed, in which Wetzel never moved and hardly breathed. The shadow had disappeared behind a tree. He fixed his keen eyes on that tree and presently a dark object glided from it and darted stealthily forward to another tree. One, two, three dark forms followed the first one. They were Indian warriors, and they moved so quickly that only the eyes of a woodsman like Wetzel could have discerned their movements at that distance.

Probably most hunters would have taken to their heels while there was yet time. The thought did not occur to Wetzel. He slowly raised the hammer of his rifle. As the Indians came into plain view he saw they did not suspect his presence, but were returning on the trail in their customary cautious manner.

When the first warrior reached a big oak tree some two hundred yards distant, the long, black barrel of the hunter's rifle began slowly, almost imperceptibly, to rise, and as it reached a level the savage stepped forward from the tree. With the sharp report of the weapon he staggered and fell.

Wetzel sprang up and knowing that his only escape was in rapid flight, with his well known yell, he bounded off at the top of his speed. The remaining Indians discharged their guns at the fleeing, dodging figure, but without effect. So rapidly did he dart in and out among the trees that an effectual aim was impossible. Then, with loud yells, the Indians, drawing their tomahawks, started in pursuit, expecting soon to overtake their victim.

In the early years of his Indian hunting, Wetzel had perfected himself in a practice which had saved his life many tunes, and had added much to his fame. He could reload his rifle while running at topmost speed. His extraordinary fleetness enabled him to keep ahead of his pursuers until his rifle was reloaded. This trick he now employed. Keeping up his uneven pace until his gun was ready, he turned quickly and shot the nearest Indian dead in his tracks. The next Indian had by this time nearly come up with him and close enough to throw his tomahawk, which whizzed dangerously near Wetzel's head. But he leaped forward again and soon his rifle was reloaded. Every time he looked around the Indians treed, afraid to face his unerring weapon. After running a mile or more in this manner, he reached an open space in the woods where he wheeled suddenly on his pursuers. The foremost Indian jumped behind a tree, but, as it did not entirely screen his body, he, too, fell a victim to the hunter's aim. The Indian must have been desperately wounded, for his companion now abandoned the chase and went to his assistance. Together they disappeared in the forest.

Wetzel, seeing that he was no longer pursued, slackened his pace and proceeded thoughtfully toward the settlement.

~

THAT SAME DAY, SEVERAL HOURS AFTER WETZEL'S DEPARTURE IN QUEST of the turkey, Alfred Clarke strolled over from the fort and found Colonel Zane in the yard. The Colonel was industriously stirring the contents of a huge copper kettle which swung over a brisk wood fire. The honeyed fragrance of apple-butter mingled with the pungent odor of burning hickory.

"Morning, Alfred, you see they have me at it," was the Colonel's salute.

"So I observe," answered Alfred, as he seated himself on the wood-pile. "What is it you are churning so vigorously?"

"Apple-butter, my boy, apple-butter. I don't allow even Bessie to help when I am making apple-butter."

"Colonel Zane, I have come over to ask a favor. Ever since you notified us that you intended sending an expedition up the river I have been worried about my horse Roger. He is too light for a pack horse, and I cannot take two horses."

"I'll let you have the bay. He is big and strong enough. That black horse of yours is a beauty. You leave Roger with me and if you never come back I'll be in a fine horse. Ha, Ha! But, seriously, Clarke, this proposed trip is a hazardous undertaking, and if you would rather stay—"

"You misunderstand me," quickly replied Alfred, who had flushed. "I do not care about myself. I'll go and take my medicine. But I do mind about my horse."

"That's right. Always think of your horses. I'll have Sam take the best of care of Roger."

"What is the nature of this excursion, and how long shall we be gone?"

"Jonathan will guide the party. He says it will take six weeks if you have pleasant weather. You are to go by way of Short Creek, where you will help put up a blockhouse. Then you go to Fort Pitt. There you will embark on a raft with the supplies I need and make the return journey by water. You will probably smell gunpowder before you get back."

"What shall we do with the horses?"

"Bring them along with you on the raft, of course."

"That is a new way to travel with horses," said Alfred, looking dubiously at the swift river. "Will there be any way to get news from Fort Henry while we are away?"

"Yes, there will be several runners."

"Mr. Clarke, I am going to feed my pets. Would you like to see them?" asked a voice which brought Alfred to his feet. He turned and saw Betty. Her dog followed her, carrying a basket.

"I shall be delighted," answered Alfred. "Have you more pets than Tige and Madcap?"

"Oh, yes, indeed. I have a bear, six squirrels, one of them white, and some pigeons."

Betty led the way to an enclosure adjoining Colonel Zane's barn. It was about twenty feet square, made of pine saplings which had been split and driven firmly into the ground. As Betty took down a bar and opened the small gate a number of white pigeons fluttered down from the roof of the barn, several of them alighting on her shoulders. A half-grown black bear came out of a kennel and shuffled toward her. He was unmistakably glad to see her, but he avoided going near Tige, and looked doubtfully at the young man. But after Alfred had stroked his head and had spoken to him he seemed disposed to be friendly, for he sniffed around Alfred's knees and then stood up and put his paws against the young man's shoulders.

"Here, Caesar, get down," said Betty. "He always wants to wrestle, especially with anyone of whom he is not suspicious. He is very tame and will do almost anything. Indeed, you would marvel at his intelligence. He never forgets an injury. If anyone plays a trick on him you may be sure that person will not get a second opportunity. The night we caught him Tige chased him up a tree and Jonathan climbed the tree and lassoed him. Ever since he has evinced a hatred of Jonathan, and if I should leave Tige alone with him there would be a terrible fight. But for that I could allow Caesar to run free about the yard."

"He looks bright and sagacious," remarked Alfred.

"He is, but sometimes he gets into mischief. I nearly died laughing one day. Bessie, my brother's wife, you know, had the big kettle on the fire, just as you saw it a moment ago, only this time she was boiling down maple syrup. Tige was out with some of the men and I let Caesar loose awhile. If there is anything he loves it is maple sugar, so when he smelled the syrup he pulled down the kettle and the hot syrup went all over his nose. Oh, his howls were dreadful to hear. The funniest part about it was he seemed to think it was intentional, for he remained sulky and cross with me for two weeks."

"I can understand your love for animals," said Alfred. "I think there are many interesting things about wild creatures. There are comparatively few animals down in Virginia where I used to live, and my opportunities to study them have been limited."

"Here are my squirrels," said Betty, unfastening the door of a cage. A number of squirrels ran out. Several jumped to the ground. One perched on top of the box. Another sprang on Betty's shoulder. "I fasten them up every night, for I'm afraid the weasels and foxes will get them. The white squirrel is the only albino we have seen around here. It took Jonathan weeks to trap him, but once captured he soon grew tame. Is he not pretty?"

"He certainly is. I never saw one before; in fact, I did not know such a beautiful little animal existed," answered Alfred, looking in admiration at the graceful creature, as he leaped from the shelf to Betty's arm and ate from her hand, his great, bushy white tail arching over his back and his small pink eyes shining.

"There! Listen," said Betty. "Look at the fox squirrel, the big brownish red one. I call him the Captain, because he always wants to boss the others. I had another fox squirrel, older than this fellow, and he ran things to suit himself, until one day the grays united their forces and routed him. I think they would have killed him had I not freed him. Well, this one is commencing the same way. Do you hear that odd clicking noise? That comes from the Captain's teeth, and he is angry and jealous because I show so much attention to this one. He always does that, and he would fight too if I were not careful. It is a singular fact, though, that the white squirrel has not even a little pugnacity. He either cannot fight, or he is too well behaved. Here, Mr. Clarke, show Snowball this nut, and then hide it in your pocket, and see him find it."

Alfred did as he was told, except that while he pretended to put the nut in his pocket he really kept it concealed in his hand.

The pet squirrel leaped lightly on Alfred's shoulder, ran over his breast, peeped in all his pockets, and even pushed his cap to one side of his head. Then he ran down Alfred's arm, sniffed in his coat sleeve, and finally wedged a cold little nose between his closed fingers.

"There, he has found it, even though you did not play fair," said Betty, laughing gaily.

Alfred never forgot the picture Betty made standing there with the red cap on her dusky hair, and the loving smile upon her face as she talked to her pets. A white fan-tail pigeon had alighted on her shoulder and was picking daintily at the piece of cracker she held between her lips. The squirrels were all sitting up, each with a nut in his little paws, and each with an alert and cunning look in the corner of his eye, to prevent, no doubt, being surprised out of a portion of his nut. Caesar was lying on all fours, growling and tearing at his breakfast, while the dog looked on with a superior air, as if he knew they would not have had any breakfast but for him.

"Are you fond of canoeing and fishing?" asked Betty, as they returned to the house.

"Indeed I am. Isaac has taken me out on the river often. Canoeing may be pleasant for a girl, but I never knew one who cared for fishing."

"Now you behold one. I love dear old Izaak Walton. Of course, you have read his books?"

"I am ashamed to say I have not."

"And you say you are a fisherman? Well, you haste a great pleasure in store, as well as an opportunity to learn something of the 'contemplative man's recreation.' I shall lend you the books."

"I have not seen a book since I came to Fort Henry."

"I have a fine little library, and you are welcome to any of my books. But to return to fishing. I love it, and yet I nearly always allow the fish to go free. Sometimes I bring home a pretty sunfish, place him in a tub of water, watch him and try to tame him. But I must admit failure. It is the association which makes fishing so delightful. The canoe gliding down a swift stream, the open air, the blue sky, the birds and trees and flowers— these are what I love. Come and see my canoe."

Thus Betty rattled on as she led the way through the sitting-room and kitchen to Colonel Zane's magazine and store-house which opened into the kitchen. This little low-roofed hut contained a variety of things. Boxes, barrels and farming implements filled one corner; packs of dried skins were piled against the wall; some otter and fox pelts were stretched on the wall, and a number of powder kegs lined a shelf. A slender canoe swung from ropes thrown over the rafters. Alfred slipped it out of the loops and carried it outside.

The canoe was a superb specimen of Indian handiwork. It had a length of fourteen feet and was made of birch bark, stretched over a light framework of basswood. The bow curved gracefully upward, ending in a carved image representing a warrior's head. The sides were beautifully ornamented and decorated in fanciful Indian designs.

"My brother's Indian guide, Tomepomehala, a Shawnee chief, made it for me. You see this design on the bow. The arrow and the arm mean in Indian language, 'The race is to the swift and the strong.' The canoe is very light. See, I can easily carry it," said Betty, lifting it from the grass.

She ran into the house and presently came out with two rods, a book and a basket.

"These are Jack's rods. He cut them out of the heart of ten-year-old basswood trees, so he says. We must be careful of them."

Alfred examined the rods with the eye of a connoisseur and pronounced them perfect.

"These rods have been made by a lover of the art. Anyone with half an eye could see that. What shall we use for bait?" he said.

"Sam got me some this morning."

"Did you expect to go?" asked Alfred, looking up in surprise.

"Yes, I intended going, and as you said you were coming over, I meant to ask you to accompany me."

"That was kind of you."

"Where are you young people going?" called Colonel Zane, stopping in his task.

"We are going down to the sycamore," answered Betty.

"Very well. But be certain and stay on this side of the creek and do not go out on the river," said the Colonel.

"Why, Eb, what do you mean? One might think Mr. Clarke and I were children," exclaimed Betty.

"You certainly aren't much more. But that is not my reason. Never mind the reason. Do as I say or do not go," said Colonel Zane.

"All right, brother. I shall not forget," said Betty, soberly, looking at the Colonel. He had not spoken in his usual teasing way, and she was at a loss to understand him. "Come, Mr. Clarke, you carry the canoe and follow me down this path and look sharp for roots and stones or you may trip."

"Where is Isaac?" asked Alfred, as he lightly swung the canoe over his shoulder.

"He took his rifle and went up to the chestnut grove an hour or more ago."

A few minutes' walk down the willow skirted path and they reached the creek. Here it was a narrow stream, hardly fifty feet wide, shallow, and full of stones over which the clear brown water rushed noisily.

"Is it not rather risky going down there?" asked Alfred as he noticed the swift current and the numerous boulders poking treacherous heads just above the water.

"Of course. That is the great pleasure in canoeing," said Betty, calmly. "If you would rather walk—"

"No, I'll go if I drown. I was thinking of you."

"It is safe enough if you can handle a paddle," said Betty, with a smile at his hesitation. "And, of course, if your partner in the canoe sits trim."

"Perhaps you had better allow me to use the paddle. Where did you learn to steer a canoe?"

"I believe you are actually afraid. Why, I was born on the Potomac, and have used a paddle since I was old enough to lift one. Come, place the canoe in here and we will keep to the near shore until we reach the bend. There is a little fall just below this and I love to shoot it."

He steadied the canoe with one hand while he held out the other to help her, but she stepped nimbly aboard without his assistance.

"Wait a moment while I catch some crickets and grasshoppers."

"Gracious! What a fisherman. Don't you know we have had frost?"

"That's so," said Alfred, abashed by her simple remark.

"But you might find some crickets under those logs," said Betty. She laughed merrily at the awkward spectacle made by Alfred crawling over the ground, improvising a sort of trap out of his hat, and pouncing down on a poor little insect.

"Now, get in carefully, and give the canoe a push. There, we are off," she said, taking up the paddle.

The little bark glided slowly down stream at first hugging the bank as though reluctant to trust itself to the deeper water, and then gathering headway as a few gentle strokes of the paddle swerved it into the current.

Betty knelt on one knee and skillfully plied the paddle, using the Indian stroke in which the paddle was not removed from the water.

"This is great!" exclaimed Alfred, as he leaned back in the bow facing her. "There is nothing more to be desired. This beautiful clear stream, the air so fresh, the gold lined banks, the autumn leaves, a guide who—"

"Look," said Betty. "There is the fall over which we must pass."

He looked ahead and saw that they were swiftly approaching two huge stones that reared themselves high out of the water. They were only a few yards apart and surrounded by smaller rocks, about high the water rushed white with foam.

"Please do not move!" cried Betty, her eyes shining bright with excitement.

Indeed, the situation was too novel for Alfred to do anything but feel a keen enjoyment. He had made up his mind that he was sure to get a ducking, but, as he watched Betty's easy, yet vigorous sweeps with the paddle, and her smiling, yet resolute lips, he felt reassured. He could see that the fall was not a great one, only a few feet, but one of those glancing sheets of water like a mill race, and he well knew that if they struck a stone disaster would be theirs. Twenty feet above the white-capped wave which marked the fall, Betty gave a strong forward pull on the paddle, a deep stroke which momentarily retarded their progress even in that swift current, and then, a short backward stroke, far under the stern of the canoe, and the little vessel turned straight, almost in the middle of the course between the two rocks. As she raised her paddle into the canoe and smiled at the fascinated young man, the bow dipped, and with that peculiar downward movement, that swift, exhilarating rush so dearly loved by canoeists, they shot down the smooth incline of water, were lost for a moment in a white cloud of mist, and in another they coated into a placid pool.

"Was not that delightful?" she asked, with just a little conscious pride glowing in her dark eyes.

"Miss Zane, it was more than that. I apologize for my suspicions. You have admirable skill. I only wish that on my voyage down the River of Life I could have such a sure eye and hand to guide me through the dangerous reefs and rapids."

"You are poetical," said Betty, who laughed, and at the same time blushed slightly. "But you are right about the guide. Jonathan says 'always get a good guide,' and as guiding is his work he ought to know. But this has nothing in common with fishing, and here is my favorite place under the old sycamore."

With a long sweep of the paddle she ran the canoe alongside a stone beneath a great tree which spread its long branches over the creek and shaded the pool. It was a grand old tree and must have guarded that sylvan spot for centuries. The gnarled and knotted trunk was scarred and seamed with the ravages of time. The upper part was dead. Long limbs extended skyward, gaunt and bare, like the masts of a storm beaten vessel. The lower branches were white and shining, relieved here and there by brown patches of bark which curled up like old parchment as they shelled away from the inner bark. The ground beneath the tree was carpeted with a velvety moss with little plots of grass and clusters of maiden-hair fern growing on it. From under an overhanging rock on the bank a spring of crystal water bubbled forth.

Alfred rigged up the rods, and baiting a hook directed Betty to throw her line well out into the current and let it float down into the eddy. She complied, and hardly had the line reached the circle of the eddy, where bits of white foam floated round and round, when there was a slight splash, a scream from Betty and she was standing up in the canoe holding tightly to her rod.

"Be careful!" exclaimed Alfred. "Sit down. You will have the canoe upset in a moment. Hold your rod steady and keep the line taut. That's right. Now lead him round toward me. There," and grasping the line he lifted a fine rock bass over the side of the canoe.

"Oh! I always get so intensely excited," breathlessly cried Betty. "I can't help it. Jonathan always declares he will never take me fishing again. Let me see the fish. It's a goggle-eye. Isn't he pretty? Look how funny he bats his eyes," and she laughed gleefully as she gingerly picked up the fish by the tail and dropped him into the water. "Now, Mr. Goggle-eye, if you are wise, in future you will beware of tempting looking bugs."

For an hour they had splendid sport. The pool teemed with sunfish. The bait would scarcely touch the water when the little orange colored fellows would rush for it. Now and then a black bass darted wickedly through the school of sunfish and stole the morsel from them. Or a sharp-nosed fiery-eyed pickerel—vulture of the water—rising to the surface, and, supreme in his indifference to man or fish, would swim lazily round until he had discovered the cause of all this commotion among the smaller fishes, and then, opening wide his jaws would take the bait with one voracious snap.

Presently something took hold of Betty's line and moved out toward the middle of the pool. She struck and the next instant her rod was bent double and the tip under water.

"Pull your rod up!" shouted Alfred. "Here, hand it to me."

But it was too late. A surge right and left, a vicious tug, and Betty's line floated on the surface of the water.

"Now, isn't that too bad? He has broken my line. Goodness, I never before felt such a strong fish. What shall I do?"

"You should be thankful you were not pulled in. I have been in a state of fear ever since we commenced fishing. You move round in this canoe as though it were a raft. Let me paddle out to that little ripple and try once there; then we will stop. I know you are tired."

Near the center of the pool a half submerged rock checked the current and caused a little ripple of the water. Several times Alfred had seen the dark shadow of a large fish followed by a swirl of the water, and the frantic leaping of little bright-sided minnows in all directions. As his hook, baited with a lively shiner, floated over the spot, a long, yellow object shot from out that shaded lair. There was a splash, not unlike that made by the sharp edge of a paddle impelled by a short, powerful stroke, the minnow disappeared, and the broad tail of the fish flapped on the water. The instant Alfred struck, the water boiled and the big fish leaped clear into the air, shaking himself convulsively to get rid of the hook. He made mad rushes up and down the pool, under the canoe, into the swift current and against the rocks, but all to no avail. Steadily Alfred increased the strain on the line and gradually it began to tell, for the plunges of the fish became shorter and less frequent. Once again, in a last magnificent effort, he leaped straight into the air, and failing to get loose, gave up the struggle and was drawn gasping and exhausted to the side of the canoe.

"Are you afraid to touch him?" asked Alfred.

"Indeed I am not," answered Betty.

"Then run your hand gently down the line, slip your fingers in under his gills and lift him over the side carefully."

"Five pounds," exclaimed Alfred, when the fish lay at his feet. "This is the largest black bass I ever caught. It is pity to take such a beautiful fish out of his element."

"Let him go, then. May I?" said Betty.

"No, you have allowed them all to go, even the pickerel which I think ought to be killed. We will keep this fellow alive, and place him in that nice clear pool over in the fort-yard."

"I like to watch you play a fish," said Betty. "Jonathan always hauls them right out. You are so skillful. You let this fish run so far and then you checked him. Then you gave him a line to go the other way, and no doubt he felt free once more when you stopped him again."

"You are expressing a sentiment which has been, is, and always will be particularly pleasing to the fair sex, I believe," observed Alfred, smiling rather grimly as he wound up his line.

"Would you mind being explicit?" she questioned.

Alfred had laughed and was about to answer when the whip-like crack of a rifle came from the hillside. The echoes of the shot reverberated from hill to hill and were finally lost far down the valley.

"What can that be?" exclaimed Alfred anxiously, recalling Colonel Zane's odd manner when they were about to leave the house.

"I am not sure, but I think that is my turkey, unless Lew Wetzel happened to miss his aim," said Betty, laughing. "And that is such an unprecedented thing that it can hardly be considered. Turkeys are scarce this season. Jonathan says the foxes and wolves ate up the broods. Lew heard this turkey calling and he made little Harry Bennet, who had started out with his gun, stay at home and went after Mr. Gobbler himself."

"Is that all? Well, that is nothing to get alarmed about, is it? I actually had a feeling of fear, or a presentiment, we might say."

They beached the canoe and spread out the lunch in the shade near the spring. Alfred threw himself at length upon the grass and Betty sat leaning against the tree. She took a biscuit in one hand, a pickle in the other, and began to chat volubly to Alfred of her school life, and of Philadelphia, and the friends she had made there. At length, remarking his abstraction, she said: "You are not listening to me."

"I beg your pardon. My thoughts did wander. I was thinking of my mother. Something about you reminds me of her. I do not know what, unless it is that little mannerism you have of pursing up your lips when you hesitate or stop to think."

"Tell me of her," said Betty, seeing his softened mood.

"My mother was very beautiful, and as good as she was lovely. I never had a care until my father died. Then she married again, and as I did not get on with my step-father I ran away from home. I have not been in Virginia for four years."

"Do you get homesick?"

"Indeed I do. While at Fort Pitt I used to have spells of the blues which lasted for days. For a time I felt more contented here. But I fear the old fever of restlessness will come over me again. I can speak freely to you because I know you will understand, and I feel sure of your sympathy. My father wanted me to be a minister. He sent me to the theological seminary at Princeton, where for two years I tried to study. Then my father died. I went home and looked after things until my mother married again. That changed everything for me. I ran away and have since been a wanderer. I feel that I am not lazy, that I am not afraid of work, but four years have drifted by and I have nothing to show for it. I am discouraged. Perhaps that is wrong, but tell me how I can help it. I have not the stoicism of the hunter, Wetzel, nor have I the philosophy of your brother. I could not be content to sit on my doorstep and smoke my pipe and watch the wheat and corn grow. And then, this life of the borderman, environed as it is by untold dangers, leads me, fascinates me, and yet appalls me with the fear that here I shall fall a victim to an Indian's bullet or spear, and find a nameless grave."

A long silence ensued. Alfred had spoken quietly, but with an undercurrent of bitterness that saddened Betty. For the first time she saw a shadow of pain in his eyes. She looked away down the valley, not seeing the brown and gold hills boldly defined against the blue sky, nor the beauty of the river as the setting sun cast a ruddy glow on the water. Her companion's words had touched an unknown chord in her heart. When finally she turned to answer him a beautiful light shone in her eyes, a light that shines not on land or sea—the light of woman's hope.

"Mr. Clarke," she said, and her voice was soft and low, "I am only a girl, but I can understand. You are unhappy. Try to rise above it. Who knows what will befall this little settlement? It may be swept away by the savages, and it may grow to be a mighty city. It must take that chance. So must you, so must we all take chances. You are here. Find your work and do it cheerfully, honestly, and let the future take care of itself. And let me say—do not be offended—beware of idleness and drink. They are as great a danger—nay, greater than the Indians."

"Miss Zane, if you were to ask me not to drink I would never touch a drop again," said Alfred, earnestly.

"I did not ask that," answered Betty, flushing slightly. "But I shall remember it as a promise and some day I may ask it of you."

He looked wonderingly at the girl beside him. He had spent most of his life among educated and cultured people. He had passed several years in the backwoods. But with all his experience with people he had to confess that this young woman was as a revelation to him. She could ride like an Indian and shoot like a hunter. He had heard that she could run

78

almost as swiftly as her brothers. Evidently she feared nothing, for he had just seen an example of her courage in a deed that had tried even his own nerve, and, withal, she was a bright, happy girl, earnest and true, possessing all the softer graces of his sisters, and that exquisite touch of feminine delicacy and refinement which appeals more to men than any other virtue.

"Have you not met Mr. Miller before he came here from Fort Pitt?" asked Betty.

"Why do you ask?"

"I think he mentioned something of the kind."

"What else did he say?"

"Why—Mr. Clarke, I hardly remember."

"I see," said Alfred, his face darkening. "He has talked about me. I do not care what he said. I knew him at Fort Pitt, and we had trouble there. I venture to say he has told no one about it. He certainly would not shine in the story. But I am not a tattler."

"It is not very difficult to see that you do not like him. Jonathan does not, either. He says Mr. Miller was friendly with McKee, and the notorious Simon Girty, the soldiers who deserted from Fort Pitt and went to the Indians. The girls like him however."

"Usually if a man is good looking and pleasant that is enough for the girls. I noticed that he paid you a great deal of attention at the dance. He danced three times with you."

"Did he? How observing you are," said Betty, giving him a little sidelong glance. "Well, he is very agreeable, and he dances better than many of the young men."

"I wonder if Wetzel got the turkey. I have heard no more shots," said Alfred, showing plainly that he wished to change the subject.

"Oh, look there! Quick!" exclaimed Betty, pointing toward the hillside.

He looked in the direction indicated and saw a doe and a spotted fawn wading into the shallow water. The mother stood motionless a moment, with head erect and long ears extended. Then she drooped her graceful head and drank thirstily of the cool water. The fawn splashed playfully round while its mother was drinking. It would dash a few paces into the stream and then look back to see if its mother approved. Evidently she did not, for she would stop her drinking and call the fawn back to her side with a soft, crooning noise. Suddenly she raised her head, the long ears shot up, and she seemed to sniff the air. She waded through the deeper water to get round a rocky bluff which ran out into the creek. Then she turned and called the little one. The fawn waded until the water reached its knees, then stopped and uttered piteous little bleats. Encouraged by the soft crooning it plunged into the deep water and with great splashing and floundering managed to swim the short distance. Its slender legs shook as it staggered up the bank. Exhausted or frightened, it shrank close to its mother. Together they disappeared in the willows which fringed the side of the hill.

"Was not that little fellow cute? I have had several fawns, but have never had the heart to keep them," said Betty. Then, as Alfred made no motion to speak, she continued:

"You do not seem very talkative."

"I have nothing to say. You will think me dull. The fact is when I feel deepest I am least able to express myself."

"I will read to you." said Betty taking up the book. He lay back against the grassy bank and gazed dreamily at the many hued trees on the little hillside; at the bare rugged sides of McColloch's Rock which frowned down upon them. A silver-breasted eagle sailed slowly round and round in the blue sky, far above the bluff. Alfred wondered what mysterious power sustained that solitary bird as he floated high in the air without perceptible movement of his broad wings. He envied the king of birds his reign over that illimitable space, his far-reaching vision, and his freedom. Round and round the eagle soared, higher and higher, with each perfect circle, and at last, for an instant poising as lightly as if he were about to perch on his lonely crag, he arched his wings and swooped down through the air with the swiftness of a falling arrow.

Betty's low voice, the water rushing so musically over the falls, the great yellow leaves falling into the pool, the gentle breeze stirring the clusters of goldenrod—all came softly to Alfred as he lay there with half closed eyes.

The time slipped swiftly by as only such time can.

"I fear the melancholy spirit of the day has prevailed upon you," said Betty, half wistfully. "You did not know I had stopped reading, and I do not believe you heard my favorite poem. I have tried to give you a pleasant afternoon and have failed."

"No, no," said Alfred, looking at her with a blue flame in his eyes. "The afternoon has been perfect. I have forgotten my role, and have allowed you to see my real self, something I have tried to hide from all."

"And are you always sad when you are sincere?"

"Not always. But I am often sad. Is it any wonder? Is not all nature sad?

Listen! There is the song of the oriole. Breaking in on the stillness it is mournful. The breeze is sad, the brook is sad, this dying Indian summer day is sad. Life itself is sad."

"Oh, no. Life is beautiful."

"You are a child," said he, with a thrill in his deep voice "I hope you may always be as you are to-day, in heart, at least."

"It grows late. See, the shadows are falling. We must go."

"You know I am going away to-morrow. I don't want to go. Perhaps that is why I have been such poor company today. I have a presentiment of evil I am afraid I may never come back."

"I am sorry you must go."

"Do you really mean that?" asked Alfred, earnestly, bending toward her "You know it is a very dangerous undertaking. Would you care if I never returned?"

She looked up and their eyes met. She had raised her head haughtily, as if questioning his right to speak to her in that manner, but as she saw the unspoken appeal in his eyes her own wavered and fell while a warm color crept into her cheek.

"Yes, I would be sorry," she said, gravely. Then, after a moment: "You must portage the canoe round the falls, and from there we can paddle back to the path."

The return trip made, they approached the house. As they turned the corner they saw Colonel Zane standing at the door talking to Wetzel.

They saw that the Colonel looked pale and distressed, and the face of the hunter was dark and gloomy.

"Lew, did you get my turkey?" said Betty, after a moment of hesitation. A nameless fear filled her breast.

For answer Wetzel threw back the flaps of his coat and there at his belt hung a small tuft of black hair. Betty knew at once it was the scalplock of an Indian. Her face turned white and she placed a hand on the hunter's arm.

"What do you mean? That is an Indian's scalp. Lew, you look so strange. Tell me, is it because we went off in the canoe and have been in danger?"

"Betty, Isaac has been captured again," said the Colonel.

"Oh, no, no, no," cried Betty in agonized tones, and wringing her hands. Then, excitedly, "Something can be done; you must pursue them. Oh, Lew, Mr. Clarke, cannot you rescue him? They have not had time to go far."

"Isaac went to the chestnut grove this morning. If he had stayed there he would not have been captured. But he went far into the Black Forest. The turkey call we heard across the creek was made by a Wyandot concealed in the cave. Lewis tells me that a number of Indians have camped there for days. He shot the one who was calling and followed the others until he found where they had taken Isaac's trail."

Betty turned to the younger man with tearful eyes, and with beseeching voice implored them to save her brother.

"I am ready to follow you," said Clarke to Wetzel.

The hunter shook his head, but did not answer.

"It is that hateful White Crane," passionately burst out Betty, as the Colonel's wife led her weeping into the house.

"Did you get more than one shot at them?" asked Clarke.

The hunter nodded, and the slight, inscrutable smile flitted across his stern features. He never spoke of his deeds. For this reason many of the thrilling adventures which he must have had will forever remain unrevealed. That evening there was sadness at Colonel Zane's supper table. They felt the absence of the Colonel's usual spirits, his teasing of Betty, and his cheerful conversation. He had nothing to say. Betty sat at the table a little while, and then got up and left the room saying she could not eat. Jonathan, on hearing of his brother's recapture, did not speak, but retired in gloomy silence. Silas was the only one of the family who was not utterly depressed. He said it could have been a great deal worse; that they must make the best of it, and that the sooner Isaac married his Indian Princess the better for his scalp and for the happiness of all concerned.

"I remember Myeerah very well," he said. "It was eight years ago, and she was only a child. Even then she was very proud and willful, and the loveliest girl I ever laid eyes on."

Alfred Clarke staid late at Colonel Zane's that night. Before going away for so many weeks he wished to have a few more moments alone with Betty. But a favorable opportunity did not present itself during the evening, so when he had bade them all goodbye and goodnight, except Betty, who opened the door for him, he said softly to her:

"It is bright moonlight outside. Come, please, and walk to the gate with me."

A full moon shone serenely down on hill and dale, flooding the valley with its pure white light and bathing the pastures in its glory; at the foot of the bluff the waves of the river gleamed like myriads of stars all twinkling and dancing on a bed of snowy clouds. Thus illumined the river wound down the valley, its brilliance growing fainter and fainter until at last, resembling the shimmering of a silver thread which joined the earth to heaven, it disappeared in the horizon.

"I must say goodbye," said Alfred, as they reached the gate.

"Friends must part. I am sorry you must go, Mr. Clarke, and I trust you may return safe. It seems only yesterday that you saved my brother's life, and I was so grateful and happy. Now he is gone."

"You should not think about it so much nor brood over it," answered the young man. "Grieving will not bring him back nor do you any good. It is not nearly so bad as if he had been captured by some other tribe. Wetzel assures us that Isaac was taken alive. Please do not grieve."

"I have cried until I cannot cry any more. I am so unhappy. We were children together, and I have always loved him better than any one since my mother died. To have him back again and then to lose him! Oh! I cannot bear it."

She covered her face with her hands and a low sob escaped her.

"Don't, don't grieve," he said in an unsteady voice, as he took the little hands in his and pulled them away from her face.

Betty trembled. Something in his voice, a tone she had never heard before startled her. She looked up at him half unconscious that he still held her hands in his. Never had she appeared so lovely.

"You cannot understand my feelings."

"I loved my mother."

"But you have not lost her. That makes all the difference."

"I want to comfort you and I am powerless. I am unable to say what—I—"

He stopped short. As he stood gazing down into her sweet face, burning, passionate words came to his lips; but he was dumb; he could not speak. All day long he had been living in a dream. Now he realized that but a moment remained for him to be near the girl he loved so well. He was leaving her, perhaps never to see her again, or to return to find her another's. A fierce pain tore his heart.

"You—you are holding my hands," faltered Betty, in a doubtful, troubled voice. She looked up into his face and saw that it was pale with suppressed emotion.

Alfred was mad indeed. He forgot everything. In that moment the world held nothing for him save that fair face. Her eyes, uplifted to his in the moonlight, beamed with a soft radiance. They were honest eyes, just now filled with innocent sadness and regret, but they drew him with irresistible power. Without realizing in the least what he was doing he yielded to the impulse. Bending his head he kissed the tremulous lips.

"Oh," whispered Betty, standing still as a statue and looking at him with wonderful eyes. Then, as reason returned, a hot flush dyed her face, and wrenching her hands free she struck him across the cheek.

"For God's sake, Betty, I did not mean to do that! Wait. I have something to tell you. For pity's sake, let me explain," he cried, as the full enormity of his offence dawned upon him.

Betty was deaf to the imploring voice, for she ran into the house and slammed the door.

He called to her, but received no answer. He knocked on the door, but it remained closed. He stood still awhile, trying to collect his thoughts, and to find a way to undo the mischief he had wrought. When the real significance of his act came to him he groaned in spirit. What a fool he had been! Only a few short hours and he must start on a perilous journey, leaving the girl he loved in ignorance of his real intentions. Who was to tell her that he loved her? Who was to tell her that it was because his whole heart and soul had gone to her that he had kissed her?

With bowed head he slowly walked away toward the fort, totally oblivious of the fact that a young girl, with hands pressed tightly over her breast to try to still a madly beating heart, watched him from her window until he disappeared into the shadow of the block-house.

Alfred paced up and down his room the four remaining hours of that eventful day. When the light was breaking in at the east and dawn near at hand he heard the rough voices of men and the tramping of iron-shod hoofs. The hour of his departure was at hand.

He sat down at his table and by the aid of the dim light from a pine knot he wrote a hurried letter to Betty. A little hope revived in his heart as he thought that perhaps all might yet be well. Surely some one would be up to whom he could intrust the letter, and if no one he would run over and slip it under the door of Colonel Zane's house.

In the gray of the early morning Alfred rode out with the daring band of heavily armed men, all grim and stern, each silent with the thought of the man who knows he may never return. Soon the settlement was left far behind.

CHAPTER 5

DURING THE LAST FEW DAYS, IN WHICH THE FROST HAD CRACKED OPEN the hickory nuts, and in which the squirrels had been busily collecting and storing away their supply of nuts for winter use, it had been Isaac's wont to shoulder his rifle, walk up the hill, and spend the morning in the grove.

On this crisp autumn morning he had started off as usual, and had been called back by Col. Zane, who advised him not to wander far from the settlement. This admonition, kind and brotherly though it was, annoyed Isaac. Like all the Zanes he had born in him an intense love for the solitude of the wilderness. There were times when nothing could satisfy him but the calm of the deep woods.

One of these moods possessed him now. Courageous to a fault and daring where daring was not always the wiser part, Isaac lacked the practical sense of the Colonel and the cool judgment of Jonathan. Impatient of restraint, independent in spirit, and it must be admitted, in his persistence in doing as he liked instead of what he ought to do, he resembled Betty more than he did his brothers.

Feeling secure in his ability to take care of himself, for he knew he was an experienced hunter and woodsman, he resolved to take a long tramp in the forest. This resolution was strengthened by the fact that he did not believe what the Colonel and Jonathan had told him—that it was not improbable some of the Wyandot braves were lurking in the vicinity, bent on killing or recapturing him. At any rate he did not fear it.

Once in the shade of the great trees the fever of discontent left him, and, forgetting all except the happiness of being surrounded by the silent oaks, he penetrated deeper and deeper into the forest. The brushing of a branch against a tree, the thud of a falling nut, the dart of a squirrel, and the sight of a bushy tail disappearing round a limb—all these things which indicated that the little gray fellows were working in the tree-tops, and which would usually have brought Isaac to a standstill, now did not seem to interest him. At times he stooped to examine the tender shoots growing at the foot of a sassafras tree. Then, again, he closely examined marks he found in the soft banks of the streams.

He went on and on. Two hours of this still-hunting found him on the bank of a shallow gully through which a brook went rippling and babbling over the mossy green stones. The forest was dense here; rugged oaks and tall poplars grew high over the tops of the first growth of white oaks and beeches; the wild grapevines which coiled round the trees like gigantic serpents, spread out in the upper branches and obscured the sun; witch-hopples and laurel bushes grew thickly; monarchs of the forest, felled by some bygone storm, lay rotting on the ground; and in places the wind-falls were so thick and high as to be impenetrable.

Isaac hesitated. He realized that he had plunged far into the Black Forest. Here it was gloomy; a dreamy quiet prevailed, that deep calm of the wilderness, unbroken save for the distant note of the hermit-thrush, the strange bird whose lonely cry, given at long intervals, pierced the still-ness. Although Isaac had never seen one of these birds, he was familiar with that cry which was never heard except in the deepest woods, far from the haunts of man.

A black squirrel ran down a tree and seeing the hunter scampered away in alarm. Isaac knew the habits of the black squirrel, that it was a denizen of the wildest woods and frequented only places remote from civilization. The song of the hermit and the sight of the black squirrel caused Isaac to stop and reflect, with the result that he concluded he had gone much farther from the fort than he had intended. He turned to retrace his steps when a faint sound from down the ravine came to his sharp ears.

There was no instinct to warn him that a hideously painted face was raised a moment over the clump of laurel bushes to his left, and that a pair of keen eyes watched every move he made.

Unconscious of impending evil Isaac stopped and looked around him. Suddenly above the musical babble of the brook and the rustle of the leaves by the breeze came a repetition of the sound. He crouched close by the trunk of a tree and strained his ears. All was quiet for some moments. Then he heard the patter, patter of little hoofs coming down the stream. Nearer and nearer they came. Sometimes they were almost inaudible and again he heard them clearly and distinctly. Then there came a splashing and the faint hollow sound caused by hard hoofs striking the stones in shallow water. Finally the sounds ceased.

Cautiously peering from behind the tree Isaac saw a doe standing on the bank fifty yards down the brook. Trembling she had stopped as if in doubt or uncertainty. Her ears pointed straight upward, and she lifted one front foot from the ground like a thoroughbred pointer. Isaac knew a doe always led the way through the woods and if there were other deer they would come up unless warned by the doe. Presently the willows parted and a magnificent buck with wide spreading antlers stepped out and stood motionless on the bank. Although they were down the wind Isaac knew the deer suspected some hidden danger. They looked steadily at the clump of laurels at Isaac's left, a circumstance he remarked at the time, but did not understand the real significance of until long afterward.

Following the ringing report of Isaac's rifle the buck sprang almost across the stream, leaped convulsively up the bank, reached the top, and then his strength failing, slid down into the stream, where, in his dying struggles, his hoofs beat the water into white foam. The doe had disappeared like a brown flash.

Isaac, congratulating himself on such a fortunate shot—for rarely indeed does a deer fall dead in his tracks even when shot through the heart—rose from his crouching position and commenced to reload his rifle. With great care he poured the powder into the palm of his hand, measuring the quantity with his eye—for it was an evidence of a hunter's skill to be able to get the proper quantity for the ball. Then he put the charge into the barrel. Placing a little greased linsey rag, about half an inch square, over the muzzle, he laid a small lead bullet on it, and with the ramrod began to push the ball into the barrel.

A slight rustle behind him, which sounded to him like the gliding of a rattlesnake over the leaves, caused him to start and turn round. But he was too late. A crushing blow on the head from a club in the hand of a brawny Indian laid him senseless on the ground.

When Isaac regained his senses he felt a throbbing pain in his head, and then he opened his eyes he was so dizzy that he was unable to discern objects clearly. After a few moments his sight returned. When he had struggled to a sitting posture he discovered that his hands were bound with buckskin thongs. By his side he saw two long poles of basswood, with some strips of green bark and pieces of grapevine laced across and tied fast to the poles. Evidently this had served as a litter on which he had been carried. From his wet clothes and the position of the sun, now low in the west, he concluded he had been brought across the river and was now miles from the fort. In front of him he saw three Indians sitting before a fire. One of them was cutting thin slices from a haunch of deer meat, another was drinking from a gourd, and the third was roasting a piece of venison which he held on a sharpened stick. Isaac knew at once the Indians were Wyandots, and he saw they were in full war paint. They were not young braves, but middle aged warriors. One of them Isaac recognized as Crow, a chief of one of the Wyandot tribes, and a warrior renowned for his daring and for his ability to make his way in a straight line through the wilderness. Crow was a short, heavy Indian and his frame denoted great strength. He had a broad forehead, high cheek bones, prominent nose and his face would have been handsome and intelligent but for the scar which ran across his cheek, giving him a sinister look.

"Hugh!" said Crow, as he looked up and saw Isaac staring at him. The other Indians immediately gave vent to a like exclamation.

"Crow, you caught me again," said Isaac, in the Wyandot tongue, which he spoke fluently.

"The white chief is sure of eye and swift of foot, but he cannot escape the Huron. Crow has been five times on his trail since the moon was bright. The white chief's eyes were shut and his ears were deaf," answered the Indian loftily.

"How long have you been near the fort?"

"Two moons have the warriors of Myeerah hunted the pale face."

"Have you any more Indians with you?"

The chief nodded and said a party of nine Wyandots had been in the vicinity of Wheeling for a month. He named some of the warriors.

Isaac was surprised to learn of the renowned chiefs who had been sent to recapture him. Not to mention Crow, the Delaware chiefs Son-of-Wingenund and Wapatomeka were among the most cunning and sagacious Indians of the west. Isaac reflected that his year's absence from Myeerah had not caused her to forget him.

Crow untied Isaac's hands and gave him water and venison. Then he picked up his rifle and with a word to the Indians he stepped into the underbrush that skirted the little dale, and was lost to view.

Isaac's head ached and throbbed so that after he had satisfied his thirst and hunger he was glad to close his eyes and lean back against the tree. Engrossed in thoughts of the home he might never see again, he had lain there an hour without moving, when he was aroused from his meditations by low guttural exclamations from the Indians. Opening his eyes he saw Crow and another Indian enter the glade, leading and half supporting a third savage.

They helped this Indian to the log, where he sat down slowly and wearily, holding one hand over his breast. He was a magnificent specimen of Indian manhood, almost a giant in stature, with broad shoulders in proportion to his height. His head-dress and the gold rings which encircled his bare muscular arms indicated that he was a chief high in power. The seven eagle plumes in his scalp-lock represented seven warriors that he had killed in battle. Little sticks of wood plaited in his coal black hair and painted different colors showed to an Indian eye how many times this chief had been wounded by bullet, knife, or tomahawk.

His face was calm. If he suffered he allowed no sign of it to escape him. He gazed thoughtfully into the fire, slowly the while untying the belt which contained his knife and tomahawk. The weapons were raised and held before him, one in each hand, and then waved on high. The action was repeated three times. Then slowly and reluctantly the Indian lowered them as if he knew their work on earth was done.

It was growing dark and the bright blaze from the camp fire lighted up the glade, thus enabling Isaac to see the drooping figure on the log, and in the background Crow, holding a whispered consultation with the other Indians. Isaac heard enough of the colloquy to guess the facts. The chief had been desperately rounded; the palefaces were on their trail, and a march must be commenced at once.

Isaac knew the wounded chief. He was the Delaware Son-of-Wingenund. He married a Wyandot squaw, had spent much of his time in the Wyandot village and on warring expeditions which the two friendly nations made on other tribes. Isaac had hunted with him, slept under the same blanket with him, and had grown to like him.

As Isaac moved slightly in his position the chief saw him. He straightened up, threw back the hunting shirt and pointed to a small hole in his broad breast. A slender stream of blood issued from the wound and flowed down his chest.

"Wind-of-Death is a great white chief. His gun is always loaded," he said calmly, and a look of pride gleamed across his dark face, as though he gloried in the wound made by such a warrior.

"Deathwind" was one of the many names given to Wetzel by the savages, and a thrill of hope shot through Isaac's heart when he saw the Indians feared Wetzel was on their track. This hope was short lived, however, for when he considered the probabilities of the thing he knew that pursuit would only result in his death before the settlers could come up with the Indians, and he concluded that Wetzel, familiar with every trick of the redmen, would be the first to think of the hopelessness of rescuing him and so would not attempt it.

The four Indians now returned to the fire and stood beside the chief. It was evident to them that his end was imminent. He sang in a low, not unmusical tone the death-chant of the Hurons. His companions silently bowed their heads. When he had finished singing he slowly rose to his great height, showing a commanding figure. Slowly his features lost their stern pride, his face softened, and his dark eyes, gazing straight into the gloom of the forest, bespoke a superhuman vision.

"Wingenund has been a great chief. He has crossed his last trail. The deeds of Wingenund will be told in the wigwams of the Lenape," said the chief in a loud voice, and then sank back into the arms of his comrades. They laid him gently down.

A convulsive shudder shook the stricken warrior's frame. Then, starting up he straightened out his long arm and clutched wildly at the air with his sinewy fingers as if to grasp and hold the life that was escaping him.

Isaac could see the fixed, sombre light in the eyes, and the pallor of death stealing over the face of the chief. He turned his eyes away from the sad spectacle, and when he looked again the majestic figure lay still.

The moon sailed out from behind a cloud and shed its mellow light down on the little glade. It showed the four Indians digging a grave beneath the oak tree. No word was spoken. They worked with their toma-hawks on the soft duff and soon their task was completed. A bed of moss and ferns lined the last resting place of the chief. His weapons were placed beside him, to go with him to the Happy Hunting Ground, the eternal home of the redmen, where the redmen believe the sun will always shine, and where they will be free from their cruel white foes.

When the grave had been filled and the log rolled on it the Indians stood by it a moment, each speaking a few words in a low tone, while the night wind moaned the dead chief's requiem through the tree tops.

Accustomed as Isaac was to the bloody conflicts common to the Indi-ans, and to the tragedy that surrounded the life of a borderman, the ghastly sight had unnerved him. The last glimpse of that stern, dark face, of that powerful form, as the moon brightened up the spot in seeming pity, he felt he could never forget. His thoughts were interrupted by the harsh voice of Crow bidding him get up. He was told that the slightest inclination on his part to lag behind on the march before them, or in any way to make their trail plainer, would be the signal for his death. With that Crow cut the thongs which bound Isaac's legs and placing him between two of the Indians, led the way into the forest.

Moving like spectres in the moonlight they marched on and on for hours. Crow was well named. He led them up the stony ridges where their footsteps left no mark, and where even a dog could not find their trail; down into the valleys and into the shallow streams where the running water would soon wash away all trace of their tracks; then out on the open plain, where the soft, springy grass retained little impress of their moccasins.

Single file they marched in the leader's tracks as he led them onward through the dark forests, out under the shining moon, never slacking his rapid pace, ever in a straight line, and yet avoiding the roughest going with that unerring instinct which was this Indian's gift. Toward dawn the moon went down, leaving them in darkness, but this made no difference, for, guided by the stars, Crow kept straight on his course. Not till break of day did he come to a halt.

Then, on the banks of a narrow stream, the Indians kindled a fire and broiled some of the venison. Crow told Isaac he could rest, so he made haste to avail himself of the permission, and almost instantly was wrapped in the deep slumber of exhaustion. Three of the Indians followed suit, and Crow stood guard. Sleepless, tireless, he paced to and fro on the bank his keen eyes vigilant for signs of pursuers.

The sun was high when the party resumed their flight toward the west. Crow plunged into the brook and waded several miles before he took to the woods on the other shore. Isaac suffered severely from the sharp and slippery stones, which in no wise bothered the Indians. His feet were cut and bruised; still he struggled on without complaining. They rested part of the night, and the next day the Indians, now deeming themselves practically safe from pursuit, did not exercise unusual care to conceal their trail.

That evening about dusk they came to a rapidly flowing stream which ran northwest. Crow and one of the other Indians parted the willows on the bank at this point and dragged forth a long birch-bark canoe which they ran into the stream. Isaac recognized the spot. It was near the head of Mad River, the river which ran through the Wyandot settlements.

Two of the Indians took the bow, the third Indian and Isaac sat in the middle, back to back, and Crow knelt in the stern. Once launched on that wild ride Isaac forgot his uneasiness and his bruises. The night was beautiful; he loved the water, and was not lacking in sentiment. He gave himself up to the charm of the silver moonlight, of the changing scenery, and the musical gurgle of the water. Had it not been for the cruel face of Crow, he could have imagined himself on one of those enchanted canoes in fairyland, of which he had read when a boy. Ever varying pictures presented themselves at the range, impelled by vigorous arms, flew over the shining bosom of the stream. Here, in a sharp bend, was a narrow place where the trees on each bank interlaced their branches and hid the moon, making a dark and dim retreat. Then came a short series of ripples, with merry, bouncing waves and foamy currents; below lay a long, smooth reach of water, deep and placid, mirroring the moon and the countless stars. Noiseless as a shadow the canoe glided down this stretch, the paddle dipping regularly, flashing brightly, and scattering diamond drops in the clear moonlight.

Another turn in the stream and a sound like the roar of an approaching storm as it is borne on a rising wind, broke the silence. It was the roar of rapids or falls. The stream narrowed; the water ran swifter; rocky ledges rose on both sides, gradually getting higher and higher. Crow rose to his feet and looked ahead. Then he dropped to his knees and turned the head of the canoe into the middle of the stream. The roar became deafening. Looking forward Isaac saw that they were entering a dark gorge. In another moment the canoe pitched over a fall and shot between two high, rocky bluffs. These walls ran up almost perpendicularly two hundred feet; the space between was scarcely twenty feet wide, and the water fairly screamed as it rushed madly through its narrow passage. In the center it was like a glancing sheet of glass, weird and dark, and was bordered on the sides by white, seething foam-capped waves which tore and dashed and leaped at their stony confines.

Though the danger was great, though Death lurked in those jagged stones and in those black waits Isaac felt no fear, he knew the strength of that arm, now rigid and again moving with lightning swiftness; he knew the power of the eye which guided them.

Once more out under the starry sky; rifts, shallows, narrows, and lake-like basins were passed swiftly. At length as the sky was becoming gray in the east, they passed into the shadow of what was called the Standing Stone. This was a peculiarly shaped stone-faced bluff, standing high over the river, and taking its name from Tarhe, or Standing Stone, chief of all the Hurons.

At the first sight of that well known landmark, which stood by the Wyandot village, there mingled with Isaac's despondency and resentment some other feeling that was akin to pleasure; with a quickening of the pulse came a confusion of expectancy and bitter memories as he thought of the dark eyed maiden from whom he had fled a year ago.

"Co-wee-Co-woe," called out one of the Indians in the bow of the canoe. The signal was heard, for immediately an answering shout came from the shore.

When a few moments later the canoe grated softly on a pebbly beach. Isaac saw, indistinctly in the morning mist, the faint outlines of tepees and wigwams, and he knew he was once more in the encampment of the Wyandots.

~

LATE IN THE AFTERNOON OF THAT DAY ISAAC WAS AWAKENED FROM HIS heavy slumber and told that the chief had summoned him. He got up from the buffalo robes upon which he had flung himself that morning, stretched his aching limbs, and walked to the door of the lodge.

The view before him was so familiar that it seemed as if he had suddenly come home after being absent a long time. The last rays of the setting sun shone ruddy and bright over the top of the Standing Stone; they touched the scores of lodges and wigwams which dotted the little valley; they crimsoned the swift, narrow river, rushing noisily over its rocky bed. The banks of the stream were lined with rows of canoes; here and there a bridge made of a single tree spanned the stream. From the camp fires long, thin columns of blue smoke curled lazily upward; giant maple trees, in them garb of purple and gold, rose high above the wigwams, adding a further beauty to this peaceful scene.

As Isaac was led down a lane between two long lines of tepees the watching Indians did not make the demonstration that usually marked the capture of a paleface. Some of the old squaws looked up from their work round the campfires and steaming kettles and grinned as the prisoner passed. The braves who were sitting upon their blankets and smoking their long pipes, or lounging before the warm blazes maintained a stolid indifference; the dusky maidens smiled shyly, and the little Indian boys, with whom Isaac had always been a great favorite, manifested their joy by yelling and running after him. One youngster grasped Isaac round the leg and held on until he was pulled away.

In the center of the village were several lodges connected with one another and larger and more imposing than the surrounding tepees. These were the wigwams of the chief, and thither Isaac was conducted. The guards led him to a large and circular apartment and left him there alone. This room was the council-room. It contained nothing but a low seat and a knotted war-club.

Isaac heard the rattle of beads and bear claws, and as he turned a tall and majestic Indian entered the room. It was Tarhe, the chief of all the Wyandots. Though Tarhe was over seventy, he walked erect; his calm face, dark as a bronze mask, showed no trace of his advanced age. Every line and feature of his face had race in it; the high forehead, the square, protruding jaw, the stern mouth, the falcon eyes—all denoted the pride and unbending will of the last of the Tarhes.

"The White Eagle is again in the power of Tarhe," said the chief in his native tongue. "Though he had the swiftness of the bounding deer or the flight of the eagle it would avail him not. The wild geese as they fly north-ward are not swifter than the warriors of Tarhe. Swifter than all is the vengeance of the Huron. The young paleface has cost the lives of some great warriors. What has he to say?"

"It was not my fault," answered Isaac quickly. "I was struck down from behind and had no chance to use a weapon. I have never raised my hand against a Wyandot. Crow will tell you that. If my people and friends kill your braves I am not to blame. Yet I have had good cause to shed Huron blood. Your warriors have taken me from my home and have wounded me many times."

"The White Chief speaks well. Tarhe believes his words," answered Tarhe in his sonorous voice. "The Lenapee seek the death of the pale face. Wingenund grieves for his son. He is Tarhe's friend. Tarhe is old and wise and he is king here. He can save the White Chief from Wingenund and Cornplanter. Listen. Tarhe is old and he has no son. He will make you a great chief and give you lands and braves and honors. He shall not ask you to raise your hand against your people, but help to bring peace. Tarhe does not love this war. He wants only justice. He wants only to keep his lands, his horses, and his people. The White Chief is known to be brave; his step is light, his eye is keen, and his bullet is true. For many long moons Tarhe's daughter has been like the singing bird without its mate. She sings no more. She shall be the White Chief's wife. She has the blood of her mother and not that of the last of the Tarhes. Thus the mistakes of Tarhe's youth come to disappoint his old age. He is the friend of the young paleface. Tarhe has said. Now go and make your peace with Myeerah."

The chief motioned toward the back of the lodge. Isaac stepped forward and went through another large room, evidently the chief's, as it was fitted up with a wild and barbaric splendor. Isaac hesitated before a bearskin curtain at the farther end of the chief's lodge. He had been there many times before, but never with such conflicting emotions. What was it that made his heart beat faster? With a quick movement he lifted the curtain and passed under it.

The room which he entered was circular in shape and furnished with all the bright colors and luxuriance known to the Indian. Buffalo robes covered the smooth, hard-packed clay floor; animals, allegorical pictures, and fanciful Indian designs had been painted on the wall; bows and arrows, shields, strings of bright-colored beads and Indian scarfs hung round the room. The wall was made of dried deerskins sewed together and fastened over long poles which were planted in the ground and bent until the ends met overhead. An oval-shaped opening let in the light. Through a narrow aperture, which served as a door leading to a smaller apartment, could be seen a low couch covered with red blankets, and a glimpse of many hued garments hanging on the wall.

As Isaac entered the room a slender maiden ran impulsively to him and throwing her arms round his neck hid her face on his breast. A few broken, incoherent words escaped her lips. Isaac disengaged himself from the clinging arms and put her from him. The face raised to his was strikingly beautiful. Oval in shape, it was as white as his own, with a broad, low brow and regular features. The eyes were large and dark and they dilated and quickened with a thousand shadows of thought.

"Myeerah, I am taken again. This time there has been blood shed. The Delaware chief was killed, and I do not know how many more Indians. The chiefs are all for putting me to death. I am in great danger. Why could you not leave me in peace?"

At his first words the maiden sighed and turned sorrowfully and proudly away from the angry face of the young man. A short silence ensued.

"Then you are not glad to see Myeerah?" she said, in English. Her voice was music. It rang low, sweet, clear-toned as a bell.

"What has that to do with it? Under some circumstances I would be glad to see you. But to be dragged back here and perhaps murdered—no, I don't welcome it. Look at this mark where Crow hit me," said Isaac, passionately, bowing his head to enable her to see the bruise where the club had struck him.

"I am sorry," said Myeerah, gently.

"I know that I am in great danger from the Delawares."

"The daughter of Tarhe has saved your life before and will save it again."

"They may kill me in spite of you."

"They will not dare. Do not forget that I saved you from the Shawnees. What did my father say to you?"

"He assured me that he was my friend and that he would protect me from Wingenund. But I must marry you and become one of the tribe. I cannot do that. And that is why I am sure they will kill me."

"You are angry now. I will tell you. Myeerah tried hard to win your love, and when you ran away from her she was proud for a long time. But there was no singing of birds, no music of the waters, no beauty in anything after you left her. Life became unbearable without you. Then Myeerah remembered that she was a daughter of kings. She summoned the bravest and greatest warriors of two tribes and said to them. 'Go and bring to me the paleface, White Eagle. Bring him to me alive or dead. If alive, Myeerah will smile once more upon her warriors. If dead, she will look once upon his face and die. Ever since Myeerah was old enough to remember she has thought of you. Would you wish her to be inconstant, like the moon?'"

"It is not what I wish you to be. It is that I cannot live always without seeing my people. I told you that a year ago."

"You told me other things in that past time before you ran away. They were tender words that were sweet to the ear of the Indian maiden. Have you forgotten them?"

"I have not forgotten them. I am not without feeling. You do not understand. Since I have been home this last time, I have realized more than ever that I could not live away from my home."

"Is there any maiden in your old home whom you have learned to love more than Myeerah?"

He did not reply, but looked gloomily out of the opening in the wall.

Myeerah had placed her hold upon his arm, and as he did not answer the hand tightened its grasp.

"She shall never have you."

The low tones vibrated with intense feeling, with a deathless resolve. Isaac laughed bitterly and looked up at her. Myeerah's face was pale and her eyes burned like fire.

"I should not be surprised if you gave me up to the Delawares," said Isaac, coldly. "I am prepared for it, and I would not care very much. I have despaired of your ever becoming civilized enough to understand the misery of my sister and family. Why not let the Indians kill me?"

He knew how to wound her. A quick, shuddery cry broke from her lips. She stood before him with bowed head and wept. When she spoke again her voice was broken and pleading.

"You are cruel and unjust. Though Myeerah has Indian blood she is a white woman. She can feel as your people do. In your anger and bitterness you forget that Myeerah saved you from the knife of the Shawnees. You forget her tenderness; you forget that she nursed you when you were wounded. Myeerah has a heart to break. Has she not suffered? Is she not laughed at, scorned, called a 'paleface' by the other tribes? She thanks the Great Spirit for the Indian blood that keep her true. The white man changes his loves and his wives. That is not an Indian gift."

"No, Myeerah, I did not say so. There is no other woman. It is that I am wretched and sick at heart. Do you not see that this will end in a tragedy some day? Can you not realize that we would be happier if you would let me go? If you love me you would not want to see me dead. If I do not marry you they will kill me; if I try to escape again they win kill me. Let me go free."

"I cannot! I cannot!" she cried. "You have taught me many of the ways of your people, but you cannot change my nature."

"Why cannot you free me?"

"I love you, and I will not live without you."

"Then come and go to my home and live there with me," said Isaac, taking the weeping maiden in his arms. "I know that my people will welcome you."

"Myeerah would be pitied and scorned," she said, sadly, shaking her head.

Isaac tried hard to steel his heart against her, but he was only mortal and he failed. The charm of her presence influenced him; her love wrung tenderness from him. Those dark eyes, so proud to all others, but which gazed wistfully and yearningly into his, stirred his heart to its depths. He kissed the tear-wet cheeks and smiled upon her.

"Well, since I am a prisoner once more, I must make the best of it. Do not look so sad. We shall talk of this another day. Come, let us go and find my little friend, Captain Jack. He remembered me, for he ran out and grasped my knee and they pulled him away."

CHAPTER 6

WHEN THE FIRST FRENCH EXPLORERS INVADED THE NORTHWEST, ABOUT
the year 1615, the Wyandot Indians occupied the territory between Georgian Bay and the Muskoka Lakes in Ontario. These Frenchmen named the
tribe Huron because of the manner in which they wore their hair.

At this period the Hurons were at war with the Iroquois, and the two
tribes kept up a bitter fight until in 1649, when the Hurons suffered a decisive defeat. They then abandoned their villages and sought other hunting
grounds. They travelled south and settled in Ohio along the south and
west shores of Lake Erie. The present site of Zanesfield, named from Isaac
Zane, marks the spot where the largest tribe of Hurons once lived.

In a grove of maples on the banks of a swift little river named Mad
River, the Hurons built their lodges and their wigwams. The stately elk
and graceful deer abounded in this fertile valley, and countless herds of
bison browsed upon the uplands.

There for many years the Hurons lived a peaceful and contented life.
The long war cry was not heard. They were at peace with the neighboring
tribes. Tarhe, the Huron chief, attained great influence with the
Delawares. He became a friend of Logan, the Mingo chief.

With the invasion of the valley of the Ohio by the whites, with the
march into the wilderness of that wild-turkey breed of heroes of which
Boone, Kenton, the Zanes, and the Wetzels were the first, the Indian's
nature gradually changed until he became a fierce and relentless foe.

The Hurons had sided with the French in Pontiac's war, and in the Revolution they aided the British. They allied themselves with the Mingoes, Delawares and Shawnees and made a fierce war on the Virginian pioneers. Some powerful influence must have engendered this implacable hatred in these tribes, particularly in the Mingo and the Wyandot.

The war between the Indians and the settlers along the Pennsylvania and West Virginia borders was known as "Dunmore's War." The Hurons, Mingoes, and Delawares living in the "hunter's paradise" west of the Ohio River, seeing their land sold by the Iroquois and the occupation of their possessions by a daring band of white men naturally were filled with fierce anger and hate. But remembering the past bloody war and British punishment they slowly moved backward toward the setting sun and kept the peace. In 1774 a canoe filled with friendly Wyandots was attacked by white men below Yellow Creek and the Indians were killed. Later the same year a party of men under Colonel Cresop made an unprovoked and dastardly massacre of the family and relatives of Logan. This attack reflected the deepest dishonor upon all the white men concerned, and was the principal cause of the long and bloody war which followed. The settlers on the border sent messengers to Governor Dunmore at Williamsburg for immediate relief parties. Knowing well that the Indians would not allow this massacre to go unavenged the frontiersmen erected forts and blockhouses.

Logan, the famous Mingo chief, had been a noted friend of the white men. After the murder of his people he made ceaseless war upon them. He incited the wrath of the Hurons and the Delawares. He went on the warpath, and when his lust for vengeance had been satisfied he sent the following remarkable address to Lord Dunmore:

"I appeal to any white man to say if ever he entered Logan's cabin and he gave him not meat: if ever he came cold and naked and he clothed him not. During the course of the last long and bloody war Logan remained idle in his cabin, an advocate of peace. Such was my love for the whites that my countrymen pointed as they passed and said: 'Logan is the friend of the white man.' I had even thought to have lived with you but for the injuries of one man, Colonel Cresop, who, last spring, in cold blood and unprovoked, murdered all the relatives of Logan, not even sparing my women and children. There runs not a drop of my blood in the veins of any living creature. This called upon me for vengeance. I have sought it: I have killed many; I have glutted my vengeance. For my country I will rejoice at the beams of peace. But do not harbor a thought that mine is the joy of fear. Logan never felt fear; he could not turn upon his heel to save his life. Who is there to mourn for Logan? Not one."

The war between the Indians and the pioneers was waged for years. The settlers pushed farther and farther into the wilderness. The Indians, who at first sought only to save their farms and their stock, now fought for revenge. That is why every ambitious pioneer who went out upon those borders carried his life in his hands; why there was always the danger of being shot or tomahawked from behind every tree; why wife and children were constantly in fear of the terrible enemy.

To creep unawares upon a foe and strike him in the dark was Indian warfare; to an Indian it was not dishonorable; it was not cowardly. He was taught to hide in the long grass like a snake, to shoot from coverts, to worm his way stealthily through the dense woods and to ambush the paleface's trail. Horrible cruelties, such as torturing white prisoners and burning them at the stake were never heard of before the war made upon the Indians by the whites.

Comparatively little is known of the real character of the Indian of that time. We ourselves sit before our warm fires and talk of the deeds of the redman. We while away an hour by reading Pontiac's siege of Detroit, of the battle of Braddock's fields, and of Custer's last charge. We lay the book down with a fervent expression of thankfulness that the day of the horrible redman is past. Because little has been written on the subject, no thought is given to the long years of deceit and treachery practiced upon Pontiac; we are ignorant of the causes which led to the slaughter of Braddock's army, and we know little of the life of bitterness suffered by Sitting Bull.

Many intelligent white men, who were acquainted with the true life of the Indian before he was harassed and driven to desperation by the pioneers, said that he had been cruelly wronged. Many white men in those days loved the Indian life so well that they left the settlements and lived with the Indians. Boone, who knew the Indian nature, said the honesty and the simplicity of the Indian were remarkable. Kenton said he had been happy among the Indians. Col. Zane had many Indian friends. Isaac Zane, who lived most of his life with the Wyandots, said the American redman had been wrongfully judged a bloodthirsty savage, an ignorant, thieving wretch, capable of not one virtue. He said the free picturesque life of the Indians would have appealed to any white man; that it had a wonderful charm, and that before the war with the whites the Indians were kind to their prisoners, and sought only to make Indians of them. He told tales of how easily white boys become Indianized, so attached to the wild life and freedom of the redmen that it was impossible to get the captives to return to civilized life. The boys had been permitted to grow wild with the Indian lads; to fish and shoot and swim with them; to play the Indian games—to live idle, joyous lives. He said these white boys had been ransomed and taken from captivity and returned to their homes and, although a close watch has kept on them, they contrived to escape and return to the Indians, and that while they were back among civilized people it was difficult to keep the boys dressed. In summer time it was useless to attempt it. The strongest hemp-linen shirts, made with the strongest collar and wrist-band, would directly be torn off and the little rascals found swimming in the river or rolling on the sand.

If we may believe what these men have said—and there seems no good reason why we may not—the Indian was very different from the impression given of him. There can be little doubt that the redman once lived a noble and blameless life; that he was simple, honest and brave, that he had a regard for honor and a respect for a promise far exceeding that of most white men. Think of the beautiful poetry and legends left by these silent men: men who were a part of the woods; men whose music was the sighing of the wind, the rustling of the leaf, the murmur of the brook; men whose simple joys were the chase of the stag, and the light in the dark eye of a maiden.

If we wish to find the highest type of the American Indian we must look for him before he was driven west by the land-seeking pioneer and before he was degraded by the rum-selling French trader.

The French claimed all the land watered by the Mississippi River and its tributaries. The French Canadian was a restless, roaming adventurer and he found his vocation in the fur-trade. This fur-trade engendered a strange class of men—bush-rangers they were called—whose work was to paddle the canoe along the lakes and streams and exchange their cheap rum for the valuable furs of the Indians. To these men the Indians of the west owe their degradation. These bush-rangers or coureurs-des-bois, perverted the Indians and sank into barbarism with them.

The few travellers there in those days were often surprised to find in the wigwams of the Indians men who acknowledged the blood of France, yet who had lost all semblance to the white man. They lived in their tepee with their Indian squaws and lolled on their blankets while the squaws cooked their venison and did all the work. They let their hair grow long and wore feathers in it; they painted their faces hideously with ochre and vermilion.

These were the worthless traders and adventurers who, from the year 1748 to 1783, encroached on the hunting grounds of the Indians and explored the wilderness, seeking out the remote tribes and trading the villainous rum for the rare pelts. In 1784 the French authorities, realizing that these vagrants were demoralizing the Indians, warned them to get off the soil. Finding this course ineffectual they arrested those that could be apprehended and sent them to Canada. But it was too late: the harm had been done: the poor, ignorant savage had tasted of the terrible "fire-water," as he called the rum and his ruin was inevitable.

It was a singular fact that almost every Indian who had once tasted strong drink, was unable to resist the desire for more. When a trader came to one of the Indian hamlets the braves purchased a keg of rum and then they held a council to see who was to get drunk and who was to keep sober. It was necessary to have some sober Indians in camp, otherwise the drunken braves would kill one another. The weapons would have to be concealed. When the Indians had finished one keg of rum they would buy another, and so on until not a beaver-skin was left. Then the trader would move or when the Indians sobered up they would be much dejected, for invariably they would find that some had been wounded, others crippled, and often several had been killed.

Logan, using all his eloquence, travelled from village to village visiting the different tribes and making speeches. He urged the Indians to shun the dreaded "fire-water." He exclaimed against the whites for introducing liquor to the Indians and thus debasing them. At the same time Logan admitted his own fondness for rum. This intelligent and noble Indian was murdered in a drunken fight shortly after sending his address to Lord Dunmore.

Thus it was that the poor Indians had no chance to avert their downfall; the steadily increasing tide of land-stealing settlers rolling westward, and the insidious, debasing, soul-destroying liquor were the noble redman's doom.

∼

ISAAC ZANE DROPPED BACK NOT ALTOGETHER UNHAPPILY INTO HIS OLD place in the wigwam, in the hunting parties, and in the Indian games.

When the braves were in camp, the greatest part of the day was spent in shooting and running matches, in canoe races, in wrestling, and in the game of ball. The chiefs and the older braves who had won their laurels and the maidens of the tribe looked on and applauded.

Isaac entered into all these pastimes, partly because he had a natural love for them, and partly because he wished to win the regard of the Indians. In wrestling, and in those sports which required weight and endurance, he usually suffered defeat. In a foot race there was not a brave in the entire tribe who could keep even with him. But it was with the rifle that Isaac won his greatest distinction. The Indians never learned the finer shooting with the ride. Some few of them could shoot well, but for the most part they were poor marksmen.

Accordingly, Isaac was always taken on the fall hunt. Every autumn there were three parties sent out to bring in the supply of meat for the winter. Because of Isaac's fine marksmanship he was always taken with the bear hunters. Bear hunting was exciting and dangerous work. Before the weather got very cold and winter actually set in the bears crawled into a hole in a tree or a cave in the rocks, where they hibernated. A favorite place for them was in hollow trees. When the Indians found a tree with the scratches of a bear on it and a hole large enough to admit the body of a bear, an Indian climbed up the tree and with a long pole tried to punch Bruin out of his den. Often this was a hazardous undertaking, for the bear would get angry on being disturbed in his winter sleep and would rush out before the Indian could reach a place of safety. At times there were even two or three bears in one den. Sometimes the bear would refuse to come out, and on these occasions, which were rare, the hunters would resort to fire. A piece of dry, rotten wood was fastened to a long pole and was set on fire. When this was pushed in on the bear he would give a sniff and a growl and come out in a hurry.

The buffalo and elk were hunted with the bow and arrow. This effective weapon did not make a noise and frighten the game. The wary Indian crawled through the high grass until within easy range and sometimes killed several buffalo or elk before the herd became alarmed. The meat was then jerked. This consisted in cutting it into thin strips and drying it in the sun. Afterwards it was hung up in the lodges. The skins were stretched on poles to dry, and when cured they served as robes, clothing and wigwam-coverings.

The Indians were fond of honey and maple sugar. The finding of a hive of bees, or a good run of maple syrup was an occasion for general rejoicing. They found the honey in hollow trees, and they obtained the maple sugar in two ways. When the sap came up in the maple trees a hole was bored in the trees about a foot from the ground and a small tube, usually made from a piece of alder, was inserted in the hole. Through this the sap was carried into a vessel which was placed under the tree. This sap was boiled down in kettles. If the Indians had no kettles they made the frost take the place of heat in preparing the sugar. They used shallow vessels made of bark, and these were filled with water and the maple sap. It was left to freeze over night and in the morning the ice was broken and thrown away. The sugar did not freeze. When this process had been repeated several times the residue was very good maple sugar.

Isaac did more than his share toward the work of provisioning the village for the winter. But he enjoyed it. He was particularly fond of fishing by moonlight. Early November was the best season for this sport, and the Indians caught large numbers of fish. They placed a torch in the bow of a canoe and paddled noiselessly over the stream. In the clear water a bright light would so attract and fascinate the fish that they would lie motionless near the bottom of the shallow stream.

One cold night Isaac was in the bow of the canoe. Seeing a large fish he whispered to the Indians with him to exercise caution. His guides paddled noiselessly through the water. Isaac stood up and raised the spear, ready to strike. In another second Isaac had cast the iron, but in his eagerness he overbalanced himself and plunged head first into the icy current, making a great splash and spoiling any further fishing. Incidents like this were a source of infinite amusement to the Indians.

Before the autumn evenings grew too cold the Indian held their courting dances. All unmarried maidens and braves in the village were expected to take part in these dances. In the bright light of huge fires, and watched by the chiefs, the old men, the squaws, and the children, the maidens and the braves, arrayed in their gaudiest apparel, marched into the circle. They formed two lines a few paces apart. Each held in the right hand a dry gourd which contained pebbles. Advancing toward one another they sang the courting song, keeping time to the tune with the rattling of the pebbles. When they met in the center the braves bent forward and whispered a word to the maidens. At a certain point in the song, which was indicated by a louder note, the maidens would change their positions, and this was continued until every brave had whispered to every maiden, when the dance ended.

Isaac took part in all these pleasures; he entered into every phase of the Indian's life; he hunted, worked, played, danced, and sang with faithfulness. But when the long, dreary winter days came with their ice-laden breezes, enforcing idleness on the Indians, he became restless. Sometimes for days he would be morose and gloomy, keeping beside his own tent and not mingling with the Indians. At such times Myeerah did not question him.

Even in his happier hours his diversions were not many. He never tired of watching and studying the Indian children. When he had an opportunity without being observed, which was seldom, he amused himself with the papooses. The Indian baby was strapped to a flat piece of wood and covered with a broad flap of buckskin. The squaws hung these primitive baby carriages up on the pole of a tepee, on a branch of a tree, or threw them round anywhere. Isaac never heard a papoose cry. He often pulled down the flap of buckskin and looked at the solemn little fellow, who would stare up at him with big, wondering eyes.

Isaac's most intimate friend was a six-year-old Indian boy, whom he called Captain Jack. He was the son of Thundercloud, the war-chief of the Hurons. Jack made a brave picture in his buckskin hunting suit and his war bonnet. Already he could stick tenaciously on the back of a racing mustang and with his little bow he could place arrow after arrow in the center of the target. Knowing Captain Jack would some day be a mighty chief, Isaac taught him to speak English. He endeavored to make Jack love him, so that when the lad should grow to be a man he would remember his white brother and show mercy to the prisoners who fell into his power.

Another of Isaac's favorites was a half-breed Ottawa Indian, a distant relative of Tarhe's. This Indian was very old; no one knew how old; his face was seamed and scarred and wrinkled. Bent and shrunken was his form. He slept most of the time, but at long intervals he would brighten up and tell of his prowess when a warrior.

One of his favorite stories was of the part he had taken in the events of that fatal and memorable July 2, 1755, when Gen. Braddock and his English army were massacred by the French and Indians near Fort Duquesne.

The old chief told how Beaujeu with his Frenchmen and his five hundred Indians ambushed Braddock's army, surrounded the soldiers, fired from the ravines, the trees, the long grass, poured a pitiless hail of bullets on the bewildered British soldiers, who, unaccustomed to this deadly and unseen foe, huddled under the trees like herds of frightened sheep, and were shot down with hardly an effort to defend themselves.

The old chief related that fifteen years after that battle he went to the Kanawha settlement to see the Big Chief, Gen. George Washington, who was travelling on the Kanawha. He told Gen. Washington how he had fought in the battle of Braddock's Fields; how he had shot and killed Gen. Braddock; how he had fired repeatedly at Washington, and had killed two horses under him, and how at last he came to the conclusion that Washington was protected by the Great Spirit who destined him for a great future.

❧

MYEERAH WAS THE INDIAN NAME FOR A RARE AND BEAUTIFUL BIRD— the white crane—commonly called by the Indians, Walk-in-the-Water. It had been the name of Tarhe's mother and grandmother. The present Myeerah was the daughter of a French woman, who had been taken captive at a very early age, adopted into the Huron tribe, and married to Tarhe. The only child of this union was Myeerah. She grew to be beautiful woman and was known in Detroit and the Canadian forts as Tarhe's white daughter. The old chief often visited the towns along the lake shore, and so proud was he of Myeerah that he always had her accompany him. White men travelled far to look at the Indian beauty. Many French soldiers wooed her in vain. Once, while Tarhe was in Detroit, a noted French family tried in every way to get possession of Myeerah.

The head of this family believed he saw in Myeerah the child of his long lost daughter. Tarhe hurried away from the city and never returned to the white settlement.

Myeerah was only five years old at the time of the capture of the Zane brothers and it was at this early age that she formed the attachment for Isaac Zane which clung to her all her life. She was seven when the men came from Detroit to ransom the brothers, and she showed such grief when she learned that Isaac was to be returned to his people that Tarhe refused to accept any ransom for Isaac. As Myeerah grew older her childish fancy for the white boy deepened into an intense love.

But while this love tendered her inexorable to Isaac on the question of giving him his freedom, it undoubtedly saved his life as well as the lives of other white prisoners, on more than one occasion.

To the white captives who fell into the hands of the Hurons, she was kind and merciful; many of the wounded she had tended with her own hands, and many poor wretches she had saved from the gauntlet and the stake. When her efforts to persuade her father to save any one were unavailing she would retire in sorrow to her lodge and remain there.

Her infatuation for the White Eagle, the Huron name for Isaac, was an old story; it was known to all the tribes and had long ceased to be questioned. At first some of the Delawares and the Shawnee braves, who had failed to win Myeerah's love, had openly scorned her for her love for the pale face. The Wyandot warriors to a man worshipped her; they would have marched straight into the jaws of death at her command; they resented the insults which had been cast on their princess, and they had wiped them out in blood: now none dared taunt her.

In the spring following Isaac's recapture a very serious accident befell him. He had become expert in the Indian game of ball, which is a game resembling the Canadian lacrosse, and from which, in fact, it had been adopted. Goals were placed at both ends of a level plain. Each party of Indians chose a goal which they endeavored to defend and at the same time would try to carry the ball over their opponent's line.

A well contested game of Indian ball presented a scene of wonderful effort and excitement. Hundreds of strong and supple braves could be seen running over the plain, darting this way and that, or struggling in a yelling, kicking, fighting mass, all in a mad scramble to get the ball.

As Isaac had his share of the Zane swiftness of foot, at times his really remarkable fleetness enabled him to get control of the ball. In front of the band of yelling savages he would carry it down the field, and evading the guards at the goal, would throw it between the posts. This was a feat of which any brave could be proud.

During one of these games Red Fox, a Wyandot brave, who had long been hopelessly in love with Myeerah, and who cordially hated Isaac, used this opportunity for revenge. Red Fox, who was a swift runner, had vied with Isaac for the honors, but being defeated in the end, he had yielded to his jealous frenzy and had struck Isaac a terrible blow on the head with his bat.

It happened to be a glancing blow or Isaac's life would have been ended then and there. As it was he had a deep gash in his head. The Indians carried him to his lodge and the medicine men of the tribe were summoned.

When Isaac recovered consciousness he asked for Myeerah and entreated her not to punish Red Fox. He knew that such a course would only increase his difficulties, and, on the other hand, if he saved the life of the Indian who had struck him in such a cowardly manner such an act would appeal favorably to the Indians. His entreaties had no effect on Myeerah, who was furious, and who said that if Red Fox, who had escaped, ever returned he would pay for his unprovoked assault with his life, even if she had to kill him herself. Isaac knew that Myeerah would keep her word. He dreaded every morning that the old squaw who prepared his meals would bring him the news that his assailant had been slain. Red Fox was a popular brave, and there were many Indians who believed the blow he had struck Isaac was not intentional. Isaac worried needlessly, however, for Red Fox never came back, and nothing could be learned as to his whereabouts.

It was during his convalescence that Isaac learned really to love the Indian maiden. She showed such distress in the first days after his injury, and such happiness when he was out of danger and on the road to recovery that Isaac wondered at her. She attended him with anxious solicitude; when she bathed and bandaged his wound her every touch was a tender caress; she sat by him for hours; her low voice made soft melody as she sang the Huron love songs. The moments were sweet to Isaac when in the gathering twilight she leaned her head on his shoulder while they listened to the evening carol of the whip-poor-will. Days passed and at length Isaac was entirely well. One day when the air was laden with the warm breath of summer Myeerah and Isaac walked by the river.

"You are sad again," said Myeerah.

"I am homesick. I want to see my people. Myeerah, you have named me rightly. The Eagle can never be happy unless he is free."

"The Eagle can be happy with his mate. And what life could be freer than a Huron's? I hope always that you will grow content."

"It has been a long time now, Myeerah, since I have spoken with you of my freedom. Will you ever free me? Or must I take again those awful chances of escape? I cannot always live here in this way. Some day I shall be killed while trying to get away, and then, if you truly love me, you will never forgive yourself."

"Does not Myeerah truly love you?" she asked, gazing straight into his eyes, her own misty and sad.

"I do not doubt that, but I think sometimes that it is not the right kind of love. It is too savage. No man should be made a prisoner for no other reason than that he is loved by a woman. I have tried to teach you many things; the language of my people, their ways and thoughts, but I have failed to civilize you. I cannot make you understand that it is unwomanly—do not turn away. I am not indifferent. I have learned to care for you. Your beauty and tenderness have made anything else impossible."

"Myeerah is proud of her beauty, if it pleases the Eagle. Her beauty and her love are his. Yet the Eagle's words make Myeerah sad. She cannot tell what she feels. The pale face's words flow swiftly and smoothly like rippling waters, but Myeerah's heart is full and her lips are dumb."

Myeerah and Isaac stopped under a spreading elm tree the branches of which drooped over and shaded the river. The action of the high water had worn away the earth round the roots of the old elm, leaving them bare and dry when the stream was low. As though Nature had been jealous in the interest of lovers, she had twisted and curled the roots into a curiously shaped bench just above the water, which was secluded enough to escape all eyes except those of the beaver and the muskrat. The bank above was carpeted with fresh, dewy grass; blue bells and violets hid modestly under their dark green leaves; delicate ferns, like wonderful fairy lace, lifted their dainty heads to sway in the summer breeze. In this quiet nook the lovers passed many hours.

"Then, if my White Chief has learned to care for me, he must not try to escape," whispered Myeerah, tenderly, as she crept into Isaac's arms and laid her head on his breast. "I love you. I love you. What will become of Myeerah if you leave her? Could she ever be happy? Could she ever forget? No, no, I will keep my captive."

"I cannot persuade you to let me go?"

"If I free you I will come and lie here," cried Myeerah, pointing to the dark pool.

"Then come with me to my home and live there."

"Go with you to the village of the pale faces, where Myeerah would be scorned, pointed at as your captors laughed at and pitied? No! No!"

"But you would not be," said Isaac, eagerly. "You would be my wife. My sister and people will love you. Come, Myeerah save me from this bondage; come home with me and I will make you happy."

"It can never be," she said, sadly, after a long pause. "How would we ever reach the fort by the big river? Tarhe loves his daughter and will not give her up. If we tried to get away the braves would overtake us and then even Myeerah could not save your life. You would be killed. I dare not try. No, no, Myeerah loves too well for that."

"You might make the attempt," said Isaac, turning away in bitter disappointment. "If you loved me you could not see me suffer."

"Never say that again," cried Myeerah, pain and scorn in her dark eyes. "Can an Indian Princess who has the blood of great chiefs in her veins prove her love in any way that she has not? Some day you will know that you wrong me. I am Tarhe's daughter. A Huron does not lie."

They slowly wended their way back to the camp, both miserable at heart; Isaac longing to see his home and friends, and yet with tenderness in his heart for the Indian maiden who would not free him; Myeerah with pity and love for him and a fear that her long cherished dream could never be realized.

One dark, stormy night, when the rain beat down in torrents and the swollen river raged almost to its banks, Isaac slipped out of his lodge unobserved and under cover of the pitchy darkness he got safely between the lines of tepees to the river. He had just the opportunity for which he had been praying. He plunged into the water and floating down with the swift current he soon got out of sight of the flickering camp fires. Half a mile below he left the water and ran along the bank until he came to a large tree, a landmark he remembered, when he turned abruptly to the east and struck out through the dense woods. He travelled due east all that night and the next day without resting, and with nothing to eat except a small piece of jerked buffalo meat which he had taken the precaution to hide in his hunting shirt. He rested part of the second night and next morning pushed on toward the east. He had expected to reach the Ohio that day, but he did not and he noticed that the ground seemed to be gradually rising. He did not come across any swampy lands or saw grass or vegetation characteristic of the lowlands. He stopped and tried to get his bearings. The country was unknown to him, but he believed he knew the general lay of the ridges and the water-courses.

The fourth day found Isaac hopelessly lost in the woods. He was famished, having eaten but a few herbs and berries in the last two days; his buckskin garments were torn in tatters; his moccasins were worn out and his feet lacerated by the sharp thorns.

Darkness was fast approaching when he first realized that he was lost. He waited hopefully for the appearance of the north star—that most faithful of hunter's guides—but the sky clouded over and no stars appeared. Tired out and hopeless he dragged his weary body into a dense laurel thicket end lay down to wait for dawn. The dismal hoot of an owl nearby, the stealthy steps of some soft-footed animal prowling round the thicket, and the mournful sough of the wind in the treetops kept him awake for hours, but at last he fell asleep.

CHAPTER 7

THE CHILLING RAINS OF NOVEMBER AND DECEMBER'S FLURRY OF SNOW had passed and mid-winter with its icy blasts had set in. The Black Forest had changed autumn's gay crimson and yellow to the somber hue of winter and now looked indescribably dreary. An ice gorge had formed in the bend of the river at the head of the island and from bank to bank logs, driftwood, broken ice and giant floes were packed and jammed so tightly as to resist the action of the mighty current. This natural bridge would remain solid until spring had loosened the frozen grip of old winter. The hills surrounding Fort Henry were white with snow. The huge drifts were on a level with Col. Zane's fence and in some places the top rail had disappeared. The pine trees in the yard were weighted down and drooped helplessly with their white burden.

On this frosty January morning the only signs of life round the settlement were a man and a dog walking up Wheeling hill. The man carried a rifle, an axe, and several steel traps. His snow-shoes sank into the drifts as he labored up the steep hill. All at once he stopped. The big black dog had put his nose high in the air and had sniffed at the cold wind.

"Well, Tige, old fellow, what is it?" said Jonathan Zane, for this was he.

The dog answered with a low whine. Jonathan looked up and down the creek valley and along the hillside, but he saw no living thing. Snow, snow everywhere, its white monotony relieved here and there by a black tree trunk. Tige sniffed again and then growled. Turning his ear to the breeze

Jonathan heard faint yelps from far over the hilltop. He dropped his axe and the traps and ran the remaining short distance up the hill. When he reached the summit the clear baying of hunting wolves was borne to his ears.

The hill sloped gradually on the other side, ending in a white, unbroken plain which extended to the edge of the laurel thicket a quarter of a mile distant. Jonathan could not see the wolves, but he heard distinctly their peculiar, broken howls. They were in pursuit of something, whether quadruped or man he could not decide. Another moment and he was no longer in doubt, for a deer dashed out of the thicket. Jonathan saw that it was a buck and that he was well nigh exhausted; his head swung low from side to side; he sank slowly to his knees, and showed every indication of distress.

The next instant the baying of the wolves, which had ceased for a moment, sounded close at hand. The buck staggered to his feet; he turned this way and that. When he saw the man and the dog he started toward them without a moment's hesitation.

At a warning word from Jonathan the dog sank on the snow. Jonathan stepped behind a tree, which, however, was not large enough to screen his body. He thought the buck would pass close by him and he determined to shoot at the most favorable moment.

The buck, however, showed no intention of passing by; in his abject terror he saw in the man and the dog foes less terrible than those which were yelping on his trail. He came on in a lame uneven trot, making straight for the tree. When he reached the tree he crouched, or rather fell, on the ground within a yard of Jonathan and his dog. He quivered and twitched; his nostrils flared; at every pant drops of blood flecked the snow; his great dark eyes had a strained and awful look, almost human in its agony.

Another yelp from the thicket and Jonathan looked up in time to see five timber wolves, gaunt, hungry looking beasts, burst from the bushes. With their noses close to the snow they followed the trail. When they came to the spot where the deer had fallen a chorus of angry, thirsty howls filled the air.

"Well, if this doesn't beat me! I thought I knew a little about deer," said Jonathan. "Tige, we will save this buck from those gray devils if it costs a leg. Steady now, old fellow, wait."

When the wolves were within fifty yards of the tree and coming swiftly

Jonathan threw his rifle forward and yelled with all the power of his strong lungs:

"Hi! Hi! Hi! Take 'em, Tige!"

In trying to stop quickly on the slippery snowcrust the wolves fell all over themselves. One dropped dead and another fell wounded at the report of Jonathan's rifle. The others turned tail and loped swiftly off into the thicket. Tige made short work of the wounded one.

"Old White Tail, if you were the last buck in the valley, I would not harm you," said Jonathan, looking at the panting deer. "You need have no farther fear of that pack of cowards."

So saying Jonathan called to Tige and wended his way down the hill toward the settlement.

An hour afterward he was sitting in Col. Zane's comfortable cabin, where all was warmth and cheerfulness. Blazing hickory logs roared and crackled in the stone fireplace.

"Hello, Jack, where did you come from?" said Col. Zane, who had just come in. "Haven't seen you since we were snowed up. Come over to see about the horses? If I were you I would not undertake that trip to Fort Pitt until the weather breaks. You could go in the sled, of course, but if you care anything for my advice you will stay home. This weather will hold on for some time. Let Lord Dunmore wait."

"I guess we are in for some stiff weather."

"Haven't a doubt of it. I told Bessie last fall we might expect a hard winter. Everything indicated it. Look at the thick corn-husks. The hulls of the nuts from the shell-bark here in the yard were larger and tougher than I ever saw them. Last October Tige killed a raccoon that had the wooliest kind of a fur. I could have given you a dozen signs of a hard winter. We shall still have a month or six weeks of it. In a week will be ground-hog day and you had better wait and decide after that."

"I tell you, Eb, I get tired chopping wood and hanging round the house."

"Aha! another moody spell," said Col. Zane, glancing kindly at his brother. "Jack, if you were married you would outgrow those 'blue-devils.' I used to have them. It runs in the family to be moody. I have known our father to take his gun and go into the woods and stay there until he had fought out the spell. I have done that myself, but once I married Bessie I have had no return of the old feeling. Get married, Jack, and then you will settle down and work. You will not have time to roam around alone in the woods."

"I prefer the spells, as you call them, any day," answered Jonathan, with a short laugh. "A man with my disposition has no right to get married. This weather is trying, for it keeps me indoors. I cannot hunt because we do not need the meat. And even if I did want to hunt I should not have to go out of sight of the fort. There were three deer in front of the barn this morning. They were nearly starved. They ran off a little at sight of me, but in a few moments came back for the hay I pitched out of the loft. This afternoon Tige and I saved a big buck from a pack of wolves. The buck came right up to me. I could have touched him. This storm is sending the deer down from the hills."

"You are right. It is too bad. Severe weather like this will kill more deer than an army could. Have you been doing anything with your traps?"

"Yes, I have thirty traps out."

"If you are going, tell Sam to fetch down another load of fodder before he unhitches."

"Eb, I have no patience with your brothers," said Col. Zane's wife to him after he had closed the door. "They are all alike; forever wanting to be on the go. If it isn't Indians it is something else. The very idea of going up the river in this weather. If Jonathan doesn't care for himself he should think of the horses."

"My dear, I was just as wild and discontented as Jack before I met you," remarked Col. Zane. "You may not think so, but a home and pretty little woman will do wonders for any man. My brothers have nothing to keep them steady."

"Perhaps. I do not believe that Jonathan ever will get married. Silas may; he certainly has been keeping company long enough with Mary Bennet. You are the only Zane who has conquered that adventurous spirit and the desire to be always roaming the woods in search of something to kill. Your old boy, Noah, is growing up like all the Zanes. He fights with all the children in the settlement. I cannot break him of it. He is not a bully, for I have never known him to do anything mean or cruel. It is just sheer love of fighting."

"Ha! Ha! I fear you will not break him of that," answered Col. Zane. "It is a good joke to say he gets it all from the Zanes. How about the McCollochs? What have you to say of your father and the Major and John McColloch? They are not anything if not the fighting kind. It's the best trait the youngster could have, out here on the border. He'll need it all. Don't worry about him. Where is Betty?"

"I told her to take the children out for a sled ride. Betty needs exercise. She stays indoors too much, and of late she looks pale."

"What! Betty not looking well! She was never ill in her life. I have noticed no change in her."

"No, I daresay you have not. You men can't see anything. But I can, and I tell you, Betty is very different from the girl she used to be. Most of the time she sits and gazes out of her window. She used to be so bright, and when she was not romping with the children she busied herself with her needle. Yesterday as I entered her room she hurriedly picked up a book, and, I think, intentionally hid her face behind it. I saw she had been crying."

"Come to think of it, I believe I have missed Betty," said Col. Zane, gravely. "She seems more quiet. Is she unhappy? When did you first see this change?"

"I think it a little while after Mr. Clarke left here last fall."

"Clarke! What has he to do with Betty? What are you driving at?" exclaimed the Colonel, stopping in front of his wife. His faced had paled slightly. "I had forgotten Clarke. Bess, you can't mean—"

"Now, Eb, do not get that look on your face. You always frighten me," answered his wife, as she quietly placed her hand on his arm. "I do not mean anything much, certainly nothing against Mr. Clarke. He was a true gentleman. I really liked him."

"So did I," interrupted the Colonel.

"I believe Betty cared for Mr. Clarke. She was always different with him. He has gone away and has forgotten her. That is strange to us, because we cannot imagine any one indifferent to our beautiful Betty. Nevertheless, no matter how attractive a woman may be men sometimes love and ride away. I hear the children coming now. Do not let Betty see that we have been talking about her. She is as quick as a steel trap."

A peal of childish laughter came from without. The door opened and Betty ran in, followed by the sturdy, rosy-cheeked youngsters. All three were white with snow.

"We have had great fun," said Betty. "We went over the bank once and tumbled off the sled into the snow. Then we had a snow-balling contest, and the boys compelled me to strike my colors and fly for the house."

Col. Zane looked closely at his sister. Her cheeks were flowing with health; her eyes were sparkling with pleasure. Failing to observe any indication of the change in Betty which his wife had spoken, he concluded that women were better qualified to judge their own sex than were men.

He had to confess to himself that the only change he could see in his sister was that she grew prettier every day of her life.

"Oh, papa. I hit Sam right in the head with a big snow-ball, and I made Betty run into the house, and I slid down to all by myself. Sam was afraid," said Noah to his father.

"Noah, if Sammy saw the danger in sliding down the hill he was braver than you. Now both of you run to Annie and have these wet things taken off."

"I must go get on dry clothes myself," said Betty. "I am nearly frozen. It is growing colder. I saw Jack come in. Is he going to Fort Pitt?"

"No. He has decided to wait until good weather. I met Mr. Miller over at the garrison this afternoon and he wants you to go on the sled-ride to-night. There is to be a dance down at Watkins' place. All the young people are going. It is a long ride, but I guess it will be perfectly safe. Silas and Wetzel are going. Dress yourself warmly and go with them. You have never seen old Grandma Watkins."

"I shall be pleased to go," said Betty.

Betty's room was very cozy, considering that it was in a pioneer's cabin. It had two windows, the larger of which opened on the side toward the river. The walls had been smoothly plastered and covered with white birch-bark. They were adorned with a few pictures and Indian ornaments. A bright homespun carpet covered the floor. A small bookcase stood in the corner. The other furniture consisted of two chairs, a small table, a bureau with a mirror, and a large wardrobe. It was in this last that Betty kept the gowns which she had brought from Philadelphia, and which were the wonder of all the girls in the village.

"I wonder why Eb looked so closely at me," mused Betty, as she slipped on her little moccasins. "Usually he is not anxious to have me go so far from the fort; and now he seemed to think I would enjoy this dance to-night. I wonder what Bessie has been telling him."

Betty threw some wood on the smouldering fire in the little stone grate and sat down to think. Like every one who has a humiliating secret, Betty was eternally suspicious and feared the very walls would guess it. Swift as light came the thought that her brother and his wife had suspected her secret and had been talking about her, perhaps pitying her. With this thought came the fear that if she had betrayed herself to the Colonel's wife she might have done so to others. The consciousness that this might well be true and that even now the girls might be talking and laughing at her caused her exceeding shame and bitterness.

Many weeks had passed since that last night that Betty and Alfred Clarke had been together.

In due time Col. Zane's men returned and Betty learned from Jonathan that Alfred had left them at Ft. Pitt, saying he was going south to his old home. At first she had expected some word from Alfred, a letter, or if not that, surely an apology for his conduct on that last evening they had been together. But Jonathan brought her no word, and after hoping against hope and wearing away the long days looking for a letter that never came, she ceased to hope and plunged into despair.

The last few months had changed her life; changed it as only constant thinking, and suffering that must be hidden from the world, can change the life of a young girl. She had been so intent on her own thoughts, so deep in her dreams that she had taken no heed of other people. She did not know that those who loved her were always thinking of her welfare and would naturally see even a slight change in her. With a sudden shock of surprise and pain she realized that to-day for the first time in a month she had played with the boys. Sammy had asked her why she did not laugh any more. Now she understood the mad antics of Tige that morning; Madcap's whinney of delight; the chattering of the squirrels, and Caesar's pranks in the snow. She had neglected her pets. She had neglected her work, her friends, the boys' lessons; and her brother. For what? What would her girl friends say? That she was pining for a lover who had forgotten her. They would say that and it would be true. She did think of him constantly.

With bitter pain she recalled the first days of the acquaintance which now seemed so long past; how much she had disliked Alfred; how angry she had been with him and how contemptuously she had spurned his first proffer of friendship; how, little by little, her pride had been subdued; then the struggle with her heart. And, at last, after he had gone, came the realization that the moments spent with him had been the sweetest of her life. She thought of him as she used to see him stand before her; so good to look at; so strong and masterful, and yet so gentle.

"Oh, I cannot bear it," whispered Betty with a half sob, giving up to a rush of tender feeling. "I love him. I love him, and I cannot forget him. Oh, I am so ashamed."

Betty bowed her head on her knees. Her slight form quivered a while and then grew still. When a half hour later she raised her head her face was pale and cold. It bore the look of a girl who had suddenly become a woman; a woman who saw the battle of life before her and who was ready to fight. Stern resolve gleamed from her flashing eyes; there was no faltering in those set lips.

Betty was a Zane and the Zanes came of a fighting race. Their blood had ever been hot and passionate; the blood of men quick to love and quick to hate. It had flowed in the veins of daring, reckless men who had fought and died for their country; men who had won their sweethearts with the sword; men who had had unconquerable spirits. It was this fighting instinct that now rose in Betty; it gave her strength and pride to defend her secret; the resolve to fight against the longing in her heart.

"I will forget him! I will tear him out of my heart!" she exclaimed passionately. "He never deserved my love. He did not care. I was a little fool to let him amuse himself with me. He went away and forgot. I hate him."

At length Betty subdued her excitement, and when she went down to supper a few minutes later she tried to maintain a cheerful composure of manner and to chat with her old-time vivacity.

"Bessie, I am sure you have exaggerated things," remarked Col. Zane after Betty had gone upstairs to dress for the dance. "Perhaps it is only that Betty grows a little tired of this howling wilderness. Small wonder if she does. You know she has always been used to comfort and many young people, places to go and all that. This is her first winter on the frontier. She'll come round all right."

"Have it your way, Ebenezer," answered his wife with a look of amused contempt on her face. "I am sure I hope you are right. By the way, what do you think of this Ralfe Miller? He has been much with Betty of late."

"I do not know the fellow, Bessie. He seems agreeable. He is a good-looking young man. Why do you ask?"

"The Major told me that Miller had a bad name at Pitt, and that he had been a friend of Simon Girty before Girty became a renegade."

"Humph! I'll have to speak to Sam. As for knowing Girty, there is nothing terrible in that. All the women seem to think that Simon is the very prince of devils. I have known all the Girtys for years. Simon was not a bad fellow before he went over to the Indians. It is his brother James who has committed most of those deeds which have made the name of Girty so infamous."

"I don't like Miller," continued Mrs. Zane in a hesitating way. "I must admit that I have no sensible reason for my dislike. He is pleasant and agreeable, yes, but behind it there is a certain intensity. That man has something on his mind."

"If he is in love with Betty, as you seem to think, he has enough on his mind. I'll vouch for that," said Col. Zane. "Betty is inclined to be a coquette. If she liked Clarke pretty well, it may be a lesson to her."

"I wish she were married and settled down. It may have been no great harm for Betty to have had many admirers while in Philadelphia, but out here on the border it will never do. These men will not have it. There will be trouble come of Betty's coquettishness."

"Why, Bessie, she is only a child. What would you have her do? Marry the first man who asked her?"

"The clod-hoppers are coming," said Mrs. Zane as the jingling of sleigh bells broke the stillness.

Col. Zane sprang up and opened the door. A broad stream of light flashed from the room and lighted up the road. Three powerful teams stood before the door. They were hitched to sleds, or clod-hoppers, which were nothing more than wagon-beds fastened on wooden runners. A chorus of merry shouts greeted Col. Zane as he appeared in the doorway.

"All right! all right! Here she is," he cried, as Betty ran down the steps.

The Colonel bundled her in a buffalo robe in a corner of the foremost sled. At her feet he placed a buckskin bag containing a hot stone Mrs. Zane thoughtfully had provided.

"All ready here. Let them go," called the Colonel. "You will have clear weather. Coming back look well to the traces and keep a watch for the wolves."

The long whips cracked, the bells jingled, the impatient horses plunged forward and away they went over the glistening snow. The night was clear and cold; countless stars blinked in the black vault overhead; the pale moon cast its wintry light down on a white and frozen world. As the runners glided swiftly and smoothly onward showers of dry snow like fine powder flew from under the horses' hoofs and soon whitened the black-robed figures in the sleds. The way led down the hill past the Fort, over the creek bridge and along the road that skirted the Black Forest. The ride was long; it led up and down hills, and through a lengthy stretch of gloomy forest. Sometimes the drivers walked the horses up a steep climb and again raced them along a level bottom. Making a turn in the road they saw a bright light in the distance which marked their destination. In five minutes the horses dashed into a wide clearing. An immense log fire burned in front of a two-story structure. Streams of light poured from the small windows; the squeaking of fiddles, the shuffling of many feet, and gay laughter came through the open door.

The steaming horses were unhitched, covered carefully with robes and led into sheltered places, while the merry party disappeared into the house.

The occasion was the celebration of the birthday of old Dan Watkins' daughter. Dan was one of the oldest settlers along the river; in fact, he had located his farm several years after Col. Zane had founded the settlement. He was noted for his open-handed dealing and kindness of heart. He had loaned many a head of cattle which had never been returned, and many a sack of flour had left his mill unpaid for in grain. He was a good shot, he would lay a tree on the ground as quickly as any man who ever swung an axe, and he could drink more whiskey than any man in the valley.

Dan stood at the door with a smile of welcome upon his rugged features and a handshake and a pleasant word for everyone. His daughter Susan greeted the men with a little curtsy and kissed the girls upon the cheek. Susan was not pretty, though she was strong and healthy; her laughing blue eyes assured a sunny disposition, and she numbered her suitors by the score.

The young people lost no time. Soon the floor was covered with their whirling forms.

In one corner of the room sat a little dried-up old woman with white hair and bright dark eyes. This was Grandma Watkins. She was very old, so old that no one knew her age, but she was still vigorous enough to do her day's work with more pleasure than many a younger woman. Just now she was talking to Wetzel, who leaned upon his inseparable rifle and listened to her chatter. The hunter liked the old lady and would often stop at her cabin while on his way to the settlement and leave at her door a fat turkey or a haunch of venison.

"Lew Wetzel, I am ashamed of you." Grandmother Watkins was saying. "Put that gun in the corner and get out there and dance. Enjoy yourself. You are only a boy yet."

"I'd better look on, mother," answered the hunter.

"Pshaw! You can hop and skip around like any of then and laugh too if you want. I hope that pretty sister of Eb Zane has caught your fancy."

"She is not for the like of me," he said gently "I haven't the gifts."

"Don't talk about gifts. Not to an old woman who has lived three times and more your age," she said impatiently. "It is not gifts a woman wants out here in the West. If she does 'twill do her no good. She needs a strong arm to build cabins, a quick eye with a rifle, and a fearless heart. What border-women want are houses and children. They must bring up men,

men to drive the redskins back, men to till the soil, or else what is the good of our suffering here."

"You are right," said Wetzel thoughtfully. "But I'd hate to see a flower like Betty Zane in a rude hunter's cabin."

"I have known the Zanes for forty year' and I never saw one yet that was afraid of work. And you might win her if you would give up running mad after Indians. I'll allow no woman would put up with that. You have killed many Indians. You ought to be satisfied."

"Fightin' redskins is somethin' I can't help," said the hunter, slowly shaking his head. "If I got married the fever would come on and I'd leave home. No, I'm no good for a woman. Fightin' is all I'm good for."

"Why not fight for her, then? Don't let one of these boys walk off with her. Look at her. She likes fun and admiration. I believe you do care for her. Why not try to win her?"

"Who is that tall man with her?" continued the old lady as Wetzel did not answer. "There, they have gone into the other room. Who is he?"

"His name is Miller."

"Lewis, I don't like him. I have been watching him all evening. I'm a contrary old woman, I know, but I have seen a good many men in my time, and his face is not honest. He is in love with her. Does she care for him?"

"No, Betty doesn't care for Miller. She's just full of life and fun."

"You may be mistaken. All the Zanes are fire and brimstone and this girl is a Zane clear through. Go and fetch her to me, Lewis. I'll tell you if there's a chance for you."

"Dear mother, perhaps there's a wife in Heaven for me. There's none on earth," said the hunter, a sad smile flitting over his calm face.

Ralfe Miller, whose actions had occasioned the remarks of the old lady, would have been conspicuous in any assembly of men. There was something in his dark face that compelled interest and yet left the observer in doubt. His square chin, deep-set eyes and firm mouth denoted a strong and indomitable will. He looked a man whom it would be dangerous to cross.

Little was known of Miller's history. He hailed from Ft. Pitt, where he had a reputation as a good soldier, but a man of morose and quarrelsome disposition. It was whispered that he drank, and that he had been friendly with the renegades McKee, Elliott, and Girty. He had passed the fall and winter at Ft. Henry, serving on garrison duty. Since he had made the acquaintance of Betty he had shown her all the attention possible.

On this night a close observer would have seen that Miller was laboring under some strong feeling. A half-subdued fire gleamed from his dark eyes. A peculiar nervous twitching of his nostrils betrayed a poorly suppressed excitement.

All evening he followed Betty like a shadow. Her kindness may have encouraged him. She danced often with him and showed a certain preference for his society. Alice and Lydia were puzzled by Betty's manner. As they were intimate friends they believed they knew something of her likes and dislikes. Had not Betty told them she did not care for Mr. Miller? What was the meaning of the arch glances she bestowed upon him, if she did not care for him? To be sure, it was nothing wonderful for Betty to smile,—she was always prodigal of her smiles—but she had never been known to encourage any man. The truth was that Betty had put her new resolution into effect; to be as merry and charming as any fancy-free maiden could possibly be, and the farthest removed from a young lady pining for an absent and indifferent sweetheart. To her sorrow Betty played her part too well.

Except to Wetzel, whose keen eyes little escaped, there was no significance in Miller's hilarity one moment and sudden thoughtfulness the next. And if there had been, it would have excited no comment. Most of the young men had sampled some of old Dan's best rye and their flushed faces and unusual spirits did not result altogether from the exercise of the dance.

After one of the reels Miller led Betty, with whom he had been dancing, into one of the side rooms. Round the dimly lighted room were benches upon which were seated some of the dancers. Betty was uneasy in mind and now wished that she had remained at home. They had exchanged several commonplace remarks when the music struck up and Betty rose quickly to her feet.

"See, the others have gone. Let us return," she said.

"Wait," said Miller hurriedly. "Do not go just yet. I wish to speak to you. I have asked you many times if you will marry me. Now I ask you again."

"Mr. Miller, I thanked you and begged you not to cause us both pain by again referring to that subject," answered Betty with dignity. "If you will persist in bringing it up we cannot be friends any longer."

"Wait, please wait. I have told you that I will not take 'No' for an answer. I love you with all my heart and soul and I cannot give you up."

His voice was low and hoarse and thrilled with a strong man's passion.

Betty looked up into his face and tears of compassion filled her eyes. Her heart softened to this man, and her conscience gave her a little twinge of remorse. Could she not have averted all this? No doubt she had been much to blame, and this thought made her voice very low and sweet as she answered him.

"I like you as a friend, Mr. Miller, but we can never be more than friends. I am very sorry for you, and angry with myself that I did not try to help you instead of making it worse. Please do not speak of this again. Come, let us join the others."

They were quite alone in the room. As Betty finished speaking and started for the door Miller intercepted her. She recoiled in alarm from his white face.

"No, you don't go yet. I won't give you up so easily. No woman can play fast and loose with me! Do you understand? What have you meant all this winter? You encouraged me. You know you did," he cried passionately.

"I thought you were a gentleman. I have really taken the trouble to defend you against persons who evidently were not misled as to your real nature. I will not listen to you," said Betty coldly. She turned away from him, all her softened feeling changed to scorn.

"You shall listen to me," he whispered as he grasped her wrist and pulled her backward. All the man's brutal passion had been aroused. The fierce border blood boiled within his heart. Unmasked he showed himself in his true colors a frontier desperado. His eyes gleamed dark and lurid beneath his bent brows and a short, desperate laugh passed his lips.

"I will make you love me, my proud beauty. I shall have you yet, one way or another."

"Let me go. How dare you touch me!" cried Betty, the hot blood coloring her face. She struck him a stinging blow with her free hand and struggled with all her might to free herself; but she was powerless in his iron grasp. Closer he drew her.

"If it costs me my life I will kiss you for that blow," he muttered hoarsely.

"Oh, you coward! you ruffian! Release me or I will scream."

She had opened her lips to call for help when she saw a dark figure cross the threshold. She recognized the tall form of Wetzel. The hunter stood still in the doorway for a second and then with the swiftness of light he sprang forward. The single straightening of his arm sent Miller backward over a bench to the floor with a crashing sound. Miller rose with some difficulty and stood with one hand to his head.

"Lew, don't draw your knife," cried Betty as she saw Wetzel's hand go inside his hunting shirt. She had thrown herself in front of him as Miller got to his feet. With both little hands she clung to the brawny arm of the hunter, but she could not stay it. Wetzel's hand slipped to his belt.

"For God's sake, Lew, do not kill him," implored Betty, gazing horror-stricken at the glittering eyes of the hunter. "You have punished him enough. He only tried to kiss me. I was partly to blame. Put your knife away. Do not shed blood. For my sake, Lew, for my sake!"

When Betty found that she could not hold Wetzel's arm she threw her arms round his neck and clung to him with all her young strength. No doubt her action averted a tragedy. If Miller had been inclined to draw a weapon then he might have had a good opportunity to use it. He had the reputation of being quick with his knife, and many of his past fights testified that he was not a coward. But he made no effort to attack Wetzel. It was certain that he measured with his eye the distance to the door. Wetzel was not like other men. Irrespective of his wonderful strength and agility there was something about the Indian hunter that terrified all men. Miller shrank before those eyes. He knew that never in all his life of adventure had he been as near death as at that moment. There was nothing between him and eternity but the delicate arms of this frail girl. At a slight wave of the hunter's hand towards the door he turned and passed out.

"Oh, how dreadful!" cried Betty, dropping upon a bench with a sob of relief. "I am glad you came when you did even though you frightened me more than he did. Promise me that you will not do Miller any further harm. If you had fought it would all have been on my account; one or both of you might have been killed. Don't look at me so. I do not care for him. I never did. Now that I know him I despise him. He lost his senses and tried to kiss me. I could have killed him myself."

Wetzel did not answer. Betty had been holding his hand in both her own while she spoke impulsively.

"I understand how difficult it is for you to overlook an insult to me," she continued earnestly. "But I ask it of you. You are my best friend, almost my brother, and I promise you that if he ever speaks a word to me again that is not what it should be I will tell you."

"I reckon I'll let him go, considerin' how set on it you are."

"But remember, Lew, that he is revengeful and you must be on the lookout," said Betty gravely as she recalled the malignant gleam in Miller's eyes.

"He's dangerous only like a moccasin snake that hides in the grass."

"Am I all right? Do I look mussed or—or excited—or anything?" asked Betty.

Lewis smiled as she turned round for his benefit. Her hair was a little awry and the lace at her neck disarranged. The natural bloom had not quite returned to her cheeks. With a look in his eyes that would have mystified Betty for many a day had she but seen it he ran his gaze over the dainty figure. Then reassuring her that she looked as well as ever, he led her into the dance-room.

"So this is Betty Zane. Dear child, kiss me," said Grandmother Watkins when Wetzel had brought Betty up to her. "Now, let me get a good look at you. Well, well, you are a true Zane. Black hair and eyes; all fire and pride. Child, I knew your father and mother long before you were born. Your father was a fine man but a proud one. And how do you like the frontier? Are you enjoying yourself?"

"Oh, yes, indeed," said Betty, smiling brightly at the old lady.

"Well, dearie, have a good time while you can. Life is hard in a pioneer's cabin. You will not always have the Colonel to look after you. They tell me you have been to some grand school in Philadelphia. Learning is very well, but it will not help you in the cabin of one of these rough men."

"There is a great need of education in all the pioneers' homes. I have persuaded brother Eb to have a schoolteacher at the Fort next spring."

"First teach the boys to plow and the girls to make Johnny cake. How much you favor your brother Isaac. He used to come and see me often. So must you in summertime. Poor lad, I suppose he is dead by this time. I have seen so many brave and good lads go. There now, I did not mean to make you sad," and the old lady patted Betty's hand and sighed.

"He often spoke of you and said that I must come with him to see you. Now he is gone," said Betty.

"Yes, he is gone, Betty, but you must not be sad while you are so young. Wait until you are old like I am. How long have you known Lew Wetzel?"

"All my life. He used to carry me in his arm, when I was a baby. Of course I do not remember that, but as far back as I can go in memory I can see Lew. Oh, the many times he has saved me from disaster! But why do you ask?"

"I think Lew Wetzel cares more for you than for all the world. He is as silent as an Indian, but I am an old woman and I can read men's hearts. If he could be made to give up his wandering life he would be the best man on the border."

"Oh, indeed I think you are wrong. Lew does not care for me in that way," said Betty, surprised and troubled by the old lady's vehemence.

A loud blast from a hunting-horn directed the attention of all to the platform at the upper end of the hall, where Dan Watkins stood. The fiddlers ceased playing, the dancers stopped, and all looked expectantly. The scene was simple strong, and earnest. The light in the eyes of these maidens shone like the light from the pine cones on the walls. It beamed soft and warm. These fearless sons of the wilderness, these sturdy sons of progress, standing there clasping the hands of their partners and with faces glowing with happiness, forgetful of all save the enjoyment of the moment, were ready to go out on the morrow and battle unto the death for the homes and the lives of their loved ones.

"Friends," said Dan when the hum of voices had ceased "I never thought as how I'd have to get up here and make a speech to-night or I might have taken to the woods. Howsomever, mother and Susan says as it's gettin' late it's about time we had some supper. Somewhere in the big cake is hid a gold ring. If one of the girls gets it she can keep it as a gift from Susan, and should one of the boys find it he may make a present to his best girl. And in the bargain he gets to kiss Susan. She made some objection about this and said that part of the game didn't go, but I reckon the lucky young man will decide that for hisself. And now to the festal board."

Ample justice was done to the turkey, the venison, and the bear meat. Grandmother Watkins' delicious apple and pumpkin pies for which she was renowned, disappeared as by magic. Likewise the cakes and the sweet cider and the apple butter vanished.

When the big cake had been cut and divided among the guests, Wetzel discovered the gold ring within his share. He presented the ring to Betty, and gave his privilege of kissing Susan to George Reynolds, with the remark: "George, I calkilate Susan would like it better if you do the kissin' part." Now it was known to all that George had long been an ardent admirer of Susan's, and it was suspected that she was not indifferent to him. Nevertheless, she protested that it was not fair. George acted like a man who had the opportunity of his life. Amid uproarious laughter he ran Susan all over the room, and when he caught her he pulled her hands away from her blushing face and bestowed a right hearty kiss on her cheek. To everyone's surprise and to Wetzel's discomfiture, Susan walked up to him and saying that as he had taken such an easy way out of it she intended to punish him by kissing him. And so she did. Poor Lewis' face looked the picture of dismay. Probably he had never been kissed before in his life.

Happy hours speed away on the wings of the wind. The feasting over, the good-byes were spoken, the girls were wrapped in the warm robes, for it was now intensely cold, and soon the horses, eager to start on the long homeward journey, were pulling hard on their bits. On the party's return trip there was an absence of the hilarity which had prevailed on their coming. The bells were taken off before the sleds left the blockhouse, and the traces and the harness examined and tightened with the caution of men who were apprehensive of danger and who would take no chances.

In winter time the foes most feared by the settlers were the timber wolves. Thousands of these savage beasts infested the wild forest regions which bounded the lonely roads, and their wonderful power of scent and swift and tireless pursuit made a long night ride a thing to be dreaded. While the horses moved swiftly danger from wolves was not imminent; but carelessness or some mishap to a trace or a wheel had been the cause of more than one tragedy.

Therefore it was not remarkable that the drivers of our party breathed a sigh of relief when the top of the last steep hill had been reached. The girls were quiet, and tired out and cold they pressed close to one another; the men were silent and watchful.

When they were half way home and had just reached the outskirts of the Black Forest the keen ear of Wetzel caught the cry of a wolf. It came from the south and sounded so faint that Wetzel believed at first that he had been mistaken. A few moments passed in which the hunter turned his ear to the south. He had about made up his mind that he had only imagined he had heard something when the unmistakable yelp of a wolf came down on the wind. Then another, this time clear and distinct, caused the driver to turn and whisper to Wetzel. The hunter spoke in a low tone and the driver whipped up his horses. From out the depths of the dark woods along which they were riding came a long and mournful howl. It was a wolf answering the call of his mate. This time the horses heard it, for they threw back their ears and increased their speed. The girls heard it, for they shrank closer to the men.

There is that which is frightful in the cry of a wolf. When one is safe in camp before a roaring fire the short, sharp bark of a wolf is startling, and the long howl will make one shudder. It is so lonely and dismal. It makes no difference whether it be given while the wolf is sitting on his haunches near some cabin waiting for the remains of the settler's dinner, or while he is in full chase after his prey—the cry is equally wild, savage and blood-curdling.

Betty had never heard it and though she was brave, when the howl from the forest had its answer in another howl from the creek thicket, she slipped her little mittened hand under Wetzel's arm and looked up at him with frightened eyes.

In half an hour the full chorus of yelps, barks and howls swelled hideously on the air, and the ever increasing pack of wolves could be seen scarcely a hundred yards behind the sleds. The patter of their swiftly flying feet on the snow could be distinctly heard. The slender, dark forms came nearer and nearer every moment. Presently the wolves had approached close enough for the occupants of the sleds to see their shining eyes looking like little balls of green fire. A gaunt beast bolder than the others, and evidently the leader of the pack, bounded forward until he was only a few yards from the last sled. At every jump he opened his great jaws and uttered a quick bark as if to embolden his followers.

Almost simultaneously with the red flame that burst from Wetzel's rifle came a sharp yelp of agony from the leader. He rolled over and over. Instantly followed a horrible mingling of snarls and barks, and snapping of jaws as the band fought over the body of their luckless comrade.

This short delay gave the advantage to the horses. When the wolves again appeared they were a long way behind. The distance to the fort was now short and the horses were urged to their utmost. The wolves kept up the chase until they reached the creek bridge and the mill. Then they slowed up: the howling became desultory, and finally the dark forms disappeared in the thickets.

CHAPTER 8

Winter dragged by uneventfully for Betty. Unlike the other pioneer girls, who were kept busy all the time with their mending, and linsey weaving, and household duties, Betty had nothing to divert her but her embroidery and her reading. These she found very tiresome. Her maid was devoted to her and never left a thing undone. Annie was old Sam's daughter, and she had waited on Betty since she had been a baby. The cleaning or mending or darning—anything in the shape of work that would have helped pass away the monotonous hours for Betty, was always done before she could lift her hand.

During the day she passed hours in her little room, and most of them were dreamed away by her window. Lydia and Alice came over sometimes and whiled away the tedious moments with their bright chatter and merry laughter, their castle-building, and their romancing on heroes and love and marriage as girls always will until the end of time. They had not forgotten Mr. Clarke, but as Betty had rebuked them with a dignity which forbade any further teasing on that score, they had transferred their fun-making to the use of Mr. Miller's name.

Fearing her brothers' wrath Betty had not told them of the scene with Miller at the dance. She had learned enough of rough border justice to dread the consequence of such a disclosure. She permitted Miller to come to the house, although she never saw him alone. Miller had accepted this favor gratefully. He said that on the night of the dance he had been a little the worse for Dan Watkins' strong liquor, and that, together with his bitter disappointment, made him act in the mad way which had so grievously offended her. He exerted himself to win her forgiveness. Betty was always tender-hearted, and though she did not trust him, she said they might still be friends, but that that depended on his respect for her forbearance. Miller had promised he would never refer to the old subject and he had kept his word.

Indeed Betty welcomed any diversion for the long winter evenings. Occasionally some of the young people visited her, and they sang and danced, roasted apples, popped chestnuts, and played games. Often Wetzel and Major McColloch came in after supper. Betty would come down and sing for them, and afterward would coax Indian lore and woodcraft from Wetzel, or she would play checkers with the Major. If she succeeded in winning from him, which in truth was not often, she teased him unmercifully. When Col. Zane and the Major had settled down to their series of games, from which nothing short of Indians could have diverted them, Betty sat by Wetzel. The silent man of the woods, an appellation the hunter had earned by his reticence, talked for Betty as he would for no one else.

One night while Col. Zane, his wife and Betty were entertaining Capt. Boggs and Major McColloch and several of Betty's girls friends, after the usual music and singing, storytelling became the order of the evening. Little Noah told of the time he had climbed the apple-tree in the yard after a raccoon and got severely bitten.

"One day," said Noah, "I heard Tige barking out in the orchard and I ran out there and saw a funny little fur ball up in the tree with a black tail and white rings around it. It looked like a pretty cat with a sharp nose. Every time Tige barked the little animal showed his teeth and swelled up his back. I wanted him for a pet. I got Sam to give me a sack and I climbed the tree and the nearer I got to him the farther he backed down the limb. I followed him and put out the sack to put it over his head and he bit me. I fell from the limb, but he fell too and Tige killed him and Sam stuffed him for me."

"Noah, you are quite a valiant hunter," said Betty. "Now, Jonathan, remember that you promised to tell me of your meeting with Daniel Boone."

"It was over on the Muskingong near the mouth of the Sandusky. I was hunting in the open woods along the bank when I saw an Indian. He saw me at the same time and we both treed. There we stood a long time each afraid to change position. Finally I began to act tired and resorted to an old ruse. I put my coon-skin cap on my ramrod and cautiously poked it from behind the tree, expecting every second to hear the whistle of the redskin's bullet. Instead I heard a jolly voice yell: 'Hey, young feller, you'll have to try something better'n that.' I looked and saw a white man standing out in the open and shaking all over with laughter. I went up to him and found him to be a big strong fellow with an honest, merry face. He said: 'I'm Boone.' I was considerably taken aback, especially when I saw he knew I was a white man all the time. We camped and hunted along the river a week and at the Falls of the Muskingong he struck out for his Kentucky home."

"Here is Wetzel," said Col. Zane, who had risen and gone to the door. "Now, Betty, try and get Lew to tell us something."

"Come, Lewis, here is a seat by me," said Betty. "We have been pleasantly passing the time. We have had bear stories, snake stories, ghost stories—all kinds of tales. Will you tell us one?"

"Lewis, did you ever have a chance to kill a hostile Indian and not take it?" asked Col. Zane.

"Never but once," answered Lewis.

"Tell us about it. I imagine it will be interesting."

"Well, I ain't good at tellin' things," began Lewis. "I reckon I've seen some strange sights. I kin tell you about the only redskin I ever let off. Three years ago I was takin' a fall hunt over on the Big Sandy, and I run into a party of Shawnees. I plugged a chief and started to run. There was some good runners and I couldn't shake 'em in the open country. Comin' to the Ohio I jumped in and swum across, keepin' my rifle and powder dry by holdin' 'em up. I hid in some bulrushes and waited. Pretty soon along comes three Injuns, and when they saw where I had taken to the water they stopped and held a short pow-wow. Then they all took to the water. This was what I was waitin' for. When they got nearly acrosst I shot the first redskin, and loadin' quick got a bullet into the others. The last Injun did not sink. I watched him go floatin' down stream expectin' every minute to see him go under as he was hurt so bad he could hardly keep his head above water. He floated down a long ways and the current carried him to a pile of driftwood which had lodged against a little island. I saw the Injun crawl up on the drift. I went down stream and by keepin' the island between me and him I got out to where he was. I pulled my tomahawk and went around the head of the island and found the redskin leanin' against a big log. He was a young brave and a fine lookin strong feller. He was tryin' to stop the blood from my bullet-hole in his side. When he saw me he tried to get up, but he was too weak. He smiled, pointed to the wound and said: 'Deathwind not heap times bad shot.' Then he bowed his head and waited for the tomahawk. Well, I picked him up and carried him ashore and made a shack by a spring. I staid there with him. When he got well enough to stand a few days' travel I got him across the river and givin' him a hunk of deer meat I told him to go, and if I ever saw him again I'd make a better shot.

"A year afterwards I trailed two Shawnees into Wingenund's camp and got surrounded and captured. The Delaware chief is my great enemy. They beat me, shot salt into my legs, made me run the gauntlet, tied me on the back of a wild mustang. Then they got ready to burn me at the stake. That night they painted my face black and held the usual death dances. Some of the braves got drunk and worked themselves into a frenzy. I allowed I'd never see daylight. I seen that one of the braves left to guard me was the young feller I had wounded the year before. He never took no notice of me. In the gray of the early mornin' when all were asleep and the other watch dozin' I felt cold steel between my wrists and my buckskin thongs dropped off. Then my feet were cut loose. I looked round and in the dim light I seen my young brave. He handed me my own rifle, knife and toma-hawk, put his finger on his lips and with a bright smile, as if to say he was square with me, he pointed to the east. I was out of sight in a minute."

"How noble of him!" exclaimed Betty, her eyes all aglow. "He paid his debt to you, perhaps at the price of his life."

"I have never known an Indian to forget a promise, or a kind action, or an injury," observed Col. Zane.

"Are the Indians half as bad as they are called?" asked Betty. "I have heard as many stories of their nobility as of their cruelty."

"The Indians consider that they have been robbed and driven from their homes. What we think hideously inhuman is war to them," answered Col. Zane.

"When I came here from Fort Pitt I expected to see and fight Indians every day," said Capt. Boggs. "I have been here at Wheeling for nearly two years and have never seen a hostile Indian. There have been some Indians in the vicinity during that time but not one has shown himself to me. I'm not up to Indian tricks, I know, but I think the last siege must have been enough for them. I don't believe we shall have any more trouble from them."

"Captain," called out Col. Zane, banging his hand on the table. "I'll bet you my best horse to a keg of gunpowder that you see enough Indians before you are a year older to make you wish you had never seen or heard of the western border."

"And I'll go you the same bet," said Major McColloch.

"You see, Captain, you must understand a little of the nature of the Indian," continued Col. Zane. "We have had proof that the Delawares and the Shawnees have been preparing for an expedition for months. We shall have another siege some day and to my thinking it will be a longer and harder one than the last. What say you, Wetzel?"

"I ain't sayin' much, but I don't calkilate on goin' on any long hunts this summer," answered the hunter.

"And do you think Tarhe, Wingenund, Pipe, Cornplanter, and all those chiefs will unite their forces and attack us?" asked Betty of Wetzel.

"Cornplanter won't. He has been paid for most of his land and he ain't so bitter. Tarhe is not likely to bother us. But Pipe and Wingenund and Red Fox—they all want blood."

"Have you seen these chiefs?" said Betty.

"Yes, I know 'em all and they all know me," answered the hunter. "I've watched over many a trail waitin' for one of 'em. If I can ever get a shot at any of 'em I'll give up Injuns and go farmin'. Good night, Betty."

"What a strange man is Wetzel," mused Betty, after the visitors had gone. "Do you know, Eb, he is not at all like any one else. I have seen the girls shudder at the mention of his name and I have heard them say they could not look in his eyes. He does not affect me that way. It is not often I can get him to talk, but sometimes he tells me beautiful thing about the woods; how he lives in the wilderness, his home under the great trees; how every leaf on the trees and every blade of grass has its joy for him as well as its knowledge; how he curls up in his little bark shack and is lulled to sleep by the sighing of the wind through the pine tops. He told me he has often watched the stars for hours at a time. I know there is a waterfall back in the Black Forest somewhere that Lewis goes to, simply to sit and watch the water tumble over the precipice."

"Wetzel is a wonderful character, even to those who know him only as an Indian slayer and a man who wants no other occupation. Some day he will go off on one of these long jaunts and will never return. That is certain. The day is fast approaching when a man like Wetzel will be of no use in life. Now, he is a necessity. Like Tige he can smell Indians. Betty, I believe Lewis tells you so much and is so kind and gentle toward you because he cares for you."

"Of course Lew likes me. I know he does and I want him to," said Betty. "But he does not care as you seem to think. Grandmother Watkins said the same. I am sure both of you are wrong."

"Did Dan's mother tell you that? Well, she's pretty shrewd. It's quite likely, Betty, quite likely. It seems to me you are not so quick witted as you used to be."

"Why so?" asked Betty, quickly.

"Well, you used to be different somehow," said her brother, as he patted her hand.

"Do you mean I am more thoughtful?"

"Yes, and sometimes you seem sad."

"I have tried to be brave and—and happy," said Betty, her voice trembling slightly.

"Yes, yes, I know you have, Betty. You have done wonderfully well here in this dead place. But tell me, don't be angry, don't you think too much of some one?"

"You have no right to ask me that," said Betty, flushing and turning away toward the stairway.

"Well, well, child, don't mind me. I did not mean anything. There, good night, Betty."

Long after she had gone up-stairs Col. Zane sat by his fireside. From time to time he sighed. He thought of the old Virginia home and of the smile of his mother. It seemed only a few short years since he had promised her that he would take care of the baby sister. How had he kept that promise made when Betty was a little thing bouncing on his knee? It seemed only yesterday. How swift the flight of time! Already Betty was a woman; her sweet, gay girlhood had passed; already a shadow had fallen on her face, the shadow of a secret sorrow.

MARCH WITH ITS BLUSTERING WINDS HAD DEPARTED, AND NOW APRIL'S showers and sunshine were gladdening the hearts of the settlers. Patches of green freshened the slopes of the hills; the lilac bushes showed tiny leaves, and the maple-buds were bursting. Yesterday a blue-bird—surest harbinger of spring—had alighted on the fence-post and had sung his plaintive song. A few more days and the blossoms were out mingling their pink and white with the green; the red-bud, the hawthorne, and the dogwood were in bloom, checkering the hillsides.

"Bessie, spring is here," said Col. Zane, as he stood in the doorway. "The air is fresh, the sun shines warm, the birds are singing; it makes me feel good."

"Yes, it is pleasant to have spring with us again," answered his wife. "I think, though, that in winter I am happier. In summer I am always worried. I am afraid for the children to be out of my sight, and when you are away on a hunt I am distraught until you are home safe."

"Well, if the redskins let us alone this summer it will be something new," he said, laughing. "By the way, Bess, some new people came to the fort last night. They rafted down from the Monongahela settlements. Some of the women suffered considerably. I intend to offer them the cabin on the hill until they can cut the timber and run up a house. Sam said the cabin roof leaked and the chimney smoked, but with a little work I think they can be made more comfortable there than at the block-house."

"It is the only vacant cabin in the settlement. I can accommodate the women folks here."

"Well, we'll see about it. I don't want you and Betty inconvenienced. I'll send Sam up to the cabin and have him fix things up a bit and make it more habitable."

The door opened, admitting Col. Zane's elder boy. The lad's face was dirty, his nose was all bloody, and a big bruise showed over his right eye.

"For the land's sake!" exclaimed his mother. "Look at the boy. Noah, come here. What have you been doing?"

Noah crept close to his mother and grasping her apron with both hands hid his face. Mrs. Zane turned the boy around and wiped his discolored features with a wet towel. She gave him a little shake and said: "Noah, have you been fighting again?"

"Let him go and I'll tell you about it," said the Colonel, and when the youngster had disappeared he continued: "Right after breakfast Noah went with me down to the mill. I noticed several children playing in front of Reihart's blacksmith shop. I went in, leaving Noah outside. I got a plow-share which I had left with Reihart to be repaired. He came to the door with me and all at once he said: 'look at the kids.' I looked and saw Noah walk up to a boy and say something to him. The lad was a stranger, and I have no doubt belongs to these new people I told you about. He was bigger than Noah. At first the older boy appeared very friendly and evidently wanted to join the others in their game. I guess Noah did not approve of this, for after he had looked the stranger over he hauled away and punched the lad soundly. To make it short the strange boy gave Noah

136

the worst beating he ever got in his life. I told Noah to come straight to you and confess."

"Well, did you ever!" ejaculated Mrs. Zane. "Noah is a bad boy. And you stood and watched him fight. You are laughing about it now. Ebenezer Zane, I would not put it beneath you to set Noah to fighting. I know you used to make the little niggers fight. Anyway, it serves Noah right and I hope it will be a lesson to him."

"I'll make you a bet, Bessie," said the Colonel, with another laugh. "I'll bet you that unless we lock him up, Noah will fight that boy every day or every time he meets him."

"I won't bet," said Mrs. Zane, with a smile of resignation.

"Where's Betts? I haven't seen her this morning. I am going over to Short Creek to-morrow or next day, and think I'll take her with me. You know I am to get a commission to lay out several settlements along the river, and I want to get some work finished at Short Creek this spring. Mrs. Raymer'll be delighted to have Betty. Shall I take her?"

"By all means. A visit there will brighten her up and do her good."

"Well, what on earth have you been doing?" cried the Colonel. His remark had been called forth by a charming vision that had entered by the open door. Betty—for it was she—wore a little red cap set jauntily on her black hair. Her linsey dress was crumpled and covered with hayseed.

"I've been in the hay-mow," said Betty, waving a small basket. "For a week that old black hen has circumvented me, but at last I have conquered. I found the nest in the farthest corner under the hay."

"How did you get up in the loft?" inquired Mrs. Zane.

"Bessie, I climbed up the ladder of course. I acknowledge being unusually light-hearted and happy this morning, but I have not as yet grown wings. Sam said I could not climb up that straight ladder, but I found it easy enough."

"You should not climb up into the loft," said Mrs. Zane, in a severe tone. "Only last fall Hugh Bennet's little boy slid off the hay down into one of the stalls and the horse kicked him nearly to death."

"Oh, fiddlesticks, Bessie, I am not a baby," said Betty, with vehemence. "There is not a horse in the barn but would stand on his hind legs before he would step on me, let alone kick me."

"I don't know, Betty, but I think that black horse Mr. Clarke left here would kick any one," remarked the Colonel.

"Oh, no, he would not hurt me."

"Betty, we have had pleasant weather for about three days," said the

Colonel, gravely. "In that time you have let out that crazy bear of yours to turn everything topsy-turvy. Only yesterday I got my hands in the paint you have put on your canoe. If you had asked my advice I would have told you that painting your canoe should not have been done for a month yet. Silas told me you fell down the creek hill; Sam said you tried to drive his team over the bluff, and so on. We are happy to see you get back your old time spirits, but could you not be a little more careful? Your versatility is bewildering. We do not know what to look for next. I fully expect to see you brought to the house some day maimed for life, or all that beautiful black hair gone to decorate some Huron's lodge."

"I tell you I am perfectly delighted that the weather is again so I can go out. I am tired to death of staying indoors. This morning I could have cried for very joy. Bessie will soon be lecturing me about Madcap. I must not ride farther than the fort. Well, I don't care. I intend to ride all over."

"Betty, I do not wish you to think I am lecturing you," said the Colonel's wife. "But you are as wild as a March hare and some one must tell you things. Now listen. My brother, the Major, told me that Simon Girty, the renegade, had been heard to say that he had seen Eb Zane's little sister and that if he ever got his hands on her he would make a squaw of her. I am not teasing you. I am telling you the truth. Girty saw you when you were at Fort Pitt two years ago. Now what would you do if he caught you on one of your lonely rides and carried you off to his wigwam? He has done things like that before. James Girty carried off one of the Johnson girls. Her brothers tried to rescue her and lost their lives. It is a common trick of the Indians."

"What would I do if Mr. Simon Girty tried to make a squaw of me?" exclaimed Betty, her eyes flashing fire. "Why, I'd kill him!"

"I believe it, Betts, on my word I do," spoke up the Colonel. "But let us hope you may never see Girty. All I ask is that you be careful. I am going over to Short Creek to-morrow. Will you go with me? I know Mrs. Raymer will be pleased to see you."

"Oh, Eb, that will be delightful!"

"Very well, get ready and we shall start early in the morning."

Two weeks later Betty returned from Short Creek and seemed to have profited much by her short visit. Col. Zane remarked with satisfaction to his wife that Betty had regained all her former cheerfulness.

The morning after Betty's return was a perfect spring morning—the first in that month of May-days. The sun shone bright and warm; the mayflowers blossomed; the trailing arbutus scented the air; everywhere the grass and the leaves looked fresh and green; swallows flitted in and out of the barn door; the blue-birds twittered; a meadow-lark caroled forth his pure melody, and the busy hum of bees came from the fragrant apple-blossoms.

"Mis' Betty, Madcap 'pears powerfo' skittenish," said old Sam, when he had led the pony to where Betty stood on the hitching block. "Whoa, dar, you rascal."

Betty laughed as she leaped lightly into the saddle, and soon she was flying over the old familiar road, down across the creek bridge, past the old grist-mill, around the fort and then out on the river bluff. The Indian pony was fiery and mettlesome. He pranced and side-stepped, galloped and trotted by turns. He seemed as glad to get out again into the warm sunshine as was Betty herself. He tore down the road a mile at his best speed. Coming back Betty pulled him into a walk. Presently her musings were interrupted by a sharp switch in the face from a twig of a tree. She stopped the pony and broke off the offending branch. As she looked around the recollection of what had happened to her in that very spot flashed into her mind. It was here that she had been stopped by the man who had passed almost as swiftly out of her life as he had crossed her path that memorable afternoon. She fell to musing on the old perplexing question. After all could there not have been some mistake? Perhaps she might have misjudged him? And then the old spirit, which resented her thinking of him in that softened mood, rose and fought the old battle over again. But as often happened the mood conquered, and Betty permitted herself to sink for the moment into the sad thoughts which returned like a mournful strain of music once sung by beloved voices, now forever silent.

She could not resist the desire to ride down to the old sycamore. The pony turned into the bridle-path that led down the bluff and the sure-footed beast picked his way carefully over the roots and stones. Betty's heart beat quicker when she saw the noble tree under whose spreading branches she had spent the happiest day of her life. The old monarch of the forest was not one whit changed by the wild winds of winter. The dew sparkled on the nearly full grown leaves; the little sycamore balls were already as large as marbles.

Betty drew rein at the top of the bank and looked absently at the tree and into the foam covered pool beneath. At that moment her eyes saw nothing physical. They held the faraway light of the dreamer, the look that sees so much of the past and nothing of the present.

Presently her reflections were broken by the actions of the pony.

Madcap had thrown up her head, laid back her ears and commenced to paw the ground with her forefeet. Betty looked round to see the cause of Madcap's excitement. What was that! She saw a tall figure clad in brown leaning against the stone. She saw a long fishing-rod. What was there so familiar in the poise of that figure? Madcap dislodged a stone from the path and it went rattling down the rock, slope and fell with a splash into the water. The man heard it, turned and faced the hillside. Betty recognized Alfred Clarke. For a moment she believed she must be dreaming. She had had many dreams of the old sycamore. She looked again. Yes, it was he. Pale, worn, and older he undoubtedly looked, but the features were surely those of Alfred Clarke. Her heart gave a great bound and then seemed to stop beating while a very agony of joy surged over her and made her faint. So he still lived. That was her first thought, glad and joyous, and then memory returning, her face went white as with clenched teeth she wheeled Madcap and struck her with the switch. Once on the level bluff she urged her toward the house at a furious pace.

Col. Zane had just stepped out of the barn door and his face took on an expression of amazement when he saw the pony come tearing up the road, Betty's hair flying in the wind and with a face as white as if she were pursued by a thousand yelling Indians.

"Say, Betts, what the deuce is wrong?" cried the Colonel, when Betty reached the fence.

"Why did you not tell me that man was here again?" she demanded in intense excitement.

"That man! What man?" asked Col. Zane, considerably taken back by this angry apparition.

"Mr. Clarke, of course. Just as if you did not know. I suppose you thought it a fine opportunity for one of your jokes."

"Oh, Clarke. Well, the fact is I just found it out myself. Haven't I been away as well as you? I certainly cannot imagine how any man could create such evident excitement in your mind. Poor Clarke, what has he done now?"

"You might have told me. Somebody could have told me and saved me from making a fool of myself," retorted Betty, who was plainly on the verge of tears. "I rode down to the old sycamore tree and he saw me in, of all the places in the world, the one place where I would not want him to see me."

"Huh!" said the Colonel, who often gave vent to the Indian exclamation. "Is that all? I thought something had happened."

"All! Is it not enough? I would rather have died. He is a man and he will think I followed him down there, that I was thinking of—that—Oh!" cried Betty, passionately, and then she strode into the house, slammed the door, and left the Colonel, lost in wonder.

"Humph! These women beat me. I can't make them out, and the older I grow the worse I get," he said, as he led the pony into the stable.

Betty ran up-stairs to her room, her head in a whirl stronger than the surprise of Alfred's unexpected appearance in Fort Henry and stronger than the mortification in having been discovered going to a spot she should have been too proud to remember was the bitter sweet consciousness that his mere presence had thrilled her through and through. It hurt her and made her hate herself in that moment. She hid her face in shame at the thought that she could not help being glad to see the man who had only trifled with her, the man who had considered the acquaintance of so little consequence that he had never taken the trouble to write her a line or send her a message. She wrung her trembling hands. She endeavored to still that throbbing heart and to conquer that sweet vague feeling which had crept over her and made her weak. The tears began to come and with a sob she threw herself on the bed and buried her head in the pillow.

An hour after, when Betty had quieted herself and had seated herself by the window a light knock sounded on the door and Col. Zane entered. He hesitated and came in rather timidly, for Betty was not to be taken liberties with, and seeing her by the window he crossed the room and sat down by her side.

Betty did not remember her father or her mother. Long ago when she was a child she had gone to her brother, laid her head on his shoulder and told him all her troubles. The desire grew strong within her now. There was comfort in the strong clasp of his hand. She was not proof against it, and her dark head fell on his shoulder.

ALFRED CLARKE HAD INDEED MADE HIS REAPPEARANCE IN FORT HENRY. The preceding October when he left the settlement to go on the expedition up the Monongahela River his intention had been to return to the fort as soon as he had finished his work, but what he did do was only another illustration of that fatality which affects everything. Man hopefully makes his plans and an inexorable destiny works out what it has in store for him.

The men of the expedition returned to Fort Henry in due time, but Alfred had been unable to accompany them. He had sustained a painful injury and had been compelled to go to Fort Pitt for medical assistance. While there he had received word that his mother was lying very ill at his old home in Southern Virginia and if he wished to see her alive he must not delay in reaching her bedside. He left Fort Pitt at once and went to his home, where he remained until his mother's death. She had been the only tie that bound him to the old home, and now that she was gone he determined to leave the scene of his boyhood forever.

Alfred was the rightful heir to all of the property, but an unjust and selfish stepfather stood between him and any contentment he might have found there. He decided he would be a soldier of fortune. He loved the daring life of a ranger, and preferred to take his chances with the hardy settlers on the border rather than live the idle life of a gentleman farmer. He declared his intention to his step-father, who ill-concealed his satisfaction at the turn affairs had taken. Then Alfred packed his belongings, secured his mother's jewels, and with one sad, backward glance rode away from the stately old mansion.

It was Sunday morning and Clarke had been two days in Fort Henry. From his little room in the block-house he surveyed the well-remembered scene. The rolling hills, the broad river, the green forests seemed like old friends.

"Here I am again," he mused. "What a fool a man can be. I have left a fine old plantation, slaves, horses, a country noted for its pretty women— for what? Here there can be nothing for me but Indians, hard work, privation, and trouble. Yet I could not get here quickly enough. Pshaw! What use to speak of the possibilities of a new country. I cannot deceive myself. It is she. I would walk a thousand miles and starve myself for months just for one glimpse of her sweet face. Knowing this what care I for all the rest. How strange she should ride down to the old sycamore tree yesterday the moment I was there and thinking of her. Evidently she had just returned from her visit. I wonder if she ever cared. I wonder if she ever thinks of me. Shall I accept that incident as a happy augury? Well, I am here to find out and find out I will. Aha! there goes the church bell."

Laughing a little at his eagerness he brushed his coat, put on his cap and went down stairs. The settlers with their families were going into the meeting house. As Alfred started up the steps he met Lydia Boggs.

"Why, Mr. Clarke, I heard you had returned," she said, smiling pleasantly and extending her hand. "Welcome to the fort. I am very glad to see you."

While they were chatting her father and Col. Zane came up and both greeted the young man warmly.

"Well, well, back on the frontier," said the Colonel, in his hearty way. "Glad to see you at the fort again. I tell you, Clarke, I have taken a fancy to that black horse you left me last fall. I did not know what to think when Jonathan brought back my horse. To tell you the truth I always looked for you to come back. What have you been doing all winter?"

"I have been at home. My mother was ill all winter and she died in April."

"My lad, that's bad news. I am sorry," said Col. Zane putting his hand kindly on the young man's shoulder. "I was wondering what gave you that older and graver look. It's hard, lad, but it's the way of life."

"I have come back to get my old place with you, Col. Zane, if you will give it to me."

"I will, and can promise you more in the future. I am going to open a road through to Maysville, Kentucky, and start several new settlements along the river. I will need young men, and am more than glad you have returned."

"Thank you, Col. Zane. That is more than I could have hoped for."

Alfred caught sight of a trim figure in a gray linsey gown coming down the road. There were several young people approaching, but he saw only Betty. By some evil chance Betty walked with Ralfe Miller, and for some mysterious reason, which women always keep to themselves, she smiled and looked up into his face at a time of all times she should not have done so. Alfred's heart turned to lead.

When the young people reached the steps the eyes of the rivals met for one brief second, but that was long enough for them to understand each other. They did not speak. Lydia hesitated and looked toward Betty.

"Betty, here is—" began Col. Zane, but Betty passed them with flaming cheeks and with not so much as a glance at Alfred. It was an awkward moment for him.

"Let us go in," he said composedly, and they filed into the church.

As long as he lived Alfred Clarke never forgot that hour. His pride kept him chained in his seat. Outwardly he maintained his composure, but inwardly his brain seemed throbbing, whirling, bursting. What an idiot he had been! He understood now why his letter had never been answered. Betty loved Miller, a man who hated him, a man who would leave no stone unturned to destroy even a little liking which she might have felt for him. Once again Miller had crossed his path and worsted him. With a sudden sickening sense of despair he realized that all his fond hopes had been but dreams, a fool's dreams. The dream of that moment when he would give her his mother's jewels, the dream of that charming face uplifted to his, the dream of the little cottage to which he would hurry after his day's work and find her waiting at the gate,—these dreams must be dispelled forever. He could barely wait until the end of the service. He wanted to be alone; to fight it out with himself; to crush out of his heart that fair image. At length the hour ended and he got out before the congregation and hurried to his room.

Betty had company all that afternoon and it was late in the day when Col. Zane ascended the stairs and entered her room to find her alone.

"Betty, I wish to know why you ignored Mr. Clarke this morning?" said Col. Zane, looking down on his sister. There was a gleam in his eye and an expression about his mouth seldom seen in the Colonel's features.

"I do not know that it concerns any one but myself," answered Betty quickly, as her head went higher and her eyes flashed with a gleam not unlike that in her brother's.

"I beg your pardon. I do not agree with you," replied Col. Zane. "It does concern others. You cannot do things like that in this little place where every one knows all about you and expect it to pass unnoticed. Martin's wife saw you cut Clarke and you know what a gossip she is. Already every one is talking about you and Clarke."

"To that I am indifferent."

"But I care. I won't have people talking about you," replied the Colonel, who began to lose patience. Usually he had the best temper imaginable. "Last fall you allowed Clarke to pay you a good deal of attention and apparently you were on good terms when he went away. Now that he has returned you won't even speak to him. You let this fellow Miller run after you. In my estimation Miller is not to be compared to Clarke, and judging from the warm greetings I saw Clarke receive this morning, there are a number of folk who agree with me. Not that I am praising Clarke. I simply say this because to Bessie, to Jack, to everyone, your act is incomprehensible. People are calling you a flirt and saying that they would prefer some country manners."

"I have not allowed Mr. Miller to run after me, as you are pleased to term it," retorted Betty with indignation. "I do not like him. I never see him any more unless you or Bessie or some one else is present. You know that. I cannot prevent him from walking to church with me."

"No, I suppose not, but are you entirely innocent of those sweet glances which you gave him this morning?"

"I did not," cried Betty with an angry blush. "I won't be called a flirt by you or by anyone else. The moment I am civil to some man all these old maids and old women say I am flirting. It is outrageous."

"Now, Betty, don't get excited. We are getting from the question. Why are you not civil to Clarke?" asked Col. Zane. She did not answer and after a moment he continued. "If there is anything about Clarke that I do not know and that I should know I want you to tell me. Personally I like the fellow. I am not saying that to make you think you ought to like him because I do. You might not care for him at all, but that would be no good reason for your actions. Betty, in these frontier settlements a man is soon known for his real worth. Every one at the Fort liked Clarke. The young-sters adored him. Jessie liked him very much. You know he and Isaac became good friends. I think he acted like a man to-day. I saw the look Miller gave him. I don't like this fellow Miller, anyway. Now, I am taking the trouble to tell you my side of the argument. It is not a question of your liking Clarke—that is none of my affair. It is simply that either he is not the man we all think him or you are acting in a way unbecoming a Zane. I do not purpose to have this state of affairs continue. Now, enough of this beating about the bush."

Betty had seen the Colonel angry more than once, but never with her. It was quite certain she had angered him and she forgot her own resent-ment. Her heart had warmed with her brother's praise of Clarke. Then as she remembered the past she felt a scorn for her weakness and such a revulsion of feeling that she cried out passionately:

"He is a trifler. He never cared for me. He insulted me."

Col. Zane reached for his hat, got up without saying another word and went down stairs.

Betty had not intended to say quite what she had and instantly regretted her hasty words. She called to the Colonel, but he did not answer her, nor return.

"Betty, what in the world could you have said to my husband?" said Mrs. Zane as she entered the room. She was breathless from running up the stairs and her comely face wore a look of concern. "He was as white as that sheet and he stalked off toward the Fort without a word to me."

"I simply told him Mr. Clarke had insulted me," answered Betty calmly.

"Great Heavens! Betty, what have you done?" exclaimed Mrs. Zane. "You don't know Eb when he is angry. He is a big fool over you, anyway. He is liable to kill Clarke."

Betty's blood was up now and she said that would not be a matter of much importance.

"When did he insult you?" asked the elder woman, yielding to her natural curiosity.

"It was last October."

"Pooh! It took you a long time to tell it. I don't believe it amounted to much. Mr. Clarke did not appear to be the sort of a man to insult anyone. All the girls were crazy about him last year. If he was not all right they would not have been."

"I do not care if they were. The girls can have him and welcome. I don't want him. I never did. I am tired of hearing everyone eulogize him. I hate him. Do you hear? I hate him! And I wish you would go away and leave me alone."

"Well, Betty, all I will say is that you are a remarkable young woman," answered Mrs. Zane, who saw plainly that Betty's violent outburst was a prelude to a storm of weeping. "I don't believe a word you have said. I don't believe you hate him. There!"

Col. Zane walked straight to the Fort, entered the block-house and knocked on the door of Clarke's room. A voice bade him come in. He shoved open the door and went into the room. Clarke had evidently just returned from a tramp in the hills, for his garments were covered with burrs and his boots were dusty. He looked tired, but his face was calm.

"Why, Col. Zane! Have a seat. What can I do for you?"

"I have come to ask you to explain a remark of my sister's."

"Very well, I am at your service," answered Alfred slowly lighting his pipe, after which he looked straight into Col. Zane's face.

"My sister informs me that you insulted her last fall before you left the Fort. I am sure you are neither a liar nor a coward, and I expect you to answer as a man."

"Col. Zane, I am not a liar, and I hope I am not a coward," said Alfred coolly. He took a long pull on his pipe and blew a puff of white smoke toward the ceiling.

"I believe you, but I must have an explanation. There is something wrong somewhere. I saw Betty pass you without speaking this morning. I did not like it and I took her to task about it. She then said you had insulted her. Betty is prone to exaggerate, especially when angry, but she never told me a lie in her life. Ever since you pulled Isaac out of the river I have taken an interest in you. That's why I'd like to avoid any trouble. But this thing has gone far enough. Now be sensible, swallow your pride and let me hear your side of the story."

Alfred had turned pale at his visitor's first words. There was no mistaking Col. Zane's manner. Alfred well knew that the Colonel, if he found Betty had really been insulted, would call him out and kill him. Col. Zane spoke quietly, ever kindly, but there was an undercurrent of intense feeling in his voice, a certain deadly intent which boded ill to anyone who might cross him at that moment. Alfred's first impulse was a reckless desire to tell Col. Zane he had nothing to explain and that he stood ready to give any satisfaction in his power. But he wisely thought better of this. It struck him that this would not be fair, for no matter what the girl had done the Colonel had always been his friend. So Alfred pulled himself together and resolved to make a clean breast of the whole affair.

"Col. Zane, I do not feel that I owe your sister anything, and what I am going to tell you is simply because you have always been my friend, and I do not want you to have any wrong ideas about me. I'll tell you the truth and you can be the judge as to whether or not I insulted your sister. I fell in love with her, almost at first sight. The night after the Indians recaptured your brother, Betty and I stood out in the moonlight and she looked so bewitching and I felt so sorry for her and so carried away by my love for her that I yielded to a momentary impulse and kissed her. I simply could not help it. There is no excuse for me. She struck me across the face and ran into the house. I had intended that night to tell her of my love and place my fate in her hands, but, of course, the unfortunate occurrence made that impossible. As I was to leave at dawn next day, I remained up all night, thinking what I ought to do. Finally I decided to write. I wrote her a letter, telling her all and begging her to become my wife. I gave the letter to your slave, Sam, and told him it was a matter of life and death, and not to lose the letter nor fail to give it to Betty. I have had no answer to that letter. Today she coldly ignored me. That is my story, Col. Zane."

"Well, I don't believe she got the letter," said Col. Zane. "She has not acted like a young lady who has had the privilege of saying 'yes' or 'no' to you. And Sam never had any use for you. He disliked you from the first, and never failed to say something against you."

"I'll kill that d—n nigger if he did not deliver that letter," said Clarke, jumping up in his excitement. "I never thought of that. Good Heaven! What could she have thought of me? She would think I had gone away without a word. If she knew I really loved her she could not think so terribly of me."

"There is more to be explained, but I am satisfied with your side of it," said Col. Zane. "Now I'll go to Sam and see what has become of that letter. I am glad I am justified in thinking of you as I have. I imagine this thing has hurt you and I don't wonder at it. Maybe we can untangle the problem yet. My advice would be—but never mind that now. Anyway, I'm your friend in this matter. I'll let you know the result of my talk with Sam."

"I thought that young fellow was a gentleman," mused Col. Zane as he crossed the green square and started up the hill toward the cabins. He found the old negro seated on his doorstep.

"Sam, what did you do with a letter Mr. Clarke gave you last October and instructed you to deliver to Betty?"

"I dun recollec' no lettah, sah," replied Sam.

"Now, Sam, don't lie about it. Clarke has just told me that he gave you the letter. What did you do with it?"

"Masse Zane, I ain dun seen no lettah," answered the old darkey, taking a dingy pipe from his mouth and rolling his eyes at his master.

"If you lie again I will punish you," said Col. Zane sternly. "You are getting old, Sam, and I would not like to whip you, but I will if you do not find that letter."

Sam grumbled, and shuffled inside the cabin. Col. Zane heard him rummaging around. Presently he came back to the door and handed a very badly soiled paper to the Colonel.

"What possessed you to do this, Sam? You have always been honest. Your act has caused great misunderstanding and it might have led to worse."

"He's one of dem no good Southern white trash; he's good fer nuttin'," said Sam. "I saw yo' sistah, Mis' Betty, wit him, and I seen she was gittin' fond of him, and I says I ain't gwinter have Mis' Betty runnin' off wif him. And I'se never gibbin de lettah to her."

That was all the explanation Sam would vouchsafe, and Col. Zane, knowing it would be useless to say more to the well-meaning but ignorant and superstitious old negro, turned and wended his way back to the house. He looked at the paper and saw that it was addressed to Elizabeth Zane, and that the ink was faded until the letters were scarcely visible.

"What have you there?" asked his wife, who had watched him go up the hill to the negro's cabin. She breathed a sigh of relief when she saw that her husband's face had recovered its usual placid expression.

"It is a little letter for that young fire-brand up stairs, and, I believe it will clear up the mystery. Clarke gave it to Sam last fall and Sam never gave it to Betty."

"I hope with all my heart it may settle Betty. She worries me to death with her love affairs."

Col. Zane went up stairs and found the young lady exactly as he had left her. She gave an impatient toss of her head as he entered.

"Well, Madam, I have here something that may excite even your interest." he said cheerily.

"What?" asked Betty with a start. She flushed crimson when she saw the letter and at first refused to take it from her brother. She was at a loss to understand his cheerful demeanor. He had been anything but pleasant a few moments since.

"Here, take it. It is a letter from Mr. Clarke which you should have received last fall. That last morning he gave this letter to Sam to deliver to you, and the crazy old nigger kept it. However, it is too late to talk of that, only it does seem a great pity. I feel sorry for both of you. Clarke never will forgive you, even if you want him to, which I am sure you do not. I don't know exactly what is in this letter, but I know it will make you ashamed to think you did not trust him."

With this parting reproof the Colonel walked out, leaving Betty completely bewildered. The words "too late," "never forgive," and "a great pity" rang through her head. What did he mean? She tore the letter open with trembling hands and holding it up to the now fast-waning light, she read

"Dear Betty:

"If you had waited only a moment longer I know you would not have been so angry with me. The words I wanted so much to say choked me and I could not speak them. I love you. I have loved you from the very first moment, that blessed moment when I looked up over your pony's head to see the sweetest face the sun ever shone on. I'll be the happiest man on earth if you will say you care a little for me and promise to be my wife.

"It was wrong to kiss you and I beg your forgiveness. Could you but see your face as I saw it last night in the moonlight, I would not need to plead: you would know that the impulse which swayed me was irresistible.

In that kiss I gave you my hope, my love, my life, my all. Let it plead for me.

"I expect to return from Ft. Pitt in about six or eight weeks, but I cannot wait until then for your answer.

"With hope I sign myself,

"Yours until death,

"Alfred."

Betty read the letter through. The page blurred before her eyes; a sensation of oppression and giddiness made her reach out helplessly with both hands. Then she slipped forward and fell on the floor. For the first time in all her young life Betty had fainted. Col. Zane found her lying pale and quiet under the window.

CHAPTER 9

Yantwaia, or, as he was more commonly called, Cornplanter, was originally a Seneca chief, but when the five war tribes consolidated, forming the historical "Five Nations," he became their leader. An old historian said of this renowned chieftain: "Tradition says that the blood of a famous white man coursed through the veins of Cornplanter. The tribe he led was originally ruled by an Indian queen of singular power and beauty. She was born to govern her people by the force of her character. Many a great chief importuned her to become his wife, but she preferred to cling to her power and dignity. When this white man, then a very young man, came to the Ohio valley the queen fell in love with him, and Cornplanter was their son."

Cornplanter lived to a great age. He was a wise counsellor, a great leader, and he died when he was one hundred years old, having had more conceded to him by the white men than any other chieftain. General Washington wrote of him: "The merits of Cornplanter and his friendship for the United States are well known and shall not be forgotten."

But Cornplanter had not always been a friend to the palefaces. During Dunmore's war and for years after, he was one of the most vindictive of the savage leaders against the invading pioneers.

It was during this period of Cornplanter's activity against the whites that Isaac Zane had the misfortune to fall into the great chief's power.

We remember Isaac last when, lost in the woods, weak from hunger and exposure, he had crawled into a thicket and had gone to sleep. He was awakened by a dog licking his face. He heard Indian voices. He got up and ran as fast as he could, but exhausted as he was he proved no match for his pursuers. They came up with him and seeing that he was unable to defend himself they grasped him by the arms and led him down a well-worn bridle-path.

"D—n poor run. No good legs," said one of his captors, and at this the other two Indians laughed. Then they whooped and yelled, at which signal other Indians joined them. Isaac saw that they were leading him into a large encampment. He asked the big savage who led him what camp it was, and learned that he had fallen into the hands of Cornplanter.

While being marched through the large Indian village Isaac saw unmistakable indications of war. There was a busy hum on all sides; the squaws were preparing large quantities of buffalo meat, cutting it in long, thin strips, and were parching corn in stone vessels. The braves were cleaning rifles, sharpening tomahawks, and mixing war paints. All these things Isaac knew to be preparations for long marches and for battle. That night he heard speech after speech in the lodge next to the one in which he lay, but they were in an unknown tongue. Later he heard the yelling of the Indians and the dull thud of their feet as they stamped on the ground. He heard the ring of the tomahawks as they were struck into hard wood. The Indians were dancing the war-dance round the war-post. This continued with some little intermission all the four days that Isaac lay in the lodge rapidly recovering his strength. The fifth day a man came into the lodge. He was tall and powerful, his hair fell over his shoulders and he wore the scanty buckskin dress of the Indian. But Isaac knew at once he was a white man, perhaps one of the many French traders who passed through the Indian village.

"Your name is Zane," said the man in English, looking sharply at Isaac.

"That is my name. Who are you?" asked Isaac in great surprise.

"I am Girty. I've never seen you, but I knew Col. Zane and Jonathan well. I've seen your sister; you all favor one another."

"Are you Simon Girty?"

"Yes."

"I have heard of your influence with the Indians. Can you do anything to get me out of this?"

"How did you happen to git over here? You are not many miles from Wingenund's Camp," said Girty, giving Isaac another sharp look from his small black eyes.

"Girty, I assure you I am not a spy. I escaped from the Wyandot village on Mad River and after traveling three days I lost my way. I went to sleep in a thicket and when I awoke an Indian dog had found me. I heard voices and saw three Indians. I got up and ran, but they easily caught me."

"I know about you. Old Tarhe has a daughter who kept you from bein' ransomed."

"Yes, and I wish I were back there. I don't like the look of things."

"You are right, Zane. You got ketched at a bad time. The Indians are mad. I suppose you don't know that Col. Crawford massacred a lot of Indians a few days ago. It'll go hard with any white man that gits captured. I'm afraid I can't do nothin' for you."

A few words concerning Simon Girty, the White Savage. He had two brothers, James and George, who had been desperadoes before they were adopted by the Delawares, and who eventually became fierce and relentless savages. Simon had been captured at the same time as his brothers, but he did not at once fall under the influence of the unsettled, free-and-easy life of the Indians. It is probable that while in captivity he acquired the power of commanding the Indians' interest and learned the secret of ruling them—two capabilities few white men ever possessed. It is certain that he, like the noted French-Canadian Joucaire, delighted to sit round the camp fires and to go into the council-lodge and talk to the assembled Indians.

At the outbreak of the revolution Girty was a commissioned officer of militia at Ft. Pitt. He deserted from the Fort, taking with him the Tories McKee and Elliott, and twelve soldiers, and these traitors spread as much terror among the Delaware Indians as they did among the whites. The Delawares had been one of the few peacefully disposed tribes. In order to get them to join their forces with Governor Hamilton, the British commander, Girty declared that Gen. Washington had been killed, that Congress had been dispersed, and that the British were winning all the battles.

Girty spoke most of the Indian languages, and Hamilton employed him to go among the different Indian tribes and incite them to greater hatred of the pioneers. This proved to be just the life that suited him. He soon rose to have a great and bad influence on all the tribes. He became noted for his assisting the Indians in marauds, for his midnight forays, for his scalpings, and his efforts to capture white women, and for his devilish cunning and cruelty.

For many years Girty was the Deathshead of the frontier. The mention of his name alone created terror in any household; in every pioneer's cabin it made the children cry out in fear and paled the cheeks of the stoutest-hearted wife.

It is difficult to conceive of a white man's being such a fiend in human guise. The only explanation that can be given is that renegades rage against the cause of their own blood with the fury of insanity rather than with the malignity of a naturally ferocious temper. In justice to Simon Girty it must be said that facts not known until his death showed he was not so cruel and base as believed; that some deeds of kindness were attributed to him; that he risked his life to save Kenton from the stake, and that many of the terrible crimes laid at his door were really committed by his savage brothers.

Isaac Zane suffered no annoyance at the hands of Cornplanter's braves until the seventh day of his imprisonment. He saw no one except the squaw who brought him corn and meat. On that day two savages came for him and led him into the immense council-lodge of the Five Nations. Cornplanter sat between his right-hand chiefs, Big Tree and Half Town, and surrounded by the other chiefs of the tribes. An aged Indian stood in the center of the lodge and addressed the others. The listening savages sat immovable, their faces as cold and stern as stone masks. Apparently they did not heed the entrance of the prisoner.

"Zane, they're havin' a council," whispered a voice in Isaac's ear. Isaac turned and recognized Girty. "I want to prepare you for the worst."

"Is there, then, no hope for me?" asked Isaac.

"I'm afraid not," continued the renegade, speaking in a low whisper. "They wouldn't let me speak at the council. I told Cornplanter that killin' you might bring the Hurons down on him, but he wouldn't listen. Yester-day, in the camp of the Delawares, I saw Col. Crawford burnt at the stake. He was a friend of mine at Pitt, and I didn't dare to say one word to the frenzied Indians. I had to watch the torture. Pipe and Wingenund, both old friends of Crawford, stood by and watched him walk round the stake on the red-hot coals five hours."

Isaac shuddered at the words of the renegade, but did not answer. He had felt from the first that his case was hopeless, and that no opportunity for escape could possibly present itself in such a large encampment. He set his teeth hard and resolved to show the red devils how a white man could die.

Several speeches were made by different chiefs and then an impressive oration by Big Tree. At the conclusion of the speeches, which were in an unknown tongue to Isaac, Cornplanter handed a war-club to Half Town. This chief got up, walked to the end of the circle, and there brought the club down on the ground with a resounding thud. Then he passed the club to Big Tree. In a solemn and dignified manner every chief duplicated Half Town's performance with the club.

Isaac watched the ceremony as if fascinated. He had seen a war-club used in the councils of the Hurons and knew that striking it on the ground signified war and death.

"White man, you are a killer of Indians," said Cornplanter in good English. "When the sun shines again you die."

A brave came forward and painted Isaac's face black. This Isaac knew to indicate that death awaited him on the morrow. On his way back to his prison-lodge he saw that a war-dance was in progress.

A hundred braves with tomahawks, knives, and mallets in their hands were circling round a post and keeping time to the low music of a muffled drum. Close together, with heads bowed, they marched. At certain moments, which they led up to with a dancing on rigid legs and a stamping with their feet, they wheeled, and uttering hideous yells, started to march in the other direction. When this had been repeated three times a brave stepped from the line, advanced, and struck his knife or tomahawk into the post. Then with a loud voice he proclaimed his past exploits and great deeds in war. The other Indians greeted this with loud yells of applause and a flourishing of weapons. Then the whole ceremony was gone through again.

That afternoon many of the Indians visited Isaac in his lodge and shook their fists at him and pointed their knives at him. They hissed and groaned at him. Their vindictive faces expressed the malignant joy they felt at the expectation of putting him to the torture.

When night came Isaac's guards laced up the lodge-door and shut him from the sight of the maddened Indians. The darkness that gradually enveloped him was a relief. By and by all was silent except for the occasional yell of a drunken savage. To Isaac it sounded like a long, rolling death-cry echoing throughout the encampment and murdering his sleep. Its horrible meaning made him shiver and his flesh creep. At length even that yell ceased. The watch-dogs quieted down and the perfect stillness which ensued could almost be felt. Through Isaac's mind ran over and over again the same words. His last night to live! His last night to live! He forced himself to think of other things. He lay there in the darkness of his tent, but he was far away in thought, far away in the past with his mother and brothers before they had come to this bloodthirsty country. His thoughts wandered to the days of his boyhood when he used to drive the sows to the pasture on the hillside, and in his dreamy, disordered fancy he was once more letting down the bars of the gate. Then he was wading in the brook and whacking the green frogs with his stick. Old playmates' faces, forgotten for years, were there looking at him from the dark wall of his wigwam. There was Andrew's face; the faces of his other brothers; the laughing face of his sister; the serene face of his mother. As he lay there with the shadow of death over him sweet was the thought that soon he would be reunited with that mother. The images faded slowly away, swallowed up in the gloom. Suddenly a vision appeared to him. A radiant white light illumined the lodge and shone full on the beautiful face of the Indian maiden who had loved him so well. Myeerah's dark eyes were bright with an undying love and her lips smiled hope.

A rude kick dispelled Isaac's dreams. A brawny savage pulled him to his feet and pushed him outside of the lodge.

It was early morning. The sun had just cleared the low hills in the east and its red beams crimsoned the edges of the clouds of fog which hung over the river like a great white curtain. Though the air was warm, Isaac shivered a little as the breeze blew softly against his cheek. He took one long look toward the rising sun, toward that east he had hoped to see, and then resolutely turned his face away forever.

Early though it was the Indians were astir and their whooping rang throughout the valley. Down the main street of the village the guards led the prisoner, followed by a screaming mob of squaws and young braves and children who threw sticks and stones at the hated Long Knife.

Soon the inhabitants of the camp congregated on the green oval in the midst of the lodges. When the prisoner appeared they formed in two long lines facing each other, and several feet apart. Isaac was to run the gauntlet—one of the severest of Indian tortures. With the exception of Corn-planter and several of his chiefs, every Indian in the village was in line. Little Indian boys hardly large enough to sling a stone; maidens and squaws with switches or spears; athletic young braves with flashing toma-hawks; grim, matured warriors swinging knotted war clubs,—all were there in line, yelling and brandishing their weapons in a manner frightful to behold.

The word was given, and stripped to the waist, Isaac bounded forward fleet as a deer. He knew the Indian way of running the gauntlet. The head of that long lane contained the warriors and older braves and it was here that the great danger lay. Between these lines he sped like a flash, dodging this way and that, running close in under the raised weapons, taking what blows he could on his uplifted arms, knocking this warrior over and doubling that one up with a lightning blow in the stomach, never slacking his speed for one stride, so that it was extremely difficult for the Indians to strike him effectually. Once past that formidable array, Isaac's gauntlet was run, for the squaws and children scattered screaming before the sweep of his powerful arms.

The old chiefs grunted their approval. There was a bruise on Isaac's forehead and a few drops of blood mingled with the beads of perspiration. Several lumps and scratches showed on his bare shoulders and arms, but he had escaped any serious injury. This was a feat almost without a parallel in gauntlet running.

When he had been tied with wet buckskin thongs to the post in the center of the oval, the youths, the younger braves, and the squaws began circling round him, yelling like so many demons. The old squaws thrust sharpened sticks, which had been soaked in salt water, into his flesh. The maidens struck him with willows which left red welts on his white shoulders. The braves buried the blades of their tomahawks in the post as near as possible to his head without actually hitting him.

Isaac knew the Indian nature well. To command the respect of the savages was the only way to lessen his torture. He knew that a cry for mercy would only increase his sufferings and not hasten his death,—indeed it would prolong both. He had resolved to die without a moan. He had determined to show absolute indifference to his torture, which was the only way to appeal to the savage nature, and if anything could, make the Indians show mercy. Or, if he could taunt them into killing him at once he would be spared all the terrible agony which they were in the habit of inflicting on their victims.

One handsome young brave twirled a glittering tomahawk which he threw from a distance of ten, fifteen, and twenty feet and every time the sharp blade of the hatchet sank deep into the stake within an inch of Isaac's head. With a proud and disdainful look Isaac gazed straight before him and paid no heed to his tormentor.

"Does the Indian boy think he can frighten a white warrior?" said Isaac scornfully at length. "Let him go and earn his eagle plumes. The pale face laughs at him."

The young brave understood the Huron language, for he gave a frightful yell and cast his tomahawk again, this time shaving a lock of hair from Isaac's head.

This was what Isaac had prayed for. He hoped that one of these glittering hatchets would be propelled less skillfully than its predecessors and would kill him instantly. But the enraged brave had no other opportunity to cast his weapon, for the Indians jeered at him and pushed him from the line.

Other braves tried their proficiency in the art of throwing knives and tomahawks, but their efforts called forth only words of derision from Isaac. They left the weapons sticking in the post until round Isaac's head and shoulders there was scarcely room for another.

"The White Eagle is tired of boys," cried Isaac to a chief dancing near. "What has he done that he be made the plaything of children? Let him die the death of a chief."

The maidens had long since desisted in their efforts to torment the prisoner. Even the hardened old squaws had withdrawn. The prisoner's proud, handsome face, his upright bearing, his scorn for his enemies, his indifference to the cuts and bruises, and red welts upon his clear white skin had won their hearts.

Not so with the braves. Seeing that the pale face scorned all efforts to make him flinch, the young brave turned to Big Tree. At a command from this chief the Indians stopped their maneuvering round the post and formed a large circle. In another moment a tall warrior appeared carrying an armful of fagots.

In spite of his iron nerve Isaac shuddered with horror. He had anticipated running the gauntlet, having his nails pulled out, powder and salt shot into his flesh, being scalped alive and a host of other Indian tortures, but as he had killed no members of this tribe he had not thought of being burned alive. God, it was too horrible!

The Indians were now quiet. Their songs and dances would break out soon enough. They piled fagot after fagot round Isaac's feet. The Indian warrior knelt on the ground the steel clicked on the flint; a little shower of sparks dropped on the pieces of punk and then—a tiny flame shot up, and slender little column of blue smoke floated on the air.

Isaac shut his teeth hard and prayed with all his soul for a speedy death.

Simon Girty came hurriedly through the lines of waiting, watching Indians. He had obtained permission to speak to the man of his own color.

"Zane, you made a brave stand. Any other time but this it might have saved you. If you want I'll get word to your people." And then bending and placing his mouth close to Isaac's ear, he whispered, "I did all I could for you, but it must have been too late."

"Try and tell them at Ft. Henry," Isaac said simply.

There was a little cracking of dried wood and then a narrow tongue of red flame darted up from the pile of fagots and licked at the buckskin fringe on the prisoner's legging. At this supreme moment when the attention of all centered on that motionless figure lashed to the stake, and when only the low chanting of the death-song broke the stillness, a long, piercing yell rang out on the quiet morning air. So strong, so sudden, so startling was the break in that almost perfect calm that for a moment afterward there was a silence as of death. All eyes turned to the ridge of rising ground whence that sound had come. Now came the unmistakable thunder of horses' hoofs pounding furiously on the rocky ground. A moment of paralyzed inaction ensued. The Indians stood bewildered, petrified. Then on that ridge of rising ground stood, silhouetted against the blue sky, a great black horse with arching neck and flying mane. Astride him sat a plumed warrior, who waved his rifle high in the air. Again that shrill screeching yell came floating to the ears of the astonished Indians.

The prisoner had seen that horse and rider before; he had heard that long yell; his heart bounded with hope. The Indians knew that yell; it was the terrible war-cry of the Hurons.

A horse followed closely after the leader, and then another appeared on the crest of the hill. Then came two abreast, and then four abreast, and now the hill was black with plunging horses. They galloped swiftly down the slope and into the narrow street of the village. When the black horse entered the oval the train of racing horses extended to the top of the ridge. The plumes of the riders streamed gracefully on the breeze; their feathers shone; their weapons glittered in the bright sunlight.

Never was there more complete surprise. In the earlier morning the Hurons had crept up to within a rifle shot of the encampment, and at an opportune moment when all the scouts and runners were round the torture-stake, they had reached the hillside from which they rode into the village before the inhabitants knew what had happened. Not an Indian raised a weapon. There were screams from the women and children, a shouted command from Big Tree, and then all stood still and waited.

Thundercloud, the war chief of the Wyandots, pulled his black stallion back on his haunches not twenty feet from the prisoner at the stake. His band of painted devils closed in behind him. Full two hundred strong were they and all picked warriors tried and true. They were naked to the waist. Across their brawny chests ran a broad bar of flaming red paint; hideous designs in black and white covered their faces. Every head had been clean-shaven except where the scalp lock bristled like a porcupine's quills. Each warrior carried a plumed spear, a tomahawk, and a rifle. The shining heads, with the little tufts of hair tied tightly close to the scalp, were enough to show that these Indians were on the war-path.

From the back of one of the foremost horses a slender figure dropped and darted toward the prisoner at the stake. Surely that wildly flying hair proved this was not a warrior. Swift as a flash of light this figure reached the stake, the blazing fagots scattered right and left; a naked blade gleamed; the thongs fell from the prisoner's wrists; and the front ranks of the Hurons opened and closed on the freed man. The deliverer turned to the gaping Indians, disclosing to their gaze the pale and beautiful face of Myeerah, the Wyandot Princes.

"Summon your chief," she commanded.

The tall form of the Seneca chief moved from among the warriors and with slow and measured tread approached the maiden. His bearing fitted the leader of five nations of Indians. It was of one who knew that he was the wisest of chiefs, the hero of a hundred battles. Who dared beard him in his den? Who dared defy the greatest power in all Indian tribes? When he stood before the maiden he folded his arms and waited for her to speak.

"Myeerah claims the White Eagle," she said.

Cornplanter did not answer at once. He had never seek Myeerah, though he had heard many stories of her loveliness. Now he was face to face with the Indian Princess whose fame had been the theme of many an Indian romance, and whose beauty had been sung of in many an Indian song. The beautiful girl stood erect and fearless. Her disordered garments, torn and bedraggled and stained from the long ride, ill-concealed the grace of her form. Her hair rippled from the uncovered head and fell in dusky splendor over her shoulders; her dark eyes shone with a stern and steady fire: her bosom swelled with each deep breath. She was the daughter of great chiefs; she looked the embodiment of savage love.

"The Huron squaw is brave," said Cornplanter. "By what right does she come to free my captive?"

"He is an adopted Wyandot."

"Why does the paleface hide like a fox near the camp of Cornplanter?"

"He ran away. He lost the trail to the Fort on the river."

"Cornplanter takes prisoners to kill; not to free."

"If you will not give him up Myeerah will take him," she answered, pointing to the long line of mounted warriors. "And should harm befall Tarhe's daughter it will be avenged."

Cornplanter looked at Thundercloud. Well he knew that chief's prowess in the field. He ran his eyes over the silent, watching Hurons, and then back to the sombre face of their leader. Thundercloud sat rigid upon his stallion; his head held high; every muscle tense and strong for instant action. He was ready and eager for the fray. He, and every one of his warriors, would fight like a thousand tigers for their Princess—the pride of the proud race of Wyandots. Cornplanter saw this and he felt that on the eve of important marches he dared not sacrifice one of his braves for any reason, much less a worthless pale face; and yet to let the prisoner go galled the haughty spirit of the Seneca chief.

"The Long Knife is not worth the life of one of my dogs," he said, with scorn in his deep voice. "If Cornplanter willed he could drive the Hurons before him like leaves before the storm. Let Myeerah take the pale face back to her wigwam and there feed him and make a squaw of him. When he stings like a snake in the grass remember the chief's words. Cornplanter turns on his heel from the Huron maiden who forgets her blood."

WHEN THE SUN REACHED ITS ZENITH IT SHONE DOWN UPON A LONG line of mounted Indians riding single file along the narrow trail and like a huge serpent winding through the forest and over the plain.

They were Wyandot Indians, and Isaac Zane rode among them. Freed from the terrible fate which had menaced him, and knowing that he was once more on his way to the Huron encampment, he had accepted his destiny and quarreled no more with fate. He was thankful beyond all words for his rescue from the stake.

Coming to a clear, rapid stream, the warriors dismounted and rested while their horses drank thirstily of the cool water. An Indian touched Isaac on the arm and silently pointed toward the huge maple tree under which Thundercloud and Myeerah were sitting. Isaac turned his horse and rode the short distance intervening. When he got near he saw that Myeerah stood with one arm over her pony's neck. She raised eyes that were weary and sad, which yet held a lofty and noble resolve.

"White Eagle, this stream leads straight to the Fort on the river," she said briefly, almost coldly. "Follow it, and when the sun reaches the top of yonder hill you will be with your people. Go, you are free."

She turned her face away. Isaac's head whirled in his amazement. He could not believe his ears. He looked closely at her and saw that though her face was calm her throat swelled, and the hand which lay over the neck of her pony clenched the bridle in a fierce grasp. Isaac glanced at Thundercloud and the other Indians near by. They sat unconcerned with the invariable unreadable expression.

"Myeerah, what do you mean?" asked Isaac.

"The words of Cornplanter cut deep into the heart of Myeerah," she answered bitterly. "They were true. The Eagle does not care for Myeerah. She shall no longer keep him in a cage. He is free to fly away."

"The Eagle does not want his freedom. I love you, Myeerah. You have saved me and I am yours. If you will go home with me and marry me there as my people are married I will go back to the Wyandot village."

Myeerah's eyes softened with unutterable love. With a quick cry she was in his arms. After a few moments of forgetfulness Myeerah spoke to Thundercloud and waved her hand toward the west. The chief swung himself over his horse, shouted a single command, and rode down the bank into the water. His warriors followed him, wading their horses into the shallow creek, with never backward look. When the last rider had disappeared in the willows the lovers turned their horses eastward.

CHAPTER 10

It was near the close of a day in early summer. A small group of persons surrounded Col. Zane where he sat on his doorstep. From time to time he took the long Indian pipe from his mouth and blew great clouds of smoke over his head. Major McColloch and Capt. Boggs were there. Silas Zane half reclined on the grass. The Colonel's wife stood in the doorway, and Betty sat on the lower step with her head leaning against her brother's knee. They all had grave faces. Jonathan Zane had returned that day after an absence of three weeks, and was now answering the many questions with which he was plied.

"Don't ask me any more and I'll tell you the whole thing," he had just said, while wiping the perspiration from his brow. His face was worn; his beard ragged and unkempt; his appearance suggestive of extreme fatigue. "It was this way: Colonel Crawford had four hundred and eighty men under him, with Slover and me acting as guides. This was a large force of men and comprised soldiers from Pitt and the other forts and settlers from all along the river. You see, Crawford wanted to crush the Shawnees at one blow. When we reached the Sandusky River, which we did after an arduous march, not one Indian did we see. You know Crawford expected to surprise the Shawnee camp, and when he found it deserted he didn't know what to do. Slover and I both advised an immediate retreat. Crawford would not listen to us. I tried to explain to him that ever since the Guadenhutten massacre keen-eyed Indian scouts had been watching the border. The news of the present expedition had been carried by fleet runners to the different Indian tribes and they were working like hives of angry bees. The deserted Shawnee village meant to me that the alarm had been sounded in the towns of the Shawnees and the Delawares; perhaps also in the Wyandot towns to the north. Colonel Crawford was obdurate and insisted on resuming the march into the Indian country. The next day we met the Indians coming directly toward us. It was the combined force of the Delaware chiefs, Pipe and Wingenund. The battle had hardly commenced when the redskins were reinforced by four hundred warriors under Shanshota, the Huron chief. The enemy skulked behind trees and rocks, hid in ravines, and crawled through the long grass. They could be picked off only by Indian hunters, of whom Crawford had but few—probably fifty all told. All that day we managed to keep our position, though we lost sixty men. That night we lay down to rest by great fires which we built, to prevent night surprises.

"Early next morning we resumed the fight. I saw Simon Girty on his white horse. He was urging and cheering the Indians on to desperate fighting. Their fire became so deadly that we were forced to retreat. In the afternoon Slover, who had been out scouting, returned with the information that a mounted force was approaching, and that he believed they were the reinforcements which Col. Crawford expected. The reinforcements came up and proved to be Butler's British rangers from Detroit. This stunned Crawford's soldiers. The fire of the enemy became hotter and hotter. Our men were falling like leaves around us. They threw aside their rifles and ran, many of them right into the hands of the savages. I believe some of the experienced bordermen escaped but most of Crawford's force met death on the field. I hid in a hollow log. Next day when I felt that it could be done safely I crawled out. I saw scalped and mutilated bodies everywhere, but did not find Col. Crawford's body. The Indians had taken all the clothing, weapons, blankets and everything of value. The Wyandots took a northwest trail and the Delawares and the Shawnees traveled east. I followed the latter because their trail led toward home. Three days later I stood on the high bluff above Wingenund's camp. From there I saw Col. Crawford tied to a stake and a fire started at his feet. I was not five hundred yards from the camp. I saw the war chiefs, Pipe and Wingenund; I saw Simon Girty and a British officer in uniform. The chiefs and Girty were once Crawford's friends. They stood calmly by and watched the poor victim slowly burn to death. The Indians yelled and danced round the stake; they devised every kind of hellish torture. When at last an Indian ran in and tore off the scalp of the still living man I could bear to see no more, and I turned and ran. I have been in some tough places, but this last was the worst."

"My God! it is awful—and to think that man Girty was once a white man," cried Col. Zane.

"He came very near being a dead man," said Jonathan, with grim humor. "I got a long shot at him and killed his big white horse."

"It's a pity you missed him," said Silas Zane.

"Here comes Wetzel. What will he say about the massacre?" remarked Major McColloch.

Wetzel joined the group at that moment and shook hands with Jonathan. When interrogated about the failure of Col. Crawford's expedition Wetzel said that Slover had just made his appearance at the cabin of Hugh Bennet, and that he was without clothing and almost dead from exposure.

"I'm glad Slover got out alive. He was against the march all along. If Crawford had listened to us he would have averted this terrible affair and saved his own life. Lew, did Slover know how many men got out?" asked Jonathan.

"He said not many. The redskins killed all the prisoners exceptin' Crawford and Knight."

"I saw Col. Crawford burned at the stake. I did not see Dr. Knight. Maybe they murdered him before I reached the camp of the Delawares," said Jonathan.

"Wetzel, in your judgment, what effect will this massacre and Crawford's death have on the border?" inquired Col. Zane.

"It means another bloody year like 1777," answered Wetzel.

"We are liable to have trouble with the Indians any day. You mean that."

"There'll be war all along the river. Hamilton is hatchin' some new devil's trick with Girty. Col. Zane, I calkilate that Girty has a spy in the river settlements and knows as much about the forts and defense as you do."

"You can't mean a white spy."

"Yes, just that."

"That is a strong assertion, Lewis, but coming from you it means something. Step aside here and explain yourself," said Col. Zane, getting up and walking out to the fence.

"I don't like the looks of things," said the hunter. "A month ago I ketched this man Miller pokin' his nose round the block-house where he hadn't ought to be. And I kep' watchin' him. If my suspicions is correct he's playin' some deep game. I ain't got any proof, but things looks bad."

"That's strange, Lewis," said Col. Zane soberly. "Now that you mention it I remember Jonathan said he met Miller near the Kanawha three weeks ago. That was when Crawford's expedition was on the way to the Shawnee villages. The Colonel tried to enlist Miller, but Miller said he was in a hurry to get back to the Fort. And he hasn't come back yet."

"I ain't surprised. Now, Col. Zane, you are in command here. I'm not a soldier and for that reason I'm all the better to watch Miller. He won't suspect me. You give me authority and I'll round up his little game."

"By all means, Lewis. Go about it your own way, and report anything to me. Remember you may be mistaken and give Miller the benefit of the doubt. I don't like the fellow. He has a way of appearing and disappearing, and for no apparent reason, that makes me distrust him. But for Heaven's sake, Lew, how would he profit by betraying us?"

"I don't know. All I know is he'll bear watchin'."

"My gracious, Lew Wetzel!" exclaimed Betty as her brother and the hunter rejoined the others. "Have you come all the way over here without a gun? And you have on a new suit of buckskin."

Lewis stood a moment by Betty, gazing down at her with his slight smile. He looked exceedingly well. His face was not yet bronzed by summer suns. His long black hair, of which he was as proud as a woman could have been, and of which he took as much care as he did of his rifle, waved over his shoulders.

"Betty, this is my birthday, but that ain't the reason I've got my fine feathers on. I'm goin' to try and make an impression on you," replied Lewis, smiling.

"I declare, this is very sudden. But you have succeeded. Who made the suit? And where did you get all that pretty fringe and those beautiful beads?"

"That stuff I picked up round an Injun camp. The suit I made myself."

"I think, Lewis, I must get you to help me make my new gown," said Betty, roguishly.

"Well, I must be getting' back," said Wetzel, rising.

"Oh, don't go yet. You have not talked to me at all," said Betty petulantly. She walked to the gate with him.

"What can an Injun hunter say to amuse the belle of the border?"

"I don't want to be amused exactly. I mean I'm not used to being unnoticed, especially by you." And then in a lower tone she continued: "What did you mean about Mr. Miller? I heard his name and Eb looked worried. What did you tell him?"

"Never mind now, Betty. Maybe I'll tell you some day. It's enough for you to know the Colonel don't like Miller and that I think he is a bad man. You don't care nothin' for Miller, do you Betty?"

"Not in the least."

"Don't see him any more, Betty. Good-night, now, I must be goin' to supper."

"Lew, stop! or I shall run after you."

"And what good would your runnin' do?" said Lewis "You'd never ketch me. Why, I could give you twenty paces start and beat you to yon tree."

"You can't. Come, try it," retorted Betty, catching hold of her skirt. She could never have allowed a challenge like that to pass.

"Ha! ha! We are in for a race, Betty. if you beat him, start or no start, you will have accomplished something never done before," said Col. Zane.

"Come, Silas, step off twenty paces and make them long ones," said Betty, who was in earnest.

"We'll make it forty paces," said Silas, as he commenced taking immense strides.

"What is Lewis looking at?" remarked Col. Zane's wife.

Wetzel, in taking his position for the race, had faced the river. Mrs. Zane had seen him start suddenly, straighten up and for a moment stand like a statue. Her exclamation drew he attention of the others to the hunter.

"Look!" he cried, waving his hand toward the river.

"I declare, Wetzel, you are always seeing something. Where shall I look? Ah, yes, there is a dark form moving along the bank. By jove! I believe it's an Indian," said Col. Zane.

Jonathan darted into the house. When he reappeared second later he had three rifles.

"I see horses, Lew. What do you make out?" said Jonathan. "It's a bold manoeuvre for Indians unless they have a strong force."

"Hostile Injuns wouldn't show themselves like that. Maybe they ain't redskins at all. We'll go down to the bluff."

"Oh, yes, let us go," cried Betty, walking down the path toward Wetzel.

Col. Zane followed her, and presently the whole party were on their way to the river. When they reached the bluff they saw two horses come down the opposite bank and enter the water. Then they seemed to fade from view. The tall trees cast a dark shadow over the water and the horses had become lost in this obscurity. Col. Zane and Jonathan walked up and down the bank seeking to find a place which afforded a clearer view of the river.

"There they come," shouted Silas.

"Yes, I see them just swimming out of the shadow," said Col. Zane. "Both horses have riders. Lewis, what can you make out?"

"It's Isaac and an Indian girl," answered Wetzel.

This startling announcement created a commotion in the little group. It was followed by a chorus of exclamations.

"Heavens! Wetzel, you have wonderful eyes. I hope to God you are right. There, I see the foremost rider waving his hand," cried Col. Zane.

"Oh, Bessie, Bessie! I believe Lew is right. Look at Tige," said Betty excitedly.

Everybody had forgotten the dog. He had come down the path with Betty and had pressed close to her. First he trembled, then whined, then with a loud bark he ran down the bank and dashed into the water.

"Hel-lo, Betts," came the cry across the water. There was no mistaking that clear voice. It was Isaac's.

Although the sun had long gone down behind the hills daylight lingered. It was bright enough for the watchers to recognize Isaac Zane. He sat high on his horse and in his hand he held the bridle of a pony that was swimming beside him. The pony bore the slender figure of a girl. She was bending forward and her hands were twisted in the pony's mane.

By this time the Colonel and Jonathan were standing in the shallow water waiting to grasp the reins and lead the horses up the steep bank. Attracted by the unusual sight of a wildly gesticulating group on the river bluff, the settlers from the Fort hurried down to the scene of action. Capt. Boggs and Alfred Clarke joined the crowd. Old Sam came running down from the barn. All were intensely excited and Col. Zane and Jonathan reached for the bridles and led the horses up the slippery incline.

"Eb, Jack, Silas, here I am alive and well," cried Isaac as he leaped from his horse. "Betty, you darling, it's Isaac. Don't stand staring as if I were a ghost."

Whereupon Betty ran to him, flung her arms around his neck and clung to him. Isaac kissed her tenderly and disengaged himself from her arms.

"You'll get all wet. Glad to see me? Well, I never had such a happy moment in my life. Betty, I have brought you home one whom you must love. This is Myeerah, your sister. She is wet and cold. Take her home and make her warm and comfortable. You must forget all the past, for Myeerah has saved me from the stake."

Betty had forgotten the other. At her brother's words she turned and saw a slender form. Even the wet, mud-stained and ragged Indian costume failed to hide the grace of that figure. She saw a beautiful face, as white as her own, and dark eyes full of unshed tears.

"The Eagle is free," said the Indian girl in her low, musical voice.

"You have brought him home to us. Come," said Betty taking the hand of the trembling maiden.

The settlers crowded round Isaac and greeted him warmly while they plied him with innumerable questions. Was he free? Who was the Indian girl? Had he run off with her? Were the Indians preparing for war?

On the way to the Colonel's house Isaac told briefly of his escape from the Wyandots, of his capture by Cornplanter, and of his rescue. He also mentioned the preparations for war he had seen in Cornplanter's camp, and Girty's story of Col. Crawford's death.

"How does it come that you have the Indian girl with you?" asked Col. Zane as they left the curious settlers and entered the house.

"I am going to marry Myeerah and I brought her with me for that purpose. When we are married I will go back to the Wyandots and live with them until peace is declared."

"Humph! Will it be declared?"

"Myeerah has promised it, and I believe she can bring it about, especially if I marry her. Peace with the Hurons may help to bring about peace with the Shawnees. I shall never cease to work for that end; but even if peace cannot be secured, my duty still is to Myeerah. She saved me from a most horrible death."

"If your marriage with this Indian girl will secure the friendly offices of that grim old warrior Tarhe, it is far more than fighting will ever do. I do not want you to go back. Would we ever see you again?"

"Oh, yes, often I hope. You see, if I marry Myeerah the Hurons will allow me every liberty."

"Well, that puts a different light on the subject."

"Oh, how I wish you and Jonathan could have seen Thundercloud and his two hundred warriors ride into Cornplanter's camp. It was magnificent! The braves were all crowded near the stake where I was bound. The fire had been lighted. Suddenly the silence was shattered by an awful yell. It was Thundercloud's yell. I knew it because I had heard it before, and anyone who had once heard that yell could never forget it. In what seemed an incredibly short time Thundercloud's warriors were lined up in the middle of the camp. The surprise was so complete that, had it been necessary, they could have ridden Cornplanter's braves down, killed many, routed the others, and burned the village. Cornplanter will not get over that surprise in many a moon."

Betty had always hated the very mention of the Indian girl who had been the cause of her brother's long absence from home. But she was so happy in the knowledge of his return that she felt that it was in her power to forgive much; more over, the white, weary face of the Indian maiden touched Betty's warm heart. With her quick intuition she had divined that this was even a greater trial for Myeerah. Undoubtedly the Indian girl feared the scorn of her lover's people. She showed it in her trembling hands, in her fearful glances.

Finding that Myeerah could speak and understand English, Betty became more interested in her charge every moment. She set about to make Myeerah comfortable, and while she removed the wet and stained garments she talked all the time. She told her how happy she was that Isaac was alive and well. She said Myeerah's heroism in saving him should atone for all the past, and that Isaac's family would welcome her in his home.

Gradually Myeerah's agitation subsided under Betty's sweet graciousness, and by the time Betty had dressed her in a white gown, had brushed the dark hair and added a bright ribbon to the simple toilet, Myeerah had so far forgotten her fears as to take a shy pleasure in the picture of herself in the mirror. As for Betty, she gave vent to a little cry of delight. "Oh, you are perfectly lovely," cried Betty. "In that gown no one would know you as a Wyandot princess."

"Myeerah's mother was a white woman."

"I have heard your story, Myeerah, and it is wonderful. You must tell me all about your life with the Indians. You speak my language almost as well as I do. Who taught you?"

"Myeerah learned to talk with the White Eagle. She can speak French with the Coureurs-des-bois."

"That's more than I can do, Myeerah. And I had French teacher," said Betty, laughing.

"Hello, up there," came Isaac's voice from below.

"Come up, Isaac," called Betty.

"Is this my Indian sweetheart?" exclaimed Isaac, stopping at the door. "Betty, isn't she—"

"Yes," answered Betty, "she is simply beautiful."

"Come, Myeerah, we must go down to supper," said Isaac, taking her in his arms and kissing her. "Now you must not be afraid, nor mind being looked at."

"Everyone will be kind to you," said Betty, taking her hand. Myeerah had slipped from Isaac's arm and hesitated and hung back. "Come," continued Betty, "I will stay with you, and you need not talk if you do not wish."

Thus reassured Myeerah allowed Betty to lead her down stairs. Isaac had gone ahead and was waiting at the door.

The big room was brilliantly lighted with pine knots. Mrs. Zane was arranging the dishes on the table. Old Sam and Annie were hurrying to and fro from the kitchen. Col. Zane had just come up the cellar stairs carrying a mouldy looking cask. From its appearance it might have been a powder keg, but the merry twinkle in the Colonel's eyes showed that the cask contained something as precious, perhaps, as powder, but not quite so dangerous. It was a cask of wine over thirty years old. With Col. Zane's other effects it had stood the test of the long wagon-train journey over the Virginia mountains, and of the raft-ride down the Ohio. Col. Zane thought the feast he had arranged for Isaac would be a fitting occasion for the breaking of the cask.

Major McCullough, Capt. Boggs and Hugh Bennet had been invited. Wetzel had been persuaded to come. Betty's friends Lydia and Alice were there.

As Isaac, with an air of pride, led the two girls into the room Old Sam saw them and he exclaimed, "For de Lawd's sakes, Marsh Zane, dar's two pippins, sure can't tell 'em from one anudder."

Betty and Myeerah did resemble each other. They were of about the same size, tall and slender. Betty was rosy, bright-eyed and smiling; Myeerah was pale one moment and red the next.

"Friends, this is Myeerah, the daughter of Tarhe," said Isaac simply. "We are to be married to-morrow."

"Oh, why did you not tell me?" asked Betty in great surprise. "She said nothing about it."

"You see Myeerah has that most excellent trait in a woman—knowing when to keep silent," answered Isaac with a smile.

The door opened at this moment, admitting Will Martin and Alfred Clarke.

"Everybody is here now, Bessie, and I guess we may as well sit down to supper," said Col. Zane. "And, good friends, let me say that this is an occasion for rejoicing. It is not so much a marriage that I mean. That we might have any day if Lydia or Betty would show some of the alacrity which got a good husband for Alice. Isaac is a free man and we expect his marriage will bring about peace with a powerful tribe of Indians. To us, and particularly to you, young people, that is a matter of great importance. The friendship of the Hurons cannot but exert an influence on other tribes. I, myself, may live to see the day that my dream shall be realized—peaceful and friendly relations with the Indians, the freedom of the soil, well-tilled farms and growing settlements, and at last, the opening of this glorious country to the world. Therefore, let us rejoice; let every one be happy; let your gayest laugh ring out, and tell your best story."

Betty had blushed painfully at the entrance of Alfred and again at the Colonel's remark. To add to her embarrassment she found herself seated opposite Alfred at the table. This was the first time he had been near her since the Sunday at the meeting-house, and the incident had a singular effect on Betty. She found herself possessed, all at once, of an unaccountable shyness, and she could not lift her eyes from her plate. But at length she managed to steal a glance at Alfred. She failed to see any signs in his beaming face of the broken spirit of which her brother had hinted. He looked very well indeed. He was eating his dinner like any other healthy man, and talking and laughing with Lydia. This developed another unaccountable feeling in Betty, but this time it was resentment. Who ever heard of a man, who was as much in love as his letter said, looking well and enjoying himself with any other than the object of his affections? He had got over it, that was all. Just then Alfred turned and gazed full into Betty's eyes. She lowered them instantly, but not so quickly that she failed to see in his a reproach.

"You are going to stay with us a while, are you not?" asked Betty of Isaac.

"No, Betts, not more than a day or so. Now, do not look so distressed. I do not go back as a prisoner. Myeerah and I can often come and visit you. But just now I want to get back and try to prevent the Delawares from urging Tarhe to war."

"Isaac, I believe you are doing the wisest thing possible," said Capt.

Boggs. "And when I look at your bride-to-be I confess I do not see how you remained single so long."

"That's so, Captain," answered Isaac. "But you see, I have never been satisfied or contented in captivity, I wanted nothing but to be free."

"In other words, you were blind," remarked Alfred, smiling at Isaac.

"Yes, Alfred, was. And I imagine had you been in my place you would have discovered the beauty and virtue of my Princess long before I did. Nevertheless, please do not favor Myeerah with so many admiring glances. She is not used to it. And that reminds me that I must expect trouble tomorrow. All you fellows will want to kiss her."

"And Betty is going to be maid of honor. She, too, will have her troubles," remarked Col. Zane.

"Think of that, Alfred," said Isaac "A chance to kiss the two prettiest girls on the border—a chance of a lifetime."

"It is customary, is it not?" said Alfred coolly.

"Yes, it's a custom, if you can catch the girl," answered Col. Zane.

Betty's face flushed at Alfred's cool assumption. How dared he? In spite of her will she could not resist the power that compelled her to look at him. As plainly as if it were written there, she saw in his steady blue eyes the light of a memory—the memory of a kiss. And Betty dropped her head, her face burning, her heart on fire with shame, and love, and regret.

"It'll be a good chance for me, too," said Wetzel. His remark instantly turned attention to himself.

"The idea is absurd," said Isaac. "Why, Lew Wetzel, you could not be made to kiss any girl."

"I would not be backward about it," said Col. Zane.

"You have forgotten the fuss you made when the boys were kissing me," said Mrs. Zane with a fine scorn.

"My dear," said Col. Zane, in an aggrieved tone, "I did not make so much of a fuss, as you call it, until they had kissed you a great many times more than was reasonable."

"Isaac, tell us one thing more," said Capt. Boggs. "How did Myeerah learn of your capture by Cornplanter? Surely she could not have trailed you?"

"Will you tell us?" said Isaac to Myeerah.

"A bird sang it to me," answered Myeerah.

"She will never tell, that is certain," said Isaac. "And for that reason I believe Simon Girty got word to her that I was in the hands of Cornplanter. At the last moment when the Indians were lashing me to the stake Girty came to me and said he must have been too late."

"Yes, Girty might have done that," said Col. Zane. "I suppose, though he dared not interfere in behalf of poor Crawford."

"Isaac, Can you get Myeerah to talk? I love to hear her speak," said Betty, in an aside.

"Myeerah, will you sing a Huron love-song?" said Isaac "Or, if you do not wish to sing, tell a story. I want them to know how well you can speak our language."

"What shall Myeerah say?" she said, shyly.

"Tell them the legend of the Standing Stone."

"A beautiful Indian girl once dwelt in the pine forests," began Myeerah, with her eyes cast down and her hand seeking Isaac's. "Her voice was like rippling waters, her beauty like the rising sun. From near and from far came warriors to see the fair face of this maiden. She smiled on them all and they called her Smiling Moon. Now there lived on the Great Lake a Wyandot chief. He was young and bold. No warrior was as great as Tarhe. Smiling Moon cast a spell on his heart. He came many times to woo her and make her his wife. But Smiling Moon said: 'Go, do great deeds, an come again.'

"Tarhe searched the east and the west. He brought her strange gifts from strange lands. She said: 'Go and slay my enemies.' Tarhe went forth in his war paint and killed the braves who named her Smiling Moon. He came again to her and she said: 'Run swifter than the deer, be more cunning than the beaver, dive deeper than the loon.'

"Tarhe passed once more to the island where dwelt Smiling Moon. The ice was thick, the snow was deep. Smiling Moon turned not from her warm fire as she said: 'The chief is a great warrior, but Smiling Moon is not easily won. It is cold. Change winter into summer and then Smiling Moon will love him.'

"Tarhe cried in a loud voice to the Great Spirit: 'Make me a master.'

"A voice out of the forest answered: 'Tarhe, great warrior, wise chief, waste not thy time, go back to thy wigwam.'

"Tarhe unheeding cried 'Tarhe wins or dies. Make him a master so that he may drive the ice northward.'

"Stormed the wild tempest; thundered the rivers of ice; chill blew the north wind, the cold northwest wind, against the mild south wind; snow-spirits and hail-spirits fled before the warm raindrops; the white mountains melted, and lo! it was summer.

"On the mountain top Tarhe waited for his bride. Never wearying, ever faithful he watched many years. There he turned to stone. There he stands to-day, the Standing Stone of ages. And Smiling Moon, changed by the Great Spirit into the Night Wind, forever wails her lament at dusk through the forest trees, and moans over the mountain tops."

Myeerah's story elicited cheers and praises from all. She was entreated to tell another, but smilingly shook her head. Now that her shyness had worn off to some extent she took great interest in the jest and the general conversation.

Col. Zane's fine old wine flowed like water. The custom was to fill a guest's cup as soon as it was empty. Drinking much was rather encouraged than otherwise. But Col. Zane never allowed this custom to go too far in his house.

"Friends, the hour grows late," he said. "To-morrow, after the great event, we shall have games, shooting matches, running races, and contests of all kinds. Capt. Boggs and I have arranged to give prizes, and I expect the girls can give something to lend a zest to the competition."

"Will the girls have a chance in these races?" asked Isaac. "If so, I should like to see Betty and Myeerah run."

"Betty can outrun any woman, red or white, on the border," said Wetzel. "And she could make some of the men run their level best."

"Well, perhaps we shall give her one opportunity to-morrow," observed the Colonel. "She used to be good at running but it seems to me that of late she has taken to books and—"

"Oh, Eb! that is untrue," interrupted Betty.

Col. Zane laughed and patted his sister's cheek. "Never mind, Betty," and then, rising, he continued, "Now let us drink to the bride and groom-to-be. Capt. Boggs, I call on you."

"We drink to the bride's fair beauty; we drink to the groom's good luck," said Capt. Boggs, raising his cup.

"Do not forget the maid-of-honor," said Isaac.

"Yes, and the maid-of-honor. Mr. Clarke, will you say something appropriate?" asked Col. Zane.

Rising, Clarke said: "I would be glad to speak fittingly on this occasion, but I do not think I can do it justice. I believe as Col. Zane does, that this Indian Princess is the first link in that chain of peace which will some day unite the red men and the white men. Instead of the White Crane she should be called the White Dove. Gentlemen, rise and drink to her long life and happiness."

The toast was drunk. Then Clarke refilled his cup and holding it high over his head he looked at Betty.

"Gentlemen, to the maid-of-honor. Miss Zane, your health, your happiness, in this good old wine."

"I thank you," murmured Betty with downcast eyes. "I bid you all good-night. Come, Myeerah."

Once more alone with Betty, the Indian girl turned to her with eyes like twin stars.

"My sister has made me very happy," whispered Myeerah in her soft, low voice. "Myeerah's heart is full."

"I believe you are happy, for I know you love Isaac dearly."

"Myeerah has always loved him. She will love his sister."

"And I will love you," said Betty. "I will love you because you have saved him. Ah! Myeerah, yours has been wonderful, wonderful love."

"My sister is loved," whispered Myeerah. "Myeerah saw the look in the eyes of the great hunter. It was the sad light of the moon on the water. He loves you. And the other looked at my sister with eyes like the blue of northern skies. He, too, loves you."

"Hush!" whispered Betty, trembling and hiding her face. "Hush! Myeerah, do not speak of him."

CHAPTER 11

HE FOLLOWING AFTERNOON THE SUN SHONE FAIR AND WARM; THE sweet smell of the tan-bark pervaded the air and the birds sang their gladsome songs. The scene before the grim battle-scarred old fort was not without its picturesqueness. The low vine-covered cabins on the hill side looked more like picture houses than like real habitations of men; the mill with its burned-out roof—a reminder of the Indians—and its great wheel, now silent and still, might have been from its lonely and dilapidated appearance a hundred years old.

On a little knoll carpeted with velvety grass sat Isaac and his Indian bride. He had selected this vantage point because it afforded a fine view of the green square where the races and the matches were to take place. Admiring women stood around him and gazed at his wife. They gossiped in whispers about her white skin, her little hands, her beauty. The girls stared with wide open and wondering eyes. The youngsters ran round and round the little group; they pushed each other over, and rolled in the long grass, and screamed with delight.

It was to be a gala occasion and every man, woman and child in the settlement had assembled on the green. Col. Zane and Sam were planting a post in the center of the square. It was to be used in the shooting matches. Capt. Boggs and Major McColloch were arranging the contestants in order. Jonathan Zane, Will Martin, Alfred Clarke—all the young men were carefully charging and priming their rifles. Betty was sitting on the black stallion which Col. Zane had generously offered as first prize. She was in the gayest of moods and had just coaxed Isaac to lift her on the tall horse, from which height she purposed watching the sports. Wetzel alone did not seem infected by the spirit of gladsomeness which pervaded. He stood apart leaning on his long rifle and taking no interest in the proceedings behind him. He was absorbed in contemplating the forest on the opposite shore of the river.

"Well, boys, I guess we are ready for the fun," called Col. Zane, cheerily. "Only one shot apiece, mind you, except in case of a tie. Now, everybody shoot his best."

The first contest was a shooting match known as "driving the nail." It was as the name indicated, nothing less than shooting at the head of a nail. In the absence of a nail—for nails were scarce—one was usually fashioned from a knife blade, or an old file, or even a piece of silver. The nail was driven lightly into the stake, the contestants shot at it from a distance as great as the eyesight permitted. To drive the nail hard and fast into the wood at one hundred yards was a feat seldom accomplished. By many hunters it was deemed more difficult than "snuffing the candle," another border pastime, which consisted of placing in the dark at any distance a lighted candle, and then putting out the flame with a single rifle ball. Many settlers, particularly those who handled the plow more than the rifle, sighted from a rest, and placed a piece of moss under the rife-barrel to prevent its spring at the discharge.

The match began. Of the first six shooters Jonathan Zane and Alfred Clarke scored the best shots. Each placed a bullet in the half-inch circle round the nail.

"Alfred, very good, indeed," said Col. Zane. "You have made a decided improvement since the last shooting-match."

Six other settlers took their turns. All were unsuccessful in getting a shot inside the little circle. Thus a tie between Alfred and Jonathan had to be decided.

"Shoot close, Alfred," yelled Isaac. "I hope you beat him. He always won from me and then crowed over it."

Alfred's second shot went wide of the mark, and as Jonathan placed another bullet in the circle, this time nearer the center, Alfred had to acknowledge defeat.

"Here comes Miller," said Silas Zane. "Perhaps he will want a try."

Col. Zane looked round. Miller had joined the party. He carried his rifle and accoutrements, and evidently had just returned to the settlement. He nodded pleasantly to all.

"Miller, will you take a shot for the first prize, which I was about to award to Jonathan?" said Col. Zane.

"No. I am a little late, and not entitled to a shot. I will take a try for the others," answered Miller.

At the arrival of Miller on the scene Wetzel had changed his position to one nearer the crowd. The dog, Tige, trotted closely at his heels. No one heard Tige's low growl or Wetzel's stern word to silence him. Throwing his arm over Betty's pony, Wetzel apparently watched the shooters. In reality he studied intently Miller's every movement.

"I expect some good shooting for this prize," said Col. Zane, waving a beautifully embroidered buckskin bullet pouch, which was one of Betty's donations.

Jonathan having won his prize was out of the lists and could compete no more. This entitled Alfred to the first shot for second prize. He felt he would give anything he possessed to win the dainty trifle which the Colonel had waved aloft. Twice he raised his rifle in his exceeding earnestness to score a good shot and each time lowered the barrel. When finally he did shoot the bullet embedded itself in the second circle. It was a good shot, but he knew it would never win that prize.

"A little nervous, eh?" remarked Miller, with a half sneer on his swarthy face.

Several young settlers followed in succession, but their aims were poor. Then little Harry Bennet took his stand. Harry had won many prizes in former matches, and many of the pioneers considered him one of the best shots in the country.

"Only a few more after you, Harry," said Col. Zane. "You have a good chance."

"All right, Colonel. That's Betty's prize and somebody'll have to do some mighty tall shootin' to beat me," said the lad, his blue eyes flashing as he toed the mark.

Shouts and cheers of approval greeted his attempt. The bullet had passed into the wood so close to the nail that a knife blade could not have been inserted between.

Miller's turn came next. He was a fine marksman and he knew it. With the confidence born of long experience and knowledge of his weapon, he took a careful though quick aim and fired. He turned away satisfied that he would carry off the coveted prize. He had nicked the nail.

But Miller reckoned without his host. Betty had seen the result of his shot and the self-satisfied smile on his face. She watched several of the settlers make poor attempts at the nail, and then, convinced that not one of the other contestants could do so well as Miller, she slipped off the horse and ran around to where Wetzel was standing by her pony.

"Lew, I believe Miller will win my prize," she whispered, placing her hand on the hunter's arm. "He has scratched the nail, and I am sure no one except you can do better. I do not want Miller to have anything of mine."

"And, little girl, you want me to shoot fer you," said Lewis.

"Yes, Lew, please come and shoot for me."

It was said of Wetzel that he never wasted powder. He never entered into the races and shooting-matches of the settlers, yet it was well known that he was the fleetest runner and the most unerring shot on the frontier. Therefore, it was with surprise and pleasure that Col. Zane heard the hunter say he guessed he would like one shot anyway.

Miller looked on with a grim smile. He knew that, Wetzel or no Wetzel, it would take a remarkably clever shot to beat his.

"This shot's for Betty," said Wetzel as he stepped to the mark. He fastened his keen eyes on the stake. At that distance the head of the nail looked like a tiny black speck. Wetzel took one of the locks of hair that waved over his broad shoulders and held it up in front of his eyes a moment. He thus ascertained that there was not any perceptible breeze. The long black barrel started slowly to rise—it seemed to the interested onlookers that it would never reach a level and when, at last, it became rigid, there was a single second in which man and rifle appeared as if carved out of stone. Then followed a burst of red flame, a puff of white smoke, a clear ringing report.

Many thought the hunter had missed altogether. It seemed that the nail had not changed its position; there was no bullet hole in the white lime wash that had been smeared round the nail. But on close inspection the nail was found to have been driven to its head in the wood.

"A wonderful shot!" exclaimed Col. Zane. "Lewis, I don't remember having seen the like more than once or twice in my life."

Wetzel made no answer. He moved away to his former position and commenced to reload his rifle. Betty came running up to him, holding in her hand the prize bullet pouch.

"Oh, Lew, if I dared I would kiss you. It pleases me more for you to have won my prize than if any one else had won it. And it was the finest, straightest shot ever made."

"Betty, it's a little fancy for redskins, but it'll be a keepsake," answered Lewis, his eyes reflecting the bright smile on her face.

Friendly rivalry in feats that called for strength, speed and daring was the diversion of the youth of that period, and the pioneers conducted this good-natured but spirited sport strictly on its merits. Each contestant strove his utmost to outdo his opponent. It was hardly to be expected that Alfred would carry off any of the laurels. Used as he had been to comparative idleness he was no match for the hardy lads who had been brought up and trained to a life of action, wherein a ten mile walk behind a plow, or a cord of wood chopped in a day, were trifles. Alfred lost in the foot-race and the sackrace, but by dint of exerting himself to the limit of his strength, he did manage to take one fall out of the best wrestler. He was content to stop here, and, throwing himself on the grass, endeavored to recover his breath. He felt happier today than for some time past. Twice during the afternoon he had met Betty's eyes and the look he encountered there made his heart stir with a strange feeling of fear and hope. While he was ruminating on what had happened between Betty and himself he allowed his eyes to wander from one person to another. When his gaze alighted on Wetzel it became riveted there. The hunter's attitude struck him as singular. Wetzel had his face half turned toward the boys romping near him and he leaned carelessly against a white oak tree. But a close observer would have seen, as Alfred did, that there was a certain alertness in that rigid and motionless figure. Wetzel's eyes were fixed on the western end of the island. Almost involuntarily Alfred's eyes sought the same direction. The western end of the island ran out into a long low point covered with briars, rushes and saw-grass. As Alfred directed his gaze along the water line of this point he distinctly saw a dark form flit from one bush to another. He was positive he had not been mistaken. He got up slowly and unconcernedly, and strolled over to Wetzel.

"Wetzel, I saw an object just now," he said in a low tone. "It was moving behind those bushes at the head of the island. I am not sure whether it was an animal or an Indian."

"Injuns. Go back and be natur'l like. Don't say nothin' and watch Miller," whispered Wetzel.

Much perturbed by the developments of the last few moments, and wondering what was going to happen, Alfred turned away. He had scarcely reached the others when he heard Betty's voice raised in indignant protest.

"I tell you I did swim my pony across the river," cried Betty. "It was just even with that point and the river was higher than it is now."

"You probably overestimated your feat," said Miller, with his disagreeable, doubtful smile. "I have seen the river so low that it could be waded, and then it would be a very easy matter to cross. But now your pony could not swim half the distance."

"I'll show you," answered Betty, her black eyes flashing. She put her foot in the stirrup and leaped on Madcap.

"Now, Betty, don't try that foolish ride again," implored Mrs. Zane. "What do you care whether strangers believe or not? Eb, make her come back."

Col. Bane only laughed and made no attempt to detain Betty. He rather indulged her caprices.

"Stop her!" cried Clarke.

"Betty, where are you goin'?" said Wetzel, grabbing at Madcap's bridle. But Betty was too quick for him. She avoided the hunter, and with a saucy laugh she wheeled the fiery little pony and urged her over the bank. Almost before any one could divine her purpose she had Madcap in the water up to her knees.

"Betty, stop!" cried Wetzel.

She paid no attention to his call. In another moment the pony would be off the shoal and swimming.

"Stop! Turn back, Betty, or I'll shoot the pony," shouted Wetzel, and this time there was a ring of deadly earnestness in his voice. With the words he had cocked and thrown forward the long rifle.

Betty heard, and in alarm she turned her pony. She looked up with great surprise and concern, for she knew Wetzel was not one to trifle.

"For God's sake!" exclaimed Colonel Zane, looking in amazement at the hunter's face, which was now white and stern.

"Why, Lew, you do not mean you would shoot Madcap?" said Betty, reproachfully, as she reached the shore.

All present in that watching crowd were silent, awaiting the hunter's answer. They felt that mysterious power which portends the revelation of strange events. Col. Zane and Jonathan knew the instant they saw Wetzel that something extraordinary was coming. His face had grown cold and gray; his lips were tightly compressed; his eyes dilated and shone with a peculiar lustre.

"Where were you headin' your pony?" asked Wetzel.

"I wanted to reach that point where the water is shallow," answered Betty.

"That's what I thought. Well, Betty, hostile Injuns are hidin' and waitin' fer you in them high rushes right where you were makin' fer," said Wetzel. Then he shouldered his rifle and walked rapidly away.

"Oh, he cannot be serious!" cried Betty. "Oh, how foolish am I."

"Get back up from the river, everybody," commanded Col. Zane.

"Col. Zane," said Clarke, walking beside the Colonel up the bank, "I saw Wetzel watching the island in a manner that I thought odd, under the circumstances, and I watched too. Presently I saw a dark form dart behind a bush. I went over and told Wetzel, and he said there were Indians on the island."

"This is most d—n strange," said Col. Zane, frowning heavily. "Wetzel's suspicions, Miller turns up, teases Betty attempting that foolhardy trick, and then—Indians! It may be a coincidence, but it looks bad."

"Col. Zane, don't you think Wetzel may be mistaken?" said Miller, coming up. "I came over from the other side this morning and I did not see any Indian sign. Probably Wetzel has caused needless excitement."

"It does not follow that because you came from over the river there are no Indians there," answered Col. Zane, sharply. "Do you presume to criticise Wetzel's judgment?"

"I saw an Indian!" cried Clarke, facing Miller with blazing eyes. "And if you say I did not, you lie! What is more, I believe you know more than any one else about it. I watched you. I saw you were uneasy and that you looked across the river from time to time. Perhaps you had better explain to Col. Zane the reason you taunted his sister into attempting that ride."

With a snarl more like that of a tiger than of a human being, Miller sprang at Clarke. His face was dark with malignant hatred, as he reached for and drew an ugly knife. There were cries of fright from the children and screams from the women. Alfred stepped aside with the wonderful quickness of the trained boxer and shot out his right arm. His fist caught Miller a hard blow on the head, knocking him down and sending the knife flying in the air.

It had all happened so quickly that everyone was as if paralyzed. The settlers stood still and watched Miller rise slowly to his feet.

"Give me my knife!" he cried hoarsely. The knife had fallen at the feet of Major McColloch, who had concealed it with his foot.

"Let this end right here," ordered Col. Zane. "Clarke, you have made a very strong statement. Have you anything to substantiate your words?"

"I think I have," said Clarke. He was standing erect, his face white and his eyes like blue steel. "I knew him at Ft. Pitt. He was a liar and a drunkard there. He was a friend of the Indians and of the British. What he was there he must be here. It was Wetzel who told me to watch him. Wetzel and I both think he knew the Indians were on the island."

"Col. Zane, it is false," said Miller, huskily. "He is trying to put you against me. He hates me because your sister—"

"You cur!" cried Clarke, striking at Miller. Col. Zane struck up the infuriated young man's arm.

"Give us knives, or anything," panted Clarke.

"Yes, let us fight it out now," said Miller.

"Capt. Boggs, take Clarke to the block-house. Make him stay there if you have to lock him up," commanded Col. Zane. "Miller, as for you, I cannot condemn you without proof. If I knew positively that there were Indians on the island and that you were aware of it, you would be a dead man in less time than it takes to say it. I will give you the benefit of the doubt and twenty-four hours to leave the Fort."

The villagers dispersed and went to their homes. They were inclined to take Clarke's side. Miller had become disliked. His drinking habits and his arrogant and bold manner had slowly undermined the friendships he had made during the early part of his stay at Ft. Henry; while Clarke's good humor and willingness to help any one, his gentleness with the children, and his several acts of heroism had strengthened their regard.

"Jonathan, this looks like some of Girty's work. I wish I knew the truth," said Col. Zane, as he, his brothers and Betty and Myeerah entered the house. "Confound it! We can't have even one afternoon of enjoyment. I must see Lewis. I cannot be sure of Clarke. He is evidently bitter against Miller. That would have been a terrible fight. Those fellows have had trouble before, and I am afraid we have not seen the last of their quarrel."

"If they meet again—but how can you keep them apart?" said Silas. "If Miller leaves the Fort without killing Clarke he'll hide around in the woods and wait for a chance to shoot him."

"Not with Wetzel here," answered Col. Zane. "Betty, do you see what your—" he began, turning to his sister, but when he saw her white and miserable face he said no more.

"Don't mind, Betts. It wasn't any fault of yours," said Isaac, putting his arm tenderly round the trembling girl. "I for another believe Clarke was

184

right when he said Miller knew there were Indians over the river. It looks like a plot to abduct you. Have no fear for Alfred. He can take care of himself. He showed that pretty well."

An hour later Clarke had finished his supper and was sitting by his window smoking his pipe. His anger had cooled somewhat and his reflections were not of the pleasantest kind. He regretted that he lowered himself so far as to fight with a man little better than an outlaw. Still there was a grim satisfaction in the thought of the blow he had given Miller. He remembered he had asked for a knife and that his enemy and he be permitted to fight to the death. After all to have ended, then and there, the feud between them would have been the better course; for he well knew Miller's desperate character, that he had killed more than one white man, and that now a fair fight might not be possible. Well, he thought, what did it matter? He was not going to worry himself. He did not care much, one way or another. He had no home; he could not make one without the woman he loved. He was a Soldier of Fortune; he was at the mercy of Fate, and he would drift along and let what came be welcome. A soft footfall on the stairs and a knock on the door interrupted his thoughts.

"Come in," he said.

The door opened and Wetzel strode into the room.

"I come over to say somethin' to you," said the hunter taking the chair by the window and placing his rifle over his knee.

"I will be pleased to listen or talk, as you desire," said Alfred.

"I don't mind tellin' you that the punch you give Miller was what he deserved. If he and Girty didn't hatch up that trick to ketch Betty, I don't know nothin'. But we can't prove nothin' on him yet. Mebbe he knew about the redskins; mebbe he didn't. Personally, I think he did. But I can't kill a white man because I think somethin'. I'd have to know fer sure. What I want to say is to put you on your guard against the baddest man on the river."

"I am aware of that," answered Alfred. "I knew his record at Ft. Pitt. What would you have me do?"

"Keep close till he's gone."

"That would be cowardly."

"No, it wouldn't. He'd shoot you from behind some tree or cabin."

"Well, I'm much obliged to you for your kind advice, but for all that I won't stay in the house," said Alfred, beginning to wonder at the hunter's earnest manner.

"You're in love with Betty, ain't you?"

The question came with Wetzel's usual bluntness and it staggered Alfred. He could not be angry, and he did not know what to say. The hunter went on:

"You needn't say so, because I know it. And I know she loves you and that's why I want you to look out fer Miller."

"My God! man, you're crazy," said Alfred, laughing scornfully. "She cares nothing for me."

"That's your great failin', young feller. You fly off'en the handle too easy. And so does Betty. You both care fer each other and are unhappy about it. Now, you don't know Betty, and she keeps misunderstandin' you."

"For Heaven's sake! Wetzel, if you know anything tell me. Love her? Why, the words are weak! I love her so well that an hour ago I would have welcomed death at Miller's hands only to fall and die at her feet defending her. Your words set me on fire. What right have you to say that? How do you know?"

The hunter leaned forward and put his hand on Alfred's shoulder. On his pale face was that sublime light which comes to great souls when they give up a life long secret, or when they sacrifice what is best beloved. His broad chest heaved: his deep voice trembled.

"Listen. I'm not a man fer words, and it's hard to tell. Betty loves you. I've carried her in my arms when she was a baby. I've made her toys and played with her when she was a little girl. I know all her moods. I can read her like I do the moss, and the leaves, and the bark of the forest. I've loved her all my life. That's why I know she loves you. I can feel it. Her happiness is the only dear thing left on earth fer me. And that's why I'm your friend."

In the silence that followed his words the door opened and closed and he was gone.

~

BETTY AWOKE WITH A START. SHE WAS WIDE AWAKE IN A SECOND. THE moonbeams came through the leaves of the maple tree near her window and cast fantastic shadows on the wall of her room. Betty lay quiet, watching the fairy-like figures on the wall and listening intently. What had awakened her? The night was still; the crow of a cock in the distance proclaimed that the hour of dawn was near at hand. She waited for Tige's bark under her window, or Sam's voice, or the kicking and trampling of horses in the barn—sounds that usually broke her slumbers in the morning. But no such noises were forthcoming. Suddenly she heard a light, quick tap, tap, and then a rattling in the corner. It was like no sound but that made by a pebble striking the floor, bounding and rolling across the room. There it was again. Some one was tossing stones in at her window. She slipped out of bed, ran, and leaned on the window-sill and looked out. The moon was going down behind the hill, but there was light enough for her to distinguish objects. She saw a dark figure crouching by the fence.

"Who is it?" said Betty, a little frightened, but more curious.

"Sh-h-h, it's Miller," came the answer, spoken in low voice.

The bent form straightened and stood erect. It stepped forward under Betty's window. The light was dim, but Betty recognized the dark face of Miller. He carried a rifle in his hand and a pack on his shoulder.

"Go away, or I'll call my brother. I will not listen to you," said Betty, making a move to leave the window.

"Sh-h-h, not so loud," said Miller, in a quick, hoarse whisper. "You'd better listen. I am going across the border to join Girty. He is going to bring the Indians and the British here to burn the settlement. If you will go away with me I'll save the lives of your brothers and their families. I have aided Girty and I have influence with him. If you won't go you'll be taken captive and you'll see all your friends and relatives scalped and burned. Quick, your answer."

"Never, traitor! Monster! I'd be burned at the stake before I'd go a step with you!" cried Betty.

"Then remember that you've crossed a desperate man. If you escape the massacre you will beg on your knees to me. This settlement is doomed. Now, go to your white-faced lover. You'll find him cold. Ha! Ha! Ha!" and with a taunting laugh he leaped the fence and disappeared in the gloom.

Betty sank to the floor stunned, horrified. She shuddered at the malignity expressed in Miller's words. How had she ever been deceived in him? He was in league with Girty. At heart he was a savage, a renegade. Betty went over his words, one by one.

"Your white-faced lover. You will find him cold," whispered Betty. "What did he mean?"

Then came the thought. Miller had murdered Clarke. Betty gave one agonized quiver, as if a knife had been thrust into her side, and then her paralyzed limbs recovered the power of action. She flew out into the passage-way and pounded on her brother's door.

"Eb! Eb! Get up! Quickly, for God's sake!" she cried. A smothered exclamation, a woman's quick voice, the heavy thud of feet striking the floor followed Betty's alarm. Then the door opened.

"Hello, Betts, what's up?" said Col. Zane, in his rapid voice.

At the same moment the door at the end of the hall opened and Isaac came out.

"Eb, Betty, I heard voices out doors and in the house. What's the row?"

"Oh, Isaac! Oh, Eb! Something terrible has happened!" cried Betty, breathlessly.

"Then it is no time to get excited," said the Colonel, calmly. He placed his arm round Betty and drew her into the room. "Isaac, get down the rifles. Now, Betty, time is precious. Tell me quickly, briefly."

"I was awakened by a stone rolling on the floor. I ran to the window and saw a man by the fence. He came under my window and I saw it was Miller. He said he was going to join Girty. He said if I would go with him he would save the lives of all my relatives. If I would not they would all be killed, massacred, burned alive, and I would be taken away as his captive. I told him I'd rather die before I'd go with him. Then he said we were all doomed, and that my white-faced lover was already cold. With that he gave a laugh which made my flesh creep and ran on toward the river. Oh! he has murdered Mr. Clarke."

"Hell! What a fiend!" cried Col. Zane, hurriedly getting into his clothes. "Betts, you had a gun in there. Why didn't you shoot him? Why didn't I pay more attention to Wetzel's advice?"

"You should have allowed Clarke to kill him yesterday," said Isaac. "Like as not he'll have Girty here with a lot of howling devils. What's to be done?"

"I'll send Wetzel after him and that'll soon wind up his ball of yarn," answered Col. Zane.

"Please—go—and find—if Mr. Clarke—"

"Yes, Betty, I'll go at once. You must not lose courage, Betty. It's quite probable that Miller has killed Alfred and that there's worse to follow."

"I'll come, Eb, as soon as I have told Myeerah. She is scared half to death," said Isaac, starting for the door.

"All right, only hurry," said Col. Zane, grabbing his rifle. Without wasting more words, and lacing up his hunting shirt as he went he ran out of the room.

The first rays of dawn came streaking in at the window. The chill gray light brought no cheer with its herald of the birth of another day. For what might the morning sun disclose? It might shine on a long line of painted Indians. The fresh breeze from over the river might bring the long war whoop of the savage.

No wonder Noah and his brother, awakened by the voice of their father, sat up in their little bed and looked about with frightened eyes. No wonder Mrs. Zane's face blanched. How many times she had seen her husband grasp his rifle and run out to meet danger!

"Bessie," said Betty. "If it's true I will not be able to bear it. It's all my fault."

"Nonsense! You heard Eb say Miller and Clarke had quarreled before. They hated each other before they ever saw you."

A door banged, quick footsteps sounded on the stairs, and Isaac came rushing into the room. Betty, deathly pale, stood with her hands pressed to her bosom, and looked at Isaac with a question in her eyes that her tongue could not speak.

"Betty, Alfred's badly hurt, but he's alive. I can tell you no more now," said Isaac. "Bessie, bring your needle, silk linen, liniment—everything you need for a bad knife wound, and come quickly."

Betty's haggard face changed as if some warm light had been reflected on it; her lips moved, and with a sob of thankfulness she fled to her room.

Two hours later, while Annie was serving breakfast to Betty and Myeerah, Col. Zane strode into the room.

"Well, one has to eat whatever happens," he said, his clouded face brightening somewhat. "Betty, there's been bad work, bad work. When I got to Clarke's room I found him lying on the bed with a knife sticking in him. As it is we are doubtful about pulling him through."

"May I see him?" whispered Betty, with pale lips.

"If the worst comes to the worst I'll take you over. But it would do no good now and would surely unnerve you. He still has a fighting chance."

"Did they fight, or was Mr. Clarke stabbed in his sleep?"

"Miller climbed into Clarke's window and knifed him in the dark. As I came over I met Wetzel and told him I wanted him to trail Miller and find if there is any truth in his threat about Girty and the Indians. Sam just now found Tige tied fast in the fence corner back of the barn. That explains the mystery of Miller's getting so near the house. You know he always took pains to make friends with Tige. The poor dog was helpless; his legs were tied and his jaws bound fast. Oh, Miller is as cunning as an Indian! He has had this all planned out, and he has had more than one arrow to his bow. But, if I mistake not he has shot his last one."

"Miller must be safe from pursuit by this time," said Betty.

"Safe for the present, yes," answered Col. Zane, "but while Jonathan and Wetzel live I would not give a snap of my fingers for Miller's chances. Hello, I hear some one talking. I sent for Jack and the Major."

The Colonel threw open the door. Wetzel, Major McColloch, Jonathan and Silas Zane were approaching. They were all heavily armed. Wetzel was equipped for a long chase. Double leggins were laced round his legs. A buckskin knapsack was strapped to his shoulders.

"Major, I want you and Jonathan to watch the river," said Col. Zane. "Silas, you are to go to the mouth of Yellow Creek and reconnoiter. We are in for a siege. It may be twenty-four hours and it may be ten days. In the meantime I will get the Fort in shape to meet the attack. Lewis, you have your orders. Have you anything to suggest?"

"I'll take the dog," answered Wetzel. "He'll save time for me. I'll stick to Miller's trail and find Girty's forces. I've believed all along that Miller was helpin' Girty, and I'm thinkin' that where Miller goes there I'll find Girty and his redskins. If it's night when I get back I'll give the call of the hoot-owl three times, quick, so Jack and the Major will know I want to get back across the river."

"All right, Lewis, we'll be expecting you any time," said Col. Zane.

"Betty, I'm goin' now and I want to tell you somethin'," said Wetzel, as Betty appeared. "Come as far as the end of the path with me."

"I'm sorry you must go. But Tige seems delighted," said Betty, walking beside Wetzel, while the dog ran on before.

"Betty, I wanted to tell you to stay close like to the house, fer this feller Miller has been layin' traps fer you, and the Injuns is on the war-path. Don't ride your pony, and stay home now."

"Indeed, I shall never again do anything as foolish as I did yesterday. I have learned my lesson. And Oh! Lew, I am so grateful to you for saving me. When will you return to the Fort?"

"Mebbe never, Betty."

"Oh, no. Don't say that. I know all this Indian talk will blow over, as it always does, and you will come back and everything will be all right again."

"I hope it'll be as you say, Betty, but there's no tellin', there's no tellin'."

"You are going to see if the Indians are making preparations to besiege the Fort?"

"Yes, I am goin' fer that. And if I happen to find Miller on my way I'll give him Betty's regards."

Betty shivered at his covert meaning. Long ago in a moment of playfulness, Betty had scratched her name on the hunter's rifle. Ever after that Wetzel called his fatal weapon by her name.

"If you were going simply to avenge I would not let you go. That wretch will get his just due some day, never fear for that."

"Betty, 'taint likely he'll get away from me, and if he does there's Jonathan. This mornin' when we trailed Miller down to the river bank Jonathan points across the river and says: 'You or me,' and I says: 'Me,' so it's all settled."

"Will Mr. Clarke live?" said Betty, in an altered tone, asking the question which was uppermost in her mind.

"I think so, I hope so. He's a husky young chap and the cut wasn't bad. He lost so much blood. That's why he's so weak. If he gets well he'll have somethin' to tell you."

"Lew, what do you mean?" demanded Betty, quickly.

"Me and him had a long talk last night and—"

"You did not go to him and talk of me, did you?" said Betty, reproachfully.

They had now reached the end of the path. Wetzel stopped and dropped the butt of his rifle on the ground. Tige looked on and wagged his tail. Presently the hunter spoke.

"Yes, we talked about you."

"Oh! Lewis. What did—could you have said?" faltered Betty.

"You think I hadn't ought to speak to him of you?"

"I do not see why you should. Of course you are my good friend, but he—it is not like you to speak of me."

"Fer once I don't agree with you. I knew how it was with him so I told him. I knew how it was with you so I told him, and I know how it is with me, so I told him that too."

"With you?" whispered Betty.

"Yes, with me. That kind of gives me a right, don't it, considerin' it's all fer your happiness?"

"With you?" echoed Betty in a low tone. She was beginning to realize that she had not known this man. She looked up at him. His eyes were misty with an unutterable sadness.

"Oh, no! No! Lew. Say it is not true," she cried, piteously. All in a moment Betty's burdens became too heavy for her. She wrung her little hands. Her brother's kindly advice, Bessie's warnings, and old Grandmother Watkins' words came back to her. For the first time she believed what they said—that Wetzel loved her. All at once the scales fell from her eyes and she saw this man as he really was. All the thousand and one things he had done for her, his simple teaching, his thoughtfulness, his faithfulness, and his watchful protection—all came crowding on her as debts that she could never pay. For now what could she give this man to whom she owed more than her life? Nothing. It was too late. Her love could have reclaimed him, could have put an end to that solitary wandering, and have made him a good, happy man.

"Yes, Betty, it's time to tell it. I've loved you always," he said softly.

She covered her face and sobbed. Wetzel put his arm round her and drew her to him until the dark head rested on his shoulder. Thus they stood a moment.

"Don't cry, little one," he said, tenderly. "Don't grieve fer me. My love fer you has been the only good in my life. It's been happiness to love you. Don't think of me. I can see you and Alfred in a happy home, surrounded by bright-eyed children. There'll be a brave lad named fer me, and when I come, if I ever do, I'll tell him stories, and learn him the secrets of the woods, and how to shoot, and things I know so well."

"I am so wretched—so miserable. To think I have been so—so blind, and I have teased you—and—it might have been—only now it's too late," said Betty, between her sobs.

"Yes, I know, and it's better so. This man you love rings true. He has learnin' and edication. I have nothin' but muscle and a quick eye. And that'll serve you and Alfred when you are in danger. I'm goin' now. Stand here till I'm out of sight."

"Kiss me goodbye," whispered Betty.

The hunter bent his head and kissed her on the brow. Then he turned and with a rapid step went along the bluff toward the west. When he reached the laurel bushes which fringed the edge of the forest he looked back. He saw the slender gray clad figure standing motionless in the narrow path. He waved his hand and then turned and plunged into the forest. The dog looked back, raised his head and gave a long, mournful howl. Then, he too disappeared.

A mile west of the settlement Wetzel abandoned the forest and picked his way down the steep bluff to the river. Here he prepared to swim to the western shore. He took off his buckskin garments, spread them out on the ground, placed his knapsack in the middle, and rolling all into a small bundle tied it round his rifle. Grasping the rifle just above the hammer he waded into the water up to his waist and then, turning easily on his back he held the rifle straight up, allowing the butt to rest on his breast. This left his right arm unhampered. With a powerful back-arm stroke he rapidly swam the river, which was deep and narrow at this point. In a quarter of an hour he was once more in his dry suit.

He was now two miles below the island, where yesterday the Indians had been concealed, and where this morning Miller had crossed. Wetzel knew Miller expected to be trailed, and that he would use every art and cunning of woodcraft to elude his pursuers, or to lead them into a death-trap. Wetzel believed Miller had joined the Indians, who had undoubtedly been waiting for him, or for a signal from him, and that he would use them to ambush the trail.

Therefore Wetzel decided he would try to strike Miller's tracks far west of the river. He risked a great deal in attempting this because it was possible he might fail to find any trace of the spy. But Wetzel wasted not one second. His course was chosen. With all possible speed, which meant with him walking only when he could not run, he traveled northwest. If Miller had taken the direction Wetzel suspected, the trails of the two men would cross about ten miles from the Ohio. But the hunter had not traversed more than a mile of the forest when the dog put his nose high in the air and growled. Wetzel slowed down into a walk and moved cautiously onward, peering through the green aisles of the woods. A few rods farther on Tige uttered another growl and put his nose to the ground. He found a trail. On examination Wetzel discovered in the moss two moccasin tracks. Two Indians had passed that point that morning. They were going northwest directly toward the camp of Wingenund. Wetzel stuck close to the trail all that day and an hour before dusk he heard the sharp crack of a rifle. A moment afterward a doe came crashing through the thicket to Wetzel's right and bounding across a little brook she disappeared.

A tree with a bushy, leafy top had been uprooted by a storm and had fallen across the stream at this point. Wetzel crawled among the branches. The dog followed and lay down beside him. Before darkness set in Wetzel saw that the clear water of the brook had been roiled; therefore, he concluded that somewhere upstream Indians had waded into the brook. Probably they had killed a deer and were getting their evening meal.

Hours passed. Twilight deepened into darkness. One by one the stars appeared; then the crescent moon rose over the wooded hill in the west, and the hunter never moved. With his head leaning against the log he sat quiet and patient. At midnight he whispered to the dog, and crawling from his hiding place glided stealthily up the stream. Far ahead from the dark depths of the forest peeped the flickering light of a camp-fire. Wetzel consumed a half hour in approaching within one hundred feet of this light. Then he got down on his hands and knees and crawled behind a tree on top of the little ridge which had obstructed a view of the camp scene.

From this vantage point Wetzel saw a clear space surrounded by pines and hemlocks. In the center of this glade a fire burned briskly. Two Indians lay wrapped in their blankets, sound asleep. Wetzel pressed the dog close to the ground, laid aside his rifle, drew his tomahawk, and lying flat on his breast commenced to work his way, inch by inch, toward the sleeping savages. The tall ferns trembled as the hunter wormed his way among them, but there was no sound, not a snapping of a twig nor a rustling of a leaf. The nightwind sighed softly through the pines; it blew the bright sparks from the burning logs, and fanned the embers into a red glow; it swept caressingly over the sleeping savages, but it could not warn them that another wind, the Wind-of-Death, was near at hand.

A quarter of an hour elapsed. Nearer and nearer; slowly but surely drew the hunter. With what wonderful patience and self-control did this cold-blooded Nemesis approach his victims! Probably any other Indian slayer would have fired his rifle and then rushed to combat with a knife or a tomahawk. Not so Wetzel. He scorned to use powder. He crept forward like a snake gliding upon its prey. He slid one hand in front of him and pressed it down on the moss, at first gently, then firmly, and when he had secured a good hold he slowly dragged his body forward the length of his arm. At last his dark form rose and stood over the unconscious Indians, like a minister of Doom. The tomahawk flashed once, twice in the fire-light, and the Indians, without a moan, and with a convulsive quivering and straightening of their bodies, passed from the tired sleep of nature to the eternal sleep of death.

Foregoing his usual custom of taking the scalps, Wetzel hurriedly left the glade. He had found that the Indians were Shawnees and he had expected they were Delawares. He knew Miller's red comrades belonged to the latter tribe. The presence of Shawnees so near the settlement confirmed his belief that a concerted movement was to be made on the whites in the near future. He would not have been surprised to find the woods full of redskins. He spent the remainder of that night close under the side of a log with the dog curled up beside him.

Next morning Wetzel ran across the trail of a white man and six Indians. He tracked them all that day and half of the night before he again rested. By noon of the following day he came in sight of the cliff from which Jonathan Zane had watched the sufferings of Col. Crawford. Wetzel now made his favorite move, a wide detour, and came up on the other side of the encampment.

From the top of the bluff he saw down into the village of the Delawares. The valley was alive with Indians; they were working like beavers; some with weapons, some painting themselves, and others dancing war-dances. Packs were being strapped on the backs of ponies. Everywhere was the hurry and bustle of the preparation for war. The dancing and the singing were kept up half the night.

At daybreak Wetzel was at his post. A little after sunrise he heard a long yell which he believed announced the arrival of an important party. And so it turned out. Amid thrill yelling and whooping, the like of which Wetzel had never before heard, Simon Girty rode into Wingenund's camp at the head of one hundred Shawnee warriors and two hundred British Rangers from Detroit. Wetzel recoiled when he saw the red uniforms of the Britishers and their bayonets. Including Pipe's and Wingenund's braves the total force which was going to march against the Fort exceeded six hundred. An impotent frenzy possessed Wetzel as he watched the orderly marching of the Rangers and the proud bearing of the Indian warriors. Miller had spoken the truth. Ft. Henry vas doomed.

"Tige, there's one of them struttin' turkey cocks as won't see the Ohio," said Wetzel to the dog.

Hurriedly slipping from round his neck the bullet-pouch that Betty had given him, he shook out a bullet and with the point of his knife he scratched deep in the soft lead the letter W. Then he cut the bullet half through. This done he detached the pouch from the cord and running the cord through the cut in the bullet he bit the lead. He tied the string round the neck of the dog and pointing eastward he said: "Home."

The intelligent animal understood perfectly. His duty was to get that warning home. His clear brown eyes as much as said: "I will not fail." He wagged his tail, licked the hunter's hand, bounded away and disappeared in the forest.

Wetzel rested easier in mind. He knew the dog would stop for nothing, and that he stood a far better chance of reaching the Fort in safety than did he himself.

With a lurid light in his eyes Wetzel now turned to the Indians. He would never leave that spot without sending a leaden messenger into the heart of someone in that camp. Glancing on all sides he at length selected a place where it was possible he might approach near enough to the camp to get a shot. He carefully studied the lay of the ground, the trees, rocks, bushes, grass,—everything that could help screen him from the keen eye of savage scouts. When he had marked his course he commenced his perilous descent. In an hour he had reached the bottom of the cliff. Dropping flat on the ground, he once more started his snail-like crawl. A stretch of swampy ground, luxuriant with rushes and saw-grass, made a part of the way easy for him, though it led through mud, and slime, and stagnant water. Frogs and turtles warming their backs in the sunshine scampered in alarm from their logs. Lizards blinked at him. Moccasin snakes darted wicked forked tongues at him and then glided out of reach of his tomahawk. The frogs had stopped their deep bass notes. A swamp-blackbird rose in fright from her nest in the saw-grass, and twittering plaintively fluttered round and round over the pond. The flight of the bird worried Wetzel. Such little things as these might attract the attention of some Indian scout. But he hoped that in the excitement of the war preparations these unusual disturbances would escape notice. At last he gained the other side of the swamp. At the end of the corn-field before him was the clump of laurel which he had marked from the cliff as his objective point. The Indian corn was now about five feet high. Wetzel passed through this field unseen. He reached the laurel bushes, where he dropped to the ground and lay quiet a few minutes. In the dash which he would soon make to the forest he needed all his breath and all his fleetness. He looked to the right to see how far the woods was from where he lay. Not more than one hundred feet. He was safe. Once in the dark shade of those trees, and with his foes behind him, he could defy the whole race of Delawares. He looked to his rifle, freshened the powder in the pan, carefully adjusted the flint, and then rose quietly to his feet.

Wetzel's keen gaze, as he swept it from left to right, took in every detail of the camp. He was almost in the village. A tepee stood not twenty feet from his hiding-place. He could have tossed a stone in the midst of squaws, and braves, and chiefs. The main body of Indians was in the center of the camp. The British were lined up further on. Both Indians and soldiers were resting on their arms and waiting. Suddenly Wetzel started and his heart leaped. Under a maple tree not one hundred and fifty yards distant stood four men in earnest consultation. One was an Indian. Wetzel recognized the fierce, stern face, the haughty, erect figure. He knew that long, trailing war-bonnet. It could have adorned the head of but one chief—Wingenund, the sachem of the Delawares. A British officer, girdled and epauletted, stood next to Wingenund. Simon Girty, the renegade, and Miller, the traitor, completed the group.

Wetzel sank to his knees. The perspiration poured from his face. The mighty hunter trembled, but it was from eagerness. Was not Girty, the white savage, the bane of the poor settlers, within range of a weapon that never failed? Was not the murderous chieftain, who had once whipped and tortured him, who had burned Crawford alive, there in plain sight? Wetzel revelled a moment in fiendish glee. He passed his hands tenderly over the long barrel of his rifle. In that moment as never before he gloried in his power—a power which enabled him to put a bullet in the eye of a squirrel at the distance these men were from him. But only for an instant did the hunter yield to this feeling. He knew too well the value of time and opportunity.

He rose again to his feet and peered out from under the shading laurel branches. As he did so the dark face of Miller turned full toward him. A tremor, like the intense thrill of a tiger when he is about to spring, ran over Wetzel's frame. In his mad gladness at being within rifle-shot of his great Indian foe, Wetzel had forgotten the man he had trailed for two days. He had forgotten Miller. He had only one shot—and Betty was to be avenged. He gritted his teeth. The Delaware chief was as safe as though he were a thousand miles away. This opportunity for which Wetzel had waited so many years, and the successful issue of which would have gone so far toward the fulfillment of a life's purpose, was worse than useless. A great temptation assailed the hunter.

Wetzel's face was white when he raised the rifle; his dark eye, gleaming vengefully, ran along the barrel. The little bead on the front sight first covered the British officer, and then the broad breast of Girty. It moved reluctantly and searched out the heart of Wingenund, where it lingered for a fleeting instant. At last it rested upon the swarthy face of Miller.

"Fer Betty," muttered the hunter, between his clenched teeth as he pressed the trigger.

The spiteful report awoke a thousand echoes. When the shot broke the stillness Miller was talking and gesticulating. His hand dropped inertly; he stood upright for a second, his head slowly bowing and his body swaying perceptibly. Then he plunged forward like a log, his face striking the sand. He never moved again. He was dead even before he struck the ground.

Blank silence followed this tragic denouement. Wingenund, a cruel and relentless Indian, but never a traitor, pointed to the small bloody hole in the middle of Miller's forehead, and then nodded his head solemnly. The wondering Indians stood aghast. Then with loud yells the braves ran to the cornfield; they searched the laurel bushes. But they only discovered several moccasin prints in the sand, and a puff of white smoke wafting away upon the summer breeze.

CHAPTER 12

ALFRED CLARKE LAY BETWEEN LIFE AND DEATH. MILLER'S KNIFE-thrust, although it had made a deep and dangerous wound, had not pierced any vital part; the amount of blood lost made Alfred's condition precarious. Indeed, he would not have lived through that first day but for a wonderful vitality. Col. Zane's wife, to whom had been consigned the delicate task of dressing the wound, shook her head when she first saw the direction of the cut. She found on a closer examination that the knife-blade had been deflected by a rib, and had just missed the lungs. The wound was bathed, sewed up, and bandaged, and the greatest precaution taken to prevent the sufferer from loosening the linen. Every day when Mrs. Zane returned from the bedside of the young man she would be met at the door by Betty, who, in that time of suspense, had lost her bloom, and whose pale face showed the effects of sleepless nights.

"Betty, would you mind going over to the Fort and relieving Mrs. Martin an hour or two?" said Mrs. Zane one day as she came home, looking worn and weary. "We are both tired to death, and Nell Metzar was unable to come. Clarke is unconscious, and will not know you, besides he is sleeping now."

Betty hurried over to Capt. Boggs' cabin, next the blockhouse, where Alfred lay, and with a palpitating heart and a trepidation wholly out of keeping with the brave front she managed to assume, she knocked gently on the door.

"Ah, Betty, 'tis you, bless your heart," said a matronly little woman who opened the door. "Come right in. He is sleeping now, poor fellow, and it's the first real sleep he has had. He has been raving crazy forty-eight hours."

"Mrs. Martin, what shall I do?" whispered Betty.

"Oh, just watch him, my dear," answered the elder woman.

"If you need me send one of the lads up to the house for me. I shall return as soon as I can. Keep the flies away—they are bothersome—and bathe his head every little while. If he wakes and tries to sit up, as he does sometimes, hold him back. He is as weak as a cat. If he raves, soothe him by talking to him. I must go now, dearie."

Betty was left alone in the little room. Though she had taken a seat near the bed where Alfred lay, she had not dared to look at him. Presently conquering her emotion, Betty turned her gaze on the bed. Alfred was lying easily on his back, and notwithstanding the warmth of the day he was covered with a quilt. The light from the window shone on his face. How deathly white it was! There was not a vestige of color in it; the brow looked like chiseled marble; dark shadows underlined the eyes, and the whole face was expressive of weariness and pain.

There are times when a woman's love is all motherliness. All at once this man seemed to Betty like a helpless child. She felt her heart go out to the poor sufferer with a feeling before unknown. She forgot her pride and her fears and her disappointments. She remembered only that this strong man lay there at death's door because he had resented an insult to her. The past with all its bitterness rolled away and was lost, and in its place welled up a tide of forgiveness strong and sweet and hopeful. Her love, like a fire that had been choked and smothered, smouldering but never extinct, and which blazes up with the first breeze, warmed and quickened to life with the touch of her hand on his forehead.

An hour passed. Betty was now at her ease and happier than she had been for months. Her patient continued to sleep peacefully and dreamlessly. With a feeling of womanly curiosity Betty looked around the room. Over the rude mantelpiece were hung a sword, a brace of pistols, and two pictures. These last interested Betty very much. They were portraits; one of them was a likeness of a sweet-faced woman who Betty instinctively knew was his mother. Her eyes lingered tenderly on that face, so like the one lying on the pillow. The other portrait was of a beautiful girl whose dark, magnetic eyes challenged Betty. Was this his sister or—someone else? She could not restrain a jealous twinge, and she felt annoyed to find herself comparing that face with her own. She looked no longer at that portrait, but recommenced her survey of the room. Upon the door hung a broad-brimmed hat with eagle plumes stuck in the band. A pair of high-topped riding-boots, a saddle, and a bridle lay on the floor in the corner. The table was covered with Indian pipes, tobacco pouches, spurs, silk stocks, and other articles.

Suddenly Betty felt that some one was watching her. She turned timidly toward the bed and became much frightened when she encountered the intense gaze from a pair of steel-blue eyes. She almost fell from the chair; but presently she recollected that Alfred had been unconscious for days, and that he would not know who was watching by his bedside.

"Mother, is that you?" asked Alfred, in a weak, low voice.

"Yes, I am here," answered Betty, remembering the old woman's words about soothing the sufferer.

"But I thought you were ill."

"I was, but I am better now, and it is you who are ill."

"My head hurts so."

"Let me bathe it for you."

"How long have I been home?"

Betty bathed and cooled his heated brow. He caught and held her hands, looking wonderingly at her the while.

"Mother, somehow I thought you had died. I must have dreamed it. I am very happy; but tell me, did a message come for me to-day?"

Betty shook her head, for she could not speak. She saw he was living in the past, and he was praying for the letter which she would gladly have written had she but known.

"No message, and it is now so long."

"It will come to-morrow," whispered Betty.

"Now, mother, that is what you always say," said the invalid, as he began to toss his head wearily to and fro. "Will she never tell me? It is not like her to keep me in suspense. She was the sweetest, truest, loveliest girl in all the world. When I get well, mother, I ant going to find out if she loves me."

"I am sure she does. I know she loves you," answered Betty.

"It is very good of you to say that," he went on in his rambling talk. "Some day I'll bring her to you and we'll make her a queen here in the old home. I'll be a better son now and not run away from home again. I've given the dear old mother many a heartache, but that's all past now. The wanderer has come home. Kiss me good-night, mother."

Betty looked down with tear-blurred eyes on the haggard face. Unconsciously she had been running her fingers through the fair hair that lay so damp over his brow. Her pity and tenderness had carried her far beyond herself, and at the last words she bent her head and kissed him on the lips.

"Who are you? You are not my mother. She is dead," he cried, starting up wildly, and looking at her with brilliant eyes.

Betty dropped the fan and rose quickly to her feet. What had she done? A terrible thought had flashed into her mind. Suppose he were not delirious, and had been deceiving her. Oh! for a hiding-place, or that the floor would swallow her. Oh! if some one would only come.

Footsteps sounded on the stairs and Betty ran to the door. To her great relief Mrs. Martin was coming up.

"You can run home now, there's a dear," said the old lady. "We have several watchers for to-night. It will not be long now when he will commence to mend, or else he will die. Poor boy, please God that he gets well. Has he been good? Did he call for any particular young lady? Never fear, Betty, I'll keep the secret. He'll never know you were here unless you tell him yourself."

Meanwhile the days had been busy ones for Col. Zane. In anticipation of an attack from the Indians, the settlers had been fortifying their refuge and making the block-house as nearly impregnable as possible. Everything that was movable and was of value they put inside the stockade fence, out of reach of the destructive redskins. All the horses and cattle were driven into the inclosure. Wagon-loads of hay, grain and food were stored away in the block-house.

Never before had there been such excitement on the frontier. Runners from Ft. Pitt, Short Creek, and other settlements confirmed the rumor that all the towns along the Ohio were preparing for war. Not since the outbreak of the Revolution had there been so much confusion and alarm among the pioneers. To be sure, those on the very verge of the frontier, as at Ft. Henry, had heretofore little to fear from the British. During most of this time there had been comparative peace on the western border, excepting those occasional murders, raids, and massacres perpetrated by the different Indian tribes, and instigated no doubt by Girty and the British at Detroit. Now all kinds of rumors were afloat: Washington was defeated; a close alliance between England and the confederated western tribes had been formed; Girty had British power and wealth back of him. These and many more alarming reports travelled from settlement to settlement.

The death of Col. Crawford had been a terrible shock to the whole country. On the border spread an universal gloom, and the low, sullen mutterings of revengeful wrath. Crawford had been so prominent a man, so popular, and, except in his last and fatal expedition, such an efficient leader that his sudden taking off was almost a national calamity. In fact no one felt it more keenly than did Washington himself, for Crawford was his esteemed friend.

Col. Zane believed Ft. Henry had been marked by the British and the Indians. The last runner from Ft. Pitt had informed him that the description of Miller tallied with that of one of the ten men who had deserted from Ft. Pitt in 1778 with the tories Girth, McKee, and Elliott. Col. Zane was now satisfied that Miller was an agent of Girty and therefore of the British. So since all the weaknesses of the Fort, the number of the garrison, and the favorable conditions for a siege were known to Girty, there was nothing left for Col. Zane and his men but to make a brave stand.

Jonathan Zane and Major McColloch watched the river. Wetzel had disappeared as if the earth had swallowed him. Some pioneers said he would never return. But Col. Zane believed Wetzel would walk into the Fort, as he had done many times in the last ten years, with full information concerning the doings of the Indians. However, the days passed and nothing happened. Their work completed, the settlers waited for the first sign of an enemy. But as none came, gradually their fears were dispelled and they began to think the alarm had been a false one.

All this time Alfred Clarke was recovering his health and strength. The day came when he was able to leave his bed and sit by the window. How glad it made him feel to look out on the green woods and the broad, winding river; how sweet to his ears were the songs of the birds; how soothing was the drowsy hum of the bees in the fragrant honeysuckle by his window. His hold on life had been slight and life was good. He smiled in pitying derision as he remembered his recklessness. He had not been in love with life. In his gloomy moods he had often thought life was hardly worth the living. What sickly sentiment! He had been on the brink of the grave, but he had been snatched back from the dark river of Death. It needed but this to show him the joy of breathing, the glory of loving, the sweetness of living. He resolved that for him there would be no more drifting, no more purposelessness. If what Wetzel had told him was true, if he really had not loved in vain, then his cup of happiness was overflowing. Like a far-off and almost forgotten strain of music some memory struggled to take definite shape in his mind; but it was so hazy, so vague, so impalpable, that he could remember nothing clearly.

Isaac Zane and his Indian bride called on Alfred that afternoon.

"Alfred, I can't tell you how glad I am to see you up again," said Isaac, earnestly, as he wrung Alfred's hand. "Say, but it was a tight squeeze! It has been a bad time for you."

Nothing could have been more pleasing than Myeerah's shy yet eloquent greeting. She gave Alfred her little hand and said in her figurative style of speaking, "Myeerah is happy for you and for others. You are strong like the West Wind that never dies."

"Myeerah and I are going this afternoon, and we came over to say good-bye to you. We intend riding down the river fifteen miles and then crossing, to avoid running into any band of Indians."

"And how does Myeerah like the settlement by this time?"

"Oh, she is getting on famously. Betty and she have fallen in love with each other. It is amusing to hear Betty try to talk in the Wyandot tongue, and to see Myeerah's consternation when Betty gives her a lesson in deportment."

"I rather fancy it would be interesting, too. Are you not going back to the Wyandots at a dangerous time?"

"As to that I can't say. I believe, though, it is better that I get back to Tarhe's camp before we have any trouble with the Indians. I am anxious to get there before Girty or some of his agents."

"Well, if you must go, good luck to you, and may we meet again."

"It will not be long, I am sure. And, old man," he continued, with a bright smile, "when Myeerah and I come again to Ft. Henry we expect to find all well with you. Cheer up, and good-bye."

All the preparations had been made for the departure of Isaac and Myeerah to their far-off Indian home. They were to ride the Indian ponies on which they had arrived at the Fort. Col. Zane had given Isaac one of his pack horses. This animal carried blankets, clothing, and food which insured comparative comfort in the long ride through the wilderness.

"We will follow the old trail until we reach the hickory swale," Isaac was saying to the Colonel, "and then we will turn off and make for the river. Once across the Ohio we can make the trip in two days."

"I think you'll make it all right," said Col. Zane.

"Even if I do meet Indians I shall have no fear, for I have a protector here," answered Isaac as he led Myeerah's pony to the step.

"Good-bye, Myeerah; he is yours, but do not forget he is dear to us," said Betty, embracing and kissing the Indian girl.

"My sister does not know Myeerah. The White Eagle will return."

"Good-bye, Betts, don't cry. I shall come home again. And when I do I hope I shall be in time to celebrate another event, this time with you as the heroine. Good-bye. Goodbye."

The ponies cantered down the road. At the bend Isaac and Myeerah turned and waved their hands until the foliage of the trees hid them from view.

"Well, these things happen naturally enough. I suppose they must be. But I should much have preferred Isaac staying here. Hello! What the deuce is that? By Lord! It's Tige!"

The exclamation following Col. Zane's remarks had been called forth by Betty's dog. He came limping painfully up the road from the direction of the river. When he saw Col. Zane he whined and crawled to the Colonel's feet. The dog was wet and covered with burrs, and his beautiful glossy coat, which had been Betty's pride, was dripping with blood.

"Silas, Jonathan, come here," cried Col. Zane. "Here's Tige, back without Wetzel, and the poor dog has been shot almost to pieces. What does it mean?"

"Indians," said Jonathan, coming out of the house with Silas, and Mrs. Zane and Betty, who had heard the Colonel's call.

"He has come a long way. Look at his feet. They are torn and bruised," continued Jonathan. "And he has been near Wingenund's camp. You see that red clay on his paws. There is no red clay that I know of round here, and there are miles of it this side of the Delaware camp."

"What is the matter with Tige?" asked Betty.

"He is done for. Shot through, poor fellow. How did he ever reach home?" said Silas.

"Oh, I hope not! Dear old Tige," said Betty as she knelt and tenderly placed the head of the dog in her lap. "Why, what is this? I never put that there. Eb, Jack, look here. There is a string around his neck," and Betty pointed excitedly to a thin cord which was almost concealed in the thick curly hair.

"Good gracious! Eb, look! It is the string off the prize bullet pouch I made, and that Wetzel won on Isaac's wedding day. It is a message from Lew," said Betty.

"Well, by Heavens! This is strange. So it is. I remember that string. Cut it off, Jack," said Col. Zane.

When Jonathan had cut the string and held it up they all saw the lead bullet. Col. Zane examined it and showed them what had been rudely scratched on it.

"A letter W. Does that mean Wetzel?" asked the Colonel.

"It means war. It's a warning from Wetzel—not the slightest doubt of that," said Jonathan. "Wetzel sends this because he knows we are to be attacked, and because there must have been great doubt of his getting back to tell us. And Tige has been shot on his way home."

This called the attention to the dog, which had been momentarily forgotten. His head rolled from Betty's knee; a quiver shook his frame; he struggled to rise to his feet, but his strength was too far spent; he crawled close to Betty's feet; his eyes looked up at her with almost human affection; then they closed, and he lay still. Tige was dead.

"It is all over, Betty. Tige will romp no more. He will never be forgotten, for he was faithful to the end. Jonathan, tell the Major of Wetzel's warning, and both of you go back to your posts on the river. Silas, send Capt. Boggs to me."

An hour after the death of Tige the settlers were waiting for the ring of the meeting-house bell to summon them to the Fort.

Supper at Col. Zane's that night was not the occasion of good-humored jest and pleasant conversation. Mrs. Zane's face wore a distressed and troubled look; Betty was pale and quiet; even the Colonel was gloomy; and the children, missing the usual cheerfulness of the evening meal, shrank close to their mother.

Darkness slowly settled down; and with it came a feeling of relief, at least for the night, for the Indians rarely attacked the settlements after dark. Capt. Boggs came over and he and Col. Zane conversed in low tones.

"The first thing in the morning I want you to ride over to Short Creek for reinforcements. I'll send the Major also and by a different route. I expect to hear tonight from Wetzel. Twelve times has he crossed that threshold with the information which made an Indian surprise impossible. And I feel sure he will come again."

"What was that?" said Betty, who was sitting on the doorstep.

"Sh-h!" whispered Col. Zane, holding up his finger.

The night was warm and still. In the perfect quiet which followed the Colonel's whispered exclamation the listeners heard the beating of their hearts. Then from the river bank came the cry of an owl; low but clear it came floating to their ears, its single melancholy note thrilling them. Faint and far off in the direction of the island sounded the answer.

"I knew it. I told you. We shall know all presently," said Col. Zane. "The first call was Jonathan's, and it was answered."

The moments dragged away. The children had fallen asleep on the bearskin rug. Mrs. Zane and Betty had heard the Colonel's voice, and sat with white faces, waiting, waiting for they knew not what.

A familiar, light-moccasined tread sounded on the path, a tall figure loomed up from the darkness; it came up the path, passed up the steps, and crossed the threshold.

"Wetzel!" exclaimed Col. Zane and Capt. Boggs. It was indeed the hunter. How startling was his appearance! The buckskin hunting coat and leggins were wet, torn and bespattered with mud; the water ran and dripped from him to form little muddy pools on the floor; only his rifle and powder horn were dry. His face was ghastly white except where a bullet wound appeared on his temple, from which the blood had oozed down over his cheek. An unearthly light gleamed from his eyes. In that moment Wetzel was an appalling sight.

"Col. Zane, I'd been here days before, but I run into some Shawnees, and they gave me a hard chase. I have to report that Girty, with four hundred Injuns and two hundred Britishers, are on the way to Ft. Henry."

"My God!" exclaimed Col. Zane. Strong man as he was the hunter's words had unnerved him.

The loud and clear tone of the church-bell rang out on the still night air. Only once it sounded, but it reverberated among the hills, and its single deep-toned ring was like a knell. The listeners almost expected to hear it followed by the fearful war-cry, that cry which betokened for many desolation and death.

CHAPTER 13

MORNING FOUND THE SETTLERS, WITH THE EXCEPTION OF COL. ZANE, his brother Jonathan, the negro Sam, and Martin Wetzel, all within the Fort. Col. Zane had determined, long before, that in the event of another siege, he would use his house as an outpost. Twice it had been destroyed by fire at the hands of the Indians. Therefore, surrounding himself by these men, who were all expert marksmen, Col. Zane resolved to protect his property and at the same time render valuable aid to the Fort.

Early that morning a pirogue loaded with cannon balls, from Ft. Pitt and bound for Louisville, had arrived and Captain Sullivan, with his crew of three men, had demanded admittance. In the absence of Capt. Boggs and Major McColloch, both of whom had been dispatched for reinforcements, Col. Zane had placed his brother Silas in command of the Fort. Sullivan informed Silas that he and his men had been fired on by Indians and that they sought the protection of the Fort. The services of himself and men, which he volunteered, were gratefully accepted.

All told, the little force in the block-house did not exceed forty-two, and that counting the boys and the women who could handle rifles. The few preparations had been completed and now the settlers were awaiting the appearance of the enemy. Few words were spoken. The children were secured where they would be out of the way of flying bullets. They were huddled together silent and frightened; pale-faced but resolute women passed up and down the length of the block-house; some carried buckets of water and baskets of food; others were tearing bandages; grim-faced men peered from the portholes; all were listening for the war-cry.

They had not long to wait. Before noon the well-known whoop came from the wooded shore of the river, and it was soon followed by the appearance of hundreds of Indians. The river, which was low, at once became a scene of great animation. From a placid, smoothly flowing stream it was turned into a muddy, splashing, turbulent torrent. The mounted warriors urged their steeds down the bank and into the water; the unmounted improvised rafts and placed their weapons and ammunition upon them; then they swam and pushed, kicked and yelled their way across; other Indians swam, holding the bridles of the pack-horses. A detachment of British soldiers followed the Indians. In an hour the entire army appeared on the river bluff not three hundred yards from the Fort. They were in no hurry to begin the attack. Especially did the Indians seem to enjoy the lull before the storm, and as they stalked to and fro in plain sight of the garrison, or stood in groups watching the Fort, they were seen in all their hideous war-paint and formidable battle-array. They were exultant. Their plumes and eagle feathers waved proudly in the morning breeze. Now and then the long, peculiarly broken yell of the Shawnees rang out clear and strong. The soldiers were drawn off to one side and well out of range of the settlers' guns. Their red coats and flashing bayonets were new to most of the little band of men in the blockhouse.

"Ho, the Fort!"

It was a strong, authoritative voice and came from a man mounted on a black horse.

"Well, Girty, what is it?" shouted Silas Zane.

"We demand unconditional surrender," was the answer.

"You will never get it," replied Silas.

"Take more time to think it over. You see we have a force here large enough to take the Fort in an hour."

"That remains to be seen," shouted some one through porthole.

An hour passed. The soldiers and the Indians lounged around on the grass and walked to and fro on the bluff. At intervals a taunting Indian yell, horrible in its suggestiveness came floating on the air. When the hour was up three mounted men rode out in advance of the waiting Indians. One was clad in buckskin, another in the uniform of a British officer, and the third was an Indian chief whose powerful form was naked except for his buckskin belt and legging.

"Will you surrender?" came in the harsh and arrogant voice of the renegade.

"Never! Go back to your squaws!" yelled Sullivan.

"I am Capt. Pratt of the Queen's Rangers. If you surrender I will give you the best protection King George affords," shouted the officer.

"To hell with lying George! Go back to your hair-buying Hamilton and tell him the whole British army could not make us surrender," roared Hugh Bennet.

"If you do not give up, the Fort will be attacked and burned. Your men will be massacred and your women given to the Indians," said Girty.

"You will never take a man, woman or child alive," yelled Silas. "We remember Crawford, you white traitor, and we are not going to give up to be butchered. Come on with your red-jackets and your red-devils. We are ready."

"We have captured and killed the messenger you sent out, and now all hope of succor must be abandoned. Your doom is sealed."

"What kind of a man was he?" shouted Sullivan.

"A fine, active young fellow," answered the outlaw.

"That's a lie," snapped Sullivan, "he was an old, gray haired man."

As the officer and the outlaw chief turned, apparently to consult their companion, a small puff of white smoke shot forth from one of the portholes of the block-house. It was followed by the ringing report of a rifle. The Indian chief clutched wildly at his breast, fell forward on his horse, and after vainly trying to keep his seat, slipped to the ground. He raised himself once, then fell backward and lay still. Full two hundred yards was not proof against Wetzel's deadly smallbore, and Red Fox, the foremost war chieftain of the Shawnees, lay dead, a victim to the hunter's vengeance. It was characteristic of Wetzel that he picked the chief, for he could have shot either the British officer or the renegade. They retreated out of range, leaving the body of the chief where it had fallen, while the horse, giving a frightened snort, galloped toward the woods. Wetzel's yell coming quickly after his shot, excited the Indians to a very frenzy, and they started on a run for the Fort, discharging their rifles and screeching like so many demons.

In the cloud of smoke which at once enveloped the scene the Indians spread out and surrounded the Fort. A tremendous rush by a large party of Indians was made for the gate of the Fort. They attacked it fiercely with their tomahawks, and a log which they used as a battering-ram. But the stout gate withstood their united efforts, and the galling fire from the portholes soon forced them to fall back and seek cover behind the trees and the rocks. From these points of vantage they kept up an uninterrupted fire.

The soldiers had made a dash at the stockade-fence, yelling derision at the small French cannon which was mounted on top of the block-house. They thought it a "dummy" because they had learned that in the 1777 siege the garrison had no real cannon, but had tried to utilize a wooden one. They yelled and hooted and mocked at this piece and dared the garrison to fire it. Sullivan, who was in charge of the cannon, bided his time. When the soldiers were massed closely together and making another rush for the stockade-fence Sullivan turned loose the little "bulldog," spreading consternation and destruction in the British ranks.

"Stand back! Stand back!" Capt. Pratt was heard to yell. "By God! there's no wood about that gun."

After this the besiegers withdrew for a breathing spell. At this early stage of the siege the Indians were seen to board Sullivan's pirogue, and it was soon discovered they were carrying the cannon balls from the boat to the top of the bluff. In their simple minds they had conceived a happy thought. They procured a white-oak log probably a foot in diameter, split it through the middle and hollowed out the inside with their tomahawks. Then with iron chains and bars, which they took from Reihart's black-smith shop, they bound and securely fastened the sides together. They dragged the improvised cannon nearer to the Fort, placed it on two logs and weighted it down with stones. A heavy charge of powder and ball was then rammed into the wooden gun. The soldiers, though much interested in the manoeuvre, moved back to a safe distance, while many of the Indians crowded round the new weapon. The torch was applied; there was a red flash—boom! The hillside was shaken by the tremendous explosion, and when the smoke lifted from the scene the naked forms of the Indians could be seen writhing in agony on the ground. Not a vestige of the wooden gun remained. The iron chains had proved terrible death-dealing missiles to the Indians near the gun. The Indians now took to their natural methods of warfare. They hid in the long grass, in the deserted cabins, behind the trees and up in the branches. Not an Indian was visible, but the rain of bullets pattered steadily against the block-house. Every bush and every tree spouted little puffs of white smoke, and the leaden messengers of Death whistled through the air.

After another unsuccessful effort to destroy a section of the stockade-fence the soldiers had retired. Their red jackets made them a conspicuous mark for the sharp-eyed settlers. Capt. Pratt had been shot through the thigh. He suffered great pain, and was deeply chagrined by the surprising and formidable defense of the garrison which he had been led to believe would fall an easy prey to the King's soldiers. He had lost one-third of his men. Those who were left refused to run straight in the face of certain death. They had not been drilled to fight an unseen enemy. Capt. Pratt was compelled to order a retreat to the river bluff, where he conferred with Girty.

Inside the block-house was great activity, but no confusion. That little band of fighters might have been drilled for a king's bodyguard. Kneeling before each porthole on the river side of the Fort was a man who would fight while there was breath left in him. He did not discharge his weapon aimlessly as the Indians did, but waited until he saw the outline of an Indian form, or a red coat, or a puff of white smoke; then he would thrust the rifle-barrel forward, take a quick aim and fire. By the side of every man stood a heroic woman whose face was blanched, but who spoke never a word as she put the muzzle of the hot rifle into a bucket of water, cooled the barrel, wiped it dry and passed it back to the man beside her.

Silas Zane had been wounded at the first fire. A glancing ball had struck him on the head, inflicting a painful scalp wound. It was now being dressed by Col. Zane's wife, whose skilled fingers were already tired with the washing and the bandaging of the injuries received by the defenders. In all that horrible din of battle, the shrill yells of the savages, the hoarse shouts of the settlers, the boom of the cannon overhead, the cracking of rifles and the whistling of bullets; in all that din of appalling noise, and amid the stifling smoke, the smell of burned powder, the sickening sight of the desperately wounded and the already dead, the Colonel's brave wife had never faltered. She was here and there; binding the wounds, helping Lydia and Betty mould bullets, encouraging the men, and by her example, enabling those women to whom border war was new to bear up under the awful strain.

Sullivan, who had been on top of the block-house, came down the ladder almost without touching it. Blood was running down his bare arm and dripping from the ends of his fingers.

"Zane, Martin has been shot," he said hoarsely. "The same Indian who shot away these fingers did it. The bullets seem to come from some elevation. Send some scout up there and find out where that damned Indian is hiding."

"Martin shot? God, his poor wife! Is he dead?" said Silas.

"Not yet. Bennet is bringing him down. Here, I want this hand tied up, so that my gun won't be so slippery."

Wetzel was seen stalking from one porthole to another. His fearful yell sounded above all the others. He seemed to bear a charmed life, for not a bullet had so much as scratched him. Silas communicated to him what Sullivan had said. The hunter mounted the ladder and went up on the roof. Soon he reappeared, descended into the room and ran into the west end of the block-house. He kneeled before a porthole through which he pushed the long black barrel of his rifle. Silas and Sullivan followed him and looked in the direction indicated by his weapon. It pointed toward the bushy top of a tall poplar tree which stood on the hill west of the Fort. Presently a little cloud of white smoke issued from the leafy branches, and it was no sooner seen than Wetzel's rifle was discharged. There was a great commotion among the leaves, the branches swayed and thrashed, and then a dark body plunged downward to strike on the rocky slope of the bluff and roll swiftly out of sight. The hunter's unnatural yell pealed out.

"Great God! The man's crazy," cried Sullivan, staring at Wetzel's demon-like face.

"No, no. It's his way," answered Silas.

At that moment the huge frame of Bennet filled up the opening in the roof and started down the ladder. In one arm he carried the limp body of a young man. When he reached the floor he laid the body down and beckoned to Mrs. Zane. Those watching saw that the young man was Will Martin, and that he was still alive. But it was evident that he had not long to live. His face had a leaden hue and his eyes were bright and glassy. Alice, his wife, flung herself on her knees beside him and tenderly raised the drooping head. No words could express the agony in her face as she raised it to Mrs. Zane. In it was a mute appeal, an unutterable prayer for hope. Mrs. Zane turned sorrowfully to her task. There was no need of her skill here. Alfred Clarke, who had been ordered to take Martin's place on top of the block-house, paused a moment in silent sympathy. When he saw that little hole in the bared chest, from which the blood welled up in an awful stream, he shuddered and passed on. Betty looked up from her work and then turned away sick and faint. Her mute lips moved as if in prayer.

Alice was left alone with her dying husband. She tenderly supported his head on her bosom, leaned her face against his and kissed the cold, numb lips. She murmured into his already deaf ear the old tender names. He knew her, for he made a feeble effort to pass his arm round her neck. A smile illumined his face. Then death claimed him. With wild, distended eyes and with hands pressed tightly to her temples Alice rose slowly to her feet.

"Oh, God! Oh, God!" she cried.

Her prayer was answered. In a momentary lull in the battle was heard the deadly hiss of a bullet as it sped through one of the portholes. It ended with a slight sickening spat as the lead struck the flesh. Then Alice, without a cry, fell on the husband's breast. Silas Zane found her lying dead with the body of her husband clasped closely in her arms. He threw a blanket over them and went on his wearying round of the bastions.

THE BESIEGERS HAD BEEN GREATLY HARASSED AND HAMPERED BY THE continual fire from Col. Zane's house. It was exceedingly difficult for the Indians, and impossible for the British, to approach near enough to the Colonel's house to get an effective shot. Col. Zane and his men had the advantage of being on higher ground. Also they had four rifles to a man, and they used every spare moment for reloading. Thus they were enabled to pour a deadly fire into the ranks of the enemy, and to give the impression of being much stronger in force than they really were.

About dusk the firing ceased and the Indians repaired to the river bluff. Shortly afterward their camp-fires were extinguished and all became dark and quiet. Two hours passed. Fortunately the clouds, which had at first obscured the moon, cleared away somewhat and enough light was shed on the scene to enable the watchers to discern objects near by.

Col. Zane had just called together his men for a conference. He suspected some cunning deviltry on part of the Indians.

"Sam, take what stuff to eat you can lay your hands on and go up to the loft. Keep a sharp lookout and report anything to Jonathan or me," said the Colonel.

All afternoon Jonathan Zane had loaded and fired his rifles in sullen and dogged determination. He had burst one rifle and disabled another. The other men were fine marksmen, but it was undoubtedly Jonathan's unerring aim that made the house so unapproachable. He used an extremely heavy, large bore rifle. In the hands of a man strong enough to stand its fierce recoil it was a veritable cannon. The Indians had soon learned to respect the range of that rifle, and they gave the cabin a wide berth.

But now that darkness had enveloped the valley the advantage lay with the savages. Col. Zane glanced apprehensively at the blackened face of his brother.

"Do you think the Fort can hold out?" he asked in a husky voice. He was a bold man, but he thought now of his wife and children.

"I don't know," answered Jonathan. "I saw that big Shawnee chief today. His name is Fire. He is well named. He is a fiend. Girty has a picked band."

"The Fort has held out surprisingly well against such combined and fierce attacks. The Indians are desperate. You can easily see that in the way in which they almost threw their lives away. The green square is covered with dead Indians."

"If help does not come in twenty-four hours not one man will escape alive. Even Wetzel could not break through that line of Indians. But if we can hold the Indians off a day longer they will get tired and discouraged. Girty will not be able to hold them much longer. The British don't count. It's not their kind of war. They can't shoot, and so far as I can see they haven't done much damage."

"To your posts, men, and every man think of the women and children in the block-house."

For a long time, which seemed hours to the waiting and watching settlers, not a sound could be heard, nor any sign of the enemy seen. Thin clouds had again drifted over the moon, allowing only a pale, wan light to shine down on the valley. Time dragged on and the clouds grew thicker and denser until the moon and the stars were totally obscured. Still no sign or sound of the savages.

"What was that?" suddenly whispered Col. Zane.

"It was a low whistle from Sam. We'd better go up," said Jonathan.

They went up the stairs to the second floor from which they ascended to the loft by means of a ladder. The loft was as black as pitch. In that Egyptian darkness it was no use to look for anything, so they crawled on their hands and knees over the piles of hides and leather which lay on the floor. When they reached the small window they made out the form of the negro.

"What is it, Sam?" whispered Jonathan.

"Look, see thar, Massa Zane," came the answer in a hoarse whisper from the negro and at the same time he pointed down toward the ground.

Col. Zane put his head alongside Jonathan's and all three men peered out into the darkness.

"Jack, can you see anything?" said Col. Zane.

"No, but wait a minute until the moon throws a light."

A breeze had sprung up. The clouds were passing rapidly over the moon, and at long intervals a rift between the clouds let enough light through to brighten the square for an instant.

"Now, Massa Zane, thar!" exclaimed the slave.

"I can't see a thing. Can you, Jack?"

"I am not sure yet. I can see something, but whether it is a log or not I don't know."

Just then there was a faint light like the brightening of a firefly, or like the blowing of a tiny spark from a stick of burning wood. Jonathan uttered a low curse.

"D—n 'em! At their old tricks with fire. I thought all this quiet meant something. The grass out there is full of Indians, and they are carrying lighted arrows under them so as to cover the light. But we'll fool the red devils this time"

"I can see 'em, Massa Zane."

"Sh-h-h! no more talk," whispered Col. Zane.

The men waited with cocked rifles. Another spark rose seemingly out of the earth. This time it was nearer the house. No sooner had its feeble light disappeared than the report of the negro's rifle awoke the sleeping echoes. It was succeeded by a yell which seemed to come from under the window. Several dark forms rose so suddenly that they appeared to spring out of the ground. Then came the peculiar twang of Indian bows. There were showers of sparks and little streaks of fire with long tails like comets winged their parabolic flight toward the cabin. Falling short they hissed and sputtered in the grass. Jonathan's rifle spoke and one of the fleeing forms tumbled to the earth. A series of long yells from all around the Fort greeted this last shot, but not an Indian fired a rifle.

Fire-tipped arrows were now shot at the block-house, but not one took effect, although a few struck the stockade-fence. Col. Zane had taken the precaution to have the high grass and the clusters of goldenrod cut down all round the Fort. The wisdom of this course now became evident, for the wily savages could not crawl near enough to send their fiery arrows on the roof of the block-house. This attempt failing, the Indians drew back to hatch up some other plot to burn the Fort.

"Look!" suddenly exclaimed Jonathan.

Far down the road, perhaps five hundred yards from the Fort, a point of light had appeared. At first it was still, and then it took an odd jerky motion, to this side and to that, up and down like a jack-o-lantern.

"What the hell?" muttered Col. Zane, sorely puzzled. "Jack, by all that's strange it's getting bigger."

Sure enough the spark of fire, or whatever it was, grew larger and larger. Col. Zane thought it might be a light carried by a man on horseback. But if this were true where was the clatter of the horse's hoofs? On that rocky blur no horse could run noiselessly. It could not be a horse. Fascinated and troubled by this new mystery which seemed to presage evil to them the watchers waited with that patience known only to those accustomed to danger. They knew that whatever it was, it was some satanic stratagem of the savages, and that it would come all too soon.

The light was now zigzagging back and forth across the road, and approaching the Fort with marvelous rapidity. Now its motion was like the wide swinging of a lighted lantern on a dark night. A moment more of breathless suspense and the lithe form of an Indian brave could be seen behind the light. He was running with almost incredible swiftness down the road in the direction of the Fort. Passing at full speed within seventy-five yards of the stockade-fence the Indian shot his arrow. Like a fiery serpent flying through the air the missile sped onward in its graceful flight, going clear over the block-house, and striking with a spiteful thud the roof of one of the cabins beyond. Unhurt by the volley that was fired at him, the daring brave passed swiftly out of sight.

Deeds like this were dear to the hearts of the savages. They were deeds which made a warrior of a brave, and for which honor any Indian would risk his life over and over again. The exultant yells which greeted this performance proclaimed its success.

The breeze had already fanned the smouldering arrow into a blaze and the dry roof of the cabin had caught fire and was burning fiercely.

"That infernal redskin is going to do that again," ejaculated Jonathan.

It was indeed true. That same small bright light could be seen coming down the road gathering headway with every second. No doubt the same Indian, emboldened by his success, and maddened with that thirst for glory so often fatal to his kind, was again making the effort to fire the block-house.

The eyes of Col. Zane and his companions were fastened on the light as it came nearer and nearer with its changing motion. The burning cabin brightened the square before the Fort. The slender, shadowy figure of the Indian could be plainly seen emerging from the gloom. So swiftly did he run that he seemed to have wings. Now he was in the full glare of the light. What a magnificent nerve, what a terrible assurance there was in his action! It seemed to paralyze all. The red arrow emitted a shower of sparks as it was discharged. This time it winged its way straight and true and imbedded itself in the roof of the block-house.

Almost at the same instant a solitary rifle shot rang out and the daring warrior plunged headlong, sliding face downward in the dust of the road, while from the Fort came that demoniac yell now grown so familiar.

"Wetzel's compliments," muttered Jonathan. "But the mischief is done. Look at that damned burning arrow. If it doesn't blow out the Fort will go."

The arrow was visible, but it seemed a mere spark. It alternately paled and glowed. One moment it almost went out, and the next it gleamed brightly. To the men, compelled to look on and powerless to prevent the burning of the now apparently doomed block-house, that spark was like the eye of Hell.

"Ho, the Fort," yelled Col. Zane with all the power of his strong lungs. "Ho, Silas, the roof is on fire!"

Pandemonium had now broken out among the Indians. They could be plainly seen in the red glare thrown by the burning cabin. It had been a very dry season, the rough shingles were like tinder, and the inflammable material burst quickly into great flames, lighting up the valley as far as the edge of the forest. It was an awe-inspiring and a horrible spectacle. Columns of yellow and black smoke rolled heavenward; every object seemed dyed a deep crimson; the trees assumed fantastic shapes; the river veiled itself under a red glow. Above the roaring and crackling of the flames rose the inhuman yelling of the savages. Like demons of the inferno they ran to and fro, their naked painted bodies shining in the glare. One group of savages formed a circle and danced hands-around a stump as gayly as a band of school-girls at a May party. They wrestled with and hugged one another; they hopped, skipped and jumped, and in every possible way manifested their fiendish joy.

The British took no part in this revelry. To their credit it must be said they kept in the background as though ashamed of this horrible fire-war on people of their own blood.

"Why don't they fire the cannon?" impatiently said Col. Zane. "Why don't they do something?"

"Perhaps it is disabled, or maybe they are short of ammunition," suggested Jonathan.

"The block-house will burn down before our eyes. Look! The hell-hounds have set fire to the fence. I see men running and throwing water."

"I see something on the roof of the block-house," cried Jonathan. "There, down towards the east end of the roof and in the shadow of the chimney. And as I'm a living sinner it's a man crawling towards that blazing arrow. The Indians have not discovered him yet. He is still in the shadow. But they'll see him. God! What a nervy thing to do in the face of all those redskins. It is almost certain death!"

"Yes, and they see him," said the Colonel.

With shrill yells the Indians bounded forward and aimed and fired their rifles at the crouching figure of the man. Some hid behind the logs they had rolled toward the Fort; others boldly faced the steady fire now pouring from the portholes. The savages saw in the movement of that man an attempt to defeat their long-cherished hope of burning the Fort. Seeing he was discovered, the man did not hesitate, nor did he lose a second. Swiftly he jumped and ran toward the end of the roof where the burning arrow, now surrounded by blazing shingles, was sticking in the roof. How he ever ran along that slanting roof and with a pail in his hand was incomprehensible. In moments like that men become superhuman. It all happened in an instant. He reached the arrow, kicked it over the wall, and then dashed the bucket of water on the blazing shingles. In that single instant, wherein his tall form was outlined against the bright light behind him, he presented the fairest kind of a mark for the Indians. Scores of rifles were levelled and discharged at him. The bullets pattered like hail on the roof of the block-house, but apparently none found their mark, for the man ran back and disappeared.

"It was Clarke!" exclaimed Col. Zane. "No one but Clarke has such light hair. Wasn't that a plucky thing?"

"It has saved the block-house for to-night," answered Jonathan. "See, the Indians are falling back. They can't stand in the face of that shooting. Hurrah! Look at them fall! It could not have happened better. The light from the cabin will prevent any more close attacks for an hour and daylight is near."

CHAPTER 14

THE SUN ROSE RED. ITS RUDDY RAYS PEEPED OVER THE EASTERN HILLS, kissed the tree-tops, glinted along the stony bluffs, and chased away the gloom of night from the valley. Its warm gleams penetrated the portholes of the Fort and cast long bright shadows on the walls; but it brought little cheer to the sleepless and almost exhausted defenders. It brought to many of the settlers the familiar old sailor's maxim: "Redness 'a the morning, sailor's warning." Rising in its crimson glory the sun flooded the valley, dyeing the river, the leaves, the grass, the stones, tingeing everything with that awful color which stained the stairs, the benches, the floor, even the portholes of the block-house.

Historians call this the time that tried men's souls. If it tried the men think what it must have been to those grand, heroic women. Though they had helped the men load and fire nearly forty-eight hours; though they had worked without a moment's rest and were now ready to succumb to exhaustion; though the long room was full of stifling smoke and the sickening odor of burned wood and powder, and though the row of silent, covered bodies had steadily lengthened, the thought of giving up never occurred to the women. Death there would be sweet compared to what it would be at the hands of the redmen.

At sunrise Silas Zane, bare-chested, his face dark and fierce, strode into the bastion which was connected with the blockhouse. It was a small shedlike room, and with portholes opening to the river and the forest.

This bastion had seen the severest fighting. Five men had been killed here. As Silas entered four haggard and powder-begrimed men, who were kneeling before the portholes, looked up at him. A dead man lay in one corner.

"Smith's dead. That makes fifteen," said Silas. "Fifteen out of forty-two, that leaves twenty-seven. We must hold out. Len, don't expose yourselves recklessly. How goes it at the south bastion?"

"All right. There's been firin' over there all night," answered one of the men. "I guess it's been kinder warm over that way. But I ain't heard any shootin' for some time."

"Young Bennet is over there, and if the men needed anything they would send him for it," answered Silas. "I'll send some food and water. Anything else?"

"Powder. We're nigh out of powder," replied the man addressed. "And we might jes as well make ready fer a high old time. The red devils hadn't been quiet all this last hour fer nothin'."

Silas passed along the narrow hallway which led from the bastion into the main room of the block-house. As he turned the corner at the head of the stairway he encountered a boy who was dragging himself up the steps.

"Hello! Who's this? Why, Harry!" exclaimed Silas, grasping the boy and drawing him into the room. Once in the light Silas saw that the lad was so weak he could hardly stand. He was covered with blood. It dripped from a bandage wound tightly about his arm; it oozed through a hole in his hunting shirt, and it flowed from a wound over his temple. The shadow of death was already stealing over the pallid face, but from the grey eyes shone an indomitable spirit, a spirit which nothing but death could quench.

"Quick!" the lad panted. "Send men to the south wall. The redskins are breakin' in where the water from the spring runs under the fence."

"Where are Metzar and the other men?"

"Dead! Killed last night. I've been there alone all night. I kept on shootin'. Then I gets plugged here under the chin. Knowin' it's all up with me I deserted my post when I heard the Injuns choppin' on the fence where it was on fire last night. But I only—run—because—they're gettin' in."

"Wetzel, Bennet, Clarke!" yelled Silas, as he laid the boy on the bench.

Almost as Silas spoke the tall form of the hunter confronted him. Clarke and the other men were almost as prompt.

"Wetzel, run to the south wall. The Indians are cutting a hole through the fence."

Wetzel turned, grabbed his rifle and an axe and was gone like a flash.

"Sullivan, you handle the men here. Bessie, do what you can for this brave lad. Come, Bennet, Clarke, we must follow Wetzel," commanded Silas.

Mrs. Zane hastened to the side of the fainting lad. She washed away the blood from the wound over his temple. She saw that a bullet had glanced on the bone and that the wound was not deep or dangerous. She unlaced the hunting shirt at the neck and pulled the flaps apart. There on the right breast, on a line with the apex of the lung, was a horrible gaping wound. A murderous British slug had passed through the lad. From the hole at every heart-beat poured the dark, crimson life-tide. Mrs. Zane turned her white face away for a second; then she folded a small piece of linen, pressed it tightly over the wound, and wrapped a towel round the lad's breast.

"Don't waste time on me. It's all over," he whispered. "Will you call Betty here a minute?"

Betty came, white-faced and horror-stricken. For forty hours she had been living in a maze of terror. Her movements had almost become mechanical. She had almost ceased to hear and feel. But the light in the eyes of this dying boy brought her back to the horrible reality of the present.

"Oh, Harry! Harry! Harry!" was all Betty could whisper.

"I'm goin', Betty. And I wanted—you to say a little prayer for me—and say good-bye to me," he panted.

Betty knelt by the bench and tried to pray.

"I hated to run, Betty, but I waited and waited and nobody came, and the Injuns was getting' in. They'll find dead Injuns in piles out there. I was shootin' fer you, Betty, and every time I aimed I thought of you."

The lad rambled on, his voice growing weaker and weaker and finally ceasing. The hand which had clasped Betty's so closely loosened its hold. His eyes closed. Betty thought he was dead, but no! he still breathed. Suddenly his eyes opened. The shadow of pain was gone. In its place shone a beautiful radiance.

"Betty, I've cared a lot for you—and I'm dyin'—happy because I've fought fer you—and somethin' tells me—you'll—be saved. Good-bye." A smile transformed his face and his gray eyes gazed steadily into hers. Then his head fell back. With a sigh his brave spirit fled.

Hugh Bennet looked once at the pale face of his son, then he ran down the stairs after Silas and Clarke. When the three men emerged from behind Capt. Boggs' cabin, which was adjacent to the block-house, and which hid the south wall from their view, they were two hundred feet from Wetzel. They heard the heavy thump of a log being rammed against the fence; then a splitting and splintering of one of the six-inch oak planks. Another and another smashing blow and the lower half of one of the planks fell inwards, leaving an aperture large enough to admit an Indian. The men dashed forward to the assistance of Wetzel, who stood by the hole with upraised axe. At the same moment a shot rang out. Bennet stumbled and fell headlong. An Indian had shot through the hole in the fence. Silas and Alfred sheered off toward the fence, out of line. When within twenty yards of Wetzel they saw a swarthy-faced and athletic savage squeeze through the narrow crevice. He had not straightened up before the axe, wielded by the giant hunter, descended on his head, cracking his skull as if it were an eggshell. The savage sank to the earth without even a moan. Another savage naked and powerful, slipped in. He had to stoop to get through. He raised himself, and seeing Wetzel, he tried to dodge the lightning sweep of the axe. It missed his head, at which it had been aimed, but struck just over the shoulders, and buried itself in flesh and bone. The Indian uttered an agonizing yell which ended in a choking, gurgling sound as the blood spurted from his throat. Wetzel pulled the weapon from the body of his victim, and with the same motion he swung it around. This time the blunt end met the next Indian's head with a thud like that made by the butcher when he strikes the bullock to the ground. The Indian's rifle dropped, his tomahawk flew into the air, while his body rolled down the little embankment into the spring. Another and another Indian met the same fate. Then two Indians endeavored to get through the aperture. The awful axe swung by those steel arms, dispatched both of than in the twinkling of an eye. Their bodies stuck in the hole.

Silas and Alfred stood riveted to the spot. Just then Wetzel in all his horrible glory was a sight to freeze the marrow of any man. He had cast aside his hunting shirt in that run to the fence and was now stripped to the waist. He was covered with blood. The muscles of his broad back and his brawny arms swelled and rippled under the brown skin. At every swing of the gory axe he let out a yell the like of which had never before been heard by the white men. It was the hunter's mad yell of revenge. In his thirst for vengeance he had forgotten that he was defending the

Fort with its women and its children; he was fighting because he loved to kill.

Silas Zane heard the increasing clamor outside and knew that hundreds of Indians were being drawn to the spot. Something must be done at once. He looked around and his eyes fell on a pile of white-oak logs that had been hauled inside the Fort. They had been placed there by Col. Zane, with wise forethought. Silas grabbed Clarke and pulled him toward the pile of logs, at the same time communicating his plan. Together they carried a log to the fence and dropped it in front of the hole. Wetzel immediately stepped on it and took a vicious swing at an Indian who was trying to poke his rifle sideways through the hole. This Indian had discharged his weapon twice. While Wetzel held the Indians at bay, Silas and Clarke piled the logs one upon another, until the hole was closed. This effectually fortified and barricaded the weak place in the stockade fence. The settlers in the bastions were now pouring such a hot fire into the ranks of the savage that they were compelled to retreat out of range.

While Wetzel washed the blood from his arms and his shoulders Silas and Alfred hurried back to where Bennet had fallen. They expected to find him dead, and were overjoyed to see the big settler calmly sitting by the brook binding up a wound in his shoulder.

"It's nothin' much. Jest a scratch, but it tumbled me over," he said. "I was comin' to help you. That was the wust Injun scrap I ever saw. Why didn't you keep on lettin' 'em come in? The red varmints would'a kept on comin' and Wetzel was good fer the whole tribe. All you'd had to do was to drag the dead Injuns aside and give him elbow room."

Wetzel joined them at this moment, and they hurried back to the block-house. The firing had ceased on the bluff. They met Sullivan at the steps of the Fort. He was evidently coming in search of them.

"Zane, the Indians and the Britishers are getting ready for more determined and persistent effort than any that has yet been made," said Sullivan.

"How so?" asked Silas.

"They have got hammers from the blacksmith's shop, and they boarded my boat and found a keg of nails. Now they are making a number of ladders. If they make a rush all at once and place ladders against the fence we'll have the Fort full of Indians in ten minutes. They can't stand in the face of a cannon charge. We *must* use the cannon."

"Clarke, go into Capt. Boggs' cabin and fetch out two kegs of powder," said Silas.

The young man turned in the direction of the cabin, while Silas and the others ascended the stairs.

"The firing seems to be all on the south side," said Silas, "and is not so heavy as it was."

"Yes, as I said, the Indians on the river front are busy with their new plans," answered Sullivan.

"Why does not Clarke return?" said Silas, after waiting a few moments at the door of the long room. "We have no time to lose. I want to divide one keg of that powder among the men."

Clarke appeared at the moment. He was breathing heavily as though he had run up the stairs, or was laboring under a powerful emotion. His face was gray.

"I could not find any powder!" he exclaimed. "I searched every nook and corner in Capt. Boggs' house. There is no powder there."

A brief silence ensued. Everyone in the block-house heard the young man's voice. No one moved. They all seemed waiting for someone to speak. Finally Silas Zane burst out:

"Not find it? You surely could not have looked well. Capt. Boggs himself told me there were three kegs of powder in the storeroom. I will go and find it myself."

Alfred did not answer, but sat down on a bench with an odd numb feeling round his heart. He knew what was coming. He had been in the Captain's house and had seen those kegs of powder. He knew exactly where they had been. Now they were not on the accustomed shelf, nor at any other place in the storeroom. While he sat there waiting for the awful truth to dawn on the garrison, his eyes roved from one end of the room to the other. At last they found what they were seeking. A young woman knelt before a charcoal fire which she was blowing with a bellows. It was Betty. Her face was pale and weary, her hair dishevelled, her shapely arms blackened with charcoal, but notwithstanding she looked calm, resolute, self-contained. Lydia was kneeling by her side holding a bullet-mould on a block of wood. Betty lifted the ladle from the red coals and poured the hot metal with a steady hand and an admirable precision. Too much or too little lead would make an imperfect ball. The little missile had to be just so for those soft-metal, smooth-bore rifles. Then Lydia dipped the mould in a bucket of water, removed it and knocked it on the floor. A small, shiny lead bullet rolled out. She rubbed it with a greasy rag and then dropped it in a jar. For nearly forty hours, without sleep or rest, almost without food, those brave girls had been at their post.

Silas Zane came running into the room. His face was ghastly, even his lips were white and drawn.

"Sullivan, in God's name, what can we do? The powder is gone!" he cried in a strident voice.

"Gone?" repeated several voices.

"Gone?" echoed Sullivan. "Where?"

"God knows. I found where the kegs stood a few days ago. There were marks in the dust. They have been moved."

"Perhaps Boggs put them here somewhere," said Sullivan. "We will look."

"No use. No use. We were always careful to keep the powder out of here on account of fire. The kegs are gone, gone."

"Miller stole them," said Wetzel in his calm voice.

"What difference does that make now?" burst out Silas, turning passionately on the hunter, whose quiet voice in that moment seemed so unfeeling. "They're gone!"

In the silence which ensued after these words the men looked at each other with slowly whitening faces. There was no need of words. Their eyes told one another what was coming. The fate which had overtaken so many border forts was to be theirs. They were lost! And every man thought not of himself, cared not for himself, but for those innocent children, those brave young girls and heroic women.

A man can die. He is glorious when he calmly accepts death; but when he fights like a tiger, when he stands at bay his back to the wall, a broken weapon in his hand, bloody, defiant, game to the end, then he is sublime. Then he wrings respect from the souls of even his bitterest foes. Then he is avenged even in his death.

But what can women do in times of war? They help, they cheer, they inspire, and if their cause is lost they must accept death or worse. Few women have the courage for self-destruction. "To the victor belong the spoils," and women have ever been the spoils of war.

No wonder Silas Zane and his men weakened in that moment. With only a few charges for their rifles and none for the cannon how could they hope to hold out against the savages? Alone they could have drawn their tomahawks and have made a dash through the lines of Indians, but with the women and the children that was impossible.

"Wetzel, what can we do? For God's sake, advise us!" said Silas hoarsely.

"We cannot hold the Fort without powder. We cannot leave the women here. We had better tomahawk every woman in the block-house than let her fall into the hands of Girty."

"Send someone fer powder," answered Wetzel.

"Do you think it possible," said Silas quickly, a ray of hope lighting up his haggard features. "There's plenty of powder in Eb's cabin. Whom shall we send? Who will volunteer?"

Three men stepped forward, and others made a movement.

"They'd plug a man full of lead afore he'd get ten foot from the gate," said Wetzel. "I'd go myself, but it wouldn't do no good. Send a boy, and one as can run like a streak."

"There are no lads big enough to carry a keg of powder. Harry Bennett might go," said Silas. "How is he, Bessie?"

"He is dead," answered Mrs. Zane.

Wetzel made a motion with his hands and turned away. A short, intense silence followed this indication of hopelessness from him. The women understood, for some of them covered their faces, while others sobbed.

"I will go."

It was Betty's voice, and it rang clear and vibrant throughout the room. The miserable women raised their drooping heads, thrilled by that fresh young voice. The men looked stupefied. Clarke seemed turned to stone. Wetzel came quickly toward her.

"Impossible!" said Sullivan.

Silas Zane shook his head as if the idea were absurd.

"Let me go, brother, let me go?" pleaded Betty as she placed her little hands softly, caressingly on her brother's bare arm. "I know it is only a forlorn chance, but still it is a chance. Let me take it. I would rather die that way than remain here and wait for death."

"Silas, it ain't a bad plan," broke in Wetzel. "Betty can run like a deer. And bein' a woman they may let her get to the cabin without shootin'."

Silas stood with arms folded across his broad chest. As he gazed at his sister great tears coursed down his dark cheeks and splashed on the hands which so tenderly clasped his own. Betty stood before him transformed; all signs of weariness had vanished; her eyes shone with a fateful resolve; her white and eager face was surpassingly beautiful with its light of hope, of prayer, of heroism.

"Let me go, brother. You know I can run, and oh! I will fly today. Every moment is precious. Who knows? Perhaps Capt. Boggs is already near at hand with help. You cannot spare a man. Let me go."

"Betty, Heaven bless and save you, you shall go," said Silas.

"No! No! Do not let her go!" cried Clarke, throwing himself before them. He was trembling, his eyes were wild, and he had the appearance of a man suddenly gone mad.

"She shall not go," he cried.

"What authority have you here?" demanded Silas Zane, sternly. "What right have you to speak?"

"None, unless it is that I love her and I will go for her," answered Alfred desperately.

"Stand back!" cried Wetzel, placing his powerful hard on Clarke's breast and pushing him backward. "If you love her you don't want to have her wait here for them red devils," and he waved his hand toward the river. "If she gets back she'll save the Fort. If she fails she'll at least escape Girty."

Betty gazed into the hunter's eyes and then into Alfred's. She understood both men. One was sending her out to her death because he knew it would be a thousand times more merciful than the fate which awaited her at the hands of the Indians. The other had not the strength to watch her go to her death. He had offered himself rather than see her take such fearful chances.

"I know. If it were possible you would both save me," said Betty, simply. "Now you can do nothing but pray that God may spare my life long enough to reach the gate. Silas, I am ready."

Downstairs a little group of white-faced men were standing before the gateway. Silas Zane had withdrawn the iron bar. Sullivan stood ready to swing in the ponderous gate. Wetzel was speaking with a clearness and a rapidity which were wonderful under the circumstances.

"When we let you out you'll have a clear path. Run, but not very fast. Save your speed. Tell the Colonel to empty a keg of powder in a table cloth. Throw it over your shoulder and start back. Run like you was racin' with me, and keep on comin' if you do get hit. Now go!"

The huge gate creaked and swung in. Betty ran out, looking straight before her. She had covered half the distance between the Fort and the Colonel's house when long taunting yells filled the air.

"Squaw! Waugh! Squaw! Waugh!" yelled the Indians in contempt.

Not a shot did they fire. The yells ran all along the river front, showing that hundreds of Indians had seen the slight figure running up the gentle slope toward the cabin.

Betty obeyed Wetzel's instructions to the letter. She ran easily and not at all hurriedly, and was as cool as if there had not been an Indian within miles.

Col. Zane had seen the gate open and Betty come forth. When she bounded up the steps he flung open that door and she ran into his arms.

"Betts, for God's sake! What's this?" he cried.

"We are out of powder. Empty a keg of powder into a table cloth. Quick! I've not a second to lose," she answered, at the same time slipping off her outer skirt. She wanted nothing to hinder that run for the block-house.

Jonathan Zane heard Betty's first words and disappeared into the magazine-room. He came out with a keg in his arms. With one blow of an axe he smashed in the top of the keg. In a twinkling a long black stream of the precious stuff was piling up in a little hill in the center of the table. Then the corners of the table cloth were caught up, turned and twisted, and the bag of powder was thrown over Betty's shoulder.

"Brave girl, so help me God, you are going to do it!" cried Col. Zane, throwing open the door. "I know you can. Run as you never ran in all your life."

Like an arrow sprung from a bow Betty flashed past the Colonel and out on the green. Scarcely ten of the long hundred yards had been covered by her flying feet when a roar of angry shouts and yells warned Betty that the keen-eyed savages saw the bag of powder and now knew they had been deceived by a girl. The cracking of rifles began at a point on the bluff nearest Col. Zane's house, and extended in a half circle to the eastern end of the clearing. The leaden messengers of Death whistled past Betty. They sped before her and behind her, scattering pebbles in her path, striking up the dust, and ploughing little furrows in the ground. A quarter of the distance covered! Betty had passed the top of the knoll now and she was going down the gentle slope like the wind. None but a fine marksman could have hit that small, flitting figure. The yelling and screeching had become deafening. The reports of the rifles blended in a roar. Yet above it all Betty heard Wetzel's stentorian yell. It lent wings to her feet. Half the distance covered! A hot, stinging pain shot through Betty's arm, but she heeded it not. The bullets were raining about her. They sang over her head; hissed close to her ears, and cut the grass in front of her; they pattered like hail on the stockade-fence, but still untouched, unharmed, the slender brown figure sped toward the gate. Three-fourths of the distance covered! A tug at the flying hair, and a long, black tress cut off by a bullet, floated away on the breeze. Betty saw the big gate swing; she saw the tall figure of the hunter; she saw her brother. Only a few more yards! On! On! On! A blinding red mist obscured her sight. She lost the opening in the fence, but unheeding she rushed on. Another second and she stumbled; she felt herself grasped by eager arms; she heard the gate slam and the iron bar shoot into place; then she felt and heard no more.

Silas Zane bounded up the stairs with a doubly precious burden in his arms. A mighty cheer greeted his entrance. It aroused Alfred Clarke, who had bowed his head on the bench and had lost all sense of time and place. What were the women sobbing and crying over? To whom belonged that white face? Of course, it was the face of the girl he loved. The face of the girl who had gone to her death. And he writhed in his agony.

Then something wonderful happened. A warm, living flush swept over that pale face. The eyelids fluttered; they opened, and the dark eyes, radiant, beautiful, gazed straight into Alfred's.

Still Alfred could not believe his eyes. That pale face and the wonderful eyes belonged to the ghost of his sweetheart. They had come back to haunt him. Then he heard a voice.

"O-h! but that brown place burns!"

Alfred saw a bare and shapely arm. Its beauty was marred by a cruel red welt. He heard that same sweet voice laugh and cry together. Then he came back to life and hope. With one bound he sprang to a porthole.

"God, what a woman!" he said between his teeth, as he thrust the rifle forward.

It was indeed not a time for inaction. The Indians, realizing they had been tricked and had lost a golden opportunity, rushed at the Fort with renewed energy. They attacked from all sides and with the persistent fury of savages long disappointed in their hopes. They were received with a scathing, deadly fire. Bang! roared the cannon, and the detachment of savages dropped their ladders and fled. The little "bull dog" was turned on its swivel and directed at another rush of Indians. Bang! and the bullets, chainlinks, and bits of iron ploughed through the ranks of the enemy. The Indians never lived who could stand in the face of well-aimed cannon-shot. They fell back. The settlers, inspired, carried beyond themselves by the heroism of a girl, fought as they had never fought before. Every shot went to a redskin's heart, impelled by the powder for which a brave girl had offered her life, guided by hands and arms of iron, and aimed by eyes as fixed and stern as Fate, every bullet shed the life-blood of a warrior.

Slowly and sullenly the red men gave way before that fire. Foot by foot they retired. Girty was seen no more. Fire, the Shawnee chief, lay dead in the road almost in the same spot where two days before his brother chief, Red Fox, had bit the dust. The British had long since retreated.

When night came the exhausted and almost famished besiegers sought rest and food.

The moon came out clear and beautiful, as if ashamed at her traitor's part of the night before, and brightened up the valley, bathing the Fort, the river, and the forest in her silver light.

Shortly after daybreak the next morning the Indians, despairing of success, held a pow-wow. While they were grouped in plain view of the garrison, and probably conferring over the question of raising the siege, the long, peculiar whoop of an Indian spy, who had been sent out to watch for the approach of a relief party, rang out. This seemed a signal for retreat. Scarcely had the shrill cry ceased to echo in the hills when the Indians and the British, abandoning their dead, moved rapidly across the river.

After a short interval a mounted force was seen galloping up the creek road. It proved to be Capt. Boggs, Swearengen, and Williamson with seventy men. Great was the rejoicing. Capt. Boggs had expected to find only the ashes of the Fort. And the gallant little garrison, although saddened by the loss of half its original number, rejoiced that it had repulsed the united forces of braves and British.

CHAPTER 15

PEACE AND QUIET REIGNED ONES MORE AT FT. HENRY. BEFORE THE glorious autumn days had waned, the settlers had repaired the damage done to their cabins, and many of them were now occupied with the fall plowing. Never had the Fort experienced such busy days. Many new faces were seen in the little meeting-house. Pioneers from Virginia, from Ft. Pitt, and eastward had learned that Fort Henry had repulsed the biggest force of Indians and soldiers that Governor Hamilton and his minions could muster. Settlers from all points along the river were flocking to Col. Zane's settlement. New cabins dotted the hillside; cabins and barns in all stages of construction could be seen. The sounds of hammers, the ringing stroke of the axe, and the crashing down of mighty pines or poplars were heard all day long.

Col. Zane sat oftener and longer than ever before in his favorite seat on his doorstep. On this evening he had just returned from a hard day in the fields, and sat down to rest a moment before going to supper. A few days previous Isaac Zane and Myeerah had come to the settlement. Myeerah brought a treaty of peace signed by Tarhe and the other Wyandot chieftains. The once implacable Huron was now ready to be friendly with the white people. Col. Zane and his brothers signed the treaty, and Betty, by dint of much persuasion, prevailed on Wetzel to bury the hatchet with the Hurons. So Myeerah's love, like the love of many other women, accomplished more than years of war and bloodshed.

The genial and happy smile never left Col. Zane's face, and as he saw the well-laden rafts coming down the river, and the air of liveliness and animation about the growing settlement, his smile broadened into one of pride and satisfaction. The prophecy that he had made twelve years before was fulfilled. His dream was realized. The wild, beautiful spot where he had once built a bark shack and camped half a year without seeing a white man was now the scene of a bustling settlement; and he believed he would live to see that settlement grow into a prosperous city. He did not think of the thousands of acres which would one day make him a wealthy man. He was a pioneer at heart; he had opened up that rich new country; he had conquered all obstacles, and that was enough to make him content.

"Papa, when shall I be big enough to fight bars and bufflers and Injuns?" asked Noah, stopping in his play and straddling his father's knee.

"My boy, did you not have Indians enough a short time ago?"

"But, papa, I did not get to see any. I heard the shooting and yelling. Sammy was afraid, but I wasn't. I wanted to look out of the little holes, but they locked us up in the dark room."

"If that boy ever grows up to be like Jonathan or Wetzel it will be the death of me," said the Colonel's wife, who had heard the lad's chatter.

"Don't worry, Bessie. When Noah grows to be a man the Indians will be gone."

Col. Zane heard the galloping of a horse and looking up saw Clarke coming down the road on his black thoroughbred. The Colonel rose and walked out to the hitching-block, where Clarke had reined in his fiery steed.

"Ah, Alfred. Been out for a ride?"

"Yes, I have been giving Roger a little exercise."

"That's a magnificent animal. I never get tired watching him move. He's the best bit of horseflesh on the river. By the way, we have not seen much of you since the siege. Of course you have been busy. Getting ready to put on the harness, eh? Well, that's what we want the young men to do. Come over and see us."

"I have been trying to come. You know how it is with me—about Betty, I mean. Col. Zane, I—I love her. That's all."

"Yes, I know, Alfred, and I don't wonder at your fears. But I have always liked you, and now I guess it's about time for me to put a spoke in your wheel of fortune. If Betty cares for you—and I have a sneaking idea she does—I will give her to you."

"I have nothing. I gave up everything when I left home."

"My lad, never mind about that," said the Colonel, laying his hand on Clarke's knee. "We don't need riches. I have so often said that we need nothing out here on the border but honest hearts and strong, willing hands. These you have. That is enough for me and for my people, and as for land, why, I have enough for an army of young men. I got my land cheap. That whole island there I bought from Cornplanter. You can have that island or any tract of land along the river. Some day I shall put you at the head of my men. It will take you years to cut that road through to Maysville. Oh, I have plenty of work for you."

"Col. Zane, I cannot thank you," answered Alfred, with emotion. "I shall try to merit your friendship and esteem. Will you please tell your sister I shall come over in the morning and beg to see her alone."

"That I will, Alfred. Goodnight."

Col. Zane strode across his threshold with a happy smile on his face. He loved to joke and tease, and never lost an opportunity.

"Things seem to be working out all right. Now for some fun with Her Highness," he said to himself.

As the Colonel surveyed the pleasant home scene he felt he had nothing more to wish for. The youngsters were playing with a shaggy little pup which had already taken Tige's place in their fickle affections. His wife was crooning a lullaby as she gently rocked the cradle to and fro. A wonderful mite of humanity peacefully slumbered in that old cradle. Annie was beginning to set the table for the evening meal. Isaac lay with a contented smile on his face, fast asleep on the couch, where, only a short time before, he had been laid bleeding and almost dead. Betty was reading to Myeerah, whose eyes were rapturously bright as she leaned her head against her sister and listened to the low voice.

"Well, Betty, what do you think?" said Col. Zane, stopping before the girls.

"What do I think?" retorted Betty. "Why, I think you are very rude to interrupt me. I am reading to Myeerah her first novel."

"I have a very important message for you."

"For me? What! From whom?"

"Guess."

Betty ran through a list of most of her acquaintances, but after each name her brother shook his head.

"Oh, well, I don't care," she finally said. The color in her cheeks had heightened noticeably.

"Very well. If you do not care, I will say nothing more," said Col. Zane.

At this juncture Annie called them to supper. Later, when Col. Zane sat on the doorstep smoking, Betty came and sat beside him with her head resting against his shoulder. The Colonel smoked on in silence. Presently the dusky head moved restlessly.

"Eb, tell me the message," whispered Betty.

"Message? What message?" asked Col. Zone. "What are you talking about?"

"Do not tease—not now. Tell me." There was an undercurrent of wistfulness in Betty's voice which touched the kindhearted brother.

"Well, to-day a certain young man asked me if he could relieve me of the responsibility of looking after a certain young lady."

"Oh——"

"Wait a moment. I told him I would be delighted."

"Eb, that was unkind."

"Then he asked me to tell her he was coming over to-morrow morning to fix it up with her."

"Oh, horrible!" cried Betty. "Were those the words he used?"

"Betts, to tell the honest truth, he did not say much of anything. He just said: 'I love her,' and his eyes blazed."

Betty uttered a half articulate cry and ran to her room. Her heart was throbbing. What could she do? She felt that if she looked once into her lover's eyes she would have no strength. How dared she allow herself to be so weak! Yet she knew this was the end. She could deceive him no longer. For she felt a stir in her heart, stronger than all, beyond all resistance, an exquisite agony, the sweet, blind, tumultuous exultation of the woman who loves and is loved.

"Bess, what do you think?" said Col. Zane, going into the kitchen next morning, after he had returned from the pasture. "Clarke just came over and asked for Betty. I called her. She came down looking as sweet and cool as one of the lilies out by the spring. She said: 'Why, Mr. Clarke, you are almost a stranger. I am pleased to see you. Indeed, we are all very glad to know you have recovered from your severe burns.' She went on talking like that for all the world like a girl who didn't care a snap for him. And she knows as well as I do. Not only that, she has been actually breaking her heart over him all these months. How did she do it? Oh, you women beat me all hollow!"

"Would you expect Betty to fall into his arms?" asked the Colonel's worthy spouse, indignantly.

"Not exactly. But she was too cool, too friendly. Poor Alfred looked as if he hadn't slept. He was nervous and scared to death. When Betty ran up stairs I put a bug in Alfred's ear. He'll be all right now, if he follows my advice."

"Humph! What did Colonel Ebenezer Zane tell him?" asked Bessie, in disgust.

"Oh, not much. I simply told him not to lose his nerve; that a woman never meant 'no'; that she often says it only to be made say 'yes.' And I ended up with telling him if she got a little skittish, as thoroughbreds do sometimes, to try a strong arm. That was my way."

"Col. Zane, if my memory does not fail me, you were as humble and beseeching as the proudest girl could desire."

"I beseeching? Never!"

"I hope Alfred's wooing may go well. I like him very much. But I'm afraid. Betty has such a spirit that it is quite likely she will refuse him for no other reason than that he built his cabin before he asked her."

"Nonsense. He asked her long ago. Never fear, Bess, my sister will come back as meek as a lamb."

Meanwhile Betty and Alfred were strolling down the familiar path toward the river. The October air was fresh with a suspicion of frost. The clear notes of a hunter's horn came floating down from the hills. A flock of wild geese had alighted on the marshy ground at the end of the island where they kept up a continual honk! honk! The brown hills, the red forest, and the yellow fields were now at the height of their autumnal beauty. Soon the November north wind would thrash the trees bare, and bow the proud heads of the daisies and the goldenrod; but just now they flashed in the sun, and swayed back and forth in all their glory.

"I see you limp. Are you not entirely well?" Betty was saying.

"Oh, I am getting along famously, thank you," said Alfred. "This one foot was quite severely burned and is still tender."

"You have had your share of injuries. I heard my brother say you had been wounded three times within a year."

"Four times."

"Jonathan told of the axe wound; then the wound Miller gave you, and finally the burns. These make three, do they not?"

"Yes, but you see, all three could not be compared to the one you forgot to mention."

"Let us hurry past here," said Betty, hastening to change the subject. "This is where you had the dreadful fight with Miller."

"As Miller did go to meet Girty, and as he did not return to the Fort with the renegade, we must believe he is dead. Of course, we do not know this to be actually a fact. But something makes me think so. Jonathan and Wetzel have not said anything; I can't get any satisfaction on that score from either; but I am sure neither of them would rest until Miller was dead."

"I think you are right. But we may never know. All I can tell you is that Wetzel and Jack trailed Miller to the river, and then they both came back. I was the last to see Lewis that night before he left on Miller's trail. It isn't likely I shall forget what Lewis said and how he looked. Miller was a wicked man; yes, a traitor."

"He was a bad man, and he nearly succeeded in every one of his plans. I have not the slightest doubt that had he refrained from taking part in the shooting match he would have succeeded in abducting you, in killing me, and in leading Girty here long before he was expected."

"There are many things that may never be explained, but one thing Miller did always mystify us. How did he succeed in binding Tige?"

"To my way of thinking that was not so difficult as climbing into my room and almost killing me, or stealing the powder from Capt. Boggs' room."

"The last, at least, gave me a chance to help," said Betty, with a touch of her odd roguishness.

"That was the grandest thing a woman ever did," said Alfred, in a low tone.

"Oh, no, I only ran fast."

"I would have given the world to have seen you, but I was lying on the bench wishing I were dead. I did not have strength to look out of a port-hole. Oh! that horrible time! I can never forget it. I lie awake at night and hear the yelling and shooting. Then I dream of running over the burning roofs and it all comes back so vividly I can almost feel the flames and smell the burnt wood. Then I wake up and think of that awful moment when you were carried into the blockhouse white, and, as I thought, dead."

"But I wasn't. And I think it best for us to forget that horrible siege. It is past. It is a miracle that any one was spared. Ebenezer says we should not grieve for those who are gone; they were heroic; they saved the Fort. He says too, that we shall never again be troubled by Indians. Therefore let us forget and be happy. I have forgotten Miller. You can afford to do the same."

"Yes, I forgive him." Then, after a long silence, Alfred continued, "Will you go down to the old sycamore?"

Down the winding path they went. Coming to a steep place in the rocky bank Alfred jumped down and then turned to help Betty. But she avoided his gaze, pretended to not see his outstretched hands, and leaped lightly down beside him. He looked at her with perplexity and anxiety in his eyes. Before he could speak she ran on ahead of him and climbed down the bank to the pool. He followed slowly, thoughtfully. The supreme moment had come. He knew it, and somehow he did not feel the confidence the Colonel had inspired in him. It had been easy for him to think of subduing this imperious young lady; but when the time came to assert his will he found he could not remember what he had intended to say, and his feelings were divided between his love for her and the horrible fear that he should lose her.

When he reached the sycamore tree he found her sitting behind it with a cluster of yellow daisies in her lap. Alfred gazed at her, conscious that all his hopes of happiness were dependent on the next few words that would issue from her smiling lips. The little brown hands, which were now rather nervously arranging the flowers, held more than his life.

"Are they not sweet?" asked Betty, giving him a fleeting glance. "We call them 'black-eyed Susans.' Could anything be lovelier than that soft, dark brown?"

"Yes," answered Alfred, looking into her eyes.

"But—but you are not looking at my daisies at all," said Betty, lowering her eyes.

"No, I am not," said Alfred. Then suddenly: "A year ago this very day we were here."

"Here? Oh, yes, I believe I do remember. It was the day we came in my canoe and had such fine fishing."

"Is that all you remember?"

"I can recollect nothing in particular. It was so long ago."

"I suppose you will say you had no idea why I wanted you to come to this spot in particular."

"I supposed you simply wanted to take a walk, and it is very pleasant here."

"Then Col. Zane did not tell you?" demanded Alfred. Receiving no reply he went on.

"Did you read my letter?"

"What letter?"

"The letter old Sam should have given you last fall. Did you read it?"

"Yes," answered Betty, faintly.

"Did your brother tell you I wanted to see you this morning?"

"Yes, he told me, and it made me very angry," said Betty, raising her head. There was a bright red spot in each cheek. "You—you seemed to think you—that I—well—I did not like it."

"I think I understand; but you are entirely wrong. I have never thought you cared for me. My wildest dreams never left me any confidence. Col. Zane and Wetzel both had some deluded notion that you cared—"

"But they had no right to say that or to think it," said Betty, passionately. She sprang to her feet, scattering the daisies over the grass. "For them to presume that I cared for you is absurd. I never gave them any reason to think so, for—for I—I don't."

"Very well, then, there is nothing more to be said," answered Alfred, in a voice that was calm and slightly cold. "I'm sorry if you have been annoyed. I have been mad, of course, but I promise you that you need fear no further annoyance from me. Come, I think we should return to the house."

And he turned and walked slowly up the path. He had taken perhaps a dozen steps when she called him.

"Mr. Clarke, come back."

Alfred retraced his steps and stood before her again. Then he saw a different Betty. The haughty poise had disappeared. Her head was bowed. Her little hands were tightly pressed over a throbbing bosom.

"Well," said Alfred, after a moment.

"Why—why are you in such a hurry to go?"

"I have learned what I wanted to know. And after that I do not imagine I would be very agreeable. I am going back. Are you coming?"

"I did not mean quite what I said," whispered Betty.

"Then what did you mean?" asked Alfred, in a stern voice.

"I don't know. Please don't speak so."

"Betty, forgive my harshness. Can you expect a man to feel as I do and remain calm? You know I love you. You must not trifle any longer. You must not fight any longer."

"But I can't help fighting."

"Look at me," said Alfred, taking her hands. "Let me see your eyes. I

239

believe you care a little for me, or else you wouldn't have called me back. I love you. Can you understand that?"

"Yes, I can; and I think you should love me a great deal to make up for what you made me suffer."

"Betty, look at me."

Slowly she raised her head and lifted the downcast eyes. Those telltale traitors no longer hid her secret. With a glad cry Alfred caught her in his arms. She tried to hide her face, but he got his hand under her chin and held it firmly so that the sweet crimson lips were very near his own. Then he slowly bent his head.

Betty saw his intention, closed her eyes and whispered.

"Alfred, please don't—it's not fair—I beg of you—Oh!"

That kiss was Betty's undoing. She uttered a strange little cry. Then her dark head found a hiding place over his heart, and her slender form, which a moment before had resisted so fiercely, sank yielding into his embrace.

"Betty, do you dare tell me now that you do not care for me?" Alfred whispered into the dusky hair which rippled over his breast.

Betty was brave even in her surrender. Her hands moved slowly upward along his arms, slipped over his shoulders, and clasped round his neck. Then she lifted a flushed and tearstained face with tremulous lips and wonderful shining eyes.

"Alfred, I do love you—with my whole heart I love you. I never knew until now."

The hours flew apace. The prolonged ringing of the dinner bell brought the lovers back to earth, and to the realization that the world held others than themselves. Slowly they climbed the familiar path, but this time as never before. They walked hand in hand. From the blur they looked back. They wanted to make sure they were not dreaming. The water rushed over the fall more musically than ever before; the white patches of foam floated round and round the shady pool; the leaves of the sycamore rustled cheerily in the breeze. On a dead branch a wood-pecker hammered industriously.

"Before we get out of sight of that dear old tree I want to make a confession," said Betty, as she stood before Alfred. She was pulling at the fringe on his hunting-coat.

"You need not make confessions to me."

"But this was dreadful; it preys on my conscience."

"Very well, I will be your judge. Your punishment shall be slight."

"One day when you were lying unconscious from your wound, Bessie sent me to watch you. I nursed you for hours; and—and—do not think badly of me—I—I kissed you."

"My darling," cried the enraptured young man.

When they at last reached the house they found Col. Zane on the doorstep.

"Where on earth have you been?" he said. "Wetzel was here. He said he would not wait to see you. There he goes up the hill. He is behind that laurel."

They looked and presently saw the tall figure of the hunter emerge from the bushes. He stopped and leaned on his rifle. For a minute he remained motionless. Then he waved his hand and plunged into the thicket. Betty sighed and Alfred said:

"Poor Wetzel! ever restless, ever roaming."

"Hello, there!" exclaimed a gay voice. The lovers turned to see the smiling face of Isaac, and over his shoulder Myeerah's happy face beaming on them. "Alfred, you are a lucky dog. You can thank Myeerah and me for this; because if I had not taken to the river and nearly drowned myself to give you that opportunity you would not wear that happy face to-day. Blush away, Betts, it becomes you mightily."

"Bessie, here they are!" cried Col. Zane, in his hearty voice. "She is tamed at last. No excuses, Alfred, in to dinner you go."

Col. Zane pushed the young people up the steps before him, and stopping on the threshold while he knocked the ashes from his pipe, he smiled contentedly.

AFTERWORD

Betty lived all her after life on the scene of her famous exploit. She became a happy wife and mother. When she grew to be an old lady, with her grandchildren about her knee, she delighted to tell them that when a girl she had run the gauntlet of the Indians.

Col. Zane became the friend of all redmen. He maintained a trading-post for many years, and his dealings were ever kind and honorable. After the country got settled he received from time to time various marks of distinction from the State, Colonial, and National governments. His most noted achievement was completed about 1796. President Washington, desiring to open a National road from Fort Henry to Maysville, Kentucky, paid a great tribute to Col. Zane's ability by employing him to undertake the arduous task. His brother Jonathan and the Indian guide, Tomepome-hala, rendered valuable aid in blazing out the path through the wilderness. This road, famous for many years as Zane's Trace, opened the beautiful Ohio valley to the ambitious pioneer. For this service Congress granted Col. Zane the privilege of locating military warrants upon three sections of land, each a square mile in extent, which property the government eventually presented to him. Col. Zane was the founder of Wheeling, Zanesville, Martin's Ferry, and Bridgeport. He died in 1811.

Isaac Zane received from the government a patent of ten thousand acres of land on Mad river. He established his home in the center of this tract, where he lived with the Wyandot until his death. A white settlement sprang up, prospered, and grew, and today it is the thriving city of Zanesfield.

Jonathan Zane settled down after peace was declared with the Indians, found himself a wife, and eventually became an influential citizen. However, he never lost his love for the wild woods. At times he would take down the old rifle and disappear for two or three days. He always returned cheerful and happy from these lonely hunts.

Wetzel alone did not take kindly to the march of civilization; but then he was a hunter, not a pioneer. He kept his word of peace with his old enemies, the Hurons, though he never abandoned his wandering and vengeful quests after the Delawares.

As the years passed Wetzel grew more silent and taciturn. From time to time he visited Ft. Henry, and on these visits he spent hours playing with Betty's children. But he was restless in the settlement, and his sojourns grew briefer and more infrequent as time rolled on. True to his conviction that no wife existed on earth for him, he never married. His home was the trackless wilds, where he was true to his calling—a foe to the redman.

Wonderful to relate his long, black hair never adorned the walls of an Indian's lodge, where a warrior might point with grim pride and say: "No more does the Deathwind blow over the hills and vales." We could tell of how his keen eye once again saw Wingenund over the sights of his fatal rifle, and how he was once again a prisoner in the camp of that lifelong foe, but that's another story, which, perhaps, we may tell some day.

To-day the beautiful city of Wheeling rises on the banks of the Ohio, where the yells of the Indians once blanched the cheeks of the pioneers. The broad, winding river rolls on as of yore; it alone remains unchanged. What were Indians and pioneers, forts and cities to it? Eons of time before human beings lived it flowed slowly toward the sea, and ages after men and their works are dust, it will roll on placidly with its eternal scheme of nature.

Upon the island still stand noble beeches, oaks, and chestnuts—trees that long ago have covered up their bullet-scars, but they could tell, had they the power to speak, many a wild thrilling tale. Beautiful parks and stately mansions grace the island; and polished equipages roll over the ground that once knew naught save the soft tread of the deer and the moccasin.

McColloch's Rock still juts boldly out over the river as deep and rugged as when the brave Major leaped to everlasting fame. Wetzel's Cave, so named to this day, remains on the side of the bluff overlooking the creek. The grapevines and wild rose-bushes still cluster round the cavern-entrance, where, long ago, the wily savage was wont to lie in wait for the settler, lured there by the false turkey-call. The boys visit the cave on Saturday afternoons and play "Injuns."

Not long since the writer spent a quiet afternoon there, listening to the musical flow of the brook, and dreaming of those who had lived and loved, fought and died by that stream one hundred and twenty years ago. The city with its long blocks of buildings, its spires and bridges, faded away, leaving the scene as it was in the days of Fort Henry—unobscured by smoke, the river undotted by pulling boats, and everywhere the green and verdant forest.

Nothing was wanting in that dream picture: Betty tearing along on her pony; the pioneer plowing in the field; the stealthy approach of the savage; Wetzel and Jonathan watching the river; the deer browsing with the cows in the pasture, and the old fort, grim and menacing on the bluff—all were there as natural as in those times which tried men's souls.

And as the writer awoke to the realities of life, that his dreams were of long ago, he was saddened by the thought that the labor of the pioneer is ended; his faithful, heroic wife's work is done. That beautiful country, which their sacrifices made ours, will ever be a monument to them.

Sad, too, is the thought that the poor Indian is unmourned. He is almost forgotten; he is in the shadow; his songs are sung; no more will he sing to his dusky bride: his deeds are done; no more will he boast of his all-conquering arm or of his speed like the Northwind; no more will his heart bound at the whistle of the stag, for he sleeps in the shade of the oaks, under the moss and the ferns.

THE SPIRIT OF THE BORDER

A ROMANCE OF THE EARLY SETTLERS IN THE OHIO VALLEY

CONTENTS

TO MY BROTHER

With many fond recollections of days spent in the solitude of the forests where only can be satisfied that wild fever of freedom of which this book tells; where to hear the whirr of a wild duck in his rapid flight is joy; where the quiet of an autumn afternoon swells the heart, and where one may watch the fragrant wood-smoke curl from the campfire, and see the stars peep over dark, wooded hills as twilight deepens, and know a happiness that dwells in the wilderness alone.

INTRODUCTION

The author does not intend to apologize for what many readers may call the "brutality" of the story; but rather to explain that its wild spirit is true to the life of the Western border as it was known only a little more than one hundred years ago.

The writer is the fortunate possessor of historical material of undoubted truth and interest. It is the long-lost journal of Colonel Ebenezer Zane, one of the most prominent of the hunter-pioneer, who labored in the settlement of the Western country.

The story of that tragic period deserves a higher place in historical literature than it has thus far been given, and this unquestionably because of a lack of authentic data regarding the conquering of the wilderness. Considering how many years the pioneers struggled on the border of this country, the history of their efforts is meager and obscure.

If the years at the close of the eighteenth and the beginning of the nineteenth century were full of stirring adventure on the part of the colonists along the Atlantic coast, how crowded must they have been for the almost forgotten pioneers who daringly invaded the trackless wilds! None there was to chronicle the fight of these sturdy, travelers toward the setting sun. The story of their stormy lives, of their heroism, and of their sacrifice for the benefit of future generations is too little known.

It is to a better understanding of those days that the author has labored to draw from his ancestor's notes a new and striking portrayal of the frontier; one which shall paint the fever of freedom, that powerful impulse which lured so many to unmarked graves; one which shall show his work, his love, the effect of the causes which rendered his life so hard, and surely one which does not forget the wronged Indian.

The frontier in 1777 produced white men so savage as to be men in name only. These outcasts and renegades lived among the savages, and during thirty years harassed the border, perpetrating all manner of fiendish cruelties upon the settlers. They were no less cruel to the redmen whom they ruled, and at the height of their bloody careers made futile the Moravian missionaries' long labors, and destroyed the beautiful hamlet of the Christian Indians, called Gnaddenhutten, or Village of Peace.

And while the border produced such outlaws so did it produce hunters Eke Boone, the Zanes, the McCollochs, and Wetzel, that strange, silent man whose deeds are still whispered in the country where he once roamed in his insatiate pursuit of savages and renegades, and who was purely a product of the times. Civilization could not have brought forth a man like Wetzel. Great revolutions, great crises, great moments come, and produce the men to deal with them.

The border needed Wetzel. The settlers would have needed many more years in which to make permanent homes had it not been for him. He was never a pioneer; but always a hunter after Indians. When not on the track of the savage foe, he was in the settlement, with his keen eye and ear ever alert for signs of the enemy. To the superstitious Indians he was a shadow; a spirit of the border, which breathed menace from the dark forests. To the settlers he was the right arm of defense, a fitting leader for those few implacable and unerring frontiersmen who made the settlement of the West a possibility.

And if this story of one of his relentless pursuits shows the man as he truly was, loved by pioneers, respected and feared by redmen, and hated by renegades; if it softens a little the ruthless name history accords him, the writer will have been well repaid.

Z. G.

CHAPTER 1

"NELL, I'M GROWING POWERFUL FOND OF YOU."

"So you must be, Master Joe, if often telling makes it true."

The girl spoke simply, and with an absence of that roguishness which was characteristic of her. Playful words, arch smiles, and a touch of coquetry had seemed natural to Nell; but now her grave tone and her almost wistful glance disconcerted Joe.

During all the long journey over the mountains she had been gay and bright, while now, when they were about to part, perhaps never to meet again, she showed him the deeper and more earnest side of her character. It checked his boldness as nothing else had done. Suddenly there came to him the real meaning of a woman's love when she bestows it without reservation. Silenced by the thought that he had not understood her at all, and the knowledge that he had been half in sport, he gazed out over the wild country before them.

The scene impressed its quietness upon the young couple and brought more forcibly to their minds the fact that they were at the gateway of the unknown West; that somewhere beyond this rude frontier settlement, out there in those unbroken forests stretching dark and silent before them, was to be their future home.

From the high bank where they stood the land sloped and narrowed gradually until it ended in a sharp point which marked the last bit of land between the Allegheny and Monongahela rivers. Here these swift streams merged and formed the broad Ohio. The new-born river, even here at its beginning proud and swelling as if already certain of its far-away grandeur, swept majestically round a wide curve and apparently lost itself in the forest foliage.

On the narrow point of land commanding a view of the rivers stood a long, low structure enclosed by a stockade fence, on the four corners of which were little box-shaped houses that bulged out as if trying to see what was going on beneath. The massive timbers used in the construction of this fort, the square, compact form, and the small, dark holes cut into the walls, gave the structure a threatening, impregnable aspect.

Below Nell and Joe, on the bank, were many log cabins. The yellow clay which filled the chinks between the logs gave these a peculiar striped appearance. There was life and bustle in the vicinity of these dwellings, in sharp contrast with the still grandeur of the neighboring forests. There were canvas-covered wagons around which curly-headed youngsters were playing. Several horses were grazing on the short grass, and six red and white oxen munched at the hay that had been thrown to them. The smoke of many fires curled upward, and near the blaze hovered ruddy-faced women who stirred the contents of steaming kettles. One man swung an axe with a vigorous sweep, and the clean, sharp strokes rang on the air; another hammered stakes into the ground on which to hang a kettle. Before a large cabin a fur-trader was exhibiting his wares to three Indians. A second redskin was carrying a pack of pelts from a canoe drawn up on the river bank. A small group of persons stood near; some were indifferent, and others gazed curiously at the savages. Two children peeped from behind their mother's skirts as if half-curious, half-frightened.

From this scene, the significance of which had just dawned on him, Joe turned his eyes again to his companion. It was a sweet face he saw; one that was sedate, but had a promise of innumerable smiles. The blue eyes could not long hide flashes of merriment. The girl turned, and the two young people looked at each other. Her eyes softened with a woman's gentleness as they rested upon him, for, broad of shoulder, and lithe and strong as a deer stalker, he was good to look at.

"Listen," she said. "We have known each other only three weeks. Since you joined our wagon-train, and have been so kind to me and so helpful to make that long, rough ride endurable, you have won my regard. I—I cannot say more, even if I would. You told me you ran away from your Virginian home to seek adventure on the frontier, and that you knew no one in all this wild country. You even said you could not, or would not, work at farming. Perhaps my sister and I are as unfitted as you for this life; but we must cling to our uncle because he is the only relative we have. He has come out here to join the Moravians, and to preach the gospel to these Indians. We shall share his life, and help him all we can. You have been telling me you—you cared for me, and now that we are about to part I—I don't know what to say to you—unless it is: Give up this intention of yours to seek adventure, and come with us. It seems to me you need not hunt for excitement here; it will come unsought."

"I wish I were Jim," said he, suddenly.

"Who is Jim?"

"My brother."

"Tell me of him."

"There's nothing much to tell. He and I are all that are left of our people, as are you and Kate of yours. Jim's a preacher, and the best fellow —oh! I cared a lot for Jim."

"Then, why did you leave him?"

"I was tired of Williamsburg—I quarreled with a fellow, and hurt him. Besides, I wanted to see the West; I'd like to hunt deer and bear and fight Indians. Oh, I'm not much good."

"Was Jim the only one you cared for?" asked Nell, smiling. She was surprised to find him grave.

"Yes, except my horse and dog, and I had to leave them behind," answered Joe, bowing his head a little.

"You'd like to be Jim because he's a preacher, and could help uncle convert the Indians?"

"Yes, partly that, but mostly because—somehow—something you've said or done has made me care for you in a different way, and I'd like to be worthy of you."

"I don't think I can believe it, when you say you are 'no good,'" she replied.

"Nell," he cried, and suddenly grasped her hand.

She wrenched herself free, and leaped away from him. Her face was bright now, and the promise of smiles was made good.

"Behave yourself, sir." She tossed her head with a familiar backward motion to throw the chestnut hair from her face, and looked at him with eyes veiled slightly under their lashes. "You will go with Kate and me?"

Before he could answer, a cry from some one on the plain below attracted their attention. They turned and saw another wagon-train pulling into the settlement. The children were shooting and running alongside the weary oxen; men and women went forward expectantly.

"That must be the train uncle expected. Let us go down," said Nell.

Joe did not answer; but followed her down the path. When they gained a clump of willows near the cabins he bent forward and took her hand. She saw the reckless gleam in his eyes.

"Don't. They'll see," she whispered.

"If that's the only reason you have, I reckon I don't care," said Joe.

"What do you mean? I didn't say—I didn't tell—oh! let me go!" implored Nell.

She tried to release the hand Joe had grasped in his broad palm, but in vain; the more she struggled the firmer was his hold. A frown wrinkled her brow and her eyes sparkled with spirit. She saw the fur-trader's wife looking out of the window, and remembered laughing and telling the good woman she did not like this young man; it was, perhaps, because she feared those sharp eyes that she resented his audacity. She opened her mouth to rebuke him; but no words came. Joe had bent his head and softly closed her lips with his own.

For the single instant during which Nell stood transfixed, as if with surprise, and looking up at Joe, she was dumb. Usually the girl was ready with sharp or saucy words and impulsive in her movements; but now the bewilderment of being kissed, particularly within view of the trader's wife, confused her. Then she heard voices, and as Joe turned away with a smile on his face, the unusual warmth in her heart was followed by an angry throbbing.

Joe's tall figure stood out distinctly as he leisurely strolled toward the incoming wagon-train without looking backward. Flashing after him a glance that boded wordy trouble in the future, she ran into the cabin.

As she entered the door it seemed certain the grizzled frontiersman sitting on the bench outside had grinned knowingly at her, and winked as if to say he would keep her secret. Mrs. Wentz, the fur-trader's wife, was seated by the open window which faced the fort; she was a large woman, strong of feature, and with that calm placidity of expression common to people who have lived long in sparsely populated districts. Nell glanced furtively at her and thought she detected the shadow of a smile in the gray eyes.

"I saw you and your sweetheart makin' love behind the willow," Mrs. Wentz said in a matter-of-fact voice. "I don't see why you need hide to do it. We folks out here like to see the young people sparkin'. Your young man is a fine-appearin' chap. I felt certain you was sweethearts, for all you allowed you'd known him only a few days. Lize Davis said she saw he was sweet on you. I like his face. Jake, my man, says as how he'll make a good husband for you, and he'll take to the frontier like a duck does to water. I'm sorry you'll not tarry here awhile. We don't see many lasses, especially any as pretty as you, and you'll find it more quiet and lonesome the farther West you get. Jake knows all about Fort Henry, and Jeff Lynn, the hunter outside, he knows Eb and Jack Zane, and Wetzel, and all those Fort Henry men. You'll be gettin' married out there, won't you?"

"You are—quite wrong," said Nell, who all the while Mrs. Wentz was speaking grew rosier and rosier. "We're not anything—"

Then Nell hesitated and finally ceased speaking. She saw that denials or explanations were futile; the simple woman had seen the kiss, and formed her own conclusions. During the few days Nell had spent at Fort Pitt, she had come to understand that the dwellers on the frontier took everything as a matter of course. She had seen them manifest a certain pleasure; but neither surprise, concern, nor any of the quick impulses so common among other people. And this was another lesson Nell took to heart. She realized that she was entering upon a life absolutely different from her former one, and the thought caused her to shrink from the ordeal. Yet all the suggestions regarding her future home; the stories told about Indians, renegades, and of the wild border-life, fascinated her. These people who had settled in this wild region were simple, honest and brave; they accepted what came as facts not to be questioned, and believed what looked true. Evidently the fur-trader's wife and her female neighbors had settled in their minds the relation in which the girl stood to Joe.

This latter reflection heightened Nell's resentment toward her lover. She stood with her face turned away from Mrs. Wentz; the little frown deepened, and she nervously tapped her foot on the floor.

"Where is my sister?" she presently asked.

"She went to see the wagon-train come in. Everybody's out there."

Nell deliberated a moment and then went into the open air. She saw a number of canvas-covered wagons drawn up in front of the cabins; the vehicles were dusty and the wheels encrusted with yellow mud. The grizzled frontiersman who had smiled at Nell stood leaning on his gun, talking to three men, whose travel-stained and worn homespun clothes suggested a long and toilsome journey. There was the bustle of excitement incident to the arrival of strangers; to the quick exchange of greetings, the unloading of wagons and unharnessing of horses and oxen.

Nell looked here and there for her sister. Finally she saw her standing near her uncle while he conversed with one of the teamsters. The girl did not approach them; but glanced quickly around in search of some one else. At length she saw Joe unloading goods from one of the wagons; his back was turned toward her, but she at once recognized the challenge conveyed by the broad shoulders. She saw no other person; gave heed to nothing save what was to her, righteous indignation.

Hearing her footsteps, the young man turned, glancing at her admiringly, said:

"Good evening, Miss."

Nell had not expected such a matter-of-fact greeting from Joe. There was not the slightest trace of repentance in his calm face, and he placidly continued his labor.

"Aren't you sorry you—you treated me so?" burst out Nell.

His coolness was exasperating. Instead of the contrition and apology she had expected, and which was her due, he evidently intended to tease her, as he had done so often.

The young man dropped a blanket and stared.

"I don't understand," he said, gravely. "I never saw you before."

This was too much for quick-tempered Nell. She had had some vague idea of forgiving him, after he had sued sufficiently for pardon; but now, forgetting her good intentions in the belief that he was making sport of her when he should have pleaded for forgiveness, she swiftly raised her hand and slapped him smartly.

The red blood flamed to the young man's face; as he staggered backward with his hand to his cheek, she heard a smothered exclamation behind her, and then the quick, joyous barking of a dog.

When Nell turned she was amazed to see Joe standing beside the wagon, while a big white dog was leaping upon him. Suddenly she felt faint. Bewildered, she looked from Joe to the man she had just struck; but could not say which was the man who professed to love her.

"Jim! So you followed me!" cried Joe, starting forward and flinging his arms around the other.

"Yes, Joe, and right glad I am to find you," answered the young man, while a peculiar expression of pleasure came over his face.

"It's good to see you again! And here's my old dog Mose! But how on earth did you know? Where did you strike my trail? What are you going to do out here on the frontier? Tell me all. What happened after I left—"

Then Joe saw Nell standing nearby, pale and distressed, and he felt something was amiss. He glanced quickly from her to his brother; she seemed to be dazed, and Jim looked grave.

"What the deuce—? Nell, this is my brother Jim, the one I told you about. Jim, this is my friend, Miss Wells."

"I am happy to meet Miss Wells," said Jim, with a smile, "even though she did slap my face for nothing."

"Slapped you? What for?" Then the truth dawned on Joe, and he laughed until the tears came into his eyes. "She took you for me! Ha, ha, ha! Oh, this is great!"

Nell's face was now rosy red and moisture glistened in her eyes; but she tried bravely to stand her ground. Humiliation had taken the place of anger.

"I—I—am sorry, Mr. Downs. I did take you for him. He—he has insulted me." Then she turned and ran into the cabin.

CHAPTER 2

JOE AND JIM WERE SINGULARLY ALIKE. THEY WERE NEARLY THE SAME size, very tall, but so heavily built as to appear of medium height, while their grey eyes and, indeed, every feature of their clean-cut faces corresponded so exactly as to proclaim them brothers.

"Already up to your old tricks?" asked Jim, with his hand on Joe's shoulder, as they both watched Nell's flight.

"I'm really fond of her, Jim, and didn't mean to hurt her feelings. But tell me about yourself; what made you come West?"

"To teach the Indians, and I was, no doubt, strongly influenced by your being here."

"You're going to do as you ever have—make some sacrifice. You are always devoting yourself; if not to me, to some other. Now it's your life you're giving up. To try to convert the redskins and influence me for good is in both cases impossible. How often have I said there wasn't any good in me! My desire is to kill Indians, not preach to them, Jim. I'm glad to see you; but I wish you hadn't come. This wild frontier is no place for a preacher."

"I think it is," said Jim, quietly.

"What of Rose—the girl you were to marry?"

Joe glanced quickly at his brother. Jim's face paled slightly as he turned away.

"I'll speak once more of her, and then, never again," he answered. "You knew Rose better than I did. Once you tried to tell me she was too fond of admiration, and I rebuked you; but now I see that your wider experience of women had taught you things I could not then understand. She was untrue. When you left Williamsburg, apparently because you had gambled with Jewett and afterward fought him, I was not misled. You made the game of cards a pretense; you sought it simply as an opportunity to wreak your vengeance on him for his villainy toward me. Well, it's all over now. Though you cruelly beat and left him disfigured for life, he will live, and you are saved from murder, thank God! When I learned of your departure I yearned to follow. Then I met a preacher who spoke of having intended to go West with a Mr. Wells, of the Moravian Mission. I immediately said I would go in his place, and here I am. I'm fortunate in that I have found both him and you."

"I'm sorry I didn't kill Jewett; I certainly meant to. Anyway, there's some comfort in knowing I left my mark on him. He was a sneaking, cold-blooded fellow, with his white hair and pale face, and always fawning round the girls. I hated him, and gave it to him good." Joe spoke musingly and complacently as though it was a trivial thing to compass the killing of a man.

"Well, Jim, you're here now, and there's no help for it. We'll go along with this Moravian preacher and his nieces. If you haven't any great regrets for the past, why, all may be well yet. I can see that the border is the place for me. But now, Jim, for once in your life take a word of advice from me. We're out on the frontier, where every man looks after himself. Your being a minister won't protect you here where every man wears a knife and a tomahawk, and where most of them are desperadoes. Cut out that soft voice and most of your gentle ways, and be a little more like your brother. Be as kind as you like, and preach all you want to; but when some of these buckskin-legged frontiermen try to walk all over you, as they will, take your own part in a way you have never taken it before. I had my lesson the first few days out with that wagon-train. It was a case of four fights; but I'm all right now."

"Joe, I won't run, if that's what you mean," answered Jim, with a laugh. "Yes, I understand that a new life begins here, and I am content. If I can find my work in it, and remain with you, I shall be happy."

"Ah! old Mose! I'm glad to see you," Joe cried to the big dog who came nosing round him. "You've brought this old fellow; did you bring the horses?"

"Look behind the wagon."

With the dog bounding before him, Joe did as he was directed, and there found two horses tethered side by side. Little wonder that his eyes gleamed with delight. One was jet-black; the other iron-gray and in every line the clean-limbed animals showed the thoroughbred. The black threw up his slim head and whinnied, with affection clearly shining in his soft, dark eyes as he recognized his master.

"Lance, old fellow, how did I ever leave you!" murmured Joe, as he threw his arm over the arched neck. Mose stood by looking up, and wagging his tail in token of happiness at the reunion of the three old friends. There were tears in Joe's eyes when, with a last affectionate caress, he turned away from his pet.

"Come, Jim, I'll take you to Mr. Wells."

They stated across the little square, while Mose went back under the wagon; but at a word from Joe he bounded after them, trotting contentedly at their heels. Half way to the cabins a big, raw-boned teamster, singing in a drunken voice, came staggering toward them. Evidently he had just left the group of people who had gathered near the Indians.

"I didn't expect to see drunkenness out here," said Jim, in a low tone.

"There's lots of it. I saw that fellow yesterday when he couldn't walk. Wentz told me he was a bad customer."

The teamster, his red face bathed in perspiration, and his sleeves rolled up, showing brown, knotty arms, lurched toward them. As they met he aimed a kick at the dog; but Mose leaped nimbly aside, avoiding the heavy boot. He did not growl, nor show his teeth; but the great white head sank forward a little, and the lithe body crouched for a spring.

"Don't touch that dog; he'll tear your leg off!" Joe cried sharply.

"Say, pard, cum an' hev' a drink," replied the teamster, with a friendly leer.

"I don't drink," answered Joe, curtly, and moved on.

The teamster growled something of which only the word "parson" was intelligible to the brothers. Joe stopped and looked back. His gray eyes seemed to contract; they did not flash, but shaded and lost their warmth. Jim saw the change, and, knowing what it signified, took Joe's arm as he gently urged him away. The teamster's shrill voice could be heard until they entered the fur-trader's cabin.

An old man with long, white hair flowing from beneath his wide-brimmed hat, sat near the door holding one of Mrs. Wentz's children on his knee. His face was deep-lined and serious; but kindness shone from his mild blue eyes.

"Mr. Wells, this is my brother James. He is a preacher, and has come in place of the man you expected from Williamsburg."

The old minister arose, and extended his hand, gazing earnestly at the new-comer meanwhile. Evidently he approved of what he saw in his quick scrutiny of the other's face, for his lips were wreathed with a smile of welcome.

"Mr. Downs, I am glad to meet you, and to know you will go with me. I thank God I shall take into the wilderness one who is young enough to carry on the work when my days are done."

"I will make it my duty to help you in whatsoever way lies in my power," answered Jim, earnestly.

"We have a great work before us. I have heard many scoffers who claim that it is worse than folly to try to teach these fierce savages Christianity; but I know it can be done, and my heart is in the work. I have no fear; yet I would not conceal from you, young man, that the danger of going among these hostile Indians must be great."

"I will not hesitate because of that. My sympathy is with the redman. I have had an opportunity of studying Indian nature and believe the race inherently noble. He has been driven to make war, and I want to help him into other paths."

Joe left the two ministers talking earnestly and turned toward Mrs. Wentz. The fur-trader's wife was glowing with pleasure. She held in her hand several rude trinkets, and was explaining to her listener, a young woman, that the toys were for the children, having been brought all the way from Williamsburg.

"Kate, where's Nell?" Joe asked of the girl.

"She went on an errand for Mrs. Wentz."

Kate Wells was the opposite of her sister. Her motions were slow, easy and consistent with her large, full, form. Her brown eyes and hair contrasted sharply with Nell's. The greatest difference in the sisters lay in that Nell's face was sparkling and full of the fire of her eager young life, while Kate's was calm, like the unruffled surface of a deep lake.

"That's Jim, my brother. We're going with you," said Joe.

"Are you? I'm glad," answered the girl, looking at the handsome earnest face of the young minister.

"Your brother's like you for all the world," whispered Mrs. Wentz.

"He does look like you," said Kate, with her slow smile.

"Which means you think, or hope, that that is all," retorted Joe laughingly. "Well, Kate, there the resemblance ends, thank God for Jim!"

He spoke in a sad, bitter tone which caused both women to look at him wonderingly. Joe had to them ever been full of surprises; never until then had they seen evidences of sadness in his face. A moment's silence ensued. Mrs. Wentz gazed lovingly at the children who were playing with the trinkets; while Kate mused over the young man's remark, and began studying his, half-averted face. She felt warmly drawn to him by the strange expression in the glance he had given his brother. The tenderness in his eyes did not harmonize with much of this wild and reckless boy's behavior. To Kate he had always seemed so bold, so cold, so different from other men, and yet here was proof that Master Joe loved his brother.

The murmured conversation of the two ministers was interrupted by a low cry from outside the cabin. A loud, coarse laugh followed, and then a husky voice:

"Hol' on, my purty lass."'

Joe took two long strides, and was on the door-step. He saw Nell struggling violently in the grasp of the half-drunken teamster.

"I'll jes' hev' to kiss this lassie fer luck," he said in a tone of good humor.

At the same instant Joe saw three loungers laughing, and a fourth, the grizzled frontiersman, starting forward with a yell.

"Let me go!" cried Nell.

Just when the teamster had pulled her close to him, and was bending his red, moist face to hers, two brown, sinewy hands grasped his neck with an angry clutch. Deprived thus of breath, his mouth opened, his tongue protruded; his eyes seemed starting from their sockets, and his arms beat the air. Then he was lifted and flung with a crash against the cabin wall. Falling, he lay in a heap on the grass, while the blood flowed from a cut on his temple.

"What's this?" cried a man, authoritatively. He had come swiftly up, and arrived at the scene where stood the grizzled frontiersman.

"It was purty handy, Wentz. I couldn't hev' did better myself, and I was comin' for that purpose," said the frontiersman. "Leffler was tryin' to kiss the lass. He's been drunk fer two days. That little girl's sweetheart kin handle himself some, now you take my word on it."

"I'll agree Leff's bad when he's drinkin'," answered the fur-trader, and to Joe he added, "He's liable to look you up when he comes around."

"Tell him if I am here when he gets sober, I'll kill him," Joe cried in a sharp voice. His gaze rested once more on the fallen teamster, and again an odd contraction of his eyes was noticeable. The glance was cutting, as if with the flash of cold gray steel. "Nell, I'm sorry I wasn't round sooner," he said, apologetically, as if it was owing to his neglect the affair had happened.

As they entered the cabin Nell stole a glance at him. This was the third time he had injured a man because of her. She had on several occasions seen that cold, steely glare in his eyes, and it had always frightened her. It was gone, however, before they were inside the building. He said something which she did not hear distinctly, and his calm voice allayed her excitement. She had been angry with him; but now she realized that her resentment had disappeared. He had spoken so kindly after the outburst. Had he not shown that he considered himself her protector and lover? A strange emotion, sweet and subtle as the taste of wine, thrilled her, while a sense of fear because of his strength was mingled with her pride in it. Any other girl would have been only too glad to have such a champion; she would, too, hereafter, for he was a man of whom to be proud.

"Look here, Nell, you haven't spoken to me," Joe cried suddenly, seeming to understand that she had not even heard what he said, so engrossed had she been with her reflections. "Are you mad with me yet?" he continued. "Why, Nell, I'm in—I love you!"

Evidently Joe thought such fact a sufficient reason for any act on his part. His tender tone conquered Nell, and she turned to him with flushed cheeks and glad eyes.

"I wasn't angry at all," she whispered, and then, eluding the arm he extended, she ran into the other room.

CHAPTER 3

JOE LOUNGED IN THE DOORWAY OF THE CABIN, THOUGHTFULLY contemplating two quiet figures that were lying in the shade of a maple tree. One he recognized as the Indian with whom Jim had spent an earnest hour that morning; the red son of the woods was wrapped in slumber. He had placed under his head a many-hued homespun shirt which the young preacher had given him; but while asleep his head had rolled off this improvised pillow, and the bright garment lay free, attracting the eye. Certainly it had led to the train of thought which had found lodgment in Joe's fertile brain.

The other sleeper was a short, stout man whom Joe had seen several times before. This last fellow did not appear to be well-balanced in his mind, and was the butt of the settlers' jokes, while the children called him "Loorey." He, like the Indian, was sleeping off the effects of the previous night's dissipation.

During a few moments Joe regarded the recumbent figures with an expression on his face which told that he thought in them were great possibilities for sport. With one quick glance around he disappeared within the cabin, and when he showed himself at the door, surveying the village square with mirthful eyes, he held in his hand a small basket of Indian design. It was made of twisted grass, and simply contained several bits of soft, chalky stone such as the Indians used for painting, which collection Joe had discovered among the fur-trader's wares.

He glanced around once more, and saw that all those in sight were busy with their work. He gave the short man a push, and chuckled when there was no response other than a lazy grunt. Joe took the Indians' gaudy shirt, and, lifting Loorey, slipped it around him, shoved the latter's arms through the sleeves, and buttoned it in front. He streaked the round face with red and white paint, and then, dexterously extracting the eagle plume from the Indian's head-dress, stuck it in Loorey's thick shock of hair. It was all done in a moment, after which Joe replaced the basket, and went down to the river.

Several times that morning he had visited the rude wharf where Jeff Lynn, the grizzled old frontiersman, busied himself with preparations for the raft-journey down the Ohio. Lynn had been employed to guide the missionary's party to Fort Henry, and, as the brothers had acquainted him with their intention of accompanying the travelers, he had constructed a raft for them and their horses.

Joe laughed when he saw the dozen two-foot logs fastened together, upon which a rude shack had been erected for shelter. This slight protection from sun and storm was all the brothers would have on their long journey.

Joe noted, however, that the larger raft had been prepared with some thought for the comfort of the girls. The floor of the little hut was raised so that the waves which broke over the logs could not reach it. Taking a peep into the structure, Joe was pleased to see that Nell and Kate would be comfortable, even during a storm. A buffalo robe and two red blankets gave to the interior a cozy, warm look. He observed that some of the girls' luggage was already on board.

"When'll we be off?" he inquired.

"Sun-up," answered Lynn, briefly.

"I'm glad of that. I like to be on the go in the early morning," said Joe, cheerfully.

"Most folks from over Eastways ain't in a hurry to tackle the river," replied Lynn, eyeing Joe sharply.

"It's a beautiful river, and I'd like to sail on it from here to where it ends, and then come back to go again," Joe replied, warmly.

"In a hurry to be a-goin'? I'll allow you'll see some slim red devils, with feathers in their hair, slipping among the trees along the bank, and mebbe you'll hear the ping which's made when whistlin' lead hits. Perhaps you'll want to be back here by termorrer sundown."

"Not I," said Joe, with his short, cool laugh.

The old frontiersman slowly finished his task of coiling up a rope of wet cowhide, and then, producing a dirty pipe, he took a live ember from the fire and placed it on the bowl. He sucked slowly at the pipe-stem, and soon puffed out a great cloud of smoke. Sitting on a log, he deliberately surveyed the robust shoulders and long, heavy limbs of the young man, with a keen appreciation of their symmetry and strength. Agility, endurance and courage were more to a borderman than all else; a newcomer on the frontier was always "sized-up" with reference to these "points," and respected in proportion to the measure in which he possessed them.

Old Jeff Lynn, riverman, hunter, frontiersman, puffed slowly at his pipe while he mused thus to himself: "Mebbe I'm wrong in takin' a likin' to this youngster so sudden. Mebbe it's because I'm fond of his sunny-haired lass, an' ag'in mebbe it's because I'm gettin' old an' likes young folks better'n I onct did. Anyway, I'm kinder thinkin, if this young feller gits worked out, say fer about twenty pounds less, he'll lick a whole raft-load of wild-cats."

Joe walked to and fro on the logs, ascertained how the raft was put together, and took a pull on the long, clumsy steering-oar. At length he seated himself beside Lynn. He was eager to ask questions; to know about the rafts, the river, the forest, the Indians—everything in connection with this wild life; but already he had learned that questioning these frontiersmen is a sure means of closing their lips.

"Ever handle the long rifle?" asked Lynn, after a silence.

"Yes," answered Joe, simply.

"Ever shoot anythin'?" the frontiersman questioned, when he had taken four or five puffs at his pipe.

"Squirrels."

"Good practice, shootin' squirrels," observed Jeff, after another silence, long enough to allow Joe to talk if he was so inclined. "Kin ye hit one—say, a hundred yards?"

"Yes, but not every time in the head," returned Joe. There was an apologetic tone in his answer.

Another interval followed in which neither spoke. Jeff was slowly pursuing his line of thought. After Joe's last remark he returned his pipe to his pocket and brought out a tobacco-pouch. He tore off a large portion of the weed and thrust it into his mouth. Then he held out the little buck-skin sack to Joe.

"Hev' a chaw," he said.

To offer tobacco to anyone was absolutely a borderman's guarantee of friendliness toward that person.

Jeff expectorated half a dozen times, each time coming a little nearer the stone he was aiming at, some five yards distant. Possibly this was the borderman's way of oiling up his conversational machinery. At all events, he commenced to talk.

"Yer brother's goin' to preach out here, ain't he? Preachin' is all right, I'll allow; but I'm kinder doubtful about preachin' to redskins. Howsumever, I've knowed Injuns who are good fellows, and there's no tellin'. What are ye goin' in fer—farmin'?"

"No, I wouldn't make a good farmer."

"Jest cum out kinder wild like, eh?" rejoined Jeff, knowingly.

"I wanted to come West because I was tired of tame life. I love the forest; I want to fish and hunt; and I think I'd like to—to see Indians."

"I kinder thought so," said the old frontiersman, nodding his head as though he perfectly understood Joe's case. "Well, lad, where you're goin' seein' Injuns ain't a matter of choice. You has to see 'em, and fight 'em, too. We've had bad times for years out here on the border, and I'm thinkin' wuss is comin'. Did ye ever hear the name Girty?"

"Yes; he's a renegade."

"He's a traitor, and Jim and George Girty, his brothers, are p'isin rattlesnake Injuns. Simon Girty's bad enough; but Jim's the wust. He's now wusser'n a full-blooded Delaware. He's all the time on the lookout to capture white wimen to take to his Injun teepee. Simon Girty and his pals, McKee and Elliott, deserted from that thar fort right afore yer eyes. They're now livin' among the redskins down Fort Henry way, raisin' as much hell fer the settlers as they kin."

"Is Fort Henry near the Indian towns?" asked Joe.

"There's Delawares, Shawnees and Hurons all along the Ohio below Fort Henry."

"Where is the Moravian Mission located?"

"Why, lad, the Village of Peace, as the Injuns call it, is right in the midst of that Injun country. I 'spect it's a matter of a hundred miles below and cross-country a little from Fort Henry."

"The fort must be an important point, is it not?"

"Wal, I guess so. It's the last place on the river," answered Lynn, with a grim smile. "There's only a stockade there, an' a handful of men. The Injuns hev swarmed down on it time and ag'in, but they hev never burned it. Only such men as Colonel Zane, his brother Jack, and Wetzel could hev kept that fort standin' all these bloody years. Eb Zane's got but a few men, yet he kin handle 'em some, an' with such scouts as Jack Zane and Wetzel, he allus knows what's goin' on among the Injuns."

"I've heard of Colonel Zane. He was an officer under Lord Dunmore. The hunters here speak often of Jack Zane and Wetzel. What are they?"

"Jack Zane is a hunter an' guide. I knowed him well a few years back. He's a quiet, mild chap; but a streak of chain-lightnin' when he's riled. Wetzel is an Injun-killer. Some people say as how he's crazy over scalp-huntin'; but I reckon that's not so. I've seen him a few times. He don't hang round the settlement 'cept when the Injuns are up, an' nobody sees him much. At home he sets round silent-like, an' then mebbe next mornin' he'll be gone, an' won't show up fer days or weeks. But all the frontier knows of his deeds. Fer instance, I've hearn of settlers gettin' up in the mornin' an' findin' a couple of dead and scalped Injuns right in front of their cabins. No one knowed who killed 'em, but everybody says 'Wetzel.' He's allus warnin' the settlers when they need to flee to the fort, and sure he's right every time, because when these men go back to their cabins they find nothin' but ashes. There couldn't be any farmin' done out there but fer Wetzel."

"What does he look like?" questioned Joe, much interested.

"Wetzel stands straight as the oak over thar. He'd hev' to go sideways to git his shoulders in that door, but he's as light of foot an' fast as a deer. An' his eyes—why, lad, ye kin hardly look into 'em. If you ever see Wetzel you'll know him to onct."

"I want to see him," Joe spoke quickly, his eyes lighting with an eager flash. "He must be a great fighter."

"Is he? Lew Wetzel is the heftiest of 'em all, an' we hev some as kin fight out here. I was down the river a few years ago and joined a party to go out an' hunt up some redskins as had been reported. Wetzel was with us. We soon struck Injun sign, and then come on to a lot of the pesky varmints. We was all fer goin' home, because we had a small force. When we started to go we finds Wetzel sittin' calm-like on a log. We said: 'Ain't ye goin' home?' and he replied, 'I cum out to find redskins, an' now as we've found 'em, I'm not goin' to run away.' An' we left him settin' thar. Oh, Wetzel is a fighter!"

"I hope I shall see him," said Joe once more, the warm light, which made him look so boyish, still glowing in his face.

"Mebbe ye'll git to; and sure ye'll see redskins, an' not tame ones, nuther."

At this moment the sound of excited voices near the cabins broke in on the conversation. Joe saw several persons run toward the large cabin and disappear behind it. He smiled as he thought perhaps the commotion had been caused by the awakening of the Indian brave.

Rising to his feet, Joe went toward the cabin, and soon saw the cause of the excitement. A small crowd of men and women, all laughing and talking, surrounded the Indian brave and the little stout fellow. Joe heard some one groan, and then a deep, guttural voice:

"Paleface—big steal—ugh! Injun mad—heap mad—kill paleface."

After elbowing his way into the group, Joe saw the Indian holding Loorey with one hand, while he poked him on the ribs with the other. The captive's face was the picture of dismay; even the streaks of paint did not hide his look of fear and bewilderment. The poor half-witted fellow was so badly frightened that he could only groan.

"Silvertip scalp paleface. Ugh!" growled the savage, giving Loorey another blow on the side. This time he bent over in pain. The bystanders were divided in feeling; the men laughed, while the women murmured sympathetically.

"This's not a bit funny," muttered Joe, as he pushed his way nearly to the middle of the crowd. Then he stretched out a long arm that, bare and brawny, looked as though it might have been a blacksmith's, and grasped the Indian's sinewy wrist with a force that made him loosen his hold on Loorey instantly.

"I stole the shirt—fun—joke," said Joe. "Scalp me if you want to scalp anyone."

The Indian looked quickly at the powerful form before him. With a twist he slipped his arm from Joe's grasp.

"Big paleface heap fun—all squaw play," he said, scornfully. There was a menace in his somber eyes as he turned abruptly and left the group.

"I'm afraid you've made an enemy," said Jake Wentz to Joe. "An Indian never forgets an insult, and that's how he regarded your joke. Silvertip has been friendly here because he sells us his pelts. He's a Shawnee chief. There he goes through the willows!"

By this time Jim and Mr. Wells, Mrs. Wentz and the girls had joined the group. They all watched Silvertip get into his canoe and paddle away.

"A bad sign," said Wentz, and then, turning to Jeff Lynn, who joined the party at that moment, he briefly explained the circumstances.

"Never did like Silver. He's a crafty redskin, an' not to be trusted," replied Jeff.

"He has turned round and is looking back," Nell said quickly.

"So he has," observed the fur-trader.

The Indian was now several hundred yards down the swift river, and for an instant had ceased paddling. The sun shone brightly on his eagle plumes. He remained motionless for a moment, and even at such a distance the dark, changeless face could be discerned. He lifted his hand and shook it menacingly.

"If ye don't hear from that redskin ag'in Jeff Lynn don't know nothin'," calmly said the old frontiersman.

CHAPTER 4

As the rafts drifted with the current the voyagers saw the settlers on the landing-place diminish until they had faded from indistinct figures to mere black specks against the green background. Then came the last wave of a white scarf, faintly in the distance, and at length the dark outline of the fort was all that remained to their regretful gaze. Quickly that, too, disappeared behind the green hill, which, with its bold front, forces the river to take a wide turn.

The Ohio, winding in its course between high, wooded bluffs, rolled on and on into the wilderness.

Beautiful as was the ever-changing scenery, rugged gray-faced cliffs on one side contrasting with green-clad hills on the other, there hovered over land and water something more striking than beauty. Above all hung a still atmosphere of calmness—of loneliness.

And this penetrating solitude marred somewhat the pleasure which might have been found in the picturesque scenery, and caused the voyagers, to whom this country was new, to take less interest in the gaily-feathered birds and stealthy animals that were to be seen on the way. By the forms of wild life along the banks of the river, this strange intruder on their peace was regarded with attention. The birds and beasts evinced little fear of the floating rafts. The sandhill crane, stalking along the shore, lifted his long neck as the unfamiliar thing came floating by, and then stood still and silent as a statue until the rafts disappeared from view. Blueherons feeding along the bars, saw the unusual spectacle, and, uttering surprised "booms," they spread wide wings and lumbered away along the shore. The crows circled above the voyagers, cawing in not unfriendly excitement. Smaller birds alighted on the raised poles, and several—a robin, a catbird and a little brown wren—ventured with hesitating boldness to peck at the crumbs the girls threw to them. Deer waded knee-deep in the shallow water, and, lifting their heads, instantly became motionless and absorbed. Occasionally a buffalo appeared on a level stretch of bank, and, tossing his huge head, seemed inclined to resent the coming of this stranger into his domain.

All day the rafts drifted steadily and swiftly down the river, presenting to the little party ever-varying pictures of densely wooded hills, of jutting, broken cliffs with scant evergreen growth; of long reaches of sandy bar that glistened golden in the sunlight, and over all the flight and call of wildfowl, the flitting of woodland songsters, and now and then the whistle and bellow of the horned watchers in the forest.

The intense blue of the vault above began to pale, and low down in the west a few fleecy clouds, gorgeously golden for a fleeting instant, then crimson-crowned for another, shaded and darkened as the setting sun sank behind the hills. Presently the red rays disappeared, a pink glow suffused the heavens, and at last, as gray twilight stole down over the hill-tops, the crescent moon peeped above the wooded fringe of the western bluffs.

"Hard an' fast she is," sang out Jeff Lynn, as he fastened the rope to a tree at the head of a small island. "All off now, and' we'll hev' supper. Thar's a fine spring under yon curly birch, an' I fetched along a leg of deer-meat. Hungry, little 'un?"

He had worked hard all day steering the rafts, yet Nell had seen him smiling at her many times during the journey, and he had found time before the early start to arrange for her a comfortable seat. There was now a solicitude in the frontiersman's voice that touched her.

"I am famished," she replied, with her bright smile. "I am afraid I could eat a whole deer."

They all climbed the sandy slope, and found themselves on the summit of an oval island, with a pretty glade in the middle surrounded by birches. Bill, the second raftsman, a stolid, silent man, at once swung his axe upon a log of driftwood. Mr. Wells and Jim walked to and fro under the birches, and Kate and Nell sat on the grass watching with great interest the old helmsman as he came up from the river, his brown hands and face shining from the scrubbing he had given them. Soon he had a fire cheerfully blazing, and after laying out the few utensils, he addressed himself to Joe:

"I'll tell ye right here, lad, good venison kin be spoiled by bad cuttin' and cookin'. You're slicin' it too thick. See—thar! Now salt good, an' keep outen the flame; on the red coals is best."

With a sharpened stick Jeff held the thin slices over the fire for a few moments. Then he laid them aside on some clean white-oak chips Bill's axe had provided. The simple meal of meat, bread, and afterward a drink of the cold spring water, was keenly relished by the hungry voyagers. When it had been eaten, Jeff threw a log on the fire and remarked:

"Seein' as how we won't be in redskin territory fer awhile yit, we kin hev a fire. I'll allow ye'll all be chilly and damp from river-mist afore long, so toast yerselves good."

"How far have we come to-day?" inquired Mr. Wells, his mind always intent on reaching the scene of his cherished undertaking.

"'Bout thirty-odd mile, I reckon. Not much on a trip, thet's sartin, but we'll pick up termorrer. We've some quicker water, an' the rafts hev to go separate."

"How quiet!" exclaimed Kate, suddenly breaking the silence that followed the frontiersman's answer.

"Beautiful!" impetuously said Nell, looking up at Joe. A quick flash from his gray eyes answered her; he did not speak; indeed he had said little to her since the start, but his glance showed her how glad he was that she felt the sweetness and content of this wild land.

"I was never in a wilderness before," broke in the earnest voice of the young minister. "I feel an almost overpowering sense of loneliness. I want to get near to you all; I feel lost. Yet it is grand, sublime!"

"Here is the promised land—the fruitful life—Nature as it was created by God," replied the old minister, impressively.

"Tell us a story," said Nell to the old frontiersman, as he once more joined the circle round the fire.

"So, little 'un, ye want a story?" queried Jeff, taking up a live coal and placing it in the bowl of his pipe. He took off his coon-skin cap and carefully laid it aside. His weather-beaten face beamed in answer to the girl's request. He drew a long and audible pull at his black pipe, and send forth slowly a cloud of white smoke. Deliberately poking the fire with a stick, as if stirring into life dead embers of the past, he sucked again at his pipe, and emitted a great puff of smoke that completely enveloped the grizzled head. From out that white cloud came his drawling voice.

"Ye've seen thet big curly birch over thar—thet 'un as bends kind of sorrowful like. Wal, it used to stand straight an' proud. I've knowed thet tree all the years I've navigated this river, an' it seems natural like to me thet it now droops dyin', fer it shades the grave of as young, an' sweet, an' purty a lass as yerself, Miss Nell. Rivermen called this island George's Island, 'cause Washington onct camped here; but of late years the name's got changed, an' the men say suthin' like this: 'We'll try an' make Milly's birch afore sundown,' jest as Bill and me hev done to-day. Some years agone I was comin' up from Fort Henry, an' had on board my slow old scow a lass named Milly—we never learned her other name. She come to me at the fort, an' tells as how her folks hed been killed by Injuns, an' she wanted to git back to Pitt to meet her sweetheart. I was ag'in her comin' all along, an' fust off I said 'No.' But when I seen tears in her blue eyes, an' she puts her little hand on mine, I jest wilted, an' says to Jim Blair, 'She goes.' Wal, jest as might hev been expected—an' fact is I looked fer it—we wus tackled by redskins. Somehow, Jim Girty got wind of us hevin' a lass aboard, an' he ketched up with us jest below here. It's a bad place, called Shawnee Rock, an' I'll show it to ye termorrer. The renegade, with his red devils, attacked us thar, an' we had a time gittin' away. Milly wus shot. She lived fer awhile, a couple of days, an' all the time wus so patient, an' sweet, an' brave with thet renegade's bullet in her—fer he shot her when he seen he couldn't capture her—thet thar wusn't a blame man of us who wouldn't hev died to grant her prayer, which wus that she could live to onct more see her lover."

There was a long silence, during which the old frontiersman sat gazing into the fire with sad eyes.

"We couldn't do nuthin', an' we buried her thar under thet birch, where she smiled her last sad, sweet smile, an' died. Ever since then the river has been eatn' away at this island. It's only half as big as it wus onct, an' another flood will take away this sand-bar, these few birches—an' Milly's grave."

The old frontiersman's story affected all his listeners. The elder minister bowed his head and prayed that no such fate might overtake his nieces. The young minister looked again, as he had many times that day, at Nell's winsome face. The girls cast grave glances at the drooping birch, and their bright tears glistened in the fire-glow. Once more Joe's eyes glinted with that steely flash, and as he gazed out over the wide, darkening expanse of water his face grew cold and rigid.

"I'll allow I might hev told a more cheerful story, an' I'll do so next time; but I wanted ye all, particular the lasses, to know somethin' of the kind of country ye're goin' into. The frontier needs women; but jist yit it deals hard with them. An' Jim Girty, with more of his kind, ain't dead yit."

"Why don't some one kill him?" was Joe's sharp question.

"Easier said than done, lad. Jim Girty is a white traitor, but he's a cunnin' an' fierce redskin in his ways an' life. He knows the woods as a crow does, an' keeps outer sight 'cept when he's least expected. Then ag'in, he's got Simon Girty, his brother, an' almost the whole redskin tribe behind him. Injuns stick close to a white man that has turned ag'inst his own people, an' Jim Girty hain't ever been ketched. Howsumever, I heard last trip thet he'd been tryin' some of his tricks round Fort Henry, an' thet Wetzel is on his trail. Wal, if it's so thet Lew Wetzel is arter him, I wouldn't give a pinch o' powder fer the white-redskin's chances of a long life."

No one spoke, and Jeff, after knocking the ashes from his pipe, went down to the raft, returning shortly afterward with his blanket. This he laid down and rolled himself in it. Presently from under his coon-skin cap came the words:

"Wal, I've turned in, an' I advise ye all to do the same."

All save Joe and Nell acted on Jeff's suggestion. For a long time the young couple sat close together on the bank, gazing at the moonlight on the river.

The night was perfect. A cool wind fanned the dying embers of the fire and softly stirred the leaves. Earlier in the evening a single frog had voiced his protest against the loneliness; but now his dismal croak was no longer heard. A snipe, belated in his feeding, ran along the sandy shore uttering his tweet-tweet, and his little cry, breaking in so softly on the silence, seemed only to make more deeply felt the great vast stillness of the night.

Joe's arm was around Nell. She had demurred at first, but he gave no heed to her slight resistance, and finally her head rested against his shoulder. There was no need of words.

Joe had a pleasurable sense of her nearness, and there was a delight in the fragrance of her hair as it waved against his cheek; but just then love was not uppermost in his mind. All day he had been silent under the force of an emotion which he could not analyze. Some power, some feeling in which the thought of Nell had no share, was drawing him with irresistible strength. Nell had just begun to surrender to him in the sweetness of her passion; and yet even with that knowledge knocking reproachfully at his heart, he could not help being absorbed in the shimmering water, in the dark reflection of the trees, the gloom and shadow of the forest.

Presently he felt her form relax in his arms; then her soft regular breathing told him she had fallen asleep and he laughed low to himself. How she would pout on the morrow when he teased her about it! Then, realizing that she was tired with her long day's journey, he reproached himself for keeping her from the needed rest, and instantly decided to carry her to the raft. Yet such was the novelty of the situation that he yielded to its charm, and did not go at once. The moonlight found bright threads in her wavy hair; it shone caressingly on her quiet face, and tried to steal under the downcast lashes.

Joe made a movement to rise with her, when she muttered indistinctly as if speaking to some one. He remembered then she had once told him that she talked in her sleep, and how greatly it annoyed her. He might hear something more with which to tease her; so he listened.

"Yes—uncle—I will go—Kate, we must—go. . ."

Another interval of silence, then more murmurings. He distinguished his own name, and presently she called clearly, as if answering some inward questioner.

"I—love him—yes—I love Joe—he has mastered me. Yet I wish he were—like Jim—Jim who looked at me—so—with his deep eyes—and I. . . ."

Joe lifted her as if she were a baby, and carrying her down to the raft, gently laid her by her sleeping sister.

The innocent words which he should not have heard were like a blow. What she would never have acknowledged in her waking hours had been revealed in her dreams. He recalled the glance of Jim's eyes as it had rested on Nell many times that day, and now these things were most significant.

He found at the end of the island a great, mossy stone. On this he climbed, and sat where the moonlight streamed upon him. Gradually that cold bitterness died out from his face, as it passed from his heart, and once more he became engrossed in the silver sheen on the water, the lapping of the waves on the pebbly beach, and in that speaking, mysterious silence of the woods.

WHEN THE FIRST FAINT RAYS OF RED STREAKED OVER THE EASTERN hill-tops, and the river mist arose from the water in a vapory cloud, Jeff

Lynn rolled out of his blanket, stretched his long limbs, and gave a hearty call to the morning. His cheerful welcome awakened all the voyagers except Joe, who had spent the night in watching and the early morning in fishing.

"Wal, I'll be darned," ejaculated Jeff as he saw Joe. "Up afore me, an' ketched a string of fish."

"What are they?" asked Joe, holding up several bronze-backed fish.

"Bass—black bass, an' thet big feller is a lammin' hefty 'un. How'd ye ketch 'em?"

"I fished for them."

"Wal, so it 'pears," growled Jeff, once more reluctantly yielding to his admiration for the lad. "How'd ye wake up so early?"

"I stayed up all night. I saw three deer swim from the mainland, but nothing else came around."

"Try yer hand at cleanin' 'em fer breakfast," continued Jeff, beginning to busy himself with preparations for that meal. "Wal, wal, if he ain't surprisin'! He'll do somethin' out here on the frontier, sure as I'm a born sinner," he muttered to himself, wagging his head in his quaint manner.

Breakfast over, Jeff transferred the horses to the smaller raft, which he had cut loose from his own, and, giving a few directions to Bill, started down-stream with Mr. Wells and the girls.

The rafts remained close together for a while, but as the current quickened and was more skillfully taken advantage of by Jeff, the larger raft gained considerable headway, gradually widening the gap between the two.

All day they drifted. From time to time Joe and Jim waved their hands to the girls; but the greater portion of their attention was given to quieting the horses. Mose, Joe's big white dog, retired in disgust to the hut, where he watched and dozed by turns. He did not fancy this kind of voyaging. Bill strained his sturdy arms all day on the steering-oar.

About the middle of the afternoon Joe observed that the hills grew more rugged and precipitous, and the river ran faster. He kept a constant lookout for the wall of rock which marked the point of danger. When the sun had disappeared behind the hills, he saw ahead a gray rock protruding from the green foliage. It was ponderous, overhanging, and seemed to frown down on the river. This was Shawnee Rock. Joe looked long at the cliff, and wondered if there was now an Indian scout hidden behind the pines that skirted the edge. Prominent on the top of the bluff a large, dead tree projected its hoary, twisted branches.

Bill evidently saw the landmark, for he stopped in his monotonous walk to and fro across the raft, and pushing his oar amidships he looked ahead for the other raft. The figure of the tall frontiersman could be plainly seen as he labored at the helm.

The raft disappeared round a bend, and as it did so Joe saw a white scarf waved by Nell.

Bill worked the clumsy craft over toward the right shore where the current was more rapid. He pushed with all his strength, and when the oar had reached its widest sweep, he lifted it and ran back across the raft for another push. Joe scanned the river ahead. He saw no rapids; only rougher water whirling over some rocks. They were where the channel narrowed and ran close to the right-hand bank. Under a willow-flanked ledge was a sand-bar. To Joe there seemed nothing hazardous in drifting through this pass.

"Bad place ahead," said Bill, observing Joe's survey of the river.

"It doesn't look so," replied Joe.

"A raft ain't a boat. We could pole a boat. You has to hev water to float logs, an' the river's run out considerable. I'm only afeerd fer the horses. If we hit or drag, they might plunge around a bit."

When the raft passed into the head of the bend it struck the rocks several times, but finally gained the channel safely, and everything seemed propitious for an easy passage.

But, greatly to Bill's surprise, the wide craft was caught directly in the channel, and swung round so that the steering-oar pointed toward the opposite shore. The water roared a foot deep over the logs.

"Hold hard on the horses!" yelled Bill. "Somethin's wrong. I never seen a snag here."

The straining mass of logs, insecurely fastened together, rolled and then pitched loose again, but the short delay had been fatal to the steering apparatus.

Joe would have found keen enjoyment in the situation, had it not been for his horse, Lance. The thoroughbred was difficult to hold. As Bill was making strenuous efforts to get in a lucky stroke of the oar, he failed to see a long length of grapevine floating like a brown snake of the water below. In the excitement they heeded not the barking of Mose. Nor did they see the grapevine straighten and become taut just as they drifted upon it; but they felt the raft strike and hold on some submerged object. It creaked and groaned and the foamy water surged, gurgling, between the logs.

Jim's mare snorted with terror, and rearing high, pulled her halter loose and plunged into the river. But Jim still held her, at risk of being drawn overboard.

"Let go! She'll drag you in!" yelled Joe, grasping him with his free hand. Lance trembled violently and strained at the rope, which his master held with a strong grip.

CRACK!

The stinging report of a rifle rang out above the splashing of the water.

Without a cry, Bill's grasp on the oar loosened; he fell over it limply, his head striking the almost submerged log. A dark-red fluid colored the water; then his body slipped over the oar and into the river, where it sank.

"My God! Shot!" cried Jim, in horrified tones.

He saw a puff of white smoke rising above the willows. Then the branches parted, revealing the dark forms of several Indian warriors. From the rifle in the foremost savage's hand a slight veil of smoke rose. With the leap of a panther the redskin sprang from the strip of sand to the raft.

"Hold, Jim! Drop that ax! We're caught!" cried Joe.

"It's that Indian from the fort!" gasped Jim.

The stalwart warrior was indeed Silvertip. But how changed! Stripped of the blanket he had worn at the settlement, now standing naked but for his buckskin breech-cloth, with his perfectly proportioned form disclosed in all its sinewy beauty, and on his swarthy, evil face an expression of savage scorn, he surely looked a warrior and a chief.

He drew his tomahawk and flashed a dark glance at Joe. For a moment he steadily regarded the young man; but if he expected to see fear in the latter's face he was mistaken, for the look was returned coolly.

"Paleface steal shirt," he said in his deep voice. "Fool paleface play— Silvertip no forget."

CHAPTER 5

SILVERTIP TURNED TO HIS BRAVES, AND GIVING A BRIEF COMMAND, sprang from the raft. The warriors closed in around the brothers; two grasping each by the arms, and the remaining Indian taking care of the horse. The captives were then led ashore, where Silvertip awaited them.

When the horse was clear of the raft, which task necessitated considerable labor on the part of the Indians, the chief seized the grapevine, that was now plainly in sight, and severed it with one blow of his tomahawk. The raft dashed forward with a lurch and drifted downstream.

In the clear water Joe could see the cunning trap which had caused the death of Bill, and insured the captivity of himself and his brother. The crafty savages had trimmed a six-inch sapling and anchored it under the water. They weighted the heavy end, leaving the other pointing upstream. To this last had been tied the grapevine. When the drifting raft reached the sapling, the Indians concealed in the willows pulled hard on the improvised rope; the end of the sapling stuck up like a hook, and the aft was caught and held. The killing of the helmsman showed the Indians' foresight; even had the raft drifted on downstream the brothers would have been helpless on a craft they could not manage. After all, Joe thought, he had not been so far wrong when he half fancied that an Indian lay behind Shawnee Rock, and he marveled at this clever trick which had so easily effected their capture.

But he had little time to look around at the scene of action. There was a moment only in which to study the river to learn if the unfortunate rafts-man's body had appeared. It was not to be seen. The river ran swiftly and hid all evidence of the tragedy under its smooth surface. When the brave who had gone back to the raft for the goods joined his companion the two hurried Joe up the bank after the others.

Once upon level ground Joe saw before him an open forest. On the border of this the Indians stopped long enough to bind the prisoners' wrists with thongs of deerhide. While two of the braves performed this office, Silvertip leaned against a tree and took no notice of the brothers. When they were thus securely tied one of their captors addressed the chief, who at once led the way westward through the forest. The savages followed in single file, with Joe and Jim in the middle of the line. The last Indian tried to mount Lance; but the thoroughbred would have none of him, and after several efforts the savage was compelled to desist. Mose trotted reluctantly along behind the horse.

Although the chief preserved a dignified mien, his braves were disposed to be gay. They were in high glee over their feat of capturing the palefaces, and kept up an incessant jabbering. One Indian, who walked directly behind Joe, continually prodded him with the stock of a rifle; and whenever Joe turned, the brawny redskin grinned as he grunted, "Ugh!" Joe observed that this huge savage had a broad face of rather a lighter shade of red than his companions. Perhaps he intended those rifle-prods in friendliness, for although they certainly amused him, he would allow no one else to touch Joe; but it would have been more pleasing had he shown his friendship in a gentle manner. This Indian carried Joe's pack, much to his own delight, especially as his companions evinced an envious curiosity. The big fellow would not, however, allow them to touch it.

"He's a cheerful brute," remarked Joe to Jim.

"Ugh!" grunted the big Indian, jamming Joe with his rifle-stock.

Joe took heed to the warning and spoke no more. He gave all his attention to the course over which he was being taken. Here was his first opportunity to learn something of Indians and their woodcraft. It occurred to him that his captors would not have been so gay and careless had they not believed themselves safe from pursuit, and he concluded they were leisurely conducting him to one of the Indian towns. He watched the supple figure before him, wondering at the quick step, light as the fall of a leaf, and tried to walk as softly. He found, however, that where the Indian readily avoided the sticks and brush, he was unable to move without snapping twigs. Now and then he would look up and study the lay of the land

ahead; and as he came nearer to certain rocks and trees he scrutinized
them closely, in order to remember their shape and general appearance.
He believed he was blazing out in his mind this woodland trail, so that
should fortune favor him and he contrive to escape, he would be able to
find his way back to the river. Also, he was enjoying the wild scenery.

This forest would have appeared beautiful, even to one indifferent to
such charms, and Joe was far from that. Every moment he felt steal
stronger over him a subtle influence which he could not define. Half
unconsciously he tried to analyze it, but it baffled him. He could no more
explain what fascinated him than he could understand what caused the
melancholy quiet which hung over the glades and hollows. He had
pictured a real forest so differently from this. Here was a long lane paved
with springy moss and fenced by bright-green sassafras; there a secluded
dale, dotted with pale-blue blossoms, over which the giant cottonwoods
leaned their heads, jealously guarding the delicate flowers from the sun.
Beech trees, growing close in clanny groups, spread their straight limbs
gracefully; the white birches gleamed like silver wherever a stray sunbeam
stole through the foliage, and the oaks, monarchs of the forest, rose over
all, dark, rugged, and kingly.

Joe soon understood why the party traveled through such open forest.
The chief, seeming hardly to deviate from his direct course, kept clear of
broken ground, matted thickets and tangled windfalls. Joe got a glimpse of
dark ravines and heard the music of tumbling waters; he saw gray cliffs
grown over with vines, and full of holes and crevices; steep ridges, covered
with dense patches of briar and hazel, rising in the way. Yet the Shawnee
always found an easy path.

The sun went down behind the foliage in the west, and shadows
appeared low in the glens; then the trees faded into an indistinct mass; a
purple shade settled down over the forest, and night brought the party to
a halt.

The Indians selected a sheltered spot under the lee of a knoll, at the
base of which ran a little brook. Here in this inclosed space were the
remains of a camp-fire. Evidently the Indians had halted there that same
day, for the logs still smouldered. While one brave fanned the embers,
another took from a neighboring branch a haunch of deer meat. A blaze
was soon coaxed from the dull coals, more fuel was added, and presently a
cheerful fire shone on the circle of dusky forms.

It was a picture which Joe had seen in many a boyish dream; now that
he was a part of it he did not dwell on the hopelessness of the situation,

nor of the hostile chief whose enmity he had incurred. Almost, it seemed, he was glad of this chance to watch the Indians and listen to them. He had been kept apart from Jim, and it appeared to Joe that their captors treated his brother with a contempt which they did not show him. Silvertip had, no doubt, informed them that Jim had been on his way to teach the Indians of the white man's God.

Jim sat with drooping head; his face was sad, and evidently he took the most disheartening view of his capture. When he had eaten the slice of venison given him he lay down with his back to the fire.

Silvertip, in these surroundings, showed his real character. He had appeared friendly in the settlement; but now he was the relentless savage, a son of the wilds, free as an eagle. His dignity as a chief kept him aloof from his braves. He had taken no notice of the prisoners since the capture. He remained silent, steadily regarding the fire with his somber eyes. At length, glancing at the big Indian, he motioned toward the prisoners and with a single word stretched himself on the leaves.

Joe noted the same changelessness of expression in the other dark faces as he had seen in Silvertip's. It struck him forcibly. When they spoke in their soft, guttural tones, or burst into a low, not unmusical laughter, or sat gazing stolidly into the fire, their faces seemed always the same, inscrutable, like the depths of the forest now hidden in night. One thing Joe felt rather than saw—these savages were fierce and untamable. He was sorry for Jim, because, as he believed, it would be as easy to teach the panther gentleness toward his prey as to instill into one of these wild creatures a belief in Christ.

The braves manifested keen pleasure in anticipation as to what they would get out of the pack, which the Indian now opened. Time and again the big brave placed his broad hand on the shoulder of a comrade Indian and pushed him backward.

Finally the pack was opened. It contained a few articles of wearing apparel, a pair of boots, and a pipe and pouch of tobacco. The big Indian kept the latter articles, grunting with satisfaction, and threw the boots and clothes to the others. Immediately there was a scramble. One brave, after a struggle with another, got possession of both boots. He at once slipped off his moccasins and drew on the white man's foot-coverings. He strutted around in them a few moments, but his proud manner soon changed to disgust.

Cowhide had none of the soft, yielding qualities of buckskin, and hurt the Indian's feet. Sitting down, he pulled one off, not without difficulty, for the boots were wet; but he could not remove the other. He hesitated a moment, being aware of the subdued merriment of his comrades, and then held up his foot to the nearest one. This chanced to be the big Indian, who evidently had a keen sense of humor. Taking hold of the boot with both hands, he dragged the luckless brave entirely around the camp-fire. The fun, however, was not to be all one-sided. The big Indian gave a more strenuous pull, and the boot came off suddenly. Unprepared for this, he lost his balance and fell down the bank almost into the creek. He held on to the boot, nevertheless, and getting up, threw it into the fire.

The braves quieted down after that, and soon lapsed into slumber, leaving the big fellow, to whom the chief had addressed his brief command, acting, as guard. Observing Joe watching him as he puffed on his new pipe, he grinned, and spoke in broken English that was intelligible, and much of a surprise to the young man.

"Paleface—tobac'—heap good."

Then, seeing that Joe made no effort to follow his brother's initiative, for Jim was fast asleep, he pointed to the recumbent figures and spoke again.

"Ugh! Paleface sleep—Injun wigwams—near setting sun."

On the following morning Joe was awakened by the pain in his legs, which had been bound all night. He was glad when the bonds were cut and the party took up its westward march.

The Indians, though somewhat quieter, displayed the same carelessness: they did not hurry, nor use particular caution, but selected the most open paths through the forest. They even halted while one of their number crept up on a herd of browsing deer. About noon the leader stopped to drink from a spring; his braves followed suit and permitted the white prisoners to quench their thirst.

When they were about to start again the single note of a bird far away in the woods sounded clearly on the quiet air. Joe would not have given heed to it had he been less attentive. He instantly associated this peculiar bird-note with the sudden stiffening of Silvertip's body and his attitude of intense listening. Low exclamations came from the braves as they bent to catch the lightest sound. Presently, above the murmur of the gentle fall of water over the stones, rose that musical note once more. It was made by a bird, Joe thought, and yet, judged by the actions of the Indians, how potent with meaning beyond that of the simple melody of the woodland songster! He turned, half expecting to see somewhere in the tree-tops the bird which had wrought so sudden a change in his captors. As he did so from close at hand came the same call, now louder, but identical with the one that had deceived him. It was an answering signal, and had been given by Silvertip.

It flashed into Joe's mind that other savages were in the forest; they had run across the Shawnees' trail, and were thus communicating with them. Soon dark figures could be discerned against the patches of green thicket; they came nearer and nearer, and now entered the open glade where Silvertip stood with his warriors.

Joe counted twelve, and noted that they differed from his captors. He had only time to see that this difference consisted in the head-dress, and in the color and quantity of paint on their bodies, when his gaze was attracted and riveted to the foremost figures.

The first was that of a very tall and stately chief, toward whom Silvertip now advanced with every show of respect. In this Indian's commanding stature, in his reddish-bronze face, stern and powerful, there were readable the characteristics of a king. In his deep-set eyes, gleaming from under a ponderous brow; in his mastiff-like jaw; in every feature of his haughty face were visible all the high intelligence, the consciousness of past valor, and the power and authority that denote a great chieftain.

The second figure was equally striking for the remarkable contrast it afforded to the chief's. Despite the gaudy garments, the paint, the fringed and beaded buckskin leggins—all the Indian accouterments and garments which bedecked this person, he would have been known anywhere as a white man. His skin was burned to a dark bronze, but it had not the red tinge which characterizes the Indian. This white man had, indeed, a strange physiognomy. The forehead was narrow and sloped backward from the brow, denoting animal instincts. The eyes were close together, yellow-ish-brown in color, and had a peculiar vibrating movement, as though they were hung on a pivot, like a compass-needle. The nose was long and hooked, and the mouth set in a thin, cruel line. There was in the man's aspect an extraordinary combination of ignorance, vanity, cunning and ferocity.

While the two chiefs held a short consultation, this savage-appearing white man addressed the brothers.

"Who're you, an' where you goin'?" he asked gruffly, confronting Jim.

"My name is Downs. I am a preacher, and was on my way to the Moravian Mission to preach to the Indians. You are a white man; will you help us?"

If Jim expected the information would please his interrogator, he was mistaken.

"So you're one of 'em? Yes, I'll do suthin' fer you when I git back from this hunt. I'll cut your heart out, chop it up, an' feed it to the buzzards," he said fiercely, concluding his threat by striking Jim a cruel blow on the head.

Joe paled deathly white at this cowardly action, and his eyes, as they met the gaze of the ruffian, contracted with their characteristic steely glow, as if some powerful force within the depths of his being were at white heat and only this pale flash came to the surface.

"You ain't a preacher?" questioned the man, meeting something in Joe's glance that had been absent from Jim's.

Joe made no answer, and regarded questioner steadily.

"Ever see me afore? Ever hear of Jim Girty?" he asked boastfully.

"Before you spoke I knew you were Girty," answered Joe quietly.

"How d'you know? Ain't you afeared?"

"Of what?"

"Me—me?"

Joe laughed in the renegades face.

"How'd you knew me?" growled Girty. "I'll see thet you hev cause to remember me after this."

"I figured there was only one so-called white man in these woods who is coward enough to strike a man whose hands are tied."

"Boy, ye're too free with your tongue. I'll shet off your wind." Girty's hand was raised, but it never reached Joe's neck.

The big Indian had an hour or more previous cut Joe's bonds, but he still retained the thong which was left attached to Joe's left wrist. This allowed the young man free use of his right arm, which, badly swollen or not, he brought into quick action.

When the renegade reached toward him Joe knocked up the hand, and, instead of striking, he grasped the hooked nose with all the powerful grip of his fingers. Girty uttered a frightful curse; he writhed with pain, but could not free himself from the vise-like clutch. He drew his tomahawk and with a scream aimed a vicious blow at Joe. He missed his aim, however, for Silvertip had intervened and turned the course of the keen hatchet. But the weapon struck Joe a glancing blow, inflicting a painful, though not dangerous wound.

The renegade's nose was skinned and bleeding profusely. He was frantic with fury, and tried to get at Joe; but Silvertip remained in front of his captive until some of the braves led Girty into the forest, where the tall chief had already disappeared.

The nose-pulling incident added to the gayety of the Shawnees, who evidently were pleased with Girty's discomfiture. They jabbered among themselves and nodded approvingly at Joe, until a few words spoken by Silvertip produced a sudden change.

What the words were Joe could not understand, but to him they sounded like French. He smiled at the absurdity of imagining he had heard a savage speak a foreign language. At any rate, whatever had been said was trenchant with meaning. The Indians changed from gay to grave; they picked up their weapons and looked keenly on every side; the big Indian at once retied Joe, and then all crowded round the chief.

"Did you hear what Silvertip said, and did you notice the effect it had?" whispered Jim, taking advantage of the moment.

"It sounded like French, but of course it wasn't," replied Joe.

"It was French. 'Le Vent de la Mort.'"

"By Jove, that's it. What does it mean?" asked Joe, who was not a scholar.

"The Wind of Death."

"That's English, but I can't apply it here. Can you?"

"No doubt it is some Indian omen."

The hurried consultation over, Silvertip tied Joe's horse and dog to the trees, and once more led the way; this time he avoided the open forest and kept on low ground. For a long time he traveled in the bed of the brook, wading when the water was shallow, and always stepping where there was the least possibility of leaving a footprint. Not a word was spoken. If either of the brothers made the lightest splash in the water, or tumbled a stone into the brook, the Indian behind rapped him on the head with a tomahawk handle.

At certain places, indicated by the care which Silvertip exercised in walking, the Indian in front of the captives turned and pointed where they were to step. They were hiding the trail. Silvertip hurried them over the stony places; went more slowly through the water, and picked his way carefully over the soft ground it became necessary to cross. At times he stopped, remaining motionless many seconds.

This vigilance continued all the afternoon. The sun sank; twilight spread its gray mantle, and soon black night enveloped the forest. The Indians halted, but made no fire; they sat close together on a stony ridge, silent and watchful.

Joe pondered deeply over this behavior. Did the Shawnees fear pursuit? What had that Indian chief told Silvertip? To Joe it seemed that they acted as if believing foes were on all sides. Though they hid their tracks, it was, apparently, not the fear of pursuit alone which made them cautious.

Joe reviewed the afternoon's march and dwelt upon the possible meaning of the cat-like steps, the careful brushing aside of branches, the roving eyes, suspicious and gloomy, the eager watchfulness of the advance as well as to the rear, and always the strained effort to listen, all of which gave him the impression of some grave, unseen danger.

And now as he lay on the hard ground, nearly exhausted by the long march and suffering from the throbbing wound, his courage lessened somewhat, and he shivered with dread. The quiet and gloom of the forest; these fierce, wild creatures, free in the heart of their own wilderness yet menaced by a foe, and that strange French phrase which kept recurring in his mind—all had the effect of conjuring up giant shadows in Joe's fanciful mind. During all his life, until this moment, he had never feared anything; now he was afraid of the darkness. The spectral trees spread long arms overhead, and phantom forms stalked abroad; somewhere out in that dense gloom stirred this mysterious foe—the "Wind of Death."

Nevertheless, he finally slept. In the dull-gray light of early morning the Indians once more took up the line of march toward the west. They marched all that day, and at dark halted to eat and rest. Silvertip and another Indian stood watch.

Some time before morning Joe suddenly awoke. The night was dark, yet it was lighter than when he had fallen asleep. A pale, crescent moon shown dimly through the murky clouds. There was neither movement of the air nor the chirp of an insect. Absolute silence prevailed.

Joe saw the Indian guard leaning against a tree, asleep. Silvertip was gone. The captive raised his head and looked around for the chief. There were only four Indians left, three on the ground and one against the tree.

He saw something shining near him. He looked more closely, and made out the object to be an eagle plume Silvertip had worn, in his head-dress. It lay on the ground near the tree. Joe made some slight noise which awakened the guard. The Indian never moved a muscle; but his eyes roved everywhere. He, too, noticed the absence of the chief.

At this moment from out of the depths of the woods came a swelling sigh, like the moan of the night wind. It rose and died away, leaving the silence apparently all the deeper.

A shudder ran over Joe's frame. Fascinated, he watched the guard. The

Indian uttered a low gasp; his eyes started and glared wildly; he rose very slowly to his full height and stood waiting, listening. The dark hand which held the tomahawk trembled so that little glints of moonlight glanced from the bright steel.

From far back in the forest-deeps came that same low moaning:

"Um-m-mm-woo-o-o-o!"

It rose from a faint murmur and swelled to a deep moan, soft but clear, and ended in a wail like that of a lost soul.

The break it made in that dead silence was awful. Joe's blood seemed to have curdled and frozen; a cold sweat oozed from his skin, and it was as if a clammy hand clutched at his heart. He tried to persuade himself that the fear displayed by the savage was only superstition, and that that moan was but the sigh of the night wind.

The Indian sentinel stood as if paralyzed an instant after that weird cry, and then, swift as a flash, and as noiseless, he was gone into the gloomy forest. He had fled without awakening his companions.

Once more the moaning cry arose and swelled mournfully on the still night air. It was close at hand!

"The Wind of Death," whispered Joe.

He was shaken and unnerved by the events of the past two days, and dazed from his wound. His strength deserted him, and he lost consciousness.

CHAPTER 6

ONE EVENING, SEVERAL DAY PREVIOUS TO THE CAPTURE OF THE brothers, a solitary hunter stopped before a deserted log cabin which stood on the bank of a stream fifty miles or more inland from the Ohio River. It was rapidly growing dark; a fine, drizzling rain had set in, and a rising wind gave promise of a stormy night.

Although the hunter seemed familiar with his surroundings, he moved cautiously, and hesitated as if debating whether he should seek the protection of this lonely hut, or remain all night under dripping trees. Feeling of his hunting frock, he found that it was damp and slippery. This fact evidently decided him in favor of the cabin, for he stooped his tall figure and went in. It was pitch dark inside; but having been there before, the absence of a light did not trouble him. He readily found the ladder leading to the loft, ascended it, and lay down to sleep.

During the night a noise awakened him. For a moment he heard nothing except the fall of the rain. Then came the hum of voices, followed by the soft tread of moccasined feet. He knew there was an Indian town ten miles across the country, and believed some warriors, belated on a hunting trip, had sought the cabin for shelter.

The hunter lay perfectly quiet, awaiting developments. If the Indians had flint and steel, and struck a light, he was almost certain to be discovered. He listened to their low conversation, and understood from the language that they were Delawares.

A moment later he heard the rustling of leaves and twigs, accompanied by the metallic click of steel against some hard substance. The noise was repeated, and then followed by a hissing sound, which he knew to be the burning of a powder on a piece of dry wood, after which rays of light filtered through cracks of the unstable floor of the loft.

The man placed his eye to one of these crevices, and counted eleven Indians, all young braves, with the exception of the chief. The Indians had been hunting; they had haunches of deer and buffalo tongues, together with several packs of hides. Some of them busied themselves drying their weapons; others sat down listlessly, plainly showing their weariness, and two worked over the smouldering fire. The damp leaves and twigs burned faintly, yet there was enough to cause the hunter fear that he might be discovered. He believed he had not much to worry about from the young braves, but the hawk-eyed chief was dangerous.

And he was right. Presently the stalwart chief heard, or saw, a drop of water fall from the loft. It came from the hunter's wet coat. Almost any one save an Indian scout would have fancied this came from the roof. As the chief's gaze roamed everywhere over the interior of the cabin his expression was plainly distrustful. His eye searched the wet clay floor, but hardly could have discovered anything there, because the hunter's moccasined tracks had been obliterated by the footprints of the Indians. The chief's suspicions seemed to be allayed.

But in truth this chief, with the wonderful sagacity natural to Indians, had observed matters which totally escaped the young braves, and, like a wily old fox, he waited to see which cub would prove the keenest. Not one of them, however, noted anything unusual. They sat around the fire, ate their meat and parched corn, and chatted volubly.

The chief arose and, walking to the ladder, ran his hand along one of the rungs.

"Ugh!" he exclaimed.

Instantly he was surrounded by ten eager, bright-eyed braves. He extended his open palm; it was smeared with wet clay like that under his feet. Simultaneously with their muttered exclamations the braves grasped their weapons. They knew there was a foe above them. It was a paleface, for an Indian would have revealed himself.

The hunter, seeing he was discovered, acted with the unerring judgment and lightning-like rapidity of one long accustomed to perilous situations. Drawing his tomahawk and noiselessly stepping to the hole in the loft, he leaped into the midst of the astounded Indians.

Rising from the floor like the rebound of a rubber ball, his long arm with the glittering hatchet made a wide sweep, and the young braves scattered like frightened sheep.

He made a dash for the door and, incredible as it may seem, his movements were so quick he would have escaped from their very midst without a scratch but for one unforeseen circumstance. The clay floor was wet and slippery; his feet were hardly in motion before they slipped from under him and he fell headlong.

With loud yells of triumph the band jumped upon him. There was a convulsive, heaving motion of the struggling mass, one frightful cry of agony, and then hoarse commands. Three of the braves ran to their packs, from which they took cords of buckskin. So exceedingly powerful was the hunter that six Indians were required to hold him while the others tied his hands and feet. Then, with grunts and chuckles of satisfaction, they threw him into a corner of the cabin.

Two of the braves had been hurt in the brief struggle, one having a badly wrenched shoulder and the other a broken arm. So much for the hunter's power in that single moment of action.

The loft was searched, and found to be empty. Then the excitement died away, and the braves settled themselves down for the night. The injured ones bore their hurts with characteristic stoicism; if they did not sleep, both remained quiet and not a sigh escaped them.

The wind changed during the night, the storm abated, and when daylight came the sky was cloudless. The first rays of the sun shone in the open door, lighting up the interior of the cabin.

A sleepy Indian who had acted as guard stretched his limbs and yawned. He looked for the prisoner, and saw him sitting up in the corner. One arm was free, and the other nearly so. He had almost untied the thongs which bound him; a few moments more and he would have been free.

"Ugh!" exclaimed the young brave, awakening his chief and pointing to the hunter.

The chief glanced at his prisoner; then looked more closely, and with one spring was on his feet, a drawn tomahawk in his hand. A short, shrill yell issued from his lips. Roused by that clarion call, the young braves jumped up, trembling in eager excitement. The chief's summons had been the sharp war-cry of the Delawares.

He manifested as intense emotion as could possibly have been betrayed by a matured, experienced chieftain, and pointing to the hunter, he spoke a single word.

~

AT NOONDAY THE INDIANS ENTERED THE FIELDS OF CORN WHICH marked the outskirts of the Delaware encampment.

"Kol-loo—kol-loo—kol-loo."

The long signal, heralding the return of the party with important news, pealed throughout the quiet valley; and scarcely had the echoes died away when from the village came answering shouts.

Once beyond the aisles of waving corn the hunter saw over the shoulders of his captors the home of the redmen. A grassy plain, sloping gradually from the woody hill to a winding stream, was brightly beautiful with chestnut trees and long, well-formed lines of lodges. Many-hued blankets hung fluttering in the sun, and rising lazily were curling columns of blue smoke. The scene was picturesque and reposeful; the vivid hues suggesting the Indians love of color and ornament; the absence of life and stir, his languorous habit of sleeping away the hot noonday hours.

The loud whoops, however, changed the quiet encampment into a scene of animation. Children ran from the wigwams, maidens and braves dashed here and there, squaws awakened from their slumber, and many a doughty warrior rose from his rest in the shade. French fur traders came curiously from their lodges, and renegades hurriedly left their blankets, roused to instant action by the well-known summons.

The hunter, led down the lane toward the approaching crowd, presented a calm and fearless demeanor. When the Indians surrounded him one prolonged, furious yell rent the air, and then followed an extraordinary demonstration of fierce delight. The young brave's staccato yell, the maiden's scream, the old squaw's screech, and the deep war-cry of the warriors intermingled in a fearful discordance.

Often had this hunter heard the name which the Indian called him; he had been there before, a prisoner; he had run the gauntlet down the lane; he had been bound to a stake in front of the lodge where his captors were now leading him. He knew the chief, Wingenund, sachem of the Delawares. Since that time, now five years ago, when Wingenund had tortured him, they had been bitterest foes.

If the hunter heard the hoarse cries, or the words hissed into his ears;

if he saw the fiery glances of hatred, and sudden giving way to ungovernable rage, unusual to the Indian nature; if he felt in their fierce exultation the hopelessness of succor or mercy, he gave not the slightest sign.

"Atelang! Atelang! Atelang!" rang out the strange Indian name.

The French traders, like real savages, ran along with the procession, their feathers waving, their paint shining, their faces expressive of as much excitement as the Indians' as they cried aloud in their native tongue:

"Le Vent de la Mort! Le Vent de la Mort! La Vent de la Mort!"

The hunter, while yet some paces distant, saw the lofty figure of the chieftain standing in front of his principal men. Well he knew them all. There were the crafty Pipe, and his savage comrade, the Half King; there was Shingiss, who wore on his forehead a scar—the mark of the hunter's bullet; there were Kotoxen, the Lynx, and Misseppa, the Source, and Winstonah, the War-cloud, chiefs of sagacity and renown. Three renegades completed the circle; and these three traitors represented a power which had for ten years left an awful, bloody trail over the country. Simon Girty, the so-called White Indian, with his keen, authoritative face turned expectantly; Elliott, the Tory deserter, from Fort Pitt, a wiry, spider-like little man; and last, the gaunt and gaudily arrayed form of the demon of the frontier—Jim Girty.

The procession halted before this group, and two brawny braves pushed the hunter forward. Simon Girty's face betrayed satisfaction; Elliott's shifty eyes snapped, and the dark, repulsive face of the other Girty exhibited an exultant joy. These desperadoes had feared this hunter.

Wingenund, with a majestic wave of his arm, silenced the yelling horde of frenzied savages and stepped before the captive.

The deadly foes were once again face to face. The chieftain's lofty figure and dark, sleek head, now bare of plumes, towered over the other Indians, but he was not obliged to lower his gaze in order to look straight into the hunter's eyes.

Verily this hunter merited the respect which shone in the great chieftain's glance. Like a mountain-ash he stood, straight and strong, his magnificent frame tapering wedge-like from his broad shoulders. The bulging line of his thick neck, the deep chest, the knotty contour of his bared forearm, and the full curves of his legs—all denoted a wonderful muscular development.

The power expressed in this man's body seemed intensified in his features. His face was white and cold, his jaw square and set; his coal-black eyes glittered with almost a superhuman fire. And his hair, darker than the wing of a crow, fell far below his shoulders; matted and tangled as it was, still it hung to his waist, and had it been combed out, must have reached his knees.

One long moment Wingenund stood facing his foe, and then over the multitude and through the valley rolled his sonorous voice:

"Deathwind dies at dawn!"

The hunter was tied to a tree and left in view of the Indian populace. The children ran fearfully by; the braves gazed long at the great foe of their race; the warriors passed in gloomy silence. The savages' tricks of torture, all their diabolical ingenuity of inflicting pain was suppressed, awaiting the hour of sunrise when this hated Long Knife was to die.

Only one person offered an insult to the prisoner; he was a man of his own color. Jim Girty stopped before him, his yellowish eyes lighted by a tigerish glare, his lips curled in a snarl, and from between them issuing the odor of the fir traders' vile rum.

"You'll soon be feed fer the buzzards," he croaked, in his hoarse voice. He had so often strewed the plains with human flesh for the carrion birds that the thought had a deep fascination for him. "D'ye hear, scalp-hunter? Feed for buzzards!" He deliberately spat in the hunter's face. "D'ye hear?" he repeated.

There was no answer save that which glittered in the hunter's eye. But the renegade could not read it because he did not meet that flaming glance. Wild horses could not have dragged him to face this man had he been free. Even now a chill crept over Girty. For a moment he was enthralled by a mysterious fear, half paralyzed by a foreshadowing of what would be this hunter's vengeance. Then he shook off his craven fear. He was free; the hunter's doom was sure. His sharp face was again wreathed in a savage leer, and he spat once more on the prisoner.

His fierce impetuosity took him a step too far. The hunter's arms and waist were fastened, but his feet were free. His powerful leg was raised suddenly; his foot struck Girty in the pit of the stomach. The renegade dropped limp and gasping. The braves carried him away, his gaudy feathers trailing, his long arms hanging inertly, and his face distorted with agony.

The maidens of the tribe, however, showed for the prisoner an interest that had in it something of veiled sympathy. Indian girls were always fascinated by white men. Many records of Indian maidens' kindness, of love, of heroism for white prisoners brighten the dark pages of frontier history.

These girls walked past the hunter, averting their eyes when within his range of vision, but stealing many a sidelong glance at his impressive face and noble proportions. One of them, particularly, attracted the hunter's eye.

This was because, as she came by with her companions, while they all turned away, she looked at him with her soft, dark eyes. She was a young girl, whose delicate beauty bloomed fresh and sweet as that of a wild rose. Her costume, fringed, beaded, and exquisitely wrought with fanciful design, betrayed her rank, she was Wingenund's daughter. The hunter had seen her when she was a child, and he recognized her now. He knew that the beauty of Aola, of Whispering Winds Among the Leaves, had been sung from the Ohio to the Great Lakes.

Often she passed him that afternoon. At sunset, as the braves untied him and led him away, he once more caught the full, intense gaze of her lovely eyes.

That night as he lay securely bound in the corner of a lodge, and the long hours wore slowly away, he strained at his stout bonds, and in his mind revolved different plans of escape. It was not in this man's nature to despair; while he had life he would fight. From time to time he expanded his muscles, striving to loosen the wet buckskin thongs.

The dark hours slowly passed, no sound coming to him save the distant bark of a dog and the monotonous tread of his guard; a dim grayness pervaded the lodge. Dawn was close at hand—his hour was nearly come.

Suddenly his hearing, trained to a most acute sensibility, caught a faint sound, almost inaudible. It came from without on the other side of the lodge. There it was again, a slight tearing sound, such as is caused by a knife when it cuts through soft material.

Some one was slitting the wall of the lodge.

The hunter rolled noiselessly over and over until he lay against the skins. In the dim grayness he saw a bright blade moving carefully upward through the deer-hide. Then a long knife was pushed into the opening; a small, brown hand grasped the hilt. Another little hand followed and felt of the wall and floor, reaching out with groping fingers.

The, hunter rolled again so that his back was against the wall and his wrists in front of the opening. He felt the little hand on his arm; then it slipped down to his wrists. The contact of cold steel set a tremor of joy through his heart. The pressure of his bonds relaxed, ceased; his arms were free. He turned to find the long-bladed knife on the ground. The little hands were gone.

In a tinkling he rose unbound, armed, desperate. In another second an Indian warrior lay upon the ground in his death-throes, while a fleeing form vanished in the gray morning mist.

THE SPIRIT OF THE BORDER

CHAPTER 7

Joe felt the heavy lethargy rise from him like the removal of a blanket; his eyes became clear, and he saw the trees and the forest gloom; slowly he realized his actual position.

He was a prisoner, lying helpless among his sleeping captors. Silvertip and the guard had fled into the woods, frightened by the appalling moan which they believed sounded their death-knell. And Joe believed he might have fled himself had he been free. What could have caused that sound? He fought off the numbing chill that once again began to creep over him. He was wide-awake now; his head was clear, and he resolved to retain his senses. He told himself there could be nothing supernatural in that wind, or wail, or whatever it was, which had risen murmuring from out the forest-depths.

Yet, despite his reasoning, Joe could not allay his fears. That thrilling cry haunted him. The frantic flight of an Indian brave—nay, of a cunning, experienced chief—was not to be lightly considered. The savages were at home in these untracked wilds. Trained from infancy to scent danger and to fight when they had an equal chance they surely would not run without good cause.

Joe knew that something moved under those dark trees. He had no idea what. It might be the fretting night wind, or a stealthy, prowling, soft-footed beast, or a savage alien to these wild Indians, and wilder than they by far. The chirp of a bird awoke the stillness. Night had given way to morning. Welcoming the light that was chasing away the gloom, Joe raised his head with a deep sigh of relief. As he did so he saw a bush move; then a shadow seemed to sink into the ground. He had seen an object lighter than the trees, darker than the gray background. Again, that strange sense of the nearness of something thrilled him.

Moments, passed—to him long as hours. He saw a tall fern waver and tremble. A rabbit, or perhaps a snake, had brushed it. Other ferns moved, their tops agitated, perhaps, by a faint breeze. No; that wavering line came straight toward him; it could not be the wind; it marked the course of a creeping, noiseless thing. It must be a panther crawling nearer and nearer.

Joe opened his lips to awaken his captors, but could not speak; it was as if his heart had stopped beating. Twenty feet away the ferns were parted to disclose a white, gleaming face, with eyes that seemingly glittered. Brawny shoulders were upraised, and then a tall, powerful man stood revealed. Lightly he stepped over the leaves into the little glade. He bent over the sleeping Indians. Once, twice, three times a long blade swung high. One brave shuddered another gave a sobbing gasp, and the third moved two fingers—thus they passed from life to death.

"Wetzel!" cried Joe.

"I reckon so," said the deliverer, his deep, calm voice contrasting strangely with what might have been expected from his aspect. Then, seeing Joe's head covered with blood, he continued: "Able to get up?"

"I'm not hurt," answered Joe, rising when his bonds had been cut.

"Brothers, I reckon?" Wetzel said, bending over Jim.

"Yes, we're brothers. Wake up, Jim, wake up! We're saved!"

"What? Who's that?" cried Jim, sitting up and staring at Wetzel.

"This man has saved our lives! See, Jim, the Indians are dead! And, Jim, it's Wetzel, the hunter. You remember, Jeff Lynn said I'd know him if I ever saw him and——"

"What happened to Jeff?" inquired Wetzel, interrupting. He had turned from Jim's grateful face.

"Jeff was on the first raft, and for all we know he is now safe at Fort Henry. Our steersman was shot, and we were captured."

"Has the Shawnee anythin' ag'inst you boys?"

"Why, yes, I guess so. I played a joke on him—took his shirt and put it on another fellow."

"Might jes' as well kick an' Injun. What has he ag'in you?"

"I don't know. Perhaps he did not like my talk to him," answered Jim. "I am a preacher, and have come west to teach the gospel to the Indians."

"They're good Injuns now," said Wetzel, pointing to the prostrate figures.

"How did you find us?" eagerly asked Joe.

"Run acrost yer trail two days back."

"And you've been following us?"

The hunter nodded.

"Did you see anything of another band of Indians? A tall chief and Jim Girty were among them."

"They've been arter me fer two days. I was followin' you when Silvertip got wind of Girty an' his Delawares. The big chief was Wingenund. I seen you pull Girty's nose. Arter the Delawares went I turned loose yer dog an' horse an' lit out on yer trail."

"Where are the Delawares now?"

"I reckon there nosin' my back trail. We must be gittin'. Silvertip'll soon hev a lot of Injuns here."

Joe intended to ask the hunter about what had frightened the Indians, but despite his eager desire for information, he refrained from doing so.

"Girty nigh did fer you," remarked Wetzel, examining Joe's wound. "He's in a bad humor. He got kicked a few days back, and then hed the skin pulled offen his nose. Somebody'll hev to suffer. Wal, you fellers grab yer rifles, an' we'll be startin' fer the fort."

Joe shuddered as he leaned over one of the dusky forms to detach powder and bullet horn. He had never seen a dead Indian, and the tense face, the sightless, vacant eyes made him shrink. He shuddered again when he saw the hunter scalp his victims. He shuddered the third time when he saw Wetzel pick up Silvertip's beautiful white eagle plume, dabble it in a pool of blood, and stick it in the bark of a tree. Bereft of its graceful beauty, drooping with its gory burden, the long leather was a deadly message. It had been Silvertip's pride; it was now a challenge, a menace to the Shawnee chief.

"Come," said Wetzel, leading the way into the forest.

~

SHORTLY AFTER DAYLIGHT ON THE SECOND DAY FOLLOWING THE RELEASE of the Downs brothers the hunter brushed through a thicket of alder and said: "Thar's Fort Henry."

The boys were on the summit of a mountain from which the land sloped in a long incline of rolling ridges and gentle valleys like a green, billowy sea, until it rose again abruptly into a peak higher still than the one upon which they stood. The broad Ohio, glistening in the sun, lay at the base of the mountain.

Upon the bluff overlooking the river, and under the brow of the mountain, lay the frontier fort. In the clear atmosphere it stood out in bold relief. A small, low structure surrounded by a high stockade fence was all, and yet it did not seem unworthy of its fame. Those watchful, forbidding loopholes, the blackened walls and timbers, told the history of ten long, bloody years. The whole effect was one of menace, as if the fort sent out a defiance to the wilderness, and meant to protect the few dozen log cabins clustered on the hillside.

"How will we ever get across that big river?" asked Jim, practically.

"Wade—swim," answered the hunter, laconically, and began the descent of the ridge. An hour's rapid walking brought the three to the river. Depositing his rifle in a clump of willows, and directing the boys to do the same with their guns, the hunter splashed into the water. His companions followed him into the shallow water, and waded a hundred yards, which brought them near the island that they now perceived hid the fort. The hunter swam the remaining distance, and, climbing the bank, looked back for the boys. They were close behind him. Then he strode across the island, perhaps a quarter of a mile wide.

"We've a long swim here," said Wetzel, waving his hand toward the main channel of the river. "Good fer it?" he inquired of Joe, since Jim had not received any injuries during the short captivity and consequently showed more endurance.

"Good for anything," answered Joe, with that coolness Wetzel had been quick to observe in him.

The hunter cast a sharp glance at the lad's haggard face, his bruised temple, and his hair matted with blood. In that look he read Joe thoroughly. Had the young man known the result of that scrutiny, he would have been pleased as well as puzzled, for the hunter had said to himself: "A brave lad, an' the border fever's on him."

"Swim close to me," said Wetzel, and he plunged into the river. The task was accomplished without accident.

"See the big cabin, thar, on the hillside? Thar's Colonel Zane in the door," said Wetzel.

As they neared the building several men joined the one who had been pointed out as the colonel. It was evident the boys were the subject of their conversation. Presently Zane left the group and came toward them. The brothers saw a handsome, stalwart man, in the prime of life.

"Well, Lew, what luck?" he said to Wetzel.

"Not much. I treed five Injuns, an' two got away," answered the hunter as he walked toward the fort.

"Lads, welcome to Fort Henry," said Colonel Zane, a smile lighting his dark face. "The others of your party arrived safely. They certainly will be overjoyed to see you."

"Colonel Zane, I had a letter from my uncle to you," replied Jim; "but the Indians took that and everything else we had with us."

"Never mind the letter. I knew your uncle, and your father, too. Come into the house and change those wet clothes. And you, my lad, have got an ugly knock on the head. Who gave you that?"

"Jim Girty."

"What?" exclaimed the colonel.

"Jim Girty did that. He was with a party of Delawares who ran across us. They were searching for Wetzel."

"Girty with the Delawares! The devil's to pay now. And you say hunting Wetzel? I must learn more about this. It looks bad. But tell me, how did Girty come to strike you?"

"I pulled his nose."

"You did? Good! Good!" cried Colonel Zane, heartily. "By George, that's great! Tell me—but wait until you are more comfortable. Your packs came safely on Jeff's raft, and you will find them inside."

As Joe followed the colonel he heard one of the other men say:

"Like as two peas in a pod."

Farther on he saw an Indian standing a little apart from the others. Hearing Joe's slight exclamation of surprise, he turned, disclosing a fine, manly countenance, characterized by calm dignity. The Indian read the boy's thought.

"Ugh! Me friend," he said in English.

"That's my Shawnee guide, Tomepomehala. He's a good fellow, although Jonathan and Wetzel declare the only good Indian is a dead one. Come right in here. There are your packs, and you'll find water outside the door."

Thus saying, Colonel Zane led the brothers into a small room, brought out their packs, and left them. He came back presently with a couple of soft towels.

"Now you lads fix up a bit; then come out and meet my family and tell us all about your adventure. By that time dinner will be ready."

"Geminy! Don't that towel remind you of home?" said Joe, when the colonel had gone. "From the looks of things, Colonel Zane means to have comfort here in the wilderness. He struck me as being a fine man."

The boys were indeed glad to change the few articles of clothing the Indians had left them, and when they were shaved and dressed they presented an entirely different appearance. Once more they were twin brothers, in costume and feature. Joe contrived, by brushing his hair down on his forehead, to conceal the discolored bump.

"I think I saw a charming girl," observed Joe.

"Suppose you did—what then?" asked Jim, severely.

"Why—nothing—see here, mayn't I admire a pretty girl if I want?"

"No, you may not. Joe, will nothing ever cure you? I should think the thought of Miss Wells—"

"Look here, Jim; she don't care—at least, it's very little she cares. And I'm—I'm not worthy of her."

"Turn around here and face me," said the young minister sharply.

Joe turned and looked in his brother's eyes.

"Have you trifled with her, as you have with so many others? Tell me. I know you don't lie."

"No."

"Then what do you mean?"

"Nothing much, Jim, except I'm really not worthy of her. I'm no good, you know, and she ought to get a fellow like—like you."

"Absurd! You ought to be ashamed of yourself."

"Never mind me. See here; don't you admire her?"

"Why—why, yes," stammered Jim, flushing a dark, guilty red at the direct question. "Who could help admiring her?"

"That's what I thought. And I know she admires you for qualities which I lack. Nell's like a tender vine just beginning to creep around and cling to something strong. She cares for me; but her love is like the vine. It may hurt her a little to tear that love away, but it won't kill her; and in the end it will be best for her. You need a good wife. What could I do with a woman? Go in and win her, Jim."

"Joe, you're sacrificing yourself again for me," cried Jim, white to the lips. "It's wrong to yourself and wrong to her. I tell you—"

"Enough!" Joe's voice cut in cold and sharp. "Usually you influence me; but sometimes you can't; I say this: Nell will drift into your arms as surely as the leaf falls. It will not hurt her—will be best for her. Remember, she is yours for the winning."

"You do not say whether that will hurt you," whispered Jim.

"Come—we'll find Colonel Zane," said Joe, opening the door.

They went out in the hallway which opened into the yard as well as the larger room through which the colonel had first conducted them. As Jim, who was in advance, passed into this apartment a trim figure entered from the yard. It was Nell, and she ran directly against him. Her face was flushed, her eyes were beaming with gladness, and she seemed the incarnation of girlish joy.

"Oh, Joe," was all she whispered. But the happiness and welcome in that whisper could never have been better expressed in longer speech. Then slightly, ever so slightly, she tilted her sweet face up to his.

It all happened with the quickness of thought. In a single instant Jim saw the radiant face, the outstretched hands, and heard the glad whisper. He knew that she had a again mistaken him for Joe; but for his life he could not draw back his head. He had kissed her, and even as his lips thrilled with her tremulous caress he flushed with the shame of his deceit.

"You're mistaken again—I'm Jim," he whispered.

For a moment they stood staring into each other's eyes, slowly awakening to what had really happened, slowly conscious of a sweet, alluring power. Then Colonel Zane's cheery voice rang in their ears.

"Ah, here's Nellie and your brother! Now, lads, tell me which is which?'

"That's Jim, and I'm Joe," answered the latter. He appeared not to notice his brother, and his greeting to Nell was natural and hearty. For the moment she drew the attention of the others from them.

Joe found himself listening to the congratulations of a number of people. Among the many names he remembered were those of Mrs. Zane, Silas Zane, and Major McColloch. Then he found himself gazing at the most beautiful girl he had ever seen in his life.

"My only sister, Mrs. Alfred Clarke—once Betty Zane, and the heroine of Fort Henry," said Colonel Zane proudly, with his arm around the slender, dark-eyed girl.

"I would brave the Indians and the wilderness again for this pleasure," replied Joe gallantly, as he bowed low over the little hand she cordially extended.

"Bess, is dinner ready?" inquired Colonel Zane of his comely wife. She nodded her head, and the colonel led the way into the adjoining room. "I know you boys must be hungry as bears."

During the meal Colonel Zane questioned his guests about their jour-ney, and as to the treatment they had received at the hands of the Indians. He smiled at the young minister's earnestness in regard to the conversion of the redmen, and he laughed outright when Joe said "he guessed he came to the frontier because it was too slow at home."

"I am sure your desire for excitement will soon be satisfied, if indeed it be not so already," remarked the colonel. "But as to the realization of your brother's hopes I am not so sanguine. Undoubtedly the Moravian mission-aries have accomplished wonders with the Indians. Not long ago I visited the Village of Peace—the Indian name for the mission—and was struck by the friendliness and industry which prevailed there. Truly it was a village of peace. Yet it is almost to early to be certain of permanent success of this work. The Indian's nature is one hard to understand. He is naturally roving and restless, which, however, may be owing to his habit of moving from place to place in search of good hunting grounds. I believe—though I must confess I haven't seen any pioneers who share my belief—that the savage has a beautiful side to his character. I know of many noble deeds done by them, and I believe, if they are honestly dealt with, they will return good for good. There are bad ones, of course; but the French traders, and men like the Girtys, have caused most of this long war. Jonathan and Wetzel tell me the Shawnees and Chippewas have taken the warpath again. Then the fact that the Girtys are with the Delawares is reason for alarm. We have been comparatively quiet here of late. Did you boys learn to what tribe your captors belong? Did Wetzel say?"

"He did not; he spoke little, but I will say he was exceedingly active," answered Joe, with a smile.

"To have seen Wetzel fight Indians is something you are not likely to forget," said Colonel Zane grimly. "Now, tell me, how did those Indians wear their scalp-lock?"

"Their heads were shaved closely, with the exception of a little place on top. The remaining hair was twisted into a tuft, tied tightly, and into this had been thrust a couple of painted pins. When Wetzel scalped the Indians the pins fell out. I picked one up, and found it to be bone."

"You will make a woodsman, that's certain," replied Colonel Zane. "The Indians were Shawnee on the warpath. Well, we will not borrow trouble, for when it comes in the shape of redskins it usually comes quickly. Mr. Wells seemed anxious to resume the journey down the river; but I shall try to persuade him to remain with us awhile. Indeed, I am sorry I cannot keep you all here at Fort Henry, and more especially the girls. On the border we need young people, and, while I do not want to frighten the women, I fear there will be more than Indians fighting for them."

"I hope not; but we have come prepared for anything," said Kate, with a quiet smile. "Our home was with uncle, and when he announced his intention of going west we decided our duty was to go with him."

"You were right, and I hope you will find a happy home," rejoined Colonel Zane. "If life among the Indians, proves to be too hard, we shall welcome you here. Betty, show the girls your pets and Indian trinkets. I am going to take the boys to Silas' cabin to see Mr. Wells, and then show them over the fort."

As they went out Joe saw the Indian guide standing in exactly the same position as when they entered the building.

"Can't that Indian move?" he asked curiously.

"He can cover one hundred miles in a day, when he wants to," replied Colonel Zane. "He is resting now. An Indian will often stand or sit in one position for many hours."

"He's a fine-looking chap," remarked Joe, and then to himself: "but I don't like him. I guess I'm prejudiced."

"You'll learn to like Tome, as we call him."

"Colonel Zane, I want a light for my pipe. I haven't had a smoke since the day we were captured. That blamed redskin took my tobacco. It's lucky I had some in my other pack. I'd like to meet him again; also Silvertip and that brute Girty."

"My lad, don't make such wishes," said Colonel Zane, earnestly. "You were indeed fortunate to escape, and I can well understand your feelings. There is nothing I should like better than to see Girty over the sights of my rifle; but I never hunt after danger, and to look for Girty is to court death."

"But Wetzel——"

"Ah, my lad, I know Wetzel goes alone in the woods; but then, he is different from other men. Before you leave I will tell you all about him."

Colonel Zane went around the corner of the cabin and returned with a live coal on a chip of wood, which Joe placed in the bowl of his pipe, and because of the strong breeze stepped close to the cabin wall. Being a keen observer, he noticed many small, round holes in the logs. They were so near together that the timbers had an odd, speckled appearance, and there was hardly a place where he could have put his thumb without covering a hole. At first he thought they were made by a worm or bird peculiar to that region; but finally lie concluded that they were bullet-holes. He thrust his knife blade into one, and out rolled a leaden ball.

"I'd like to have been here when these were made," he said.

"Well, at the time I wished I was back on the Potomac," replied Colonel Zane.

They found the old missionary on the doorstep of the adjacent cabin. He appeared discouraged when Colonel Zane interrogated him, and said that he was impatient because of the delay.

"Mr. Wells, is it not possible that you underrate the danger of your enterprise?"

"I fear naught but the Lord," answered the old man.

"Do you not fear for those with you?" went on the colonel earnestly. "I am heart and soul with you in your work, but want to impress upon you that the time is not propitious. It is a long journey to the village, and the way is beset with dangers of which you have no idea. Will you not remain here with me for a few weeks, or, at least, until my scouts report?"

"I thank you; but go I will."

"Then let me entreat you to remain here a few days, so that I may send my brother Jonathan and Wetzel with you. If any can guide you safely to the Village of Peace it will be they."

At this moment Joe saw two men approaching from the fort, and recognized one of them as Wetzel. He doubted not that the other was Lord Dunmore's famous guide and hunter, Jonathan Zane. In features he resembled the colonel, and was as tall as Wetzel, although not so muscular or wide of chest.

Joe felt the same thrill he had experienced while watching the frontiersmen at Fort Pitt. Wetzel and Jonathan spoke a word to Colonel Zane and then stepped aside. The hunters stood lithe and erect, with the easy, graceful poise of Indians.

"We'll take two canoes, day after to-morrow," said Jonathan, decisively, to Colonel Zane. "Have you a rifle for Wetzel? The Delawares got his."

Colonel Zane pondered over the question; rifles were not scarce at the fort, but a weapon that Wetzel would use was hard to find.

"The hunter may have my rifle," said the old missionary. "I have no use for a weapon with which to destroy God's creatures. My brother was a frontiersman; he left this rifle to me. I remember hearing him say once that if a man knew exactly the weight of lead and powder needed, it would shoot absolutely true."

He went into the cabin, and presently came out with a long object wrapped in linsey cloths. Unwinding the coverings, he brought to view a rifle, the proportions of which caused Jonathan's eyes to glisten, and brought an exclamation from Colonel Zane. Wetzel balanced the gun in his hands. It was fully six feet long; the barrel was large, and the dark steel finely polished; the stock was black walnut, ornamented with silver trimmings. Using Jonathan's powder-flask and bullet-pouch, Wetzel proceeded to load the weapon. He poured out a quantity of powder into the palm of his hand, performing the action quickly and dexterously, but was so slow while measuring it that Joe wondered if he were counting the grains. Next he selected a bullet out of a dozen which Jonathan held toward him. He examined it carefully and tried it in the muzzle of the rifle. Evidently it did not please him, for he took another. Finally he scraped a bullet with his knife, and placing it in the center of a small linsey rag, deftly forced it down. He adjusted the flint, dropped a few grains of powder in the pan, and then looked around for a mark at which to shoot.

Joe observed that the hunters and Colonel Zane were as serious regarding the work as if at that moment some important issue depended upon the accuracy of the rifle.

"There, Lew; there's a good shot. It's pretty far, even for you, when you don't know the gun," said Colonel Zane, pointing toward the river.

Joe saw the end of a log, about the size of a man's head, sticking out of the water, perhaps an hundred and fifty yards distant. He thought to hit it would be a fine shot; but was amazed when he heard Colonel Zane say to several men who had joined the group that Wetzel intended to shoot at a turtle on the log. By straining his eyes Joe succeeded in distinguishing a small lump, which he concluded was the turtle.

Wetzel took a step forward; the long, black rifle was raised with a stately sweep. The instant it reached a level a thread of flame burst forth, followed by a peculiarly clear, ringing report.

"Did he hit?" asked Colonel Zane, eagerly as a boy.

"I allow he did," answered Jonathan.

"I'll go and see," said Joe. He ran down the bank, along the beach, and stepped on the log. He saw a turtle about the size of an ordinary saucer. Picking it up, he saw a bullet-hole in the shell near the middle. The bullet had gone through the turtle, and it was quite dead. Joe carried it to the waiting group.

"I allowed so," declared Jonathan.

Wetzel examined the turtle, and turning to the old missionary, said:

"Your brother spoke the truth, an' I thank you fer the rifle."

CHAPTER 8

"So you want to know all about Wetzel?" inquired Colonel Zane of Joe, when, having left Jim and Mr. Wells, they returned to the cabin.

"I am immensely interested in him," replied Joe.

"Well, I don't think there's anything singular in that. I know Wetzel better, perhaps, than any man living; but have seldom talked about him. He doesn't like it. He is by birth a Virginian; I should say, forty years old. We were boys together, and and I am a little beyond that age. He was like any of the lads, except that he excelled us all in strength and agility. When he was nearly eighteen years old a band if Indians—Delawares, I think—crossed the border on a marauding expedition far into Virginia. They burned the old Wetzel homestead and murdered the father, mother, two sisters, and a baby brother. The terrible shock nearly killed Lewis, who for a time was very ill. When he recovered he went in search of his brothers, Martin and John Wetzel, who were hunting, and brought them back to their desolated home. Over the ashes of the home and the graves of the loved ones the brothers swore sleepless and eternal vengeance. The elder brothers have been devoted all these twenty years and more to the killing of Indians; but Lewis has been the great foe of the redman. You have already seen an example of his deeds, and will hear of more. His name is a household word on the border. Scores of times he has saved, actually saved, this fort and settlement. His knowledge of savage ways surpasses by far Boone's, Major McColloch's, Jonathan's, or any of the hunters'."

"Then hunting Indians is his sole occupation?"

"He lives for that purpose alone. He is very seldom in the settlement. Sometimes he stays here a few days, especially if he is needed; but usually he roams the forests."

"What did Jeff Lynn mean when he said that some people think Wetzel is crazy?"

"There are many who think the man mad; but I do not. When the passion for Indian hunting comes upon him he is fierce, almost frenzied, yet perfectly sane. While here he is quiet, seldom speaks except when spoken to, and is taciturn with strangers. He often comes to my cabin and sits beside the fire for hours. I think he finds pleasure in the conversation and laughter of friends. He is fond of the children, and would do anything for my sister Betty."

"His life must be lonely and sad," remarked Joe.

"The life of any borderman is that; but Wetzel's is particularly so."

"What is he called by the Indians?"

"They call him Atelang, or, in English, Deathwind."

"By George! That's what Silvertip said in French—'Le Vent de la Mort.'"

"Yes; you have it right. A French fur trader gave Wetzel that name years ago, and it has clung to him. The Indians say the Deathwind blows through the forest whenever Wetzel stalks on their trail."

"Colonel Zane, don't you think me superstitious," whispered Joe, leaning toward the colonel, "but I heard that wind blow through the forest."

"What!" ejaculated Colonel Zane. He saw that Joe was in earnest, for the remembrance of the moan had more than once paled his cheek and caused beads of perspiration to collect on his brow.

Joe related the circumstances of that night, and at the end of his narrative Colonel Zane sat silent and thoughtful.

"You don't really think it was Wetzel who moaned?" he asked, at length.

"No, I don't," replied Joe quickly; "but, Colonel Zane, I heard that moan as plainly as I can hear your voice. I heard it twice. Now, what was it?"

"Jonathan said the same thing to me once. He had been out hunting with Wetzel; they separated, and during the night Jonathan heard the wind. The next day he ran across a dead Indian. He believes Wetzel makes the noise, and so do the hunters; but I think it is simply the moan of the night wind through the trees. I have heard it at times, when my very blood seemingly ran cold."

"I tried to think it was the wind soughing through the pines, but am afraid I didn't succeed very well. Anyhow, I knew Wetzel instantly, just as Jeff Lynn said I would. He killed those Indians in an instant, and he must have an iron arm."

"Wetzel excels in strength and speed any man, red or white, on the frontier. He can run away from Jonathan, who is as swift as an Indian. He's stronger than any of the other men. I remember one day old Hugh Bennet's wagon wheels stuck in a bog down by the creek. Hugh tried, as several others did, to move the wheels; but they couldn't be made to budge. Along came Wetzel, pushed away the men, and lifted the wagon unaided. It would take hours to tell you about him. In brief, among all the border scouts and hunters Wetzel stands alone. No wonder the Indians fear him. He is as swift as an eagle, strong as mountain-ash, keen as a fox, and absolutely tireless and implacable."

"How long have you been here, Colonel Zane?"

"More than twelve years, and it has been one long fight."

"I'm afraid I'm too late for the fun," said Joe, with his quiet laugh.

"Not by about twelve more years," answered Colonel Zane, studying the expression on Joe's face. "When I came out here years ago I had the same adventurous spirit which I see in you. It has been considerably quelled, however. I have seen many a daring young fellow get the border fever, and with it his death. Let me advise you to learn the ways of the hunters; to watch some one skilled in woodcraft. Perhaps Wetzel himself will take you in hand. I don't mind saying that he spoke of you to me in a tone I never heard Lew use before."

"He did?" questioned Joe, eagerly, flushing with pleasure. "Do you think he'd take me out? Dare I ask him?"

"Don't be impatient. Perhaps I can arrange it. Come over here now to Metzar's place. I want to make you acquainted with him. These boys have all been cutting timber; they've just come in for dinner. Be easy and quiet with them; then you'll get on."

Colonel Zane introduced Joe to five sturdy boys and left him in their company. Joe sat down on a log outside a cabin and leisurely surveyed the young men. They all looked about the same: strong without being heavy, light-haired and bronze-faced. In their turn they carefully judged Joe. A newcomer from the East was always regarded with some doubt. If they expected to hear Joe talk much they were mistaken. He appeared good-natured, but not too friendly.

"Fine weather we're havin'," said Dick Metzar.

"Fine," agreed Joe, laconically.

"Like frontier life?"

"Sure."

A silence ensued after this breaking of the ice. The boys were awaiting their turn at a little wooden bench upon which stood a bucket of water and a basin.

"Hear ye got ketched by some Shawnees?" remarked another youth, as he rolled up his shirt-sleeves. They all looked at Joe now. It was not improbably their estimate of him would be greatly influenced by the way he answered this question.

"Yes; was captive for three days."

"Did ye knock any redskins over?" This question was artfully put to draw Joe out. Above all things, the bordermen detested boastfulness; tried on Joe the ruse failed signally.

"I was scared speechless most of the time," answered Joe, with his pleasant smile.

"By gosh, I don't blame ye!" burst out Will Metzar. "I hed that experience onct, an' onct's enough."

The boys laughed and looked in a more friendly manner at Joe. Though he said he had been frightened, his cool and careless manner belied his words. In Joe's low voice and clear, gray eye there was something potent and magnetic, which subtly influenced those with whom he came in contact.

While his new friends were at dinner Joe strolled over to where Colonel Zane sat on the doorstep of his home.

"How did you get on with the boys?" inquired the colonel.

"All right, I hope. Say, Colonel Zane, I'd like to talk to your Indian guide."

Colonel Zane spoke a few words in the Indian language to the guide, who left his post and came over to them. The colonel then had a short conversation with him, at the conclusion of which he pointed toward Joe.

"How do—shake," said Tome, extending his hand.

Joe smiled, and returned the friendly hand-pressure.

"Shawnee—ketch'um?" asked the Indian, in his fairly intelligible English.

Joe nodded his head, while Colonel Zane spoke once more in Shawnee, explaining the cause of Silvertip's emnity.

"Shawnee—chief—one—bad—Injun," replied Tome, seriously. "Silvertip—mad—thunder-mad. Ketch'um paleface—scalp'um sure."

After giving this warning the chief returned to his former position near the corner of the cabin.

"He can talk in English fairly well, much better than the Shawnee brave who talked with me the other day," observed Joe.

"Some of the Indians speak the language almost fluently," said Colonel Zane. "You could hardly have distinguished Logan's speech from a white man's. Corn-planter uses good English, as also does my brother's wife, a Wyandot girl."

"Did your brother marry an Indian?" and Joe plainly showed his surprise.

"Indeed he did, and a most beautiful girl she is. I'll tell you Isaac's story some time. He was a captive among the Wyandots for ten years. The chief's daughter, Myeerah, loved him, kept him from being tortured, and finally saved him from the stake."

"Well, that floors me," said Joe; "yet I don't see why it should. I'm just surprised. Where is your brother now?"

"He lives with the tribe. He and Myeerah are working hard for peace. We are now on more friendly terms with the great Wyandots, or Hurons, as we call them, than ever before."

"Who is this big man coming from the the fort?" asked Joe, suddenly observing a stalwart frontiersman approaching.

"Major Sam McColloch. You have met him. He's the man who jumped his horse from yonder bluff."

"Jonathan and he have the same look, the same swing," observed Joe, as he ran his eye over the major. His faded buckskin costume, beaded, fringed, and laced, was similar to that of the colonel's brother. Powder-flask and bullet-pouch were made from cow-horns and slung around his neck on deerhide strings. The hunting coat was unlaced, exposing, under the long, fringed borders, a tunic of the same well-tanned, but finer and softer, material. As he walked, the flaps of his coat fell back, showing a belt containing two knives, sheathed in heavy buckskin, and a bright tomahawk. He carried a long rifle in the hollow of his arm.

"These hunters have the same kind of buckskin suits," continued Joe; "still, it doesn't seem to me the clothes make the resemblance to each other. The way these men stand, walk and act is what strikes me particularly, as in the case of Wetzel."

"I know what you mean. The flashing eye, the erect poise of expectation, and the springy step—those, my lad, come from a life spent in the woods. Well, it's a grand way to live."

"Colonel, my horse is laid up," said Major McColloch, coming to the steps. He bowed pleasantly to Joe.

"So you are going to Short Creek? You can have one of my horses; but first come inside and we'll talk over you expedition."

The afternoon passed uneventfully for Joe. His brother and Mr. Wells were absorbed in plans for their future work, and Nell and Kate were resting; therefore he was forced to find such amusement or occupation as was possible in or near the stockade.

CHAPTER 9

JOE WENT TO BED THAT NIGHT WITH A PROMISE TO HIMSELF TO RISE early next morning, for he had been invited to take part in a "raising," which term meant that a new cabin was to be erected, and such task was ever an event in the lives of the settlers.

The following morning Joe rose early, dressing himself in a complete buckskin suit, for which he had exchanged his good garments of cloth. Never before had he felt so comfortable. He wanted to hop, skip and jump. The soft, undressed buckskin was as warm and smooth as silk-plush; the weight so light, the moccasins so well-fitting and springy, that he had to put himself under considerable restraint to keep from capering about like a frolicsome colt.

The possession of this buckskin outfit, and the rifle and accouterments which went with the bargain, marked the last stage in Joe's surrender to the border fever. The silent, shaded glens, the mystery of the woods, the breath of this wild, free life claimed him from this moment entirely and forever.

He met the others, however, with a serene face, showing no trace of the emotion which welled up strongly from his heart. Nell glanced shyly at him; Kate playfully voiced her admiration; Jim met him with a brotherly ridicule which bespoke his affection as well as his amusement; but Colonel Zane, having once yielded to the same burning, riotous craving for freedom which now stirred in the boy's heart, understood, and felt warmly drawn toward the lad. He said nothing, though as he watched Joe his eyes were grave and kind. In his long frontier life, where many a day measured the life and fire of ordinary years, he had seen lad after lad go down before this forest fever. It was well, he thought, because the freedom of the soil depended on these wild, light-footed boys; yet it always made him sad. How many youths, his brother among them, lay under the fragrant pine-needle carpet of the forest, in their last earthly sleep!

The "raising" brought out all the settlement—the women to look on and gossip, while the children played; the men to bend their backs in the moving of the heavy timbers. They celebrated the erection of a new cabin as a noteworthy event. As a social function it had a prominent place in the settlers' short list of pleasures.

Joe watched the proceeding with the same pleasure and surprise he had felt in everything pertaining to border life.

To him this log-raising appeared the hardest kind of labor. Yet it was plain these hardy men, these low-voiced women, and merry children regarded the work as something far more significant than the mere building of a cabin. After a while he understood the meaning of the scene. A kindred spirit, the spirit of the pioneer, drew them all into one large family. This was another cabin; another home; another advance toward the conquering of the wilderness, for which these brave men and women were giving their lives. In the bright-eyed children's glee, when they clapped their little hands at the mounting logs, Joe saw the progress, the march of civilization.

"Well, I'm sorry you're to leave us to-night," remarked Colonel Zane to Joe, as the young man came over to where he, his wife, and sister watched the work. "Jonathan said all was ready for your departure at sundown."

"Do we travel by night?"

"Indeed, yes, my lad. There are Indians everywhere on the river. I think, however, with Jack and Lew handling the paddles, you will slip by safely. The plan is to keep along the south shore all night; then cross over at a place called Girty's Point, where you are to remain in hiding during daylight. From there you paddle up Yellow Creek; then portage across country to the head of the Tuscarwawas. Another night's journey will then bring you to the Village of Peace."

Jim and Mr. Wells, with his nieces, joined the party now, and all stood watching as the last logs were put in place.

"Colonel Zane, my first log-raising is an education to me," said the young minister, in his earnest manner. "This scene is so full of life. I never saw such goodwill among laboring men. Look at that brawny-armed giant standing on the topmost log. How he whistles as he swings his ax! Mr. Wells, does it not impress you?"

"The pioneers must be brothers because of their isolation and peril; to be brothers means to love one another; to love one another is to love God. What you see in this fraternity is God. And I want to see this same beautiful feeling among the Indians."

"I have seen it," said Colonel Zane, to the old missionary. "When I came out here alone twelve years ago the Indians were peaceable. If the pioneers had paid for land, as I paid Cornplanter, there would never have been a border war. But no; the settlers must grasp every acre they could. Then the Indians rebelled; then the Girtys and their allies spread discontent, and now the border is a bloody warpath."

"Have the Jesuit missionaries accomplished anything with these war tribes?" inquired Jim.

"No; their work has been chiefly among the Indians near Detroit and northward. The Hurons, Delawares, Shawnees and other western tribes have been demoralized by the French traders' rum, and incited to fierce hatred by Girty and his renegades. Your work at Gnaddenhutten must be among these hostile tribes, and it is surely a hazardous undertaking."

"My life is God's," murmured the old minister. No fear could assail his steadfast faith.

"Jim, it strikes me you'd be more likely to impress these Indians Colonel Zane spoke of if you'd get a suit like mine and wear a knife and tomahawk," interposed Joe, cheerfully. "Then, if you couldn't convert, you could scalp them."

"Well, well, let us hope for the best," said Colonel Zane, when the laughter had subsided. "We'll go over to dinner now. Come, all of you. Jonathan, bring Wetzel. Betty, make him come, if you can."

As the party slowly wended its way toward the colonel's cabin Jim and Nell found themselves side by side. They had not exchanged a word since the evening previous, when Jim had kissed her. Unable to look at each other now, and finding speech difficult, they walked in embarrassed silence.

"Doesn't Joe look splendid in his hunting suit?" asked Jim, presently.

"I hadn't noticed. Yes; he looks well," replied Nell, carelessly. She was too indifferent to be natural.

"Are you angry with him?"

"Certainly not."

Jim was always simple and frank in his relations with women. He had none of his brother's fluency of speech, with neither confidence, boldness nor understanding of the intricate mazes of a woman's moods.

"But—you are angry with—me?" he whispered.

Nell flushed to her temples, yet she did not raise her eyes nor reply.

"It was a terrible thing for me to do," went on Jim, hesitatingly. "I don't know why I took advantage—of—of your mistaking me for Joe. If you only hadn't held up your mouth. No—I don't mean that—of course you didn't. But—well, I couldn't help it. I'm guilty. I have thought of little else. Some wonderful feeling has possessed me ever since—since—"

"What has Joe been saying about me?" demanded Nell, her eyes burning like opals.

"Why, hardly anything," answered Jim, haltingly. "I took him to task about—about what I considered might be wrong to you. Joe has never been very careful of young ladies' feelings, and I thought—well, it was none of my business. He said he honestly cared for you, that you had taught him how unworthy he was of a good woman. But he's wrong there. Joe is wild and reckless, yet his heart is a well of gold. He is a diamond in the rough. Just now he is possessed by wild notions of hunting Indians and roaming through the forests; but he'll come round all right. I wish I could tell you how much he has done for me, how much I love him, how I know him! He can be made worthy of any woman. He will outgrow this fiery, daring spirit, and then—won't you help him?"

"I will, if he will let me," softly whispered Nell, irresistibly drawn by the strong, earnest love thrilling in his voice.

CHAPTER 10

ONCE MORE OUT UNDER THE BLUE-BLACK VAULT OF HEAVEN, WITH ITS myriads of twinkling stars, the voyagers resumed their westward journey. Whispered farewells of new but sincere friends lingered in their ears. Now the great looming bulk of the fort above them faded into the obscure darkness, leaving a feeling as if a protector had gone—perhaps forever. Admonished to absolute silence by the stern guides, who seemed indeed to have embarked upon a dark and deadly mission, the voyagers lay back in the canoes and thought and listened. The water eddied with soft gurgles in the wake of the racing canoes; but that musical sound was all they heard. The paddles might have been shadows, for all the splash they made; they cut the water swiftly and noiselessly. Onward the frail barks glided into black space, side by side, close under the overhanging willows. Long moments passed into long hours, as the guides paddled tirelessly as if their sinews were cords of steel.

With gray dawn came the careful landing of the canoes, a cold breakfast eaten under cover of a willow thicket, and the beginning of a long day while they were lying hidden from the keen eyes of Indian scouts, waiting for the friendly mantle of night.

The hours dragged until once more the canoes were launched, this time not on the broad Ohio, but on a stream that mirrored no shining stars as it flowed still and somber under the dense foliage.

The voyagers spoke not, nor whispered, nor scarcely moved, so menacing had become the slow, listening caution of Wetzel and Zane. Snapping of twigs somewhere in the inscrutable darkness delayed them for long moments. Any movement the air might resound with the horrible Indian war-whoop. Every second was heavy with fear. How marvelous that these scouts, penetrating the wilderness of gloom, glided on surely, silently, safely! Instinct, or the eyes of the lynx, guide their course. But another dark night wore on to the tardy dawn, and each of its fearful hours numbered miles past and gone.

The sun was rising in ruddy glory when Wetzel ran his canoe into the bank just ahead of a sharp bend in the stream.

"Do we get out here?" asked Jim, seeing Jonathan turn his canoe toward Wetzel's.

"The village lies yonder, around the bend," answered the guide. "Wetzel cannot go there, so I'll take you all in my canoe."

"There's no room; I'll wait," replied Joe, quietly. Jim noted his look—a strange, steady glance it was—and then saw him fix his eyes upon Nell, watching her until the canoe passed around the green-bordered bend in the stream.

Unmistakable signs of an Indian town were now evident. Dozens of graceful birchen canoes lay upon the well-cleared banks; a log bridge spanned the stream; above the slight ridge of rising ground could be seen the poles of Indian teepees.

As the canoe grated upon the sandy beach a little Indian boy, who was playing in the shallow water, raised his head and smiled.

"That's an Indian boy," whispered Kate.

"The dear little fellow!" exclaimed Nell.

The boy came running up to them, when they were landed, with pleasure and confidence shining in his dusky eyes. Save for tiny buckskin breeches, he was naked, and his shiny skin gleamed gold-bronze in the sunlight. He was a singularly handsome child.

"Me—Benny," he lisped in English, holding up his little hand to Nell.

The action was as loving and trusting as any that could have been manifested by a white child. Jonathan Zane stared with a curious light in his dark eyes; Mr. Wells and Jim looked as though they doubted the evidence of their own sight. Here, even in an Indian boy, was incontestable proof that the savage nature could be tamed and civilized.

With a tender exclamation Nell bent over the child and kissed him.

Jonathan Zane swung his canoe up-stream for the purpose of bringing Joe. The trim little bark slipped out of sight round the bend. Presently its gray, curved nose peeped from behind the willows; then the canoe swept into view again. There was only one person in it, and that the guide.

"Where is my brother?" asked Jim, in amazement.

"Gone," answered Zane, quietly.

"Gone! What do you mean? Gone? Perhaps you have missed the spot where you left him."

"They're both gone."

Nell and Jim gazed at each other with slowly whitening faces.

"Come, I'll take you up to the village," said Zane, getting out of his canoe. All noticed that he was careful to take his weapons with him.

"Can't you tell us what it means—this disappearance?" asked Jim, his voice low and anxious.

"They're gone, canoe and all. I knew Wetzel was going, but I didn't calkilate on the lad. Mebbe he followed Wetzel, mebbe he didn't," answered the taciturn guide, and he spoke no more.

In his keen expectation and wonder as to what the village would be like, Jim momentarily forgot his brother's disappearance, and when he arrived at the top of the bank he surveyed the scene with eagerness. What he saw was more imposing than the Village of Peace which he had conjured up in his imagination. Confronting him was a level plain, in the center of which stood a wide, low structure surrounded by log cabins, and these in turn encircled by Indian teepees. A number of large trees, mostly full-foliaged maples, shaded the clearing. The settlement swarmed with Indians. A few shrill halloes uttered by the first observers of the newcomers brought braves, maidens and children trooping toward the party with friendly curiosity.

Jonathan Zane stepped before a cabin adjoining the large structure, and called in at the open door. A short, stoop-shouldered white man, clad in faded linsey, appeared on the threshold. His serious, lined face had the unmistakable benevolent aspect peculiar to most teachers of the gospel.

"Mr. Zeisberger, I've fetched a party from Fort Henry," said Zane, indicating those he had guided. Then, without another word, never turning his dark face to the right or left, he hurried down the lane through the throng of Indians.

Jim remembered, as he saw the guide vanish over the bank of the creek, that he had heard Colonel Zane say that Jonathan, as well as

Wetzel, hated the sight of an Indian. No doubt long years of war and bloodshed had rendered these two great hunters callous. To them there could be no discrimination—an Indian was an Indian.

"Mr. Wells, welcome to the Village of Peace!" exclaimed Mr. Zeisberger, wringing the old missionary's hand. "The years have not been so long but that I remember you."

"Happy, indeed, am I to get here, after all these dark, dangerous journeys," returned Mr. Wells. "I have brought my nieces, Nell and Kate, who were children when you left Williamsburg, and this young man, James Downs, a minister of God, and earnest in his hope for our work."

"A glorious work it is! Welcome, young ladies, to our peaceful village. And, young man, I greet you with heartfelt thankfulness. We need young men. Come in, all of your, and share my cabin. I'll have your luggage brought up. I have lived in this hut alone. With some little labor, and the magic touch women bring to the making of a home, we can be most comfortable here."

Mr. Zeisberger gave his own room to the girls, assuring them with a smile that it was the most luxurious in the village. The apartment contained a chair, a table, and a bed of Indian blankets and buffalo robes. A few pegs driven in the chinks between the logs completed the furnishings. Sparse as were the comforts, they appealed warmly to the girls, who, weary from their voyage, lay down to rest.

"I am not fatigued," said Mr. Wells, to his old friend. "I want to hear all about your work, what you have done, and what you hope to do."

"We have met with wonderful success, far beyond our wildest dreams," responded Mr. Zeisberger. "Certainly we have been blessed of God."

Then the missionary began a long, detailed account of the Moravian Mission's efforts among the western tribes. The work lay chiefly among the Delawares, a noble nation of redmen, intelligent, and wonderfully susceptible to the teaching of the gospel. Among the eastern Delawares, living on the other side of the Allegheny Mountains, the missionaries had succeeded in converting many; and it was chiefly through the western explorations of Frederick Post that his Church decided the Indians of the west could as well be taught to lead Christian lives. The first attempt to convert the western redmen took place upon the upper Allegheny, where many Indians, including Allemewi, a blind Delaware chief, accepted the faith. The mission decided, however, it would be best to move farther west, where the Delawares had migrated and were more numerous.

In April, 1770, more than ten years before, sixteen canoes, filled with converted Indians and missionaries, drifted down the Allegheny to Fort Pitt; thence down the Ohio to the Big Beaver; up that stream and far into the Ohio wilderness.

Upon a tributary of the Muskingong, called the Tuscarwawas, a settlement was founded. Near and far the news was circulated. Redmen from all tribes came flocking to the new colony. Chiefs and warriors, squaws and maidens, were attracted by the new doctrine of the converted Indians. They were astonished at the missionaries' teachings. Many doubted, some were converted, all listened. Great excitement prevailed when old Glickhican, one of the wisest chiefs of the Turtle tribe of the Delawares, became a convert to the palefaces' religion.

The interest widened, and in a few years a beautiful, prosperous town arose, which was called Village of Peace. The Indians of the warlike tribes bestowed the appropriate name. The vast forests were rich in every variety of game; the deep, swift streams were teeming with fish. Meat and grain in abundance, buckskin for clothing, and soft furs for winter garments were to be had for little labor. At first only a few wigwams were erected. Soon a large log structure was thrown up and used as a church. Then followed a school, a mill, and a workshop. The verdant fields were cultivated and surrounded by rail fences. Horses and cattle grazed with the timid deer on the grassy plains.

The Village of Peace blossomed as a rose. The reports of the love and happiness existing in this converted community spread from mouth to mouth, from town to town, with the result that inquisitive savages journeyed from all points to see this haven. Peaceful and hostile Indians were alike amazed at the change in their brethren. The good-fellowship and industry of the converts had a widespread and wonderful influence. More, perhaps, than any other thing, the great fields of waving corn, the hills covered with horses and cattle, those evidences of abundance, impressed the visitors with the well-being of the Christians. Bands of traveling Indians, whether friendly or otherwise, were treated with hospitality, and never sent away empty-handed. They were asked to partake of the abundance and solicited to come again.

A feature by no means insignificant in the popularity of the village was the church bell. The Indians loved music, and this bell charmed them. On still nights the savages in distant towns could hear at dusk the deep-toned, mellow notes of the bell summoning the worshipers to the evening service. Its ringing clang, so strange, so sweet, so solemn, breaking the vast dead wilderness quiet, haunted the savage ear as though it were a call from a woodland god.

"You have arrived most opportunely," continued Mr. Zeisberger. "Mr. Edwards and Mr. Young are working to establish other missionary posts. Heckewelder is here now in the interest of this branching out."

"How long will it take me to learn the Delaware language?" inquired Jim.

"Not long. You do not, however, need to speak the Indian tongue, for we have excellent interpreters."

"We heard much at Fort Pitt and Fort Henry about the danger, as well as uselessness, of our venture," Jim continued. "The frontiersmen declared that every rod of the way was beset with savage foes, and that, even in the unlikely event of our arriving safely at the Village of Peace, we would then be hemmed in by fierce, vengeful tribes."

"Hostile savages abound here, of course; but we do not fear them. We invite them. Our work is to convert the wicked, to teach them to lead good, useful lives. We will succeed."

Jim could not help warming to the minister for his unswervable faith, his earnest belief that the work of God could not fail; nevertheless, while he felt no fear and intended to put all his heart in the work, he remembered with disquietude Colonel Zane's warnings. He thought of the wonderful precaution and eternal vigilance of Jonathan and Wetzel—men of all men who most understood Indian craft and cunning. It might well be possible that these good missionaries, wrapped up in saving the souls of these children of the forest, so full of God's teachings as to have little mind for aught else, had no knowledge of the Indian nature beyond what the narrow scope of their work invited. If what these frontiersmen asserted was true, then the ministers' zeal had struck them blind.

Jim had a growing idea of the way in which the savages could be best taught. He resolved to go slowly; to study the redmen's natures; not to preach one word of the gospel to them until he had mastered their language and could convey to their simple minds the real truth. He would make Christianity as clear to them as were the deer-trails on the moss and leaves of the forest.

"Ah, here you are. I hope you have rested well," said Mr. Zeisberger, when at the conclusion of this long recital Nell and Kate came into the room.

"Thank you, we feel much better," answered Kate. The girls certainly looked refreshed. The substitution of clean gowns for their former travel-stained garments made a change that called forth the minister's surprise and admiration.

"My! My! Won't Edwards and Young beg me to keep them here now!" he exclaimed, his pleased eyes resting on Nell's piquant beauty and Kate's noble proportions and rich coloring. "Come; I will show you over the Village of Peace."

"Are all these Indians Christians?" asked Jim.

"No, indeed. These Indians you see here, and out yonder under the shade, though they are friendly, are not Christians. Our converts employ themselves in the fields or shops. Come; take a peep in here. This is where we preach in the evenings and during inclement weather. On pleasant days we use the maple grove yonder."

Jim and the others looked in at the door of the large log structure. They saw an immense room, the floor covered with benches, and a raised platform at one end. A few windows let in the light. Spacious and barn-like was this apartment; but undoubtedly, seen through the beaming eyes of the missionary, it was a grand amphitheater for worship. The hard-packed clay floor was velvet carpet; the rude seats soft as eiderdown; the platform with its white-oak cross, an altar of marble and gold.

"This is one of our shops," said Mr. Zeisberger, leading them to a cabin. "Here we make brooms, harness for the horses, farming implements —everything useful that we can. We have a forge here. Behold an Indian blacksmith!"

The interior of the large cabin presented a scene of bustling activity. Twenty or more Indians bent their backs in earnest employment. In one corner a savage stood holding a piece of red-hot iron on an anvil, while a brawny brave wielded a sledge-hammer. The sparks flew; the anvil rang. In another corner a circle of braves sat around a pile of dried grass and flags. They were twisting and fashioning these materials into baskets. At a bench three Indian carpenters were pounding and sawing. Young braves ran back and forth, carrying pails, rough-hewn boards and blocks of wood.

Instantly struck by two things, Jim voiced his curiosity:

"Why do these Indians all wear long hair, smooth and shiny, without adornment?"

"They are Christians. They wear neither headdress, war-bonnet, nor scalp-lock," replied Mr. Zeisberger, with unconscious pride.

"I did not expect to see a blacksmith's anvil out here in the wilderness. Where did you procure these tools?"

"We have been years getting them here. Some came by way of the Ohio River; others overland from Detroit. That anvil has a history. It was lost once, and lay for years in the woods, until some Indians found it again. It is called the Ringing Stone, and Indians come from miles around to see and hear it."

The missionary pointed out wide fields of corn, now growing yellow, and hillsides doted with browsing cattle, droves of sturdy-limbed horses, and pens of fat, grunting pigs—all of which attested to the growing prosperity of the Village of Peace.

On the way back to the cabin, while the others listened to and questioned Mr. Zeisberger, Jim was silent and thoughtful, for his thoughts reverted to his brother.

Later, as he walked with Nell by the golden-fringed stream, he spoke of Joe.

"Joe wanted so much to hunt with Wetzel. He will come back; surely he will return to us when he has satisfied his wild craving for adventure. Do you not think so?"

There was an eagerness that was almost pleading in Jim's voice. What he so much hoped for—that no harm had befallen Joe, and that he would return—he doubted. He needed the encouragement of his hope.

"Never," answered Nell, solemnly.

"Oh, why—why do you say that?"

"I saw him look at you—a strange, intent glance. He gazed long at me as we separated. Oh! I can feel his eyes. No; he will never come back."

"Nell, Nell, you do not mean he went away deliberately—because, oh! I cannot say it."

"For no reason, except that the wilderness called him more than love for you or—me."

"No, no," returned Jim, his face white. "You do not understand. He really loved you—I know it. He loved me, too. Ah, how well! He has gone because—I can't tell you."

"Oh, Jim, I hope—he loved—me," sobbed Nell, bursting into tears. "His coldness—his neglect those—last few days—hurt me—so. If he cared —as you say—I won't be—so—miserable."

"We are both right—you when you say he will never return, and I when I say he loved us both," said Jim sadly, as the bitter certainty forced itself into his mind.

As she sobbed softly, and he gazed with set, stern face into the darkening forest, the deep, mellow notes of the church bell pealed out. So thrilled, so startled were they by this melody wondrously breaking the twilight stillness, that they gazed mutely at each other. Then they remembered. It was the missionary's bell summoning the Christian Indians to the evening service.

CHAPTER 11

THE, SULTRY, DROWSY, SUMMER DAYS PASSED WITH NO UNTOWARD EVENT to mar their slumbering tranquillity. Life for the newcomers to the Village of Peace brought a content, the like of which they had never dreamed of. Mr. Wells at once began active work among the Indians, preaching to them through an interpreter; Nell and Kate, in hours apart from household duties, busied themselves brightening their new abode, and Jim entered upon the task of acquainting himself with the modes and habits of the redmen. Truly, the young people might have found perfect happiness in this new and novel life, if only Joe had returned. His disappearance and subsequent absence furnished a theme for many talks and many a quiet hour of dreamy sadness. The fascination of his personality had been so impelling that long after it was withdrawn a charm lingered around everything which reminded them of him; a subtle and sweet memory, with perverse and half bitter persistence, returned hauntingly. No trace of Joe had been seen by any of the friendly Indian runners. He was gone into the mazes of deep-shadowed forests, where to hunt for him would be like striving to trail the flight of a swallow. Two of those he had left behind always remembered him, and in their thoughts followed him in his wanderings.

Jim settled down to his study of Indians with single-heartedness of purpose. He spent part of every morning with the interpreters, with whose assistance he rapidly acquired the Delaware language. He went freely among the Indians, endeavoring to win their good-will. There were always fifty to an hundred visiting Indians at the village; sometimes, when the missionaries had advertised a special meeting, there were assembled in the shady maple grove as many as five hundred savages. Jim had, therefore, opportunities to practice his offices of friendliness.

Fortunately for him, he at once succeeded in establishing himself in the good graces of Glickhican, the converted Delaware chief. The wise old Indian was of inestimable value to Jim. Early in their acquaintance he evinced an earnest regard for the young minister, and talked with him for hours.

From Glickhican Jim learned the real nature of the redmen. The Indian's love of freedom and honor, his hatred of subjection and deceit, as explained by the good old man, recalled to Jim Colonel Zane's estimate of the savage character. Surely, as the colonel had said, the Indians had reason for their hatred of the pioneers. Truly, they were a blighted race.

Seldom had the rights of the redmen been thought of. The settler pushed onward, plodding, as it were, behind his plow with a rifle. He regarded the Indian as little better than a beast; he was easier to kill than to tame. How little the settler knew the proud independence, the wisdom, the stainless chastity of honor, which belonged so truly to many Indian chiefs!

The redmen were driven like hounded deer into the untrodden wilds. From freemen of the forests, from owners of the great boundless plains, they passed to stern, enduring fugitives on their own lands. Small wonder that they became cruel where once they had been gentle! Stratagem and cunning, the night assault, the daylight ambush took the place of their one-time open warfare. Their chivalrous courage, that sublime inheritance from ancestors who had never known the paleface foe, degenerated into a savage ferocity.

Interesting as was this history to Jim, he cared more for Glickhican's rich portrayal of the redmen's domestic life, for the beautiful poetry of his tradition and legends. He heard with delight the exquisite fanciful Indian lore. From these romantic legends, beautiful poems, and marvelous myths he hoped to get ideas of the Indian's religion. Sweet and simple as childless dreams were these quaint tales—tales of how the woodland fairies dwelt in fern-carpeted dells; how at sunrise they came out to kiss open the flowers; how the forest walks were spirit-haunted paths; how the leaves whispered poetry to the winds; how the rocks harbored Indian gods and masters who watched over their chosen ones.

Glickhican wound up his long discourses by declaring he had never lied in the whole course of his seventy years, had never stolen, never betrayed, never murdered, never killed, save in self-defence. Gazing at the chief's fine features, now calm, yet showing traces of past storms, Jim believed he spoke the truth.

When the young minister came, however, to study the hostile Indians that flocked to the village, any conclusive delineation of character, or any satisfactory analysis of their mental state in regard to the paleface religion, eluded him. Their passive, silent, sphinx-like secretiveness was baffling. Glickhican had taught him how to propitiate the friendly braves, and with these he was successful. Little he learned, however, from the unfriendly ones. When making gifts to these redmen he could never be certain that his offerings were appreciated. The jewels and gold he had brought west with him went to the French traders, who in exchange gave him trinkets, baubles, bracelets and weapons. Jim made hundreds of presents. Boldly going up to befeathered and befringed chieftains, he offered them knives, hatchets, or strings of silvery beads. Sometimes his kindly offerings were repelled with a haughty stare; at other times they would be accepted coldly, suspiciously, as if the gifts brought some unknown obligation.

For a white man it was a never-to-be-forgotten experience to see eight or ten of these grim, slowly stepping forest kings, arrayed in all the rich splendor of their costume, stalking among the teepees of the Village of Peace. Somehow, such a procession always made Jim shiver. The singing, praying and preaching they heard unmoved. No emotion was visible on their bronzed faces; nothing changed their unalterable mien. Had they not moved, or gazed with burning eyes, they would have been statues. When these chieftains looked at the converted Indians, some of whom were braves of their nations, the contempt in their glances betrayed that they now regarded these Christian Indians as belonging to an alien race.

Among the chiefs Glickhican pointed out to Jim were Wingenund, the Delaware; Tellane, the Half-King; Shingiss and Kotoxen—all of the Wolf tribe of the Delawares.

Glickhican was careful to explain that the Delaware nation had been divided into the Wolf and Turtle tribes, the former warlike people, and the latter peaceable. Few of the Wolf tribe had gone over to the new faith, and those who had were scorned. Wingenund, the great power of the Delawares—indeed, the greatest of all the western tribes—maintained a neutral attitude toward the Village of Peace. But it was well known that his right-hand war-chiefs, Pipe and Wishtonah, remained coldly opposed.

Jim turned all he had learned over and over in his mind, trying to construct part of it to fit into a sermon that would be different from any the Indians had ever heard. He did not want to preach far over their heads. If possible, he desired to keep to their ideals—for he deemed them more beautiful than his own—and to conduct his teaching along the simple lines of their belief, so that when he stimulated and developed their minds he could pass from what they knew to the unknown Christianity of the white man.

His first address to the Indians was made one day during the indisposition of Mr. Wells—who had been over-working himself—and the absence of the other missionaries. He did not consider himself at all ready for preaching, and confined his efforts to simple, earnest talk, a recital of the thoughts he had assimilated while living here among the Indians.

Amazement would not have described the state of his feelings when he learned that he had made a powerful impression. The converts were loud in his praise; the unbelievers silent and thoughtful. In spite of himself, long before he had been prepared, he was launched on his teaching. Every day he was called upon to speak; every day one savage, at least, was convinced; every day the throng of interested Indians was augmented. The elder missionaries were quite overcome with joy; they pressed him day after day to speak, until at length he alone preached during the afternoon service.

The news flew apace; the Village of Peace entertained more redmen than ever before. Day by day the faith gained a stronger foothold. A kind of religious trance affected some of the converted Indians, and this greatly influenced the doubting ones. Many of them half believed the Great Manitou had come.

Heckewelder, the acknowledged leader of the western Moravian Mission, visited the village at this time, and, struck by the young missionary's success, arranged a three days' religious festival. Indian runners were employed to carry invitations to all the tribes. The Wyandots in the west, the Shawnees in the south, and the Delawares in the north were especially requested to come. No deception was practiced to lure the distant savages to the Village of Peace. They were asked to come, partake of the feasts, and listen to the white man's teaching.

CHAPTER 12

"THE GROVES WERE GOD'S FIRST TEMPLES."

From dawn until noon on Sunday bands of Indians arrived at the Village of Peace. Hundreds of canoes glided down the swift stream and bumped their prows into the pebbly beach. Groups of mounted warriors rode out of the forests into the clearing; squaws with papooses, maidens carrying wicker baskets, and children playing with rude toys, came trooping along the bridle-paths.

Gifts were presented during the morning, after which the visitors were feasted. In the afternoon all assembled in the grove to hear the preaching.

The maple grove wherein the service was to be conducted might have been intended by Nature for just such a purpose as it now fulfilled. These trees were large, spreading, and situated far apart. Mossy stones and the thick carpet of grass afforded seats for the congregation.

Heckewelder—a tall, spare, and kindly appearing man—directed the arranging of the congregation. He placed the converted Indians just behind the knoll upon which the presiding minister was to stand. In a half circle facing the knoll he seated the chieftains and important personages of the various tribes. He then made a short address in the Indian language, speaking of the work of the mission, what wonders it had accomplished, what more good work it hoped to do, and concluded by introducing the young missionary.

While Heckewelder spoke, Jim, who stood just behind, employed the few moments in running his eye over the multitude. The sight which met his gaze was one he thought he would never forget. An involuntary word escaped him.

"Magnificent!" he exclaimed.

The shady glade had been transformed into a theater, from which gazed a thousand dark, still faces. A thousand eagle plumes waved, and ten thousand bright-hued feathers quivered in the soft breeze. The fantastically dressed scalps presented a contrast to the smooth, unadorned heads of the converted redmen. These proud plumes and defiant feathers told the difference between savage and Christian.

In front of the knoll sat fifty chiefs, attentive and dignified. Representatives of every tribe as far west as the Scioto River were numbered in that circle. There were chiefs renowned for war, for cunning, for valor, for wisdom. Their stately presence gave the meeting tenfold importance. Could these chiefs be interested, moved, the whole western world of Indians might be civilized.

Hepote, a Maumee chief, of whom it was said he had never listened to words of the paleface, had the central position in this circle. On his right and left, respectively, sat Shaushoto and Pipe, implacable foes of all white men. The latter's aspect did not belie his reputation. His copper-colored, repulsive visage compelled fear; it breathed vindictiveness and malignity. A singular action of his was that he always, in what must have been his arrogant vanity, turned his profile to those who watched him, and it was a remarkable one; it sloped in an oblique line from the top of his forehead to his protruding chin, resembling somewhat the carved bowl of his pipe, which was of flint and a famed inheritance from his ancestors. From it he took his name. One solitary eagle plume, its tip stained vermilion, stuck from his scalp-lock. It slated backward on a line with his profile.

Among all these chiefs, striking as they were, the figure of Wingenund, the Delaware, stood out alone.

His position was at the extreme left of the circle, where he leaned against a maple. A long, black mantle, trimmed with spotless white, enveloped him. One bronzed arm, circled by a heavy bracelet of gold, held the mantle close about his lofty form. His headdress, which trailed to the ground, was exceedingly beautiful. The eagle plumes were of uniform length and pure white, except the black-pointed tips.

At his feet sat his daughter, Whispering Winds. Her maidens were gathered round her. She raised her soft, black eyes, shining with a wondrous light of surprise and expectation, to the young missionary's face.

Beyond the circle the Indians were massed together, even beyond the limits of the glade. Under the trees on every side sat warriors astride their steeds; some lounged on the green turf; many reclined in the branches of low-spreading maples.

As Jim looked out over the sea of faces he started in surprise. The sudden glance of fiery eyes had impelled his gaze. He recognized Silvertip, the Shawnee chief. The Indian sat motionless on a powerful black horse. Jim started again, for the horse was Joe's thoroughbred, Lance. But Jim had no further time to think of Joe's enemy, for Heckewelder stepped back.

Jim took the vacated seat, and, with a far-reaching, resonant voice began his discourse to the Indians.

"Chieftains, warriors, maidens, children of the forest, listen, and your ears shall hear no lie. I am come from where the sun rises to tell you of the Great Spirit of the white man.

"Many, many moons ago, as many as blades of grass grow on yonder plain, the Great Spirit of whom I shall speak created the world. He made the sparkling lakes and swift rivers, the boundless plains and tangled forests, over which He caused the sun to shine and the rain to fall. He gave life to the kingly elk, the graceful deer, the rolling bison, the bear, the fox —all the beasts and birds and fishes. But He was not content; for nothing He made was perfect in His sight. He created the white man in His own image, and from this first man's rib He created his mate—a woman. He turned them free in a beautiful forest.

"Life was fair in the beautiful forest. The sun shone always, the birds sang, the waters flowed with music, the flowers cast sweet fragrance on the air. In this forest, where fruit bloomed always, was one tree, the Tree of Life, the apple of which they must not eat. In all this beautiful forest of abundance this apple alone was forbidden them.

"Now evil was born with woman. A serpent tempted her to eat of the apple of Life, and she tempted the man to eat. For their sin the Great Spirit commanded the serpent to crawl forever on his belly, and He drove them from the beautiful forest. The punishment for their sin was to be visited on their children's children, always, until the end of time. The two went afar into the dark forest, to learn to live as best they might. From them all tribes descended. The world is wide. A warrior might run all his days and not reach the setting sun, where tribes of yellow-skins live. He might travel half his days toward the south-wind, where tribes of black-skins abound. People of all colors inhabited the world. They lived in hatred toward one another. They shed each other's blood; they stole each other's lands, gold, and women. They sinned.

"Many moons ago the Great Spirit sorrowed to see His chosen tribe, the palefaces, living in ignorance and sin. He sent His only Son to redeem them, and said if they would listen and believe, and teach the other tribes, He would forgive their sin and welcome them to the beautiful forest.

"That was moons and moons ago, when the paleface killed his brother for gold and lands, and beat his women slaves to make them plant his corn. The Son of the Great Spirit lifted the cloud from the palefaces' eyes, and they saw and learned. So pleased was the Great Spirit that He made the palefaces wiser and wiser, and master of the world. He bid them go afar to teach the ignorant tribes.

"To teach you is why the young paleface journeyed from the rising sun. He wants no lands or power. He has given all that he had. He walks among you without gun or knife. He can gain nothing but the happiness of opening the redmen's eyes.

"The Great Spirit of whom I teach and the Great Manitou, your idol, are the same; the happy hunting ground of the Indian and the beautiful forest of the paleface are the same; the paleface and the redman are the same. There is but one Great Spirit, that is God; but one eternal home, that is heaven; but one human being, that is man.

"The Indian knows the habits of the beaver; he can follow the paths of the forests; he can guide his canoe through the foaming rapids; he is honest, he is brave, he is great; but he is not wise. His wisdom is clouded with the original sin. He lives in idleness; he paints his face; he makes his squaw labor for him, instead of laboring for her; he kills his brothers. He worships the trees and rocks. If he were wise he would not make gods of the swift arrow and bounding canoe; of the flowering ash and the flaming flint. For these things have not life. In his dreams he sees his arrow speed to the reeling deer; in his dreams he sees his canoe shoot over the crest of shining waves; and in his mind he gives them life. When his eyes are opened he will see they have no spirit. The spirit is in his own heart. It guides the arrow to the running deer, and steers the canoe over the swirling current. The spirit makes him find the untrodden paths, and do brave deeds, and love his children and his honor. It makes him meet his foe face to face, and if he is to die it gives him strength to die—a man. The spirit is what makes him different from the arrow, the canoe, the mountain, and all the birds and beasts. For it is born of the Great Spirit, the creator of all. Him you must worship.

339

"Redmen, this worship is understanding your spirit and teaching it to do good deeds. It is called Christianity. Christianity is love. If you will love the Great Spirit you will love your wives, your children, your brothers, your friends, your foes—you will love the palefaces. No more will you idle in winter and wage wars in summer. You will wear your knife and tomahawk only when you hunt for meat. You will be kind, gentle, loving, virtuous—you will have grown wise. When your days are done you will meet all your loved ones in the beautiful forest. There, where the flowers bloom, the fruits ripen always, where the pleasant water glides and the summer winds whisper sweetly, there peace will dwell forever.

"Comrades, be wise, think earnestly. Forget the wicked paleface; for there are many wicked palefaces. They sell the serpent firewater; they lie and steal and kill. These palefaces' eyes are still clouded. If they do not open they will never see the beautiful forest. You have much to forgive, but those who forgive please the Great Spirit; you must give yourselves to love, but those who love are loved; you must work, but those who work are happy.

"Behold the Village of Peace! Once it contained few; now there are many. Where once the dark forest shaded the land, see the cabins, the farms, the horses, the cattle! Field on field of waving, golden grain shine there under your eyes. The earth has blossomed abundance. Idling and fighting made not these rich harvests. Belief made love; love made wise eyes; wise eyes saw, and lo! there came plenty.

"The proof of love is happiness. These Christian Indians are happy. They are at peace with the redman and the paleface. They till the fields and work in the shops. In days to come cabins and farms and fields of corn will be theirs. They will bring up their children, not to hide in the forest to slay, but to walk hand in hand with the palefaces as equals.

"Oh, open your ears! God speaks to you; peace awaits you! Cast the bitterness from your hearts; it is the serpent-poison. While you hate, God shuts His eyes. You are great on the trail, in the council, in war; now be great in forgiveness. Forgive the palefaces who have robbed you of your lands. Then will come peace. If you do not forgive, the war will go on; you will lose lands and homes, to find unmarked graves under the forest leaves. Revenge is sweet; but it is not wise. The price of revenge is blood and life. Root it out of your hearts. Love these Christian Indians; love the missionaries as they love you; love all living creatures. Your days are but few; therefore, cease the the strife. Let us say, 'Brothers, that is God's word,

His law; that is love; that is Christianity!' If you will say from your heart, brother, you are a Christian.

"Brothers, the paleface teacher beseeches you. Think not of this long, bloody war, of your dishonored dead, of your silenced wigwams, of your nameless graves, of your homeless children. Think of the future. One word from you will make peace over all this broad land. The paleface must honor a Christian. He can steal no Christian's land. All the palefaces, as many as the stars of the great white path, dare not invade the Village of Peace. For God smiles here. Listen to His words: 'Come unto me all that are weary and heavy laden, and I will give you rest.'"

Over the multitude brooded an impressive, solemn silence. Then an aged Delaware chief rose, with a mien of profound thought, and slowly paced before the circle of chiefs. Presently he stopped, turned to the awaiting Indians, and spoke:

"Netawatwees is almost persuaded to be a Christian." He resumed his seat.

Another interval of penetrating quiet ensued. At length a venerable-looking chieftain got up:

"White Eyes hears the rumbling thunder in his ears. The smoke blows from his eyes. White Eyes is the oldest chief of the Lenni-Lenape. His days are many; they are full; they draw near the evening of his life; he rejoices that wisdom is come before his sun is set.

"White Eyes believes the young White Father. The ways of the Great Spirit are many as the fluttering leaves; they are strange and secret as the flight of a loon; White Eyes believes the redman's happy hunting grounds need not be forgotten to love the palefaces' God. As a young brave pants and puzzles over his first trail, so the grown warrior feels in his understanding of his God. He gropes blindly through dark ravines.

"White Eyes speaks few words to-day, for he is learning wisdom; he bids his people hearken to the voice of the White Father. War is wrong; peace is best. Love is the way to peace. The paleface advances one step nearer his God. He labors for his home; he keeps the peace; he asks but little; he frees his women. That is well. White Eyes has spoken."

The old chief slowly advanced toward the Christian Indians. He laid aside his knife and tomahawk, and then his eagle plumes and war-bonnet. Bareheaded, he seated himself among the converted redmen. They began chanting in low, murmuring tones.

Amid the breathless silence that followed this act of such great significance, Wingenund advanced toward the knoll with slow, stately step. His dark eye swept the glade with lightning scorn; his glance alone revealed the passion that swayed him.

"Wingenund's ears are keen; they have heard a feather fall in the storm; now they hear a soft-voiced thrush. Wingenund thunders to his people, to his friends, to the chiefs of other tribes: 'Do not bury the hatchet!' The young White Father's tongue runs smooth like the gliding brook; it sings as the thrush calls its mate. Listen; but wait, wait! Let time prove his beautiful tale; let the moons go by over the Village of Peace.

"Wingenund does not flaunt his wisdom. He has grown old among his warriors; he loves them; he fears for them. The dream of the palefaces' beautiful forest glimmers as the rainbow glows over the laughing falls of the river. The dream of the paleface is too beautiful to come true. In the days of long ago, when Wingenund's forefathers heard not the paleface's ax, they lived in love and happiness such as the young White Father dreams may come again. They waged no wars. A white dove sat in every wigwam. The lands were theirs and they were rich. The paleface came with his leaden death, his burning firewater, his ringing ax, and the glory of the redmen faded forever.

"Wingenund seeks not to inflame his braves to anger. He is sick of blood-spilling—not from fear; for Wingenund cannot feel fear. But he asks his people to wait. Remember, the gifts of the paleface ever contained a poisoned arrow. Wingenund's heart is sore. The day of the redman is gone. His sun is setting. Wingenund feels already the gray shades of evening."

He stopped one long moment as if to gather breath for his final charge to his listeners. Then with a magnificent gesture he thundered:

"Is the Delaware a fool? When Wingenund can cross unarmed to the Big Water he shall change his mind. When Deathwind ceases to blow his bloody trail over the fallen leaves Wingenund will believe."

CHAPTER 13

As the summer waned, each succeeding day, with its melancholy calm, its changing lights and shades, its cool, damp evening winds, growing more and more suggestive of autumn, the little colony of white people in the Village of Peace led busy, eventful lives.

Upwards of fifty Indians, several of them important chiefs, had become converted since the young missionary began preaching. Heckewelder declared that this was a wonderful showing, and if it could be kept up would result in gaining a hold on the Indian tribes which might not be shaken. Heckewelder had succeeded in interesting the savages west of the Village of Peace to the extent of permitting him to establish missionary posts in two other localities—one near Goshhocking, a Delaware town; and one on the Muskingong, the principal river running through central Ohio. He had, with his helpers, Young and Edwards, journeyed from time to time to these points, preaching, making gifts, and soliciting help from chiefs.

The most interesting feature, perhaps, of the varied life of the missionary party was a rivalry between Young and Edwards for the elder Miss Wells. Usually Nell's attractiveness appealed more to men than Kate's; however, in this instance, although the sober teachers of the gospel admired Nell's winsome beauty, they fell in love with Kate. The missionaries were both under forty, and good, honest men, devoted to the work which had engrossed them for years. Although they were ardent lovers,

343

certainly they were not picturesque. Two homelier men could hardly have been found. Moreover, the sacrifice of their lives to missionary work had taken them far from the companionship of women of their own race, so that they lacked the ease of manner which women like to see in men. Young and Edwards were awkward, almost uncouth. Embarrassment would not have done justice to their state of feeling while basking in the shine of Kate's quiet smile. They were happy, foolish, and speechless.

If Kate shared in the merriment of the others—Heckewelder could not conceal his, and Nell did not try very hard to hide hers—she never allowed a suspicion of it to escape. She kept the easy, even tenor of her life, always kind and gracious in her quaint way, and precisely the same to both her lovers. No doubt she well knew that each possessed, under all his rough exterior, a heart of gold.

One day the genial Heckewelder lost, or pretended to lose, his patience.

"Say, you worthy gentlemen are becoming ornamental instead of useful. All this changing of coats, trimming of mustaches, and eloquent sighing doesn't seem to have affected the young lady. I've a notion to send you both to Maumee town, one hundred miles away. This young lady is charming, I admit, but if she is to keep on seriously hindering the work of the Moravian Mission I must object. As for that matter, I might try conclusions myself. I'm as young as either of you, and, I flatter myself, much handsomer. You'll have a dangerous rival presently. Settle it! You can't both have her; settle it!"

This outburst from their usually kind leader placed the earnest but awkward gentlemen in a terrible plight.

On the afternoon following the crisis Heckewelder took Mr. Wells to one of the Indian shops, and Jim and Nell went canoeing. Young and Edwards, after conferring for one long, trying hour, determined on settling the question.

Young was a pale, slight man, very homely except when he smiled. His smile not only broke up the plainness of his face, but seemed to chase away a serious shadow, allowing his kindly, gentle spirit to shine through. He was nervous, and had a timid manner. Edwards was his opposite, being a man of robust frame, with a heavy face, and a manner that would have suggested self-confidence in another man.

They were true and tried friends.

"Dave, I couldn't ask her," said Young, trembling at the very thought. "Besides, there's no hope for me. I know it. That's why I'm afraid, why I don't want to ask her. What'd such a glorious creature see in a poor, puny little thing like me?"

"George, you're not over-handsome," admitted Dave, shaking his head. "But you can never tell about women. Sometimes they like even little, insignificant fellows. Don't be too scared about asking her. Besides, it will make it easier for me. You might tell her about me—you know, sort of feel her out, so I'd—"

Dave's voice failed him here; but he had said enough, and that was most discouraging to poor George. Dave was so busy screwing up his courage that he forgot all about his friend.

"No; I couldn't," gasped George, falling into a chair. He was ghastly pale. "I couldn't ask her to accept me, let alone do another man's wooing. She thinks more of you. She'll accept you."

"You really think so?" whispered Dave, nervously.

"I know she will. You're such a fine, big figure of a man. She'll take you, and I'll be glad. This fever and fretting has about finished me. When she's yours I'll not be so bad. I'll be happy in your happiness. But, Dave, you'll let me see her occasionally, won't you? Go! Hurry—get it over!"

"Yes; we must have it over," replied Dave, getting up with a brave, effort. Truly, if he carried that determined front to his lady-love he would look like a masterful lover. But when he got to the door he did not at all resemble a conqueror.

"You're sure she—cares for me?" asked Dave, for the hundredth time. This time, as always, his friend was faithful and convincing.

"I know she does. Go—hurry. I tell you I can't stand this any longer," cried George, pushing Dave out of the door.

"You won't go—first?" whispered Dave, clinging to the door.

"I won't go at all. I couldn't ask her—I don't want her—go! Get out!"

Dave started reluctantly toward the adjoining cabin, from the open window of which came the song of the young woman who was responsible for all this trouble. George flung himself on his bed. What a relief to feel it was all over! He lay there with eyes shut for hours, as it seemed. After a time Dave came in. George leaped to his feet and saw his friend stumbling over a chair. Somehow, Dave did not look as usual. He seemed changed, or shrunken, and his face wore a discomfited, miserable expression.

"Well?" cried George, sharply. Even to his highly excited imagination this did not seem the proper condition for a victorious lover.

"She refused—refused me," faltered Dave. "She was very sweet and

345

kind; said something about being my sister—I don't remember just what—but she wouldn't have me."

"What did you say to her?" whispered George, a paralyzing hope almost rendering him speechless.

"I—I told her everything I could think of," replied Dave, despondently; "even what you said."

"What I said? Dave, what did you tell her I said?"

"Why, you know—about she cared for me—that you were sure of it, and that you didn't want her——"

"Jackass!" roared George, rising out of his meekness like a lion roused from slumber.

"Didn't you—say so?" inquired Dave, weakly.

"No! No! No! Idiot!"

As one possessed, George rushed out of the cabin, and a moment later stood disheveled and frantic before Kate.

"Did that fool say I didn't love you?" he demanded.

Kate looked up, startled; but as an understanding of George's wild aspect and wilder words dawned upon her, she resumed her usual calm demeanor. Looking again to see if this passionate young man was indeed George, she turned her face as she said:

"If you mean Mr. Edwards, yes; I believe he did say as much. Indeed, from his manner, he seemed to have monopolized all the love near the Village of Peace."

"But it's not true. I do love you. I love you to distraction. I have loved you ever since I first saw you. I told Dave that. Heckewelder knows it; even the Indians know it," cried George, protesting vehemently against the disparaging allusion to his affections. He did not realize he was making a most impassioned declaration of love. When he was quite out of breath he sat down and wiped his moist brow.

A pink bloom tinged Kate's cheeks, and her eyes glowed with a happy light; but George never saw these womanly evidences of pleasure.

"Of course I know you don't care for me——"

"Did Mr. Edwards tell you so?" asked Kate, glancing up quickly.

"Why, yes, he has often said he thought that. Indeed, he always seemed to regard himself as the fortunate object of your affections. I always believed he was."

"But it wasn't true."

"What?"

"It's not true."

"What's not true?"

"Oh—about my—not caring."

"Kate!" cried George, quite overcome with rapture. He fell over two chairs getting to her; but he succeeded, and fell on his knees to kiss her hand.

"Foolish boy! It has been you all the time," whispered Kate, with her quiet smile.

~

"Look here, Downs; come to the door. See there," said Heckewelder to Jim.

Somewhat surprised at Heckewelder's grave tone, Jim got up from the supper-table and looked out of the door. He saw two tall Indians pacing to and fro under the maples. It was still early twilight and light enough to see clearly. One Indian was almost naked; the lithe, graceful symmetry of his dark figure standing out in sharp contrast to the gaunt, gaudily-costumed form of the other.

"Silvertip! Girty!" exclaimed Jim, in a low voice.

"Girty I knew, of course; but I was not sure the other was the Shawnee who captured you and your brother," replied Heckewelder, drawing Jim into another room.

"What do they mean by loitering around the village? Inquired Jim, apprehensively. Whenever he heard Girty's name mentioned, or even thought of him, he remembered with a shudder the renegade's allusion to the buzzards. Jim never saw one of these carrion birds soaring overhead but his thoughts instantly reverted to the frontier ruffian and his horrible craving.

"I don't know," answered Heckewelder. "Girty has been here several times of late. I saw him conferring with Pipe at Goshhocking. I hope there's no deviltry afoot. Pipe is a relentless enemy of all Christians, and Girty is a fiend, a hyena. I think, perhaps, it will be well for you and the girls to stay indoors while Girty and Silvertip are in the village."

That evening the entire missionary party were gathered in Mr. Wells' room. Heckewelder told stories of Indian life; Nell sang several songs, and Kate told many amusing things said and done by the little Indian boys in her class at the school. Thus the evening passed pleasantly for all.

"So next Wednesday I am to perform the great ceremony," remarked

Heckewelder, laying his hand kindly on Young's knee. "We'll celebrate the first white wedding in the Village of Peace."

Young looked shyly down at his boots; Edwards crossed one leg over the other, and coughed loudly to hide his embarrassment. Kate wore, as usual, her pensive smile; Nell's eyes twinkled, and she was about to speak, when Heckewelder's quizzical glance in her direction made her lips mute.

"I hope I'll have another wedding on my hands soon," he said placidly.

This ordinary remark had an extraordinary effect. Nell turned with burning cheeks and looked out of the window. Jim frowned fiercely and bit his lips. Edwards began to laugh, and even Mr. Wells' serious face lapsed into a smile.

"I mean I've picked out a nice little Delaware squaw for Dave," said Heckewelder, seeing his badinage had somehow gone amiss.

"Oh-h!" suddenly cried Nell, in shuddering tones.

They all gazed at her in amazement. Every vestige of color had receded from her face, leaving it marblelike. Her eyes were fixed in startled horror. Suddenly she relaxed her grasp on the windowsill and fell back limp and senseless.

Heckewelder ran to the door to look out, while the others bent over the unconscious girl, endeavoring to revive her. Presently a fluttering breath and a quivering of her dark lashes noted a return of suspended life. Then her beautiful eyes opened wide to gaze with wonder and fear into the grave faces bent so anxiously over her.

"Nell, dearest, you are safe. What was it? What frightened you so?" said Kate, tenderly.

"Oh, it was fearful!" gasped Nell, sitting up. She clung to her sister with one hand, while the other grasped Jim's sleeve.

"I was looking out into the dark, when suddenly I beheld a face, a terrible face!" cried Nell. Those who watched her marveled at the shrinking, awful fear in her eyes. "It was right by the window. I could have touched it. Such a greedy, wolfish face, with a long, hooked nose! The eyes, oh! the eyes! I'll never forget them. They made me sick; they paralyzed me. It wasn't an Indian's face. It belonged to that white man, that awful white man! I never saw him before; but I knew him."

"Girty!" said Heckewelder, who had come in with his quiet step. "He looked in at the window. Calm yourself, Nellie. The renegade has gone."

The incident worried them all at the time, and made Nell nervous for several days; but as Girty had disappeared, and nothing more was heard of him, gradually they forgot. Kate's wedding day dawned with all the little party well and happy. Early in the afternoon Jim and Nell, accompanied by Kate and her lover, started out into the woods just beyond the clearing for the purpose of gathering wild flowers to decorate the cabin.

"We are both thinking of—him," Jim said, after he and Nell had walked some little way in silence.

"Yes," answered Nell, simply.

"I hope—I pray Joe comes back, but if he doesn't—Nell—won't you care a little for me?"

He received no answer. But Nell turned her face away.

"We both loved him. If he's gone forever our very love for him should bring us together. I know—I know he would have wished that."

"Jim, don't speak of love to me now," she whispered. Then she turned to the others. "Come quickly; here are great clusters of wild clematis and goldenrod. How lovely! Let us gather a quantity."

The young men had almost buried the girls under huge masses of the beautiful flowers, when the soft tread of moccasined feet caused them all to turn in surprise. Six savages stood waist-deep in the bushes, where they had lain concealed. Fierce, painted visages scowled from behind leveled rifles.

"Don't yell!" cried a hoarse voice in English. Following the voice came a snapping of twigs, and then two other figures came into view. They were Girty and Silvertip.

"Don't yell, er I'll leave you layin' here fer the buzzards," said the renegade. He stepped forward and grasped Young, at the same time speaking in the Indian language and pointing to a nearby tree. Strange to relate, the renegade apparently wanted no bloodshed. While one of the savages began to tie Young to the tree, Girty turned his gaze on the girls. His little, yellow eyes glinted; he stroked his chin with a bony hand, and his dark, repulsive face was wreathed in a terrible, meaning smile.

"I've been layin' fer you," he croaked, eyeing Nell. "Ye're the purtiest lass, 'ceptin' mebbe Bet Zane, I ever seed on the border. I got cheated outen her, but I've got you; arter I feed yer Injun preacher to ther buzzards mebbe ye'll larn to love me."

Nell gazed one instant into the monster's face. Her terror-stricken eyes were piteous to behold. She tried to speak; but her voice failed. Then, like stricken bird, she fell on the grass.

CHAPTER 14

Not many miles from the Village of Peace rose an irregular chain of hills, the first faint indications of the grand Appalachian Mountain system. These ridges were thickly wooded with white oak, poplar and hickory, among which a sentinel pine reared here and there its evergreen head. There were clefts in the hills, passes lined by gray-stoned cliffs, below which ran clear brooks, tumbling over rocks in a hurry to meet their majestic father, the Ohio.

One of these valleys, so narrow that the sun seldom brightened the merry brook, made a deep cut in the rocks. The head of this valley tapered until the walls nearly met; it seemed to lose itself in the shade of fern-faced cliffs, shadowed as they were by fir trees leaning over the brink, as though to search for secrets of the ravine. So deep and dark and cool was this sequestered nook that here late summer had not dislodged early spring. Everywhere was a soft, fresh, bright green. The old gray cliffs were festooned with ferns, lichens and moss. Under a great, shelving rock, damp and stained by the copper-colored water dripping down its side, was a dewy dell into which the sunshine had never peeped. Here the swift brook tarried lovingly, making a wide turn under the cliff, as though loth to leave this quiet nook, and then leaped once more to enthusiasm in its murmuring flight.

Life abounded in this wild, beautiful, almost inaccessible spot. Little brown and yellow birds flitted among the trees; thrushes ran along the leaf-strewn ground; orioles sang their melancholy notes; robins and flickers darted beneath the spreading branches. Squirrels scurried over the leaves like little whirlwinds, and leaped daringly from the swinging branches or barked noisily from woody perches. Rabbits hopped inquisitively here and there while nibbling at the tender shoots of sassafras and laurel.

Along this flower-skirted stream a tall young man, carrying a rifle cautiously stepped, peering into the branches overhead. A gray flash shot along a limb of a white oak; then the bushy tail of a squirrel flitted into a well-protected notch, from whence, no doubt, a keen little eye watched the hunter's every movement.

The rifle was raised; then lowered. The hunter walked around the tree. Presently up in the tree top, snug under a knotty limb, he spied a little ball of gray fur. Grasping a branch of underbush, he shook it vigorously. The thrashing sound worried the gray squirrel, for he slipped from his retreat and stuck his nose over the limb. CRACK! With a scratching and tearing of bark the squirrel loosened his hold and then fell; alighting with a thump. As the hunter picked up his quarry a streak of sunshine glinting through the tree top brightened his face.

The hunter was Joe.

He was satisfied now, for after stowing the squirrel in the pocket of his hunting coat he shouldered his rifle and went back up the ravine. Presently a dull roar sounded above the babble of the brook. It grew louder as he threaded his way carefully over the stones. Spots of white foam flecked the brook. Passing under the gray, stained cliff, Joe turned around a rocky corner, and came to an abrupt end of the ravine. A waterfall marked the spot where the brook entered. The water was brown as it took the leap, light green when it thinned out; and below, as it dashed on the stones, it became a beautiful, sheeny white.

Upon a flat rock, so near the cascade that spray flew over him, sat another hunter. The roaring falls drowned all other sounds, yet the man roused from his dreamy contemplation of the waterfall when Joe rounded the corner.

"I heerd four shots," he said, as Joe came up.

"Yes; I got a squirrel for every shot."

Wetzel led the way along a narrow foot trail which gradually wound toward the top of the ravine. This path emerged presently, some distance above the falls, on the brink of a bluff. It ran along the edge of the precipice a few yards, then took a course back into densely wooded thickets. Just before stepping out on the open cliff Wetzel paused and peered keenly on all sides. There was no living thing to be seen; the silence was the deep, unbroken calm of the wilderness.

Wetzel stepped to the bluff and looked over. The stony wall opposite was only thirty feet away, and somewhat lower. From Wetzel's action it appeared as if he intended to leap the fissure. In truth, many a band of Indians pursuing the hunter into this rocky fastness had come out on the bluff, and, marveling at what they thought Wetzel's prowess, believed he had made a wonderful leap, thus eluding them. But he had never attempted that leap, first, because he knew it was well-nigh impossible, and secondly, there had never been any necessity for such risk.

Any one leaning over this cliff would have observed, perhaps ten feet below, a narrow ledge projecting from the face of the rock. He would have imagined if he were to drop on that ledge there would be no way to get off and he would be in a worse predicament.

Without a moment's hesitation Wetzel swung himself over the ledge. Joe followed suit. At one end of this lower ledge grew a hardy shrub of the ironwood species, and above it a scrub pine leaned horizontally out over the ravine. Laying his rifle down, Wetzel grasped a strong root and cautiously slid over the side. When all of his body had disappeared, with the exception of his sinewy fingers, they loosened their hold on the root, grasped the rifle, and dragged it down out of sight. Quietly, with similar caution, Joe took hold of the same root, let himself down, and when at full length swung himself in under the ledge. His feet found a pocket in the cliff. Letting go of the root, he took his rifle, and in another second was safe.

Of all Wetzel's retreats—for he had many—he considered this one the safest. The cavern under the ledge he had discovered by accident. One day, being hotly pursued by Shawnees, he had been headed off on this cliff, and had let himself down on the ledge, intending to drop from it to the tops of the trees below. Taking advantage of every little aid, he hung over by means of the shrub, and was in the act of leaping when he saw that the cliff shelved under the ledge, while within reach of his feet was the entrance to a cavern. He found the cave to be small with an opening at the back into a split in the rock. Evidently the place had been entered from the rear by bears, who used the hole for winter sleeping quarters. By crawling on his hands and knees, Wetzel found the rear opening. Thus he had established a hiding place where it was almost impossible to locate him. He provisioned his retreat, which he always entered by the cliff and left by the rear.

An evidence of Wetzel's strange nature, and of his love for this wild home, manifested itself when he bound Joe to secrecy. It was unlikely, even if the young man ever did get safely out of the wilderness, that any stories he might relate would reveal the hunter's favorite rendezvous. But Wetzel seriously demanded this secrecy, as earnestly as if the forest were full of Indians and white men, all prowling in search of his burrow.

Joe was in the seventh heaven of delight, and took to the free life as a wild gosling takes to the water. No place had ever appealed to him as did this dark, silent hole far up on the side of a steep cliff. His interest in Wetzel soon passed into a great admiration, and from that deepened to love.

This afternoon, when they were satisfied that all was well within their refuge, Joe laid aside his rifle, and, whistling softly, began to prepare supper. The back part of the cave permitted him to stand erect, and was large enough for comparative comfort. There was a neat, little stone fireplace, and several cooking utensils and gourds. From time to time Wetzel had brought these things. A pile of wood and a bundle of pine cones lay in one corner. Haunches of dried beef, bear and buffalo meat hung from pegs; a bag of parched corn, another of dried apples lay on a rocky shelf. Nearby hung a powder-horn filled with salt and pepper. In the cleft back of the cave was a spring of clear, cold water.

The wants of woodsmen are few and simple. Joe and Wetzel, with appetites whetted by their stirring outdoor life, relished the frugal fare as they could never have enjoyed a feast. As the shadows of evening entered the cave, they lighted their pipes to partake of the hunter's sweetest solace, a quiet smoke.

Strange as it may appear, this lonely, stern Indian-hunter and the reckless, impulsive boy were admirably suited for companionship. Wetzel had taken a liking to the young man when he led the brothers to Fort Henry. Subsequent events strengthened his liking, and now, many days after, Joe having followed him into the forest, a strong attachment had been insensibly forged between them.

Wetzel understood Joe's burning desire to roam the forests; but he half expected the lad would soon grow tired of this roving life, but exactly the opposite symptoms were displayed. The hunter had intended to take his comrade on a hunting trip, and to return with him, after that was over, to Fort Henry. They had now been in the woods for weeks and every day in some way had Joe showed his mettle. Wetzel finally admitted him into the secrets of his most cherished hiding place. He did not want to hurt the lad's feelings by taking him back to the settlement; he could not send him back. So the days wore on swiftly; full of heart-satisfying incident and life, with man and boy growing closer in an intimacy that was as warm as it was unusual.

Two reasons might account for this: First, there is no sane human being who is not better off for companionship. An exile would find something of happiness in one who shared his misery. And, secondly, Joe was a most acceptable comrade, even for a slayer of Indians. Wedded as Wetzel was to the forest trails, to his lonely life, to the Nemesis-pursuit he had followed for eighteen long years, he was still a white man, kind and gentle in his quiet hours, and because of this, though he knew it not, still capable of affection. He had never known youth; his manhood had been one pitiless warfare against his sworn foes; but once in all those years had his sore, cold heart warmed; and that was toward a woman who was not for him. His life had held only one purpose—a bloody one. Yet the man had a heart, and he could not prevent it from responding to another. In his simple ignorance he rebelled against this affection for anything other than his forest homes. Man is weak against hate; what can he avail against love? The dark caverns of Wetzel's great heart opened, admitting to their gloomy depths this stranger. So now a new love was born in that cheerless heart, where for so long a lonely inmate, the ghost of old love, had dwelt in chill seclusion.

The feeling of comradeship which Wetzel had for Joe was something altogether new in the hunter's life. True he had hunted with Jonathan Zane, and accompanied expeditions where he was forced to sleep with another scout; but a companion, not to say friend, he had never known. Joe was a boy, wilder than an eagle, yet he was a man. He was happy and enthusiastic, still his good spirits never jarred on the hunter; they were restrained. He never asked questions, as would seem the case in any eager lad; he waited until he was spoken to. He was apt; he never forgot anything; he had the eye of a born woodsman, and lastly, perhaps what went far with Wetzel, he was as strong and supple as a young lynx, and absolutely fearless.

On this evening Wetzel and Joe followed their usual custom; they smoked a while before lying down to sleep. Tonight the hunter was even more silent than usual, and the lad, tired out with his day's tramp, lay down on a bed of fragrant boughs.

Wetzel sat there in the gathering gloom while he pulled slowly on his pipe. The evening was very quiet; the birds had ceased their twittering; the wind had died away; it was too early for the bay of a wolf, the wail of a panther, or hoot of an owl; there was simply perfect silence.

The lad's deep, even breathing caught Wetzel's ear, and he found himself meditating, as he had often of late, on this new something that had crept into his life. For Joe loved him; he could not fail to see that. The lad had preferred to roam with the lonely Indian-hunter through the forests, to encounter the perils and hardships of a wild life, rather than accept the smile of fortune and of love. Wetzel knew that Colonel Zane had taken a liking to the boy, and had offered him work and a home; and, also, the hunter remembered the warm light he had seen in Nell's hazel eyes. Musing thus, the man felt stir in his heart an emotion so long absent that it was unfamiliar. The Avenger forgot, for a moment his brooding plans. He felt strangely softened. When he laid his head on the rude pillow it was with some sense of gladness that, although he had always desired a lonely life, and wanted to pass it in the fulfillment of his vow, his loneliness was now shared by a lad who loved him.

Joe was awakened by the merry chirp of a chipmunk that every morning ran along the seamy side of the opposite wall of the gorge. Getting up, he went to the back of the cave, where he found Wetzel combing out his long hair. The lad thrust his hands into the cold pool, and bathed his face. The water was icy cold, and sent an invigorating thrill through him. Then he laughed as he took a rude comb Wetzel handed to him.

"My scalp is nothing to make an Indian very covetous, is it?" said he, eyeing in admiration the magnificent black hair that fell over the hunter's shoulders.

"It'll grow," answered Wetzel.

Joe did not wonder at the care Wetzel took of his hair, nor did he misunderstand the hunter's simple pride. Wetzel was very careful of his rifle, he was neat and clean about his person, he brushed his buckskin costume, he polished his knife and tomahawk; but his hair received more attention than all else. It required much care. When combed out it reached fully to his knees. Joe had seen him, after he returned from a long hunt, work patiently for an hour with his wooden comb, and not stop until every little burr was gone, or tangle smoothed out. Then he would comb it again in the morning—this, of course, when time permitted—and twist and tie it up so as to offer small resistance to his slipping through the underbush. Joe knew the hunter's simplicity was such, that if he cut off his hair it would seem he feared the Indians—for that streaming black hair the Indians had long coveted and sworn to take. It would make any brave a famous chief, and was the theme of many a savage war tale.

After breakfast Wetzel said to Joe:

"You stay here, an' I'll look round some; mebbe I'll come back soon, and we'll go out an' kill a buffalo. Injuns sometimes foller up a buffalo trail, an' I want to be sure none of the varlets are chasin' that herd we saw to-day."

Wetzel left the cave by the rear. It took him fifteen minutes to crawl to the head of the tortuous, stony passage. Lifting the stone which closed up the aperture, he looked out and listened. Then, rising, he replaced the stone, and passed down the wooded hillside.

It was a beautiful morning; the dew glistened on the green leaves, the sun shone bright and warm, the birds warbled in the trees. The hunter's moccasins pressed so gently on the moss and leaves that they made no more sound than the soft foot of a panther. His trained ear was alert to catch any unfamiliar noise; his keen eyes sought first the remoter open glades and glens, then bent their gaze on the mossy bluff beneath his feet. Fox squirrels dashed from before him into bushy retreats; grouse whirred away into the thickets; startled deer whistled, and loped off with their white-flags upraised. Wetzel knew from the action of these denizens of the woods that he was the only creature, not native to these haunts, who had disturbed them this morning. Otherwise the deer would not have been grazing, but lying low in some close thicket; fox squirrels seldom or never were disturbed by a hunter twice in one day, for after being frightened these little animals, wilder and shyer than gray squirrels, remained hidden for hours, and grouse that have been flushed a little while before, always get up unusually quick, and fly very far before alighting.

Wetzel circled back over the hill, took a long survey from a rocky eminence, and then reconnoitered the lowland for several miles. He located the herd of buffalo, and satisfying himself there were no Indians near—for the bison were grazing quietly—he returned to the cave. A soft whistle into the back door of the rocky home told Joe that the hunter was waiting.

"Coast clear?" whispered the lad, thrusting his head out of the entrance. His gray eyes gleamed brightly, showing his eager spirit.

The hunter nodded, and, throwing his rifle in the hollow of his arm, proceeded down the hill. Joe followed closely, endeavoring, as Wetzel had trained him, to make each step precisely in the hunter's footprints. The lad had soon learned to step nimbly and softly as a cat. When half way down the bill Wetzel paused.

"See anythin'?" he whispered.

Joe glanced on all sides. Many mistakes had taught him to be cautious. He had learned from experience that for every woodland creature he saw, there were ten watching his every move. Just now he could not see even a little red squirrel. Everywhere were sturdy hickory and oak trees, thickets and hazelnuts, slender ash saplings, and, in the open glades, patches of sumach. Rotting trees lay on the ground, while ferns nodded long, slender heads over the fallen monarchs. Joe could make out nothing but the colors of the woods, the gray of the tree trunks, and, in the openings through the forest-green, the dead purple haze of forests farther on. He smiled, and, shaking his head at the hunter, by his action admitted failure.

"Try again. Dead ahead," whispered Wetzel.

Joe bent a direct gaze on the clump of sassafras one hundred feet ahead. He searched the open places, the shadows—even the branches. Then he turned his eyes slowly to the right. Whatever was discernible to human vision he studied intently. Suddenly his eye became fixed on a small object protruding from behind a beech tree. It was pointed, and in color darker than the gray bark of the beech. It had been a very easy matter to pass over this little thing; but now that the lad saw it, he knew to what it belonged.

"That's a buck's ear," he replied.

Hardly had he finished speaking when Wetzel intentionally snapped a twig. There was a crash and commotion in the thicket; branches moved and small saplings waved; then out into the open glade bounded a large buck with a whistle of alarm. Throwing his rifle to a level, Joe was trying to cover the bounding deer, when the hunter struck up his piece.

"Lad, don't kill fer the sake of killin'," he said, quietly. "We have plenty of venison. We'll go arter a buffalo. I hev a hankerin' fer a good rump steak."

Half an hour later, the hunters emerged from the forest into a wide plain of waving grass. It was a kind of oval valley, encircled by hills, and had been at one time, perhaps, covered with water. Joe saw a herd of large animals browsing, like cattle, in a meadow. His heart beat high, for until that moment the only buffalo he had seen were the few which stood on the river banks as the raft passed down the Ohio. He would surely get a shot at one of these huge fellows.

Wetzel bade Joe do exactly as he did, whereupon he dropped on his hands and knees and began to crawl through the long grass. This was easy for the hunter, but very hard for the lad to accomplish. Still, he managed to keep his comrade in sight, which was a matter for congratulation, because the man crawled as fast as he walked. At length, after what to Joe seemed a very long time, the hunter paused.

"Are we near enough?" whispered Joe, breathlessly.

"Nope. We're just circlin' on 'em. The wind's not right, an' I'm afeered they'll get our scent."

Wetzel rose carefully and peeped over the top of the grass; then, dropping on all fours, he resumed the advance.

He paused again, presently and waited for Joe to come up.

"See here, young fellar, remember, never hurry unless the bizness calls fer speed, an' then act like lightnin'."

Thus admonishing the eager lad, Wetzel continued to crawl. It was easy for him. Joe wondered how those wide shoulders got between the weeds and grasses without breaking, or, at least, shaking them. But so it was.

"Flat now," whispered Wetzel, putting his broad hand on Joe's back and pressing him down. "Now's yer time fer good practice. Trail yer rifle over yer back—if yer careful it won't slide off—an' reach out far with one arm an' dig yer fingers in deep. Then pull yerself forrard."

Wetzel slipped through the grass like a huge buckskin snake. His long, lithe body wormed its way among the reeds. But for Joe, even with the advantage of having the hunter's trail to follow, it was difficult work. The dry reeds broke under him, and the stalks of saw-grass shook. He worked persistently at it, learning all the while, and improving with every rod. He was surprised to hear a swish, followed by a dull blow on the ground. Raising his head, he looked forward. He saw the hunter wipe his toma-hawk on the grass.

"Snake," whispered Wetzel.

Joe saw a huge blacksnake squirming in the grass. Its head had been severed. He caught glimpses of other snakes gliding away, and glossy round moles darting into their holes. A gray rabbit started off with a leap.

"We're near enough," whispered Wetzel, stopping behind a bush. He rose and surveyed the plain; then motioned Joe to look.

Joe raised himself on his knees. As his gaze reached the level of the grassy plain his heart leaped. Not fifty yards away was a great, shaggy, black buffalo. He was the king of the herd; but ill at ease, for he pawed the grass and shook his huge head. Near him were several cows and a half-grown calf. Beyond was the main herd, extending as far as Joe could see—a great sea of black humps! The lad breathed hard as he took in the grand sight.

"Pick out the little fellar—the reddish-brown one—an' plug him behind the shoulder. Shoot close now, fer if we miss, mebbe I can't hit one, because I'm not used to shootin' at sich small marks."

Wetzel's rare smile lighted up his dark face. Probably he could have shot a fly off the horn of the bull, if one of the big flies or bees, plainly visible as they swirled around the huge head, had alighted there.

Joe slowly raised his rifle. He had covered the calf, and was about to pull the trigger, when, with a sagacity far beyond his experience as hunter, he whispered to Wetzel:

"If I fire they may run toward us."

"Nope; they'll run away," answered Wetzel, thinking the lad was as keen as an Indian.

Joe quickly covered the calf again, and pulled the trigger. Bellowing loud the big bull dashed off. The herd swung around toward the west, and soon were galloping off with a lumbering roar. The shaggy humps bobbed up and down like hot, angry waves on a storm-blackened sea.

Upon going forward, Wetzel and Joe found the calf lying dead in the grass.

"You might hev did better'n that," remarked the hunter, as he saw where the bullet had struck. "You went a little too fer back, but mebbe thet was 'cause the calf stepped as you shot."

CHAPTER 15

So the days passed swiftly, dreamily, each one bringing Joe a keener delight. In a single month he was as good a woodsman as many pioneers who had passed years on the border, for he had the advantage of a teacher whose woodcraft was incomparable. Besides, he was naturally quick in learning, and with all his interest centered upon forest lore, it was no wonder he assimilated much of Wetzel's knowledge. He was ever willing to undertake anything whereby he might learn. Often when they were miles away in the dense forest, far from their cave, he asked Wetzel to let him try to lead the way back to camp. And he never failed once, though many times he got off a straight course, thereby missing the easy travelling.

Joe did wonderfully well, but he lacked, as nearly all white men do, the subtler, intuitive forest-instinct, which makes the Indian as much at home in the woods as in his teepee. Wetzel had this developed to a high degree. It was born in him. Years of training, years of passionate, unrelenting search for Indians, had given him a knowledge of the wilds that was incomprehensible to white men, and appalling to his red foes.

Joe saw how Wetzel used this ability, but what it really was baffled him. He realized that words were not adequate to explain fully this great art. Its possession required a marvelously keen vision, an eye perfectly familiar with every creature, tree, rock, shrub and thing belonging to the forest; an eye so quick in flight as to detect instantly the slightest change in nature, or anything unnatural to that environment. The hearing must be delicate, like that of a deer, and the finer it is, the keener will be the woodsman. Lastly, there is the feeling that prompts the old hunter to say: "No game to-day." It is something in him that speaks when, as he sees a night-hawk circling low near the ground, he says: "A storm to-morrow." It is what makes an Indian at home in any wilderness. The clouds may hide the guiding star; the northing may be lost; there may be no moss on the trees, or difference in their bark; the ridges may be flat or lost altogether, and there may be no water-courses; yet the Indian brave always goes for his teepee, straight as a crow flies. It was this voice which rightly bade Wetzel, when he was baffled by an Indian's trail fading among the rocks, to cross, or circle, or advance in the direction taken by his wily foe.

Joe had practiced trailing deer and other hoofed game, until he was true as a hound. Then he began to perfect himself in the art of following a human being through the forest. Except a few old Indian trails, which the rain had half obliterated, he had no tracks to discover save Wetzel's, and these were as hard to find as the airy course of a grosbeak. On soft ground or marshy grass, which Wetzel avoided where he could, he left a faint trail, but on a hard surface, for all the traces he left, he might as well not have gone over the ground at all.

Joe's persistence stood him in good stead; he hung on, and the more he failed, the harder he tried. Often he would slip out of the cave after Wetzel had gone, and try to find which way he had taken. In brief, the lad became a fine marksman, a good hunter, and a close, persevering student of the wilderness. He loved the woods, and all they contained. He learned the habits of the wild creatures. Each deer, each squirrel, each grouse that he killed, taught him some lesson.

He was always up with the lark to watch the sun rise red and grand over the eastern hills, and chase away the white mist from the valleys. Even if he was not hunting, or roaming the woods, if it was necessary for him to lie low in camp awaiting Wetzel's return, he was always content. Many hours he idled away lying on his back, with the west wind blowing softly over him, his eye on the distant hills, where the cloud shadows swept across with slow, majestic movement, like huge ships at sea.

If Wetzel and Joe were far distant from the cave, as was often the case, they made camp in the open woods, and it was here that Joe's contentment was fullest. Twilight shades stealing down over the camp-fire; the cheery glow of red embers; the crackling of dry stocks; the sweet smell of wood smoke, all had for the lad a subtle, potent charm.

The hunter would broil a venison steak, or a partridge, on the coals. Then they would light their pipes and smoke while twilight deepened. The oppressive stillness of the early evening hour always brought to the younger man a sensation of awe. At first he attributed this to the fact that he was new to this life; however, as the days passed and the emotion remained, nay, grew stronger, he concluded it was imparted by this close communion with nature. Deep solemn, tranquil, the gloaming hour brought him no ordinary fullness of joy and clearness of perception.

"Do you ever feel this stillness?" he asked Wetzel one evening, as they sat near their flickering fire.

The hunter puffed his pipe, and, like an Indian, seemed to let the question take deep root.

"I've scalped redskins every hour in the day, 'ceptin' twilight," he replied.

Joe wondered no longer whether the hunter was too hardened to feel this beautiful tranquillity. That hour which wooed Wetzel from his implacable pursuit was indeed a bewitching one.

There was never a time, when Joe lay alone in camp waiting for Wetzel, that he did not hope the hunter would return with information of Indians. The man never talked about the savages, and if he spoke at all it was to tell of some incident of his day's travel. One evening he came back with a large black fox that he had killed.

"What beautiful, glossy fur!" said Joe. "I never saw a black fox before."

"I've been layin' fer this fellar some time," replied Wetzel, as he began his first evening task, that of combing his hair. "Jest back here in a clump of cottonwoods there's a holler log full of leaves. Happenin' to see a black-snake sneakin' round, I thought mebbe he was up to somethin', so I investigated, an' found a nest full of young rabbits. I killed the snake, an' arter that took an interest in 'em. Every time I passed I'd look in at the bunnies, an' each time I seen signs that some tarnal varmint had been prowlin' round. One day I missed a bunny, an' next day another; so on until only one was left, a peart white and gray little scamp. Somethin' was stealin' of 'em, an' it made me mad. So yistidday an' to-day I watched, an' finally I plugged this black thief. Yes, he's got a glossy coat; but he's a bad un fer all his fine looks. These black foxes are bigger, stronger an' cunniner than red ones. In every litter you'll find a dark one, the black sheep of the family. Because he grows so much faster, an' steals all the food from the others, the mother jest takes him by the nape of the neck an' chucks him out in the world to shift fer hisself. An' it's a good thing."

The next day Wetzel told Joe they would go across country to seek new game fields. Accordingly the two set out, and tramped industriously until evening. They came upon a country no less beautiful than the one they had left, though the picturesque cliffs and rugged hills had given way to a rolling land, the luxuriance of which was explained by the abundant springs and streams. Forests and fields were thickly interspersed with bubbling springs, narrow and deep streams, and here and there a small lake with a running outlet.

Wetzel had said little concerning this region, but that little was enough to rouse all Joe's eagerness, for it was to the effect that they were now in a country much traversed by Indians, especially runners and hunting parties travelling from north to south. The hunter explained that through the center of this tract ran a buffalo road; that the buffalo always picked out the straightest, lowest and dryest path from one range to another, and the Indians followed these first pathfinders.

Joe and Wetzel made camp on the bank of a stream that night, and as the lad watched the hunter build a hidden camp-fire, he peered furtively around half expecting to see dark forms scurrying through the forest. Wetzel was extremely cautious. He stripped pieces of bark from fallen trees and built a little hut over his firewood. He rubbed some powder on a piece of punk, and then with flint and steel dropped two or three sparks on the inflammable substance. Soon he had a blaze. He arranged the covering so that not a ray of light escaped. When the flames had subsided, and the wood had burned down to a glowing bed of red, he threw aside the bark, and broiled the strips of venison they had brought with them.

They rested on a bed of boughs which they had cut and arranged alongside a huge log. For hours Joe lay awake, he could not sleep. He listened to the breeze rustling the leaves, and shivered at the thought of the sighing wind he had once heard moan through the forest. Presently he turned over. The slight noise instantly awakened Wetzel who lifted his dark face while he listened intently. He spoke one word: "Sleep," and lay back again on the leaves. Joe forced himself to be quiet, relaxed all his muscles and soon slumbered.

On the morrow Wetzel went out to look over the hunting prospects. About noon he returned. Joe was surprised to find some slight change in the hunter. He could not tell what it was.

"I seen Injun sign," said Wetzel. "There's no tellin' how soon we may run agin the sneaks. We can't hunt here. Like as not there's Hurons and Delawares skulkin' round. I think I'd better take you back to the village."

"It's all on my account you say that," said Joe.

"Sure," Wetzel replied.

"If you were alone what would you do?"

"I calkilate I'd hunt fer some red-skinned game."

The supreme moment had come. Joe's heart beat hard. He could not miss this opportunity; he must stay with the hunter. He looked closely at Wetzel.

"I won't go back to the village," he said.

The hunter stood in his favorite position, leaning on his long rifle, and made no response.

"I won't go," continued Joe, earnestly. "Let me stay with you. If at any time I hamper you, or can not keep the pace, then leave me to shift for myself; but don't make me go until I weaken. Let me stay."

Fire and fearlessness spoke in Joe's every word, and his gray eyes contracted with their peculiar steely flash. Plain it was that, while he might fail to keep pace with Wetzel, he did not fear this dangerous country, and, if it must be, would face it alone.

Wetzel extended his broad hand and gave his comrade's a viselike squeeze. To allow the lad to remain with him was more than he would have done for any other person in the world. Far better to keep the lad under his protection while it was possible, for Joe was taking that war-trail which had for every hunter, somewhere along its bloody course, a bullet, a knife, or a tomahawk. Wetzel knew that Joe was conscious of this inevitable conclusion, for it showed in his white face, and in the resolve in his big, gray eyes.

So there, in the shade of a towering oak, the Indian-killer admitted the boy into his friendship, and into a life which would no longer be play, but eventful, stirring, hazardous.

"Wal, lad, stay," he said, with that rare smile which brightened his dark face like a ray of stray sunshine. "We'll hang round these diggins a few days. First off, we'll take in the lay of the land. You go down stream a ways an' scout round some, while I go up, an' then circle down. Move slow, now, an' don't miss nothin'."

Joe followed the stream a mile or more. He kept close in the shade of willows, and never walked across an open glade without first waiting and watching. He listened to all sounds; but none were unfamiliar. He closely examined the sand along the stream, and the moss and leaves under the trees. When he had been separated from Wetzel several hours, and concluded he would slowly return to camp, he ran across a well-beaten path winding through the forest. This was, perhaps, one of the bridle-trails Wetzel had referred to. He bent over the worn grass with keen scrutiny.

CRACK!

The loud report of a heavily charged rifle rang out. Joe felt the zip of a bullet as it fanned his cheek. With an agile leap he gained the shelter of a tree, from behind which he peeped to see who had shot at him. He was just in time to detect the dark form of an Indian dart behind the foliage an hundred yards down the path. Joe expected to see other Indians, and to hear more shots, but he was mistaken. Evidently the savage was alone, for the tree Joe had taken refuge behind was scarcely large enough to screen his body, which disadvantage the other Indians would have been quick to note.

Joe closely watched the place where his assailant had disappeared, and presently saw a dark hand, then a naked elbow, and finally the ramrod of a rifle. The savage was reloading. Soon a rifle-barrel protruded from behind the tree. With his heart beating like a trip-hammer, and the skin tight-ening on his face, Joe screened his body as best he might. The tree was small, but it served as a partial protection. Rapidly he revolved in his mind plans to outwit the enemy. The Indian was behind a large oak with a low limb over which he could fire without exposing his own person to danger.

"Bang!" The Indian's rifle bellowed; the bullet crumbled the bark close to Joe's face. The lad yelled loudly, staggered to his knees, and then fell into the path, where he lay quiet.

The redskin gave an exultant shout. Seeing that the fallen figure remained quite motionless he stepped forward, drawing his knife as he came. He was a young brave, quick and eager in his movements, and came nimbly up the path to gain his coveted trophy, the paleface's scalp.

Suddenly Joe sat up, raised his rifle quickly as thought, and fired point-blank at the Indian.

But he missed.

The redskin stopped aghast when he saw the lad thus seemingly come back to life. Then, realizing that Joe's aim had been futile, he bounded forward, brandishing his knife, and uttering infuriated yells.

Joe rose to his feet with rifle swung high above his head.

When the savage was within twenty feet, so near that his dark face, swollen with fierce passion, could be plainly discerned, a peculiar whistling noise sounded over Joe's shoulder. It was accompanied, rather than followed, by a clear, ringing rifleshot.

The Indian stopped as if he had encountered a heavy shock from a tree or stone barring his way. Clutching at his breast, he uttered a weird cry, and sank slowly on the grass.

Joe ran forward to bend over the prostrate figure. The Indian, a slender, handsome young brave, had been shot through the breast. He held his hand tightly over the wound, while bright red blood trickled between his fingers, flowed down his side, and stained the grass.

The brave looked steadily up at Joe. Shot as he was, dying as he knew himself to be, there was no yielding in the dark eye—only an unquenchable hatred. Then the eyes glazed; the fingers ceased twitching.

Joe was bending over a dead Indian.

It flashed into his mind, of course, that Wetzel had come up in time to save his life, but he did not dwell on the thought; he shrank from this violent death of a human being. But it was from the aspect of the dead, not from remorse for the deed. His heart beat fast, his fingers trembled, yet he felt only a strange coldness in all his being. The savage had tried to kill him, perhaps, even now, had it not been for the hunter's unerring aim, would have been gloating over a bloody scalp.

Joe felt, rather than heard, the approach of some one, and he turned to see Wetzel coming down the path.

"He's a lone Shawnee runner," said the hunter, gazing down at the dead Indian. "He was tryin' to win his eagle plumes. I seen you both from the hillside."

"You did!" exclaimed Joe. Then he laughed. "It was lucky for me. I tried the dodge you taught me, but in my eagerness I missed."

"Wal, you hadn't no call fer hurry. You worked the trick clever, but you missed him when there was plenty of time. I had to shoot over your shoulder, or I'd hev plugged him sooner."

"Where were you?" asked Joe.

"Up there by that bit of sumach!" and Wetzel pointed to an open ridge on a hillside not less than one hundred and fifty yards distant.

Joe wondered which of the two bullets, the death-seeking one fired by the savage, or the life-saving missile from Wetzel's fatal weapon, had passed nearest to him.

"Come," said the hunter, after he had scalped the Indian.

"What's to be done with this savage?" inquired Joe, as Wetzel started up the path.

"Let him lay."

They returned to camp without further incident. While the hunter busied himself reinforcing their temporary shelter—for the clouds looked threatening—Joe cut up some buffalo meat, and then went down to the brook for a gourd of water. He came hurriedly back to where Wetzel was working, and spoke in a voice which he vainly endeavors to hold steady:

"Come quickly. I have seen something which may mean a good deal."

He led the way down to the brookside.

"Look!" Joe said, pointing at the water.

Here the steam was about two feet deep, perhaps twenty wide, and had just a noticeable current. Shortly before, it had been as clear as a bright summer sky; it was now tinged with yellow clouds that slowly floated downstream, each one enlarging and becoming fainter as the clear water permeated and stained. Grains of sand glided along with the current, little pieces of bark floated on the surface, and minnows darted to and fro nibbling at these drifting particles.

"Deer wouldn't roil the water like that. What does it mean?" asked Joe.

"Injuns, an' not fer away."

Wetzel returned to the shelter and tore it down. Then he bent the branch of a beech tree low over the place. He pulled down another branch over the remains of the camp-fire. These precautions made the spot less striking. Wetzel knew that an Indian scout never glances casually; his roving eyes survey the forest, perhaps quickly, but thoroughly. An unnatural position of bush or log always leads to an examination.

This done, the hunter grasped Joe's hand and led him up the knoll. Making his way behind a well-screened tree, which had been uprooted, he selected a position where, hidden themselves, they could see the creek.

Hardly had Wetzel, admonished Joe to lie perfectly still, when from a short distance up the stream came the sound of splashing water; but nothing could be seen above the open glade, as in that direction willows lined the creek in dense thickets. The noise grew more audible.

Suddenly Joe felt a muscular contraction pass over the powerful frame lying close beside him. It was a convulsive thrill such as passes through a tiger when he is about to spring upon his quarry. So subtle and strong was its meaning, so clearly did it convey to the lad what was coming, that he felt it himself; save that in his case it was a cold, chill shudder.

Breathless suspense followed. Then into the open space along the creek glided a tall Indian warrior. He was knee-deep in the water, where he waded with low, cautious steps. His garish, befrilled costume seemed familiar to Joe. He carried a rifle at a low trail, and passed slowly ahead with evident distrust. The lad believed he recognized that head, with its tangled black hair, and when he saw the swarthy, villainous countenance turned full toward him, he exclaimed:

"Girty! by——"

Wetzel's powerful arm forced him so hard against the log that he could not complete the exclamation; but he could still see. Girty had not heard that stifled cry, for he continued his slow wading, and presently his tall, gaudily decorated form passed out of sight.

Another savage appeared in the open space, and then another. Close between them walked a white man, with hands bound behind him. The prisoner and guards disappeared down stream among the willows.

The splashing continued—grew even louder than before. A warrior came into view, then another, and another. They walked close together. Two more followed. They were wading by the side of a raft made of several logs, upon which were two prostrate figures that closely resembled human beings.

Joe was so intent upon the lithe forms of the Indians that he barely got a glimpse of their floating prize, whatever it might have been. Bringing up the rear was an athletic warrior, whose broad shoulders, sinewy arms, and shaved, polished head Joe remembered well. It was the Shawnee chief, Silvertip.

When he, too, passed out of sight in the curve of willows, Joe found himself trembling. He turned eagerly to Wetzel; but instantly recoiled.

Terrible, indeed, had been the hunter's transformation. All calmness of facial expression was gone; he was now stern, somber. An intense emotion was visible in his white face; his eyes seemed reduced to two dark shining points, and they emitted so fierce, so piercing a flash, so deadly a light, that Joe could not bear their glittering gaze.

"Three white captives, two of 'em women," uttered the hunter, as if weighing in his mind the importance of this fact.

"Were those women on the raft?" questioned Joe, and as Wetzel only nodded, he continued, "A white man and two women, six warriors, Silvertip, and that renegade, Jim Girty!"

Wetzel deigned not to answer Joe's passionate outburst, but maintained silence and his rigid posture. Joe glanced once more at the stern face.

"Considering we'd go after Girty and his redskins if they were alone, we're pretty likely to go quicker now that they've got white women prisoners, eh?" and Joe laughed fiercely between his teeth.

The lad's heart expanded, while along every nerve tingled an exquisite thrill of excitement. He had yearned for wild, border life. Here he was in it, with the hunter whose name alone was to the savages a symbol for all that was terrible.

Wetzel evidently decided quickly on what was to be done, for in few words he directed Joe to cut up so much of the buffalo meat as they could stow in their pockets. Then, bidding the lad to follow, he turned into the woods, walking rapidly, and stopping now and then for a brief instant. Soon they emerged from the forest into more open country. They faced a wide plain skirted on the right by a long, winding strip of bright green willows which marked the course of the stream. On the edge of this plain Wetzel broke into a run. He kept this pace for a distance of an hundred yards, then stopped to listen intently as he glanced sharply on all sides, after which he was off again.

Half way across this plain Joe's wind began to fail, and his breathing became labored; but he kept close to the hunter's heels. Once he looked back to see a great wide expanse of waving grass. They had covered perhaps four miles at a rapid pace, and were nearing the other side of the plain. The lad felt as if his head was about to burst; a sharp pain seized upon his side; a blood-red film obscured his sight. He kept doggedly on, and when utterly exhausted fell to the ground.

When, a few minutes later, having recovered his breath, he got up, they had crossed the plain and were in a grove of beeches. Directly in front of him ran a swift stream, which was divided at the rocky head of what appeared to be a wooded island. There was only a slight ripple and fall of the water, and, after a second glance, it was evident that the point of land was not an island, but a portion of the mainland which divided the stream. The branches took almost opposite courses.

Joe wondered if they had headed off the Indians. Certainly they had run fast enough. He was wet with perspiration. He glanced at Wetzel, who was standing near. The man's broad breast rose and fell a little faster; that was the only evidence of exertion. The lad had a painful feeling that he could never keep pace with the hunter, if this five-mile run was a sample of the speed he would be forced to maintain.

"They've got ahead of us, but which crick did they take?" queried Wetzel, as though debating the question with himself.

"How do you know they've passed?"

"We circled," answered Wetzel, as he shook his head and pointed into the bushes. Joe stepped over and looked into the thicket. He found a quantity of dead leaves, sticks, and litter thrown aside, exposing to light a long, hollowed place on the ground. It was what would be seen after rolling over a log that had lain for a long time. Little furrows in the ground, holes, mounds, and curious winding passages showed where grubs and crickets had made their homes. The frightened insects were now running round wildly.

"What was here? A log?"

"A twenty-foot canoe was hid under thet stuff. The Injuns has taken one of these streams."

"How can we tell which one?"

"Mebbe we can't; but we'll try. Grab up a few of them bugs, go below thet rocky point, an' crawl close to the bank so you can jest peep over. Be keerful not to show the tip of your head, an' don't knock nothin' off'en the bank into the water. Watch fer trout. Look everywheres, an' drop in a bug now and then. I'll do the same fer the other stream. Then we'll come back here an' talk over what the fish has to say about the Injuns."

Joe walked down stream a few paces, and, dropping on his knees, crawled carefully to the edge of the bank. He slightly parted the grass so he could peep through, and found himself directly over a pool with a narrow shoal running out from the opposite bank. The water was so clear he could see the pebbly bottom in all parts, except a dark hole near a bend in the shore close by. He did not see a living thing in the water, not a crawfish, turtle, nor even a frog. He peered round closely, then flipped in one of the bugs he had brought along. A shiny yellow fish flared up from the depths of the deep hole and disappeared with the cricket; but it was a bass or a pike, not a trout. Wetzel had said there were a few trout living near the cool springs of these streams. The lad tried again to coax one to the surface. This time the more fortunate cricket swam and hopped across the stream to safety.

When Joe's eyes were thoroughly accustomed to the clear water, with its deceiving lights and shades, he saw a fish lying snug under the side of a stone. The lad thought he recognized the snub-nose, the hooked, wolfish jaw, but he could not get sufficient of a view to classify him. He crawled to a more advantageous position farther down stream, and then he peered again through the woods. Yes, sure enough, he had espied a trout. He well knew those spotted silver sides, that broad, square tail. Such a monster! In his admiration for the fellow, and his wish for a hook and line to try conclusions with him, Joe momentarily forgot his object. Remembering, he tossed out a big, fat cricket, which alighted on the water just above the fish. The trout never moved, nor even blinked. The lad tried again, with no better success. The fish would not rise. Thereupon Joe returned to the point where he had left Wetzel.

"I couldn't see nothin' over there," said the hunter, who was waiting. "Did you see any?'

"One, and a big fellow."

"Did he see you?"

"No."

"Did he rise to a bug?"

"No, he didn't; but then maybe he wasn't hungry" answered Joe, who could not understand what Wetzel was driving at.

"Tell me exactly what he did."

"That's just the trouble; he didn't do anything," replied Joe, thoughtfully. "He just lay low, stifflike, under a stone. He never batted an eye. But his side-fins quivered like an aspen leaf."

"Them side-fins tell us the story. Girty, an' his redskins hev took this branch," said Wetzel, positively. "The other leads to the Huron towns. Girty's got a place near the Delaware camp somewheres. I've tried to find it a good many times. He's took more'n one white lass there, an' nobody ever seen her agin."

"Fiend! To think of a white woman, maybe a girl like Nell Wells, at the mercy of those red devils!"

"Young fellar, don't go wrong. I'll allow Injuns is bad enough; but I never hearn tell of one abusin' a white woman, as mayhap you mean. Injuns marry white women sometimes; kill an' scalp 'em often, but that's all. It's men of our own color, renegades like this Girty, as do worse'n murder."

Here was the amazing circumstance of Lewis Wetzel, the acknowledged unsatiable foe of all redmen, speaking a good word for his enemies. Joe was so astonished he did not attempt to answer.

"Here's where they got in the canoe. One more look, an' then we're off," said Wetzel. He strode up and down the sandy beach; examined the willows, and scrutinized the sand. Suddenly he bent over and picked up an object from the water. His sharp eyes had caught the glint of something white, which, upon being examined, proved to be a small ivory or bone buckle with a piece broken out. He showed it to Joe.

"By heavens! Wetzel, that's a buckle off Nell Well's shoe. I've seen it too many times to mistake it."

"I was afeared Girty hed your friends, the sisters, an' mebbe your brother, too. Jack Zane said the renegade was hangin' round the village, an' that couldn't be fer no good."

"Come on. Let's kill the fiend!" cried Joe, white to the lips.

"I calkilate they're about a mile down stream, makin' camp fer the night. I know the place. There's a fine spring, an, look! D'ye see them crows flyin' round thet big oak with the bleached top? Hear them cawin'? You might think they was chasin' a hawk, or king-birds were arter 'em, but thet fuss they're makin' is because they see Injuns."

"Well?" asked Joe, impatiently.

"It'll be moonlight a while arter midnight. We'll lay low an' wait, an' then—"

The sharp click of his teeth, like the snap of a steel trap, completed the sentence. Joe said no more, but followed the hunter into the woods. Stopping near a fallen tree, Wetzel raked up a bundle of leaves and spread them on the ground. Then he cut a few spreading branches from a beech, and leaned them against a log. Bidding the lad crawl in before he took one last look around and then made his way under the shelter.

It was yet daylight, which seemed a strange time to creep into this little nook; but, Joe thought, it was not to sleep, only to wait, wait, wait for the long hours to pass. He was amazed once more, because, by the time twilight had given place to darkness, Wetzel was asleep. The lad said then to himself that he would never again be surprised at the hunter. He assumed once and for all that Wetzel was capable of anything. Yet how could he lose himself in slumber? Feeling, as he must, over the capture of the girls; eager to draw a bead on the black-hearted renegade; hating Indians with all his soul and strength, and lying there but a few hours before what he knew would be a bloody battle, Wetzel calmly went to sleep. Knowing the hunter to be as bloodthirsty as a tiger, Joe had expected he would rush to a combat with his foes; but, no, this man, with his keen sagacity, knew when to creep upon his enemy; he bided that time, and, while he waited, slept.

Joe could not close his eyes in slumber. Through the interstices in the branches he saw the stars come out one by one, the darkness deepened, and the dim outline of tall trees over the dark hill came out sharply. The moments dragged, each one an hour. He heard a whippoorwill call, lonely and dismal; then an owl hoot monotonously. A stealthy footed animal ran along the log, sniffed at the boughs, and then scurried away over the dry leaves. By and by the dead silence of night fell over all. Still Joe lay there wide awake, listening—his heart on fire. He was about to rescue Nell; to kill that hawk-nosed renegade; to fight Silvertip to the death.

The hours passed, but not Joe's passionate eagerness. When at last he saw the crescent moon gleam silver-white over the black hilltop he knew the time was nigh, and over him ran thrill on thrill.

CHAPTER 16

Wʜᴇɴ ᴛʜᴇ ᴡᴀɴɪɴɢ ᴍᴏᴏɴ ʀᴏsᴇ ʜɪɢʜ ᴇɴᴏᴜɢʜ ᴛᴏ sʜᴇᴅ ᴀ ᴘᴀʟᴇ ʟɪɢʜᴛ over forest and field, two dark figures, moving silently from the shade of the trees, crossed the moonlit patches of ground, out to the open plain where low on the grass hung silver mists.

A timber wolf, gray and gaunt, came loping along with lowered nose. A new scent brought the animal to a standstill. His nose went up, his fiery eyes scanned the plain. Two men had invaded his domain, and, with a short, dismal bark, he dashed away.

Like spectres, gliding swiftly with noiseless tread, the two vanished. The long grass had swallowed them.

Deserted once again seemed the plain. It became unutterably lonely. No stir, no sound, no life; nothing but a wide expanse bathed in sad, gray light.

The moon shone steadily; the silver radiance mellowed; the stars paled before this brighter glory.

Slowly the night hours wore away.

On the other side of the plain, near where the adjoining forest loomed darkling, the tall grass parted to disclose a black form. Was it only a deceiving shade cast by a leafy branch—only a shadow? Slowly it sank, and was lost. Once more the gray, unwavering line of silver-crested grass tufts was unbroken.

Only the night breeze, wandering caressingly over the grass, might have told of two dark forms gliding, gliding, gliding so softly, so surely, so surely toward the forest. Only the moon and the pale stars had eyes to see these creeping figures.

Like avengers they moved, on a mission to slay and to save!

On over the dark line where plain merged into forest they crawled. No whispering, no hesitating; but a silent, slow, certain progress showed their purpose. In single file they slipped over the moss, the leader clearing the path. Inch by inch they advanced. Tedious was this slow movement, difficult and painful this journey which must end in lightninglike speed. They rustled no leaf, nor snapped a twig, nor shook a fern, but passed onward slowly, like the approach of Death. The seconds passed as minutes; minutes as hours; an entire hour was spent in advancing twenty feet!

At last the top of the knoll was reached. The Avenger placed his hand on his follower's shoulder. The strong pressure was meant to remind, to warn, to reassure. Then, like a huge snake, the first glided away.

He who was left behind raised his head to look into the open place called the glade of the Beautiful Spring. An oval space lay before him, exceedingly lovely in the moonlight; a spring, as if a pearl, gemmed the center. An Indian guard stood statuelike against a stone. Other savages lay in a row, their polished heads shining. One slumbering form was bedecked with feathers and frills. Near him lay an Indian blanket, from the border of which peered two faces, gleaming white and sad in the pitying moonlight.

The watcher quivered at the sight of those pale faces; but he must wait while long moments passed. He must wait for the Avenger to creep up, silently kill the guard, and release the prisoners without awakening the savages. If that plan failed, he was to rush into the glade, and in the excitement make off with one of the captives.

He lay there waiting, listening, wrought up to the intensest pitch of fierce passion. Every nerve was alert, every tendon strung, and every muscle strained ready for the leap.

Only the faint rustling of leaves, the low swish of swaying branches, the soft murmur of falling water, and over all the sigh of the night wind, proved to him that this picture was not an evil dream. His gaze sought the quiet figures, lingered hopefully on the captives, menacingly on the sleeping savages, and glowered over the gaudily arrayed form. His glance sought the upright guard, as he stood a dark blot against the gray stone. He saw the Indian's plume, a single feather waving silver-white. Then it became riveted on the bubbling, refulgent spring. The pool was round, perhaps five feet across, and shone like a burnished shield. It mirrored the moon, the twinkling stars, the spectre trees.

An unaccountable horror suddenly swept over the watching man. His hair stood straight up; a sensation as of cold stole chillingly over him. Whether it was the climax of this long night's excitement, or anticipation of the bloody struggle soon to come, he knew not. Did this boiling spring, shimmering in the sliver moon-rays, hold in its murky depths a secret? Did these lonesome, shadowing trees, with their sad drooping branches, harbor a mystery? If a future tragedy was to be enacted here in this quiet glade, could the murmuring water or leaves whisper its portent? No; they were only silent, only unintelligible with nature's mystery.

The waiting man cursed himself for a craven coward; he fought back the benumbing sense; he steeled his heart. Was this his vaunted willingness to share the Avenger's danger? His strong spirit rose up in arms; once more he was brave and fierce.

He fastened a piercing gaze on the plumed guard. The Indian's lounging posture against the rock was the same as it had been before, yet now it seemed to have a kind of strained attention. The savage's head was poised, like that of a listening deer. The wary Indian scented danger.

A faint moan breathed low above the sound of gently splashing water somewhere beyond the glade.

"Woo-o-oo."

The guard's figure stiffened, and became rigidly erect; his blanket slowly slid to his feet.

"Ah-oo-o," sighed the soft breeze in the tree tops.

Louder then, with a deep wail, a moan arose out of the dark gray shadows, swelled thrilling on the still air, and died away mournfully.

"Um-m-mmwoo-o-o-o!"

The sentinel's form melted into the shade. He was gone like a phantom.

Another Indian rose quickly, and glanced furtively around the glade. He bent over a comrade and shook him. Instantly the second Indian was on his feet. Scarcely had he gained a standing posture when an object, bounding like a dark ball, shot out of the thicket and hurled both warriors to the earth. A moonbeam glinted upon something bright. It flashed again on a swift, sweeping circle. A short, choking yell aroused the other savages. Up they sprang, alarmed, confused.

The shadow-form darted among them. It moved with inconceivable rapidity; it became a monster. Terrible was the convulsive conflict. Dull blows, the click of steel, angry shouts, agonized yells, and thrashing, wrestling sounds mingled together and half drowned by an awful roar like that of a mad bull. The strife ceased as suddenly as it had begun. Warriors lay still on the grass; others writhed in agony. For an instant a fleeting shadow crossed the open lane leading out of the glade; then it vanished.

Three savages had sprung toward their rifles. A blinding flash, a loud report burst from the thicket overhead. The foremost savage sank life-lessly. The others were intercepted by a giant shadow with brandished rifle. The watcher on the knoll had entered the glade. He stood before the stacked rifles and swung his heavy gun. Crash! An Indian went down before that sweep, but rose again. The savages backed away from this threatening figure, and circled around it.

The noise of the other conflict ceased. More savages joined the three who glided to and fro before their desperate foe. They closed in upon him, only to be beaten back. One savage threw a glittering knife, another hurled a stone, a third flung his tomahawk, which struck fire from the swinging rifle.

He held them at bay. While they had no firearms he was master of the situation. With every sweep of his arms he brought the long rifle down and knocked a flint from the firelock of an enemy's weapon. Soon the Indians' guns were useless. Slowly then he began to edge away from the stone, toward the opening where he had seen the fleeting form vanish.

His intention was to make a dash for life, for he had heard a noise behind the rock, and remembered the guard. He saw the savages glance behind him, and anticipated danger from that direction, but he must not turn. A second there might be fatal. He backed defiantly along the rock until he gained its outer edge. But too late! The Indians glided before him, now behind him; he was surrounded. He turned around and around, with the ever-circling rifle whirling in the faces of the baffled foe.

Once opposite the lane leading from the glade he changed his tactics, and plunged with fierce impetuosity into the midst of the painted throng. Then began a fearful conflict. The Indians fell before the sweep of his powerful arms; but grappled with him from the ground. He literally plowed his way through the struggling mass, warding off an hundred vicious blows. Savage after savage he flung off, until at last he had a clear path before him. Freedom lay beyond that shiny path. Into it he bounded.

As he left the glade the plumed guard stepped from behind a tree near the entrance of the path, and cast his tomahawk.

A white, glittering flash, it flew after the fleeing runner; its aim was true.

Suddenly the moonlight path darkened in the runner's sight; he saw a million flashing stars; a terrible pain assailed him; he sank slowly, slowly down; then all was darkness.

CHAPTER 17

JOE AWOKE AS FROM A FEARSOME NIGHTMARE. RETURNING consciousness brought a vague idea that he had been dreaming of clashing weapons, of yelling savages, of a conflict in which he had been clutched by sinewy fingers. An acute pain pulsed through his temples; a bloody mist glazed his eyes; a sore pressure cramped his arms and legs. Surely he dreamed this distress, as well as the fight. The red film cleared from his eyes. His wandering gaze showed the stern reality.

The bright sun, making the dewdrops glisten on the leaves, lighted up a tragedy. Near him lay an Indian whose vacant, sightless eyes were fixed in death. Beyond lay four more savages, the peculiar, inert position of whose limbs, the formlessness, as it were, as if they had been thrown from a great height and never moved again, attested that here, too, life had been extinguished. Joe took in only one detail—the cloven skull of the nearest—when he turned away sickened. He remembered it all now. The advance, the rush, the fight—all returned. He saw again Wetzel's shadowy form darting like a demon into the whirl of conflict; he heard again that hoarse, booming roar with which the Avenger accompanied his blows. Joe's gaze swept the glade, but found no trace of the hunter.

He saw Silvertip and another Indian bathing a wound on Girty's head. The renegade groaned and writhed in pain. Near him lay Kate, with white face and closed eyes. She was unconscious, or dead. Jim sat crouched under a tree to which he was tied.

"Joe, are you badly hurt?" asked the latter, in deep solicitude.

"No, I guess not; I don't know," answered Joe. "Is poor Kate dead?"

"No, she has fainted."

"Where's Nell?"

"Gone," replied Jim, lowering his voice, and glancing at the Indians. They were too busy trying to bandage Girty's head to pay any attention to their prisoners. "That whirlwind was Wetzel, wasn't it?"

"Yes; how'd you know?"

"I was awake last night. I had an oppressive feeling, perhaps a presentiment. Anyway, I couldn't sleep. I heard that wind blow through the forest, and thought my blood would freeze. The moan is the same as the night wind, the same soft sigh, only louder and somehow pregnant with superhuman power. To speak of it in broad daylight one seems superstitious, but to hear it in the darkness of this lonely forest, it is fearful! I hope I am not a coward; I certainly know I was deathly frightened. No wonder I was scared! Look at these dead Indians, all killed in a moment. I heard the moan; I saw Silvertip disappear, and the other two savages rise. Then something huge dropped from the rock; a bright object seemed to circle round the savages; they uttered one short yell, and sank to rise no more. Somehow at once I suspected that this shadowy form, with its lightning-like movements, its glittering hatchet, was Wetzel. When he plunged into the midst of the other savages I distinctly recognized him, and saw that he had a bundle, possibly his coat, wrapped round his left arm, and his right hand held the glittering tomahawk. I saw him strike that big Indian there, the one lying with split skull. His wonderful daring and quickness seemed to make the savages turn at random. He broke through the circle, swung Nell under his arm, slashed at my bonds as he passed by, and then was gone as he had come. Not until after you were struck, and Silvertip came up to me, was I aware my bonds were cut. Wetzel's hatchet had severed them; it even cut my side, which was bleeding. I was free to help, to fight, and I did not know it. Fool that I am!"

"I made an awful mess of my part of the rescue," groaned Joe. "I wonder if the savages know it was Wetzel."

"Do they? Well, I rather think so. Did you not hear them scream that French name? As far as I am able to judge, only two Indians were killed instantly. The others died during the night. I had to sit here, tied and helpless, listening as they groaned and called the name of their slayer, even in their death-throes. Deathwind! They have named him well."

"I guess he nearly killed Girty."

"Evidently, but surely the evil one protects the renegade."

"Jim Girty's doomed," whispered Joe, earnestly. "He's as good as dead already. I've lived with Wetzel, and know him. He told me Girty had murdered a settler, a feeble old man, who lived near Fort Henry with his son. The hunter has sworn to kill the renegade; but, mind you, he did not tell me that. I saw it in his eyes. It wouldn't surprise me to see him jump out of these bushes at any moment. I'm looking for it. If he knows there are only three left, he'll be after them like a hound on a trail. Girty must hurry. Where's he taking you?"

"To the Delaware town."

"I don't suppose the chiefs will let any harm befall you; but Kate and I would be better off dead. If we can only delay the march, Wetzel will surely return."

"Hush! Girty's up."

The renegade staggered to an upright position, and leaned on the Shawnee's arm. Evidently he had not been seriously injured, only stunned. Covered with blood from a swollen, gashed lump on his temple, he certainly presented a savage appearance.

"Where's the yellow-haired lass?" he demanded, pushing away Silver-tip's friendly arm. He glared around the glade. The Shawnee addressed him briefly, whereupon he raged to and fro under the tree, cursing with foam-flecked lips, and actually howling with baffled rage. His fury was so great that he became suddenly weak, and was compelled to sit down.

"She's safe, you villainous renegade!" cried Joe.

"Hush, Joe! Do not anger him. It can do no good," interposed Jim.

"Why not? We couldn't be worse off," answered Joe.

"I'll git her, I'll git her agin," panted Girty. "I'll keep her, an' she'll love me."

The spectacle of this perverted wretch speaking as if he had been cheated out of love was so remarkable, so pitiful, so monstrous, that for a moment Joe was dumbfounded.

"Bah! You white-livered murderer!" Joe hissed. He well knew it was not wise to give way to his passion; but he could not help it. This beast in human guise, whining for love, maddened him. "Any white woman on earth would die a thousand deaths and burn for a million years afterward rather than love you!"

"I'll see you killed at the stake, beggin' fer mercy, an' be feed fer buzzards," croaked the renegade.

"Then kill me now, or you may slip up on one of your cherished buzzard-feasts," cried Joe, with glinting eye and taunting voice. "Then go sneaking back to your hole like a hyena, and stay there. Wetzel is on your trail! He missed you last night; but it was because of the girl. He's after you, Girty; he'll get you one of these days, and when he does—My God!—"

Nothing could be more revolting than that swarthy, evil face turned pale with fear. Girty's visage was a ghastly, livid white. So earnest, so intense was Joe's voice, that it seemed to all as if Wetzel was about to dart into the glade, with his avenging tomahawk uplifted to wreak an awful vengeance on the abductor. The renegade's white, craven heart contained no such thing as courage. If he ever fought it was like a wolf, backed by numbers. The resemblance ceased here, for even a cornered wolf will show his teeth, and Girty, driven to bay, would have cringed and cowered. Even now at the mention of Wetzel's enmity he trembled.

"I'll shet yer wind," he cried, catching up his tomahawk and making for Joe.

Silvertip intervened, and prevented the assault. He led Girty back to his seat and spoke low, evidently trying to soothe the renegade's feelings.

"Silvertip, give me a tomahawk, and let me fight him," implored Joe.

"Paleface brave—like Injun chief. Paleface Shawnee's prisoner—no speak more," answered Silvertip, with respect in his voice.

"Oh, where's Nellie?"

A grief-stricken whisper caught Jim's ear. He turned to see Kate's wide, questioning eyes fixed upon him.

"Nell was rescued."

"Thank God!" murmured the girl.

"Come along," shouted Girty, in his harsh voice, as, grasping Kate's arm, he pulled the girl violently to her feet. Then, picking up his rifle, he led her into the forest. Silvertip followed with Joe, while the remaining Indian guarded Jim.

THE GREAT COUNCIL-LODGE OF THE DELAWARES RANG WITH SAVAGE and fiery eloquence. Wingenund paced slowly before the orators. Wise as he was, he wanted advice before deciding what was to be done with the missionary. The brothers had been taken to the chief, who immediately called a council. The Indians sat in a half circle around the lodge. The prisoners, with hands bound, guarded by two brawny braves, stood in one corner gazing with curiosity and apprehension at this formidable array. Jim knew some of the braves, but the majority of those who spoke bitterly against the palefaces had never frequented the Village of Peace. Nearly all were of the Wolf tribe of Delawares. Jim whispered to Joe, interpreting that part of the speeches bearing upon the disposal to be made of them. Two white men, dressed in Indian garb, held prominent positions before Wingenund. The boys saw a resemblance between one of these men and Jim Girty, and accordingly concluded he was the famous renegade, or so-called white Indian, Simon Girty. The other man was probably Elliott, the Tory, with whom Girty had deserted from Fort Pitt. Jim Girty was not present. Upon nearing the encampment he had taken his captive and disappeared in a ravine.

Shingiss, seldom in favor of drastic measures with prisoners, eloquently urged initiating the brothers into the tribe. Several other chiefs were favorably inclined, though not so positive as Shingiss. Kotoxen was for the death penalty; the implacable Pipe for nothing less than burning at the stake. Not one was for returning the missionary to his Christian Indians. Girty and Elliott, though requested to speak, maintained an ominous silence.

Wingenund strode with thoughtful mien before his council. He had heard all his wise chiefs and his fiery warriors. Supreme was his power. Freedom or death for the captives awaited the wave of his hand. His impassive face gave not the slightest inkling of what to expect. Therefore the prisoners were forced to stand there with throbbing hearts while the chieftain waited the customary dignified interval before addressing the council.

"Wingenund has heard the Delaware wise men and warriors. The white Indian opens not his lips; his silence broods evil for the palefaces. Pipe wants the blood of the white men; the Shawnee chief demands the stake. Wingenund says free the white father who harms no Indian. Wingenund hears no evil in the music of his voice. The white father's brother should die. Kill the companion of Deathwind!"

A plaintive murmur, remarkable when coming from an assembly of stern-browed chiefs, ran round the circle at the mention of the dread appellation.

"The white father is free," continued Wingenund. "Let one of my runners conduct him to the Village of Peace."

A brave entered and touched Jim on the shoulder.

Jim shook his head and pointed to Joe. The runner touched Joe.

"No, no. I am not the missionary," cried Joe, staring aghast at his brother. "Jim, have you lost your senses?"

Jim sadly shook his head, and turning to Wingenund made known in a broken Indian dialect that his brother was the missionary, and would sacrifice himself, taking this opportunity to practice the Christianity he had taught.

"The white father is brave, but he is known," broke in Wingenund's deep voice, while he pointed to the door of the lodge. "Let him go back to his Christian Indians."

The Indian runner cut Joe's bonds, and once more attempted to lead him from the lodge. Rage and misery shown in the lad's face. He pushed the runner aside. He exhausted himself trying to explain, to think of Indian words enough to show he was not the missionary. He even implored Girty to speak for him. When the renegade sat there stolidly silent Joe's rage burst out.

"Curse you all for a lot of ignorant redskins. I am not a missionary. I am Deathwind's friend. I killed a Delaware. I was the companion of Le Vent de la Mort!"

Joe's passionate vehemence, and the truth that spoke from his flashing eyes compelled the respect, if not the absolute belief of the Indians. The savages slowly shook their heads. They beheld the spectacle of two brothers, one a friend, the other an enemy of all Indians, each willing to go to the stake, to suffer an awful agony, for love of the other. Chivalrous deeds always stir an Indian's heart. It was like a redman to die for his brother. The indifference, the contempt for death, won their admiration.

"Let the white father stand forth," sternly called Wingenund.

A hundred somber eyes turned on the prisoners. Except that one wore a buckskin coat, the other a linsey one, there was no difference. The strong figures were the same, the white faces alike, the stern resolve in the gray eyes identical—they were twin brothers.

Wingenund once more paced before his silent chiefs. To deal rightly with this situation perplexed him. To kill both palefaces did not suit him. Suddenly he thought of a way to decide.

"Let Wingenund's daughter come," he ordered.

A slight, girlish figure entered. It was Whispering Winds. Her beautiful face glowed while she listened to her father.

"Wingenund's daughter has her mother's eyes, that were beautiful as a doe's, keen as a hawk's, far-seeing as an eagle's. Let the Delaware maiden show her blood. Let her point out the white father."

Shyly but unhesitatingly Whispering Winds laid her hand Jim's arm.

"Missionary, begone!" came the chieftain's command. "Thank Winge-nund's daughter for your life, not the God of your Christians!"

He waved his hand to the runner. The brave grasped Jim's arm.

"Good-by, Joe," brokenly said Jim.

"Old fellow, good-by," came the answer.

They took one last, long look into each others' eyes. Jim's glance betrayed his fear—he would never see his brother again. The light in Joe's eyes was the old steely flash, the indomitable spirit—while there was life there was hope.

"Let the Shawnee chief paint his prisoner black," commanded Wingenund.

When the missionary left the lodge with the runner, Whispering Winds had smiled, for she had saved him whom she loved to hear speak; but the dread command that followed paled her cheek. Black paint meant hideous death. She saw this man so like the white father. Her piteous gaze tried to turn from that white face; but the cold, steely eyes fascinated her.

She had saved one only to be the other's doom!

She had always been drawn toward white men. Many prisoners had she rescued. She had even befriended her nation's bitter foe, Deathwind. She had listened to the young missionary with rapture; she had been his savior. And now when she looked into the eyes of this young giant, whose fate had rested on her all unwitting words, she resolved to save him.

She had been a shy, shrinking creature, fearing to lift her eyes to a pale-face's, but now they were raised clear and steadfast.

As she stepped toward the captive and took his hand, her whole person radiated with conscious pride in her power. It was the knowledge that she could save. When she kissed his hand, and knelt before him, she expressed a tender humility.

She had claimed questionable right of an Indian maiden; she asked what no Indian dared refuse a chief's daughter; she took the paleface for her husband.

Her action was followed by an impressive silence. She remained kneeling. Wingenund resumed his slow march to and fro. Silvertip retired to his corner with gloomy face. The others bowed their heads as if the maiden's decree was irrevocable.

Once more the chieftain's sonorous command rang out. An old Indian, wrinkled and worn, weird of aspect, fanciful of attire, entered the lodge and waved his wampum wand. He mumbled strange words, and departed chanting a long song.

Whispering Winds arose, a soft, radiant smile playing over her face, and, still holding Joe's hand, she led him out of the lodge, through long rows of silent Indians, down a land bordered by teepees, he following like one in a dream.

He expected to awaken at any minute to see the stars shining through the leaves. Yet he felt the warm, soft pressure of a little hand. Surely this slender, graceful figure was real.

She bade him enter a lodge of imposing proportions. Still silent, in amazement and gratitude, he obeyed.

The maiden turned to Joe. Though traces of pride still lingered, all her fire had vanished. Her bosom rose with each quick-panting breath; her lips quivered, she trembled like a trapped doe.

But at last the fluttering lashes rose. Joe saw two velvety eyes dark with timid fear, yet veiling in their lustrous depths an unuttered hope and love.

"Whispering Winds—save—paleface," she said, in a voice low and tremulous. "Fear—father. Fear—tell—Wingenund—she—Christian."

～

INDIAN SUMMER, THAT ENCHANTED TIME, UNFOLDED ITS GOLDEN, dreamy haze over the Delaware village. The forests blazed with autumn fire, the meadows boomed in rich luxuriance. All day low down in the valleys hung a purple smoke which changed, as the cool evening shades crept out of the woodland, into a cloud of white mist. All day the asters along the brooks lifted golden-brown faces to the sun as if to catch the warning warmth of his smile. All day the plains and forests lay in melancholy repose. The sad swish of the west wind over the tall grass told that he was slowly dying away before his enemy, the north wind. The sound of dropping nuts was heard under the motionless trees.

For Joe the days were days of enchantment. His wild heart had found its mate. A willing captive he was now. All his fancy for other women, all his memories faded into love for his Indian bride.

Whispering Winds charmed the eye, mind, and heart. Every day her beauty seemed renewed. She was as apt to learn as she was quick to turn her black-crowned head, but her supreme beauty was her loving, innocent soul. Untainted as the clearest spring, it mirrored the purity and simplicity of her life. Indian she might be, one of a race whose morals and manners were alien to the man she loved, yet she would have added honor to the proudest name.

When Whispering Winds raised her dark eyes they showed radiant as a lone star; when she spoke low her voice made music.

"Beloved," she whispered one day to him, "teach the Indian maiden more love for you, and truth, and God. Whispering Winds yearns to go to the Christians, but she fears her stern father. Wingenund would burn the Village of Peace. The Indian tribes tremble before the thunder of his wrath. Be patient, my chief. Time changes the leaves, so it will the anger of the warriors. Whispering Winds will set you free, and be free herself to go far with you toward the rising sun, where dwell your people. She will love, and be constant, as the northern star. Her love will be an eternal spring where blossoms bloom ever anew, and fresh, and sweet. She will love your people, and raise Christian children, and sit ever in the door of your home praying for the west wind to blow. Or, if my chief wills, we shall live the Indian life, free as two eagles on their lonely crag."

Although Joe gave himself up completely to his love for his bride, he did not forget that Kate was in the power of the renegade, and that he must rescue her. Knowing Girty had the unfortunate girls somewhere near the Delaware encampment, he resolved to find the place. Plans of all kinds he resolved in his mind. The best one he believed lay through Whispering Winds. First to find the whereabouts of Girty; kill him if possible, or at least free Kate, and then get away with her and his Indian bride. Sanguine as he invariably was, he could not but realize the peril of this undertaking. If Whispering Winds betrayed her people, it meant death to her as well as to him. He would far rather spend the remaining days of his life in the Indian village, than doom the maiden whose love had saved him. Yet he thought he might succeed in getting away with her, and planned to that end. His natural spirit, daring, reckless, had gained while he was associated with Wetzel.

Meanwhile he mingled freely with the Indians, and here, as elsewhere, his winning personality, combined with his athletic prowess, soon made him well liked. He was even on friendly terms with Pipe. The swarthy war chief liked Joe because, despite the animosity he had aroused in some former lovers of Whispering Winds, he actually played jokes on them. In fact, Joe's pranks raised many a storm; but the young braves who had been suitors for Wingenund's lovely daughter, feared the muscular paleface, and the tribe's ridicule more; so he continued his trickery unmolested. Joe's idea was to lead the savages to believe he was thoroughly happy in his new life, and so he was, but it suited him better to be free. He succeeded in misleading the savages. At first he was closely watched, the the vigilance relaxed, and finally ceased.

This last circumstance was owing, no doubt, to a ferment of excitement that had suddenly possessed the Delawares. Council after council was held in the big lodge. The encampment was visited by runner after runner. Some important crisis was pending.

Joe could not learn what it all meant, and the fact that Whispering Winds suddenly lost her gladsome spirit and became sad caused him further anxiety. When he asked her the reason for her unhappiness, she was silent. Moreover, he was surprised to learn, when he questioned her upon the subject of their fleeing together, that she was eager to go immediately. While all this mystery puzzled Joe, it did not make any difference to him or in his plans. It rather favored the latter. He understood that the presence of Simon Girty and Elliott, with several other renegades unknown to him, was significant of unrest among the Indians. These presagers of evil were accustomed to go from village to village, exciting the savages to acts of war. Peace meant the downfall and death of these men. They were busy all day and far into the night. Often Joe heard Girty's hoarse voice lifted in the council lodge. Pipe thundered incessantly for war. But Joe could not learn against whom. Elliott's suave, oily oratory exhorted the Indians to vengeance. But Joe could not guess upon whom. He was, however, destined to learn.

The third day of the councils a horseman stopped before Whispering Winds' lodge, and called out. Stepping to the door, Joe saw a white man, whose dark, keen, handsome face seemed familiar. Yet Joe knew he had never seen this stalwart man.

"A word with you," said the stranger. His tone was curt, authoritative, as that of a man used to power.

"As many as you like. Who are you?"

"I am Isaac Zane. Are you Wetzel's companion, or the renegade Deering?"

"I am not a renegade any more than you are. I was rescued by the Indian girl, who took me as her husband," said Joe coldly. He was surprised, and did not know what to make of Zane's manner.

"Good! I'm glad to meet you," instantly replied Zane, his tone and expression changing. He extended his hand to Joe. "I wanted to be sure. I never saw the renegade Deering. He is here now. I am on my way to the Wyandot town. I have been to Fort Henry, where my brother told me of you and the missionaries. When I arrived here I heard your story from Simon Girty. If you can, you must get away from here. If I dared I'd take you to the Huron village, but it's impossible. Go, while you have a chance."

"Zane, I thank you. I've suspected something was wrong. What is it?"

"Couldn't be worse," whispered Zane, glancing round to see if they were overheard. "Girty and Elliott, backed by this Deering, are growing jealous of the influence of Christianity on the Indians. They are plotting against the Village of Peace. Tarhe, the Huron chief, has been approached, and asked to join in a concerted movement against religion. Seemingly it is not so much the missionaries as the converted Indians, that the renegades are fuming over. They know if the Christian savages are killed, the strength of the missionaries' hold will be forever broken. Pipe is wild for blood. These renegades are slowly poisoning the minds of the few chiefs who are favorably disposed. The outlook is bad! bad!"

"What can I do?"

"Cut out for yourself. Get away, if you can, with a gun. Take the creek below, follow the current down to the Ohio, and then make east for Fort Henry."

"But I want to rescue the white girl Jim Girty has concealed here somewhere."

"Impossible! Don't attempt it unless you want to throw your life away. Buzzard Jim, as we call Girty, is a butcher; he has probably murdered the girl."

"I won't leave without trying. And there's my wife, the Indian girl who saved me. Zane, she's a Christian. She wants to go with me. I can't leave her."

"I am warning you, that's all. If I were you I'd never leave without a try to find the white girl, and I'd never forsake my Indian bride. I've been through the same thing. You must be a good woodsman, or Wetzel wouldn't have let you stay with him. Pick out a favorable time and make the attempt. I suggest you make your Indian girl show you where Girty is. She knows, but is afraid to tell you, for she fears Girty. Get your dog and horse from the Shawnee. That's a fine horse. He can carry you both to safety. Take him away from Silvertip."

"How?"

"Go right up and demand your horse and dog. Most of these Delawares are honest, for all their blood-shedding and cruelty. With them might is right. The Delawares won't try to get your horse for you; but they'll stick to you when you assert your rights. They don't like the Shawnee, anyhow. If Silvertip refuses to give you the horse, grab him before he can draw a weapon, and beat him good. You're big enough to do it. The Delawares will be tickled to see you pound him. He's thick with Girty; that's why he lays round here. Take my word, it's the best way. Do it openly, and no one will interfere."

"By Heavens, Zane, I'll give him a drubbing. I owe him one, and am itching to get hold of him."

"I must go now. I shall send a Wyandot runner to your brother at the village. They shall be warned. Good-by. Good luck. May we meet again."

Joe watched Zane ride swiftly down the land and disappear in the shrubbery. Whispering Winds came to the door of the lodge. She looked anxiously at him. He went within, drawing her along with him, and quickly informed her that he had learned the cause of the council, that he had resolved to get away, and she must find out Girty's hiding place. Whispering Winds threw herself into his arms, declaring with an energy and passion unusual to her, that she would risk anything for him. She informed Joe that she knew the direction from which Girty always returned to the village. No doubt she could find his retreat. With a cunning that showed her Indian nature, she suggested a plan which Joe at once saw was excellent. After Joe got his horse, she would ride around the village, then off into the woods, where she could leave the horse and return to say he had run away from her. As was their custom during afternoons, they would walk leisurely along the brook, and, trusting to the excitement created by the councils, get away unobserved. Find the horse, if possible rescue the prisoner, and then travel east with all speed.

Joe left the lodge at once to begin the working out of the plan. Luck favored him at the outset, for he met Silvertip before the council lodge. The Shawnee was leading Lance, and the dog followed at his heels. The spirit of Mose had been broken. Poor dog, Joe thought, he had been beaten until he was afraid to wag his tail at his old master. Joe's resentment blazed into fury, but he kept cool outwardly.

Right before a crowd of Indians waiting for the council to begin, Joe planted himself in front of the Shawnee, barring his way.

"Silvertip has the paleface's horse and dog," said Joe, in a loud voice.

The chief stared haughtily while the other Indians sauntered nearer. They all knew how the Shawnee had got the animals, and now awaited the outcome of the white man's challenge.

"Paleface—heap—liar," growled the Indian. His dark eyes glowed craftily, while his hand dropped, apparently in careless habit, to the haft of his tomahawk.

Joe swung his long arm; his big fist caught the Shawnee on the jaw, sending him to the ground. Uttering a frightful yell, Silvertip drew his weapon and attempted to rise, but the moment's delay in seizing the hatchet, was fatal to his design. Joe was upon him with tigerlike suddenness. One kick sent the tomahawk spinning, another landed the Shawnee again on the ground. Blind with rage, Silvertip leaped up, and without a weapon rushed at his antagonist; but the Indian was not a boxer, and he failed to get his hands on Joe. Shifty and elusive, the lad dodged around the struggling savage. One, two, three hard blows staggered Silvertip, and a fourth, delivered with the force of Joe's powerful arm, caught the Indian when he was off his balance, and felled him, battered and bloody, on the grass. The surrounding Indians looked down at the vanquished Shawnee, expressing their approval in characteristic grunts.

With Lance prancing proudly, and Mose leaping lovingly beside him, Joe walked back to his lodge. Whispering Winds sprang to meet him with joyful face. She had feared the outcome of trouble with the Shawnee, but no queen ever bestowed upon returning victorious lord a loftier look of pride, a sweeter glance of love, than the Indian maiden bent upon her lover.

Whispering Winds informed Joe that an important council was to be held that afternoon. It would be wise for them to make the attempt to get away immediately after the convening of the chiefs. Accordingly she got upon Lance and rode him up and down the village lane, much to the pleasure of the watching Indians. She scattered the idle crowds on the grass plots, she dashed through the side streets, and let every one in the encampment see her clinging to the black stallion. Then she rode him out along the creek. Accustomed to her imperious will, the Indians thought nothing unusual. When she returned an hour later, with flying hair and disheveled costume, no one paid particular attention to her.

That afternoon Joe and his bride were the favored of fortune. With Mose running before them, they got clear of the encampment and into the woods. Once in the forest Whispering Winds rapidly led the way east. When they climbed to the top of a rocky ridge she pointed down into a thicket before her, saying that somewhere in this dense hollow was Girty's hut. Joe hesitated about taking Mose. He wanted the dog, but in case he had to run it was necessary Whispering Winds should find his trail, and for this he left the dog with her.

He started down the ridge, and had not gone a hundred paces when over some gray boulders he saw the thatched roof of a hut. So wild and secluded was the spot, that he would never have discovered the cabin from any other point than this, which he had been so fortunate as to find.

His study and practice under Wetzel now stood him in good stead. He picked out the best path over the rough stones and through the brambles, always keeping under cover. He stepped as carefully as if the hunter was behind him. Soon he reached level ground. A dense laurel thicket hid the cabin, but he knew the direction in which it lay. Throwing himself flat on the ground, he wormed his way through the thicket, carefully, yet swiftly, because he knew there was no time to lose. Finally the rear of the cabin stood in front of him.

It was made of logs, rudely hewn, and as rudely thrown together. In several places clay had fallen from chinks between the timbers, leaving small holes. Like a snake Joe slipped close to the hut. Raising his head he looked through one of the cracks.

Instantly he shrank back into the grass, shivering with horror. He almost choked in his attempt to prevent an outcry.

CHAPTER 18

The sight which Joe had seen horrified him, for several moments, into helpless inaction. He lay breathing heavily, impotent, in an awful rage. As he remained there stunned by the shock, he gazed up through the open space in the leaves, trying to still his fury, to realize the situation, to make no hasty move. The soft blue of the sky, the fleecy clouds drifting eastward, the fluttering leaves and the twittering birds—all assured him he was wide awake. He had found Girty's den where so many white women had been hidden, to see friends and home no more. He had seen the renegade sleeping, calmly sleeping like any other man. How could the wretch sleep! He had seen Kate. It had been the sight of her that had paralyzed him. To make a certainty of his fears, he again raised himself to peep into the hole. As he did so a faint cry came from within.

Girty lay on a buffalo robe near a barred door. Beyond him sat Kate, huddled in one corner of the cabin. A long buckskin thong was knotted round her waist, and tied to a log. Her hair was matted and tangled, and on her face and arms were many discolored bruises. Worse still, in her plaintive moaning, in the meaningless movement of her head, in her vacant expression, was proof that her mind had gone. She was mad. Even as an agonizing pity came over Joe, to be followed by the surging fire of rage, blazing up in his breast, he could not but thank God that she was mad! It was merciful that Kate was no longer conscious of her suffering.

Like leaves in a storm wavered Joe's hands as he clenched them until the nails brought blood. "Be calm, be cool," whispered his monitor, Wetzel, ever with him in spirit. But God! Could he be cool? Bounding with lion-spring he hurled his heavy frame against the door.

Crash! The door was burst from its fastenings.

Girty leaped up with startled yell, drawing his knife as he rose. It had not time to descend before Joe's second spring, more fierce even than the other, carried him directly on top of the renegade. As the two went down Joe caught the villain's wrist with a grip that literally cracked the bones. The knife fell and rolled away from the struggling men. For an instant they tumbled about on the floor, clasped in a crushing embrace. The renegade was strong, supple, slippery as an eel. Twice he wriggled from his foe. Gnashing his teeth, he fought like a hyena. He was fighting for life—life, which is never so dear as to a coward and a murderer. Doom glared from Joe's big eyes, and scream after scream issued from the renegade's white lips.

Terrible was this struggle, but brief. Joe seemingly had the strength of ten men. Twice he pulled Girty down as a wolf drags a deer. He dashed him against the wall, throwing him nearing and nearer the knife. Once within reach of the blade Joe struck the renegade a severe blow on the temple and the villain's wrestling became weaker. Planting his heavy knee on Girty's breast, Joe reached for the knife, and swung it high. Exultantly he cried, mad with lust for the brute's blood.

But the slight delay saved Girty's life.

The knife was knocked from Joe's hand and he leaped erect to find himself confronted by Silvertip. The chief held a tomahawk with which he had struck the weapon from the young man's grasp, and, to judge from his burning eyes and malignant smile, he meant to brain the now defenseless paleface.

In a single fleeting instant Joe saw that Girty was helpless for the moment, that Silvertip was confident of his revenge, and that the situation called for Wetzel's characteristic advice, "act like lightnin'."

Swifter than the thought was the leap he made past Silvertip. It carried him to a wooden bar which lay on the floor. Escape was easy, for the door was before him and the Shawnee behind, but Joe did not flee! He seized the bar and rushed at the Indian. Then began a duel in which the savage's quickness and cunning matched the white man's strength and fury. Silvertip dodged the vicious swings Joe aimed at him; he parried many blows, any one of which would have crushed his skull. Nimble as a cat, he avoided every rush, while his dark eyes watched for an opening. He fought wholly on the defensive, craftily reserving his strength until his opponent should tire.

At last, catching the bar on his hatchet, he broke the force of the blow, and then, with agile movement, dropped to the ground and grappled Joe's legs. Long before this he had drawn his knife, and now he used it, plunging the blade into the young man's side.

Cunning and successful as was the savage's ruse, it failed signally, for to get hold of the Shawnee was all Joe wanted. Feeling the sharp pain as they fell together, he reached his hand behind him and caught Silvertip's wrist. Exerting all his power, he wrenched the Indian's arm so that it was not only dislocated, but the bones cracked.

Silvertip saw his fatal mistake, but he uttered no sound. Crippled, though he was, he yet made a supreme effort, but it was as if he had been in the hands of a giant. The lad handled him with remorseless and resistless fury. Suddenly he grasped the knife, which Silvertip had been unable to hold with his crippled hand, and thrust it deeply into the Indian's side.

All Silvertip's muscles relaxed as if a strong tension had been removed. Slowly his legs straightened, his arms dropped, and from his side gushed a dark flood. A shadow crept over his face, not dark nor white, but just a shadow. His eyes lost their hate; they no longer saw the foe, they looked beyond with gloomy question, and then were fixed cold in death. Silvertip died as he had lived—a chief.

Joe glared round for Girty. He was gone, having slipped away during the fight. The lad turned to release the poor prisoner, when he started back with a cry of fear. Kate lay bathed in a pool of blood—dead. The renegade, fearing she might be rescued, had murdered her, and then fled from the cabin.

Almost blinded by horror, and staggering with weakness, Joe turned to leave the cabin. Realizing that he was seriously, perhaps dangerously, wounded he wisely thought he must not leave the place without weapons. He had marked the pegs where the renegade's rifle hung, and had been careful to keep between that and his enemies. He took down the gun and horns, which were attached to it, and, with one last shuddering glance at poor Kate, left the place.

He was conscious of a queer lightness in his head, but he suffered no pain. His garments were dripping with blood. He did not know how much of it was his, or the Indian's. Instinct rather than sight was his guide. He grew weaker and weaker; his head began to whirl, yet he kept on, knowing that life and freedom were his if he found Whispering Winds. He gained the top of the ridge; his eyes were blurred, his strength gone. He called aloud, and then plunged forward on his face. He heard dimly, as though the sound were afar off, the whine of a dog. He felt something soft and wet on his face. Then consciousness left him.

When he regained his senses he was lying on a bed of ferns under a projecting rock. He heard the gurgle of running water mingling with the song of birds. Near him lay Mose, and beyond rose a wall of green thicket. Neither Whispering Winds nor his horse was visible.

He felt a dreamy lassitude. He was tired, but had no pain. Finding he could move without difficulty, he concluded his weakness was more from loss of blood than a dangerous wound. He put his hand on the place where he had been stabbed, and felt a soft, warm compress such as might have been made by a bunch of wet leaves. Some one had unlaced his hunting-shirt—for he saw the strings were not as he usually tied them—and had dressed the wound. Joe decided, after some deliberation, that Whispering Winds had found him, made him as comfortable as possible, and, leaving Mose on guard, had gone out to hunt for food, or perhaps back to the Indian encampment. The rifle and horns he had taken from Girty's hut, together with Silvertip's knife, lay beside him.

As Joe lay there hoping for Whispering Winds' return, his reflections were not pleasant. Fortunate, indeed, he was to be alive; but he had no hope he could continue to be favored by fortune. Odds were now against his escape. Girty would have the Delawares on his trail like a pack of hungry wolves. He could not understand the absence of Whispering Winds. She would have died sooner than desert him. Girty had, perhaps, captured her, and was now scouring the woods for him.

"I'll get him next time, or he'll get me," muttered Joe, in bitter wrath. He could never forgive himself for his failure to kill the renegade.

The recollection of how nearly he had forever ended Girty's brutal career brought before Joe's mind the scene of the fight. He saw again Buzzard Jim's face, revolting, unlike anything human. There stretched Silvertip's dark figure, lying still and stark, and there was Kate's white form in its winding, crimson wreath of blood. Hauntingly her face returned, sad, stern in its cold rigidity.

"Poor girl, better for her to be dead," he murmured. "Not long will she be unavenged!"

His thoughts drifted to the future. He had no fear of starvation, for Mose could catch a rabbit or woodchuck at any time. When the strips of meat he had hidden in his coat were gone, he could start a fire and roast more. What concerned him most was pursuit. His trail from the cabin had been a bloody one, which would render it easily followed. He dared not risk exertion until he had given his wound time to heal. Then, if he did escape from Girty and the Delawares, his future was not bright. His experiences of the last few days had not only sobered, but brought home to him this real border life. With all his fire and daring he new he was no fool. He had eagerly embraced a career which, at the present stage of his training, was beyond his scope—not that he did not know how to act in sudden crises, but because he had not had the necessary practice to quickly and surely use his knowledge.

Bitter, indeed, was his self-scorn when he recalled that of the several critical positions he had been in since his acquaintance with Wetzel, he had failed in all but one. The exception was the killing of Silvertip. Here his fury had made him fight as Wetzel fought with only his every day incentive. He realized that the border was no place for any save the boldest and most experienced hunters—men who had become inured to hardship, callous as to death, keen as Indians. Fear was not in Joe nor lack of confidence; but he had good sense, and realized he would have done a wiser thing had he stayed at Fort Henry. Colonel Zane was right. The Indians were tigers, the renegades vultures, the vast untrammeled forests and plains their covert. Ten years of war had rendered this wilderness a place where those few white men who had survived were hardened to the spilling of blood, stern even in those few quiet hours which peril allowed them, strong in their sacrifice of all for future generations.

A low growl from Mose broke into Joe's reflections. The dog had raised his nose from his paws and sniffed suspiciously at the air. The lad heard a slight rustling outside, and in another moment was overjoyed at seeing Whispering Winds. She came swiftly, with a lithe, graceful motion, and flying to him like a rush of wind, knelt beside him. She kissed him and murmured words of endearment.

"Winds, where have you been?" he asked her, in the mixed English and Indian dialect in which they conversed.

She told him the dog had led her to him two evenings before. He was insensible. She had bathed and bandaged his wound, and remained with him all that night. The next day, finding he was ill and delirious, she decided to risk returning to the village. If any questions arose, she could say he had left her. Then she would find a way to get back to him, bringing healing herbs for his wound and a soothing drink. As it turned out Girty had returned to the camp. He was battered and bruised, and in a white heat of passion. Going at once to Wingenund, the renegade openly accused Whispering Winds of aiding her paleface lover to escape. Wingenund called his daughter before him, and questioned her. She confessed all to her father.

"Why is the daughter of Wingenund a traitor to her race?" demanded the chief.

"Whispering Winds is a Christian."

Wingenund received this intelligence as a blow. He dismissed Girty and sent his braves from his lodge, facing his daughter alone. Gloomy and stern, he paced before her.

"Wingenund's blood might change, but would never betray. Wingenund is the Delaware chief," he said. "Go. Darken no more the door of Wingenund's wigwam. Let the flower of the Delawares fade in alien pastures. Go. Whispering Winds is free!"

Tears shone brightly in the Indian girl's eyes while she told Joe her story. She loved her father, and she would see him no more.

"Winds is free," she whispered. "When strength returns to her master she can follow him to the white villages. Winds will live her life for him."

"Then we have no one to fear?" asked Joe.

"No redman, now that the Shawnee chief is dead."

"Will Girty follow us? He is a coward; he will fear to come alone."

"The white savage is a snake in the grass."

Two long days followed, during which the lovers lay quietly in hiding. On the morning of the third day Joe felt that he might risk the start for the Village of Peace. Whispering Winds led the horse below a stone upon which the invalid stood, thus enabling him to mount. Then she got on behind him.

The sun was just gilding the horizon when they rode out of the woods into a wide plain. No living thing could be seen. Along the edge of the forest the ground was level, and the horse traveled easily. Several times during the morning Joe dismounted beside a pile of stones or a fallen tree. The miles were traversed without serious inconvenience to the invalid, except that he grew tired. Toward the middle of the afternoon, when they had ridden perhaps twenty-five miles, they crossed a swift, narrow brook. The water was a beautiful clear brown. Joe made note of this, as it was an unusual circumstance. Nearly all the streams, when not flooded, were green in color. He remembered that during his wanderings with Wetzel they had found one stream of this brown, copper-colored water. The lad knew he must take a roundabout way to the village so that he might avoid

Indian runners or scouts, and he hoped this stream would prove to be the one he had once camped upon.

As they were riding toward a gentle swell or knoll covered with trees and shrubbery, Whispering Winds felt something warm on her hand, and, looking, was horrified to find it covered with blood. Joe's wound had opened. She told him they must dismount here, and remain until he was stronger. The invalid himself thought this conclusion was wise. They would be practically safe now, since they must be out of the Indian path, and many miles from the encampment. Accordingly he got off the horse, and sat down on a log, while Whispering Winds searched for a suitable place in which to erect a temporary shelter.

Joe's wandering gaze was arrested by a tree with a huge knotty formation near the ground. It was like many trees, but this peculiarity was not what struck Joe. He had seen it before. He never forgot anything in the woods that once attracted his attention. He looked around on all sides. Just behind him was an opening in the clump of trees. Within this was a perpendicular stone covered with moss and lichens; above it a beech tree spread long, graceful branches. He thrilled with the remembrance these familiar marks brought. This was Beautiful Spring, the place where Wetzel rescued Nell, where he had killed the Indians in that night attack he would never forget.

CHAPTER 19

One evening a week or more after the disappearance of Jim and the girls, George Young and David Edwards, the missionaries, sat on the cabin steps, gazing disconsolately upon the forest scenery. Hard as had been the ten years of their labor among the Indians, nothing had shaken them as the loss of their young friends.

"Dave, I tell you your theory about seeing them again is absurd," asserted George. "I'll never forget that wretch, Girty, as he spoke to Nell. Why, she just wilted like a flower blasted by fire. I can't understand why he let me go, and kept Jim, unless the Shawnee had something to do with it. I never wished until now that I was a hunter. I'd go after Girty. You've heard as well as I of his many atrocities. I'd rather have seen Kate and Nell dead than have them fall into his power. I'd rather have killed them myself!"

Young had aged perceptibly in these last few days. The blue veins showed at his temples; his face had become thinner and paler, his eyes had a look of pain. The former expression of patience, which had sat so well on him, was gone.

"George, I can't account for my fancies or feelings, else, perhaps, I'd be easier in mind," answered Dave. His face, too, showed the ravages of grief. "I've had queer thoughts lately, and dreams such as I never had before. Perhaps it's this trouble which has made me so nervous. I don't seem able to pull myself together. I can neither preach nor work."

"Neither can I! This trouble has hit you as hard as it has me. But, Dave, we've still our duty. To endure, to endure—that is our life. Because a beam of sunshine brightened, for a brief time, the gray of our lives, and then faded away, we must not shirk nor grow sour and discontented."

"But how cruel is this border life!"

"Nature itself is brutal."

"Yes, I know, and we have elected to spend our lives here in the midst of this ceaseless strife, to fare poorly, to have no pleasure, never to feel the comfort of a woman's smiles, nor the joy of a child's caress, all because out in the woods are ten or twenty or a hundred savages we may convert."

"That is why, and it is enough. It is hard to give up the women you love to a black-souled renegade, but that is not for my thought. What kills me is the horror for her—for her."

"I, too, suffer with that thought; more than that, I am morbid and depressed. I feel as if some calamity awaited us here. I have never been superstitious, nor have I had presentiments, but of late there are strange fears in my mind."

At this juncture Mr. Wells and Heckewelder came out of the adjoining cabin.

"I had word from a trustworthy runner to-day. Girty and his captives have not been seen in the Delaware towns," said Heckewelder.

"It is most unlikely that he will take them to the towns," replied Edwards. "What do you make of his capturing Jim?"

"For Pipe, perhaps. The Delaware Wolf is snapping his teeth. Pipe is particularly opposed to Christianity, and—what's that?"

A low whistle from the bushes near the creek bank attracted the attention of all. The younger men got up to investigate, but Heckewelder detained them.

"Wait," he added. "There is no telling what that signal may mean."

They waited with breathless interest. Presently the whistle was repeated, and an instant later the tall figure of a man stepped from behind a thicket. He was a white man, but not recognizable at that distance, even if a friend. The stranger waved his hand as if asking them to be cautious, and come to him.

They went toward the thicket, and when within a few paces of the man Mr. Wells exclaimed:

"It's the man who guided my party to the village. It is Wetzel!"

The other missionaries had never seen the hunter though, of course, they were familiar with his name, and looked at him with great curiosity. The hunter's buckskin garments were wet, torn, and covered with burrs. Dark spots, evidently blood stains, showed on his hunting-shirt.

"Wetzel?" interrogated Heckewelder.

The hunter nodded, and took a step behind the bush. Bending over he lifted something from the ground. It was a girl. It was Nell! She was very white—but alive. A faint, glad smile lighted up her features.

Not a word was spoken. With an expression of tender compassion Mr. Wells received her into his arms. The four missionaries turned fearful, questioning eyes upon the hunter, but they could not speak.

"She's well, an' unharmed," said Wetzel, reading their thoughts, "only worn out. I've carried her these ten miles."

"God bless you, Wetzel!" exclaimed the old missionary. "Nellie, Nellie, can you speak?"

"Uncle dear—I'm—all right," came the faint answer.

"Kate? What—of her?" whispered George Young with lips as dry as corn husks.

"I did my best," said the hunter with a simple dignity. Nothing but the agonized appeal in the young man's eyes could have made Wetzel speak of his achievement.

"Tell us," broke in Heckewelder, seeing that fear had stricken George dumb.

"We trailed 'em an' got away with the golden-haired lass. The last I saw of Joe he was braced up agin a rock fightin' like a wildcat. I tried to cut Jim loose as I was goin' by. I s'pect the wust fer the brothers an' the other lass."

"Can we do nothing?" asked Mr. Wells.

"Nothin'!"

"Wetzel, has the capturing of James Downs any significance to you?" inquired Heckewelder.

"I reckon so."

"What?"

"Pipe an' his white-redskin allies are agin Christianity."

"Do you think we are in danger?"

"I reckon so."

"What do you advise?"

"Pack up a few of your traps, take the lass, an' come with me. I'll see you back in Fort Henry."

Heckewelder nervously walked up to the tree and back again. Young and Edwards looked blankly at one another. They both remembered Edward's presentiment. Mr. Wells uttered an angry exclamation.

"You ask us to fail in our duty? No, never! To go back to the white settlements and acknowledge we were afraid to continue teaching the Gospel to the Indians! You can not understand Christianity if you advise that. You have no religion. You are a killer of Indians."

A shadow that might have been one of pain flitted over the hunter's face.

"No, I ain't a Christian, an' I am a killer of Injuns," said Wetzel, and his deep voice had a strange tremor. "I don't know nothin' much 'cept the woods an' fields, an' if there's a God fer me He's out thar under the trees an' grass. Mr. Wells, you're the first man as ever called me a coward, an' I overlook it because of your callin'. I advise you to go back to Fort Henry, because if you don't go now the chances are aginst your ever goin'. Christianity or no Christianity, such men as you hev no bisness in these woods."

"I thank you for your advice, and bless you for your rescue of this child; but I can not leave my work, nor can I understand why all this good work we have done should be called useless. We have converted Indians, saved their souls. Is that not being of some use, of some good here?"

"It's accordin' to how you look at it. Now I know the bark of an oak is different accordin' to the side we see from. I'll allow, hatin' Injuns as I do, is no reason you oughtn't to try an' convert 'em. But you're bringin' on a war. These Injuns won't allow this Village of Peace here with its big fields of corn, an' shops an' workin' redskins. It's agin their nature. You're only sacrificin' your Christian Injuns."

"What do you mean?" asked Mr. Wells, startled by Wetzel's words.

"Enough. I'm ready to guide you to Fort Henry."

"I'll never go."

Wetzel looked at the other men. No one would have doubted him. No one could have failed to see he knew that some terrible anger hovered over the Village of Peace.

"I believe you, Wetzel, but I can not go," said Heckewelder, with white face.

"I will stay," said George, steadily.

"And I," said Dave.

Wetzel nodded, and turned to depart when George grasped his arm. The young missionary's face was drawn and haggard; he fixed an intense gaze upon the hunter.

"Wetzel, listen;" his voice was low and shaken with deep feeling. "I am a teacher of God's word, and I am as earnest in that purpose as you are in your life-work. I shall die here; I shall fill an unmarked grave; but I shall have done the best I could. This is the life destiny has marked out for me, and I will live it as best I may; but in this moment, preacher as I am, I would give all I have or hope to have, all the little good I may have done, all my life, to be such a man as you. For I would avenge the woman I loved. To torture, to kill Girty! I am only a poor, weak fellow who would be lost a mile from this village, and if not, would fall before the youngest brave. But you with your glorious strength, your incomparable woodcraft, you are the man to kill Girty. Rid the frontier of this fiend. Kill him! Wetzel, kill him! I beseech you for the sake of some sweet girl who even now may be on her way to this terrible country, and who may fall into Girty's power—for her sake, Wetzel, kill him. Trail him like a bloodhound, and when you find him remember my broken heart, remember Nell, remember, oh, God! remember poor Kate!"

Young's voice broke into dry sobs. He had completely exhausted himself, so that he was forced to lean against the tree for support.

Wetzel spoke never a word. He stretched out his long, brawny arm and gripped the young missionary's shoulder. His fingers clasped hard. Simple, without words as the action was, it could not have been more potent. And then, as he stood, the softer look faded slowly from his face. A ripple seemed to run over his features, which froze, as it subsided, into a cold, stone rigidity.

His arm dropped; he stepped past the tree, and, bounding lightly as a deer, cleared the creek and disappeared in the bushes.

Mr. Wells carried Nell to his cabin where she lay for hours with wan face and listless languor. She swallowed the nourishing drink an old Indian nurse forced between her teeth; she even smiled weakly when the missionaries spoke to her; but she said nothing nor seemed to rally from her terrible shock. A dark shadow lay always before her, conscious of nothing present, living over again her frightful experience. Again she seemed sunk in dull apathy.

"Dave, we're going to loose Nell. She's fading slowly," said George, one evening, several days after the girl's return. "Wetzel said she was unharmed, yet she seems to have received a hurt more fatal than a physical one. It's her mind—her mind. If we cannot brighten her up to make her forget, she'll die."

"We've done all within our power. If she could only be brought out of this trance! She lies there all day long with those staring eyes. I can't look into them. They are the eyes of a child who has seen murder."

"We must try in some way to get her out of this stupor, and I have an idea. Have you noticed that Mr. Wells has failed very much in the last few weeks?"

"Indeed I have, and I'm afraid he's breaking down. He has grown so thin, eats very little, and doesn't sleep. He is old, you know, and, despite his zeal, this border life is telling on him."

"Dave, I believe he knows it. Poor, earnest old man! He never says a word about himself, yet he must know he is going down hill. Well, we all begin, sooner or later, that descent which ends in the grave. I believe we might stir Nellie by telling her Mr. Wells' health is breaking."

"Let us try."

A hurried knock on the door interrupted their conversation.

"Come in," said Edwards.

The door opened to admit a man, who entered eagerly.

"Jim! Jim!" exclaimed both missionaries, throwing themselves upon the newcomer.

It was, indeed, Jim, but no answering smile lighted his worn, distressed face while he wrung his friends' hands.

"You're not hurt?" asked Dave.

"No, I'm uninjured."

"Tell us all. Did you escape? Did you see your brother? Did you know Wetzel rescued Nell?"

"Wingenund set me free in spite of many demands for my death. He kept Joe a prisoner, and intends to kill him, for the lad was Wetzel's companion. I saw the hunter come into the glade where we camped, break through the line of fighting Indians and carry Nell off."

"Kate?" faltered Young, with ashen face.

"George, I wish to God I could tell you she is dead," answered Jim, nervously pacing the room. "But she was well when I last saw her. She endured the hard journey better than either Nell or I. Girty did not carry her into the encampment, as Silvertip did Joe and me, but the renegade left us on the outskirts of the Delaware town. There was a rocky ravine with dense undergrowth where he disappeared with his captive. I suppose he has his den somewhere in that ravine."

George sank down and buried his face in his arms; neither movement nor sound betokened consciousness.

"Has Wetzel come in with Nell? Joe said he had a cave where he might have taken her in case of illness or accident."

"Yes, he brought her back," answered Edwards, slowly.

"I want to see her," said Jim, his haggard face expressing a keen anxiety. "She's not wounded? hurt? ill?"

"No, nothing like that. It's a shock which she can't get over, can't forget."

"I must see her," cried Jim, moving toward the door.

"Don't go," replied Dave, detaining him. "Wait. We must see what's best to be done. Wait till Heckewelder comes. He'll be here soon. Nell thinks you're dead, and the surprise might be bad for her."

Heckewelder came in at that moment, and shook hands warmly with Jim.

"The Delaware runner told me you were here. I am overjoyed that Wingenund freed you," said the missionary. "It is a most favorable sign. I have heard rumors from Goshocking and Sandusky that have worried me. This good news more than offsets the bad. I am sorry about your brother. Are you well?"

"Well, but miserable. I want to see Nell. Dave tells me she is not exactly ill, but something is wrong with her. Perhaps I ought not to see her just yet."

"It'll be exactly the tonic for her," replied Heckewelder. "She'll be surprised out of herself. She is morbid, apathetic, and, try as we may, we can't interest her. Come at once."

Heckewelder had taken Jim's arm and started for the door when he caught sight of Young, sitting bowed and motionless. Turning to Jim he whispered:

"Kate?"

"Girty did not take her into the encampment," answered Jim, in a low voice. "I hoped he would, because the Indians are kind, but he didn't. He took her to his den."

Just then Young raised his face. The despair in it would have melted a heart of stone. It had become the face of an old man.

"If only you'd told me she had died," he said to Jim, "I'd have been man enough to stand it, but—this—this kills me—I can't breathe!"

He staggered into the adjoining room, where he flung himself upon a bed.

"It's hard, and he won't be able to stand up under it, for he's not strong," whispered Jim.

Heckewelder was a mild, pious man, in whom no one would ever expect strong passion; but now depths were stirred within his heart that had ever been tranquil. He became livid, and his face was distorted with rage.

"It's bad enough to have these renegades plotting and working against our religion; to have them sow discontent, spread lies, make the Indians think we have axes to grind, to plant the only obstacle in our path—all this is bad; but to doom an innocent white woman to worse than death! What can I call it!"

"What can we do?" asked Jim.

"Do? That's the worst of it. We can do nothing, nothing. We dare not move."

"Is there no hope of getting Kate back?"

"Hope? None. That villain is surrounded by his savages. He'll lie low now for a while. I've heard of such deeds many a time, but it never before came so close home. Kate Wells was a pure, loving Christian woman. She'll live an hour, a day, a week, perhaps, in that snake's clutches, and then she'll die. Thank God!"

"Wetzel has gone on Girty's trail. I know that from his manner when he left us," said Edwards.

"Wetzel may avenge her, but he can never save her. It's too late. Hello—"

The exclamation was called forth by the appearance of Young, who entered with a rifle in his hands.

"George, where are you going with that gun?" asked Edwards, grasping his friend by the arm.

"I'm going after her," answered George wildly. He tottered as he spoke, but wrenched himself free from Dave.

"Come, George, listen, listen to reason," interposed Heckewelder, laying hold of Young. "You are frantic with grief now. So are all of us. But calm yourself. Why, man, you're a preacher, not a hunter. You'd be lost, you'd starve in the woods before getting half way to the Indian town. This is terrible enough; don't make it worse by throwing your life away. Think of us, your friends; think of your Indian pupils who rely so much on you. Think of the Village of Peace. We can pray, but we can't prevent these border crimes. With civilization, with the spread of Christianity, they will pass away. Bear up under this blow for the sake of your work. Remember we alone can check such barbarity. But we must not fight. We must sacrifice all that men hold dear, for the sake of the future."

He took the rifle away from George, and led him back into the little, dark room. Closing the door he turned to Jim and Dave.

"He is in a bad way, and we must carefully watch him for a few days."

"Think of George starting out to kill Girty!" exclaimed Dave. "I never fired a gun, but yet I'd go too."

"So would we all, if we did as our hearts dictate," retorted Heckewelder, turning fiercely upon Dave as if stung. "Man! we have a village full of Christians to look after. What would become of them? I tell you we've all we can do here to outwit these border ruffians. Simon Girty is plotting our ruin. I heard it to-day from the Delaware runner who is my friend. He is jealous of our influence, when all we desire is to save these poor Indians. And, Jim, Girty has killed our happiness. Can we ever recover from the misery brought upon us by poor Kate's fate?"

The missionary raised his hand as if to exhort some power above.

"Curse the Girty's!" he exclaimed in a sudden burst of uncontrollable passion. "Having conquered all other obstacles, must we fail because of wicked men of our own race? Oh, curse them!"

"Come," he said, presently, in a voice which trembled with the effort he made to be calm. "We'll go in to Nellie."

The three men entered Mr. Wells' cabin. The old missionary, with bowed head and hands clasped behind his back, was pacing to and fro. He greeted Jim with glad surprise.

"We want Nellie to see him," whispered Heckewelder. "We think the surprise will do her good."

"I trust it may," said Mr. Wells.

"Leave it to me."

They followed Heckewelder into an adjoining room. A torch flickered over the rude mantle-shelf, lighting up the room with fitful flare. It was a warm night, and the soft breeze coming in the window alternately paled and brightened the flame.

Jim saw Nell lying on the bed. Her eyes were closed, and her long, dark lashes seemed black against the marble paleness of her skin.

"Stand behind me," whispered Heckewelder to Jim.

"Nellie," he called softly, but only a faint flickering of her lashes answered him.

"Nellie, Nellie," repeated Heckewelder, his deep, strong voice thrilling.

Her eyes opened. They gazed at Mr. Wells on one side, at Edwards standing at the foot of the bed, at Heckewelder leaning over her, but there was no recognition or interest in her look.

"Nellie, can you understand me?" asked Heckewelder, putting into his voice all the power and intensity of feeling of which he was capable.

An almost imperceptible shadow of understanding shone in her eyes.

"Listen. You have had a terrible shock, and it has affected your mind. You are mistaken in what you think, what you dream of all the time. Do you understand? You are wrong!"

Nell's eyes quickened with a puzzled, questioning doubt. The minister's magnetic, penetrating voice had pierced her dulled brain.

"See, I have brought you Jim!"

Heckewelder stepped aside as Jim fell on his knees by the bed. He took her cold hands in his and bent over her. For the moment his voice failed.

The doubt in Nell's eyes changed to a wondrous gladness. It was like the rekindling of a smoldering fire.

"Jim?" she whispered.

"Yes, Nellie, it's Jim alive and well. It's Jim come back to you."

A soft flush stained her white face. She slipped her arm tenderly around his neck, and held her cheek close to his.

"Jim," she murmured.

"Nellie, don't you know me?" asked Mr. Wells, trembling, excited. This was the first word she had spoken in four days.

"Uncle!" she exclaimed, suddenly loosening her hold on Jim, and sitting up in bed, then she gazed wildly at the others.

"Was it all a horrible dream?"

Mr. Wells took her hand soothingly, but he did not attempt to answer her question. He looked helplessly at Heckewelder, but that missionary was intently studying the expression on Nell's face.

"Part of it was a dream," he answered, impressively.

"Then that horrible man did take us away?"

"Yes."

"Oh-h! but we're free now? This is my room. Oh, tell me?"

"Yes, Nellie, you're safe at home now."

"Tell—tell me," she cried, shudderingly, as she leaned close to Jim and raised a white, imploring face to his. "Where is Kate?—Oh! Jim—say, say she wasn't left with Girty?"

"Kate is dead," answered Jim, quickly. He could not endure the horror in her eyes. He deliberately intended to lie, as had Heckewelder.

It was as if the tension of Nell's nerves was suddenly relaxed. The relief from her worst fear was so great that her mind took in only the one impression. Then, presently, a choking cry escaped her, to be followed by a paroxysm of sobs.

CHAPTER 20

EARLY ON THE FOLLOWING DAY HECKEWELDER, ASTRIDE HIS HORSE, appeared at the door of Edwards' cabin.

"How is George?" he inquired of Dave, when the latter had opened the door.

"He had a bad night, but is sleeping now. I think he'll be all right after a time," answered Dave.

"That's well. Nevertheless keep a watch on him for a few days."

"I'll do so."

"Dave, I leave matters here to your good judgment. I'm off to Goshocking to join Zeisberger. Affairs there demand our immediate attention, and we must make haste."

"How long do you intend to be absent?"

"A few days; possibly a week. In case of any unusual disturbance among the Indians, the appearance of Pipe and his tribe, or any of the opposing factions, send a fleet runner at once to warn me. Most of my fears have been allayed by Wingenund's attitude toward us. His freeing Jim in face of the opposition of his chiefs is a sure sign of friendliness. More than once I have suspected that he was interested in Christianity. His daughter, Whispering Winds, exhibited the same intense fervor in religion as has been manifested by all our converts. It may be that we have not appealed in vain to Wingenund and his daughter; but their high position in the Delaware tribe makes it impolitic for them to reveal a change of heart. If we could win over those two we'd have every chance to convert the whole tribe. Well, as it is we must be thankful for Wingenund's friendship. We have two powerful allies now. Tarhe, the Wyandot chieftain, remains neutral, to be sure, but that's almost as helpful as his friendship."

"I, too, take a hopeful view of the situation," replied Edwards.

"We'll trust in Providence, and do our best," said Heckewelder, as he turned his horse. "Good-by."

"Godspeed!" called Edwards, as his chief rode away.

The missionary resumed his work of getting breakfast. He remained in doors all that day, except for the few moments when he ran over to Mr. Wells' cabin to inquire regarding Nell's condition. He was relieved to learn she was so much better that she had declared her intention of moving about the house. Dave kept a close watch on Young. He, himself, was suffering from the same blow which had prostrated his friend, but his physical strength and fortitude were such that he did not weaken. He was overjoyed to see that George rallied, and showed no further indications of breaking down.

True it was, perhaps, that Heckewelder's earnest prayer on behalf of the converted Indians had sunk deeply into George's heart and thus kept it from breaking. No stronger plea could have been made than the allusion to those gentle, dependent Christians. No one but a missionary could realize the sweetness, the simplicity, the faith, the eager hope for a good, true life which had been implanted in the hearts of these Indians. To bear it in mind, to think of what he, as a missionary and teacher, was to them, relieved him of half his burden, and for strength to bear the remainder he went to God. For all worry there is a sovereign cure, for all suffering there is a healing balm; it is religious faith. Happiness had suddenly flashed with a meteor-like radiance into Young's life only to be snuffed out like a candle in a windy gloom, but his work, his duty remained. So in his trial he learned the necessity of resignation. He chaffed no more at the mysterious, seemingly brutal methods of nature; he questioned no more. He wondered no more at the apparent indifference of Providence. He had one hope, which was to be true to his faith, and teach it to the end.

Nell mastered her grief by an astonishing reserve of strength. Undoubtedly it was that marvelously merciful power which enables a person, for the love of others, to bear up under a cross, or even to fight death himself. As Young had his bright-eyed Indian boys and girls, who had learned Christianity from him, and whose future depended on him, so Nell had her aged and weakening uncle to care for and cherish.

Jim's attentions to her before the deep affliction had not been slight, but now they were so marked as to be unmistakable. In some way Jim seemed changed since he had returned from the Delaware encampment. Although he went back to the work with his old aggressiveness, he was not nearly so successful as he had been before. Whether or not this was his fault, he took his failure deeply to heart. There was that in his tenderness which caused Nell to regard him, in one sense, as she did her uncle. Jim, too, leaned upon her, and she accepted his devotion where once she had repelled it. She had unconsciously betrayed a great deal when she had turned so tenderly to him in the first moments after her recognition, and he remembered it. He did not speak of love to her; he let a thousand little acts of kindness, a constant thoughtfulness of her plead his cause.

The days succeeding Heckewelder's departure were remarkable for several reasons. Although the weather was enticing, the number of visiting Indians gradually decreased. Not a runner from any tribe came into the village, and finally the day dawned when not a single Indian from the outlying towns was present to hear the preaching.

Jim spoke, as usual. After several days had passed and none but converted Indians made up the congregation, the young man began to be uneasy in mind.

Young and Edwards were unable to account for the unusual absence from worship, yet they did not see in it anything to cause especial concern. Often there had been days without visitation to the Village of Peace.

Finally Jim went to consult Glickhican. He found the Delaware at work in the potato patch. The old Indian dropped his hoe and bowed to the missionary. A reverential and stately courtesy always characterized the attitude of the Indians toward the young white father.

"Glickhican, can you tell me why no Indians have come here lately?"

The old chief shook his head.

"Does their absence signify ill to the Village of Peace?"

"Glickhican saw a blackbird flitting in the shadow of the moon. The bird hovered above the Village of Peace, but sang no song."

The old Delaware vouchsafed no other than this strange reply.

Jim returned to his cabin decidedly worried. He did not at all like Glickhican's answer. The purport of it seemed to be that a cloud was rising on the bright horizon of the Christian village. He confided his fears to Young and Edwards. After discussing the situation, the three missionaries decided to send for Heckewelder. He was the leader of the Mission; he knew more of Indian craft than any of them, and how to meet it. If this calm in the heretofore busy life of the Mission was the lull before a storm, Heckewelder should be there with his experience and influence.

"For nearly ten years Heckewelder has anticipated trouble from hostile savages," said Edwards, "but so far he has always averted it. As you know, he has confined himself mostly to propitiating the Indians, and persuading them to be friendly, and listen to us. We'll send for him."

Accordingly they dispatched a runner to Goshocking. In due time the Indian returned with the startling news that Heckewelder had left the Indian village days before, as had, in fact, all the savages except the few converted ones. The same held true in the case of Sandusky, the adjoining town. Moreover, it had been impossible to obtain any news in regard to Zeisberger.

The missionaries were now thoroughly alarmed, and knew not what to do. They concealed the real state of affairs from Nell and her uncle, desiring to keep them from anxiety as long as possible. That night the three teachers went to bed with heavy hearts.

The following morning at daybreak, Jim was awakened from a sound sleep by some one calling at his window. He got up to learn who it was, and, in the gray light, saw Edwards standing outside.

"What's the matter?" questioned Jim, hurriedly.

"Matter enough. Hurry. Get into your clothes," replied Edwards. "As soon as you are dressed, quietly awaken Mr. Wells and Nellie, but do not frighten them."

"But what's the trouble?" queried Jim, as he began to dress.

"The Indians are pouring into the village as thickly as flying leaves in autumn."

Edwards' exaggerated assertion proved to be almost literally true. No sooner had the rising sun dispelled the mist, than it shone on long lines of marching braves, mounted warriors, hundreds of packhorses approaching from the forests. The orderly procession was proof of a concerted plan on the part of the invaders.

From their windows the missionaries watched with bated breath; with wonder and fear they saw the long lines of dusky forms. When they were in the clearing the savages busied themselves with their packs. Long rows of teepees sprung up as if by magic. The savages had come to stay! The number of incoming visitors did not lessen until noon, when a few straggling groups marked the end of the invading host. Most significant of all was the fact that neither child, maiden, nor squaw accompanied this army.

Jim appraised the number at six or seven hundred, more than had ever before visited the village at one time. They were mostly Delawares, with many Shawnees, and a few Hurons among them. It was soon evident, however, that for the present, at least, the Indians did not intend any hostile demonstration. They were quiet in manner, and busy about their teepees and camp-fires, but there was an absence of the curiosity that had characterized the former sojourns of Indians at the peaceful village.

After a brief consultation with his brother missionaries, who all were opposed to his preaching that afternoon, Jim decided he would not deviate from his usual custom. He held the afternoon service, and spoke to the largest congregation that had ever sat before him. He was surprised to find that the sermon, which heretofore so strongly impressed the savages, did not now arouse the slightest enthusiasm. It was followed by a brooding silence of a boding, ominous import.

Four white men, dressed in Indian garb, had been the most attentive listeners to Jim's sermon. He recognized three as Simon Girty, Elliott and Deering, the renegades, and he learned from Edwards that the other was the notorious McKee. These men went through the village, stalking into the shops and cabins, and acting as do men who are on a tour of inspection.

So intrusive was their curiosity that Jim hurried back to Mr. Well's cabin and remained there in seclusion. Of course, by this time Nell and her uncle knew of the presence of the hostile savages. They were frightened, and barely regained their composure when the young man assured them he was certain they had no real cause for fear.

Jim was sitting at the doorstep with Mr. Wells and Edwards when Girty, with his comrades, came toward them. The renegade leader was a tall, athletic man, with a dark, strong face. There was in it none of the brutality and ferocity which marked his brother's visage. Simon Girty appeared keen, forceful, authoritative, as, indeed, he must have been to have attained the power he held in the confederated tribes. His companions presented wide contrasts. Elliott was a small, spare man of cunning, vindictive aspect; McKee looked, as might have been supposed from his reputation, and Deering was a fit mate for the absent Girty. Simon appeared to be a man of some intelligence, who had used all his power to make that position a great one. The other renegades were desperadoes.

"Where's Heckewelder?" asked Girty, curtly, as he stopped before the missionaries.

"He started out for the Indian towns on the Muskingong," answered Edwards. "But we have had no word from either him or Zeisberger."

"When d'ye expect him?"

"I can't say. Perhaps to-morrow, and then, again, maybe not for a week."

"He is in authority here, ain't he?"

"Yes; but he left me in charge of the Mission. Can I serve you in any way?"

"I reckon not," said the renegade, turning to his companions. They conversed in low tones for a moment. Presently McKee, Elliott and Deering went toward the newly erected teepees.

"Girty, do you mean us any ill will?" earnestly asked Edwards. He had met the man on more than one occasion, and had no hesitation about questioning him.

"I can't say as I do," answered the renegade, and those who heard him believed him. "But I'm agin this redskin preachin', an' hev been all along. The injuns are mad clear through, an' I ain't sayin' I've tried to quiet 'em any. This missionary work has got to be stopped, one way or another. Now what I waited here to say is this: I ain't quite forgot I was white once, an' believe you fellars are honest. I'm willin' to go outer my way to help you git away from here."

"Go away?" echoed Edwards.

"That's it," answered Girty, shouldering his rifle.

"But why? We are perfectly harmless; we are only doing good and hurt no one. Why should we go?"

"'Cause there's liable to be trouble," said the renegade, significantly.

Edwards turned slowly to Mr. Wells and Jim. The old missionary was trembling visibly. Jim was pale; but more with anger than fear.

"Thank you, Girty, but we'll stay," and Jim's voice rang clear.

CHAPTER 21

"Jim, come out here," called Edwards at the window of Mr. Wells' cabin.

The young man arose from the breakfast table, and when outside found Edwards standing by the door with an Indian brave. He was a Wyandot lightly built, lithe and wiry, easily recognizable as an Indian runner. When Jim appeared the man handed him a small packet. He unwound a few folds of some oily skin to find a square piece of birch bark, upon which were scratched the following words:

"Rev. J. Downs. Greeting.

"Your brother is alive and safe. Whispering Winds rescued him by taking him as her husband. Leave the Village of Peace. Pipe and Half King have been influenced by Girty.

"Zane."

"Now, what do you think of that?" exclaimed Jim, handing the message to Edwards. "Thank Heaven, Joe was saved!"

"Zane? That must be the Zane who married Tarhe's daughter," answered Edwards, when he had read the note. "I'm rejoiced to hear of your brother."

"Joe married to that beautiful Indian maiden! Well, of all wonderful things," mused Jim. "What will Nell say?"

"We're getting warnings enough. Do you appreciate that?" asked

Edwards. "'Pipe and Half King have been influenced by Girty.' Evidently the writer deemed that brief sentence of sufficient meaning."

"Edwards, we're preachers. We can't understand such things. I am learning, at least something every day. Colonel Zane advised us not to come here. Wetzel said, 'Go back to Fort Henry.' Girty warned us, and now comes this peremptory order from Isaac Zane."

"Well?"

"It means that these border men see what we will not admit. We ministers have such hope and trust in God that we can not realize the dangers of this life. I fear that our work has been in vain."

"Never. We have already saved many souls. Do not be discouraged."

All this time the runner had stood near at hand straight as an arrow. Presently Edwards suggested that the Wyandot was waiting to be questioned, and accordingly he asked the Indian if he had anything further to communicate.

"Huron—go by—paleface." Here he held up both hands and shut his fists several times, evidently enumerating how many white men he had seen. "Here—when—high—sun."

With that he bounded lightly past them, and loped off with an even, swinging stride.

"What did he mean?" asked Jim, almost sure he had not heard the runner aright.

"He meant that a party of white men are approaching, and will be here by noon. I never knew an Indian runner to carry unreliable information. We have joyful news, both in regard to your brother, and the Village of Peace. Let us go in to tell the others."

The Huron runner's report proved to be correct. Shortly before noon signals from Indian scouts proclaimed the approach of a band of white men. Evidently Girty's forces had knowledge beforehand of the proximity of this band, for the signals created no excitement. The Indians expressed only a lazy curiosity. Soon several Delaware scouts appeared, escorting a large party of frontiersmen.

These men turned out to be Captain Williamson's force, which had been out on an expedition after a marauding tribe of Chippewas. This last named tribe had recently harried the remote settlers, and committed depredations on the outskirts of the white settlements eastward. The company was composed of men who had served in the garrison at Fort Pitt, and hunters and backwoodsmen from Yellow Creek and Fort Henry. The captain himself was a typical borderman, rough and bluff, hardened by long years of border life, and, like most pioneers, having no more use for an Indian than for a snake. He had led his party after the marauders, and surprised and slaughtered nearly all of them. Returning eastward he had passed through Goshocking, where he learned of the muttering storm rising over the Village of Peace, and had come more out of curiosity than hope to avert misfortune.

The advent of so many frontiersmen seemed a godsend to the perplexed and worried missionaries. They welcomed the newcomers most heartily. Beds were made in several of the newly erected cabins; the village was given over for the comfort of the frontiersmen. Edwards conducted Captain Williamson through the shops and schools, and the old border-man's weather-beaten face expressed a comical surprise.

"Wal, I'll be durned if I ever expected to see a redskin work," was his only comment on the industries.

"We are greatly alarmed by the presence of Girty and his followers," said Edwards. "We have been warned to leave, but have not been actually threatened. What do you infer from the appearance here of these hostile savages?"

"It hardly 'pears to me they'll bother you preachers. They're agin the Christian redskins, that's plain."

"Why have we been warned to go?"

"That's natural, seein' they're agin the preachin'."

"What will they do with the converted Indians?"

"Mighty onsartin. They might let them go back to the tribes, but 'pears to me these good Injuns won't go. Another thing, Girty is afeered of the spread of Christianity."

"Then you think our Christians will be made prisoners?"

"'Pears likely."

"And you, also, think we'd do well to leave here."

"I do, sartin. We're startin' for Fort Henry soon. You'd better come along with us."

"Captain Williamson, we're going to stick it out, Girty or no Girty."

"You can't do no good stayin' here. Pipe and Half King won't stand for the singin', prayin' redskins, especially when they've got all these cattle and fields of grain."

"Wetzel said the same."

"Hev you seen Wetzel?"

"Yes; he rescued a girl from Jim Girty, and returned her to us."

"That so? I met Wetzel and Jack Zane back a few miles in the woods.

They're layin' for somebody, because when I asked them to come along they refused, sayin' they had work as must be done. They looked like it, too. I never hern tell of Wetzel advisin' any one before; but I'll say if he told me to do a thing, by Gosh! I'd do it."

"As men, we might very well take the advice given us, but as preachers we must stay here to do all we can for these Christian Indians. One thing more: will you help us?"

"I reckon I'll stay here to see the thing out," answered Williamson. Edwards made a mental note of the frontiersman's evasive answer.

Jim had, meanwhile, made the acquaintance of a young minister, John Christy by name, who had lost his sweetheart in one of the Chippewa raids, and had accompanied the Williamson expedition in the hope he might rescue her.

"How long have you been out?" asked Jim.

"About four weeks now," answered Christy. "My betrothed was captured five weeks ago yesterday. I joined Williamson's band, which made up at Short Creek to take the trail of the flying Chippewas, in the hope I might find her. But not a trace! The expedition fell upon a band of redskins over on the Walhonding, and killed nearly all of them. I learned from a wounded Indian that a renegade had made off with a white girl about a week previous. Perhaps it was poor Lucy."

Jim related the circumstances of his own capture by Jim Girty, the rescue of Nell, and Kate's sad fate.

"Could Jim Girty have gotten your girl?" inquired Jim, in conclusion.

"It's fairly probable. The description doesn't tally with Girty's. This renegade was short and heavy, and noted especially for his strength. Of course, an Indian would first speak of some such distinguishing feature. There are, however, ten or twelve renegades on the border, and, excepting Jim Girty, one's as bad as another."

"Then it's a common occurrence, this abducting girls from the settlements?"

"Yes, and the strange thing is that one never hears of such doings until he gets out on the frontier."

"For that matter, you don't hear much of anything, except of the wonderful richness and promise of the western country."

"You're right. Rumors of fat, fertile lands induce the colonist to become a pioneer. He comes west with his family; two out of every ten lose their scalps, and in some places the average is much greater. The wives, daughters and children are carried off into captivity. I have been on the border two years, and know that the rescue of any captive, as Wetzel rescued your friend, is a remarkable exception."

"If you have so little hope of recovering your sweetheart, what then is your motive for accompanying this band of hunters?"

"Revenge!"

"And you are a preacher?" Jim's voice did not disguise his astonishment.

"I was a preacher, and now I am thirsting for vengeance," answered Christy, his face clouding darkly. "Wait until you learn what frontier life means. You are young here yet; you are flushed with the success of your teaching; you have lived a short time in this quiet village, where, until the last few days, all has been serene. You know nothing of the strife, of the necessity of fighting, of the cruelty which makes up this border existence. Only two years have hardened me so that I actually pant for the blood of the renegade who has robbed me. A frontiersman must take his choice of succumbing or cutting his way through flesh and bone. Blood will be spilled; if not yours, then your foe's. The pioneers run from the plow to the fight; they halt in the cutting of corn to defend themselves, and in winter must battle against cold and hardship, which would be less cruel if there was time in summer to prepare for winter, for the savages leave them hardly an opportunity to plant crops. How many pioneers have given up, and gone back east? Find me any who would not return home to-morrow, if they could. All that brings them out here is the chance for a home, and all that keeps them out here is the poor hope of finally attaining their object. Always there is a possibility of future prosperity. But this generation, if it survives, will never see prosperity and happiness. What does this border life engender in a pioneer who holds his own in it? Of all things, not Christianity. He becomes a fighter, keen as the redskin who steals through the coverts."

THE SERENE DAYS OF THE VILLAGE OF PEACE HAD PASSED INTO HISTORY. Soon that depraved vagabond, the French trader, with cheap trinkets and vile whisky, made his appearance. This was all that was needed to inflame the visitors. Where they had been only bold and impudent, they became insulting and abusive. They execrated the Christian indians for their neutrality; scorned them for worshiping this unknown God, and denounced a religion which made women of strong men.

The slaughtering of cattle commenced; the despoiling of maize fields, and robbing of corn-cribs began with the drunkenness.

All this time it was seen that Girty and Elliott consulted often with Pipe and Half King. The latter was the only Huron chief opposed to neutrality toward the Village of Peace, and he was, if possible, more fierce in his hatred than Pipe. The future of the Christian settlement rested with these two chiefs. Girty and Elliott, evidently, were the designing schemers, and they worked diligently on the passions of these simple-minded, but fierce, warlike chiefs.

Greatly to the relief of the distracted missionaries, Heckewelder returned to the village. Jaded and haggard, he presented a travel-worn appearance. He made the astonishing assertions that he had been thrice waylaid and assaulted on his way to Goshocking; then detained by a roving band of Chippewas, and soon after his arrival at their camping ground a renegade had run off with a white woman captive, while the Indians west of the village were in an uproar. Zeisberger, however, was safe in the Moravian town of Salem, some miles west of Goshocking. Heckewelder had expected to find the same condition of affairs as existed in the Village of Peace; but he was bewildered by the great array of hostile Indians. Chiefs who had once extended friendly hands to him, now drew back coldly, as they said:

"Washington is dead. The American armies are cut to pieces. The few thousands who had escaped the British are collecting at Fort Pitt to steal the Indian's land."

Heckewelder vigorously denied all these assertions, knowing they had been invented by Girty and Elliott. He exhausted all his skill and patience in the vain endeavor to show Pipe where he was wrong. Half King had been so well coached by the renegades that he refused to listen. The other chiefs maintained a cold reserve that was baffling and exasperating. Wingenund took no active part in the councils; but his presence apparently denoted that he had sided with the others. The outlook was altogether discouraging.

"I'm completely fagged out," declared Heckewelder, that night when he returned to Edwards' cabin. He dropped into a chair as one whose strength is entirely spent, whose indomitable spirit has at last been broken.

"Lie down to rest," said Edwards.

"Oh, I can't. Matters look so black."

"You're tired out and discouraged. You'll feel better to-morrow. The situation is not, perhaps, so hopeless. The presence of these frontiersmen should encourage us."

"What will they do? What can they do?" cried Heckewelder, bitterly. "I tell you never before have I encountered such gloomy, stony Indians. It seems to me that they are in no vacillating state. They act like men whose course is already decided upon, and who are only waiting."

"For what?" asked Jim, after a long silence.

"God only knows! Perhaps for a time; possibly for a final decision, and, it may be, for a reason, the very thought of which makes me faint."

"Tell us," said Edwards, speaking quietly, for he had ever been the calmest of the missionaries.

"Never mind. Perhaps it's only my nerves. I'm all unstrung, and could suspect anything to-night."

"Heckewelder, tell us?" Jim asked, earnestly.

"My friends, I pray I am wrong. God help us if my fears are correct. I believe the Indians are waiting for Jim Girty."

CHAPTER 22

Simon Girty lolled on a blanket in Half King's teepee. He was alone, awaiting his allies. Rings of white smoke curled lazily from his lips as he puffed on a long Indian pipe, and gazed out over the clearing that contained the Village of Peace.

Still water has something in its placid surface significant of deep channels, of hidden depths; the dim outline of the forest is dark with meaning, suggestive of its wild internal character. So Simon Girty's hard, bronzed face betrayed the man. His degenerate brother's features were revolting; but his own were striking, and fell short of being handsome only because of their craggy hardness. Years of revolt, of bitterness, of consciousness of wasted life, had graven their stern lines on that copper, masklike face. Yet despite the cruelty there, the forbidding shade on it, as if a reflection from a dark soul, it was not wholly a bad countenance. Traces still lingered, faintly, of a man in whom kindlier feelings had once predominated.

In a moment of pique Girty had deserted his military post at Fort Pitt, and become an outlaw of his own volition. Previous to that time he had been an able soldier, and a good fellow. When he realized that his step was irrevocable, that even his best friends condemned him, he plunged, with anger and despair in his heart, into a war upon his own race. Both of his brothers had long been border ruffians, whose only protection from the outraged pioneers lay in the faraway camps of hostile tribes. George Girty had so sunk his individuality into the savage's that he was no longer a

white man. Jim Girty stalked over the borderland with a bloody tomahawk, his long arm outstretched to clutch some unfortunate white woman,
and with his hideous smile of death. Both of these men were far lower
than the worst savages, and it was almost wholly to their deeds of darkness
that Simon Girty owed his infamous name.

To-day White Chief, as Girty was called, awaited his men. A slight
tremor of the ground caused him to turn his gaze. The Huron chief, Half
King, resplendent in his magnificent array, had entered the teepee. He
squatted in a corner, rested the bowl of his great pipe on his knee, and
smoked in silence. The habitual frown of his black brow, like a shaded,
overhanging cliff; the fire flashing from his eyes, as a shining light is
reflected from a dark pool; his closely-shut, bulging jaw, all bespoke a
nature, lofty in its Indian pride and arrogance, but more cruel than death.

Another chief stalked into the teepee and seated himself. It was Pipe.
His countenance denoted none of the intelligence that made Wingenund's
face so noble; it was even coarser than Half King's, and his eyes, resembling live coals in the dark; the long, cruel lines of his jaw; the thin, tightly-
closed lips, which looked as if they could relax only to utter a savage
command, expressed fierce cunning and brutality.

"White Chief is idle to-day," said Half King, speaking in the Indian
tongue.

"King, I am waiting. Girty is slow, but sure," answered the renegade.

"The eagle sails slowly round and round, up and up," replied Half King,
with majestic gestures, "until his eye sees all, until he knows his time; then
he folds his wings and swoops down from the blue sky like the forked fire.
So does White Chief. But Half King is impatient."

"To-day decides the fate of the Village of Peace," answered Girty,
imperturbably.

"Ugh!" grunted Pipe.

Half King vented his approval in the same meaning exclamation.

An hour passed; the renegade smoked in silence; the chiefs did
likewise.

A horseman rode up to the door of the teepee, dismounted, and came
in. It was Elliott. He had been absent twenty hours. His buckskin suit
showed the effect of hard riding through the thickets.

"Hullo, Bill, any sign of Jim?" was Girty's greeting to his lieutenant.

"Nary. He's not been seen near the Delaware camp. He's after that
chap who married Winds."

"I thought so. Jim's roundin' up a tenderfoot who will be a bad man to handle if he has half a chance. I saw as much the day he took his horse away from Silver. He finally did fer the Shawnee, an' almost put Jim out. My brother oughtn't to give rein to personal revenge at a time like this." Girty's face did not change, but his tone was one of annoyance.

"Jim said he'd be here to-day, didn't he?"

"To-day is as long as we allowed to wait."

"He'll come. Where's Jake and Mac?"

"They're here somewhere, drinkin' like fish, an' raisin' hell."

Two more renegades appeared at the door, and, entering the teepee, squatted down in Indian fashion. The little wiry man with the wizened face was McKee; the other was the latest acquisition to the renegade force, Jake Deering, deserter, thief, murderer—everything that is bad. In appearance he was of medium height, but very heavily, compactly built, and evidently as strong as an ox. He had a tangled shock of red hair, a broad, bloated face; big, dull eyes, like the openings of empty furnaces, and an expression of beastliness.

Deering and McKee were intoxicated.

"Bad time fer drinkin'," said Girty, with disapproval in his glance.

"What's that ter you?" growled Deering. "I'm here ter do your work, an' I reckon it'll be done better if I'm drunk."

"Don't git careless," replied Girty, with that cool tone and dark look such as dangerous men use. "I'm only sayin' it's a bad time fer you, because if this bunch of frontiersmen happen to git onto you bein' the renegade that was with the Chippewas an' got thet young feller's girl, there's liable to be trouble."

"They ain't agoin' ter find out."

"Where is she?"

"Back there in the woods."

"Mebbe it's as well. Now, don't git so drunk you'll blab all you know. We've lots of work to do without havin' to clean up Williamson's bunch," rejoined Girty. "Bill, tie up the tent flaps an' we'll git to council."

Elliott arose to carry out the order, and had pulled in the deer-hide flaps, when one of them was jerked outward to disclose the befrilled person of Jim Girty. Except for a discoloration over his eye, he appeared as usual.

"Ugh!" grunted Pipe, who was glad to see his renegade friend.

Half King evinced the same feeling.

"Hullo," was Simon Girty's greeting.

"'Pears I'm on time fer the picnic," said Jim Girty, with his ghastly leer.

Bill Elliott closed the flaps, after giving orders to the guard to prevent any Indians from loitering near the teepee.

"Listen," said Simon Girty, speaking low in the Delaware language. "The time is ripe. We have come here to break forever the influence of the white man's religion. Our councils have been held; we shall drive away the missionaries, and burn the Village of Peace."

He paused, leaning forward in his exceeding earnestness, with his bronzed face lined by swelling veins, his whole person made rigid by the murderous thought. Then he hissed between his teeth: "What shall we do with these Christian Indians?"

Pipe raised his war-club, struck it upon the ground; then handed it to Half King.

Half King took the club and repeated the action.

Both chiefs favored the death penalty.

"Feed 'em to ther buzzards," croaked Jim Girty.

Simon Girty knitted his brow in thought. The question of what to do with the converted Indians had long perplexed him.

"No," said he; "let us drive away the missionaries, burn the village, and take the Indians back to camp. We'll keep them there; they'll soon forget."

"Pipe does not want them," declared the Delaware.

"Christian Indians shall never sit round Half King's fire," cried the Huron.

Simon Girty knew the crisis had come; that but few moments were left him to decide as to the disposition of the Christians; and he thought seriously. Certainly he did not want the Christians murdered. However cruel his life, and great his misdeeds, he was still a man. If possible, he desired to burn the village and ruin the religious influence, but without shedding blood. Yet, with all his power, he was handicapped, and that by the very chiefs most nearly under his control. He could not subdue this growing Christian influence without the help of Pipe and Half King. To these savages a thing was either right or wrong. He had sown the seed of unrest and jealousy in the savage breasts, and the fruit was the decree of death. As far as these Indians were concerned, this decision was unalterable.

On the other hand, if he did not spread ruin over the Village of Peace, the missionaries would soon get such a grasp on the tribes that their hold would never be broken. He could not allow that, even if he was forced to sacrifice the missionaries along with their converts, for he saw in the growth of this religion his own downfall. The border must be hostile to the whites, or it could no longer be his home. To be sure, he had aided the

British in the Revolution, and could find a refuge among them; but this did not suit him.

He became an outcast because of failure to win the military promotion which he had so much coveted. He had failed among his own people. He had won a great position in an alien race, and he loved his power. To sway men—Indians, if not others—to his will; to avenge himself for the fancied wrong done him; to be great, had been his unrelenting purpose.

He knew he must sacrifice the Christians, or eventually lose his own power. He had no false ideas about the converted Indians. He knew they were innocent; that they were a thousand times better off than the pagan Indians; that they had never harmed him, nor would they ever do so; but if he allowed them to spread their religion there was an end of Simon Girty.

His decision was characteristic of the man. He would sacrifice any one, or all, to retain his supremacy. He knew the fulfillment of the decree as laid down by Pipe and Half King would be known as his work. His name, infamous now, would have an additional horror, and ever be remembered by posterity in unspeakable loathing, in unsoftening wrath. He knew this, and deep down in his heart awoke a numbed chord of humanity that twinged with strange pain. What awful work he must sanction to keep his vaunted power! More bitter than all was the knowledge that to retain this hold over the indians he must commit a deed which, so far as the whites were concerned, would take away his great name, and brand him a coward.

He briefly reviewed his stirring life. Singularly fitted for a leader, in a few years he had risen to the most powerful position on the border. He wielded more influence than any chief. He had been opposed to the invasion of the pioneers, and this alone, without his sagacity or his generalship, would have given him control of many tribes. But hatred for his own people, coupled with unerring judgment, a remarkable ability to lead expeditions, and his invariable success, had raised him higher and higher until he stood alone. He was the most powerful man west of the Alleghenies. His fame was such that the British had importuned him to help them, and had actually, in more than one instance, given him command over British subjects.

All of which meant that he had a great, even though an infamous name. No matter what he was blamed for; no matter how many dastardly deeds had been committed by his depraved brothers and laid to his door, he knew he had never done a cowardly act. That which he had committed while he was drunk he considered as having been done by the liquor, and not by the man. He loved his power, and he loved his name.

In all Girty's eventful, ignoble life, neither the alienation from his people, the horror they ascribed to his power, nor the sacrifice of his life to stand high among the savage races, nor any of the cruel deeds committed while at war, hurt him a tithe as much as did this sanctioning the massacre of the Christians.

Although he was a vengeful, unscrupulous, evil man, he had never acted the coward.

Half King waited long for Girty to speak; since he remained silent, the wily Huron suggested they take a vote on the question.

"Let us burn the Village of Peace, drive away the missionaries, and take the Christians back to the Delaware towns—all without spilling blood," said Girty, determined to carry his point, if possible.

"I say the same," added Elliott, refusing the war-club held out to him by Half King.

"Me, too," voted McKee, not so drunk but that he understood the lightninglike glance Girty shot at him.

"Kill 'em all; kill everybody," cried Deering in drunken glee. He took the club and pounded with it on the ground.

Pipe repeated his former performance, as also did Half King, after which he handed the black, knotted symbol of death to Jim Girty.

Three had declared for saving the Christians, and three for the death penalty.

Six pairs of burning eyes were fastened on the Deaths-head.

Pipe and Half King were coldly relentless; Deering awoke to a brutal earnestness; McKee and Elliott watched with bated breath. These men had formed themselves into a tribunal to decide on the life or death of many, and the situation, if not the greatest in their lives, certainly was one of vital importance.

Simon Girty cursed all the fates. He dared not openly oppose the voting, and he could not, before those cruel but just chiefs, try to influence his brother's vote.

As Jim Girty took the war-club, Simon read in his brother's face the doom of the converted Indians and he muttered to himself:

"Now tremble an' shrink, all you Christians!"

Jim was not in a hurry. Slowly he poised the war-club. He was playing as a cat plays with a mouse; he was glorying in his power. The silence was that of death. It signified the silence of death. The war-club descended with violence.

"Feed the Christians to ther buzzards!"

CHAPTER 23

"I have been here before," said Joe to Whispering Winds. "I remember that vine-covered stone. We crawled over it to get at Girty and Silvertip. There's the little knoll; here's the very spot where I was hit by a flying tomahawk. Yes, and there's the spring. Let me see, what did Wetzel call this spot?"

"Beautiful Spring," answered the Indian girl.

"That's it, and it's well named. What a lovely place!"

Nature had been lavish in the beautifying of this inclosed dell. It was about fifty yards wide, and nestled among little, wooded knolls and walls of gray, lichen-covered stone. Though the sun shone brightly into the opening, and the rain had free access to the mossy ground, no stormy winds ever entered this well protected glade.

Joe reveled in the beauty of the scene, even while he was too weak to stand erect. He suffered no pain from his wound, although he had gradually grown dizzy, and felt as if the ground was rising before him. He was glad to lie upon the mossy ground in the little cavern under the cliff.

Upon examination his wound was found to have opened, and was bleeding. His hunting coat was saturated with blood. Whispering Winds washed the cut, and dressed it with cooling leaves. Then she rebandaged it tightly with Joe's linsey handkerchiefs, and while he rested comfortable she gathered bundles of ferns, carrying them to the little cavern. When she had a large quantity of these she sat down near Joe, and began to weave the long stems into a kind of screen. The fern stalks were four feet long and half a foot wide; these she deftly laced together, making broad screens which would serve to ward off the night dews. This done, she next built a fireplace with flat stones. She found wild apples, plums and turnips on the knoll above the glade. Then she cooked strips of meat which had been brought with them. Lance grazed on the long grass just without the glade, and Mose caught two rabbits. When darkness settled down Whispering Winds called the dog within the cavern, and hung the screens before the opening.

Several days passed. Joe rested quietly, and began to recover strength. Besides the work of preparing their meals, Whispering Winds had nothing to do save sit near the invalid and amuse or interest him so that he would not fret or grow impatient, while his wound was healing.

They talked about their future prospects. After visiting the Village of Peace, they would go to Fort Henry, where Joe could find employment. They dwelt upon the cabin they would build, and passed many happy moments planning a new home. Joe's love of the wilderness had in no wise diminished; but a blow on his head from a heavy tomahawk, and a vicious stab in the back, had lessened his zeal so far that he understood it was not wise to sacrifice life for the pleasures of the pathless woods. He could have the last without the danger of being shot at from behind every tree. He reasoned that it would be best for him to take his wife to Fort Henry, there find employment, and devote his leisure time to roaming in the forest.

"Will the palefaces be kind to an Indian who has learned to love them?" Whispering Winds asked wistfully of Joe.

"Indeed they will," answered Joe, and he told her the story of Isaac Zane; how he took his Indian bride home; how her beauty and sweetness soon won all the white people's love. "It will be so with you, my wife."

"Whispering Winds knows so little," she murmured.

"Why, you are learning every day, and even if such was not the case, you know enough for me."

"Whispering Winds will be afraid; she fears a little to go."

"I'll be glad when we can be on the move," said Joe, with his old impatient desire for action. "How soon, Winds, can we set off?"

"As many days," answered the Indian girl, holding up five fingers.

"So long? I want to leave this place."

"Leave Beautiful Spring?"

"Yes, even this sweet place. It has a horror for me. I'll never forget the night I first saw that spring shining in the moonlight. It was right above the rock that I looked into the glade. The moon was reflected in the dark pool, and as I gazed into the shadowy depths of the dark water I suddenly felt an unaccountable terror; but I oughtn't to have the same feeling now. We are safe, are we not?"

"We are safe," murmured Whispering Winds.

"Yet I have the same chill of fear whenever I look at the beautiful spring, and at night as I awake to hear the soft babble of running water, I freeze until my heart feels like cold lead. Winds, I'm not a coward; but I can't help this feeling. Perhaps, it's only the memory of that awful night with Wetzel."

"An Indian feels so when he passes to his unmarked grave," answered Winds, gazing solemnly at him. "Whispering Winds does not like this fancy of yours. Let us leave Beautiful Spring. You are almost well. Ah! if Whispering Winds should lose you! I love you!"

"And I love you, my beautiful wild flower," answered Joe, stroking the dark head so near his own.

A tender smile shone on his face. He heard a slight noise without the cave, and, looking up, saw that which caused the smile to fade quickly.

"Mose!" he called, sharply. The dog was away chasing rabbits.

Whispering Winds glanced over her shoulder with a startled cry, which ended in a scream.

Not two yards behind her stood Jim Girty.

Hideous was his face in its triumphant ferocity. He held a long knife in his hand, and, snarling like a mad wolf, he made a forward lunge.

Joe raised himself quickly; but almost before he could lift his hand in defense, the long blade was sheathed in his breast.

Slowly he sank back, his gray eyes contracting with the old steely flash. The will to do was there, but the power was gone forever.

"Remember, Girty, murderer! I am Wetzel's friend," he cried, gazing at his slayer with unutterable scorn.

Then the gray eyes softened, and sought the blanched face of the stricken maiden.

"Winds," he whispered faintly.

She was as one frozen with horror.

The gray eyes gazed into hers with lingering tenderness; then the film of death came upon them.

The renegade raised his bloody knife, and bent over the prostrate form.

Whispering Winds threw herself upon Girty with the blind fury of a maddened lioness. Cursing fiercely, he stabbed her once, twice, three times. She fell across the body of her lover, and clasped it convulsively.

Girty gave one glance at his victims; deliberately wiped the gory knife on Wind's leggins, and, with another glance, hurried and fearful, around the glade, he plunged into the thicket.

An hour passed. A dark stream crept from the quiet figures toward the spring. It dyed the moss and the green violet leaves. Slowly it wound its way to the clear water, dripping between the pale blue flowers. The little fall below the spring was no longer snowy white; blood had tinged it red.

A dog came bounding into the glade. He leaped the brook, hesitated on the bank, and lowered his nose to sniff at the water. He bounded up the bank to the cavern.

A long, mournful howl broke the wilderness's quiet.

Another hour passed. The birds were silent; the insects still. The sun sank behind the trees, and the shades of evening gathered.

The ferns on the other side of the glade trembled. A slight rustle of dead leaves disturbed the stillness. The dog whined, then barked. The tall form of a hunter rose out of the thicket, and stepped into the glade with his eyes bent upon moccasin tracks in the soft moss.

The trail he had been following led him to this bloody spring.

"I might hev knowed it," he muttered.

Wetzel, for it was he, leaned upon his long rifle while his keen eyes took in the details of the tragedy. The whining dog, the bloody water, the motionless figures lying in a last embrace, told the sad story.

"Joe an' Winds," he muttered.

Only a moment did he remain lost in sad reflection. A familiar moccasin-print in the sand on the bank pointed westward. He examined it carefully.

"Two hours gone," he muttered. "I might overtake him."

Then his motions became swift. With two blows of his tomahawk he secured a long piece of grapevine. He took a heavy stone from the bed of the brook. He carried Joe to the spring, and, returning for Winds, placed her beside her lover. This done, he tied one end of the grapevine around the stone, and wound the other about the dead bodies.

He pushed them off the bank into the spring. As the lovers sank into the deep pool they turned, exposing first Winds' sad face, and then Joe's. Then they sank out of sight. Little waves splashed on the shore of the pool; the ripple disappeared, and the surface of the spring became tranquil.

Wetzel stood one moment over the watery grave of the maiden who had saved him, and the boy who had loved him. In the gathering gloom his stalwart form assumed gigantic proportions, and when he raised his long arm and shook his clenched fist toward the west, he resembled a magnificent statue of dark menace.

With a single bound he cleared the pool, and then sped out of the glade. He urged the dog on Girty's trail, and followed the eager beast toward the west. As he disappeared, a long, low sound like the sigh of the night wind swelled and moaned through the gloom.

CHAPTER 24

WHEN THE FIRST RUDDY RAYS OF THE RISING SUN CRIMSONED THE
eastern sky, Wetzel slowly wound his way down a rugged hill far west of
Beautiful Spring. A white dog, weary and footsore, limped by his side.
Both man and beast showed evidence of severe exertion.

The hunter stopped in a little cave under a projecting stone, and,
laying aside his rifle, began to gather twigs and sticks. He was particular
about selecting the wood, and threw aside many pieces which would have
burned well; but when he did kindle a flame it blazed hotly, yet made no
smoke.

He sharpened a green stick, and, taking some strips of meat from his
pocket, roasted them over the hot flame. He fed the dog first. Mose had
crouched close on the ground with his head on his paws, and his brown
eyes fastened upon the hunter.

"He had too big a start fer us," said Wetzel, speaking as if the dog were
human. It seemed that Wetzel's words were a protest against the meaning
in those large, sad eyes.

Then the hunter put out the fire, and, searching for a more secluded
spot, finally found one on top of the ledge, where he commanded a good
view of his surroundings. The weary dog was asleep. Wetzel settled
himself to rest, and was soon wrapped in slumber.

About noon he awoke. He arose, stretched his limbs, and then took an
easy position on the front of the ledge, where he could look below.

Evidently the hunter was waiting for something. The dog slept on. It was the noonday hour, when the stillness of the forest almost matched that of midnight. The birds were more quiet than at any other time during daylight.

Wetzel reclined there with his head against the stone, and his rifle resting across his knees.

He listened now to the sounds of the forest. The soft breeze fluttering among the leaves, the rain-call of the tree frog, the caw of crows from distant hilltops, the sweet songs of the thrush and oriole, were blended together naturally, harmoniously.

But suddenly the hunter raised his head. A note, deeper than the others, a little too strong, came from far down the shaded hollow. To Wetzel's trained ear it was a discord. He manifested no more than this attention, for the birdcall was the signal he had been awaiting. He whistled a note in answer that was as deep and clear as the one which had roused him.

Moments passed. There was no repetition of the sound. The songs of the other birds had ceased. Besides Wetzel there was another intruder in the woods.

Mose lifted his shaggy head and growled. The hunter patted the dog. In a few minutes the figure of a tall man appeared among the laurels down the slope. He stopped while gazing up at the ledge. Then, with noiseless step, he ascended the ridge, climbed the rocky ledge, and turned the corner of the stone to face Wetzel. The newcomer was Jonathan Zane.

"Jack, I expected you afore this," was Wetzel's greeting.

"I couldn't make it sooner," answered Zane. "After we left Williamson and separated, I got turned around by a band of several hundred redskins makin' for the Village of Peace. I went back again, but couldn't find any sign of the trail we're huntin'. Then I makes for this meetin' place. I've been goin' for some ten hours, and am hungry."

"I've got some bar ready cooked," said Wetzel, handing Zane several strips of meat.

"What luck did you have?"

"I found Girty's trail, an old one, over here some eighteen or twenty miles, an' follered it until I went almost into the Delaware town. It led to a hut in a deep ravine. I ain't often surprised, but I wus then. I found the dead body of that girl, Kate Wells, we fetched over from Fort Henry. Thet's sad, but it ain't the surprisin' part. I also found Silvertip, the Shawnee I've been lookin' fer. He was all knocked an' cut up, deader'n a stone. There'd been somethin' of a scrap in the hut. I calkilate Girty murdered Kate, but I couldn't think then who did fer Silver, though I allowed the renegade might hev done thet, too. I watched round an' seen Girty come back to the hut. He had ten Injuns with him, an' presently they all made fer the west. I trailed them, but didn't calkilate it'd be wise to tackle the bunch single-handed, so laid back. A mile or so from the hut I came across hoss tracks minglin' with the moccasin-prints. About fifteen mile or from the Delaware town, Girty left his buckskins, an' they went west, while he stuck to the hoss tracks. I was onto his game in a minute. I cut across country fer Beautiful Spring, but I got there too late. I found the warm bodies of Joe and thet Injun girl, Winds. The snake hed murdered them."

"I allow Joe won over Winds, got away from the Delaware town with her, tried to rescue Kate, and killed Silver in the fight. Girty probably was surprised, an' run after he had knifed the girl."

"'Pears so to me. Joe had two knife cuts, an' one was an old wound."

"You say it was a bad fight?"

"Must hev been. The hut was all knocked in, an' stuff scattered about. Wal, Joe could go some if he onct got started."

"I'll bet he could. He was the likeliest lad I've seen for many a day."

"If he'd lasted, he'd been somethin' of a hunter an' fighter."

"Too bad. But Lord! you couldn't keep him down, no more than you can lots of these wild young chaps that drift out here."

"I'll allow he had the fever bad."

"Did you hev time to bury them?"

"I hedn't time fer much. I sunk them in the spring."

"It's a pretty deep hole," said Zane, reflectively. "Then, you and the dog took Girty's trail, but couldn't catch up with him. He's now with the renegade cutthroats and hundreds of riled Indians over there in the Village of Peace."

"I reckon you're right."

A long silence ensued. Jonathan finished his simple repast, drank from the little spring that trickled under the stone, and, sitting down by the dog, smoothed out his long silken hair.

"Lew, we're pretty good friends, ain't we?" he asked, thoughtfully.

"Jack, you an' the colonel are all the friends I ever hed, 'ceptin' that boy lyin' quiet back there in the woods."

"I know you pretty well, and ain't sayin' a word about your runnin' off from me on many a hunt, but I want to speak plain about this fellow Girty."

"Wal?" said Wetzel, as Zane hesitated.

"Twice in the last few years you and I have had it in for the same men, both white-livered traitors. You remember? First it was Miller, who tried to ruin my sister Betty, and next it was Jim Girty, who murdered our old friend, as good an old man as ever wore moccasins. Wal, after Miller ran off from the fort, we trailed him down to the river, and I points across and says, 'You or me?' and you says, 'Me.' You was Betty's friend, and I knew she'd be avenged. Miller is lyin' quiet in the woods, and violets have blossomed twice over his grave, though you never said a word; but I know it's true because I know you."

Zane looked eagerly into the dark face of his friend, hoping perhaps to get some verbal assurance there that his belief was true. But Wetzel did not speak, and he continued:

"Another day not so long ago we both looked down at an old friend, and saw his white hair matted with blood. He'd been murdered for nothin'. Again you and me trailed a coward and found him to be Jim Girty. I knew you'd been huntin' him for years, and so I says, 'Lew, you or me?' and you says, 'Me.' I give in to you, for I knew you're a better man than me, and because I wanted you to have the satisfaction. Wal, the months have gone by, and Jim Girty's still livin' and carryin' on. Now he's over there after them poor preachers. I ain't sayin', Lew, that you haven't more agin him than me, but I do say, let me in on it with you. He always has a gang of redskins with him; he's afraid to travel alone, else you'd had him long ago. Two of us'll have more chance to get him. Let me go with you. When it comes to a finish, I'll stand aside while you give it to him. I'd enjoy seein' you cut him from shoulder to hip. After he leaves the Village of Peace we'll hit his trail, camp on it, and stick to it until it ends in his grave."

The earnest voice of the backwoodsman ceased. Both men rose and stood facing each other. Zane's bronzed face was hard and tense, expressive of an indomitable will; Wetzel's was coldly dark, with fateful resolve, as if his decree of vengeance, once given, was as immutable as destiny. The big, horny hands gripped in a viselike clasp born of fierce passion, but no word was spoken.

Far to the west somewhere, a befrilled and bedizened renegade pursued the wild tenor of his ways; perhaps, even now steeping his soul in more crime, or staining his hands a deeper red, but sleeping or waking, he dreamed not of this deadly compact that meant his doom.

The two hunters turned their stern faces toward the west, and passed silently down the ridge into the depths of the forest. Darkness found them within rifle-shot of the Village of Peace. With the dog creeping between them, they crawled to a position which would, in daylight, command a view of the clearing. Then, while one stood guard, the other slept.

When morning dawned they shifted their position to the top of a low, fern-covered cliff, from which they could see every movement in the village. All the morning they watched with that wonderful patience of men who knew how to wait. The visiting savages were quiet, the missionaries moved about in and out of the shops and cabins; the Christian indians worked industriously in the fields, while the renegades lolled before a prominent teepee.

"This quiet looks bad," whispered Jonathan to Wetzel. No shouts were heard; not a hostile Indian was seen to move.

"They've come to a decision," whispered Jonathan, and Wetzel answered him:

"If they hev, the Christians don't know it."

An hour later the deep pealing of the church bell broke the silence. The entire band of Christian Indians gathered near the large log structure, and then marched in orderly form toward the maple grove where the service was always held in pleasant weather. This movement brought the Indians within several hundred yards of the cliff where Zane and Wetzel lay concealed.

"There's Heckewelder walking with old man Wells," whispered Jonathan. "There's Young and Edwards, and, yes, there's the young missionary, brother of Joe. 'Pears to me they're foolish to hold service in the face of all those riled Injuns."

"Wuss'n foolish," answered Wetzel.

"Look! By gum! As I'm a livin' sinner there comes the whole crowd of hostile redskins. They've got their guns, and—by Gum! they're painted. Looks bad, bad! Not much friendliness about that bunch!"

"They ain't intendin' to be peaceable."

"By gum! You're right. There ain't one of them settin' down. 'Pears to me I know some of them redskins. There's Pipe, sure enough, and Kotoxen. By gum! If there ain't Shingiss; he was friendly once."

"None of them's friendly."

"Look! Lew, look! Right behind Pipe. See that long war-bonnet. As I'm a born sinner, that's your old friend, Wingenund. 'Pears to me we've rounded up all our acquaintances."

The two bordermen lay close under the tall ferns and watched the proceedings with sharp eyes. They saw the converted Indians seat themselves before the platform. The crowd of hostile Indians surrounded the glade on all sides, except on, which, singularly enough, was next to the woods.

"Look thar!" exclaimed Wetzel, under his breath. He pointed off to the right of the maple glade. Jonathan gazed in the direction indicated, and saw two savages stealthily slipping through the bushes, and behind trees. Presently these suspicious acting spies, or scouts, stopped on a little knoll perhaps an hundred yards from the glade.

Wetzel groaned.

"This ain't comfortable," growled Zane, in a low whisper. "Them red devils are up to somethin' bad. They'd better not move round over here."

The hunters, satisfied that the two isolated savages meant mischief, turned their gaze once more toward the maple grove.

"Ah! Simon you white traitor! See him, Lew, comin' with his precious gang," said Jonathan. "He's got the whole thing fixed, you can plainly see that. Bill Elliott, McKee; and who's that renegade with Jim Girty? I'll allow he must be the fellar we heard was with the Chippewas. Tough lookin' customer; a good mate fer Jim Girty! A fine lot of border-hawks!"

"Somethin' comin' off," whispered Wetzel, as Zane's low growl grew unintelligible.

Jonathan felt, rather than saw, Wetzel tremble.

"The missionaries are consultin'. Ah! there comes one! Which? I guess it's Edwards. By gum! who's that Injun stalkin' over from the hostile bunch. Big chief, whoever he is. Blest if it ain't Half King!"

The watchers saw the chief wave his arm and speak with evident arrogance to Edwards, who, however, advanced to the platform and raised his hand to address the Christians.

"Crack!"

A shot rang out from the thicket. Clutching wildly at his breast, the missionary reeled back, staggered, and fell.

"One of those skulkin' redskins has killed Edwards," said Zane. "But, no; he's not dead! He's gettin' up! Mebbe he ain't hurt bad. By gum! there's Young comin' forward. Of all the fools!"

It was indeed true that Young had faced the Indians. Half King

440

addressed him as he had the other; but Young raised his hand and began speaking.

"Crack!"

Another shot rang out. Young threw up his hands and fell heavily. The missionaries rushed toward him. Mr. Wells ran round the group, wringing his hands as if distracted.

"He's hard hit," hissed Zane, between his teeth. "You can tell that by the way he fell."

Wetzel did not answer. He lay silent and motionless, his long body rigid, and his face like marble.

"There comes the other young fellar—Joe's brother. He'll get plugged, too," continued Zane, whispering rather to himself than to his companion. "Oh, I hoped they'd show some sense! It's noble for them to die for Christianity, but it won't do no good. By gum! Heckewelder has pulled him back. Now, that's good judgment!"

Half King stepped before the Christians and addressed them. He held in his hand a black war-club, which he wielded as he spoke.

Jonathan's attention was now directed from the maple grove to the hunter beside him. He had heard a slight metallic click, as Wetzel cocked his rifle. Then he saw the black barrel slowly rise.

"Listen, Lew. Mebbe it ain't good sense. We're after Girty, you remember; and it's a long shot from here—full three hundred yards."

"You're right, Jack, you're right," answered Wetzel, breathing hard.

"Let's wait, and see what comes off."

"Jack, I can't do it. It'll make our job harder; but I can't help it. I can put a bullet just over the Huron's left eye, an' I'm goin' to do it."

"You can't do it, Lew; you can't! It's too far for any gun. Wait! Wait!" whispered Jonathan, laying his hand on Wetzel's shoulder.

"Wait? Man, can't you see what the unnamable villain is doin'?"

"What?" asked Zane, turning his eyes again to the glade.

The converted Indians sat with bowed heads. Half King raised his war-club, and threw it on the ground in front of them.

"He's announcin' the death decree!" hissed Wetzel.

"Well! if he ain't!"

Jonathan looked at Wetzel's face. Then he rose to his knees, as had Wetzel, and tightened his belt. He knew that in another instant they would be speeding away through the forest.

"Lew, my rifle's no good fer that distance. But mebbe yours is. You ought to know. It's not sense, because there's Simon Girty, and there's Jim, the men we're after. If you can hit one, you can another. But go ahead, Lew. Plug that cowardly redskin!"

Wetzel knelt on one knee, and thrust the black rifle forward through the fern leaves. Slowly the fatal barrel rose to a level, and became as motionless as the immovable stones.

Jonathan fixed his keen gaze on the haughty countenance of Half King as he stood with folded arms and scornful mien in front of the Christians he had just condemned.

Even as the short, stinging crack of Wetzel's rifle broke the silence, Jonathan saw the fierce expression of Half King's dark face change to one of vacant wildness. His arms never relaxed from their folded position. He fell, as falls a monarch of the forest trees, a dead weight.

CHAPTER 25

"PLEASE DO NOT PREACH TO-DAY," SAID NELL, RAISING HER EYES imploringly to Jim's face.

"Nellie, I must conduct the services as usual. I can not shirk my duty, nor let these renegades see I fear to face them."

"I have such a queer feeling. I am afraid. I don't want to be left alone. Please do not leave me."

Jim strode nervously up and down the length of the room. Nell's worn face, her beseeching eyes and trembling hands touched his heart. Rather than almost anything else, he desired to please her, to strengthen her; yet how could he shirk his duty?

"Nellie, what is it you fear?" he asked, holding her hands tightly.

"Oh, I don't know what—everything. Uncle is growing weaker every day. Look at Mr. Young; he is only a shadow of his former self, and this anxiety is wearing Mr. Heckewelder out. He is more concerned than he dares admit. You needn't shake your head, for I know it. Then those Indians who are waiting, waiting—for God only knows what! Worse than all to me, I saw that renegade, that fearful beast who made way with poor dear Kate!"

Nell burst into tears, and leaned sobbing on Jim's shoulder.

"Nell, I've kept my courage only because of you," replied Jim, his voice trembling slightly.

She looked up quickly. Something in the pale face which was bent over

443

her told that now, if ever, was the time for a woman to forget herself, and to cheer, to inspire those around her.

"I am a silly baby, and selfish!" she cried, freeing herself from his hold. "Always thinking of myself." She turned away and wiped the tears from her eyes. "Go, Jim, do you duty; I'll stand by and help you all a woman can."

THE MISSIONARIES WERE CONSULTING IN HECKEWELDER'S CABIN. Zeisberger had returned that morning, and his aggressive, dominating spirit was just what they needed in an hour like this. He raised the downcast spirits of the ministers.

"Hold the service? I should say we will," he declared, waving his hands. "What have we to be afraid of?"

"I do not know," answered Heckewelder, shaking his head doubtfully. "I do not know what to fear. Girty himself told me he bore us no ill will; but I hardly believe him. All this silence, this ominous waiting perplexes, bewilders me."

"Gentlemen, our duty at least is plain," said Jim, impressively. "The faith of these Christian Indians in us is so absolute that they have no fear. They believe in God, and in us. These threatening savages have failed signally to impress our Christians. If we do not hold the service they will think we fear Girty, and that might have a bad influence."

"I am in favor of postponing the preaching for a few days. I tell you I am afraid of Girty's Indians, not for myself, but for these Christians whom we love so well. I am afraid." Heckewelder's face bore testimony to his anxious dread.

"You are our leader; we have but to obey," said Edwards. "Yet I think we owe it to our converts to stick to our work until we are forced by violence to desist."

"Ah! What form will that violence take?" cried Heckewelder, his face white. "You cannot tell what these savages mean. I fear! I fear!"

"Listen, Heckewelder, you must remember we had this to go through once before," put in Zeisberger earnestly. "In '78 Girty came down on us like a wolf on the fold. He had not so many Indians at his beck and call as now; but he harangued for days, trying to scare us and our handful of Christians. He set his drunken fiends to frighten us, and he failed. We stuck it out and won. He's trying the same game. Let us stand against him, and hold our services as usual. We should trust in God!"

"Never give up!" cried Jim.

"Gentlemen, you are right; you shame me, even though I feel that I understand the situation and its dread possibilities better than any one of you. Whatever befalls we'll stick to our post. I thank you for reviving the spirit in my cowardly heart. We will hold the service to-day as usual and to make it more impressive, each shall address the congregation in turn."

"And, if need be, we will give our lives for our Christians," said Young, raising his pale face.

THE DEEP MELLOW PEALS OF THE CHURCH BELL AWOKE THE SLUMBERING echoes. Scarcely had its melody died away in the forest when a line of Indians issued from the church and marched toward the maple grove. Men, women, youths, maidens and children.

Glickhican, the old Delaware chief, headed the line. His step was firm, his head erect, his face calm in its noble austerity. His followers likewise expressed in their countenances the steadfastness of their belief. The maidens' heads were bowed, but with shyness, not fear. The children were happy, their bright faces expressive of the joy they felt in the anticipation of listening to their beloved teachers.

This procession passed between rows of painted savages, standing immovable, with folded arms, and somber eyes.

No sooner had the Christians reached the maple grove, when from all over the clearing appeared hostile Indians, who took positions near the knoll where the missionaries stood.

Heckewelder's faithful little band awaited him on the platform. The converted Indians seated themselves as usual at the foot of the knoll. The other savages crowded closely on both sides. They carried their weapons, and maintained the same silence that had so singularly marked their mood of the last twenty-four hours. No human skill could have divined their intention. This coldness might be only habitual reserve, and it might be anything else.

Heckewelder approached at the same time that Simon Girty and his band of renegades appeared. With the renegades were Pipe and Half King. These two came slowly across the clearing, passed through the opening in the crowd, and stopped close to the platform.

Heckewelder went hurriedly up to his missionaries. He seemed beside himself with excitement, and spoke with difficulty.

"Do not preach to-day. I have been warned again," he said, in a low voice.

"Do you forbid it?" inquired Edwards.

"No, no. I have not that authority, but I implore it. Wait, wait until the Indians are in a better mood."

Edwards left the group, and, stepping upon the platform, faced the Christians.

At the same moment Half King stalked majestically from before his party. He carried no weapon save a black, knotted war-club. A surging forward of the crowd of savages behind him showed the intense interest which his action had aroused. He walked forward until he stood half way between the platform and the converts. He ran his evil glance slowly over the Christians, and then rested it upon Edwards.

"Half King's orders are to be obeyed. Let the paleface keep his mouth closed," he cried in the Indian tongue. The imperious command came as a thunderbolt from a clear sky. The missionaries behind Edwards stood bewildered, awaiting the outcome.

But Edwards, without a moment's hesitation, calmly lifted his hand and spoke.

"Beloved Christians, we meet to-day as we have met before, as we hope to meet in——"

"Spang!"

The whistling of a bullet over the heads of the Christians accompanied the loud report of a rifle. All presently plainly heard the leaden missile strike. Edwards wheeled, clutching his side, breathed hard, and then fell heavily without uttering a cry. He had been shot by an Indian concealed in the thicket.

For a moment no one moved, nor spoke. The missionaries were stricken with horror; the converts seemed turned to stone, and the hostile throng waited silently, as they had for hours.

"He's shot! He's shot! Oh, I feared this!" cried Heckewelder, running forward. The missionaries followed him. Edwards was lying on his back, with a bloody hand pressed to his side.

"Dave, Dave, how is it with you?" asked Heckewelder, in a voice low with fear.

"Not bad. It's too far out to be bad, but it knocked me over," answered Edwards, weakly. "Give me——water."

They carried him from the platform, and laid him on the grass under a tree.

Young pressed Edwards' hand; he murmured something that sounded like a prayer, and then walked straight upon the platform, as he raised his face, which was sublime with a white light.

"Paleface! Back!" roared Half King, as he waved his war-club.

"You Indian dog! Be silent!"

Young's clear voice rolled out on the quiet air so imperiously, so powerful in its wonderful scorn and passion, that the hostile savages were overcome by awe, and the Christians thrilled anew with reverential love.

Young spoke again in a voice which had lost its passion, and was singularly sweet in its richness.

"Beloved Christians, if it is God's will that we must die to prove our faith, then as we have taught you how to live, so we can show you how to die——"

"Spang!"

Again a whistling sound came with the bellow of an overcharged rifle; again the sickening thud of a bullet striking flesh.

Young fell backwards from the platform.

The missionaries laid him beside Edwards, and then stood in shuddering silence. A smile shone on Young's pale face; a stream of dark blood welled from his breast. His lips moved; he whispered:

"I ask no more—God's will."

Jim looked down once at his brother missionaries; then with blanched face, but resolute and stern, he marched toward the platform.

Heckewelder ran after him, and dragged him back.

"No! no! no! My God! Would you be killed? Oh! I tried to prevent this!" cried Heckewelder, wringing his hands.

One long, fierce, exultant yell pealed throughout the grove. It came from those silent breasts in which was pent up hatred; it greeted this action which proclaimed victory over the missionaries.

All eyes turned on Half King. With measured stride he paced to and fro before the Christian Indians.

Neither cowering nor shrinking marked their manner; to a man, to a child, they rose with proud mien, heads erect and eyes flashing. This mighty chief with his blood-thirsty crew could burn the Village of Peace, could annihilate the Christians, but he could never change their hope and trust in God.

"Blinded fools!" cried Half King. "The Huron is wise; he tells no lies.

Many moons ago he told the Christians they were sitting half way between two angry gods, who stood with mouths open wide and looking ferociously at each other. If they did not move back out of the road they would be ground to powder by the teeth of one or the other, or both. Half King urged them to leave the peaceful village, to forget the paleface God; to take their horses, and flocks, and return to their homes. The Christians scorned the Huron King's counsel. The sun has set for the Village of Peace. The time has come. Pipe and the Huron are powerful. They will not listen to the paleface God. They will burn the Village of Peace. Death to the Christians!"

Half King threw the black war-club with a passionate energy on the grass before the Indians.

They heard this decree of death with unflinching front. Even the children were quiet. Not a face paled, not an eye was lowered.

Half King cast their doom in their teeth. The Christians eyed him with unspoken scorn.

"My God! My God! It is worse than I thought!" moaned Heckewelder. "Utter ruin! Murder! Murder!"

In the momentary silence which followed his outburst, a tiny cloud of blue-white smoke came from the ferns overhanging a cliff.

Crack!

All heard the shot of a rifle; all noticed the difference between its clear, ringing intonation and the loud reports of the other two. All distinctly heard the zip of a bullet as it whistled over their heads.

All? No, not all. One did not hear that speeding bullet. He who was the central figure in this tragic scene, he who had doomed the Christians might have seen that tiny puff of smoke which heralded his own doom, but before the ringing report could reach his ears a small blue hole appeared, as if by magic, over his left eye, and pulse, and sense, and life had fled forever.

Half King, great, cruel chieftain, stood still for an instant as if he had been an image of stone; his haughty head lost its erect poise, the fierceness seemed to fade from his dark face, his proud plume waved gracefully as he swayed to and fro, and then fell before the Christians, inert and lifeless.

No one moved; it was as if no one breathed. The superstitious savages awaited fearfully another rifle shot; another lightning stroke, another visitation from the paleface's God.

But Jim Girty, with a cunning born of his terrible fear, had recognized the ring of that rifle. He had felt the zip of a bullet which could just as readily have found his brain as Half King's. He had stood there as fair a mark as the cruel Huron, yet the Avenger had not chosen him. Was he reserved for a different fate? Was not such a death too merciful for the frontier Deathshead? He yelled in his craven fear:

"Le vent de la Mort!"

The well known, dreaded appellation aroused the savages from a fearful stupor into a fierce manifestation of hatred. A tremendous yell rent the air. Instantly the scene changed.

CHAPTER 26

In the confusion the missionaries carried Young and Edwards into Mr. Wells' cabin. Nell's calm, white face showed that she had expected some such catastrophe as this, but she of all was the least excited. Heckewelder left them at the cabin and hurried away to consult Captain Williamson. While Zeisberger, who was skilled in surgery, attended to the wounded men, Jim barred the heavy door, shut the rude, swinging windows, and made the cabin temporarily a refuge from prowling savages.

Outside the clamor increased. Shrill yells rent the air, long, rolling war-cries sounded above all the din. The measured stamp of moccasined feet, the rush of Indians past the cabin, the dull thud of hatchets struck hard into the trees—all attested to the excitement of the savages, and the imminence of terrible danger.

In the front room of Mr. Wells' cabin Edwards lay on a bed, his face turned to the wall, and his side exposed. There was a bloody hole in his white skin. Zeisberger was probing for the bullet. He had no instruments, save those of his own manufacture, and they were darning needles with bent points, and a long knife-blade ground thin.

"There, I have it," said Zeisberger. "Hold still, Dave. There!" As Edwards moaned Zeisberger drew forth the bloody bullet. "Jim, wash and dress this wound. It isn't bad. Dave will be all right in a couple of days. Now I'll look at George."

Zeisberger hurried into the other room. Young lay with quiet face and closed eyes, breathing faintly. Zeisberger opened the wounded man's shirt and exposed the wound, which was on the right side, rather high up. Nell, who had followed Zeisberger that she might be of some assistance if needed, saw him look at the wound and then turn a pale face away for a second. That hurried, shuddering movement of the sober, practical missionary was most significant. Then he bent over Young and inserted on of the probes into the wound. He pushed the steel an inch, two, three, four inches into Young's breast, but the latter neither moved nor moaned. Zeisberger shook his head, and finally removed the instrument. He raised the sufferer's shoulder to find the bed saturated with blood. The bullet wound extended completely through the missionary's body, and was bleeding from the back. Zeisberger folded strips of linsey cloth into small pads and bound them tightly over both apertures of the wound.

"How is he?" asked Jim, when the amateur surgeon returned to the other room, and proceeded to wash the blood from his hands.

Zeisberger shook his head gloomily.

"How is George?" whispered Edwards, who had heard Jim's question.

"Shot through the right lung. Human skill can not aid him! Only God can save."

"Didn't I hear a third shot?" whispered Dave, gazing round with sad, questioning eyes. "Heckewelder?"

"Is safe. He has gone to see Williamson. You did hear a third shot. Half King fell dead with a bullet over his left eye. He had just folded his arms in a grand pose after his death decree to the Christians."

"A judgment of God!"

"It does seem so, but it came in the form of leaden death from Wetzel's unerring rifle. Do you hear all that yelling? Half King's death has set the Indians wild."

There was a gentle knock at the door, and then the word, "Open," in Heckewelder's voice.

Jim unbarred the door. Heckewelder came in carrying over his shoulder what apparently was a sack of meal. He was accompanied by young Christy. Heckewelder put the bag down, opened it, and lifted out a little Indian boy. The child gazed round with fearful eyes.

"Save Benny! Save Benny!" he cried, running to Nell, and she clasped him closely in her arms.

Heckewelder's face was like marble as he asked concerning Edwards' condition.

"I'm not badly off," said the missionary with a smile.

"How's George?" whispered Heckewelder.

No one answered him. Zeisberger raised his hands. All followed Heckewelder into the other room, where Young lay in the same position as when first brought in. Heckewelder stood gazing down into the wan face with its terribly significant smile.

"I brought him out here. I persuaded him to come!" whispered Heckewelder. "Oh, Almighty God!" he cried. His voice broke, and his prayer ended with the mute eloquence of clasped hands and uplifted, appealing face.

"Come out," said Zeisberger, leading him into the larger room. The others followed, and Jim closed the door.

"What's to be done?" said Zeisberger, with his practical common sense. "What did Williamson say? Tell us what you learned?"

"Wait—directly," answered Heckewelder, sitting down and covering his face with his hands. There was a long silence. At length he raised his white face and spoke calmly:

"Gentlemen, the Village of Peace is doomed. I entreated Captain Williamson to help us, but he refused. Said he dared not interfere. I prayed that he would speak at least a word to Girty, but he denied my request."

"Where are the converts?"

"Imprisoned in the church, every one of them except Benny. Mr. Christy and I hid the child in the meal sack and were thus able to get him here. We must save him."

"Save him?" asked Nell, looking from Heckewelder to the trembling Indian boy.

"Nellie, the savages have driven all our Christians into the church, and shut them up there, until Girty and his men shall give the word to complete their fiendish design. The converts asked but one favor—an hour in which to pray. It was granted. The savages intend to murder them all."

"Oh! Horrible! Monstrous!" cried Nell. "How can they be so inhuman?" She lifted Benny up in her arms. "They'll never get you, my boy. We'll save you—I'll save you!" The child moaned and clung to her neck.

"They are scouring the clearing now for Christians, and will search all the cabins. I'm positive."

"Will they come here?" asked Nell, turning her blazing eyes on Heckewelder.

"Undoubtedly. We must try to hide Benny. Let me think; where would be a good place? We'll try a dark corner of the loft."

"No, no," cried Nell.

"Put Benny in Young's bed," suggested Jim.

"No, no," cried Nell.

"Put him in a bucket and let him down in the well," whispered Edwards, who had listened intently to the conversation.

"That's a capital place," said Heckewelder. "But might he not fall out and drown?"

"Tie him in the bucket," said Jim.

"No, no, no," cried Nell.

"But Nellie, we must decide upon a hiding place, and in a hurry."

"I'll save Benny."

"You? Will you stay here to face those men? Jim Girty and Deering are searching the cabins. Could you bear it to see them? You couldn't."

"Oh! No, I believe it would kill me! That man! that beast! will he come here?" Nell grew ghastly pale, and looked as if about to faint. She shrunk in horror at the thought of again facing Girty. "For God's sake, Heckewelder, don't let him see me! Don't let him come in! Don't!"

Even as the imploring voice ceased a heavy thump sounded on the door.

"Who's there?" demanded Heckewelder.

Thump! Thump!

The heavy blows shook the cabin. The pans rattled on the shelves. No answer came from without.

"Quick! Hide Benny! It's as much as our lives are worth to have him found here," cried Heckewelder in a fierce whisper, as he darted toward the door.

"All right, all right, in a moment," he called out, fumbling over the bar.

He opened the door a moment later and when Jim Girty and Deering entered he turned to his friends with a dread uncertainty in his haggard face.

Edwards lay on the bed with wide-open eyes staring at the intruders. Mr. Wells sat with bowed head. Zeisberger calmly whittled a stick, and Jim stood bolt upright, with a hard light in his eyes.

Nell leaned against the side of a heavy table. Wonderful was the change that had transformed her from a timid, appealing, fear-agonized girl to a woman whose only evidence of unusual excitement were the flame in her eyes and the peculiar whiteness of her face.

Benny was gone!

Heckewelder's glance returned to the visitors. He thought he had never seen such brutal, hideous men.

"Wal, I reckon a preacher ain't agoin' to lie. Hev you seen any Injun Christians round here?" asked Girty, waving a heavy sledge-hammer.

"Girty, we have hidden no Indians here," answered Heckewelder, calmly.

"Wal, we'll hev a look, anyway," answered the renegade.

Girty surveyed the room with wolfish eyes. Deering was so drunk that he staggered. Both men, in fact, reeked with the vile fumes of rum. Without another word they proceeded to examine the room, by looking into every box, behind a stone oven, and in the cupboard. They drew the bedclothes from the bed, and with a kick demolished a pile of stove wood. Then the ruffians passed into the other apartments, where they could be heard making thorough search. At length both returned to the large room, when Girty directed Deering to climb a ladder leading to the loft, but because Deering was too much under the influence of liquor to do so, he had to go himself. He rummaged around up there for a few minutes, and then came down.

"Wal, I reckon you wasn't lyin' about it," said Girty, with his ghastly leer.

He and his companion started to go out. Deering had stood with bloodshot eyes fixed on Nell while Girty searched the loft, and as they passed the girl on their way to the open air, the renegade looked at Girty as he motioned with his head toward her. His besotted face expressed some terrible meaning.

Girty had looked at Nell when he first entered, but had not glanced twice at her. As he turned now, before going out of the door, he fixed on her his baleful glance. His aspect was more full of meaning than could have been any words. A horrible power, of which he was boastfully conscious, shone from his little, pointed eyes. His mere presence was deadly. Plainly as if he had spoken was the significance of his long gaze. Any one could have translated that look.

Once before Nell had faced it, and fainted when its dread meaning grew clear to her. But now she returned his gaze with one in which flashed lightning scorn, and repulsion, in which glowed a wonderful defiance.

The cruel face of this man, the boastful barbarity of his manner, the long, dark, bloody history which his presence recalled, was, indeed, terrifying without the added horror of his intent toward her, but now the self-forgetfulness of a true woman sustained her.

Girty and Deering backed out of the door. Heckewelder closed it, and dropped the bar in place.

Nell fell over the table with a long, low gasp. Then with one hand she lifted her skirt. Benny walked from under it. His big eyes were bright. The young woman clasped him again in her arms. Then she released him, and, laboring under intense excitement, ran to the window.

"There he goes! Oh, the horrible beast! If I only had a gun and could shoot! Oh, if only I were a man! I'd kill him. To think of poor Kate! Ah! he intends the same for me!"

Suddenly she fell upon the floor in a faint. Mr. Wells and Jim lifted her on the bed beside Edwards, where they endeavored to revive her. It was some moments before she opened her eyes.

Jim sat holding Nell's hand. Mr. Wells again bowed his head. Zeisberger continued to whittle a stick, and Heckewelder paced the floor. Christy stood by with every evidence of sympathy for this distracted group. Outside the clamor increased.

"Just listen!" cried Heckewelder. "Did you ever hear the like? All drunk, crazy, fiendish! They drank every drop of liquor the French traders had. Curses on the vagabond dealers! Rum has made these renegades and savages wild. Oh! my poor, innocent Christians!"

Heckewelder leaned his head against the mantle-shelf. He had broken down at last. Racking sobs shook his frame.

"Are you all right again?" asked Jim of Nell.

"Yes."

"I am going out, first to see Williamson, and then the Christians," he said, rising very pale, but calm.

"Don't go!" cried Heckewelder. "I have tried everything. It was all of no use."

"I will go," answered Jim.

"Yes, Jim, go," whispered Nell, looking up into his eyes. It was an earnest gaze in which a faint hope shone.

Jim unbarred the door and went out.

"Wait, I'll go along," cried Zeisberger, suddenly dropping his knife and stick.

As the two men went out a fearful spectacle met their eyes. The clearing was alive with Indians. But such Indians! They were painted demons, maddened by rum. Yesterday they had been silent; if they moved at all it had been with deliberation and dignity. To-day they were a yelling, running, blood-seeking mob.

"Awful! Did you ever see human beings like these?" asked Zeisberger.

"No, no!"

"I saw such a frenzy once before, but, of course, only in a small band of savages. Many times have I seen Indians preparing for the war-path, in search of both white men and redskins. They were fierce then, but nothing like this. Every one of these frenzied fiends is honest. Think of that! Every man feels it his duty to murder these Christians. Girty has led up to this by cunning, and now the time is come to let them loose."

"It means death for all."

"I have given up any thought of escaping," said Zeisberger, with the calmness that had characterized his manner since he returned to the village. "I shall try to get into the church."

"I'll join you there as soon as I see Williamson."

Jim walked rapidly across the clearing to the cabin where Captain Williamson had quarters. The frontiersmen stood in groups, watching the savages with an interest which showed little or no concern.

"I want to see Captain Williamson," said Jim to a frontiersman on guard at the cabin door.

"Wal, he's inside," drawled the man.

Jim thought the voice familiar, and he turned sharply to see the sun-burnt features of Jeff Lynn, the old riverman who had taken Mr. Wells' party to Fort Henry.

"Why, Lynn! I'm glad to see you," exclaimed Jim.

"Purty fair to middlin'," answered Jeff, extending his big hand. "Say, how's the other one, your brother as wus called Joe?"

"I don't know. He ran off with Wetzel, was captured by Indians, and when I last heard of him he had married Wingenund's daughter."

"Wal, I'll be dog-goned!" Jeff shook his grizzled head and slapped his leg. "I jest knowed he'd raise somethin'."

"I'm in a hurry. Do you think Captain Williamson will stand still and let all this go on?"

"I'm afeerd so."

Evidently the captain heard the conversation, for he appeared at the cabin door, smoking a long pipe.

"Captain Williamson, I have come to entreat you to save the Christians from this impending massacre."

"I can't do nuthin'," answered Williamson, removing his pipe to puff forth a great cloud of smoke.

"You have eighty men here!"

"If we interfered Pipe would eat us alive in three minutes. You preacher fellows don't understand this thing. You've got Pipe and Girty to deal with. If you don't know them, you'll be better acquainted by sundown."

"I don't care who they are. Drunken ruffians and savages! That's enough. Will you help us? We are men of your own race, and we come to you for help. Can you withhold it?"

"I won't hev nuthin' to do with this bizness. The chiefs hev condemned the village, an' it'll hev to go. If you fellars hed been careful, no white blood would hev been spilled. I advise you all to lay low till it's over."

"Will you let me speak to your men, to try and get them to follow me?"

"Heckewelder asked that same thing. He was persistent, and I took a vote fer him just to show how my men stood. Eighteen of them said they'd follow him; the rest wouldn't interfere."

"Eighteen! My God!" cried Jim, voicing the passion which consumed him. "You are white men, yet you will stand by and see these innocent people murdered! Man, where's your humanity? Your manhood? These converted Indians are savages no longer, they are Christians. Their children are as good, pure, innocent as your own. Can you remain idle and see these little ones murdered?"

Williamson made no answer, the men who had crowded round were equally silent. Not one lowered his head. Many looked at the impassioned missionary; others gazed at the savages who were circling around the trees brandishing their weapons. If any pitied the unfortunate Christians, none showed it. They were indifferent, with the indifference of men hardened to cruel scenes.

Jim understood, at last, as he turned from face to face to find everywhere that same imperturbability. These bordermen were like Wetzel and Jonathan Zane. The only good Indian was a dead Indian. Years of war and bloodshed, of merciless cruelty at the hands of redmen, of the hard, border life had rendered these frontiersmen incapable of compassion for any savage.

Jim no longer restrained himself.

"Bordermen you may be, but from my standpoint, from any man's, from

God's, you are a lot of coldly indifferent cowards!" exclaimed Jim, with white, quivering lips. "I understand now. Few of you will risk anything for Indians. You will not believe a savage can be a Christian. You don't care if they are all murdered. Any man among you—any man, I say—would step out before those howling fiends and boldly demand that there be no bloodshed. A courageous leader with a band of determined followers could avert this tragedy. You might readily intimidate yonder horde of drunken demons. Captain Williamson, I am only a minister, far removed from a man of war and leader, as you claim to be, but, sir, I curse you as a miserable coward. If I ever get back to civilization I'll brand this inhuman coldness of yours, as the most infamous and dastardly cowardice that ever disgraced a white man. You are worse than Girty!"

Williamson turned a sickly yellow; he fumbled a second with the handle of his tomahawk, but made no answer. The other bordermen maintained the same careless composure. What to them was the raving of a mad preacher?

Jim saw it and turned baffled, fiercely angry, and hopeless. As he walked away Jeff Lynn took his arm, and after they were clear of the crowd of frontiersmen he said:

"Young feller, you give him pepper, an' no mistake. An' mebbe you're right from your side the fence. But you can't see the Injuns from our side. We hunters hevn't much humanity—I reckon that's what you called it— but we've lost so many friends an' relatives, an' hearn of so many murders by the reddys that we look on all of 'em as wild varmints that should be killed on sight. Now, mebbe it'll interest you to know I was the feller who took the vote Williamson told you about, an' I did it 'cause I had an interest in you. I wus watchin' you when Edwards and the other missionary got shot. I like grit in a man, an' I seen you had it clear through. So when Heckewelder comes over I talked to the fellers, an' all I could git interested was eighteen, but they wanted to fight simply fer fightin' sake. Now, ole Jeff Lynn is your friend. You just lay low until this is over."

Jim thanked the old riverman and left him. He hardly knew which way to turn. He would make one more effort. He crossed the clearing to where the renegades' teepee stood. McKee and Elliott were sitting on a log. Simon Girty stood beside them, his hard, keen, roving eyes on the scene. The missionary was impressed by the white leader. There was a difference in his aspect, a wilder look than the others wore, as if the man had suddenly awakened to the fury of his Indians. Nevertheless the young man went straight toward him.

"Girty, I come——"

"Git out! You meddlin' preacher!" yelled the renegade, shaking his fist at Jim.

Simon Girty was drunk.

Jim turned from the white fiends. He knew his life to them was not worth a pinch of powder.

"Lost! Lost! All lost!" he exclaimed in despair.

As he went toward the church he saw hundreds of savages bounding over the grass, brandishing weapons and whooping fiendishly. They were concentrating around Girty's teepee, where already a great throng had congregated. Of all the Indians to be seen not one walked. They leaped by Jim, and ran over the grass nimble as deer.

He saw the eager, fire in their dusky eyes, and the cruelly clenched teeth like those of wolves when they snarl. He felt the hissing breath of many savages as they raced by him. More than one whirled a tomahawk close to Jim's head, and uttered horrible yells in his ear. They were like tigers lusting for blood.

Jim hurried to the church. Not an Indian was visible near the log structure. Even the savage guards had gone. He entered the open door to be instantly struck with reverence and awe.

The Christians were singing.

Miserable and full of sickening dread though Jim was, he could not but realize that the scene before him was one of extraordinary beauty and pathos. The doomed Indians lifted up their voices in song. Never had they sung so feelingly, so harmoniously.

When the song ended Zeisberger, who stood upon a platform, opened his Bible and read:

"In a little wrath I hid my face from thee for a moment, but with everlasting kindness will I have mercy on thee, saith the Lord, thy Redeemer."

In a voice low and tremulous the venerable missionary began his sermon.

The shadow of death hovered over these Christian martyrs; it was reflected in their somber eyes, yet not one was sullen or sad. The children who were too young to understand, but instinctively feeling the tragedy soon to be enacted there, cowered close to their mothers.

Zeisberger preached a touching and impressive, though short, sermon. At its conclusion the whole congregation rose and surrounded the missionary. The men shook his hands, the women kissed them, the children clung to his legs. It was a wonderful manifestation of affection.

Suddenly Glickhican, the old Delaware chief, stepped on the platform, raised his hand and shouted one Indian word.

A long, low wail went up from the children and youths; the women slowly, meekly bowed their heads. The men, due to the stoicism of their nature and the Christianity they had learned, stood proudly erect awaiting the death that had been decreed.

Glickhican pulled the bell rope.

A deep, mellow tone pealed out.

The sound transfixed all the Christians. No one moved.

Glickhican had given the signal which told the murderers the Christians were ready.

"Come, man, my God! We can't stay here!" cried Jim to Zeisberger.

As they went out both men turned to look their last on the martyrs. The death knell which had rung in the ears of the Christians, was to them the voice of God. Stern, dark visages of men and the sweet, submissive faces of women were uplifted with rapt attention. A light seemed to shine from these faces as if the contemplation of God had illumined them.

As Zeisberger and Jim left the church and hurried toward the cabins, they saw the crowd of savages in a black mass round Girty's teepee. The yelling and leaping had ceased.

Heckewelder opened the door. Evidently he had watched for them.

"Jim! Jim!" cried Nell, when he entered the cabin. "Oh-h! I was afraid. Oh! I am glad you're back safe. See, this noble Indian has come to help us."

Wingenund stood calm and erect by the door.

"Chief, what will you do?"

"Wingenund will show you the way to the big river," answered the chieftain, in his deep bass.

"Run away? No, never! That would be cowardly. Heckewelder, you would not go? Nor you, Zeisberger? We may yet be of use, we may yet save some of the Christians."

"Save the yellow-hair," sternly said Wingenund.

"Oh, Jim, you don't understand. The chief has come to warn me of Girty. He intends to take me as he has others, as he did poor Kate. did you not see the meaning in his eyes to-day? How they scorched me! Ho! Jim, take me away! Save me! Do not leave me here to that horrible fate? Oh! Jim, take me away!"

"Nell, I will take you," cried Jim, grasping her hands.

"Hurry! There's a blanket full of things I packed for you," said Heckewelder. "Lose no time. Ah! hear that! My Heavens! what a yell!" Heck-ewelder rushed to the door and looked out. "There they go, a black mob of imps; a pack of hungry wolves! Jim Girty is in the lead. How he leaps! How he waves his sledge! He leads the savages toward the church. Oh! it's the end!"

"Benny? Where's Benny?" cried Jim, hurriedly lacing the hunting coat he had flung about him.

"Benny's safe. I've hidden him. I'll get him away from here," answered young Christy. "Go! Now's your time. Godspeed you!"

"I'm ready," declared Mr. Wells. "I—have—finished!"

"There goes Wingenund! He's running. Follow him, quick! Good-by! Good-by! God be with you!" cried Heckewelder.

"Good-by! Good-by!"

Jim hurried Nell toward the bushes where Wingenund's tall form could dimly be seen. Mr. Wells followed them. On the edge of the clearing Jim and Nell turned to look back.

They saw a black mass of yelling, struggling, fighting savages crowding around the church.

"Oh! Jim, look back! Look back!" cried Nell, holding hard to his hand. "Look back! See if Girty is coming!"

CHAPTER 27

At last the fugitives breathed free under the gold and red cover of the woods. Never speaking, never looking back, the guide hurried eastward with long strides. His followers were almost forced to run in order to keep him in sight. He had waited at the edge of the clearing for them, and, relieving Jim of the heavy pack, which he swung slightly over his shoulder, he set a pace that was most difficult to maintain. The young missionary half led, half carried Nell over the stones and rough places. Mr. Wells labored in the rear.

"Oh! Jim! Look back! Look back! See if we are pursued!" cried Nell frequently, with many a earful glance into the dense thickets.

The Indian took a straight course through the woods. He leaped the brooks, climbed the rough ridges, and swiftly trod the glades that were free of windfalls. His hurry and utter disregard for the plain trail left behind, proved his belief in the necessity of placing many miles between the fugitives and the Village of Peace. Evidently they would be followed, and it would be a waste of valuable time to try to conceal their trail. Gradually the ground began to rise, the way become more difficult, but Wingenund never slackened his pace. Nell was strong, supple, and light of foot. She held her own with Jim, but time and time again they were obliged to wait for her uncle. Once he was far behind. Wingenund halted for them at the height of a ridge where the forest was open.

"Ugh!" exclaimed the chieftain, as they finished the ascent. He stretched a long arm toward the sun; his falcon eye gleamed.

Far in the west a great black and yellow cloud of smoke rolled heavenward. It seemed to rise from out the forest, and to hang low over the trees; then it soared aloft and grew thinner until it lost its distinct line far in the clouds. The setting sun stood yet an hour high over a distant hill, and burned dark red through the great pall of smoke.

"Is it a forest fire?" asked Nell, fearfully.

"Fire, of course, but——" Jim did not voice his fear; he looked closely at Wingenund.

The chieftain stood silent a moment as was his wont when addressed. The dull glow of the sun was reflected in the dark eyes that gazed far away over forest and field.

"Fire," said Wingenund, and it seemed that as he spoke a sterner shadow flitted across his bronzed face. "The sun sets to-night over the ashes of the Village of Peace."

He resumed his rapid march eastward. With never a backward glance the saddened party followed. Nell kept close beside Jim, and the old man tramped after them with bowed head. The sun set, but Wingenund never slackened his stride. Twilight deepened, yet he kept on.

"Indian, we can go no further to-night, we must rest," cried Jim, as Nell stumbled against him, and Mr. Wells panted wearily in the rear.

"Rest soon," replied the chief, and kept on.

Darkness had settled down when Wingenund at last halted. The fugitives could see little in the gloom, but they heard the music of running water, and felt soft moss beneath their feet.

They sank wearily down upon a projecting stone. The moss was restful to their tired limbs. Opening the pack they found food with which to satisfy the demands of hunger. Then, close under the stone, the fugitives sank into slumber while the watchful Indian stood silent and motionless.

Jim thought he had but just closed his eyes when he felt a gentle pressure on his arm.

"Day is here," said the Indian.

Jim opened his eyes to see the bright red sun crimsoning the eastern hills, and streaming gloriously over the colored forests. He raised himself on his elbow to look around. Nell was still asleep. The blanket was tucked close to her chin. Her chestnut hair was tumbled like a schoolgirl's; she looked as fresh and sweet as the morning.

"Nell, Nell, wake up," said Jim, thinking the while how he would love to kiss those white eyelids.

Nell's eyes opened wide; a smile lay deep in their hazel shadows.

"Where a I? Oh, I remember," she cried, sitting up. "Oh, Jim, I had such a sweet dream. I was at home with mother and Kate. Oh, to wake and find it all a dream! I am fleeing for life. But, Jim, we are safe, are we not?"

"Another day, and we'll be safe."

"Let us fly," she cried, leaping up and shaking out her crumpled skirt. "Uncle, come!"

Mr. Wells lay quietly with his mild blue eyes smiling up at her. He neither moved nor spoke.

"Eat, drink," said the chief, opening the pack.

"What a beautiful place," exclaimed Nell, taking the bread and meat handed to her. "This is a lovely little glade. Look at those golden flowers, the red and purple leaves, the brown shining moss, and those lichen-covered stones. Why! Some one has camped here. See the little cave, the screens of plaited ferns, and the stone fireplace."

"It seems to me this dark spring and those gracefully spreading branches are familiar," said Jim.

"Beautiful Spring," interposed Wingenund.

"Yes, I know this place," cried Nell excitedly. "I remember this glade though it was moonlight when I saw it. Here Wetzel rescued me from Girty."

"Nell, you're right," replied Jim. "How strange we should run across this place again."

Strange fate, indeed, which had brought them again to Beautiful Spring! It was destined that the great scenes of their lives were to be enacted in this mossy glade.

"Come, uncle, you are lazy," cried Nell, a touch of her old roguishness making playful her voice.

Mr. Wells lay still, and smiled up at them.

"You are not ill?" cried Nell, seeing for the first time how pallid was his face.

"Dear Nellie, I am not ill. I do not suffer, but I am dying," he answered, again with that strange, sweet smile.

"Oh-h-h!" breathed Nell, falling on her knees.

"No, no, Mr. Wells, you are only weak; you will be all right again soon," cried Jim.

"Jim, Nellie, I have known all night. I have lain here wakeful. My heart never was strong. It gave out yesterday, and now it is slowly growing weaker. Put your hand on my breast. Feel. Ah! you see! My life is flickering. God's will be done. I am content. My work is finished. My only regret is that I brought you out to this terrible borderland. But I did not know. If only I could see you safe from the peril of this wilderness, at home, happy, married."

Nell bent over him blinded by her tears, unable to see or speak, crushed by this last overwhelming blow. Jim sat on the other side of the old missionary, holding his hand. For many moments neither spoke. They glanced at the pale face, watching with eager, wistful eyes for a smile, or listening for a word.

"Come," said the Indian.

Nell silently pointed toward her uncle.

"He is dying," whispered Jim to the Indian.

"Go, leave me," murmured Mr. Wells. "You are still in danger."

"We'll not leave you," cried Jim.

"No, no, no," sobbed Nell, bending over to kiss him.

"Nellie, may I marry you to Jim?" whispered Mr. Wells into her ear. "He has told me how it is with him. He loves you, Nellie. I'd die happier knowing I'd left you with him."

Even at that moment, with her heart almost breaking, Nell's fair face flushed.

"Nell, will you marry me?" asked Jim, softly. Low though it was, he had heard Mr. Wells' whisper.

Nell stretched a little trembling hand over her uncle to Jim, who inclosed it in his own. Her eyes met his. Through her tears shone faintly a light, which, but for the agony that made it dim, would have beamed radiant.

"Find the place," said Mr. Wells, handing Jim a Bible. It was the one he always carried in his pocket.

With trembling hand Jim turned the leaves. At last he found the lines, and handed the book back to the old man.

Simple, sweet and sad was that marriage service. Nell and Jim knelt with hands clasped over Mr. Wells. The old missionary's voice was faint; Nell's responses were low, and Jim answered with deep and tender feeling. Beside them stood Wingenund, a dark, magnificent figure.

"There! May God bless you!" murmured Mr. Wells, with a happy smile, closing the Bible.

"Nell, my wife!" whispered Jim, kissing her hand.

"Come!" broke in Wingenund's voice, deep, strong, like that of a bell.

Not one of them had observed the chief as he stood erect, motionless, poised like a stag scenting the air. His dark eyes seemed to pierce the purple-golden forest, his keen ear seemed to drink in the singing of the birds and the gentle rustling of leaves. Native to these haunts as were the wild creatures, they were no quicker than the Indian to feel the approach of foes. The breeze had borne faint, suspicious sounds.

"Keep—the—Bible," said Mr. Wells, "remember—its—word." His hand closely clasped Nell's, and then suddenly loosened. His pallid face was lighted by a meaning, tender smile which slowly faded—faded, and was gone. The venerable head fell back. The old missionary was dead.

Nell kissed the pale, cold brow, and then rose, half dazed and shuddering. Jim was vainly trying to close the dead man's eyes. She could no longer look. On rising she found herself near the Indian chief. He took her fingers in his great hand, and held them with a strong, warm pressure. Strangely thrilled, she looked up at Wingenund. His somber eyes, fixed piercingly on the forest, and his dark stern face, were, as always, inscrutable. No compassion shone there; no emotion unbefitting a chieftain would ever find expression in that cold face, but Nell felt a certain tenderness in this Indian, a response in his great heart. Felt it so surely, so powerfully that she leaned her head against him. She knew he was her friend.

"Come," said the chief once more. He gently put Nell aside before Jim arose from his sad task.

"We can not leave him unburied," expostulated Jim.

Wingenund dragged aside a large stone which formed one wall of the cavern. Then he grasped a log which was half covered by dirt, and, exerting his great strength, pulled it from its place. There was a crash, a rumble, the jar of a heavy weight striking the earth, then the rattling of gravel, and, before Nell and Jim realized what had happened, the great rock forming the roof of the cavern slipped down the bank followed by a small avalanche. The cavern was completely covered. Mr. Wells was buried. A mossy stone marked the old missionary's grave.

Nell and Jim were lost in wonder and awe.

"Ugh!" cried the chief, looking toward the opening in the glade.

Fearfully Nell and Jim turned, to be appalled by four naked, painted savages standing with leveled rifles. Behind them stood Deering and Jim Girty.

"Oh, God! We are lost! Lost! Lost!" exclaimed Jim, unable to command himself. Hope died in his heart.

No cry issued from Nell's white lips. She was dazed by this final blow. Having endured so much, this last misfortune, apparently the ruin of her life, brought no added suffering, only a strange, numb feeling.

"Ah-huh! Thought you'd give me the slip, eh?" croaked Girty, striding forward, and as he looked at Wingenund his little, yellow eyes flared like flint. "Does a wolf befriend Girty's captives? Chief you hev led me a hard chase."

Wingenund deigned no reply. He stood as he did so often, still and silent, with folded arms, and a look that was haughty, unresponsive.

The Indians came forward into the glade, and one of them quickly bound Jim's hands behind his back. The savages wore a wild, brutish look. A feverish ferocity, very near akin to insanity, possessed them. They were not quiet a moment, but ran here and there, for no apparent reason, except, possibly, to keep in action with the raging fire in their hearts. The cleanliness which characterized the normal Indian was absent in them; their scant buckskin dress was bedraggled and stained. They were still drunk with rum and the lust for blood. Murder gleamed from the glance of their eyes.

"Jake, come over here," said Girty to his renegade friend. "Ain't she a prize?"

Girty and Deering stood before the poor, stricken girl, and gloated over her fair beauty. She stood as when first transfixed by the horror from which she had been fleeing. Her pale face was lowered, her hands clenched tightly in the folds of her skirt.

Never before had two such coarse, cruel fiends as Deering and Girty encumbered the earth. Even on the border, where the best men were bad, they were the worst. Deering was yet drunk, but Girty had recovered somewhat from the effects of the rum he had absorbed. The former rolled his big eyes and nodded his shaggy head. He was passing judgment, from his point of view, on the fine points of the girl.

"She cer'aintly is," he declared with a grin. "She's a little beauty. Beats any I ever seen!"

Jim Girty stroked his sharp chin with dirty fingers. His yellow eyes, his burnt saffron skin, his hooked nose, his thin lips—all his evil face seemed to shine with an evil triumph. To look at him was painful. To have him gaze at her was enough to drive any woman mad.

Dark stains spotted the bright frills of his gaudy dress, his buckskin coat and leggins, and dotted his white eagle plumes. Dark stains, horribly suggestive, covered him from head to foot. Blood stains! The innocent blood of Christians crimsoned his renegade's body, and every dark red blotch cried murder.

"Girl, I burned the Village of Peace to git you," growled Girty. "Come here!"

With a rude grasp that tore open her dress, exposing her beautiful white shoulder and bosom, the ruffian pulled her toward him. His face was transfixed with a fierce joy, a brutal passion.

Deering looked on with a drunken grin, while his renegade friend hugged the almost dying girl. The Indians paced the glade with short strides like leashed tigers. The young missionary lay on the moss with closed eyes. He could not endure the sight of Nell in Girty's arms.

No one noticed Wingenund. He stood back a little, half screened by drooping branches. Once again the chief's dark eyes gleamed, his head turned a trifle aside, and, standing in the statuesque position habitual with him when resting, he listened, as one who hears mysterious sounds. Suddenly his keen glance was riveted on the ferns above the low cliff. He had seen their graceful heads quivering. Then two blinding sheets of flame burst from the ferns.

Spang! Spang!

The two rifle reports thundered through the glade. Two Indians staggered and fell in their tracks—dead without a cry.

A huge yellow body, spread out like a panther in his spring, descended with a crash upon Deering and Girty. The girl fell away from the renegade as he went down with a shrill screech, dragging Deering with him. Instantly began a terrific, whirling, wrestling struggle.

A few feet farther down the cliff another yellow body came crashing down to alight with a thud, to bound erect, to rush forward swift as a leaping deer. The two remaining Indians had only time to draw their weapons before this lithe, threatening form whirled upon them. Shrill cries, hoarse yells, the clash of steel and dull blows mingled together. One savage went down, twisted over, writhed and lay still. The other staggered, warded off lightninglike blows until one passed under his guard, and crashed dully on his head. Then he reeled, rose again, but only to have his skull cloven by a bloody tomahawk.

The victor darted toward the whirling mass.

"Lew, shake him loose! Let him go!" yelled Jonathan Zane, swinging his bloody weapon.

High above Zane's cry, Deering's shouts and curses, Girty's shrieks of fear and fury, above the noise of wrestling bodies and dull blows, rose a deep booming roar.

It was Wetzel's awful cry of vengeance.

"Shake him loose," yelled Jonathan.

Baffled, he ran wildly around the wrestlers. Time and time again his gory tomahawk was raised only to be lowered. He found no opportunity to strike. Girty's ghastly countenance gleamed at him from the whirl of legs, and arms and bodies. Then Wetzel's dark face, lighted by merciless eyes, took its place, and that gave way to Deering's broad features. The men being clad alike in buckskin, and their motions so rapid, prevented Zane from lending a helping hand.

Suddenly Deering was propelled from the mass as if by a catapult. His body straightened as it came down with a heavy thud. Zane pounced upon it with catlike quickness. Once more he swung aloft the bloody hatchet; then once more he lowered it, for there was no need to strike. The renegade's side was torn open from shoulder to hip. A deluge of blood poured out upon the moss. Deering choked, a bloody froth formed on his lips. His fingers clutched at nothing. His eyes rolled violently and then were fixed in an awful stare.

The girl lying so quiet in the woods near the old hut was avenged!

Jonathan turned again to Wetzel and Girty, not with any intention to aid the hunter, but simply to witness the end of the struggle.

Without the help of the powerful Deering, how pitifully weak was the Deathshead of the frontier in the hands of the Avenger!

Jim Girty's tomahawk was thrown in one direction and his knife in another. He struggled vainly in the iron grip that held him.

Wetzel rose to his feet clutching the renegade. With his left arm, which had been bared in the fight, he held Girty by the front of his buckskin shirt, and dragged him to that tree which stood alone in the glade. He pushed him against it, and held him there.

The white dog leaped and snarled around the prisoner.

Girty's hands pulled and tore at the powerful arm which forced him hard against the beech. It was a brown arm, and huge with its bulging, knotted, rigid muscles. A mighty arm, strong as the justice which ruled it.

"Girty, thy race is run!" Wetzel's voice cut the silence like a steel whip.

The terrible, ruthless smile, the glittering eyes of doom seemed literally to petrify the renegade.

The hunter's right arm rose slowly. The knife in his hand quivered as if with eagerness. The long blade, dripping with Deering's blood, pointed toward the hilltop.

"Look thar! See 'em! Thar's yer friends!" cried Wetzel.

On the dead branches of trees standing far above the hilltop, were many great, dark birds. They sat motionless as if waiting.

"Buzzards! Buzzards!" hissed Wetzel.

Girty's ghastly face became an awful thing to look upon. No living countenance ever before expressed such fear, such horror, such agony. He foamed at the mouth, he struggled, he writhed. With a terrible fascination he watched that quivering, dripping blade, now poised high.

Wetzel's arm swung with the speed of a shooting star. He drove the blade into Girty's groin, through flesh and bone, hard and fast into the tree. He nailed the renegade to the beech, there to await his lingering doom.

"Ah-h! Ah-h! Ah-h!" shrieked Girty, in cries of agony. He fumbled and pulled at the haft of the knife, but could not loosen it. He beat his breast, he tore his hair. His screams were echoed from the hilltop as if in mockery.

The white dog stood near, his hair bristling, his teeth snapping.

The dark birds sat on the dead branches above the hilltop, as if waiting for their feast.

CHAPTER 28

ZANE TURNED AND CUT THE YOUNG MISSIONARY'S BONDS. JIM RAN TO where Nell was lying on the ground, and tenderly raised her head, calling to her that they were saved. Zane bathed the girl's pale face. Presently she sighed and opened her eyes.

Then Zane looked from the statuelike form of Wingenund to the motionless figure of Wetzel. The chief stood erect with his eyes on the distant hills. Wetzel remained with folded arms, his cold eyes fixed upon the writhing, moaning renegade.

"Lew, look here," said Zane, unhesitatingly, and pointed toward the chief.

Wetzel quivered as if sharply stung; the cold glitter in his eyes changed to lurid fire. With upraised tomahawk he bounded across the brook.

"Lew, wait a minute!" yelled Zane.

"Wetzel! wait, wait!" cried Jim, grasping the hunter's arm; but the latter flung him off, as the wind tosses a straw.

"Wetzel, wait, for God's sake, wait!" screamed Nell. She had risen at Zane's call, and now saw the deadly resolve in the hunter's eyes. Fearlessly she flung herself in front of him; bravely she risked her life before his mad rush; frantically she threw her arms around him and clung to his hands desperately.

Wetzel halted; frenzied as he was at the sight of his foe, he could not hurt a woman.

"Girl, let go!" he panted, and his broad breast heaved.

"No, no, no! Listen, Wetzel, you must not kill the chief. He is a friend."

"He is my great foe!"

"Listen, oh! please listen!" pleaded Nell. "He warned me to flee from Girty; he offered to guide us to Fort Henry. He has saved my life. For my sake, Wetzel, do not kill him! Don't let me be the cause of his murder! Wetzel, Wetzel, lower your arm, drop your hatchet. For pity's sake do not spill more blood. Wingenund is a Christian!"

Wetzel stepped back breathing heavily. His white face resembled chiseled marble. With those little hands at his breast he hesitated in front of the chief he had hunted for so many long years.

"Would you kill a Christian?" pleaded Nell, her voice sweet and earnest.

"I reckon not, but this Injun ain't one," replied Wetzel slowly.

"Put away your hatchet. Let me have it. Listen, and I will tell you, after thanking you for this rescue. Do you know of my marriage? Come, please listen! Forget for a moment your enmity. Oh! you must be merciful! Brave men are always merciful!"

"Injun, are you a Christian?" hissed Wetzel.

"Oh! I know he is! I know he is!" cried Nell, still standing between Wetzel and the chief.

Wingenund spoke no word. He did not move. His falcon eyes gazed tranquilly at his white foe. Christian or pagan, he would not speak one word to save his life.

"Oh! tell him you are a Christian," cried Nell, running to the chief.

"Yellow-hair, the Delaware is true to his race."

As he spoke gently to Nell a noble dignity shone upon his dark face.

"Injun, my back bears the scars of your braves' whips," hissed Wetzel, once more advancing.

"Deathwind, your scars are deep, but the Delaware's are deeper," came the calm reply. "Wingenund's heart bears two scars. His son lies under the moss and ferns; Deathwind killed him; Deathwind alone knows his grave. Wingenund's daughter, the delight of his waning years, freed the Delaware's great foe, and betrayed her father. Can the Christian God tell Wingenund of his child?"

Wetzel shook like a tree in a storm. Justice cried out in the Indian's deep voice. Wetzel fought for mastery of himself.

"Delaware, your daughter lays there, with her lover," said Wetzel firmly, and pointed into the spring.

"Ugh!" exclaimed the Indian, bending over the dark pool. He looked long into its murky depths. Then he thrust his arm down into the brown water.

"Deathwind tells no lie," said the chief, calmly, and pointed toward Girty. The renegade had ceased struggling, his head was bowed upon his breast. "The white serpent has stung the Delaware."

"What does it mean?" cried Jim.

"Your brother Joe and Whispering Winds lie in the spring," answered Jonathan Zane. "Girty murdered them, and Wetzel buried the two there."

"Oh, is it true?" cried Nell.

"True, lass," whispered Jim, brokenly, holding out his arms to her. Indeed, he needed her strength as much as she needed his. The girl gave one shuddering glance at the spring, and then hid her face on her husband's shoulder.

"Delaware, we are sworn foes," cried Wetzel.

"Wingenund asks no mercy."

"Are you a Christian?"

"Wingenund is true to his race."

"Delaware, begone! Take these weapons an' go. When your shadow falls shortest on the ground, Deathwind starts on your trail."

"Deathwind is the great white chief; he is the great Indian foe; he is as sure as the panther in his leap; as swift as the wild goose in his northern flight. Wingenund never felt fear." The chieftain's sonorous reply rolled through the quiet glade. "If Deathwind thirsts for Wingenund's blood, let him spill it now, for when the Delaware goes into the forest his trail will fade."

"Begone!" roared Wetzel. The fever for blood was once more rising within him.

The chief picked up some weapons of the dead Indians, and with haughty stride stalked from the glade.

"Oh, Wetzel, thank you, I knew——" Nell's voice broke as she faced the hunter. She recoiled from this changed man.

"Come, we'll go," said Jonathan Zane. "I'll guide you to Fort Henry." He lifted the pack, and led Nell and Jim out of the glade.

They looked back once to picture forever in their minds the lovely spot with its ghastly quiet bodies, the dark, haunting spring, the renegade nailed to the tree, and the tall figure of Wetzel as he watched his shadow on the ground.

~

WHEN WETZEL ALSO HAD GONE, ONLY TWO LIVING CREATURES remained in the glade—the doomed renegade, and the white dog. The gaunt beast watched the man with hungry, mad eyes.

A long moan wailed through the forest. It swelled mournfully on the air, and died away. The doomed man heard it. He raised his ghastly face; his dulled senses seemed to revive. He gazed at the stiffening bodies of the Indians, at the gory corpse of Deering, at the savage eyes of the dog.

Suddenly life seemed to surge strong within him.

"Hell's fire! I'm not done fer yet," he gasped. "This damned knife can't kill me; I'll pull it out."

He worked at the heavy knife hilt. Awful curses passed his lips, but the blade did not move. Retribution had spoken his doom.

Suddenly he saw a dark shadow moving along the sunlit ground. It swept past him. He looked up to see a great bird with wide wings sailing far above. He saw another still higher, and then a third. He looked at the hilltop. The quiet, black birds had taken wing. They were floating slowly, majestically upward. He watched their graceful flight. How easily they swooped in wide circles. He remembered that they had fascinated him when a boy, long, long ago, when he had a home. Where was that home? He had one once. Ah! the long, cruel years have rolled back. A youth blotted out by evil returned. He saw a little cottage, he saw the old Virginia homestead, he saw his brothers and his mother.

"Ah-h!" A cruel agony tore his heart. He leaned hard against the knife. With the pain the present returned, but the past remained. All his youth, all his manhood flashed before him. The long, bloody, merciless years faced him, and his crimes crushed upon him with awful might.

Suddenly a rushing sound startled him. He saw a great bird swoop down and graze the tree tops. Another followed, and another, and then a flock of them. He saw their gray, spotted breasts and hooked beaks.

"Buzzards," he muttered, darkly eyeing the dead savages. The carrion birds were swooping to their feast.

"By God! He's nailed me fast for buzzards!" he screamed in sudden, awful frenzy. "Nailed fast! Ah-h! Ah-h! Ah-h! Eaten alive by buzzards! Ah-h! Ah-h! Ah-h!"

He shrieked until his voice failed, and then he gasped.

Again the buzzards swooped overhead, this time brushing the leaves. One, a great grizzled bird, settled upon a limb of the giant oak, and stretched its long neck. Another alighted beside him. Others sailed round and round the dead tree top.

The leader arched his wings, and with a dive swooped into the glade. He alighted near Deering's dead body. He was a dark, uncanny bird, with long, scraggy, bare neck, a wreath of white, grizzled feathers, a cruel, hooked beak, and cold eyes.

The carrion bird looked around the glade, and put a great claw on the dead man's breast.

"Ah-h! Ah-h!" shrieked Girty. His agonized yell of terror and horror echoed mockingly from the wooded bluff.

The huge buzzard flapped his wings and flew away, but soon returned to his gruesome feast. His followers, made bold by their leader, floated down into the glade. Their black feathers shone in the sun. They hopped over the moss; they stretched their grizzled necks, and turned their heads sideways.

Girty was sweating blood. It trickled from his ghastly face. All the suffering and horror he had caused in all his long career was as nothing to that which then rended him. He, the renegade, the white Indian, the Deathshead of the frontier, panted and prayed for a merciful breath. He was exquisitely alive. He was human.

Presently the huge buzzard, the leader, raised his hoary head. He saw the man nailed to the tree. The bird bent his head wisely to one side, and then lightly lifted himself into the air. He sailed round the glade, over the fighting buzzards, over the spring, and over the doomed renegade. He flew out of the glade, and in again. He swooped close to Girty. His broad wings scarcely moved as he sailed along.

Girty tried to strike the buzzard as he sailed close by, but his arm fell useless. He tried to scream, but his voice failed.

Slowly the buzzard king sailed by and returned. Every time he swooped a little nearer, and bent his long, scraggy neck.

Suddenly he swooped down, light and swift as a hawk; his wide wings fanned the air; he poised under the tree, and then fastened sharp talons in the doomed man's breast.

CHAPTER 29

The fleeting human instinct of Wetzel had given way to the habit of years. His merciless quest for many days had been to kill the frontier fiend. Now that it had been accomplished, he turned his vengeance into its accustomed channel, and once more became the ruthless Indian-slayer.

A fierce, tingling joy surged through him as he struck the Delaware's trail. Wingenund had made little or no effort to conceal his tracks; he had gone northwest, straight as a crow flies, toward the Indian encampment. He had a start of sixty minutes, and it would require six hours of rapid traveling to gain the Delaware town.

"Reckon he'll make fer home," muttered Wetzel, following the trail with all possible speed.

The hunter's method of trailing an Indian was singular. Intuition played as great a part as sight. He seemed always to divine his victim's intention. Once on the trail he was as hard to shake off as a bloodhound. Yet he did not, by any means, always stick to the Indian's footsteps. With Wetzel the direction was of the greatest importance.

For half a mile he closely followed the Delaware's plainly marked trail. Then he stopped to take a quick survey of the forest before him. He abruptly left the trail, and, breaking into a run, went through the woods as fleetly and noiselessly as a deer, running for a quarter of a mile, when he stopped to listen. All seemed well, for he lowered his head, and walked

476

slowly along, examining the moss and leaves. Presently he came upon a little open space where the soil was a sandy loam. He bent over, then rose quickly. He had come upon the Indian's trail. Cautiously he moved forward, stopping every moment to listen. In all the close pursuits of his maturer years he had never been a victim of that most cunning of Indian tricks, an ambush. He relied solely on his ear to learn if foes were close by. The wild creatures of the forest were his informants. As soon as he heard any change in their twittering, humming or playing—whichever way they manifested their joy or fear of life—he became as hard to see, as difficult to hear as a creeping snake.

The Delaware's trail led to a rocky ridge and there disappeared. Wetzel made no effort to find the chief's footprints on the flinty ground, but halted a moment and studied the ridge, the lay of the land around, a ravine on one side, and a dark impenetrable forest on the other. He was calculating his chances of finding the Delaware's trail far on the other side. Indian woodcraft, subtle, wonderful as it may be, is limited to each Indian's ability. Savages, as well as other men, were born unequal. One might leave a faint trail through the forest, while another could be readily traced, and a third, more cunning and skillful than his fellows, have flown under the shady trees, for all the trail he left. But redmen followed the same methods of woodcraft from tradition, as Wetzel had learned after long years of study and experience.

And now, satisfied that he had divined the Delaware's intention, he slipped down the bank of the ravine, and once more broke into a run. He leaped lightly, sure-footed as a goat, from stone to stone, over fallen logs, and the brawling brook. At every turn of the ravine, at every open place, he stopped to listen.

Arriving on the other side of the ridge, he left the ravine and passed along the edge of the rising ground. He listened to the birds, and searched the grass and leaves. He found not the slightest indication of a trail where he had expected to find one. He retraced his steps patiently, carefully, scrutinizing every inch of the ground. But it was all in vain. Wingenund had begun to show his savage cunning. In his warrior days for long years no chief could rival him. His boast had always been that, when Wingenund sought to elude his pursuers, his trail faded among the moss and the ferns.

Wetzel, calm, patient, resourceful, deliberated a moment. The Delaware had not crossed this rocky ridge. He had been cunning enough to make his pursuer think such was his intention. The hunter hurried to the eastern end of the ridge for no other reason than apparently that course was the one the savage had the least reason to take. He advanced hurriedly because every moment was precious. Not a crushed blade of grass, a brushed leaf, an overturned pebble nor a snapped twig did he find. He saw that he was getting near to the side of the ridge where the Delaware's trail had abruptly ended. Ah! what was there? A twisted bit of fern, with the drops of dew brushed off. Bending beside the fern, Wetzel examined the grass; it was not crushed. A small plant with triangular leaves of dark green, lay under the fern. Breaking off one of these leaves, he exposed its lower side to the light. The fine, silvery hair of fuzz that grew upon the leaf had been crushed. Wetzel knew that an Indian could tread so softly as not to break the springy grass blades, but the under side of one of these leaves, if a man steps on it, always betrays his passage through the woods. To keen eyes this leaf showed that it had been bruised by a soft moccasin. Wetzel had located the trail, but was still ignorant of its direction. Slowly he traced the shaken ferns and bruised leaves down over the side of the ridge, and at last, near a stone, he found a moccasin-print in the moss. It pointed east. The Delaware was traveling in exactly the opposite direction to that which he should be going. He was, moreover, exercising wonderful sagacity in hiding his trail. This, however, did not trouble Wetzel, for if it took him a long time to find the trail, certainly the Delaware had expended as much, or more, in choosing hard ground, logs or rocks on which to tread.

Wetzel soon realized that his own cunning was matched. He trusted no more to his intuitive knowledge, but stuck close to the trail, as a hungry wolf holds to the scent of his quarry.

The Delaware trail led over logs, stones and hard-baked ground, up stony ravines and over cliffs. The wily chief used all of his old skill; he walked backward over moss and sand where his footprints showed plainly; he leaped wide fissures in stony ravines, and then jumped back again; he let himself down over ledges by branches; he crossed creeks and gorges by swinging himself into trees and climbing from one to another; he waded brooks where he found hard bottom, and avoided swampy, soft ground.

With dogged persistence and tenacity of purpose Wetzel stuck to this gradually fading trail. Every additional rod he was forced to go more slowly, and take more time in order to find any sign of his enemy's passage through the forests. One thing struck him forcibly. Wingenund was gradually circling to the southwest, a course that took him farther and farther from the Delaware encampment.

Slowly it dawned upon Wetzel that the chief could hardly have any reason for taking this circling course save that of pride and savage joy in misleading, in fooling the foe of the Delawares, in deliberately showing Deathwind that there was one Indian who could laugh at and loose him in the forests. To Wetzel this was bitter as gall. To be led a wild goose chase! His fierce heart boiled with fury. His dark, keen eyes sought the grass and moss with terrible earnestness. Yet in spite of the anger that increased to the white heat of passion, he became aware of some strange sensation creeping upon him. He remembered that the Delawares had offered his life. Slowly, like a shadow, Wetzel passed up and down the ridges, through the brown and yellow aisles of the forest, over the babbling brooks, out upon the golden-flecked fields—always close on the trail.

At last in an open part of the forest, where a fire had once swept away the brush and smaller timber, Wetzel came upon the spot where the Delaware's trail ended.

There in the soft, black ground was a moccasin-print. The forest was not dense; there was plenty of light; no logs, stones or trees were near, and yet over all that glade no further evidence of the Indian's trail was visible.

It faded there as the great chief had boasted it would.

Wetzel searched the burnt ground; he crawled on his hands and knees; again and again he went over the surroundings. The fact that one moccasin-print pointed west and the other east, showed that the Delaware had turned in his tracks, was the most baffling thing that had ever crossed the hunter in all his wild wanderings.

For the first time in many years he had failed. He took his defeat hard, because he had been successful for so long he thought himself almost infallible, and because the failure lost him the opportunity to kill his great foe. In his passion he cursed himself for being so weak as to let the prayer of a woman turn him from his life's purpose.

With bowed head and slow, dragging steps he made his way westward. The land was strange to him, but he knew he was going toward familiar ground. For a time he walked quietly, all the time the fierce fever in his veins slowly abating. Calm he always was, except when that unnatural lust for Indians' blood overcame him.

On the summit of a high ridge he looked around to ascertain his bearings. He was surprised to find he had traveled in a circle. A mile or so below him arose the great oak tree which he recognized as the landmark of Beautiful Spring. He found himself standing on the hill, under the very dead tree to which he had directed Girty's attention a few hours previous.

With the idea that he would return to the spring to scalp the dead Indians, he went directly toward the big oak tree. Once out of the forest a wide plain lay between him and the wooded knoll which marked the glade of Beautiful Spring. He crossed this stretch of verdant meadow-land, and entered the copse.

Suddenly he halted. His keen sense of the usual harmony of the forest, with its innumerable quiet sounds, had received a severe shock. He sank into the tall weeds and listened. Then he crawled a little farther. Doubt became certainty. A single note of an oriole warned him, and it needed not the quick notes of a catbird to tell him that near at hand, somewhere, was human life.

Once more Wetzel became a tiger. The hot blood leaped from his heart, firing all his veins and nerves. But calmly noiseless, certain, cold, deadly as a snake he began the familiar crawling method of stalking his game.

On, on under the briars and thickets, across the hollows full of yellow leaves, up over stony patches of ground to the fern-covered cliff overhanging the glade he glided—lithe, sinuous, a tiger in movement and in heart.

He parted the long, graceful ferns and gazed with glittering eyes down into the beautiful glade.

He saw not the shining spring nor the purple moss, nor the ghastly white bones—all that the buzzards had left of the dead—nor anything, save a solitary Indian standing erect in the glade.

There, within range of his rifle, was his great Indian foe, Wingenund.

Wetzel sank back into the ferns to still the furious exultations which almost consumed him during the moment when he marked his victim. He lay there breathing hard, gripping tightly his rifle, slowly mastering the passion that alone of all things might render his aim futile.

For him it was the third great moment of his life, the last of three moments in which the Indian's life had belonged to him. Once before he had seen that dark, powerful face over the sights of his rifle, and he could not shoot because his one shot must be for another. Again had that lofty, haughty figure stood before him, calm, disdainful, arrogant, and he yielded to a woman's prayer.

The Delaware's life was his to take, and he swore he would have it! He trembled in the ecstasy of his triumphant passion; his great muscles rippled and quivered, for the moment was entirely beyond his control. Then his passion calmed. Such power for vengeance had he that he could almost still the very beats of his heart to make sure and deadly his fatal aim. Slowly he raised himself; his eyes of cold fire glittered; slowly he raised the black rifle.

Wingenund stood erect in his old, grand pose, with folded arms, but his eyes, instead of being fixed on the distant hills, were lowered to the ground.

An Indian girl, cold as marble, lay at his feet. Her garments were wet, and clung to her slender form. Her sad face was frozen into an eternal rigidity.

By her side was a newly dug grave.

The bead on the front sight of the rifle had hardly covered the chief's dark face when Wetzel's eye took in these other details. He had been so absorbed in his purpose that he did not dream of the Delaware's reason for returning to the Beautiful Spring.

Slowly Wetzel's forefinger stiffened; slowly he lowered the black rifle.

Wingenund had returned to bury Whispering Winds.

Wetzel's teethe clenched, an awful struggle tore his heart. Slowly the rifle rose, wavered and fell. It rose again, wavered and fell. Something terrible was wrong with him; something awful was awakening in his soul.

Wingenund had not made a fool of him. The Delaware had led him a long chase, had given him the slip in the forest, not to boast of it, but to hurry back to give his daughter Christian burial.

Wingenund was a Christian!

Had he not been, once having cast his daughter from him, he would never have looked upon her face again.

Wingenund was true to his race, but he was a Christian.

Suddenly Wetzel's terrible temptation, his heart-racking struggle ceased. He lowered the long, black rifle. He took one last look at the chieftain's dark, powerful face.

Then the Avenger fled like a shadow through the forest.

CHAPTER 30

IT WAS LATE AFTERNOON AT FORT HENRY. THE RUDDY SUN HAD already sunk behind the wooded hill, and the long shadows of the trees lengthened on the green square in front of the fort.

Colonel Zane stood in his doorway watching the river with eager eyes. A few minutes before a man had appeared on the bank of the island and hailed. The colonel had sent his brother Jonathan to learn what was wanted. The latter had already reached the other shore in his flatboat, and presently the little boat put out again with the stranger seated at the stern.

"I thought, perhaps, it might be Wetzel," mused the colonel, "though I never knew of Lew's wanting a boat."

Jonathan brought the man across the river, and up the winding path to where Colonel Zane was waiting.

"Hello! It's young Christy!" exclaimed the colonel, jumping off the steps, and cordially extending his hand. "Glad to see you! Where's Williamson. How did you happen over here?"

"Captain Williamson and his men will make the river eight or ten miles above," answered Christy. "I came across to inquire about the young people who left the Village of Peace. Was glad to learn from Jonathan they got out all right."

"Yes, indeed, we're all glad. Come and sit down. Of course you'll stay over night. You look tired and worn. Well, no wonder, when you saw that Moravian massacre. You must tell me about it. I saw Sam Brady yesterday, and he spoke of seeing you over there. Sam told me a good deal. Ah! here's Jim now."

The young missionary came out of the open door, and the two young men greeted each other warmly.

"How is she?" asked Christy, when the first greetings had been exchanged.

"Nell's just beginning to get over the shock. She'll be glad to see you."

"Jonathan tells me you got married just before Girty came up with you at Beautiful Spring."

"Yes; it is true. In fact, the whole wonderful story is true, yet I cannot believe as yet. You look thin and haggard. When we last met you were well."

"That awful time pulled me down. I was an unwilling spectator of all that horrible massacre, and shall never get over it. I can still see the fiendish savages running about with the reeking scalps of their own people. I actually counted the bodies of forty-nine grown Christians and twenty-seven children. An hour after you left us the church was in ashes, and the next day I saw the burned bodies. Oh! the sickening horror of the scene! It haunts me! That monster Jim Girty killed fourteen Christians with his sledge-hammer."

"Did you hear of his death?" asked Colonel Zane.

"Yes, and a fitting end it was to the frontier 'Skull and Cross-bones'."

"It was like Wetzel to think of such a vengeance."

"Has Wetzel come in since?"

"No. Jonathan says he went after Wingenund, and there's no telling when he'll return."

"I hoped he would spare the Delaware."

"Wetzel spare an Indian!"

"But the chief was a friend. He surely saved the girl."

"I am sorry, too, because Wingenund was a fine Indian. But Wetzel is implacable."

"Here's Nell, and Mrs. Clarke too. Come out, both of you," cried Jim.

Nell appeared in the doorway with Colonel Zane's sister. The two girls came down the steps and greeted the young man. The bride's sweet face was white and thin, and there was a shadow in her eyes.

"I am so glad you got safely away from—from there," said Christy, earnestly.

"Tell me of Benny?" asked Nell, speaking softly.

"Oh, yes, I forgot. Why, Benny is safe and well. He was the only Christian Indian to escape the Christian massacre. Heckewelder hid him until it was all over. He is going to have the lad educated."

"Thank Heaven!" murmured Nell.

"And the missionaries?" inquired Jim, earnestly.

"Were all well when I left, except, of course, Young. He was dying. The others will remain out there, and try to get another hold, but I fear it's impossible."

"It is impossible, not because the Indian does not want Christianity, but because such white men as the Girty's rule. The beautiful Village of Peace owes its ruin to the renegades," said Colonel Zane impressively.

"Captain Williamson could have prevented the massacre," remarked Jim.

"Possibly. It was a bad place for him, and I think he was wrong not to try," declared the colonel.

"Hullo!" cried Jonathan Zane, getting up from the steps where he sat listening to the conversation.

A familiar soft-moccasined footfall sounded on the path. All turned to see Wetzel come slowly toward them. His buckskin hunting costume was ragged and worn. He looked tired and weary, but the dark eyes were calm.

It was the Wetzel whom they all loved.

They greeted him warmly. Nell gave him her hands, and smiled up at him.

"I'm so glad you've come home safe," she said.

"Safe an' sound, lass, an' glad to find you well," answered the hunter, as he leaned on his long rifle, looking from Nell to Colonel Zane's sister. "Betty, I allus gave you first place among border lasses, but here's one as could run you most any kind of a race," he said, with the rare smile which so warmly lighted his dark, stern face.

"Lew Wetzel making compliments! Well, of all things!" exclaimed the colonel's sister.

Jonathan Zane stood closely scanning Wetzel's features. Colonel Zane, observing his brother's close scrutiny of the hunter, guessed the cause, and said:

"Lew, tell us, did you see Wingenund over the sights of your rifle?"

"Yes," answered the hunter simply.

A chill seemed to strike the hearts of the listeners. That simple answer, coming from Wetzel, meant so much. Nell bowed her head sadly. Jim turned away biting his lip. Christy looked across the valley. Colonel Zane bent over and picked up some pebbles which he threw hard at the cabin wall. Jonathan Zane abruptly left the group, and went into the house.

But the colonel's sister fixed her large, black eyes on Wetzel's face.

"Well?" she asked, and her voice rang.

Wetzel was silent for a moment. He met her eyes with that old, inscrutable smile in his own. A slight shade flitted across his face.

"Betty, I missed him," he said, calmly, and, shouldering his long rifle, he strode away.

∼

NELL AND JIM WALKED ALONG THE BLUFF ABOVE THE RIVER. TWILIGHT was deepening. The red glow in the west was slowly darkening behind the boldly defined hills.

"So it's all settled, Jim, that we stay here," said Nell.

"Yes, dear. Colonel Zane has offered me work, and a church besides. We are very fortunate, and should be contented. I am happy because you're my wife, and yet I am sad when I think of—him. Poor Joe!"

"Don't you ever think we—we wronged him?" whispered Nell.

"No, he wished it. I think he knew how he would end. No, we did not wrong him; we loved him."

"Yes, I loved him—I loved you both," said Nell softly.

"Then let us always think of him as he would have wished."

"Think of him? Think of Joe? I shall never forget. In winter, spring and summer I shall remember him, but always most in autumn. For I shall see that beautiful glade with its gorgeous color and the dark, shaded spring where he lies asleep."

∼

THE YEARS ROLLED BY WITH THEIR CHANGING SEASONS; EVERY AUTUMN the golden flowers bloomed richly, and the colored leaves fell softly upon the amber moss in the glade of Beautiful Spring.

The Indians camped there no more; they shunned the glade and called it the Haunted Spring. They said the spirit of a white dog ran there at night, and the Wind-of-Death mourned over the lonely spot.

At long intervals an Indian chief of lofty frame and dark, powerful face stalked into the glade to stand for many moments silent and motionless.

And sometimes at twilight when the red glow of the sun had faded to gray, a stalwart hunter slipped like a shadow out of the thicket, and leaned upon a long, black rifle while he gazed sadly into the dark spring, and listened to the sad murmur of the waterfall. The twilight deepened while he stood motionless. The leaves fell into the water with a soft splash, a whippoorwill caroled his melancholy song.

From the gloom of the forest came a low sigh which swelled thrillingly upon the quiet air, and then died away like the wailing of the night wind.

Quiet reigned once more over the dark, murky grave of the boy who gave his love and his life to the wilderness.

THE LAST TRAIL

CONTENTS

CHAPTER I

Twilight of a certain summer day, many years ago, shaded softly down over the wild Ohio valley bringing keen anxiety to a traveler on the lonely river trail. He had expected to reach Fort Henry with his party on this night, thus putting a welcome end to the long, rough, hazardous journey through the wilderness; but the swift, on-coming dusk made it imperative to halt. The narrow, forest-skirted trail, difficult to follow in broad daylight, apparently led into gloomy aisles in the woods. His guide had abandoned him that morning, making excuse that his services were no longer needed; his teamster was new to the frontier, and, altogether, the situation caused him much uneasiness.

"I wouldn't so much mind another night in camp, if the guide had not left us," he said in a low tone to the teamster.

That worthy shook his shaggy head, and growled while he began unhitching the horses.

"Uncle," said a young man, who had clambered out from the wagon, "we must be within a few miles of Fort Henry."

"How d'ye know we're near the fort?" interrupted the teamster, "or safe, either, fer thet matter? I don't know this country."

"The guide assured me we could easily make Fort Henry by sundown."

"Thet guide! I tell ye, Mr. Sheppard——"

"Not so loud. Do not alarm my daughter," cautioned the man who had been called Sheppard.

491

"Did ye notice anythin' queer about thet guide?" asked the teamster, lowering his voice. "Did ye see how oneasy he was last night? Did it strike ye he left us in a hurry, kind of excited like, in spite of his offhand manner?"

"Yes, he acted odd, or so it seemed to me," replied Sheppard. "How about you, Will?"

"Now that I think of it, I believe he was queer. He behaved like a man who expected somebody, or feared something might happen. I fancied, however, that it was simply the manner of a woodsman."

"Wal, I hev my opinion," said the teamster, in a gruff whisper. "Ye was in a hurry to be a-goin', an' wouldn't take no advice. The fur-trader at Fort Pitt didn't give this guide Jenks no good send off. Said he wasn't well-known round Pitt, 'cept he could handle a knife some."

"What is your opinion?" asked Sheppard, as the teamster paused.

"Wal, the valley below Pitt is full of renegades, outlaws an' hoss-thieves. The redskins ain't so bad as they used to be, but these white fellers are wusser'n ever. This guide Jenks might be in with them, that's all. Mebbe I'm wrong. I hope so. The way he left us looks bad."

"We won't borrow trouble. If we have come all this way without seeing either Indian or outlaw—in fact, without incident—I feel certain we can perform the remainder of the journey in safety." Then Mr. Sheppard raised his voice. "Here, Helen, you lazy girl, come out of that wagon. We want some supper. Will, you gather some firewood, and we'll soon give this gloomy little glen a more cheerful aspect."

As Mr. Sheppard turned toward the canvas-covered wagon a girl leaped lightly down beside him. She was nearly as tall as he.

"Is this Fort Henry?" she asked, cheerily, beginning to dance around him. "Where's the inn? I'm *so* hungry. How glad I am to get out of that wagon! I'd like to run. Isn't this a lonesome, lovely spot?"

A camp-fire soon crackled with hiss and sputter, and fragrant wood-smoke filled the air. Steaming kettle, and savory steaks of venison cheered the hungry travelers, making them forget for the time the desertion of their guide and the fact that they might be lost. The last glow faded entirely out of the western sky. Night enveloped the forest, and the little glade was a bright spot in the gloom.

The flickering light showed Mr. Sheppard to be a well-preserved old man with gray hair and ruddy, kindly face. The nephew had a boyish, frank expression. The girl was a splendid specimen of womanhood. Her large, laughing eyes were as dark as the shadows beneath the trees.

Suddenly a quick start on Helen's part interrupted the merry flow of conversation. She sat bolt upright with half-averted face.

"Cousin, what is the matter?" asked Will, quickly.

Helen remained motionless.

"My dear," said Mr. Sheppard sharply.

"I heard a footstep," she whispered, pointing with trembling finger toward the impenetrable blackness beyond the camp-fire.

All could hear a soft patter on the leaves. Then distinct footfalls broke the silence.

The tired teamster raised his shaggy head and glanced fearfully around the glade. Mr. Sheppard and Will gazed doubtfully toward the foliage; but Helen did not change her position. The travelers appeared stricken by the silence and solitude of the place. The faint hum of insects, and the low moan of the night wind, seemed accentuated by the almost painful stillness.

"A panther, most likely," suggested Sheppard, in a voice which he intended should be reassuring. "I saw one to-day slinking along the trail."

"I'd better get my gun from the wagon," said Will.

"How dark and wild it is here!" exclaimed Helen nervously. "I believe I was frightened. Perhaps I fancied it—there! Again—listen. Ah!"

Two tall figures emerged from the darkness into the circle of light, and with swift, supple steps gained the camp-fire before any of the travelers had time to move. They were Indians, and the brandishing of their tomahawks proclaimed that they were hostile.

"Ugh!" grunted the taller savage, as he looked down upon the defenseless, frightened group.

As the menacing figures stood in the glare of the fire gazing at the party with shifty eyes, they presented a frightful appearance. Fierce lineaments, all the more so because of bars of paint, the hideous, shaven heads adorned with tufts of hair holding a single feather, sinewy, copper-colored limbs suggestive of action and endurance, the general aspect of untamed ferocity, appalled the travelers and chilled their blood.

Grunts and chuckles manifested the satisfaction with which the Indians fell upon the half-finished supper. They caused it to vanish with astonishing celerity, and resembled wolves rather than human beings in their greediness.

Helen looked timidly around as if hoping to see those who would aid, and the savages regarded her with ill humor. A movement on the part of any member of the group caused muscular hands to steal toward the tomahawks.

Suddenly the larger savage clutched his companion's knee. Then lifting his hatchet, shook it with a significant gesture in Sheppard's face, at the same time putting a finger on his lips to enjoin silence. Both Indians became statuesque in their immobility. They crouched in an attitude of listening, with heads bent on one side, nostrils dilated, and mouths open.

One, two, three moments passed. The silence of the forest appeared to be unbroken; but ears as keen as those of a deer had detected some sound. The larger savage dropped noiselessly to the ground, where he lay stretched out with his ear to the ground. The other remained immovable; only his beady eyes gave signs of life, and these covered every point.

Finally the big savage rose silently, pointed down the dark trail, and strode out of the circle of light. His companion followed close at his heels. The two disappeared in the black shadows like specters, as silently as they had come.

"Well!" breathed Helen.

"I am immensely relieved!" exclaimed Will.

"What do you make of such strange behavior?" Sheppard asked of the teamster.

"I'spect they got wind of somebody; most likely thet guide, an'll be back again. If they ain't, it's because they got switched off by some signs or tokens, skeered, perhaps, by the scent of the wind."

Hardly had he ceased speaking when again the circle of light was invaded by stalking forms.

"I thought so! Here comes the skulkin' varmints," whispered the teamster.

But he was wrong. A deep, calm voice spoke the single word: "Friends."

Two men in the brown garb of woodsmen approached. One approached the travelers; the other remained in the background, leaning upon a long, black rifle.

Thus exposed to the glare of the flames, the foremost woodsman presented a singularly picturesque figure. His costume was the fringed buckskins of the border. Fully six feet tall, this lithe-limbed young giant had something of the wild, free grace of the Indian in his posture.

He surveyed the wondering travelers with dark, grave eyes.

"Did the reddys do any mischief?" he asked.

"No, they didn't harm us," replied Sheppard. "They ate our supper, and slipped off into the woods without so much as touching one of us. But, indeed, sir, we are mighty glad to see you."

Will echoed this sentiment, and Helen's big eyes were fastened upon the stranger in welcome and wonder.

"We saw your fire blazin' through the twilight, an' came up just in time to see the Injuns make off."

"Might they not hide in the bushes and shoot us?" asked Will, who had listened to many a border story at Fort Pitt. "It seems as if we'd make good targets in this light."

The gravity of the woodsman's face relaxed.

"You will pursue them?" asked Helen.

"They've melted into the night-shadows long ago," he replied. "Who was your guide?"

"I hired him at Fort Pitt. He left us suddenly this morning. A big man, with black beard and bushy eyebrows. A bit of his ear had been shot or cut out," Sheppard replied.

"Jenks, one of Bing Legget's border-hawks."

"You have his name right. And who may Bing Legget be?"

"He's an outlaw. Jenks has been tryin' to lead you into a trap. Likely he expected those Injuns to show up a day or two ago. Somethin' went wrong with the plan, I reckon. Mebbe he was waitin' for five Shawnees, an' mebbe he'll never see three of 'em again."

Something suggestive, cold, and grim, in the last words did not escape the listeners.

"How far are we from Fort Henry?" asked Sheppard.

"Eighteen miles as a crow flies; longer by trail."

"Treachery!" exclaimed the old man. "We were no more than that this morning. It is indeed fortunate that you found us. I take it you are from Fort Henry, and will guide us there? I am an old friend of Colonel Zane's. He will appreciate any kindness you may show us. Of course you know him?"

"I am Jonathan Zane."

Sheppard suddenly realized that he was facing the most celebrated scout on the border. In Revolutionary times Zane's fame had extended even to the far Atlantic Colonies.

"And your companion?" asked Sheppard with keen interest. He guessed what might be told. Border lore coupled Jonathan Zane with a strange and terrible character, a border Nemesis, a mysterious, shadowy, elusive man, whom few pioneers ever saw, but of whom all knew.

"Wetzel," answered Zane.

With one accord the travelers gazed curiously at Zane's silent companion. In the dim background of the glow cast by the fire, he stood a gigantic figure, dark, quiet, and yet with something intangible in his shadowy outline.

Suddenly he appeared to merge into the gloom as if he really were a phantom. A warning, "Hist!" came from the bushes.

With one swift kick Zane scattered the camp-fire.

The travelers waited with bated breaths. They could hear nothing save the beating of their own hearts; they could not even see each other. ·

"Better go to sleep," came in Zane's calm voice. What a relief it was! "We'll keep watch, an' at daybreak guide you to Fort Henry."

CHAPTER 2

COLONEL ZANE, A RUGGED, STALWART PIONEER, WITH A STRONG, DARK face, sat listening to his old friend's dramatic story. At its close a genial smile twinkled in his fine dark eyes.

"Well, well, Sheppard, no doubt it was a thrilling adventure to you," he said. "It might have been a little more interesting, and doubtless would, had I not sent Wetzel and Jonathan to look you up."

"You did? How on earth did you know I was on the border? I counted much on the surprise I should give you."

"My Indian runners leave Fort Pitt ahead of any travelers, and acquaint me with particulars."

"I remembered a fleet-looking Indian who seemed to be asking for information about us, when we arrived at Fort Pitt. I am sorry I did not take the fur-trader's advice in regard to the guide. But I was in such a hurry to come, and didn't feel able to bear the expense of a raft or boat that we might come by river. My nephew brought considerable gold, and I all my earthly possessions."

"All's well that ends well," replied Colonel Zane cheerily. "But we must thank Providence that Wetzel and Jonathan came up in the nick of time."

"Indeed, yes. I'm not likely to forget those fierce savages. How they slipped off into the darkness! I wonder if Wetzel pursued them? He disappeared last night, and we did not see him again. In fact we hardly had a fair look at him. I question if I should recognize him now, unless by his great stature."

"He was ahead of Jonathan on the trail. That is Wetzel's way. In times of danger he is seldom seen, yet is always near. But come, let us go out and look around. I am running up a log cabin which will come in handy for you."

They passed out into the shade of pine and maples. A winding path led down a gentle slope. On the hillside under a spreading tree a throng of bearded pioneers, clad in faded buckskins and wearing white-ringed coonskin caps, were erecting a log cabin.

"Life here on the border is keen, hard, invigorating," said Colonel Zane. "I tell you, George Sheppard, in spite of your gray hair and your pretty daughter, you have come out West because you want to live among men who do things."

"Colonel, I won't gainsay I've still got hot blood," replied Sheppard; "but I came to Fort Henry for land. My old home in Williamsburg has fallen into ruin together with the fortunes of my family. I brought my daughter and my nephew because I wanted them to take root in new soil."

"Well, George, right glad we are to have you. Where are your sons? I remember them, though 'tis sixteen long years since I left old Williamsburg."

"Gone. The Revolution took my sons. Helen is the last of the family."

"Well, well, indeed that's hard. Independence has cost you colonists as big a price as border-freedom has us pioneers. Come, old friend, forget the past. A new life begins for you here, and it will be one which gives you much. See, up goes a cabin; that will soon be your home."

Sheppard's eye marked the sturdy pioneers and a fast diminishing pile of white-oak logs.

"Ho-heave!" cried a brawny foreman.

A dozen stout shoulders sagged beneath a well-trimmed log.

"Ho-heave!" yelled the foreman.

"See, up she goes," cried the colonel, "and to-morrow night she'll shed rain."

They walked down a sandy lane bounded on the right by a wide, green clearing, and on the left by a line of chestnuts and maples, outposts of the thick forests beyond.

"Yours is a fine site for a house," observed Sheppard, taking in the clean-trimmed field that extended up the hillside, a brook that splashed clear and noisy over the stones to tarry in a little grass-bound lake which forced water through half-hollowed logs into a spring house.

"I think so; this is the fourth time I've put up a' cabin on this land," replied the colonel.

"How's that?"

"The redskins are keen to burn things."

Sheppard laughed at the pioneer's reply. "It's not difficult, Colonel Zane, to understand why Fort Henry has stood all these years, with you as its leader. Certainly the location for your cabin is the finest in the settlement. What a view!"

High upon a bluff overhanging the majestic, slow-winding Ohio, the colonel's cabin afforded a commanding position from which to view the picturesque valley. Sheppard's eye first caught the outline of the huge, bold, time-blackened fort which frowned protectingly over surrounding log-cabins; then he saw the wide-sweeping river with its verdant islands, golden, sandy bars, and willow-bordered shores, while beyond, rolling pastures of wavy grass merging into green forests that swept upward with slow swell until lost in the dim purple of distant mountains.

"Sixteen years ago I came out of the thicket upon yonder bluff, and saw this valley. I was deeply impressed by its beauty, but more by its wonderful promise."

"Were you alone?"

"I and my dog. There had been a few white men before me on the river; but I was the first to see this glorious valley from the bluff. Now, George, I'll let you have a hundred acres of well-cleared land. The soil is so rich you can raise two crops in one season. With some stock, and a few good hands, you'll soon be a busy man."

"I didn't expect so much land; I can't well afford to pay for it."

"Talk to me of payment when the farm yields an income. Is this young nephew of yours strong and willing?"

"He is, and has gold enough to buy a big farm."

"Let him keep his money, and make a comfortable home for some good lass. We marry our young people early out here. And your daughter, George, is she fitted for this hard border life?"

"Never fear for Helen."

"The brunt of this pioneer work falls on our women. God bless them, how heroic they've been! The life here is rough for a man, let alone a woman. But it is a man's game. We need girls, girls who will bear strong men. Yet I am always saddened when I see one come out on the border."

"I think I knew what I was bringing Helen to, and she didn't flinch," said Sheppard, somewhat surprised at the tone in which the colonel spoke.

"No one knows until he has lived on the border. Well, well, all this is discouraging to you. Ah! here is Miss Helen with my sister."

The colonel's fine, dark face lost its sternness, and brightened with a smile.

"I hope you rested well after your long ride."

"I am seldom tired, and I have been made most comfortable. I thank you and your sister," replied the girl, giving Colonel Zane her hand, and including both him and his sister in her grateful glance.

The colonel's sister was a slender, handsome young woman, whose dark beauty showed to most effective advantage by the contrast with her companion's fair skin, golden hair, and blue eyes.

Beautiful as was Helen Sheppard, it was her eyes that held Colonel Zane irresistibly. They were unusually large, of a dark purple-blue that changed, shaded, shadowed with her every thought.

"Come, let us walk," Colonel Zane said abruptly, and, with Mr. Sheppard, followed the girls down the path. He escorted them to the fort, showed a long room with little squares cut in the rough-hewn logs, many bullet holes, fire-charred timbers, and dark stains, terribly suggestive of the pain and heroism which the defense of that rude structure had cost.

Under Helen's eager questioning Colonel Zane yielded to his weakness for story-telling, and recited the history of the last siege of Fort Henry; how the renegade Girty swooped down upon the settlement with hundreds of Indians and British soldiers; how for three days of whistling bullets, flaming arrows, screeching demons, fire, smoke, and attack following attack, the brave defenders stood at their posts, there to die before yielding.

"Grand!" breathed Helen, and her eyes glowed. "It was then Betty Zane ran with the powder? Oh! I've heard the story."

"Let my sister tell you of that," said the colonel, smiling.

"You! Was it you?" And Helen's eyes glowed brighter with the light of youth's glory in great deeds.

"My sister has been wedded and widowed since then," said Colonel Zane, reading in Helen's earnest scrutiny of his sister's calm, sad face a wonder if this quiet woman could be the fearless and famed Elizabeth Zane.

Impulsively Helen's hand closed softly over her companion's. Out of the girlish sympathetic action a warm friendship was born.

"I imagine things do happen here," said Mr. Sheppard, hoping to hear more from Colonel Zane.

The colonel smiled grimly.

"Every summer during fifteen years has been a bloody one on the border. The sieges of Fort Henry, and Crawford's defeat, the biggest things we ever knew out here, are matters of history; of course you are familiar with them. But the numberless Indian forays and attacks, the women who have been carried into captivity by renegades, the murdered farmers, in fact, ceaseless war never long directed at any point, but carried on the entire length of the river, are matters known only to the pioneers. Within five miles of Fort Henry I can show you where the laurel bushes grow three feet high over the ashes of two settlements, and many a clearing where some unfortunate pioneer had staked his claim and thrown up a log cabin, only to die fighting for his wife and children. Between here and Fort Pitt there is only one settlement, Yellow Creek, and most of its inhabitants are survivors of abandoned villages farther up the river. Last summer we had the Moravian Massacre, the blackest, most inhuman deed ever committed. Since then Simon Girty and his bloody redskins have lain low."

"You must always have had a big force," said Sheppard.

"We've managed always to be strong enough, though there never were a large number of men here. During the last siege I had only forty in the fort, counting men, women and boys. But I had pioneers and women who could handle a rifle, and the best bordermen on the frontier."

"Do you make a distinction between pioneers and bordermen?" asked Sheppard.

"Indeed, yes. I am a pioneer; a borderman is an Indian hunter, or scout. For years my cabins housed Andrew Zane, Sam and John McCollock, Bill Metzar, and John and Martin Wetzel, all of whom are dead. Not one saved his scalp. Fort Henry is growing; it has pioneers, rivermen, soldiers, but only two bordermen. Wetzel and Jonathan are the only ones we have left of those great men."

"They must be old," mused Helen, with a dreamy glow still in her eyes.

"Well, Miss Helen, not in years, as you mean. Life here is old in experience; few pioneers, and no bordermen, live to a great age. Wetzel is about forty, and my brother Jonathan still a young man; but both are old in border lore."

Earnestly, as a man who loves his subject, Colonel Zane told his listeners of these two most prominent characters of the border. Sixteen years previously, when but boys in years, they had cast in their lot with his, and journeyed over the Virginian Mountains, Wetzel to devote his life to the vengeful calling he had chosen, and Jonathan to give rein to an adventurous spirit and love of the wilds. By some wonderful chance, by cunning, woodcraft, or daring, both men had lived through the years of border warfare which had brought to a close the careers of all their contemporaries.

For many years Wetzel preferred solitude to companionship; he roamed the wilderness in pursuit of Indians, his life-long foes, and seldom appeared at the settlement except to bring news of an intended raid of the savages. Jonathan also spent much time alone in the woods, or scouting along the river. But of late years a friendship had ripened between the two bordermen. Mutual interest had brought them together on the trail of a noted renegade, and when, after many long days of patient watching and persistent tracking, the outlaw paid an awful penalty for his bloody deeds, these lone and silent men were friends.

Powerful in build, fleet as deer, fearless and tireless, Wetzel's peculiar bloodhound sagacity, ferocity, and implacability, balanced by Jonathan's keen intelligence and judgment caused these bordermen to become the bane of redmen and renegades. Their fame increased with each succeeding summer, until now the people of the settlement looked upon wonderful deeds of strength and of woodcraft as a matter of course, rejoicing in the power and skill with which these men were endowed.

By common consent the pioneers attributed any mysterious deed, from the finding of a fat turkey on a cabin doorstep, to the discovery of a savage scalped and pulled from his ambush near a settler's spring, to Wetzel and Jonathan. All the more did they feel sure of this conclusion because the bordermen never spoke of their deeds. Sometimes a pioneer living on the outskirts of the settlement would be awakened in the morning by a single rifle shot, and on peering out would see a dead Indian lying almost across his doorstep, while beyond, in the dim, gray mist, a tall figure stealing away. Often in the twilight on a summer evening, while fondling his children and enjoying his smoke after a hard day's labor in the fields, this same settler would see the tall, dark figure of Jonathan Zane step noiselessly out of a thicket, and learn that he must take his family and flee at once to the fort for safety. When a settler was murdered, his children carried into captivity by Indians, and the wife given over to the power of some brutal renegade, tragedies wofully frequent on the border, Wetzel and Jonathan took the trail alone. Many a white woman was returned alive and, sometimes, unharmed to her relatives; more than one maiden lived to be captured, rescued, and returned to her lover, while almost numberless were the bones of brutal redmen lying in the deep and gloomy woods, or bleaching on the plains, silent, ghastly reminders of the stern justice meted out by these two heroes.

"Such are my two bordermen, Miss Sheppard. The fort there, and all these cabins, would be only black ashes, save for them, and as for us, our wives and children—God only knows."

"Haven't they wives and children, too?" asked Helen.

"No," answered Colonel Zane, with his genial smile. "Such joys are not for bordermen."

"Why not? Fine men like them deserve happiness," declared Helen.

"It is necessary we have such," said the colonel simply, "and they cannot be bordermen unless free as the air blows. Wetzel and Jonathan have never had sweethearts. I believe Wetzel loved a lass once; but he was an Indian-killer whose hands were red with blood. He silenced his heart, and kept to his chosen, lonely life. Jonathan does not seem to realize that women exist to charm, to please, to be loved and married. Once we twitted him about his brothers doing their duty by the border, whereupon he flashed out: 'My life is the border's: my sweetheart is the North Star!'"

Helen dreamily watched the dancing, dimpling waves that broke on the stones of the river shore. All unconscious of the powerful impression the colonel's recital had made upon her, she was feeling the greatness of the lives of these bordermen, and the glory it would now be for her to share with others the pride in their protection.

"Say, Sheppard, look here," said Colonel Zane, on the return to his cabin, "that girl of yours has a pair of eyes. I can't forget the way they flashed! They'll cause more trouble here among my garrison than would a swarm of redskins."

"No! You don't mean it! Out here in this wilderness?" queried Sheppard doubtfully.

"Well, I do."

"O Lord! What a time I've had with that girl! There was one man especially, back home, who made our lives miserable. He was rich and well born; but Helen would have none of him. He got around me, old fool that I am! Practically stole what was left of my estate, and gambled it away when Helen said she'd die before giving herself to him. It was partly on his account that I brought her away. Then there were a lot of moon-eyed beggars after her all the time, and she's young and full of fire. I hoped I'd marry her to some farmer out here, and end my days in peace."

"Peace? With eyes like those? Never on this green earth," and Colonel Zane laughed as he slapped his friend on the shoulder. "Don't worry, old fellow. You can't help her having those changing dark-blue eyes any more than you can help being proud of them. They have won me, already, suscep-tible old backwoodsman! I'll help you with this spirited young lady. I've had experience, Sheppard, and don't you forget it. First, my sister, a Zane all through, which is saying enough. Then as sweet and fiery a little Indian princess as ever stepped in a beaded moccasin, and since, more than one beautiful, impulsive creature. Being in authority, I suppose it's natural that all the work, from keeping the garrison ready against an attack, to straightening out love affairs, should fall upon me. I'll take the care off your shoulders; I'll keep these young dare-devils from killing each other over Miss Helen's favors. I certainly—Hello! There are strangers at the gate. Something's up."

Half a dozen rough-looking men had appeared from round the corner of the cabin, and halted at the gate.

"Bill Elsing, and some of his men from Yellow Creek," said Colonel Zane, as he went toward the group.

"Hullo, Kurnel," was the greeting of the foremost, evidently the leader. "We've lost six head of hosses over our way, an' are out lookin' 'em up."

"The deuce you have! Say, this horse-stealing business is getting inter-esting. What did you come in for?"

"Wal, we meets Jonathan on the ridge about sunup, an' he sent us back lickety-cut. Said he had two of the hosses corralled, an' mebbe Wetzel could git the others."

"That's strange," replied Colonel Zane thoughtfully.

"'Pears to me Jack and Wetzel hev some redskins treed, an' didn't want us to spile the fun. Mebbe there wasn't scalps enough to go round. Anyway, we come in, an' we'll hang up here to-day."

"Bill, who's doing this horse-stealing?"

"Damn if I know. It's a mighty pert piece of work. I've a mind it's some slick white fellar, with Injuns backin' him."

Helen noted, when she was once more indoors, that Colonel Zane's wife appeared worried. Her usual placid expression was gone. She put off the playful overtures of her two bright boys with unusual indifference, and turned to her husband with anxious questioning as to whether the strangers brought news of Indians. Upon being assured that such was not the case, she looked relieved, and explained to Helen that she had seen armed men come so often to consult the colonel regarding dangerous missions and expeditions, that the sight of a stranger caused her unspeakable dread.

"I am accustomed to danger, yet I can never control my fears for my husband and children," said Mrs. Zane. "The older I grow the more of a coward I am. Oh! this border life is sad for women. Only a little while ago my brother Samuel McColloch was shot and scalped right here on the river bank. He was going to the spring for a bucket of water. I lost another brother in almost the same way. Every day during the summer a husband and a father fall victim to some murderous Indian. My husband will go in the same way some day. The border claims them all."

"Bessie, you must not show your fears to our new friend. And, Miss Helen, don't believe she's the coward she would make out," said the colonel's sister smilingly.

"Betty is right, Bess, don't frighten her," said Colonel Zane. "I'm afraid I talked too much to-day. But, Miss Helen, you were so interested, and are such a good listener, that I couldn't refrain. Once for all let me say that you will no doubt see stirring life here; but there is little danger of its affecting you. To be sure I think you'll have troubles; but not with Indians or outlaws."

He winked at his wife and sister. At first Helen did not understand his sally, but then she blushed red all over her fair face.

Some time after that, while unpacking her belongings, she heard the clatter of horses' hoofs on the rocky road, accompanied by loud voices. Running to the window, she saw a group of men at the gate.

"Miss Sheppard, will you come out?" called Colonel Zane's sister from the door. "My brother Jonathan has returned."

Helen joined Betty at the door, and looked over her shoulder.

"Wal, Jack, ye got two on 'em, anyways," drawled a voice which she recognized as that of Elsing's.

A man, lithe and supple, slipped from the back of one of the horses, and, giving the halter to Elsing with a single word, turned and entered the gate. Colonel Zane met him there.

"Well, Jonathan, what's up?"

"There's hell to pay," was the reply, and the speaker's voice rang clear and sharp.

Colonel Zane laid his hand on his brother's shoulder, and thus they stood for a moment, singularly alike, and yet the sturdy pioneer was, some-how, far different from the dark-haired borderman.

"I thought we'd trouble in store from the look on your face," said the colonel calmly. "I hope you haven't very bad news on the first day, for our old friends from Virginia."

"Jonathan," cried Betty when he did not answer the colonel. At her call he half turned, and his dark eyes, steady, strained like those of a watching deer, sought his sister's face.

"Betty, old Jake Lane was murdered by horse thieves yesterday, and Mabel Lane is gone."

"Oh!" gasped Betty; but she said nothing more.

Colonel Zane cursed inaudibly.

"You know, Eb, I tried to keep Lane in the settlement for Mabel's sake. But he wanted to work that farm. I believe horse-stealing wasn't as much of an object as the girl. Pretty women are bad for the border, or any other place, I guess. Wetzel has taken the trail, and I came in because I've serious suspicions—I'll explain to you alone."

The borderman bowed gravely to Helen, with a natural grace, and yet a manner that sat awkwardly upon him. The girl, slightly flushed, and some-what confused by this meeting with the man around whom her romantic imagination had already woven a story, stood in the doorway after giving him a fleeting glance, the fairest, sweetest picture of girlish beauty ever seen.

The men went into the house; but their voices came distinctly through the door.

"Eb, if Bing Legget or Girty ever see that big-eyed lass, they'll have her even if Fort Henry has to be burned, an' in case they do get her, Wetzel an' I'll have taken our last trail."

CHAPTER 3

SUPPER OVER, COLONEL ZANE LED HIS GUESTS TO A SIDE PORCH, WHERE they were soon joined by Mrs. Zane and Betty. The host's two boys, Noah and Sammy, who had preceded them, were now astride the porch-rail and, to judge by their antics, were riding wild Indian mustangs.

"It's quite cool," said Colonel Zane; "but I want you to see the sunset in the valley. A good many of your future neighbors may come over to-night for a word of welcome. It's the border custom."

He was about to seat himself by the side of Mr. Sheppard, on a rustic bench, when a Negro maid appeared in the doorway carrying a smiling, black-eyed baby. Colonel Zane took the child and, holding it aloft, said with fatherly pride:

"This is Rebecca Zane, the first girl baby born to the Zanes, and destined to be the belle of the border."

"May I have her?" asked Helen softly, holding out her arms. She took the child, and placed it upon her knee where its look of solemnity soon changed to one of infantile delight.

"Here come Nell and Jim," said Mrs. Zane, pointing toward the fort.

"Yes, and there comes my brother Silas with his wife, too," added Colonel Zane. "The first couple are James Douns, our young minister, and Nell, his wife. They came out here a year or so ago. James had a brother Joe, the finest young fellow who ever caught the border fever. He was killed by one of the Girtys. His was a wonderful story, and some day you shall hear about the parson and his wife."

"What's the border fever?" asked Mr. Sheppard.

"It's what brought you out here," replied Colonel Zane with a hearty laugh.

Helen gazed with interest at the couple now coming into the yard, and when they gained the porch she saw that the man was big and tall, with a frank, manly bearing, while his wife was a slender little woman with bright, sunny hair, and a sweet, smiling face. They greeted Helen and her father cordially.

Next came Silas Zane, a typical bronzed and bearded pioneer, with his buxom wife. Presently a little group of villagers joined the party. They were rugged men, clad in faded buckskins, and sober-faced women who wore dresses of plain gray linsey. They welcomed the newcomers with simple, homely courtesy. Then six young frontiersmen appeared from around a corner of the cabin, advancing hesitatingly. To Helen they all looked alike, tall, awkward, with brown faces and big hands. When Colonel Zane cheerily cried out to them, they stumbled forward with evident embarrassment, each literally crushing Helen's hand in his horny palm. Afterward they leaned on the rail and stole glances at her.

Soon a large number of villagers were on the porch or in the yard. After paying their respects to Helen and her father they took part in a general conversation. Two or three girls, the latest callers, were surrounded by half a dozen young fellows, and their laughter sounded high above the hum of voices.

Helen gazed upon this company with mingled feelings of relief and pleasure. She had been more concerned regarding the young people with whom her lot might be cast, than the dangers of which others had told. She knew that on the border there was no distinction of rank. Though she came of an old family, and, during her girlhood, had been surrounded by refinement, even luxury, she had accepted cheerfully the reverses of fortune, and was determined to curb the pride which had been hers. It was necessary she should have friends. Warm-hearted, impulsive and loving, she needed to have around her those in whom she could confide. Therefore it was with sincere pleasure she understood how groundless were her fears and knew that if she did not find good, true friends the fault would be her own. She saw at a glance that the colonel's widowed sister was her equal, perhaps her superior, in education and breeding, while Nellie Douns was as well-bred and gracious a little lady as she had ever met. Then, the other girls, too, were charming, with frank wholesomeness and freedom.

Concerning the young men, of whom there were about a dozen, Helen had hardly arrived at a conclusion. She liked the ruggedness, the signs of honest worth which clung to them. Despite her youth, she had been much sought after because of her personal attractions, and had thus added experience to the natural keen intuition all women possess. The glances of several of the men, particularly the bold regard of one Roger Brandt, whom Colonel Zane introduced, she had seen before, and learned to dislike. On the whole, however, she was delighted with the prospect of new friends and future prosperity, and she felt even greater pleasure in the certainty that her father shared her gratification.

Suddenly she became aware that the conversation had ceased. She looked up to see the tall, lithe form of Jonathan Zane as he strode across the porch. She could see that a certain constraint had momentarily fallen upon the company. It was an involuntary acknowledgment of the borderman's presence, of a presence that worked on all alike with a subtle, strong magnetism.

"Ah, Jonathan, come out to see the sunset? It's unusually fine tonight," said Colonel Zane.

With hardly more than a perceptible bow to those present, the borderman took a seat near the rail, and, leaning upon it, directed his gaze westward.

Helen sat so near she could have touched him. She was conscious of the same strange feeling, and impelling sense of power, which had come upon her so strongly at first sight of him. More than that, a lively interest had been aroused in her. This borderman was to her a new and novel character. She was amused at learning that here was a young man absolutely indifferent to the charms of the opposite sex, and although hardly admitting such a thing, she believed it would be possible to win him from his indifference. On raising her eyelids, it was with the unconcern which a woman feigns when suspecting she is being regarded with admiring eyes. But Jonathan Zane might not have known of her presence, for all the attention he paid her. Therefore, having a good opportunity to gaze at this borderman of daring deeds, Helen regarded him closely.

He was clad from head to foot in smooth, soft buckskin which fitted well his powerful frame. Beaded moccasins, leggings bound high above the knees, hunting coat laced and fringed, all had the neat, tidy appearance due to good care. He wore no weapons. His hair fell in a raven mass over his shoulders. His profile was regular, with a long, straight nose, strong chin, and eyes black as night. They were now fixed intently on the valley. The whole face gave an impression of serenity, of calmness.

Helen was wondering if the sad, almost stern, tranquility of that face ever changed, when the baby cooed and held out its chubby little hands. Jonathan's smile, which came quickly, accompanied by a warm light in the eyes, relieved Helen of an unaccountable repugnance she had begun to feel toward the borderman. That smile, brief as a flash, showed his gentle kindness and told that he was not a creature who had set himself apart from human life and love.

As he took little Rebecca, one of his hands touched Helen's. If he had taken heed of the contact, as any ordinary man might well have, she would, perhaps, have thought nothing about it, but because he did not appear to realize that her hand had been almost inclosed in his, she could not help again feeling his singular personality. She saw that this man had absolutely no thought of her. At the moment this did not awaken resentment, for with all her fire and pride she was not vain; but amusement gave place to a respect which came involuntarily.

Little Rebecca presently manifested the faithlessness peculiar to her sex, and had no sooner been taken upon Jonathan's knee than she cried out to go back to Helen.

"Girls are uncommon coy critters," said he, with a grave smile in his eyes. He handed back the child, and once more was absorbed in the setting sun.

Helen looked down the valley to behold the most beautiful spectacle she had ever seen. Between the hills far to the west, the sky flamed with a red and gold light. The sun was poised above the river, and the shimmering waters merged into a ruddy horizon. Long rays of crimson fire crossed the smooth waters. A few purple clouds above caught the refulgence, until aided by the delicate rose and blue space beyond, they became many hued ships sailing on a rainbow sea. Each second saw a gorgeous transformation. Slowly the sun dipped into the golden flood; one by one the clouds changed from crimson to gold, from gold to rose, and then to gray; slowly all the tints faded until, as the sun slipped out of sight, the brilliance gave way to the soft afterglow of warm lights. These in turn slowly toned down into gray twilight.

Helen retired to her room soon afterward, and, being unusually thoughtful, sat down by the window. She reviewed the events of this first day of her new life on the border. Her impressions had been so many, so varied, that she wanted to distinguish them. First she felt glad, with a sweet, warm thankfulness, that her father seemed so happy, so encouraged by the outlook. Breaking old ties had been, she knew, no child's play for him. She realized also that it had been done solely because there had been nothing left to offer her in the old home, and in a new one were hope and possibilities. Then she was relieved at getting away from the attentions of a man whose persistence had been most annoying to her. From thoughts of her father, and the old life, she came to her new friends of the present. She was so grateful for their kindness. She certainly would do all in her power to win and keep their esteem.

Somewhat of a surprise was it to her, that she reserved for Jonathan Zane the last and most prominent place in her meditations. She suddenly asked herself how she regarded this fighting borderman. She recalled her unbounded enthusiasm for the man as Colonel Zane had told of him; then her first glimpse, and her surprise and admiration at the lithe-limbed young giant; then incredulity, amusement, and respect followed in swift order, after which an unaccountable coldness that was almost resentment. Helen was forced to admit that she did not know how to regard him, but surely he was a man, throughout every inch of his superb frame, and one who took life seriously, with neither thought nor time for the opposite sex. And this last brought a blush to her cheek, for she distinctly remembered she had expected, if not admiration, more than passing notice from this hero of the border.

Presently she took a little mirror from a table near where she sat. Holding it to catch the fast-fading light, she studied her face seriously.

"Helen Sheppard, I think on the occasion of your arrival in a new country a little plain talk will be wholesome. Somehow or other, perhaps because of a crowd of idle men back there in the colonies, possibly from your own misguided fancy, you imagined you were fair to look at. It is well to be undeceived."

Scorn spoke in Helen's voice. She was angry because of having been interested in a man, and allowed that interest to betray her into a girlish expectation that he would treat her as all other men had. The mirror, even in the dim light, spoke more truly than she, for it caught the golden tints of her luxuriant hair, the thousand beautiful shadows in her great, dark eyes, the white glory of a face fair as a star, and the swelling outline of neck and shoulders.

With a sudden fiery impetuosity she flung the glass to the floor, where it was broken into several pieces.

"How foolish of me! What a temper I have!" she exclaimed repentantly. "I'm glad I have another glass. Wouldn't Mr. Jonathan Zane, borderman, Indian fighter, hero of a hundred battles and never a sweetheart, be flattered? No, most decidedly he wouldn't. He never looked at me. I don't think I expected that; I'm sure I didn't want it; but still he might have—Oh! what am I thinking, and he a stranger?"

Before Helen lost herself in slumber on that eventful evening, she vowed to ignore the borderman; assured herself that she did not want to see him again, and, rather inconsistently, that she would cure him of his indifference.

WHEN COLONEL ZANE'S GUESTS HAD RETIRED, AND THE VILLAGERS were gone to their homes, he was free to consult with Jonathan.

"Well, Jack," he said, "I'm ready to hear about the horse thieves."

"Wetzel makes it out the man who's runnin' this hoss-stealin' is located right here in Fort Henry," answered the borderman.

The colonel had lived too long on the frontier to show surprise; he hummed a tune while the genial expression faded slowly from his face.

"Last count there were one hundred and ten men at the fort," he replied thoughtfully. "I know over a hundred, and can trust them. There are some new fellows on the boats, and several strangers hanging round Metzar's."

"'Pears to Lew an' me that this fellar is a slick customer, an' one who's been here long enough to know our hosses an' where we keep them."

"I see. Like Miller, who fooled us all, even Betty, when he stole our powder and then sold us to Girty," rejoined Colonel Zane grimly.

"Exactly, only this fellar is slicker an' more desperate than Miller."

"Right you are, Jack, for the man who is trusted and betrays us, must be desperate. Does he realize what he'll get if we ever find out, or is he underrating us?"

"He knows all right, an' is matchin' his cunnin' against our'n."

"Tell me what you and Wetzel learned."

The borderman proceeded to relate the events that had occurred during a recent tramp in the forest with Wetzel. While returning from a hunt in a swamp several miles over the ridge, back of Fort Henry, they ran across the trail of three Indians. They followed this until darkness set in, when both laid down to rest and wait for the early dawn, that time most propitious for taking the savage by surprise. On resuming the trail they found that other Indians had joined the party they were tracking. To the bordermen this was significant of some unusual activity directed toward the settlement. Unable to learn anything definite from the moccasin traces, they hurried up on the trail to find that the Indians had halted.

Wetzel and Jonathan saw from their covert that the savages had a woman prisoner. A singular feature about it all was that the Indians remained in the same place all day, did not light a camp-fire, and kept a sharp lookout. The bordermen crept up as close as safe, and remained on watch during the day and night.

Early next morning, when the air was fading from black to gray, the silence was broken by the snapping of twigs and a tremor of the ground. The bordermen believed another company of Indians was approaching; but they soon saw it was a single white man leading a number of horses. He departed before daybreak. Wetzel and Jonathan could not get a clear view of him owing to the dim light; but they heard his voice, and afterwards found the imprint of his moccasins. They did, however, recognize the six horses as belonging to settlers in Yellow Creek.

While Jonathan and Wetzel were consulting as to what it was best to do, the party of Indians divided, four going directly west, and the others north. Wetzel immediately took the trail of the larger party with the prisoner and four of the horses. Jonathan caught two of the animals which the Indians had turned loose, and tied them in the forest. He then started after the three Indians who had gone northward.

"Well?" Colonel Zane said impatiently, when Jonathan hesitated in his story.

"One got away," he said reluctantly. "I barked him as he was runnin' like a streak through the bushes, an' judged that he was hard hit. I got the hosses, an' turned back on the trail of the white man."

"Where did it end?"

"In that hard-packed path near the blacksmith shop. An' the fellar steps as light as an Injun."

"He's here, then, sure as you're born. We've lost no horses yet, but last week old Sam heard a noise in the barn, and on going there found Betty's mare out of her stall."

"Some one as knows the lay of the land had been after her," suggested Jonathan.

"You can bet on that. We've got to find him before we lose all the fine

513

horse-flesh we own. Where do these stolen animals go? Indians would steal any kind; but this thief takes only the best."

"I'm to meet Wetzel on the ridge soon, an' then we'll know, for he's goin' to find out where the hosses are taken."

"That'll help some. On the way back you found where the white girl had been taken from. Murdered father, burned cabin, the usual deviltry."

"Exactly."

"Poor Mabel! Do you think this white thief had anything to do with carrying her away?"

"No. Wetzel says that's Bing Legget's work. The Shawnees were members of his gang."

"Well, Jack, what'll I do?"

"Keep quiet an' wait," was the borderman's answer.

Colonel Zane, old pioneer and frontiersman though he was, shuddered as he went to his room. His brother's dark look, and his deadly calmness, were significant.

CHAPTER 4

To those few who saw Jonathan Zane in the village, it seemed as if he was in his usual quiet and dreamy state. The people were accustomed to his silence, and long since learned that what little time he spent in the settlement was not given to sociability. In the morning he sometimes lay with Colonel Zane's dog, Chief, by the side of a spring under an elm tree, and in the afternoon strolled aimlessly along the river bluff, or on the hillside. At night he sat on his brother's porch smoking a long Indian pipe. Since that day, now a week past, when he had returned with the stolen horses, his movements and habits were precisely what would have been expected of an unsuspicious borderman.

In reality, however, Jonathan was not what he seemed. He knew all that was going on in the settlement. Hardly a bird could have entered the clearing unobserved.

At night, after all the villagers were in bed, he stole cautiously about the stockade, silencing with familiar word the bristling watch-hounds, and went from barn to barn, ending his stealthy tramp at the corral where Colonel Zane kept his thoroughbreds.

But all this scouting by night availed nothing. No unusual event occurred, not even the barking of a dog, a suspicious rustling among the thickets, or whistling of a night-hawk had been heard.

Vainly the borderman strained ears to catch some low night-signal given by waiting Indians to the white traitor within the settlement. By day there was even less to attract the sharp-eyed watcher. The clumsy river boats, half raft, half sawn lumber, drifted down the Ohio on their first and last voyage, discharged their cargoes of grain, liquor, or merchandise, and were broken up. Their crews came back on the long overland journey to Fort Pitt, there to man another craft. The garrison at the fort performed their customary duties; the pioneers tilled the fields; the blacksmith scattered sparks, the wheelwright worked industriously at his bench, and the housewives attended to their many cares. No strangers arrived at Fort Henry. The quiet life of the village was uninterrupted.

Near sunset of a long day Jonathan strolled down the sandy, well-trodden path toward Metzar's inn. He did not drink, and consequently seldom visited the rude, dark, ill-smelling bar-room. When occasion demanded his presence there, he was evidently not welcome. The original owner, a sturdy soldier and pioneer, came to Fort Henry when Colonel Zane founded the settlement, and had been killed during Girty's last attack. His successor, another Metzar, was, according to Jonathan's belief, as bad as the whiskey he dispensed. More than one murder had been committed at the inn; countless fatal knife and tomahawk fights had stained red the hard clay floor; and more than one desperate character had been harbored there. Once Colonel Zane sent Wetzel there to invite a thief and outlaw to quit the settlement, with the not unexpected result that it became necessary the robber be carried out.

Jonathan thought of the bad name the place bore all over the frontier, and wondered if Metzar could tell anything about the horse-thieves. When the borderman bent his tall frame to enter the low-studded door he fancied he saw a dark figure disappear into a room just behind the bar. A roughly-clad, heavily-bearded man turned hastily at the same moment.

"Hullo," he said gruffly.

"H' are you, Metzar. I just dropped in to see if I could make a trade for your sorrel mare," replied Jonathan. Being well aware that the innkeeper would not part with his horse, the borderman had made this announcement as his reason for entering the bar-room.

"Nope, I'll allow you can't," replied Metzar.

As he turned to go, Jonathan's eyes roamed around the bar-room. Several strangers of shiftless aspect bleared at him.

"They wouldn't steal a pumpkin," muttered Jonathan to himself as he left the inn. Then he added suspiciously, "Metzar was talkin' to some one, an' 'peared uneasy. I never liked Metzar. He'll bear watchin'."

The borderman passed on down the path thinking of what he had heard against Metzar. The colonel had said that the man was prosperous for an innkeeper who took pelts, grain or meat in exchange for rum. The village gossips disliked him because he was unmarried, taciturn, and did not care for their company. Jonathan reflected also on the fact that Indians were frequently coming to the inn, and this made him distrustful of the proprietor. It was true that Colonel Zane had red-skinned visitors, but there was always good reason for their coming. Jonathan had seen, during the Revolution, more than one trusted man proven to be a traitor, and the conviction settled upon him that some quiet scouting would show up the innkeeper as aiding the horse-thieves if not actually in league with them.

"Good evening, Jonathan Zane."

This greeting in a woman's clear voice brought Jonathan out from his reveries. He glanced up to see Helen Sheppard standing in the doorway of her father's cabin.

"Evenin', miss," he said with a bow, and would have passed on.

"Wait," she cried, and stepped out of the door.

He waited by the gate with a manner which showed that such a summons was novel to him.

Helen, piqued at his curt greeting, had asked him to wait without any idea of what she would say. Coming slowly down the path she felt again a subtle awe of this borderman. Regretting her impulsiveness, she lost confidence.

Gaining the gate she looked up intending to speak; but was unable to do so as she saw how cold and grave was his face, and how piercing were his eyes. She flushed slightly, and then, conscious of an embarrassment new and strange to her, blushed rosy red, making, as it seemed to her, a stupid remark about the sunset. When he took her words literally, and said the sunset was fine, she felt guilty of deceitfulness. Whatever Helen's faults, and they were many, she was honest, and because of not having looked at the sunset, but only wanting him to see her as did other men, the innocent ruse suddenly appeared mean and trifling.

Then, with a woman's quick intuition, she understood that coquetries were lost on this borderman, and, with a smile, got the better of her embarrassment and humiliation by telling the truth.

"I wanted to ask a favor of you, and I'm a little afraid."

She spoke with girlish shyness, which increased as he stared at her.

"Why—why do you look at me so?"

"There's a lake over yonder which the Shawnees say is haunted by a woman they killed," he replied quietly. "You'd do for her spirit, so white an' beautiful in the silver moonlight."

"So my white dress makes me look ghostly," she answered lightly, though deeply conscious of surprise and pleasure at such an unexpected reply from him. This borderman might be full of surprises. "Such a time as I had bringing my dresses out here! I don't know when I can wear them. This is the simplest one."

"An' it's mighty new an' bewilderin' for the border," he replied with a smile in his eyes.

"When these are gone I'll get no more except linsey ones," she said brightly, yet her eyes shone with a wistful uncertainty of the future.

"Will you be happy here?"

"I am happy. I have always wanted to be of some use in the world. I assure you, Master Zane, I am not the butterfly I seem. I have worked hard all day, that is, until your sister Betty came over. All the girls have helped me fix up the cabin until it's more comfortable than I ever dreamed one could be on the frontier. Father is well content here, and that makes me happy. I haven't had time for forebodings. The young men of Fort Henry have been—well, attentive; in fact, they've been here all the time."

She laughed a little at this last remark, and looked demurely at him.

"It's a frontier custom," he said.

"Oh, indeed? Do all the young men call often and stay late?"

"They do."

"You didn't," she retorted. "You're the only one who hasn't been to see me."

"I do not wait on the girls," he replied with a grave smile.

"Oh, you don't? Do you expect them to wait on you?" she asked, feeling, now she had made this silent man talk, once more at her ease.

"I am a borderman," replied Jonathan. There was a certain dignity or sadness in his answer which reminded Helen of Colonel Zane's portrayal of a borderman's life. It struck her keenly. Here was this young giant standing erect and handsome before her, as rugged as one of the ash trees of his beloved forest. Who could tell when his strong life might be ended by an Indian's hatchet?

"For you, then, is there no such thing as friendship?" she asked.

"On the border men are serious."

This recalled his sister's conversation regarding the attentions of the young men, that they would follow her, fight for her, and give her absolutely no peace until one of them had carried her to his cabin a bride.

She could not carry on the usual conventional conversation with this borderman, but remained silent for a time. She realized more keenly than ever before how different he was from other men, and watched closely as he stood gazing out over the river. Perhaps something she had said caused him to think of the many pleasures and joys he missed. But she could not be certain what was in his mind. She was not accustomed to impassive faces and cold eyes with unlit fires in their dark depths. More likely he was thinking of matters nearer to his wild, free life; of his companion Wetzel somewhere out beyond those frowning hills. Then she remembered that the colonel had told her of his brother's love for nature in all its forms; how he watched the shades of evening fall; lost himself in contemplation of the last copper glow flushing the western sky, or became absorbed in the bright stars. Possibly he had forgotten her presence. Darkness was rapidly stealing down upon them. The evening, tranquil and gray, crept over them with all its mystery. He was a part of it. She could not hope to understand him; but saw clearly that his was no common personality. She wanted to speak, to voice a sympathy strong within her; but she did not know what to say to this borderman.

"If what your sister tells me of the border is true, I may soon need a friend," she said, after weighing well her words. She faced him modestly yet bravely, and looked him straight in the eyes. Because he did not reply she spoke again.

"I mean such a friend as you or Wetzel."

"You may count on both," he replied.

"Thank you," she said softly, giving him her hand. "I shall not forget. One more thing. Will you break a borderman's custom, for my sake?"

"How?"

"Come to see me when you are in the settlement?"

Helen said this in a low voice with just a sob in her breath; but she met his gaze fairly. Her big eyes were all aglow, alight with girlish appeal, and yet proud with a woman's honest demand for fair exchange. Promise was there, too, could he but read it, of wonderful possibilities.

"No," he answered gently.

Helen was not prepared for such a rebuff. She was interested in him, and not ashamed to show it. She feared only that he might misunderstand her; but to refuse her proffered friendship, that was indeed unexpected. Rude she thought it was, while from brow to curving throat her fair skin

crimsoned. Then her face grew pale as the moonlight. Hard on her resentment had surged the swell of some new emotion strong and sweet. He
refused her friendship because he did not dare accept it; because his life
was not his own; because he was a borderman.

While they stood thus, Jonathan looking perplexed and troubled,
feeling he had hurt her, but knowing not what to say, and Helen with a
warm softness in her eyes, the stalwart figure of a man loomed out of the
gathering darkness.

"Ah, Miss Helen! Good evening," he said.

"Is it you, Mr. Brandt?" asked Helen. "Of course you know Mr. Zane."

Brandt acknowledged Jonathan's bow with an awkwardness which had
certainly been absent in his greeting to Helen. He started slightly when
she spoke the borderman's name.

A brief pause ensued.

"Good night," said Jonathan, and left them.

He had noticed Brandt's gesture of surprise, slight though it was, and
was thinking about it as he walked away. Brandt may have been astonished
at finding a borderman talking to a girl, and certainly, as far as Jonathan
was concerned, the incident was without precedent. But, on the other
hand, Brandt may have had another reason, and Jonathan tried to study
out what it might be.

He gave but little thought to Helen. That she might like him exceedingly well, did not come into his mind. He remembered his sister Betty's
gossip regarding Helen and her admirers, and particularly Roger Brandt;
but felt no great concern; he had no curiosity to know more of her. He
admired Helen because she was beautiful, yet the feeling was much the
same he might have experienced for a graceful deer, a full-foliaged tree, or
a dark mossy-stoned bend in a murmuring brook. The girl's face and
figure, perfect and alluring as they were, had not awakened him from his
indifference.

On arriving at his brother's home, he found the colonel and Betty
sitting on the porch.

"Eb, who is this Brandt?" he asked.

"Roger Brandt? He's a French-Canadian; came here from Detroit a
year ago. Why do you ask?"

"I want to know more about him."

Colonel Zane reflected a moment, first as to this unusual request from
Jonathan, and secondly in regard to what little he really did know of Roger
Brandt.

"Well, Jack, I can't tell you much; nothing of him before he showed up here. He says he has been a pioneer, hunter, scout, soldier, trader—everything. When he came to the fort we needed men. It was just after Girty's siege, and all the cabins had been burned. Brandt seemed honest, and was a good fellow. Besides, he had gold. He started the river barges, which came from Fort Pitt. He has surely done the settlement good service, and has prospered. I never talked a dozen times to him, and even then, not for long. He appears to like the young people, which is only natural. That's all I know; Betty might tell you more, for he tried to be attentive to her."

"Did he, Betty?" Jonathan asked.

"He followed me until I showed him I didn't care for company," answered Betty.

"What kind of a man is he?"

"Jack, I know nothing against him, although I never fancied him. He's better educated than the majority of frontiersmen; he's good-natured and agreeable, and the people like him."

"Why don't you?"

Betty looked surprised at his blunt question, and then said with a laugh: "I never tried to reason why; but since you have spoken I believe my dislike was instinctive."

After Betty had retired to her room the brothers remained on the porch smoking.

"Betty's pretty keen, Jack. I never knew her to misjudge a man. Why this sudden interest in Roger Brandt?"

The borderman puffed his pipe in silence.

"Say, Jack," Colonel Zane said suddenly, "do you connect Brandt in any way with this horse-stealing?"

"No more than some, an' less than others," replied Jonathan curtly.

Nothing more was said for a time. To the brothers this hour of early dusk brought the same fullness of peace. From gray twilight to gloomy dusk quiet reigned. The insects of night chirped and chorused with low, incessant hum. From out the darkness came the peeping of frogs.

Suddenly the borderman straightened up, and, removing the pipe from his mouth, turned his ear to the faint breeze, while at the same time one hand closed on the colonel's knee with a warning clutch.

Colonel Zane knew what that clutch signified. Some faint noise, too low for ordinary ears, had roused the borderman. The colonel listened, but heard nothing save the familiar evening sounds.

"Jack, what'd you hear?" he whispered.

"Somethin' back of the barn," replied Jonathan, slipping noiselessly off the steps, lying at full length with his ear close to the ground. "Where's the dog?" he asked.

"Chief must have gone with Sam. The old nigger sometimes goes at this hour to see his daughter."

Jonathan lay on the grass several moments; then suddenly he arose much as a bent sapling springs to place.

"I hear footsteps. Get the rifles," he said in a fierce whisper.

"Damn! There is some one in the barn."

"No; they're outside. Hurry, but softly."

Colonel Zane had but just risen to his feet, when Mrs. Zane came to the door and called him by name.

Instantly from somewhere in the darkness overhanging the road, came a low, warning whistle.

"A signal!" exclaimed Colonel Zane.

"Quick, Eb! Look toward Metzar's light. One, two, three, shadows —Injuns!"

"By the Lord Harry! Now they're gone; but I couldn't mistake those round heads and bristling feathers."

"Shawnees!" said the borderman, and his teeth shut hard like steel on flint.

"Jack, they were after the horses, and some one was on the lookout! By God! right under our noses!"

"Hurry," cried Jonathan, pulling his brother off the porch.

Colonel Zane followed the borderman out of the yard, into the road, and across the grassy square.

"We might find the one who gave the signal," said the colonel. "He was near at hand, and couldn't have passed the house."

Colonel Zane was correct, for whoever had whistled would be forced to take one of two ways of escape; either down the straight road ahead, or over the high stockade fence of the fort.

"There he goes," whispered Jonathan.

"Where? I can't see a blamed thing."

"Go across the square, run around the fort, an' head him off on the road. Don't try to stop him for he'll have weapons, just find out who he is."

"I see him now," replied Colonel Zane, as he hurried off into the darkness.

During a few moments Jonathan kept in view the shadow he had seen first come out of the gloom by the stockade, and thence pass swiftly down the road. He followed swiftly, silently. Presently a light beyond threw a glare across the road. He thought he was approaching a yard where there was a fire, and the flames proved to be from pine cones burning in the yard of Helen Sheppard. He remembered then that she was entertaining some of the young people.

The figure he was pursuing did not pass the glare. Jonathan made certain it disappeared before reaching the light, and he knew his eyesight too well not to trust to it absolutely. Advancing nearer the yard, he heard the murmur of voices in gay conversation, and soon saw figures moving about under the trees.

No doubt was in his mind but that the man who gave the signal to warn the Indians, was one of Helen Sheppard's guests.

Jonathan had walked across the street then down the path, before he saw the colonel coming from the opposite direction. Halting under a maple he waited for his brother to approach.

"I didn't meet any one. Did you lose him?" whispered Colonel Zane breathlessly.

"No; he's in there."

"That's Sheppard's place. Do you mean he's hiding there?"

"No!"

Colonel Zane swore, as was his habit when exasperated. Kind and generous man that he was, it went hard with him to believe in the guilt of any of the young men he had trusted. But Jonathan had said there was a traitor among them, and Colonel Zane did not question this assertion. He knew the borderman. During years full of strife, and war, and blood had he lived beside this silent man who said little, but that little was the truth. Therefore Colonel Zane gave way to anger.

"Well, I'm not so damned surprised! What's to be done?"

"Find out what men are there?"

"That's easy. I'll go to see George and soon have the truth."

"Won't do," said the borderman decisively. "Go back to the barn, an' look after the hosses."

When Colonel Zane had obeyed Jonathan dropped to his hands and knees, and swiftly, with the agile movements of an Indian, gained a corner of the Sheppard yard. He crouched in the shade of a big plum tree. Then, at a favorable opportunity, vaulted the fence and disappeared under a clump of lilac bushes.

The evening wore away no more tediously to the borderman, than to those young frontiersmen who were whispering tender or playful words to their partners. Time and patience were the same to Jonathan Zane. He lay hidden under the fragrant lilacs, his eyes, accustomed to the dark from long practice, losing no movement of the guests. Finally it became evident that the party was at an end. One couple took the initiative, and said good night to their hostess.

"Tom Bennet, I hope it's not you," whispered the borderman to himself, as he recognized the young fellow.

A general movement followed, until the merry party were assembled about Helen near the front gate.

"Jim Morrison, I'll bet it's not you," was Jonathan's comment. "That soldier Williams is doubtful; Hart an' Johnson being strangers, are unknown quantities around here, an' then comes Brandt."

All departed except Brandt, who remained talking to Helen in low, earnest tones. Jonathan lay very quietly, trying to decide what should be his next move in the unraveling of the mystery. He paid little attention to the young couple, but could not help overhearing their conversation.

"Indeed, Mr. Brandt, you frontiersmen are not backward," Helen was saying in her clear voice. "I am surprised to learn that you love me upon such short acquaintance, and am sorry, too, for I hardly know whether I even so much as like you."

"I love you. We men of the border do things rapidly," he replied earnestly.

"So it seems," she said with a soft laugh.

"Won't you care for me?" he pleaded.

"Nothing is surer than that I never know what I am going to do," Helen replied lightly.

"All these fellows are in love with you. They can't help it any more than I. You are the most glorious creature. Please give me hope."

"Mr. Brandt, let go my hand. I'm afraid I don't like such impulsive men."

"Please let me hold your hand."

"Certainly not."

"But I will hold it, and if you look at me like that again I'll do more," he said.

"What, bold sir frontiersman?" she returned, lightly still, but in a voice which rang with a deeper note.

"I'll kiss you," he cried desperately.

"You wouldn't dare."

"Wouldn't I though? You don't know us border fellows yet. You come here with your wonderful beauty, and smile at us with that light in your eyes which makes men mad. Oh, you'll pay for it."

The borderman listened to all this love-making half disgusted, until he began to grow interested. Brandt's back was turned to him, and Helen stood so that the light from the pine cones shone on her face. Her eyes were brilliant, otherwise she seemed a woman perfectly self-possessed. Brandt held her hand despite the repeated efforts she made to free it. But she did not struggle violently, or make an outcry.

Suddenly Brandt grasped her other hand, pulling her toward him.

"These other fellows will kiss you, and I'm going to be the first!" he declared passionately.

Helen drew back, now thoroughly alarmed by the man's fierce energy. She had been warned against this very boldness in frontiersmen; but had felt secure in her own pride and dignity. Her blood boiled at the thought that she must exert strength to escape insult. She struggled violently when Brandt bent his head. Almost sick with fear, she had determined to call for help, when a violent wrench almost toppled her over. At the same instant her wrists were freed; she heard a fierce cry, a resounding blow, and then the sodden thud of a heavy body falling. Recovering her balance, she saw a tall figure beside her, and a man in the act of rising from the ground.

"You?" whispered Helen, recognizing the tall figure as Jonathan's.

The borderman did not answer. He stepped forward, slipping his hand inside his hunting frock. Brandt sprang nimbly to his feet, and with a face which, even in the dim light, could be seen distorted with fury, bent forward to look at the stranger. He, too, had his hand within his coat, as if grasping a weapon; but he did not draw it.

"Zane, a lighter blow would have been easier to forget," he cried, his voice clear and cutting. Then he turned to the girl. "Miss Helen, I got what I deserved. I crave your forgiveness, and ask you to understand a man who was once a gentleman. If I am one no longer, the frontier is to blame. I was mad to treat you as I did."

Thus speaking, he bowed low with the grace of a man sometimes used to the society of ladies, and then went out of the gate.

"Where did you come from?" asked Helen, looking up at Jonathan.

He pointed under the lilac bushes.

"Were you there?" she asked wonderingly. "Did you hear all?"

"I couldn't help hearin'."

"It was fortunate for me; but why—why were you there?"

Helen came a step nearer, and regarded him curiously with her great eyes now black with excitement.

The borderman was silent.

Helen's softened mood changed instantly. There was nothing in his cold face which might have betrayed in him a sentiment similar to that of her admirers.

"Did you spy on me?" she asked quickly, after a moment's thought.

"No," replied Jonathan calmly.

Helen gazed in perplexity at this strange man. She did not know how to explain it; she was irritated, but did her best to conceal it. He had no interest in her, yet had hidden under the lilacs in her yard. She was grateful because he had saved her from annoyance, yet could not fathom his reason for being so near.

"Did you come here to see me?" she asked, forgetting her vexation.

"No."

"What for, then?"

"I reckon I won't say," was the quiet, deliberate refusal.

Helen stamped her foot in exasperation.

"Be careful that I do not put a wrong construction on your strange action," said she coldly. "If you have reasons, you might trust me. If you are only——"

"Sh-s-sh!" he breathed, grasping her wrist, and holding it firmly in his powerful hand. The whole attitude of the man had altered swiftly, subtly. The listlessness was gone. His lithe body became rigid as he leaned forward, his head toward the ground, and turned slightly in a manner that betokened intent listening.

Helen trembled as she felt his powerful frame quiver. Whatever had thus changed him, gave her another glimpse of his complex personality. It seemed to her incredible that with one whispered exclamation this man could change from cold indifference to a fire and force so strong as to dominate her.

Statue-like she remained listening; but hearing no sound, and thrillingly conscious of the hand on her arm.

Far up on the hillside an owl hooted dismally, and an instant later, faint and far away, came an answer so low as to be almost indistinct.

The borderman raised himself erect as he released her.

"It's only an owl," she said in relief.

His eyes gleamed like stars.

"It's Wetzel, an' it means Injuns!"

Then he was gone into the darkness.

CHAPTER 5

IN THE MISTY MORNING TWILIGHT COLONEL ZANE, FULLY ARMED, paced to and fro before his cabin, on guard. All night he had maintained a watch. He had not considered it necessary to send his family into the fort, to which they had often been compelled to flee. On the previous night Jonathan had come swiftly back to the cabin, and, speaking but two words, seized his weapons and vanished into the black night. The words were "Injuns! Wetzel!" and there were none others with more power to affect hearers on the border. The colonel believed that Wetzel had signaled to Jonathan.

On the west a deep gully with precipitous sides separated the settlement from a high, wooded bluff. Wetzel often returned from his journeying by this difficult route. He had no doubt seen Indian signs, and had communicated the intelligence to Jonathan by their system of night-bird calls. The nearness of the mighty hunter reassured Colonel Zane.

When the colonel returned from his chase of the previous night, he went directly to the stable, there to find that the Indians had made off with a thoroughbred, and Betty's pony. Colonel Zane was furious, not on account of the value of the horses, but because Bess was his favorite bay, and Betty loved nothing more than her pony Madcap. To have such a march stolen on him after he had heard and seen the thieves was indeed hard. High time it was that these horse thieves be run to earth. No Indian had planned these marauding expeditions. An intelligent white man was at the bottom of the thieving, and he should pay for his treachery.

The colonel's temper, however, soon cooled. He realized after thinking over the matter, that he was fortunate it passed off without bloodshed. Very likely the intent had been to get all his horses, perhaps his neighbor's as well, and it had been partly frustrated by Jonathan's keen sagacity. These Shawnees, white leader or not, would never again run such risks.

"It's like a skulking Shawnee," muttered Colonel Zane, "to slip down here under cover of early dusk, when no one but an Indian hunter could detect him. I didn't look for trouble, especially so soon after the lesson we gave Girty and his damned English and redskins. It's lucky Jonathan was here. I'll go back to the old plan of stationing scouts at the outposts until snow flies."

While Colonel Zane talked to himself and paced the path he had selected to patrol, the white mists cleared, and a rosy hue followed the brightening in the east. The birds ceased twittering to break into gay songs, and the cock in the barnyard gave one final clarion-voiced salute to the dawn. The rose in the east deepened into rich red, and then the sun peeped over the eastern hilltops to drench the valley with glad golden light.

A blue smoke curling lazily from the stone chimney of his cabin, showed that Sam had made the kitchen fire, and a little later a rich, savory odor gave pleasing evidence that his wife was cooking breakfast.

"Any sign of Jack?" a voice called from the open door, and Betty appeared.

"Nary sign."

"Of the Indians, then?"

"Well, Betts, they left you a token of their regard," and Colonel Zane smiled as he took a broken halter from the fence.

"Madcap?" cried Betty.

"Yes, they've taken Madcap and Bess."

"Oh, the villains! Poor pony," exclaimed Betty indignantly. "Eb, I'll coax Wetzel to fetch the pony home if he has to kill every Shawnee in the valley."

"Now you're talking, Betts," Colonel Zane replied. "If you could get Lew to do that much, you'd be blessed from one end of the border to the other."

He walked up the road; then back, keeping a sharp lookout on all sides, and bestowing a particularly keen glance at the hillside across the ravine, but could see no sign of the bordermen. As it was now broad daylight he felt convinced that further watch was unnecessary, and went in to break-fast. When he came out again the villagers were astir. The sharp strokes of axes rang out on the clear morning air, and a mellow anvil-clang pealed up from the blacksmith shop. Colonel Zane found his brother Silas and Jim Douns near the gate.

"Morning, boys," he cried cheerily.

"Any glimpse of Jack or Lew?" asked Silas.

"No; but I'm expecting one of 'em any moment."

"How about the Indians?" asked Douns. "Silas roused me out last night; but didn't stay long enough to say more than 'Indians.'"

"I don't know much more than Silas. I saw several of the red devils who stole the horses; but how many, where they've gone, or what we're to expect, I can't say. We've got to wait for Jack or Lew. Silas, keep the garrison in readiness at the fort, and don't allow a man, soldier or farmer, to leave the clearing until further orders. Perhaps there were only three of those Shawnees, and then again the woods might have been full of them. I take it something's amiss, or Jack and Lew would be in by now."

"Here come Sheppard and his girl," said Silas, pointing down the lane. "'Pears George is some excited."

Colonel Zane had much the same idea as he saw Sheppard and his daughter. The old man appeared in a hurry, which was sufficient reason to believe him anxious or alarmed, and Helen looked pale.

"Ebenezer, what's this I hear about Indians?" Sheppard asked excitedly. "What with Helen's story about the fort being besieged, and this brother of yours routing honest people from their beds, I haven't had a wink of sleep. What's up? Where are the redskins?"

"Now, George, be easy," said Colonel Zane calmly. "And you, Helen, mustn't be frightened. There's no danger. We did have a visit from Indians last night; but they hurt no one, and got only two horses."

"Oh, I'm so relieved that it's not worse," said Helen.

"It's bad enough, Helen," Betty cried, her black eyes flashing, "my pony Madcap is gone."

"Colonel Zane, come here quick!" cried Douns, who stood near the gate.

With one leap Colonel Zane was at the gate, and, following with his eyes the direction indicated by Douns' trembling finger, he saw two tall, brown figures striding down the lane. One carried two rifles, and the other a long bundle wrapped in a blanket.

"It's Jack and Wetzel," whispered Colonel Zane to Jim. "They've got the girl, and by God! from the way that bundle hangs, I think she's dead. Here," he added, speaking loudly, "you women get into the house."

Mrs. Zane, Betty and Helen stared.

"Go into the house!" he cried authoritatively.

Without a protest the three women obeyed.

At that moment Nellie Douns came across the lane; Sam shuffled out from the backyard, and Sheppard arose from his seat on the steps. They joined Colonel Zane, Silas and Jim at the gate.

"I wondered what kept you so late," Colonel Zane said to Jonathan, as he and his companion came up. "You've fetched Mabel, and she's——". The good man could say no more. If he should live an hundred years on the border amid savage murderers, he would still be tender-hearted. Just now he believed the giant borderman by the side of Jonathan held a dead girl, one whom he had danced, when a child, upon his knee.

"Mabel, an' jest alive," replied Jonathan.

"By God! I'm glad!" exclaimed Colonel Zane. "Here, Lew, give her to me."

Wetzel relinquished his burden to the colonel.

"Lew, any bad Indian sign?" asked Colonel Zane as he turned to go into the house.

The borderman shook his head.

"Wait for me," added the colonel.

He carried the girl to that apartment in the cabin which served the purpose of a sitting-room, and laid her on a couch. He gently removed the folds of the blanket, disclosing to view a fragile, white-faced girl.

"Bess, hurry, hurry!" he screamed to his wife, and as she came running in, followed no less hurriedly by Betty, Helen and Nellie, he continued, "Here's Mabel Lane, alive, poor child; but in sore need of help. First see whether she has any bodily injury. If a bullet must be cut out, or a knife-wound sewed up, it's better she remained unconscious. Betty, run for Bess's instruments, and bring brandy and water. Lively now!" Then he gave vent to an oath and left the room.

Helen, her heart throbbing wildly, went to the side of Mrs. Zane, who was kneeling by the couch. She saw a delicate girl, not over eighteen years old, with a face that would have been beautiful but for the set lips, the closed eyelids, and an expression of intense pain.

"Oh! Oh!" breathed Helen.

"Nell, hand me the scissors," said Mrs. Zane, "and help me take off this dress. Why, it's wet, but, thank goodness! 'tis not with blood. I know that slippery touch too well. There, that's right. Betty, give me a spoonful of brandy. Now heat a blanket, and get one of your linsey gowns for this poor child."

Helen watched Mrs. Zane as if fascinated. The colonel's wife continued to talk while with deft fingers she forced a few drops of brandy between the girl's closed teeth. Then with the adroitness of a skilled surgeon, she made the examination. Helen had heard of this pioneer woman's skill in setting broken bones and treating injuries, and when she looked from the calm face to the steady fingers, she had no doubt as to the truth of what had been told.

"Neither bullet wound, cut, bruise, nor broken bone," said Mrs. Zane. "It's fear, starvation, and the terrible shock."

She rubbed Mabel's hands while gazing at her pale face. Then she forced more brandy between the tightly-closed lips. She was rewarded by ever so faint a color tinging the wan cheeks, to be followed by a fluttering of the eyelids. Then the eyes opened wide. They were large, soft, dark and humid with agony.

Helen could not bear their gaze. She saw the shadow of death, and of worse than death. She looked away, while in her heart rose a storm of passionate fury at the brutes who had made of this tender girl a wreck.

The room was full of women now, sober-faced matrons and grave-eyed girls, yet all wore the same expression, not alone of anger, nor fear, nor pity, but of all combined.

Helen instinctively felt that this was one of the trials of border endurance, and she knew from the sterner faces of the maturer women that such a trial was familiar. Despite all she had been told, the shock and pain were too great, and she went out of the room sobbing.

She almost fell over the broad back of Jonathan Zane who was sitting on the steps. Near him stood Colonel Zane talking with a tall man clad in faded buckskin.

"Lass, you shouldn't have stayed," said Colonel Zane kindly.

"It's—hurt—me—here," said Helen, placing her hand over her heart.

"Yes, I know, I know; of course it has," he replied, taking her hand. "But be brave, Helen, bear up, bear up. Oh! this border is a stern place! Do not think of that poor girl. Come, let me introduce Jonathan's friend, Wetzel!"

Helen looked up and held out her hand. She saw a very tall man with extremely broad shoulders, a mass of raven-black hair, and a white face.

He stepped forward, and took her hand in his huge, horny palm, pressing it, he stepped back without speaking. Colonel Zane talked to her in a soothing voice; but she failed to hear what he said. This Wetzel, this Indian-hunter whom she had heard called "Deathwind of the Border," this companion, guide, teacher of Jonathan Zane, this borderman of wonderful deeds, stood before her.

Helen saw a cold face, deathly in its pallor, lighted by eyes sloe-black but like glinting steel. Striking as were these features, they failed to fascinate as did the strange tracings which apparently showed through the white, drawn skin. This first repelled, then drew her with wonderful force. Suffering, of fire, and frost, and iron was written there, and, stronger than all, so potent as to cause fear, could be read the terrible purpose of this man's tragic life.

"You avenged her! Oh! I know you did!" cried Helen, her whole heart leaping with a blaze to her eyes.

She was answered by a smile, but such a smile! Kindly it broke over the stern face, giving a glimpse of a heart still warm beneath that steely cold. Behind it, too, there was something fateful, something deadly.

Helen knew, though the borderman spoke not, that somewhere among the grasses of the broad plains, or on the moss of the wooded hills, lay dead the perpetrators of this outrage, their still faces bearing the ghastly stamp of Deathwind.

CHAPTER 6

HEADER Happier days than she had hoped for, dawned upon Helen after the first touch of border sorrow. Mabel Lane did not die. Helen and Betty nursed the stricken girl tenderly, weeping for very joy when signs of improvement appeared. She had remained silent for several days, always with that haunting fear in her eyes, and then gradually came a change. Tender care and nursing had due effect in banishing the dark shadow. One morning after a long sleep she awakened with a bright smile, and from that time her improvement was rapid.

Helen wanted Mabel to live with her. The girl's position was pitiable. Homeless, fatherless, with not a relative on the border, yet so brave, so patient that she aroused all the sympathy in Helen's breast. Village gossip was in substance, that Mabel had given her love to a young frontiersman, by name Alex Bennet, who had an affection for her, so it was said, but as yet had made no choice between her and the other lasses of the settlement. What effect Mabel's terrible experience might have on this lukewarm lover, Helen could not even guess; but she was not hopeful as to the future. Colonel Zane and Betty approved of Helen's plan to persuade Mabel to live with her, and the latter's faint protestations they silenced by claiming she could be of great assistance in the management of the house, therefore it was settled.

Finally the day came when Mabel was ready to go with Helen. Betty had given her a generous supply of clothing, for all her belongings had been destroyed when the cabin was burned. With Helen's strong young arm around her she voiced her gratitude to Betty and Mrs. Zane and started toward the Sheppard home.

From the green square, where the ground was highest, an unobstructed view could be had of the valley. Mabel gazed down the river to where her home formerly stood. Only a faint, dark spot, like a blur on the green landscape, could be seen. Her soft eyes filled with tears; but she spoke no word.

"She's game and that's why she didn't go under," Colonel Zane said to himself as he mused on the strength and spirit of borderwomen. To their heroism, more than any other thing, he attributed the establishing of homes in this wilderness.

In the days that ensued, as Mabel grew stronger, the girls became very fond of each other. Helen would have been happy at any time with such a sweet companion, but just then, when the poor girl's mind was so sorely disturbed she was doubly glad. For several days, after Mabel was out of danger, Helen's thoughts had dwelt on a subject which caused extreme vexation. She had begun to suspect that she encouraged too many admirers for whom she did not care, and thought too much of a man who did not reciprocate. She was gay and moody in turn. During the moody hours she suspected herself, and in her gay ones, scorned the idea that she might ever care for a man who was indifferent. But that thought once admitted, had a trick of returning at odd moments, clouding her cheerful moods.

One sunshiny morning while the May flowers smiled under the hedge, when dew sparkled on the leaves, and the locust-blossoms shone creamy-white amid the soft green of the trees, the girls set about their much-planned flower gardening. Helen was passionately fond of plants, and had brought a jar of seeds of her favorites all the way from her eastern home.

"We'll plant the morning-glories so they'll run up the porch, and the dahlias in this long row and the nasturtiums in this round bed," Helen said.

"You have some trailing arbutus," added Mabel, "and must have clematis, wild honeysuckle and golden-glow, for they are all sweet flowers."

"This arbutus is so fresh, so dewy, so fragrant," said Helen, bending aside a lilac bush to see the pale, creeping flowers. "I never saw anything so beautiful. I grow more and more in love with my new home and friends.

I have such a pretty garden to look into, and I never tire of the view beyond."

Helen gazed with pleasure and pride at the garden with its fresh green and lavender-crested lilacs, at the white-blossomed trees, and the vine-covered log cabins with blue smoke curling from their stone chimneys. Beyond, the great bulk of the fort stood guard above the willow-skirted river, and far away over the winding stream the dark hills, defiant, kept their secrets.

"If it weren't for that threatening fort one could imagine this little hamlet, nestling under the great bluff, as quiet and secure as it is beautiful," said Helen. "But that charred stockade fence with its scarred bastions and these lowering port-holes, always keep me alive to the reality."

"It wasn't very quiet when Girty was here," Mabel replied thoughtfully.

"Were you in the fort then?" asked Helen breathlessly.

"Oh, yes, I cooled the rifles for the men," replied Mabel calmly.

"Tell me all about it."

Helen listened again to a story she had heard many times; but told by new lips it always gained in vivid interest. She never tired of hearing how the notorious renegade, Girty, rode around the fort on his white horse, giving the defenders an hour in which to surrender; she learned again of the attack, when the British soldiers remained silent on an adjoining hillside, while the Indians yelled exultantly and ran about in fiendish glee, when Wetzel began the battle by shooting an Indian chieftain who had ventured within range of his ever fatal rifle. And when it came to the heroic deeds of that memorable siege Helen could not contain her enthusiasm. She shed tears over little Harry Bennet's death at the south bastion where, though riddled with bullets, he stuck to his post until relieved. Clark's race, across the roof of the fort to extinguish a burning arrow, she applauded with clapping hands. Her great eyes glowed and burned, but she was silent, when hearing how Wetzel ran alone to a break in the stockade, and there, with an ax, the terrible borderman held at bay the whole infuriated Indian mob until the breach was closed. Lastly Betty Zane's never-to-be-forgotten run with the powder to the relief of the garrison and the saving of the fort was something not to cry over or applaud; but to dream of and to glorify.

"Down that slope from Colonel Zane's cabin is where Betty ran with the powder," said Mabel, pointing.

"Did you see her?" asked Helen.

"Yes, I looked out of a port-hole. The Indians stopped firing at the fort in their eagerness to shoot Betty. Oh, the banging of guns and yelling of savages was one fearful, dreadful roar! Through all that hail of bullets Betty ran swift as the wind."

"I almost wish Girty would come again," said Helen.

"Don't; he might."

"How long has Betty's husband, Mr. Clarke, been dead?" inquired Helen.

"I don't remember exactly. He didn't live long after the siege. Some say he inhaled the flames while fighting fire inside the stockade."

"How sad!"

"Yes, it was. It nearly killed Betty. But we border girls do not give up easily; we must not," replied Mabel, an unquenchable spirit showing through the sadness of her eyes.

Merry voices interrupted them, and they turned to see Betty and Nell entering the gate. With Nell's bright chatter and Betty's wit, the conversation became indeed vivacious, running from gossip to gowns, and then to that old and ever new theme, love. Shortly afterward the colonel entered the gate, with swinging step and genial smile.

"Well, now, if here aren't four handsome lasses," he said with an admiring glance.

"Eb, I believe if you were single any girl might well suspect you of being a flirt," said Betty.

"No girl ever did. I tell you I was a lady-killer in my day," replied Colonel Zane, straightening his fine form. He was indeed handsome, with his stalwart frame, dark, bronzed face and rugged, manly bearing.

"Bess said you were; but that it didn't last long after you saw her," cried Betty, mischief gleaming in her dark eye.

"Well, that's so," replied the colonel, looking a trifle crest-fallen; "but you know every dog has his day." Then advancing to the porch, he looked at Mabel with a more serious gaze as he asked, "How are you to-day?"

"Thank you, Colonel Zane, I am getting quite strong."

"Look up the valley. There's a raft coming down the river," said he softly.

Far up the broad Ohio a square patch showed dark against the green water.

Colonel Zane saw Mabel start, and a dark red flush came over her pale face. For an instant she gazed with an expression of appeal, almost fear. He knew the reason. Alex Bennet was on that raft.

"I came over to ask if I can be of any service?"

"Tell him," she answered simply.

"I say, Betts," Colonel Zane cried, "has Helen's cousin cast any more such sheep eyes at you?"

"Oh, Eb, what nonsense!" exclaimed Betty, blushing furiously.

"Well, if he didn't look sweet at you I'm an old fool."

"You're one anyway, and you're horrid," said Betty, tears of anger glistening in her eyes.

Colonel Zane whistled softly as he walked down the lane. He went into the wheelwright's shop to see about some repairs he was having made on a wagon, and then strolled on down to the river. Two Indians were sitting on the rude log wharf, together with several frontiersmen and rivermen, all waiting for the raft. He conversed with the Indians, who were friendly Chippewas, until the raft was tied up. The first person to leap on shore was a sturdy young fellow with a shock of yellow hair, and a warm, ruddy skin.

"Hello, Alex, did you have a good trip?" asked Colonel Zane of the youth.

"H'are ye, Colonel Zane. Yes, first-rate trip," replied young Bennet. "Say, I've a word for you. Come aside," and drawing Colonel Zane out of earshot of the others, he continued, "I heard this by accident, not that I didn't spy a bit when I got interested, for I did; but the way it came about was all chance. Briefly, there's a man, evidently an Englishman, at Fort Pitt whom I overheard say he was out on the border after a Sheppard girl. I happened to hear from one of Brandt's men, who rode into Pitt just before we left, that you had new friends here by that name. This fellow was a handsome chap, no common sort, but lordly, dissipated and reckless as the devil. He had a servant traveling with him, a sailor, by his gab, who was about the toughest customer I've met in many a day. He cut a fellow in bad shape at Pitt. These two will be on the next boat, due here in a day or so, according to river and weather conditions, an' I thought, considerin' how unusual the thing was, I'd better tell ye."

"Well, well," said Colonel Zane reflectively. He recalled Sheppard's talk about an Englishman. "Alex, you did well to tell me. Was the man drunk when he said he came west after a woman?"

"Sure he was," replied Alex. "But not when he spoke the name. Ye see I got suspicious, an' asked about him. It's this way: Jake Wentz, the trader, told me the fellow asked for the Sheppards when he got off the wagon-train. When I first seen him he was drunk, and I heard Jeff Lynn say as how the border was a bad place to come after a woman. That's what made me prick up my ears. Then the Englishman said: 'It is, eh? By God! I'd go to hell after a woman I wanted.' An' Colonel, he looked it, too."

Colonel Zane remained thoughtful while Alex made up a bundle and forced the haft of an ax under the string; but as the young man started away the colonel suddenly remembered his errand down to the wharf.

"Alex, come back here," he said, and wondered if the lad had good stuff in him. The boatman's face was plain, but not evil, and a close scrutiny of it rather prepossessed the colonel.

"Alex, I've some bad news for you," and then bluntly, with his keen gaze fastened on the young man's face, he told of old Lane's murder, of Mabel's abduction, and of her rescue by Wetzel.

Alex began to curse and swear vengeance.

"Stow all that," said the colonel sharply. "Wetzel followed four Indians who had Mabel and some stolen horses. The redskins quarreled over the girl, and two took the horses, leaving Mabel to the others. Wetzel went after these last, tomahawked them, and brought Mabel home. She was in a bad way, but is now getting over the shock."

"Say, what'd we do here without Wetzel?" Alex said huskily, unmindful of the tears that streamed from his eyes and ran over his brown cheeks. "Poor old Jake! Poor Mabel! Damn me! it's my fault. If I'd 'a done right an' married her as I should, as I wanted to, she wouldn't have had to suffer. But I'll marry her yet, if she'll have me. It was only because I had no farm, no stock, an' only that little cabin as is full now, that I waited."

"Alex, you know me," said Colonel Zane in kindly tones. "Look there, down the clearing half a mile. See that green strip of land along the river, with the big chestnut in the middle and a cabin beyond. There's as fine farming land as can be found on the border, eighty acres, well watered. The day you marry Mabel that farm is yours."

Alex grew red, stammered, and vainly tried to express his gratitude.

"Come along, the sooner you tell Mabel the better," said the colonel with glowing face. He was a good matchmaker. He derived more pleasure from a little charity bestowed upon a deserving person, than from a season's crops.

When they arrived at the Sheppard house the girls were still on the porch. Mabel rose when she saw Alex, standing white and still. He, poor fellow, was embarrassed by the others, who regarded him with steady eyes.

Colonel Zane pushed Alex up on the porch, and said in a low voice:

"Mabel, I've just arranged something you're to give Alex. It's a nice little farm, and it'll be a wedding present."

Mabel looked in a bewildered manner from Colonel Zane's happy face to the girls, and then at the red, joyous features of her lover. Only then did she understand, and uttering a strange little cry, put her trembling hands to her bosom as she swayed to and fro.

But she did not fall, for Alex, quick at the last, leaped forward and caught her in his arms.

~

THAT EVENING HELEN DENIED HERSELF TO MR. BRANDT AND SEVERAL other callers. She sat on the porch with her father while he smoked his pipe.

"Where's Will?" she asked.

"Gone after snipe, so he said," replied her father.

"Snipe? How funny! Imagine Will hunting! He's surely catching the wild fever Colonel Zane told us about."

"He surely is."

Then came a time of silence. Mr. Sheppard, accustomed to Helen's gladsome spirit and propensity to gay chatter, noted how quiet she was, and wondered.

"Why are you so still?"

"I'm a little homesick," Helen replied reluctantly.

"No? Well, I declare! This is a glorious country; but not for such as you, dear, who love music and gaiety. I often fear you'll not be happy here, and then I long for the old home, which reminds me of your mother."

"Dearest, forget what I said," cried Helen earnestly. "I'm only a little blue to-day; perhaps not at all homesick."

"Indeed, you always seemed happy."

"Father, I am happy. It's only—only a girl's foolish sentiment."

"I've got something to tell you, Helen, and it has bothered me since Colonel Zane spoke of it to-night. Mordaunt is coming to Fort Henry."

"Mordaunt? Oh, impossible! Who said so? How did you learn?"

"I fear 'tis true, my dear. Colonel Zane told me he had heard of an Englishman at Fort Pitt who asked after us. Moreover, the fellow answers the description of Mordaunt. I am afraid it is he, and come after you."

"Suppose he has—who cares? We owe him nothing. He cannot hurt us."

"But, Helen, he's a desperate man. Aren't you afraid of him?"

"Not I," cried Helen, laughing in scorn. "He'd better have a care. He can't run things with a high hand out here on the border. I told him I would have none of him, and that ended it."

"I'm much relieved. I didn't want to tell you; but it seemed necessary. Well, child, good night, I'll go to bed."

Long after Mr. Sheppard had retired Helen sat thinking. Memories of the past, and of the unwelcome suitor, Mordaunt, thronged upon her thick and fast. She could see him now with his pale, handsome face, and distinguished bearing. She had liked him, as she had other men, until he involved her father, with himself, in financial ruin, and had made his attention to her unpleasantly persistent. Then he had followed the fall of fortune with wild dissipation, and became a gambler and a drunkard. But he did not desist in his mad wooing. He became like her shadow, and life grew to be unendurable, until her father planned to emigrate west, when she hailed the news with joy. And now Mordaunt had tracked her to her new home. She was sick with disgust. Then her spirit, always strong, and now freer for this new, wild life of the frontier, rose within her, and she dismissed all thoughts of this man and his passion.

The old life was dead and buried. She was going to be happy here. As for the present, it was enough to think of the little border village, now her home; of her girl friends; of the quiet borderman: and, for the moment, that the twilight was somber and beautiful.

High up on the wooded bluff rising so gloomily over the village, she saw among the trees something silver-bright. She watched it rise slowly from behind the trees, now hidden, now white through rifts in the foliage, until it soared lovely and grand above the black horizon. The ebony shadows of night seemed to lift, as might a sable mantle moved by invisible hands. But dark shadows, safe from the moon-rays, lay under the trees, and a pale, misty vapor hung below the brow of the bluff.

Mysterious as had grown the night before darkness yielded to the moon, this pale, white light flooding the still valley, was even more soft and strange. To one of Helen's temperament no thought was needed; to see was enough. Yet her mind was active. She felt with haunting power the beauty of all before her; in fancy transporting herself far to those silver-tipped clouds, and peopling the dells and shady nooks under the hills with spirits and fairies, maidens and valiant knights. To her the day was as a far-off dream. The great watch stars grew wan before the radiant moon; it reigned alone. The immensity of the world with its glimmering rivers, pensive valleys and deep, gloomy forests lay revealed under the glory of the clear light.

Absorbed in this contemplation Helen remained a long time gazing with dreamy ecstasy at the moonlit valley until a slight chill disturbed her happy thoughts. She knew she was not alone. Trembling, she stood up to see, easily recognizable in the moonlight, the tall buckskin-garbed figure of Jonathan Zane.

"Well, sir," she called, sharply, yet with a tremor in her voice.

The borderman came forward and stood in front of her. Somehow he appeared changed. The long, black rifle, the dull, glinting weapons made her shudder. Wilder and more untamable he looked than ever. The very silence of the forest clung to him; the fragrance of the grassy plains came faintly from his buckskin garments.

"Evenin', lass," he said in his slow, cool manner.

"How did you get here?" asked Helen presently, because he made no effort to explain his presence at such a late hour.

"I was able to walk."

Helen observed, with a vaulting spirit, one ever ready to rise in arms, that Master Zane was disposed to add humor to his penetrating mysteriousness. She flushed hot and then paled. This borderman certainly possessed the power to vex her, and, reluctantly she admitted, to chill her soul and rouse her fear. She strove to keep back sharp words, because she had learned that this singular individual always gave good reason for his odd actions.

"I think in kindness to me," she said, choosing her words carefully, "you might tell me why you appear so suddenly, as if you had sprung out of the ground."

"Are you alone?"

"Yes. Father is in bed; so is Mabel, and Will has not yet come home. Why?"

"Has no one else been here?"

"Mr. Brandt came, as did some others; but wishing to be alone, I did not see them," replied Helen in perplexity.

"Have you seen Brandt since?"

"Since when?"

"The night I watched by the lilac bush."

"Yes, several times," replied Helen. Something in his tone made her ashamed. "I couldn't very well escape when he called. Are you surprised because after he insulted me I'd see him?"

"Yes."

Helen felt more ashamed.

"You don't love him?" he continued.

Helen was so surprised she could only look into the dark face above her. Then she dropped her gaze, abashed by his searching eyes. But, thinking of his question, she subdued the vague stirrings of pleasure in her breast, and answered coldly:

"No, I do not; but for the service you rendered me I should never have answered such a question."

"I'm glad, an' hope you care as little for the other five men who were here that night."

"I declare, Master Zane, you seem exceedingly interested in the affairs of a young woman whom you won't visit, except as you have come to-night."

He looked at her with his piercing eyes.

"You spied upon my guests," she said, in no wise abashed now that her temper was high. "Did you care so very much?"

"Care?" he asked slowly.

"Yes; you were interested to know how many of my admirers were here, what they did, and what they said. You even hint disparagingly of them."

"True, I wanted to know," he replied; "but I don't hint about any man."

"You are so interested you wouldn't call on me when I invited you," said Helen, with poorly veiled sarcasm. It was this that made her bitter; she could never forget that she had asked this man to come to see her, and he had refused.

"I reckon you've mistook me," he said calmly.

"Why did you come? Why do you shadow my friends? This is twice you have done it. Goodness knows how many times you've been here! Tell me."

The borderman remained silent.

"Answer me," commanded Helen, her eyes blazing. She actually stamped her foot. "Borderman or not, you have no right to pry into my affairs. If you are a gentleman, tell me why you came here?"

The eyes Jonathan turned on Helen stilled all the angry throbbing of her blood.

"I come here to learn which of your lovers is the dastard who plotted the abduction of Mabel Lane, an' the thief who stole our hosses. When I find the villain I reckon Wetzel an' I'll swing him to some tree."

The borderman's voice rang sharp and cold, and when he ceased speaking she sank back upon the step, shocked, speechless, to gaze up at him with staring eyes.

"Don't look so, lass; don't be frightened," he said, his voice gentle and kind as it had been hard. He took her hand in his. "You nettled me into replyin'. You have a sharp tongue, lass, and when I spoke I was thinkin' of him. I'm sorry."

"A horse-thief and worse than murderer among my friends!" murmured Helen, shuddering, yet she never thought to doubt his word.

"I followed him here the night of your company."

"Do you know which one?"

"No."

He still held her hand, unconsciously, but Helen knew it well. A sense of his strength came with the warm pressure, and comforted her. She would need that powerful hand, surely, in the evil days which seemed to darken the horizon.

"What shall I do?" she whispered, shuddering again.

"Keep this secret between you an' me."

"How can I? How can I?"

"You must," his voice was deep and low. "If you tell your father, or any one, I might lose the chance to find this man, for, lass, he's desperate cunnin'. Then he'd go free to rob others, an' mebbe help make off with other poor girls. Lass, keep my secret."

"But he might try to carry me away," said Helen in fearful perplexity.

"Most likely he might," replied the borderman with the smile that came so rarely.

"Oh! Knowing all this, how can I meet any of these men again? I'd betray myself."

"No; you've got too much pluck. It so happens you are the one to help me an' Wetzel rid the border of these hell-hounds, an' you won't fail. I know a woman when it comes to that."

"I—I help you and Wetzel?"

"Exactly."

"Gracious!" cried Helen, half-laughing, half-crying. "And poor me with more trouble coming on the next boat."

"Lass, the colonel told me about the Englishman. It'll be bad for him to annoy you."

Helen thrilled with the depth of meaning in the low voice. Fate surely was weaving a bond between her and this borderman. She felt it in his steady, piercing gaze; in her own tingling blood.

Then as her natural courage dispelled all girlish fears, she faced him, white, resolute, with a look in her eyes that matched his own.

"I will do what I can," she said.

CHAPTER 7

WESTWARD FROM FORT HENRY, FAR ABOVE THE EDDYING RIVER, Jonathan Zane slowly climbed a narrow, hazel-bordered, mountain trail. From time to time he stopped in an open patch among the thickets and breathed deep of the fresh, wood-scented air, while his keen gaze swept over the glades near by, along the wooded hillsides, and above at the timber-strewn woodland.

This June morning in the wild forest was significant of nature's brightness and joy. Broad-leaved poplars, dense foliaged oaks, and vine-covered maples shaded cool, mossy banks, while between the trees the sunshine streamed in bright spots. It shone silver on the glancing silver-leaf, and gold on the colored leaves of the butternut tree. Dewdrops glistened on the ferns; ripples sparkled in the brooks; spider-webs glowed with wondrous rainbow hues, and the flower of the forest, the sweet, pale-faced daisy, rose above the green like a white star.

Yellow birds flitted among the hazel bushes caroling joyously, and cat-birds sang gaily. Robins called; bluejays screeched in the tall, white oaks; wood-peckers hammered in the dead hard-woods, and crows cawed over-head. Squirrels chattered everywhere. Ruffed grouse rose with great bustle and a whirr, flitting like brown flakes through the leaves. From far above came the shrill cry of a hawk, followed by the wilder scream of an eagle.

Wilderness music such as all this fell harmoniously on the borderman's ear. It betokened the gladsome spirit of his wild friends, happy in the warm sunshine above, or in the cool depths beneath the fluttering leaves, and everywhere in those lonely haunts unalarmed and free.

Familiar to Jonathan, almost as the footpath near his home, was this winding trail. On the height above was a safe rendezvous, much frequented by him and Wetzel. Every lichen-covered stone, mossy bank, noisy brook and giant oak on the way up this mountain-side, could have told, had they spoken their secrets, stories of the bordermen. The fragile ferns and slender-bladed grasses peeping from the gray and amber mosses, and the flowers that hung from craggy ledges, had wisdom to impart. A borderman lived under the green tree-tops, and, therefore, all the nodding branches of sassafras and laurel, the grassy slopes and rocky cliffs, the stately ash trees, kingly oaks and dark, mystic pines, together with the creatures that dwelt among them, save his deadly red-skinned foes, he loved. Other affection as close and true as this, he had not known. Hearkening thus with single heart to nature's teachings, he learned her secrets. Certain it was, therefore, that the many hours he passed in the woods apart from savage pursuits, were happy and fruitful.

Slowly he pressed on up the ascent, at length coming into open light upon a small plateau marked by huge, rugged, weather-chipped stones. On the eastern side was a rocky promontory, and close to the edge of this cliff, an hundred feet in sheer descent, rose a gnarled, time and tempest-twisted chestnut tree. Here the borderman laid down his rifle and knapsack, and, half-reclining against the tree, settled himself to rest and wait.

This craggy point was the lonely watch-tower of eagles. Here on the highest headland for miles around where the bordermen were wont to meet, the outlook was far-reaching and grand.

Below the gray, splintered cliffs sheered down to meet the waving tree-tops, and then hill after hill, slope after slope, waved and rolled far, far down to the green river. Open grassy patches, bright little islands in that ocean of dark green, shone on the hillsides. The rounded ridges ran straight, curved, or zigzag, but shaped their graceful lines in the descent to make the valley. Long, purple-hued, shadowy depressions in the wide expanse of foliage marked deep clefts between ridges where dark, cool streams bounded on to meet the river. Lower, where the land was level, in open spaces could be seen a broad trail, yellow in the sunlight, winding along with the curves of the water-course. On a swampy meadow, blue in the distance, a herd of buffalo browsed. Beyond the river, high over the green island, Fort Henry lay peaceful and solitary, the only token of the works of man in all that vast panorama.

Jonathan Zane was as much alone as if one thousand miles, instead of five, intervened between him and the settlement. Loneliness was to him a passion. Other men loved home, the light of woman's eyes, the rattle of dice or the lust of hoarding; but to him this wild, remote promontory, with its limitless view, stretching away to the dim hazy horizon, was more than all the aching joys of civilization.

Hours here, or in the shady valley, recompensed him for the loss of home comforts, the soft touch of woman's hands, the kiss of baby lips, and also for all he suffered in his pitiless pursuits, the hard fare, the steel and blood of a borderman's life.

Soon the sun shone straight overhead, dwarfing the shadow of the chestnut on the rock.

During such a time it was rare that any connected thought came into the borderman's mind. His dark eyes, now strangely luminous, strayed lingeringly over those purple, undulating slopes. This intense watchfulness had no object, neither had his listening. He watched nothing; he hearkened to the silence. Undoubtedly in this state of rapt absorption his perceptions were acutely alert; but without thought, as were those of the savage in the valley below, or the eagle in the sky above.

Yet so perfectly trained were these perceptions that the least unnatural sound or sight brought him wary and watchful from his dreamy trance.

The slight snapping of a twig in the thicket caused him to sit erect, and reach out toward his rifle. His eyes moved among the dark openings in the thicket. In another moment a tall figure pressed the bushes apart. Jonathan let fall his rifle, and sank back against the tree once more. Wetzel stepped over the rocks toward him.

"Come from Blue Pond?" asked Jonathan as the newcomer took a seat beside him.

Wetzel nodded as he carefully laid aside his long, black rifle.

"Any Injun sign?" continued Jonathan, pushing toward his companion the knapsack of eatables he had brought from the settlement.

"Nary Shawnee track west of this divide," answered Wetzel, helping himself to bread and cheese.

"Lew, we must go eastward, over Bing Legget's way, to find the trail of the stolen horses."

"Likely, an' it'll be a long, hard tramp."

"Who's in Legget's gang now beside Old Horse, the Chippewa, an' his Shawnee pard, Wildfire? I don't know Bing; but I've seen some of his Injuns an' they remember me."

"Never seen Legget but onct," replied Wetzel, "an' that time I shot half his face off. I've been told by them as have seen him since, that he's got a nasty scar on his temple an' cheek. He's a big man an' knows the woods. I don't know who all's in his gang, nor does anybody. He works in the dark, an' for cunnin' he's got some on Jim Girty, Deerin', an' several more renegades we know of lyin' quiet back here in the woods. We never tackled as bad a gang as his'n; they're all experienced woodsmen, old fighters, an' desperate, outlawed as they be by Injuns an' whites. It wouldn't surprise me to find that it's him an' his gang who are runnin' this hoss-thievin'; but bad or no, we're goin' after 'em."

Jonathan told of his movements since he had last seen his companion.

"An' the lass Helen is goin' to help us," said Wetzel, much interested. "It's a good move. Women are keen. Betty put Miller's schemin' in my eye long 'afore I noticed it. But girls have chances we men'd never get."

"Yes, an' she's like Betts, quicker'n lightnin'. She'll find out this hoss-thief in Fort Henry; but Lew, when we do get him we won't be much better off. Where do them hosses go? Who's disposin' of 'em for this fellar?"

"Where's Brandt from?" asked Wetzel.

"Detroit; he's a French-Canadian."

Wetzel swung sharply around, his eyes glowing like wakening furnaces.

"Bing Legget's a French-Canadian, an' from Detroit. Metzar was once thick with him down Fort Pitt way 'afore he murdered a man an' became an outlaw. We're on the trail, Jack."

"Brandt an' Metzar, with Legget backin' them, an' the horses go overland to Detroit?"

"I calkilate you've hit the mark."

"What'll we do?" asked Jonathan.

"Wait; that's best. We've no call to hurry. We must know the truth before makin' a move, an' as yet we're only suspicious. This lass'll find out more in a week than we could in a year. But Jack, have a care she don't fall into any snare. Brandt ain't any too honest a lookin' chap, an' them renegades is hell for women. The scars you wear prove that well enough. She's a rare, sweet, bloomin' lass, too. I never seen her equal. I remember how her eyes flashed when she said she knew I'd avenged Mabel. Jack, they're wonderful eyes; an' that girl, however sweet an' good as she must be, is chain-lightnin' wrapped up in a beautiful form. Aren't the boys at the fort runnin' arter her?"

"Like mad; it'd make you laugh to see 'em," replied Jonathan calmly.

"There'll be some fights before she's settled for, an' mebbe arter thet. Have a care for her, Jack, an' see that she don't ketch you."

"No more danger than for you."

"I was ketched onct," replied Wetzel.

Jonathan Zane looked up at his companion. Wetzel's head was bowed; but there was no merriment in the serious face exposed to the borderman's scrutiny.

"Lew, you're jokin'."

"Not me. Some day, when you're ketched good, an' I have to go back to the lonely trail, as I did afore you an' me become friends, mebbe then, when I'm the last borderman, I'll tell you."

"Lew, 'cordin' to the way settlers are comin', in a few more years there won't be any need for a borderman. When the Injuns are all gone where'll be our work?"

"'Tain't likely either of us'll ever see them times," said Wetzel, "an' I don't want to. Wal, Jack, I'm off now, an' I'll meet you here every other day."

Wetzel shouldered his long rifle, and soon passed out of sight down the mountain-side.

Jonathan arose, shook himself as a big dog might have done, and went down into the valley. Only once did he pause in his descent, and that was when a crackling twig warned him some heavy body was moving near. Silently he sank into the bushes bordering the trail. He listened with his ear close to the ground. Presently he heard a noise as of two hard substances striking together. He resumed his walk, having recognized the grating noise of a deer-hoof striking a rock. Farther down he espied a pair grazing. The buck ran into the thicket; but the doe eyed him curiously.

Less than an hour's rapid walking brought him to the river. Here he plunged into a thicket of willows, and emerged on a sandy strip of shore. He carefully surveyed the river bank, and then pulled a small birch-bark canoe from among the foliage. He launched the frail craft, paddled across the river and beached it under a reedy, over-hanging bank.

The distance from this point in a straight line to his destination was only a mile; but a rocky bluff and a ravine necessitated his making a wide detour. While lightly leaping over a brook his keen eye fell on an imprint in the sandy loam. Instantly he was on his knees. The footprint was small, evidently a woman's, and, what was more unusual, instead of the flat, round moccasin-track, it was pointed, with a sharp, square heel. Such shoes were not worn by border girls. True Betty and Nell had them; but they never went into the woods without moccasins.

Jonathan's experienced eye saw that this imprint was not an hour old. He gazed up at the light. The day was growing short. Already shadows lay in the glens. He would not long have light enough to follow the trail; but he hurried on hoping to find the person who made it before darkness came. He had not traveled many paces before learning that the one who made it was lost. The uncertainty in those hasty steps was as plain to the borderman's eyes, as if it had been written in words on the sand. The course led along the brook, avoiding the rough places; and leading into the open glades and glens; but it drew no nearer to the settlement. A quarter of an hour of rapid trailing enabled Jonathan to discern a dark figure moving among the trees. Abandoning the trail, he cut across a ridge to head off the lost woman. Stepping out of a sassafras thicket, he came face to face with Helen Sheppard.

"Oh!" she cried in alarm, and then the expression of terror gave place to one of extreme relief and gladness. "Oh! Thank goodness! You've found me. I'm lost!"

"I reckon," answered Jonathan grimly. "The settlement's only five hundred yards over that hill."

"I was going the wrong way. Oh! suppose you hadn't come!" exclaimed Helen, sinking on a log and looking up at him with warm, glad eyes.

"How did you lose your way?" Jonathan asked. He saw neither the warmth in her eyes nor the gladness.

"I went up the hillside, only a little way, after flowers, keeping the fort in sight all the time. Then I saw some lovely violets down a little hill, and thought I might venture. I found such loads of them I forgot everything else, and I must have walked on a little way. On turning to go back I couldn't find the little hill. I have hunted in vain for the clearing. It seems as if I have been wandering about for hours. I'm so glad you've found me!"

"Weren't you told to stay in the settlement, inside the clearing?" demanded Jonathan.

"Yes," replied Helen, with her head up.

"Why didn't you?"

"Because I didn't choose."

"You ought to have better sense."

"It seems I hadn't," Helen said quietly, but her eyes belied that calm voice.

"You're a headstrong child," Jonathan added curtly.

"Mr. Zane!" cried Helen with pale face.

"I suppose you've always had your own sweet will; but out here on the border you ought to think a little of others, if not of yourself."

Helen maintained a proud silence.

"You might have run right into prowlin' Shawnees."

"That dreadful disaster would not have caused you any sorrow," she flashed out.

"Of course it would. I might have lost my scalp tryin' to get you back home," said Jonathan, beginning to hesitate. Plainly he did not know what to make of this remarkable young woman.

"Such a pity to have lost all your fine hair," she answered with a touch of scorn.

Jonathan flushed, perhaps for the first time in his life. If there was anything he was proud of, it was his long, glossy hair.

"Miss Helen, I'm a poor hand at words," he said, with a pale, grave face. "I was only speakin' for your own good."

"You are exceedingly kind; but need not trouble yourself."

"Say," Jonathan hesitated, looking half-vexed at the lovely, angry face. Then an idea occurred to him. "Well, I won't trouble. Find your way home yourself."

Abruptly he turned and walked slowly away. He had no idea of allowing her to go home alone; but believed it might be well for her to think so. If she did not call him back he would remain near at hand, and when she showed signs of anxiety or fear he could go to her.

Helen determined she would die in the woods, or be captured by Shawnees, before calling him back. But she watched him. Slowly the tall, strong figure, with its graceful, springy stride, went down the glade. He would be lost to view in a moment, and then she would be alone. How dark it had suddenly become! The gray cloak of twilight was spread over the forest, and in the hollows night already had settled down. A breathless silence pervaded the woods. How lonely! thought Helen, with a shiver. Surely it would be dark before she could find the settlement. What hill hid the settlement from view? She did not know, could not remember which he had pointed out. Suddenly she began to tremble. She had been so frightened before he had found her, and so relieved afterward; and now he was going away.

"Mr. Zane," she cried with a great effort. "Come back."

Jonathan kept slowly on.

"Come back, Jonathan, please."

The borderman retraced his steps.

"Please take me home," she said, lifting a fair face all flushed, tear-stained, and marked with traces of storm. "I was foolish, and silly to come into the woods, and so glad to see you! But you spoke to me—in—in a way no one ever used before. I'm sure I deserved it. Please take me home. Papa will be worried."

Softer eyes and voice than hers never entreated man.

"Come," he said gently, and, taking her by the hand, he led her up the ridge.

Thus they passed through the darkening forest, hand in hand, like a dusky redman and his bride. He helped her over stones and logs, but still held her hand when there was no need of it. She looked up to see him walking, so dark and calm beside her, his eyes ever roving among the trees. Deepest remorse came upon her because of what she had said. There was no sentiment for him in this walk under the dark canopy of the leaves. He realized the responsibility. Any tree might hide a treacherous foe. She would atone for her sarcasm, she promised herself, while walking, ever conscious of her hand in his, her bosom heaving with the sweet, undeniable emotion which came knocking at her heart.

Soon they were out of the thicket, and on the dusty lane. A few moments of rapid walking brought them within sight of the twinkling lights of the village, and a moment later they were at the lane leading to Helen's home. Releasing her hand, she stopped him with a light touch and said:

"Please don't tell papa or Colonel Zane."

"Child, I ought. Some one should make you stay at home."

"I'll stay. Please don't tell. It will worry papa."

Jonathan Zane looked down into her great, dark, wonderful eyes with an unaccountable feeling. He really did not hear what she asked. Something about that upturned face brought to his mind a rare and perfect flower which grew in far-off rocky fastnesses. The feeling he had was intangible, like no more than a breath of fragrant western wind, faint with tidings of some beautiful field.

"Promise me you won't tell."

"Well, lass, have it your own way," replied Jonathan, wonderingly conscious that it was the first pledge ever asked of him by a woman.

"Thank you. Now we have two secrets, haven't we?" she laughed, with eyes like stars.

"Run home now, lass. Be careful hereafter. I do fear for you with such spirit an' temper. I'd rather be scalped by Shawnees than have Bing Legget so much as set eyes on you."

"You would? Why?" Her voice was like low, soft music.

"Why?" he mused. "It'd seem like a buzzard about to light on a doe."

"Good-night," said Helen abruptly, and, wheeling, she hurried down the lane.

CHAPTER 8

"JACK," SAID COLONEL ZANE TO HIS BROTHER NEXT MORNING, "TO-DAY is Saturday and all the men will be in. There was high jinks over at Metzar's place yesterday, and I'm looking for more to-day. The two fellows Alex Bennet told me about, came on day-before-yesterday's boat. Sure enough, one's a lordly Englishman, and the other, the cussedest-looking little chap I ever saw. They started trouble immediately. The Englishman, his name is Mordaunt, hunted up the Sheppards and as near as I can make out from George's story, Helen spoke her mind very plainly. Mordaunt and Case, that's his servant, the little cuss, got drunk and raised hell down at Metzar's where they're staying. Brandt and Williams are drinking hard, too, which is something unusual for Brandt. They got chummy at once with the Englishman, who seems to have plenty of gold and is fond of gambling. This Mordaunt is a gentleman, or I never saw one. I feel sorry for him. He appears to be a ruined man. If he lasts a week out here I'll be surprised. Case looks ugly, as if he were spoiling to cut somebody. I want you to keep your eye peeled. The day may pass off as many other days of drinking bouts have, without anything serious, and on the other hand there's liable to be trouble."

Jonathan's preparations were characteristic of the borderman. He laid aside his rifle, and, removing his short coat, buckled on a second belt containing a heavier tomahawk and knife than those he had been wearing. Then he put on his hunting frock, or shirt, and wore it loose with the belts underneath, instead of on the outside. Unfastened, the frock was rather full, and gave him the appearance of a man unarmed and careless.

Jonathan Zane was not so reckless as to court danger, nor, like many frontiersmen, fond of fighting for its own sake. Colonel Zane was commandant of the fort, and, in a land where there was no law, tried to maintain a semblance of it. For years he had kept thieves, renegades and outlaws away from his little settlement by dealing out stern justice. His word was law, and his bordermen executed it as such. Therefore Jonathan and Wetzel made it their duty to have a keen eye on all that was happening. They kept the colonel posted, and never interfered in any case without orders.

The morning passed quietly. Jonathan strolled here or loitered there; but saw none of the roisterers. He believed they were sleeping off the effects of their orgy on the previous evening. After dinner he smoked his pipe. Betty and Helen passed, and Helen smiled. It struck him suddenly that she had never looked at him in such a way before. There was meaning in that warm, radiant flash. A little sense of vexation, the source of which he did not understand, stirred in him against this girl; but with it came the realization that her white face and big, dark eyes had risen before him often since the night before. He wished, for the first time, that he could understand women better.

"Everything quiet?" asked Colonel Zane, coming out on the steps.

"All quiet," answered Jonathan.

"They'll open up later, I suspect. I'm going over to Sheppard's for a while, and, later, will drop into Metzar's. I'll make him haul in a yard or two. I don't like things I hear about his selling the youngsters rum. I'd like you to be within call."

The borderman strolled down the bluff and along the path which overhung the river. He disliked Metzar more than his brother suspected, and with more weighty reason than that of selling rum to minors. Jonathan threw himself at length on the ground and mused over the situation.

"We never had any peace in this settlement, an' never will in our day. Eb is hopeful an' looks at the bright side, always expectin' to-morrow will be different. What have the past sixteen years been? One long bloody fight, an' the next sixteen won't be any better. I make out that we'll have a mix-up soon. Metzar an' Brandt with their allies, whoever they are, will be in it, an' if Bing Legget's in the gang, we've got, as Wetzel said, a long, hard trail, which may be our last. More'n that, there'll be trouble about this chain-lightnin' girl, as Wetzel predicted. Women make trouble anyways;

an' when they're winsome an' pretty they cause more; but if they're beautiful an' fiery, bent on havin' their way, as this new lass is, all hell couldn't hold a candle to them. We don't need the Shawnees an' Girtys, an' hoss thieves round this here settlement to stir up excitin' times, now we've got this dark-eyed lass. An' yet any fool could see she's sweet, an' good, an' true as gold."

Toward the middle of the afternoon Jonathan sauntered in the direction of Metzar's inn. It lay on the front of the bluff, with its main doors looking into the road. A long, one-story log structure with two doors, answered as a bar-room. The inn proper was a building more pretentious, and joined the smaller one at its western end. Several horses were hitched outside, and two great oxen yoked to a cumbersome mud-crusted wagon stood patiently by.

Jonathan bent his tall head as he entered the noisy bar-room. The dingy place reeked with tobacco smoke and the fumes of vile liquor. It was crowded with men. The lawlessness of the time and place was evident. Gaunt, red-faced frontiersmen reeled to and fro across the sawdust floor; hunters and fur-traders, raftsmen and farmers, swelled the motley crowd; young men, honest-faced, but flushed and wild with drink, hung over the bar; a group of sullen-visaged, serpent-eyed Indians held one corner. The black-bearded proprietor dealt out the rum.

From beyond the bar-room, through a door entering upon the back porch, came the rattling of dice. Jonathan crossed the bar-room apparently oblivious to the keen glance Metzar shot at him, and went out upon the porch. This also was crowded, but there was more room because of greater space. At one table sat some pioneers drinking and laughing; at another were three men playing with dice. Colonel Zane, Silas, and Sheppard were among the lookers-on at the game. Jonathan joined them, and gazed at the gamesters.

Brandt he knew well enough; he had seen that set, wolfish expression in the riverman's face before. He observed, however, that the man had flushed cheeks and trembling hands, indications of hard drinking. The player sitting next to Brandt was Williams, one of the garrison, and a good-natured fellow, but garrulous and wickedly disposed when drunk. The remaining player Jonathan at once saw was the Englishman, Mordaunt. He was a handsome man, with fair skin, and long, silken, blond mustache. Heavy lines, and purple shades under his blue eyes, were die unmistakable stamp of dissipation. Reckless, dissolute, bad as he looked, there yet clung something favorable about the man. Perhaps it was his cool, devil-may-care way as he pushed over gold piece after gold piece from the fast diminishing pile before him. His velvet frock and silken doublet had once been elegant; but were now sadly the worse for border roughing.

Behind the Englishman's chair Jonathan saw a short man with a face resembling that of a jackal. The grizzled, stubbly beard, the protruding, vicious mouth, the broad, flat nose, and deep-set, small, glittering eyes made a bad impression on the observer. This man, Jonathan concluded, was the servant, Case, who was so eager with his knife. The borderman made the reflection, that if knife-play was the little man's pastime, he was not likely to go short of sport in that vicinity.

Colonel Zane attracted Jonathan's attention at this moment. The pioneers had vacated the other table, and Silas and Sheppard now sat by it. The colonel wanted his brother to join them.

"Here, Johnny, bring drinks," he said to the serving boy. "Tell Metzar who they're for." Then turning to Sheppard he continued: "He keeps good whiskey; but few of these poor devils ever see it." At the same time Colonel Zane pressed his foot upon that of Jonathan's.

The borderman understood that the signal was intended to call attention to Brandt. The latter had leaned forward, as Jonathan passed by to take a seat with his brother, and said something in a low tone to Mordaunt and Case. Jonathan knew by the way the Englishman and his man quickly glanced up at him, that he had been the subject of the remark.

Suddenly Williams jumped to his feet with an oath.

"I'm cleaned out," he cried.

"Shall we play alone?" asked Brandt of Mordaunt.

"As you like," replied the Englishman, in a tone which showed he cared not a whit whether he played or not.

"I've got work to do. Let's have some more drinks, and play another time," said Brandt.

The liquor was served and drank. Brandt pocketed his pile of Spanish and English gold, and rose to his feet. He was a trifle unsteady; but not drunk.

"Will you gentlemen have a glass with me?" Mordaunt asked of Colonel Zane's party.

"Thank you, some other time, with pleasure. We have our drink now," Colonel Zane said courteously.

Meantime Brandt had been whispering in Case's ear. The little man laughed at something the riverman said. Then he shuffled from behind the table. He was short, his compact build gave promise of unusual strength and agility.

"What are you going to do now?" asked Mordaunt, rising also. He looked hard at Case.

"Shiver my sides, cap'n, if I don't need another drink," replied the sailor.

"You have had enough. Come upstairs with me," said Mordaunt.

"Easy with your hatch, cap'n," grinned Case. "I want to drink with that ther' Injun killer. I've had drinks with buccaneers, and bad men all over the world, and I'm not going to miss this chance."

"Come on; you will get into trouble. You must not annoy these gentlemen," said Mordaunt.

"Trouble is the name of my ship, and she's a trim, fast craft," replied the man.

His loud voice had put an end to the convention. Men began to crowd in from the bar-room. Metzar himself came to see what had caused the excitement.

The little man threw up his cap, whooped, and addressed himself to Jonathan:

"Injun-killer, bad man of the border, will you drink with a jolly old tar from England?"

Suddenly a silence reigned, like that in the depths of the forest. To those who knew the borderman, and few did not know him, the invitation was nothing less than an insult. But it did not appear to them, as to him, like a pre-arranged plot to provoke a fight.

"Will you drink, redskin-hunter?" bawled the sailor.

"No," said Jonathan in his quiet voice.

"Maybe you mean that against old England?" demanded Case fiercely.

The borderman eyed him steadily, inscrutable as to feeling or intent, and was silent.

"Go out there and I'll see the color of your insides quicker than I'd take a drink," hissed the sailor, with his brick-red face distorted and hideous to look upon. He pointed with a long-bladed knife that no one had seen him draw, to the green sward beyond the porch.

The borderman neither spoke, nor relaxed a muscle.

"Ho! ho! my brave pirate of the plains!" cried Case, and he leered with braggart sneer into the faces of Jonathan and his companions.

It so happened that Sheppard sat nearest to him, and got the full effect of the sailor's hot, rum-soaked breath. He arose with a pale face.

"Colonel, I can't stand this," he said hastily. "Let's get away from that drunken ruffian."

"Who's a drunken ruffian?" yelled Case, more angry than ever. "I'm not drunk; but I'm going to be, and cut some of you white-livered border mates. Here, you old masthead, drink this to my health, damn you!"

The ruffian had seized a tumbler of liquor from the table, and held it toward Sheppard while he brandished his long knife.

White as snow, Sheppard backed against the wall; but did not take the drink.

The sailor had the floor; no one save him spoke a word. The action had been so rapid that there had hardly been time. Colonel Zane and Silas were as quiet and tense as the borderman.

"Drink!" hoarsely cried the sailor, advancing his knife toward Sheppard's body.

When the sharp point all but pressed against the old man, a bright object twinkled through the air. It struck Case's wrist, knocked the knife from his fingers, and, bounding against the wall, fell upon the floor. It was a tomahawk.

The borderman sprang over the table like a huge catamount, and with movement equally quick, knocked Case with a crash against the wall; closed on him before he could move a hand, and flung him like a sack of meal over the bluff.

The tension relieved, some of the crowd laughed, others looked over the embankment to see how Case had fared, and others remarked that for some reason he had gotten off better than they expected.

The borderman remained silent. He leaned against a post, with broad breast gently heaving, but his eyes sparkled as they watched Brandt, Williams, Mordaunt and Metzar. The Englishman alone spoke.

"Handily done," he said, cool and suave. "Sir, yours is an iron hand. I apologize for this unpleasant affair. My man is quarrelsome when under the influence of liquor."

"Metzar, a word with you," cried Colonel Zane curtly.

"Come inside, kunnel," said the innkeeper, plainly ill at ease.

"No; listen here. I'll speak to the point. You've got to stop running this kind of a place. No words, now, you've got to stop. Understand? You know as well as I, perhaps better, the character of your so-called inn. You'll get but one more chance."

"Wal, kunnel, this is a free country," growled Metzar. "I can't help these fellars comin' here lookin' fer blood. I runs an honest place. The men want to drink an' gamble. What's law here? What can you do?"

"You know me, Metzar," Colonel Zane said grimly. "I don't waste words. 'To hell with law!' so you say. I can say that, too. Remember, the next drunken boy I see, or shady deal, or gambling spree, out you go for good."

Metzar lowered his shaggy head and left the porch. Brandt and his friends, with serious faces, withdrew into the bar-room.

The borderman walked around the corner of the inn, and up the lane. The colonel, with Silas and Sheppard, followed in more leisurely fashion. At a shout from some one they turned to see a dusty, bloody figure, with ragged clothes, stagger up from the bluff.

"There's that blamed sailor now," said Sheppard. "He's a tough nut. My! What a knock on the head Jonathan gave him. Strikes me, too, that tomahawk came almost at the right time to save me a whole skin."

"I was furious, but not at all alarmed," rejoined Colonel Zane.

"I wondered what made you so quiet."

"I was waiting. Jonathan never acts until the right moment, and then—well, you saw him. The little villain deserved killing. I could have shot him with pleasure. Do you know, Sheppard, Jonathan's aversion to shedding blood is a singular thing. He'd never kill the worst kind of a white man until driven to it."

"That's commendable. How about Wetzel?"

"Well, Lew is different," replied Colonel Zane with a shudder. "If I told him to take an ax and clean out Metzar's place—God! what a wreck he'd make of it. Maybe I'll have to tell him, and if I do, you'll see something you can never forget."

CHAPTER 9

ON SUNDAY MORNING UNDER THE BRIGHT, WARM SUN, THE LITTLE hamlet of Fort Henry lay peacefully quiet, as if no storms had ever rolled and thundered overhead, no roistering ever disturbed its stillness, and no Indian's yell ever horribly broke the quiet.

"'Tis a fine morning," said Colonel Zane, joining his sister on the porch. "Well, how nice you look! All in white for the first time since— well, you do look charming. You're going to church, of course."

"Yes, I invited Helen and her cousin to go. I've persuaded her to teach my Sunday-school class, and I'll take another of older children," replied Betty.

"That's well. The youngsters don't have much chance to learn out here. But we've made one great stride. A church and a preacher means very much to young people. Next shall come the village school."

"Helen and I might teach our classes an hour or two every afternoon."

"It would be a grand thing if you did! Fancy these tots growing up unable to read or write. I hate to think of it; but the Lord knows I've done my best. I've had my troubles in keeping them alive."

"Helen suggested the day school. She takes the greatest interest in everything and everybody. Her energy is remarkable. She simply must move, must do something. She overflows with kindness and sympathy. Yesterday she cried with happiness when Mabel told her Alex was eager to be married very soon. I tell you, Eb, Helen is a fine character."

"Yes, good as she is pretty, which is saying some," mused the colonel. "I wonder who'll be the lucky fellow to win her."

"It's hard to say. Not that Englishman, surely. She hates him. Jonathan might. You should see her eyes when he is mentioned."

"Say, Betts, you don't mean it?" eagerly asked her brother.

"Yes, I do," returned Betty, nodding her head positively. "I'm not easily deceived about those things. Helen's completely fascinated with Jack. She might be only a sixteen-year-old girl for the way she betrays herself to me."

"Betty, I have a beautiful plan."

"No doubt; you're full of them."

"We can do it, Betty, we can, you and I," he said, as he squeezed her arm.

"My dear old matchmaking brother," returned Betty, laughing, "it takes two to make a bargain. Jack must be considered."

"Bosh!" exclaimed the colonel, snapping his fingers. "You needn't tell me any young man—any man, could resist that glorious girl."

"Perhaps not; I couldn't if I were a man. But Jack's not like other people. He'd never realize that she cared for him. Besides, he's a borderman."

"I know, and that's the only serious obstacle. But he could scout around the fort, even if he was married. These long, lonely, terrible journeys taken by him and Wetzel are mostly unnecessary. A sweet wife could soon make him see that. The border will be civilized in a few years, and because of that he'd better give over hunting for Indians. I'd like to see him married and settled down, like all the rest of us, even Isaac. You know Jack's the last of the Zanes, that is, the old Zanes. The difficulty arising from his extreme modesty and bashfulness can easily be overcome."

"How, most wonderful brother?"

"Easy as pie. Tell Jack that Helen is dying of love for him, and tell her that Jack loves——"

"But, dear Eb, that latter part is not true," interposed Betty.

"True, of course it's true, or would be in any man who wasn't as blind as a bat. We'll tell her Jack cares for her; but he is a borderman with stern ideas of duty, and so slow and backward he'd never tell his love even if he had overcome his tricks of ranging. That would settle it with any girl worth her salt, and this one will fetch Jack in ten days, or less."

"Eb, you're a devil," said Betty gaily, and then she added in a more sober vein, "I understand, Eb. Your idea is prompted by love of Jack, and it's all right. I never see him go out of the clearing but I think it may be for the last time, even as on that day so long ago when brother Andrew waved his cap to us, and never came back. Jack is the best man in the world, and I, too, want to see him happy, with a wife, and babies, and a settled occupation in life. I think we might weave a pretty little romance. Shall we try?"

"Try? We'll do it! Now, Betts, you explain it to both. You can do it smoother than I, and telling them is really the finest point of our little plot. I'll help the good work along afterwards. He'll be out presently. Nail him at once."

Jonathan, all unconscious of the deep-laid scheme to make him happy, soon came out on the porch, and stretched his long arms as he breathed freely of the morning air.

"Hello, Jack, where are you bound?" asked Betty, clasping one of his powerful, buckskin-clad knees with her arm.

"I reckon I'll go over to the spring," he replied, patting her dark, glossy head.

"Do you know I want to tell you something, Jack, and it's quite serious," she said, blushing a little at her guilt; but resolute to carry out her part of the plot.

"Well, dear?" he asked as she hesitated.

"Do you like Helen?"

"That is a question," Jonathan replied after a moment.

"Never mind; tell me," she persisted.

He made no answer.

"Well, Jack, she's—she's wildly in love with you."

The borderman stood very still for several moments. Then, with one step he gained the lawn, and turned to confront her.

"What's that you say?"

Betty trembled a little. He spoke so sharply, his eyes were bent on her so keenly, and he looked so strong, so forceful that she was almost afraid. But remembering that she had said only what, to her mind, was absolutely true, she raised her eyes and repeated the words:

"Helen is wildly in love with you."

"Betty, you wouldn't joke about such a thing; you wouldn't lie to me, I know you wouldn't."

"No, Jack dear."

She saw his powerful frame tremble, even as she had seen more than one man tremble, during the siege, under the impact of a bullet.

Without speaking, he walked rapidly down the path toward the spring.

Colonel Zane came out of his hiding-place behind the porch and, with a face positively electrifying in its glowing pleasure, beamed upon his sister.

"Gee! Didn't he stalk off like an Indian chief!" he said, chuckling with satisfaction. "By George! Betts, you must have got in a great piece of work. I never in my life saw Jack look like that."

Colonel Zane sat down by Betty's side and laughed softly but heartily.

"We'll fix him all right, the lonely hill-climber! Why, he hasn't a ghost of a chance. Wait until she sees him after hearing your story! I tell you, Betty—why—damme! you're crying!"

He had turned to find her head lowered, while she shaded her face with her hand.

"Now, Betty, just a little innocent deceit like that—what harm?" he said, taking her hand. He was as tender as a woman.

"Oh, Eb, it wasn't that. I didn't mind telling him. Only the flash in his eyes reminded me of—of Alfred."

"Surely it did. Why not? Almost everything brings up a tender memory for some one we've loved and lost. But don't cry, Betty."

She laughed a little, and raised a face with its dark cheeks flushed and tear-stained.

"I'm silly, I suppose; but I can't help it. I cry at least once every day."

"Brace up. Here come Helen and Will. Don't let them see you grieved. My! Helen in pure white, too! This is a conspiracy to ruin the peace of the masculine portion of Fort Henry."

Betty went forward to meet her friends while Colonel Zane continued talking, but now to himself. "What a fatal beauty she has!" His eyes swept over Helen with the pleasure of an artist. The fair richness of her skin, the perfect lips, the wavy, shiny hair, the wondrous dark-blue, changing eyes, the tall figure, slender, but strong and swelling with gracious womanhood, made a picture he delighted in and loved to have near him. The girl did not possess for him any of that magnetism, so commonly felt by most of her admirers; but he did feel how subtly full she was of something, which for want of a better term he described in Wetzel's characteristic expression, as "chain-lightning."

He reflected that as he was so much older, that she, although always winsome and earnest, showed nothing of the tormenting, bewildering coquetry of her nature. Colonel Zane prided himself on his discernment, and he had already observed that Helen had different sides of character for different persons. To Betty, Mabel, Nell, and the children, she was

564

frank, girlish, full of fun and always lovable; to her elders quiet and earnestly solicitous to please; to the young men cold; but with a penetrating, mocking promise haunting that coldness, and sometimes sweetly agreeable, often wilful, and changeable as April winds. At last the colonel concluded that she needed, as did all other spirited young women, the taming influence of a man whom she loved, a home to care for, and children to soften and temper her spirit.

"Well, young friends, I see you count on keeping the Sabbath," he said cheerily. "For my part, Will, I don't see how Jim Douns can preach this morning, before this laurel blossom and that damask rose."

"How poetical! Which is which?" asked Betty.

"Flatterer!" laughed Helen, shaking her finger.

"And a married man, too!" continued Betty.

"Well, being married has not affected my poetical sentiment, nor impaired my eyesight."

"But it has seriously inconvenienced your old propensity of making love to the girls. Not that you wouldn't if you dared," replied Betty with mischief in her eye.

"Now, Will, what do you think of that? Isn't it real sisterly regard? Come, we'll go and look at my thoroughbreds," said Colonel Zane.

"Where is Jonathan?" Helen asked presently. "Something happened at Metzar's yesterday. Papa wouldn't tell me, and I want to ask Jonathan."

"Jack is down by the spring. He spends a great deal of his time there. It's shady and cool, and the water babbles over the stones."

"How much alone he is," said Helen.

Betty took her former position on the steps, but did not raise her eyes while she continued speaking. "Yes, he's more alone than ever lately, and quieter, too. He hardly ever speaks now. There must be something on his mind more serious than horse-thieves."

"What?" Helen asked quickly.

"I'd better not tell—you."

A long moment passed before Helen spoke.

"Please tell me!"

"Well, Helen, we think, Eb and I, that Jack is in love for the first time in his life, and with you, you adorable creature. But Jack's a borderman; he is stern in his principles, thinks he is wedded to his border life, and he knows that he has both red and white blood on his hands. He'd die before he'd speak of his love, because he cannot understand that would do any good, even if you loved him, which is, of course, preposterous."

"Loves me!" breathed Helen softly.

She sat down rather beside Betty, and turned her face away. She still held the young woman's hand which she squeezed so tightly as to make its owner wince. Betty stole a look at her, and saw the rich red blood mantling her cheeks, and her full bosom heave.

Helen turned presently, with no trace of emotion except a singular brilliance of the eyes. She was so slow to speak again that Colonel Zane and Will returned from the corral before she found her voice.

"Colonel Zane, please tell me about last night. When papa came home to supper he was pale and very nervous. I knew something had happened. But he would not explain, which made me all the more anxious. Won't you please tell me?"

Colonel Zane glanced again at her, and knew what had happened. Despite her self-possession those tell-tale eyes told her secret. Everchanging and shadowing with a bounding, rapturous light, they were indeed the windows of her soul. All the emotion of a woman's heart shone there, fear, beauty, wondering appeal, trembling joy, and timid hope.

"Tell you? Indeed I will," replied Colonel Zane, softened and a little remorseful under those wonderful eyes.

No one liked to tell a story better than Colonel Zane. Briefly and graphically he related the circumstances of the affair leading to the attack on Helen's father, and, as the tale progressed, he became quite excited, speaking with animated face and forceful gestures.

"Just as the knife-point touched your father, a swiftly-flying object knocked the weapon to the floor. It was Jonathan's tomahawk. What followed was so sudden I hardly saw it. Like lightning, and flexible as steel, Jonathan jumped over the table, smashed Case against the wall, pulled him up and threw him over the bank. I tell you, Helen, it was a beautiful piece of action; but not, of course, for a woman's eyes. Now that's all. Your father was not even hurt."

"He saved papa's life," murmured Helen, standing like a statue.

She wheeled suddenly with that swift bird-like motion habitual to her, and went quickly down the path leading to the spring.

~

JONATHAN ZANE, SOLITARY DREAMER OF DREAMS AS HE WAS, HAD NEVER been in as strange and beautiful a reverie as that which possessed him on this Sabbath morning.

Deep into his heart had sunk Betty's words. The wonder of it, the sweetness, that alone was all he felt. The glory of this girl had begun, days past, to spread its glamour round him. Swept irresistibly away now, he soared aloft in a dream-castle of fancy with its painted windows and golden walls.

For the first time in his life on the border he had entered the little glade and had no eye for the crystal water flowing over the pebbles and mossy stones, or the plot of grassy ground inclosed by tall, dark trees and shaded by a canopy of fresh green and azure blue. Nor did he hear the music of the soft rushing water, the warbling birds, or the gentle sighing breeze moving the leaves.

Gone, vanished, lost to-day was that sweet companionship of nature. That indefinable and unutterable spirit which flowed so peacefully to him from his beloved woods; that something more than merely affecting his senses, which existed for him in the stony cliffs, and breathed with life through the lonely aisles of the forest, had fled before the fateful power of a woman's love and beauty.

A long time that seemed only a moment passed while he leaned against a stone. A light step sounded on the path.

A vision in pure white entered the glade; two little hands pressed his, and two dark-blue eyes of misty beauty shed their light on him.

"Jonathan, I am come to thank you."

Sweet and tremulous, the voice sounded far away.

"Thank me? For what?"

"You saved papa's life. Oh! how can I thank you?"

No voice answered for him.

"I have nothing to give but this."

A flower-like face was held up to him; hands light as thistledown touched his shoulders; dark-blue eyes glowed upon him with all tenderness.

"May I thank you—so?"

Soft lips met his full and lingeringly.

Then came a rush as of wind, a flash of white, and the patter of flying feet. He was alone in the glade.

CHAPTER 10

J<small>UNE PASSED</small>; J<small>ULY OPENED WITH UNUSUALLY WARM WEATHER, AND</small> F<small>ORT</small> Henry had no visits from Indians or horse-thieves, nor any inconvenience except the hot sun. It was the warmest weather for many years, and seriously dwarfed the settlers' growing corn. Nearly all the springs were dry, and a drouth menaced the farmers.

The weather gave Helen an excuse which she was not slow to adopt. Her pale face and languid air perplexed and worried her father and her friends. She explained to them that the heat affected her disagreeably.

Long days had passed since that Sunday morning when she kissed the borderman. What transports of sweet hope and fear were hers then! How shame had scorched her happiness! Yet still she gloried in the act. By that kiss had she awakened to a full consciousness of her love. With insidious stealth and ever-increasing power this flood had increased to full tide, and, bursting its bonds, surged over her with irresistible strength.

During the first days after the dawning of her passion, she lived in its sweetness, hearing only melodious sounds chiming in her soul. The hours following that Sunday were like long dreams. But as all things reach fruition, so this girlish period passed, leaving her a thoughtful woman. She began to gather up the threads of her life where love had broken them, to plan nobly, and to hope and wait.

Weeks passed, however, and her lover did not come. Betty told her that Jonathan made flying trips at break of day to hold council with

Colonel Zane; that he and Wetzel were on the trail of Shawnees with stolen horses, and both bordermen were in their dark, vengeful, terrible moods. In these later days Helen passed through many stages of feeling. After the exalting mood of hot, young love, came reaction. She fell into the depths of despair. Sorrow paled her face, thinned her cheeks and lent another shadow, a mournful one, to her great eyes. The constant repression of emotion, the strain of trying to seem cheerful when she was miserable, threatened even her magnificent health. She answered the solicitude of her friends by evasion, and then by that innocent falsehood in which a sensitive soul hides its secrets. Shame was only natural, because since the borderman came not, nor sent her a word, pride whispered that she had wooed him, forgetting modesty.

Pride, anger, shame, despair, however, finally fled before affection. She loved this wild borderman, and knew he loved her in return although he might not understand it himself. His simplicity, his lack of experience with women, his hazardous life and stern duty regarding it, pleaded for him and for her love. For the lack of a little understanding she would never live unhappy and alone while she was loved. Better give a thousand times more than she had sacrificed. He would return to the village some day, when the Indians and the thieves were run down, and would be his own calm, gentle self. Then she would win him, break down his allegiance to this fearful border life, and make him happy in her love.

While Helen was going through one of the fires of life to come out sweeter and purer, if a little pensive and sad, time, which waits not for love, nor life, nor death, was hastening onward, and soon the golden fields of grain were stored. September came with its fruitful promise fulfilled.

Helen entered once more into the quiet, social life of the little settlement, taught her class on Sundays, did all her own work, and even found time to bring a ray of sunshine to more than one sick child's bed. Yet she did not forget her compact with Jonathan, and bent all her intelligence to find some clew that might aid in the capture of the horse-thief. She was still groping in the darkness. She could not, however, banish the belief that the traitor was Brandt. She blamed herself for this, because of having no good reasons for suspicion; but the conviction was there, fixed by intuition. Because a man's eyes were steely gray, sharp like those of a cat's, and capable of the same contraction and enlargement, there was no reason to believe their owner was a criminal. But that, Helen acknowledged with a smile, was the only argument she had. To be sure Brandt had looked capable of anything, the night Jonathan knocked him down; she knew he had incited Case to begin the trouble at Metzar's, and had seemed worried since that time. He had not left the settlement on short journeys, as had been his custom before the affair in the bar-room. And not a horse had disappeared from Fort Henry since that time.

Brandt had not discontinued his attentions to her; if they were less ardent it was because she had given him absolutely to understand that she could be his friend only. And she would not have allowed even so much except for Jonathan's plan. She fancied it was possible to see behind Brandt's courtesy, the real subtle, threatening man. Stripped of his kindliness, an assumed virtue, the iron man stood revealed, cold, calculating, cruel.

Mordaunt she never saw but once and then, shocking and pitiful, he lay dead drunk in the grass by the side of the road, his pale, weary, handsome face exposed to the pitiless rays of the sun. She ran home weeping over this wreck of what had once been so fine a gentleman. Ah! the curse of rum! He had learned his soft speech and courtly bearing in the refinement of a home where a proud mother adored, and gentle sisters loved him. And now, far from the kindred he had disgraced, he lay in the road like a log. How it hurt her! She almost wished she could have loved him, if love might have redeemed. She was more kind to her other admirers, more tolerant of Brandt, and could forgive the Englishman, because the pangs she had suffered through love had softened her spirit.

During this long period the growing friendship of her cousin for Betty had been a source of infinite pleasure to Helen. She hoped and believed a romance would develop between the young widow and Will, and did all in her power, slyly abetted by the matchmaking colonel, to bring the two together.

One afternoon when the sky was clear with that intense blue peculiar to bright days in early autumn, Helen started out toward Betty's, intending to remind that young lady she had promised to hunt for clematis and other fall flowers.

About half-way to Betty's home she met Brandt. He came swinging round a corner with his quick, firm step. She had not seen him for several days, and somehow he seemed different. A brightness, a flash, as of daring expectation, was in his face. The poise, too, of the man had changed.

"Well, I am fortunate. I was just going to your home," he said cheerily. "Won't you come for a walk with me?"

"You may walk with me to Betty's," Helen answered.

"No, not that. Come up the hillside. We'll get some goldenrod. I'd like to have a chat with you. I may go away—I mean I'm thinking of making a short trip," he added hurriedly.

"Please come."

"I promised to go to Betty's."

"You won't come?" His voice trembled with mingled disappointment and resentment.

"No," Helen replied in slight surprise.

"You have gone with the other fellows. Why not with me?" He was white now, and evidently laboring under powerful feelings that must have had their origin in some thought or plan which hinged on the acceptance of his invitation.

"Because I choose not to," Helen replied coldly, meeting his glance fully.

A dark red flush swelled Brandt's face and neck; his gray eyes gleamed balefully with wolfish glare; his teeth were clenched. He breathed hard and trembled with anger. Then, by a powerful effort, he conquered himself; the villainous expression left his face; the storm of rage subsided. Great incentive there must have been for him thus to repress his emotions so quickly. He looked long at her with sinister, intent regard; then, with the laugh of a desperado, a laugh which might have indicated contempt for the failure of his suit, and which was fraught with a world of meaning, of menace, he left her without so much as a salute.

Helen pondered over this sudden change, and felt relieved because she need make no further pretense of friendship. He had shown himself to be what she had instinctively believed. She hurried on toward Betty's, hoping to find Colonel Zane at home, and with Jonathan, for Brandt's hint of leaving Fort Henry, and his evident chagrin at such a slip of speech, had made her suspicious. She was informed by Mrs. Zane that the colonel had gone to a log-raising; Jonathan had not been in for several days, and Betty went away with Will.

"Where did they go?" asked Helen.

"I'm not sure; I think down to the spring."

Helen followed the familiar path through the grove of oaks into the glade. It was quite deserted. Sitting on the stone against which Jonathan had leaned the day she kissed him, she gave way to tender reflection. Suddenly she was disturbed by the sound of rapid footsteps, and looking up, saw the hulking form of Metzar, the innkeeper, coming down the path. He carried a bucket, and meant evidently to get water. Helen did not desire to be seen, and, thinking he would stay only a moment, slipped into a thicket of willows behind the stone. She could see plainly through the foliage. Metzar came into the glade, peered around in the manner of a man expecting to see some one, and then, filling his bucket at the spring, sat down on the stone.

Not a minute elapsed before soft, rapid footsteps sounded in the distance. The bushes parted, disclosing the white, set face and gray eyes of Roger Brandt. With a light spring he cleared the brook and approached Metzar.

Before speaking he glanced around the glade with the fugitive, distrustful glance of a man who suspects even the trees. Then, satisfied by the scrutiny he opened his hunting frock, taking forth a long object which he thrust toward Metzar.

It was an Indian arrow.

Metzar's dull gaze traveled from this to the ominous face of Brandt.

"See there, you! Look at this arrow! Shot by the best Indian on the border into the window of my room. I hadn't been there a minute when it came from the island. God! but it was a great shot!"

"Hell!" gasped Metzar, his dull face quickening with some awful thought.

"I guess it is hell," replied Brandt, his face growing whiter and wilder.

"Our game's up?" questioned Metzar with haggard cheek.

"Up? Man! We haven't a day, maybe less, to shake Fort Henry."

"What does it mean?" asked Metzar. He was the calmer of the two.

"It's a signal. The Shawnees, who were in hiding with the horses over by Blueberry swamp, have been flushed by those bordermen. Some of them have escaped; at least one, for no one but Ashbow could shoot that arrow across the river."

"Suppose he hadn't come?" whispered Metzar hoarsely.

Brandt answered him with a dark, shuddering gaze.

A twig snapped in the thicket. Like foxes at the click of a trap, these men whirled with fearsome glances.

"Ugh!" came a low, guttural voice from the bushes, and an Indian of magnificent proportions and somber, swarthy features, entered the glade.

CHAPTER 11

THE SAVAGE HAD JUST EMERGED FROM THE RIVER, FOR HIS GRACEFUL, copper-colored body and scanty clothing were dripping with water. He carried a long bow and a quiver of arrows.

Brandt uttered an exclamation of surprise, and Metzar a curse, as the lithe Indian leaped the brook. He was not young. His swarthy face was lined, seamed, and terrible with a dark impassiveness.

"Paleface-brother-get-arrow," he said in halting English, as his eyes flashed upon Brandt. "Chief-want-make-sure."

The white man leaned forward, grasped the Indian's arm, and addressed him in an Indian language. This questioning was evidently in regard to his signal, the whereabouts of others of the party, and why he took such fearful risks almost in the village. The Indian answered with one English word.

"Deathwind!"

Brandt drew back with drawn, white face, while a whistling breath escaped him.

"I knew it, Metz. Wetzel!" he exclaimed in a husky voice.

The blood slowly receded from Metzar's evil, murky face, leaving it haggard.

"Deathwind-on-Chief's-trail-up-Eagle Rock," continued the Indian. "Deathwind-fooled-not-for-long. Chief-wait-paleface-brothers at Two Islands."

The Indian stepped into the brook, parted the willows, and was gone as he had come, silently.

"We know what to expect," said Brandt in calmer tone as the daring cast of countenance returned to him. "There's an Indian for you! He got away, doubled like an old fox on his trail, and ran in here to give us a chance at escape. Now you know why Bing Legget can't be caught."

"Let's dig at once," replied Metzar, with no show of returning courage such as characterized his companion.

Brandt walked to and fro with bent brows, like one in deep thought. Suddenly he turned upon Metzar eyes which were brightly hard, and reckless with resolve.

"By Heaven! I'll do it! Listen. Wetzel has gone to the top of Eagle Mountain, where he and Zane have a rendezvous. Even he won't suspect the cunning of this Indian; anyway it'll be after daylight to-morrow before he strikes the trail. I've got twenty-four hours, and more, to get this girl, and I'll do it!"

"Bad move to have weight like her on a march," said Metzar.

"Bah! The thing's easy. As for you, go on, push ahead after we're started. All I ask is that you stay by me until the time to cut loose."

"I ain't agoin' to crawfish now," growled Metzar. "Strikes me, too, I'm losin' more'n you."

"You won't be a loser if you can get back to Detroit with your scalp. I'll pay you in horses and gold. Once we reach Legget's place we're safe."

"What's yer plan about gittin' the gal?" asked Metzar.

Brandt leaned forward and spoke eagerly, but in a low tone.

"Git away on hoss-back?" questioned Metzar, visibly brightening. "Wal, that's some sense. Kin ye trust ther other party?"

"I'm sure I can," rejoined Brandt.

"It'll be a good job, a good job an' all done in daylight, too. Bing Legget couldn't plan better," Metzar said, rubbing his hands.

"We've fooled these Zanes and their fruit-raising farmers for a year, and our time is about up," Brandt muttered. "One more job and we've done. Once with Legget we're safe, and then we'll work slowly back towards Detroit. Let's get out of here now, for some one may come at any moment."

The plotters separated, Brandt going through the grove, and Metzar down the path by which he had come.

HELEN, TREMBLING WITH HORROR OF WHAT SHE HAD HEARD, RAISED herself cautiously from the willows where she had lain, and watched the innkeeper's retreating figure. When it had disappeared she gave a little gasp of relief. Free now to run home, there to plan what course must be pursued, she conquered her fear and weakness, and hurried from the glade. Luckily, so far as she was able to tell, no one saw her return. She resolved that she would be cool, deliberate, clever, worthy of the borderman's confidence.

First she tried to determine the purport of this interview between Brandt and Metzar. She recalled to mind all that was said, and supplied what she thought had been suggested. Brandt and Metzar were horse-thieves, aids of Bing Legget. They had repaired to the glade to plan. The Indian had been a surprise. Wetzel had routed the Shawnees, and was now on the trail of this chieftain. The Indian warned them to leave Fort Henry and to meet him at a place called Two Islands. Brandt's plan, presumably somewhat changed by the advent of the red-man, was to steal horses, abduct a girl in broad daylight, and before tomorrow's sunset escape to join the ruffian Legget.

"I am the girl," murmured Helen shudderingly, as she relapsed momentarily into girlish fears. But at once she rose above selfish feelings.

Secondly, while it was easy to determine what the outlaws meant, the wisest course was difficult to conceive. She had promised the borderman to help him, and not speak of anything she learned to any but himself. She could not be true to him if she asked advice. The point was clear; either she must remain in the settlement hoping for Jonathan's return in time to frustrate Brandt's villainous scheme, or find the borderman. Suddenly she remembered Metzar's allusion to a second person whom Brandt felt certain he could trust. This meant another traitor in Fort Henry, another horse-thief, another desperado willing to make off with helpless women.

Helen's spirit rose in arms. She had their secret, and could ruin them. She would find the borderman.

Wetzel was on the trail at Eagle Rock. What for? Trailing an Indian who was then five miles east of that rock? Not Wetzel! He was on that track to meet Jonathan. Otherwise, with the redskins near the river, he would have been closer to them. He would meet Jonathan there at sunset to-day, Helen decided.

She paced the room, trying to still her throbbing heart and trembling hands.

"I must be calm," she said sternly. "Time is precious. I have not a moment to lose. I will find him. I've watched that mountain many a time, and can find the trail and the rock. I am in more danger here, than out there in the forest. With Wetzel and Jonathan on the mountain side, the Indians have fled it. But what about the savage who warned Brandt? Let me think. Yes, he'll avoid the river; he'll go round south of the settlement, and, therefore, can't see me cross. How fortunate that I have paddled a canoe many times across the river. How glad that I made Colonel Zane describe the course up the mountains!"

Her resolution fixed, Helen changed her skirt for one of buckskin, putting on leggings and moccasins of the same serviceable material. She filled the pockets of a short, rain-proof jacket with biscuits, and, thus equipped, sallied forth with a spirit and exultation she could not subdue. Only one thing she feared, which was that Brandt or Metzar might see her cross the river. She launched her canoe and paddled down stream, under cover of the bluff, to a point opposite the end of the island, then straight across, keeping the island between her and the settlement. Gaining the other shore, Helen pulled the canoe into the willows, and mounted the bank. A thicket of willow and alder made progress up the steep incline difficult, but once out of it she faced a long stretch of grassy meadowland. A mile beyond began the green, billowy rise of that mountain which she intended to climb.

Helen's whole soul was thrown into the adventure. She felt her strong young limbs in accord with her heart.

"Now, Mr. Brandt, horse-thief and girl-snatcher, we'll see," she said with scornful lips. "If I can't beat you now I'm not fit to be Betty Zane's friend; and am unworthy of a borderman's trust."

She traversed the whole length of meadowland close under the shadow of the fringed bank, and gained the forest. Here she hesitated. All was so wild and still. No definite course through the woods seemed to invite, and yet all was open. Trees, trees, dark, immovable trees everywhere. The violent trembling of poplar and aspen leaves, when all others were so calm, struck her strangely, and the fearful stillness awed her. Drawing a deep breath she started forward up the gently rising ground.

As she advanced the open forest became darker, and of wilder aspect. The trees were larger and closer together. Still she made fair progress without deviating from the course she had determined upon. Before her rose a ridge, with a ravine on either side, reaching nearly to the summit of the mountain. Here the underbrush was scanty, the fallen trees had slipped down the side, and the rocks were not so numerous, all of which gave her reason to be proud, so far, of her judgment.

Helen, pressing onward and upward, forgot time and danger, while she reveled in the wonder of the forestland. Birds and squirrels fled before her; whistling and wheezing of alarm, or heavy crashings in the bushes, told of frightened wild beasts. A dull, faint roar, like a distant wind, suggested tumbling waters. A single birch tree, gleaming white among the black trees, enlivened the gloomy forest. Patches of sunlight brightened the shade. Giant ferns, just tinging with autumn colors, waved tips of sculptured perfection. Most wonderful of all were the colored leaves, as they floated downward with a sad, gentle rustle.

Helen was brought to a realization of her hazardous undertaking by a sudden roar of water, and the abrupt termination of the ridge in a deep gorge. Grasping a tree she leaned over to look down. It was fully an hundred feet deep, with impassable walls, green-stained and damp, at the bottom of which a brawling, brown brook rushed on its way. Fully twenty feet wide, it presented an insurmountable barrier to further progress in that direction.

But Helen looked upon it merely as a difficulty to be overcome. She studied the situation, and decided to go to the left because higher ground was to be seen that way. Abandoning the ridge, she pressed on, keeping as close to the gorge as she dared, and came presently to a fallen tree lying across the dark cleft. Without a second's hesitation, for she knew such would be fatal, she stepped upon the tree and started across, looking at nothing but the log under her feet, while she tried to imagine herself walking across the water-gate, at home in Virginia.

She accomplished the venture without a misstep. When safely on the ground once more she felt her knees tremble and a queer, light feeling came into her head. She laughed, however, as she rested a moment. It would take more than a gorge to discourage her, she resolved with set lips, as once again she made her way along the rising ground.

Perilous, if not desperate, work was ahead of her. Broken, rocky ground, matted thicket, and seemingly impenetrable forest, rose darkly in advance. But she was not even tired, and climbed, crawled, twisted and turned on her way upward. She surmounted a rocky ledge, to face a higher ridge covered with splintered, uneven stones, and the fallen trees of many storms. Once she slipped and fell, spraining her wrist. At length this uphill labor began to weary her. To breathe caused a pain in her side and she was compelled to rest.

Already the gray light of coming night shrouded the forest. She was surprised at seeing the trees become indistinct; because the shadows hovered over the thickets, and noted that the dark, dim outline of the ridges was fading into obscurity.

She struggled on up the uneven slope with a tightening at her heart which was not all exhaustion. For the first time she doubted herself, but it was too late. She could not turn back. Suddenly she felt that she was on a smoother, easier course. Not to strike a stone or break a twig seemed unusual. It might be a path worn by deer going to a spring. Then into her troubled mind flashed the joyful thought, she had found a trail.

Soft, wiry grass, springing from a wet soil, rose under her feet. A little rill trickled alongside the trail. Mossy, soft-cushioned stones lay imbedded here and there. Young maples and hickories grew breast-high on either side, and the way wound in and out under the lowering shade of forest monarchs.

Swiftly ascending this path she came at length to a point where it was possible to see some distance ahead. The ascent became hardly noticeable. Then, as she turned a bend of the trail, the light grew brighter and brighter, until presently all was open and clear. An oval space, covered with stones, lay before her. A big, blasted chestnut stood near by. Beyond was the dim, purple haze of distance. Above, the pale, blue sky just faintly rose-tinted by the setting sun. Far to her left the scraggly trees of a low hill were tipped with orange and russet shades. She had reached the summit.

Desolate and lonely was this little plateau. Helen felt immeasurably far away from home. Yet she could see in the blue distance the glancing river, the dark fort, and that cluster of cabins which marked the location of Fort Henry. Sitting upon the roots of the big chestnut tree she gazed around. There were the remains of a small camp-fire. Beyond, a hollow under a shelving rock. A bed of dry leaves lay packed in this shelter. Some one had been here, and she doubted not that it was the borderman.

She was so tired and her wrist pained so severely that she lay back against the tree-trunk, closed her eyes and rested. A weariness, the apathy of utter exhaustion, came over her. She wished the bordermen would hurry and come before she went to sleep.

Drowsily she was sinking into slumber when a long, low rumble aroused her. How dark it had suddenly become! A sheet of pale light flared across the overcast heavens.

"A storm!" exclaimed Helen. "Alone on this mountain-top with a storm coming. Am I frightened? I don't believe it. At least I'm safe from that ruffian Brandt. Oh! if my borderman would only come!"

Helen changed her position from beside the tree, to the hollow under the stone. It was high enough to permit of her sitting upright, and offered a safe retreat from the storm. The bed of leaves was soft and comfortable. She sat there peering out at the darkening heavens.

All beneath her, southward and westward was gray twilight. The settlement faded from sight; the river grew wan and shadowy. The ruddy light in the west was fast succumbing to the rolling clouds. Darker and darker it became, until only one break in the overspreading vapors admitted the last crimson gleam of sunshine over hills and valley, brightening the river until it resembled a stream of fire. Then the light failed, the glow faded. The intense blackness of night prevailed.

Out of the ebon west came presently another flare of light, a quick, spreading flush, like a flicker from a monster candle; it was followed by a long, low, rumbling roll.

Helen felt in those intervals of unutterably vast silence, that she must shriek aloud. The thunder was a friend. She prayed for the storm to break. She had withstood danger and toilsome effort with fortitude; but could not brave this awful, boding, wilderness stillness.

Flashes of lightning now revealed the rolling, pushing, turbulent clouds, and peals of thunder sounded nearer and louder.

A long swelling moan, sad, low, like the uneasy sigh of the sea, breathed far in the west. It was the wind, the ominous warning of the storm. Sheets of light were now mingled with long, straggling ropes of fire, and the rumblings were often broken by louder, quicker detonations.

Then a period, longer than usual, of inky blackness succeeded the sharp flaring of light. A faint breeze ruffled the leaves of the thicket, and fanned Helen's hot cheek. The moan of the wind became more distinct, then louder, and in another instant like the far-off roar of a rushing river. The storm was upon her. Helen shrank closer against the stone, and pulled her jacket tighter around her trembling form.

A sudden, intense, dazzling, blinding, white light enveloped her. The rocky promontory, the weird, giant chestnut tree, the open plateau, and beyond, the stormy heavens, were all luridly clear in the flash of lightning. She fancied it was possible to see a tall, dark figure emerging from the thicket. As the thunderclap rolled and pealed overhead, she strained her eyes into the blackness waiting for the next lightning flash.

It came with brilliant, dazing splendor. The whole plateau and thicket were as light as in the day. Close by the stone where she lay crept the tall, dark figure of an Indian. With starting eyes she saw the fringed clothing, the long, flying hair, and supple body peculiar to the savage. He was creeping upon her.

Helen's blood ran cold; terror held her voiceless. She felt herself sinking slowly down upon the leaves.

CHAPTER 12

THE SUN HAD BEGUN TO CAST LONG SHADOWS THE AFTERNOON OF Helen's hunt for Jonathan, when the borderman, accompanied by Wetzel, led a string of horses along the base of the very mountain she had ascended.

"Last night's job was a good one, I ain't gainsayin'; but the redskin I wanted got away," Wetzel said gloomily.

"He's safe now as a squirrel in a hole. I saw him dartin' among the trees with his white eagle feathers stickin' up like a buck's flag," replied Jonathan. "He can run. If I'd only had my rifle loaded! But I'm not sure he was that arrow-shootin' Shawnee."

"It was him. I saw his bow. We ought'er taken more time an' picked him out," Wetzel replied, shaking his head gravely. "Though mebbe that'd been useless. I think he was hidin'. He's precious shy of his red skin. I've been after him these ten year, an' never ketched him nappin' yet. We'd have done much toward snuffin' out Legget an' his gang if we'd winged the Shawnee."

"He left a plain trail."

"One of his tricks. He's slicker on a trail than any other Injun on the border, unless mebbe it's old Wingenund, the Huron. This Shawnee'd lead us many a mile for nuthin', if we'd stick to his trail. I'm long ago used to him. He's doubled like an old fox, run harder'n a skeered fawn, an', if needs be, he'll lay low as cunnin' buck. I calkilate once over the mountain, he's made a bee-line east. We'll go on with the hosses, an' then strike across country to find his trail."

"It 'pears to me, Lew, that we've taken a long time in makin' a show against these hoss-thieves," said Jonathan.

"I ain't sayin' much; but I've felt it," replied Wetzel.

"All summer, an' nothin' done. It was more luck than sense that we run into those Injuns with the hosses. We only got three out of four, an' let the best redskin give us the slip. Here fall is nigh on us, with winter comin' soon, an' still we don't know who's the white traitor in the settlement."

"I said it's be a long, an' mebbe, our last trail."

"Why?"

"Because these fellars red or white, are in with a picked gang of the best woodsmen as ever outlawed the border. We'll get the Fort Henry hoss-thief. I'll back the bright-eyed lass for that."

"I haven't seen her lately, an' allow she'd left me word if she learned anythin'."

"Wal, mebbe it's as well you hain't seen so much of her." In silence they traveled and, arriving at the edge of the meadow, were about to mount two of the horses, when Wetzel said in a sharp tone:

"Look!"

He pointed to a small, well-defined moccasin track in the black earth on the margin of a rill.

"Lew, it's a woman's, sure's you're born," declared Jonathan.

Wetzel knelt and closely examined the footprint; "Yes, a woman's, an' no Injun."

"What?" Jonathan exclaimed, as he knelt to scrutinize the imprint.

"This ain't half a day old," added Wetzel. "An' not a redskin's moccasin near. What d'you reckon?"

"A white girl, alone," replied Jonathan as he followed the trail a short distance along the brook. "See, she's makin' upland. Wetzel, these tracks could hardly be my sister's, an' there's only one other girl on the border whose feet will match 'em! Helen Sheppard has passed here, on her way up the mountain to find you or me."

"I like your reckonin'."

"She's suddenly discovered somethin', Injuns, hoss-thieves, the Fort Henry traitor, or mebbe, an' most likely, some plottin'. Bein' bound to secrecy by me, she's not told my brother. An' it must be call for hurry. She knows we frequent this mountain-top; said Eb told her about the way we get here."

"I'd calkilate about the same."

"What'll you do? Go with me after her?" asked Jonathan.

"I'll take the hosses, an' be at the fort inside of an hour. If Helen's gone, I'll tell her father you're close on her trail. Now listen! It'll be dark soon, an' a storm's comin'. Don't waste time on her trail. Hurry up to the rock. She'll be there, if any lass could climb there. If not, come back in the mornin', hunt her trail out, an' find her. I'm thinkin', Jack, we'll find the Shawnee had somethin' to do with this. Whatever happens after I get back to the fort, I'll expect you hard on my trail."

Jonathan bounded across the brook and with an easy lope began the gradual ascent. Soon he came upon a winding path. He ran along this for perhaps a quarter of an hour, until it became too steep for rapid traveling, when he settled down to a rapid walk. The forest was already dark. A slight rustling of the leaves beneath his feet was the only sound, except at long intervals the distant rumbling of thunder.

The mere possibility of Helen's being alone on that mountain seeking him, made Jonathan's heart beat as it never had before. For weeks he had avoided her, almost forgot her. He had conquered the strange, yearning weakness which assailed him after that memorable Sunday, and once more the silent shaded glens, the mystery of the woods, the breath of his wild, free life had claimed him. But now as this evidence of her spirit, her reck-lessness, was before him, and he remembered Betty's avowal, a pain, which was almost physical, tore at his heart. How terrible it would be if she came to her death through him! He pictured the big, alluring eyes, the perfect lips, the haunting face, cold in death. And he shuddered.

The dim gloom of the woods soon darkened into blackness. The flashes of lightning, momentarily streaking the foliage, or sweeping over-head in pale yellow sheets, aided Jonathan in keeping the trail.

He gained the plateau just as a great flash illumined it, and distinctly saw the dark hollow where he had taken refuge in many a storm, and where he now hoped to find the girl. Picking his way carefully over the sharp, loose stones, he at last put his hand on the huge rock. Another blue-white, dazzling flash enveloped the scene.

Under the rock he saw a dark form huddled, and a face as white as snow, with wide, horrified eyes.

"Lass," he said, when the thunder had rumbled away. He received no answer, and called again. Kneeling, he groped about until touching Helen's dress. He spoke again; but she did not reply.

Jonathan crawled under the ledge beside the quiet figure. He touched her hands; they were very cold. Bending over, he was relieved to hear her heart beating. He called her name, but still she made no reply. Dipping his hand into a little rill that ran beside the stone, he bathed her face. Soon she stirred uneasily, moaned, and suddenly sat up.

"'Tis Jonathan," he said quickly; "don't be scared."

Another illuminating flare of lightning brightened the plateau.

"Oh! thank Heaven!" cried Helen. "I thought you were an Indian!"

Helen sank trembling against the borderman, who enfolded her in his long arms. Her relief and thankfulness were so great that she could not speak. Her hands clasped and unclasped round his strong fingers. Her tears flowed freely.

The storm broke with terrific fury. A seething torrent of rain and hail came with the rushing wind. Great heaven-broad sheets of lightning played across the black dome overhead. Zigzag ropes, steel-blue in color, shot downward. Crash, and crack, and boom the thunder split and rolled the clouds above. The lightning flashes showed the fall of rain in columns like white waterfalls, borne on the irresistible wind.

The grandeur of the storm awed, and stilled Helen's emotion. She sat there watching the lightning, listening to the peals of thunder, and thrilling with the wonder of the situation.

Gradually the roar abated, the flashes became less frequent, the thunder decreased, as the storm wore out its strength in passing. The wind and rain ceased on the mountain-top almost as quickly as they had begun, and the roar died slowly away in the distance. Far to the eastward flashes of light illumined scowling clouds, and brightened many a dark, wooded hill and valley.

"Lass, how is't I find you here?" asked Jonathan gravely.

With many a pause and broken phrase, Helen told the story of what she had seen and heard at the spring.

"Child, why didn't you go to my brother?" asked Jonathan. "You don't know what you undertook!"

"I thought of everything; but I wanted to find you myself. Besides, I was just as safe alone on this mountain as in the village."

"I don't know but you're right," replied Jonathan thoughtfully. "So Brandt planned to make off with you to-morrow?"

"Yes, and when I heard it I wanted to run away from the village."

"You've done a wondrous clever thing, lass. This Brandt is a bad man, an' hard to match. But if he hasn't shaken Fort Henry by now, his career'll end mighty sudden, an' his bad trails stop short on the hillside among the graves, for Eb will always give outlaws or Injuns decent burial."

"What will the colonel, or anyone, think has become of me?"

"Wetzel knows, lass, for he found your trail below."

"Then he'll tell papa you came after me? Oh! poor papa! I forgot him. Shall we stay here until daylight?"

"We'd gain nothin' by startin' now. The brooks are full, an' in the dark we'd make little distance. You're dry here, an' comfortable. What's more, lass, you're safe."

"I feel perfectly safe, with you," Helen said softly.

"Aren't you tired, lass?"

"Tired? I'm nearly dead. My feet are cut and bruised, my wrist is sprained, and I ache all over. But, Jonathan, I don't care. I am so happy to have my wild venture turn out successfully."

"You can lie here an' sleep while I keep watch."

Jonathan made a move to withdraw his arm, which was still between Helen and the rock but had dropped from her waist.

"I am very comfortable. I'll sit here with you, watching for daybreak. My! how dark it is! I cannot see my hand before my eyes."

Helen settled herself back upon the stone, leaned a very little against his shoulder, and tried to think over her adventure. But her mind refused to entertain any ideas, except those of the present. Mingled with the dreamy lassitude that grew stronger every moment, was a sense of delight in her situation. She was alone on a wild mountain, in the night, with this borderman, the one she loved. By chance and her own foolhardiness this had come about, yet she was fortunate to have it tend to some good beyond her own happiness. All she would suffer from her perilous climb would be aching bones, and, perhaps, a scolding from her father. What she might gain was more than she had dared hope. The breaking up of the horse-thief gang would be a boon to the harassed settlement. How proudly Colonel Zane would smile! Her name would go on that long roll of border honor and heroism. That was not, however, one thousandth part so pleasing, as to be alone with her borderman.

With a sigh of mingled weariness and content, Helen leaned her head on Jonathan's shoulder and fell asleep.

The borderman trembled. The sudden nestling of her head against him, the light caress of her fragrant hair across his cheek, revived a sweet, almost-conquered, almost-forgotten emotion. He felt an inexplicable thrill vibrate through him. No untrodden, ambushed wild, no perilous trail, no dark and bloody encounter had ever made him feel fear as had the kiss of this maiden. He had sternly silenced faint, unfamiliar, yet tender, voices whispering in his heart; and now his rigorous discipline was as if it were not, for at her touch he trembled. Still he did not move away. He knew she had succumbed to weariness, and was fast asleep. He could, gently, without awakening her, have laid her head upon the pillow of leaves; indeed, he thought of doing it, but made no effort. A woman's head softly lying against him was a thing novel, strange, wonderful. For all the power he had then, each tumbling lock of her hair might as well have been a chain linking him fast to the mountain.

With the memory of his former yearning, unsatisfied moods, and the unrest and pain his awakening tenderness had caused him, came a determination to look things fairly in the face, to be just in thought toward this innocent, impulsive girl, and be honest with himself.

Duty commanded that he resist all charm other than that pertaining to his life in the woods. Years ago he had accepted a borderman's destiny, well content to be recompensed by its untamed freedom from restraint; to be always under the trees he loved so well; to lend his cunning and woodcraft in the pioneer's cause; to haunt the savage trails; to live from day to day a menace to the foes of civilization. That was the life he had chosen; it was all he could ever have.

In view of this, justice demanded that he allow no friendship to spring up between himself and this girl. If his sister's belief was really true, if Helen really was interested in him, it must be a romantic infatuation which, not encouraged, would wear itself out. What was he, to win the love of any girl? An unlettered borderman, who knew only the woods, whose life was hard and cruel, whose hands were red with Indian blood, whose vengeance had not spared men even of his own race. He could not believe she really loved him. Wildly impulsive as girls were at times, she had kissed him. She had been grateful, carried away by a generous feeling for him as the protector of her father. When she did not see him for a long time, as he vowed should be the case after he had carried her safely home, she would forget.

Then honesty demanded that he probe his own feelings. Sternly, as if judging a renegade, he searched out in his simple way the truth. This big-eyed lass with her nameless charm would bewitch even a borderman, unless he avoided her. So much he had not admitted until now. Love he had never believed could be possible for him. When she fell asleep her hand had slipped from his arm to his fingers, and now rested there lightly as a leaf. The contact was delight. The gentle night breeze blew a tress of hair across his lips. He trembled. Her rounded shoulder pressed against him until he could feel her slow, deep breathing. He almost held his own breath lest he disturb her rest.

No, he was no longer indifferent. As surely as those pale stars blinked far above, he knew the delight of a woman's presence. It moved him to study the emotion, as he studied all things, which was the habit of his borderman's life. Did it come from knowledge of her beauty, matchless as that of the mountain-laurel? He recalled the dark glance of her challenging eyes, her tall, supple figure, and the bewildering excitement and magnetism of her presence. Beauty was wonderful, but not everything. Beauty belonged to her, but she would have been irresistible without it. Was it not because she was a woman? That was the secret. She was a woman with all a woman's charm to bewitch, to twine round the strength of men as the ivy encircles the oak; with all a woman's weakness to pity and to guard; with all a woman's wilful burning love, and with all a woman's mystery.

At last so much of life was intelligible to him. The renegade committed his worst crimes because even in his outlawed, homeless state, he could not exist without the companionship, if not the love, of a woman. The pioneer's toil and privation were for a woman, and the joy of loving her and living for her. The Indian brave, when not on the war-path, walked hand in hand with a dusky, soft-eyed maiden, and sang to her of moonlit lakes and western winds. Even the birds and beasts mated. The robins returned to their old nest; the eagles paired once and were constant in life and death. The buck followed the doe through the forest. All nature sang that love made life worth living. Love, then, was everything.

The borderman sat out the long vigil of the night watching the stars, and trying to decide that love was not for him. If Wetzel had locked a secret within his breast, and never in all these years spoke of it to his companion, then surely that companion could as well live without love. Stern, dark, deadly work must stain and blot all tenderness from his life, else it would be unutterably barren. The joy of living, of unharassed freedom he had always known. If a fair face and dark, mournful eyes were to haunt him on every lonely trail, then it were better an Indian should end his existence.

The darkest hour before dawn, as well as the darkest of doubt and longing in Jonathan's life, passed away. A gray gloom obscured the pale, winking stars; the east slowly whitened, then brightened, and at length day broke misty and fresh.

The borderman rose to stretch his cramped limbs. When he turned to the little cavern the girl's eyes were wide open. All the darkness, the shadow, the beauty, and the thought of the past night, lay in their blue depths. He looked away across the valley where the sky was reddening and a pale rim of gold appeared above the hill-tops.

"Well, if I haven't been asleep!" exclaimed Helen, with a low, soft laugh.

"You're rested, I hope," said Jonathan, with averted eyes. He dared not look at her.

"Oh, yes, indeed. I am ready to start at once. How gray, how beautiful the morning is! Shall we be long? I hope papa knows."

In silence the borderman led the way across the rocky plateau, and into the winding, narrow trail. His pale, slightly drawn and stern, face did not invite conversation, therefore Helen followed silently in his footsteps. The way was steep, and at times he was forced to lend her aid. She put her hand in his and jumped lightly as a fawn. Presently a brawling brook, over-crowding its banks, impeded further progress.

"I'll have to carry you across," said Jonathan.

"I'm very heavy," replied Helen, with a smile in her eyes.

She flushed as the borderman put his right arm around her waist. Then a clasp as of steel enclosed her; she felt herself swinging easily into the air, and over the muddy brook.

Farther down the mountain this troublesome brook again crossed the trail, this time much wider and more formidable. Helen looked with some vexation and embarrassment into the borderman's face. It was always the same, stern, almost cold.

"Perhaps I'd better wade," she said hesitatingly.

"Why? The water's deep an' cold. You'd better not get wet."

Helen flushed, but did not answer. With downcast eyes she let herself be carried on his powerful arm.

The wading was difficult this time. The water foamed furiously around his knees. Once he slipped on a stone, and nearly lost his balance. Uttering a little scream Helen grasped at him wildly, and her arm encircled his neck. What was still more trying, when he put her on her feet again, it was found that her hair had become entangled in the porcupine quills on his hunting-coat.

She stood before him while with clumsy fingers he endeavored to untangle the shimmering strands; but in vain. Helen unwound the snarl of wavy hair. Most alluring she was then, with a certain softness on her face, and light and laughter, and something warm in her eyes.

The borderman felt that he breathed a subtle exhilaration which emanated from her glowing, gracious beauty. She radiated with the gladness of life, with an uncontainable sweetness and joy. But, giving no token of his feeling, he turned to march on down through the woods.

From this point the trail broadened, descending at an easier angle. Jonathan's stride lengthened until Helen was forced to walk rapidly, and sometimes run, in order to keep close behind him. A quick journey home was expedient, and in order to accomplish this she would gladly have exerted herself to a greater extent. When they reached the end of the trail where the forest opened clear of brush, finally to merge into the broad, verdant plain, the sun had chased the mist-clouds from the eastern hilltops, and was gloriously brightening the valley.

With the touch of sentiment natural to her, Helen gazed backward for one more view of the mountain-top. The wall of rugged rock she had so often admired from her window at home, which henceforth would ever hold a tender place of remembrance in her heart, rose out of a gray-blue bank of mist. The long, swelling slope lay clear to the sunshine. With the rays of the sun gleaming and glistening upon the variegated foliage, and upon the shiny rolling haze above, a beautiful picture of autumn splendor was before her. Tall pines, here and there towered high and lonely over the surrounding trees. Their dark, green, graceful heads stood in bold relief above the gold and yellow crests beneath. Maples, tinged from faintest pink to deepest rose, added warm color to the scene, and chestnuts with their brown-white burrs lent fresher beauty to the undulating slope.

The remaining distance to the settlement was short. Jonathan spoke only once to Helen, then questioning her as to where she had left her canoe. They traversed the meadow, found the boat in the thicket of willows, and were soon under the frowning bluff of Fort Henry. Ascending the steep path, they followed the road leading to Colonel Zane's cabin.

A crowd of boys, men and women loitering near the bluff arrested Helen's attention. Struck by this unusual occurrence, she wondered what was the cause of such idleness among the busy pioneer people. They were standing in little groups. Some made vehement gestures, others conversed earnestly, and yet more were silent. On seeing Jonathan, a number shouted and pointed toward the inn. The borderman hurried Helen along the path, giving no heed to the throng.

But Helen had seen the cause of all this excitement. At first glance she thought Metzar's inn had been burned; but a second later it could be seen that the smoke came from a smoldering heap of rubbish in the road. The inn, nevertheless, had been wrecked. Windows stared with that vacantness peculiar to deserted houses. The doors were broken from their hinges. A pile of furniture, rude tables, chairs, beds, and other articles, were heaped beside the smoking rubbish. Scattered around lay barrels and kegs all with gaping sides and broken heads. Liquor had stained the road, where it had been soaked up by the thirsty dust.

Upon a shattered cellar-door lay a figure covered with a piece of rag carpet. When Helen's quick eyes took in this last, she turned away in horror. That motionless form might be Brandt's. Remorse and womanly sympathy surged over her, for bad as the man had shown himself, he had loved her.

She followed the borderman, trying to compose herself. As they neared Colonel Zane's cabin she saw her father, Will, the colonel, Betty, Nell, Mrs. Zane, Silas Zane, and others whom she did not recognize. They were all looking at her. Helen's throat swelled, and her eyes filled when she got near enough to see her father's haggard, eager face. The others were grave. She wondered guiltily if she had done much wrong.

In another moment she was among them. Tears fell as her father extended his trembling hands to clasp her, and as she hid her burning face on his breast, he cried: "My dear, dear child!" Then Betty gave her a great hug, and Nell flew about them like a happy bird. Colonel Zane's face was pale, and wore a clouded, stern expression. She smiled timidly at him through her tears. "Well! well! well!" he mused, while his gaze softened. That was all he said; but he took her hand and held it while he turned to Jonathan.

The borderman leaned on his long rifle, regarding him with expectant eyes.

"Well, Jack, you missed a little scrimmage this morning. Wetzel got in at daybreak. The storm and horses held him up on the other side of the river until daylight. He told me of your suspicions, with the additional news that he'd found a fresh Indian trail on the island just across from the inn. We went down not expecting to find any one awake; but Metzar was hurriedly packing some of his traps. Half a dozen men were there, having probably stayed all night. That little English cuss was one of them, and another, an ugly fellow, a stranger to us, but evidently a woodsman. Things looked bad. Metzar told a decidedly conflicting story. Wetzel and I went outside to talk over the situation, with the result that I ordered him to clean out the place."

Here Colonel Zane paused to indulge in a grim, meaning laugh.

"Well, he cleaned out the place all right. The ugly stranger got rattlesnake-mad, and yanked out a big knife. Sam is hitching up the team now to haul what's left of him up on the hillside. Metzar resisted arrest, and got badly hurt. He's in the guardhouse. Case, who has been drunk for a week, got in Wetzel's way and was kicked into the middle of next week. He's been spitting blood for the last hour, but I guess he's not much hurt. Brandt flew the coop last night. Wetzel found this hid in his room."

Colonel Zane took a long, feathered arrow from where it lay on a bench, and held it out to Jonathan.

"The Shawnee signal! Wetzel had it right," muttered the borderman.

"Exactly. Lew found where the arrow struck in the wall of Brandt's room. It was shot from the island at the exact spot where Lew came to an end of the Indian's trail in the water."

"That Shawnee got away from us."

"So Lew said. Well, he's gone now. So is Brandt. We're well rid of the gang, if only we never hear of them again."

The borderman shook his head. During the colonel's recital his face changed. The dark eyes had become deadly; the square jaw was shut, the lines of the cheek had grown tense, and over his usually expressive countenance had settled a chill, lowering shade.

"Lew thinks Brandt's in with Bing Legget. Well, d—— his black traitor heart! He's a good man for the worst and strongest gang that ever tracked the border."

The borderman was silent; but the furtive, restless shifting of his eyes over the river and island, hill and valley, spoke more plainly than words.

"You're to take his trail at once," added Colonel Zane. "I had Bess put you up some bread, meat and parched corn. No doubt you'll have a long, hard tramp. Good luck."

The borderman went into the cabin, presently emerging with a buckskin knapsack strapped to his shoulder. He set off eastward with a long, swinging stride.

The women had taken Helen within the house where, no doubt, they could discuss with greater freedom the events of the previous day.

"Sheppard," said Colonel Zane, turning with a sparkle in his eyes. "Brandt was after Helen sure as a bad weed grows fast. And certain as death Jonathan and Wetzel will see him cold and quiet back in the woods.

That's a border saying, and it means a good deal. I never saw Wetzel so implacable, nor Jonathan so fatally cold but once, and that was when Miller, another traitor, much like Brandt, tried to make away with Betty. It would have chilled your blood to see Wetzel go at that fool this morning. Why did he want to pull a knife on the borderman? It was a sad sight. Well, these things are justifiable. We must protect ourselves, and above all our women. We've had bad men, and a bad man out here is something you cannot yet appreciate, come here and slip into the life of the settlement, because on the border you can never tell what a man is until he proves himself. There have been scores of criminals spread over the frontier, and some better men, like Simon Girty, who were driven to outlaw life. Simon must not be confounded with Jim Girty, absolutely the most fiendish desperado who ever lived. Why, even the Indians feared Jim so much that after his death his skeleton remained unmolested in the glade where he was killed. The place is believed to be haunted now, by all Indians and many white hunters, and I believe the bones stand there yet."

"Stand?" asked Sheppard, deeply interested.

"Yes, it stands where Girty stood and died, upright against a tree, pinned, pinned there by a big knife."

"Heavens, man! Who did it?" Sheppard cried in horror.

Again Colonel Zane's laugh, almost metallic, broke grimly from his lips.

"Who? Why, Wetzel, of course. Lew hunted Jim Girty five long years. When he caught him—God! I'll tell you some other time. Jonathan saw Wetzel handle Jim and his pal, Deering, as if they were mere boys. Well, as I said, the border has had, and still has, its bad men. Simon Girty took McKee and Elliott, the Tories, from Fort Pitt, when he deserted, and ten men besides. They're all, except those who are dead, outlaws of the worst type. The other bad men drifted out here from Lord only knows where. They're scattered all over. Simon Girty, since his crowning black deed, the massacre of the Christian Indians, is in hiding. Bing Legget now has the field. He's a hard nut, a cunning woodsman, and capable leader who surrounds himself with only the most desperate Indians and renegades. Brandt is an agent of Legget's and I'll bet we'll hear from him again."

CHAPTER 13

Jonathan traveled toward the east straight as a crow flies. Wetzel's trail as he pursued Brandt had been left designedly plain. Branches of young maples had been broken by the borderman; they were glaring evidences of his passage. On open ground, or through swampy meadows he had contrived to leave other means to facilitate his comrade's progress. Bits of sumach lay strewn along the way, every red, leafy branch a bright marker of the course; crimson maple leaves served their turn, and even long-bladed ferns were scattered at intervals.

Ten miles east of Fort Henry, at a point where two islands lay opposite each other, Wetzel had crossed the Ohio. Jonathan removed his clothing, and tying these, together with his knapsack, to the rifle, held them above the water while he swam the three narrow channels. He took up the trail again, finding here, as he expected, where Brandt had joined the waiting Shawnee chief. The borderman pressed on harder to the eastward.

About the middle of the afternoon signs betokened that Wetzel and his quarry were not far in advance. Fresh imprints in the grass; crushed asters and moss, broken branches with unwithered leaves, and plots of grassy ground where Jonathan saw that the blades of grass were yet springing back to their original position, proved to the borderman's practiced eye that he was close upon Wetzel.

In time he came to a grove of yellow birch trees. The ground was nearly free from brush, beautifully carpeted with flowers and ferns, and, except where bushy windfalls obstructed the way, was singularly open to the gaze for several hundred yards ahead.

Upon entering this wood Wetzel's plain, intentional markings became manifest, then wavered, and finally disappeared. Jonathan pondered a moment. He concluded that the way was so open and clear, with nothing but grass and moss to mark a trail, that Wetzel had simply considered it waste of time for, perhaps, the short length of this grove.

Jonathan knew he was wrong after taking a dozen steps more. Wetzel's trail, known so well to him, as never to be mistaken, sheered abruptly off to the left, and, after a few yards, the distance between the footsteps widened perceptibly. Then came a point where they were so far apart that they could only have been made by long leaps.

On the instant the borderman knew that some unforeseen peril or urgent cause had put Wetzel to flight, and he now bent piercing eyes around the grove. Retracing his steps to where he had found the break in the trail, he followed up Brandt's tracks for several rods. Not one hundred paces beyond where Wetzel had quit the pursuit, were the remains of a camp fire, the embers still smoldering, and moccasin tracks of a small band of Indians. The trail of Brandt and his Shawnee guide met the others at almost right angles.

The Indian, either by accident or design, had guided Brandt to a band of his fellows, and thus led Wetzel almost into an ambush.

Evidence was not clear, however, that the Indians had discovered the keen tracker who had run almost into their midst.

While studying the forest ahead Jonathan's mind was running over the possibilities. How close was Wetzel? Was he still in flight? Had the savages an inkling of his pursuit? Or was he now working out one of his cunning tricks of woodcraft? The borderman had no other idea than that of following the trail to learn all this. Taking the desperate chances warranted under the circumstances, he walked boldly forward in his comrade's footsteps.

Deep and gloomy was the forest adjoining the birch grove. It was a heavy growth of hardwood trees, interspersed with slender ash and maples, which with their scanty foliage resembled a labyrinth of green and yellow network, like filmy dotted lace, hung on the taller, darker oaks. Jonathan felt safer in this deep wood. He could still see several rods in advance. Following the trail, he was relieved to see that Wetzel's leaps had become shorter and shorter, until they once again were about the length of a long stride. The borderman was, moreover, swinging in a curve to the northeast. This was proof that the borderman had not been pursued, but was making a wide detour to get ahead of the enemy. Five hundred yards farther on the trail turned sharply toward the birch grove in the rear.

The trail was fresh. Wetzel was possibly within signal call; surely within sound of a rifle shot. But even more stirring was the certainty that Brandt and his Indians were inside the circle Wetzel had made.

Once again in sight of the more open woodland, Jonathan crawled on his hands and knees, keeping close to the cluster of ferns, until well within the eastern end of the grove. He lay for some minutes listening. A threatening silence, like the hush before a storm, permeated the wilderness. He peered out from his covert; but, owing to its location in a little hollow, he could not see far. Crawling to the nearest tree he rose to his feet slowly, cautiously.

No unnatural sight or sound arrested his attention. Repeatedly, with the acute, unsatisfied gaze of the borderman who knew that every tree, every patch of ferns, every tangled brush-heap might harbor a foe, he searched the grove with his eyes; but the curly-barked birches, the clumps of colored ferns, the bushy windfalls kept their secrets.

For the borderman, however, the whole aspect of the birch-grove had changed. Over the forest was a deep calm. A gentle, barely perceptible wind sighed among the leaves, like rustling silk. The far-off drowsy drum of a grouse intruded on the vast stillness. The silence of the birds betokened a message. That mysterious breathing, that beautiful life of the woods lay hushed, locked in a waiting, brooding silence. Far away among the somber trees, where the shade deepened into impenetrable gloom, lay a menace, invisible and indefinable.

A wind, a breath, a chill, terribly potent, seemed to pass over the borderman. Long experience had given him intuition of danger.

As he moved slightly, with lynx-eyes fixed on the grove before him, a sharp, clear, perfect bird-note broke the ominous quiet. It was like the melancholy cry of an oriole, short, deep, suggestive of lonely forest dells. By a slight variation in the short call, Jonathan recognized it as a signal from Wetzel. The borderman smiled as he realized that with all his stealth, Wetzel had heard or seen him re-enter the grove. The signal was a warning to stand still or retreat.

Jonathan's gaze narrowed down to the particular point whence had come the signal. Some two hundred yards ahead in this direction were several large trees standing in a group. With one exception, they all had straight trunks. This deviated from the others in that it possessed an irregular, bulging trunk, or else half-shielded the form of Wetzel. So indistinct and immovable was this irregularity, that the watcher could not be certain. Out of line, somewhat, with this tree which he suspected screened his comrade, lay a huge windfall large enough to conceal in ambush a whole band of savages.

Even as he gazed a sheet of flame flashed from this covert.

Crack!

A loud report followed; then the whistle and zip of a bullet as it whizzed close by his head.

"Shawnee lead!" muttered Jonathan.

Unfortunately the tree he had selected did not hide him sufficiently. His shoulders were so wide that either one or the other was exposed, affording a fine target for a marksman.

A quick glance showed him a change in the knotty tree-trunk; the seeming bulge was now the well-known figure of Wetzel.

Jonathan dodged as some object glanced slantingly before his eyes.

Twang. Whizz. Thud. Three familiar and distinct sounds caused him to press hard against the tree.

A tufted arrow quivered in the bark not a foot from his head.

"Close shave! Damn that arrow-shootin' Shawnee!" muttered Jonathan. "An' he ain't in that windfall either." His eyes searched to the left for the source of this new peril.

Another sheet of flame, another report from the windfall. A bullet sang, close overhead, and, glancing on a branch, went harmlessly into the forest.

"Injuns all around; I guess I'd better be makin' tracks," Jonathan said to himself, peering out to learn if Wetzel was still under cover.

He saw the tall figure straighten up; a long, black rifle rise to a level and become rigid; a red fire belch forth, followed by a puff of white smoke.

Spang!

An Indian's horrible, strangely-breaking death yell rent the silence.

Then a chorus of plaintive howls, followed by angry shouts, rang through the forest. Naked, painted savages darted out of the windfall toward the tree that had sheltered Wetzel.

Quick as thought Jonathan covered the foremost Indian, and with the crack of his rifle saw the redskin drop his gun, stop in his mad run, stagger sideways, and fall. Then the borderman looked to see what had become of his ally. The cracking of the Indian's rifle told him that Wetzel had been seen by his foes.

With almost incredible fleetness a brown figure with long black hair streaming behind, darted in and out among the trees, flashed through the sunlit glade, and vanished in the dark depths of the forest.

Jonathan turned to flee also, when he heard again the twanging of an Indian's bow. A wind smote his cheek, a shock blinded him, an excruciating pain seized upon his breast. A feathered arrow had pinned his shoulder to the tree. He raised his hand to pull it out; but, slippery with blood, it afforded a poor hold for his fingers. Violently exerting himself, with both hands he wrenched away the weapon. The flint-head lacerating his flesh and scraping his shoulder bones caused sharpest agony. The pain gave away to a sudden sense of giddiness; he tried to run; a dark mist veiled his sight; he stumbled and fell. Then he seemed to sink into a great darkness, and knew no more.

When consciousness returned to Jonathan it was night. He lay on his back, and knew because of his cramped limbs that he had been securely bound. He saw the glimmer of a fire, but could not raise his head. A rustling of leaves in the wind told that he was yet in the woods, and the distant rumble of a waterfall sounded familiar. He felt drowsy; his wound smarted slightly, still he did not suffer any pain. Presently he fell asleep.

Broad daylight had come when again he opened his eyes. The blue sky was directly above, and before him he saw a ledge covered with dwarfed pine trees. He turned his head, and saw that he was in a sort of amphitheater of about two acres in extent enclosed by low cliffs. A cleft in the stony wall let out a brawling brook, and served, no doubt, as entrance to the place. Several rude log cabins stood on that side of the enclosure. Jonathan knew he had been brought to Bing Legget's retreat.

Voices attracted his attention, and, turning his head to the other side, he saw a big Indian pacing near him, and beyond, seven savages and three white men reclining in the shade.

The powerful, dark-visaged savage near him he at once recognized as Ashbow, the Shawnee chief, and noted emissary of Bing Legget. Of the other Indians, three were Delawares, and four Shawnees, all veterans, with swarthy, somber faces and glistening heads on which the scalp-locks were trimmed and tufted. Their naked, muscular bodies were painted for the war-path with their strange emblems of death. A trio of white men, nearly as bronzed as their savage comrades, completed the group.

One, a desperate-looking outlaw, Jonathan did not know. The blond-bearded giant in the center was Legget. Steel-blue, inhuman eyes, with the expression of a free but hunted animal; a set, mastiff-like jaw, brutal and coarse, individualized him. The last man was the haggard-faced Brandt.

"I tell ye, Brandt, I ain't agoin' against this Injun," Legget was saying positively. "He's the best reddy on the border, an' has saved me scores of times. This fellar Zane belongs to him, an' while I'd much rather see the scout knifed right here an' now, I won't do nothin' to interfere with the Shawnee's plans."

"Why does the redskin want to take him away to his village?" Brandt growled. "All Injun vanity and pride."

"It's Injun ways, an' we can't do nothin' to change 'em."

"But you're boss here. You could make him put this borderman out of the way."

"Wal, I ain't agoin' ter interfere. Anyways, Brandt, the Shawnee'll make short work of the scout when he gits him among the tribe. Injuns is Injuns. It's a great honor fer him to git Zane, an' he wants his own people to figger in the finish. Quite nat'r'l, I reckon."

"I understand all that; but it's not safe for us, and it's courting death for Ashbow. Why don't he keep Zane here until you can spare more than three Indians to go with him? These bordermen can't be stopped. You don't know them, because you're new in this part of the country."

"I've been here as long as you, an' agoin' some, too, I reckon," replied Legget complacently.

"But you've not been hunted until lately by these bordermen, and you've had little opportunity to hear of them except from Indians. What can you learn from these silent redskins? I tell you, letting this fellow get out of here alive, even for an hour is a fatal mistake. It's two full days' tramp to the Shawnee village. You don't suppose Wetzel will be afraid of four savages? Why, he sneaked right into eight of us, when we were ambushed, waiting for him. He killed one and then was gone like a streak. It was only a piece of pure luck we got Zane."

"I've reason to know this Wetzel, this Deathwind, as the Delawares call him. I never seen him though, an' anyways, I reckon I can handle him if ever I get the chance."

"Man, you're crazy!" cried Brandt. "He'd cut you to pieces before you'd have time to draw. He could give you a tomahawk, then take it away and split your head. I tell you I know! You remember Jake Deering? He came from up your way. Wetzel fought Deering and Jim Girty together, and killed them. You know how he left Girty."

"I'll allow he must be a fighter; but I ain't afraid of him."

"That's not the question. I am talking sense. You've got a chance now to put one of these bordermen out of the way. Do it quick! That's my advice."

Brandt spoke so vehemently that Legget seemed impressed. He stroked his yellow beard, and puffed thoughtfully on his pipe. Presently he addressed the Shawnee chief in the native tongue.

"Will Ashbow take five horses for his prisoner?"

The Indian shook his head.

"How many will he take?"

The chief strode with dignity to and fro before his captive. His dark, impassive face gave no clew to his thoughts; but his lofty bearing, his measured, stately walk were indicative of great pride. Then he spoke in his deep bass:

"The Shawnee knows the woods from the Great Lakes where the sun sets, to the Blue Hills where it rises. He has met the great paleface hunters. Only for Deathwind will Ashbow trade his captive."

"See? It ain't no use," said Legget, spreading out his hands, "Let him go. He'll outwit the bordermen if any redskin's able to. The sooner he goes the quicker he'll git back, an' we can go to work. You ought'er be satisfied to git the girl——"

"Shut up!" interrupted Brandt sharply.

"'Pears to me, Brandt, bein' in love hes kinder worked on your nerves. You used to be game. Now you're afeerd of a bound an' tied man who ain't got long to live."

"I fear no man," answered Brandt, scowling darkly. "But I know what you don't seem to have sense enough to see. If this Zane gets away, which is probable, he and Wetzel will clean up your gang."

"Haw! haw! haw!" roared Legget, slapping his knees. "Then you'd hev little chanst of gittin' the lass, eh?"

"All right. I've no more to say," snapped Brandt, rising and turning on his heel. As he passed Jonathan he paused. "Zane, if I could, I'd get even with you for that punch you once gave me. As it is, I'll stop at the Shawnee village on my way west——"

"With the pretty lass," interposed Legget.

"Where I hope to see your scalp drying in the chief's lodge."

The borderman eyed him steadily; but in silence. Words could not so well have conveyed his thought as did the cold glance of dark scorn and merciless meaning.

Brandt shuffled on with a curse. No coward was he. No man ever saw him flinch. But his intelligence was against him as a desperado. While such as these bordermen lived, an outlaw should never sleep, for he was a marked and doomed man. The deadly, cold-pointed flame which scintillated in the prisoner's eyes was only a gleam of what the border felt towards outlaws.

While Jonathan was considering all he had heard, three more Shawnees entered the retreat, and were at once called aside in consultation by Ashbow. At the conclusion of this brief conference the chief advanced to Jonathan, cut the bonds round his feet, and motioned for him to rise. The prisoner complied to find himself weak and sore, but able to walk. He concluded that his wound, while very painful, was not of a serious nature, and that he would be taken at once on the march toward the Shawnee village.

He was correct, for the chief led him, with the three Shawnees following, toward the outlet of the enclosure. Jonathan's sharp eye took in every detail of Legget's rendezvous. In a corral near the entrance, he saw a number of fine horses, and among them his sister's pony. A more inaccessible, natural refuge than Legget's, could hardly have been found in that country. The entrance was a narrow opening in the wall, and could be held by half a dozen against an army of besiegers. It opened, moreover, on the side of a barren hill, from which could be had a good survey of the surrounding forests and plains.

As Jonathan went with his captors down the hill his hopes, which while ever alive, had been flagging, now rose. The long journey to the Shawnee town led through an untracked wilderness. The Delaware villages lay far to the north; the Wyandot to the west. No likelihood was there of falling in with a band of Indians hunting, because this region, stony, barren, and poorly watered, afforded sparse pasture for deer or bison. From the prisoner's point of view this enterprise of Ashbow's was reckless and vainglorious. Cunning as the chief was, he erred in one point, a great warrior's only weakness, love of show, of pride, of his achievement. In Indian nature this desire for fame was as strong as love of life. The brave risked everything to win his eagle feathers, and the matured warrior found death while keeping bright the glory of the plumes he had won.

Wetzel was in the woods, fleet as a deer, fierce and fearless as a lion. Somewhere among those glades he trod, stealthily, with the ears of a doe and eyes of a hawk strained for sound or sight of his comrade's captors. When he found their trail he would stick to it as the wolf to that of a bleeding buck's. The rescue would not be attempted until the right moment, even though that came within rifle-shot of the Shawnee encampment. Wonderful as his other gifts, was the borderman's patience.

CHAPTER 14

"GOOD MORNING, COLONEL ZANE," SAID HELEN CHEERILY, COMING into the yard where the colonel was at work. "Did Will come over this way?"

"I reckon you'll find him if you find Betty," replied Colonel Zane dryly.

"Come to think of it, that's true," Helen said, laughing. "I've a suspicion Will ran off from me this morning."

"He and Betty have gone nutting."

"I declare it's mean of Will," Helen said petulantly. "I have been wanting to go so much, and both he and Betty promised to take me."

"Say, Helen, let me tell you something," said the colonel, resting on his spade and looking at her quizzically. "I told them we hadn't had enough frost yet to ripen hickory-nuts and chestnuts. But they went anyhow. Will did remember to say if you came along, to tell you he'd bring the colored leaves you wanted."

"How extremely kind of him. I've a mind to follow them."

"Now see here, Helen, it might be a right good idea for you not to," returned the colonel, with a twinkle and a meaning in his eye.

"Oh, I understand. How singularly dull I've been."

"It's this way. We're mighty glad to have a fine young fellow like Will come along and interest Betty. Lord knows we had a time with her after Alfred died. She's just beginning to brighten up now, and, Helen, the point is that young people on the border must get married. No, my dear, you needn't laugh, you'll have to find a husband same as the other girls. It's not here as it was back east, where a lass might have her fling, so to speak, and take her time choosing. An unmarried girl on the border is a positive menace. I saw, not many years ago, two first-rate youngsters, wild with border fire and spirit, fight and kill each other over a lass who wouldn't choose. Like as not, if she had done so, the three would have been good friends, for out here we're like one big family. Remember this, Helen, and as far as Betty and Will are concerned you will be wise to follow our example: Leave them to themselves. Nothing else will so quickly strike fire between a boy and a girl."

"Betty and Will! I'm sure I'd love to see them care for each other." Then with big, bright eyes bent gravely on him she continued, "May I ask, Colonel Zane, who you have picked out for me?"

"There, now you've said it, and that's the problem. I've looked over every marriageable young man in the settlement, except Jack. Of course you couldn't care for him, a borderman, a fighter and all that; but I can't find a fellow I think quite up to you."

"Colonel Zane, is not a borderman such as Jonathan worthy a woman's regard?" Helen asked a little wistfully.

"Bless your heart, lass, yes!" replied Colonel Zane heartily. "People out here are not as they are back east. An educated man, polished and all that, but incapable of hard labor, or shrinking from dirt and sweat on his hands, or even blood, would not help us in the winning of the West. Plain as Jonathan is, and with his lack of schooling, he is greatly superior to the majority of young men on the frontier. But, unlettered or not, he is as fine a man as ever stepped in moccasins, or any other kind of foot gear."

"Then why did you say—that—what you did?"

"Well, it's this way," replied Colonel Zane, stealing a glance at her pensive, downcast face. "Girls all like to be wooed. Almost every one I ever knew wanted the young man of her choice to outstrip all her other admirers, and then, for a spell, nearly die of love for her, after which she'd give in. Now, Jack, being a borderman, a man with no occupation except scouting, will never look at a girl, let alone make up to her. I imagine, my dear, it'd take some mighty tall courting to fetch home Helen Sheppard a bride. On the other hand, if some pretty and spirited lass, like, say for instance, Helen Sheppard, would come along and just make Jack forget Indians and fighting, she'd get the finest husband in the world. True, he's wild; but only in the woods. A simpler, kinder, cleaner man cannot be found."

"I believe that, Colonel Zane; but where is the girl who would interest him?" Helen asked with spirit. "These bordermen are unapproachable. Imagine a girl interesting that great, cold, stern Wetzel! All her flatteries, her wiles, the little coquetries that might attract ordinary men, would not be noticed by him, or Jonathan either."

"I grant it'd not be easy, but woman was made to subjugate man, and always, everlastingly, until the end of life here on this beautiful earth, she will do it."

"Do you think Jonathan and Wetzel will catch Brandt?" asked Helen, changing the subject abruptly.

"I'd stake my all that this year's autumn leaves will fall on Brandt's grave."

Colonel Zane's calm, matter-of-fact coldness made Helen shiver.

"Why, the leaves have already begun to fall. Papa told me Brandt had gone to join the most powerful outlaw band on the border. How can these two men, alone, cope with savages, as I've heard they do, and break up such an outlaw band as Legget's?"

"That's a question I've heard Daniel Boone ask about Wetzel, and Boone, though not a borderman in all the name implies, was a great Indian fighter. I've heard old frontiersmen, grown grizzled on the frontier, use the same words. I've been twenty years with that man, yet I can't answer it. Jonathan, of course, is only a shadow of him; Wetzel is the type of these men who have held the frontier for us. He was the first borderman, and no doubt he'll be the last."

"What have Jonathan and Wetzel that other men do not possess?"

"In them is united a marvelously developed woodcraft, with wonderful physical powers. Imagine a man having a sense, almost an animal instinct, for what is going on in the woods. Take for instance the fleetness of foot. That is one of the greatest factors. It is absolutely necessary to run, to get away when to hold ground would be death. Whether at home or in the woods, the bordermen retreat every day. You wouldn't think they practiced anything of the kind, would you? Well, a man can't be great in anything without keeping at it. Jonathan says he exercises to keep his feet light. Wetzel would just as soon run as walk. Think of the magnificent condition of these men. When a dash of speed is called for, when to be fleet of foot is to elude vengeance-seeking Indians, they must travel as swiftly as the deer. The Zanes were all sprinters. I could do something of the kind; Betty was fast on her feet, as that old fort will testify until the logs rot; Isaac was fleet, too, and Jonathan can get over the ground like a scared buck. But, even so, Wetzel can beat him."

"Goodness me, Helen!" exclaimed the colonel's buxom wife, from the window, "don't you ever get tired hearing Eb talk of Wetzel, and Jack, and Indians? Come in with me. I venture to say my gossip will do you more good than his stories."

Therefore Helen went in to chat with Mrs. Zane, for she was always glad to listen to the colonel's wife, who was so bright and pleasant, so helpful and kindly in her womanly way. In the course of their conversation, which drifted from weaving linsey, Mrs. Zane's occupation at the tune, to the costly silks and satins of remembered days, and then to matters of more present interest, Helen spoke of Colonel Zane's hint about Will and Betty.

"Isn't Eb a terror? He's the worst matchmatcher you ever saw," declared the colonel's good spouse.

"There's no harm in that."

"No, indeed; it's a good thing, but he makes me laugh, and Betty, he sets her furious."

"The colonel said he had designs on me."

"Of course he has, dear old Eb! How he'd love to see you happily married. His heart is as big as that mountain yonder. He has given this settlement his whole life."

"I believe you. He has such interest, such zeal for everybody. Only the other day he was speaking to me of Mr. Mordaunt, telling how sorry he was for the Englishman, and how much he'd like to help him. It does seem a pity a man of Mordaunt's blood and attainments should sink to utter worthlessness."

"Yes,'tis a pity for any man, blood or no, and the world's full of such wrecks. I always liked that man's looks. I never had a word with him, of course; but I've seen him often, and something about him appealed to me. I don't believe it was just his handsome face; still I know women are susceptible that way."

"I, too, liked him once as a friend," said Helen feelingly. "Well, I'm glad he's gone."

"Gone?"

"Yes, he left Fort Henry yesterday. He came to say good-bye to me, and, except for his pale face and trembling hands, was much as he used to be in Virginia. Said he was going home to England, and wanted to tell me he was sorry—for—for all he'd done to make papa and me suffer. Drink had broken him, he said, and surely he looked 'a broken man. I shook hands with him, and then slipped upstairs and cried."

"Poor fellow!" sighed Mrs. Zane.

"Papa said he left Fort Pitt with one of Metzar's men as a guide."

"Then he didn't take the 'little cuss,' as Eb calls his man Case?"

"No, if I remember rightly papa said Case wouldn't go."

"I wish he had. He's no addition to our village."

Voices outside attracted their attention. Mrs. Zane glanced from the window and said: "There come Betty and Will."

Helen went on the porch to see her cousin and Betty entering the yard, and Colonel Zane once again leaning on his spade.

"Gather any hickory-nuts from birch or any other kind of trees?" asked the colonel grimly.

"No," replied Will cheerily, "the shells haven't opened yet."

"Too bad the frost is so backward," said Colonel Zane with a laugh. "But I can't see that it makes any difference."

"Where are my leaves?" asked Helen, with a smile and a nod to Betty.

"What leaves?" inquired that young woman, plainly mystified.

"Why, the autumn leaves Will promised to gather with me, then changed his mind, and said he'd bring them."

"I forgot," Will replied a little awkwardly.

Colonel Zane coughed, and then, catching Betty's glance, which had begun to flash, he plied his spade vigorously.

Betty's face had colored warmly at her brother's first question; it toned down slightly when she understood that he was not going to tease her as usual, and suddenly, as she looked over his head, it paled white as snow.

"Eb, look down the lane!" she cried.

Two tall men were approaching with labored tread, one half-supporting his companion.

"Wetzel! Jack! and Jack's hurt!" cried Betty.

"My dear, be calm," said Colonel Zane, in that quiet tone he always used during moments of excitement. He turned toward the bordermen, and helped Wetzel lead Jonathan up the walk into the yard.

From Wetzel's clothing water ran, his long hair was disheveled, his aspect frightful. Jonathan's face was white and drawn. His buckskin hunting coat was covered with blood, and the hand which he held tightly against his left breast showed dark red stains.

Helen shuddered. Almost fainting, she leaned against the porch, too horrified to cry out, with contracting heart and a chill stealing through her veins.

"Jack! Jack!" cried Betty, in agonized appeal.

"Betty, it's nothin'," said Wetzel.

"Now, Betts, don't be scared of a little blood," Jonathan said with a faint smile flitting across his haggard face.

"Bring water, shears an' some linsey cloth," added Wetzel, as Mrs. Zane came running out.

"Come inside," cried the colonel's wife, as she disappeared again immediately.

"No," replied the borderman, removing his coat, and, with the assistance of his brother, he unlaced his hunting shirt, pulling it down from a wounded shoulder. A great gory hole gaped just beneath his left collar-bone.

Although stricken with fear, when Helen saw the bronzed, massive shoulder, the long, powerful arm with its cords of muscles playing under the brown skin, she felt a thrill of admiration.

"Just missed the lung," said Mrs. Zane. "Eb, no bullet ever made that hole."

Wetzel washed the bloody wound, and, placing on it a wad of leaves he took from his pocket, bound up the shoulder tightly.

"What made that hole?" asked Colonel Zane.

Wetzel lifted the quiver of arrows Jonathan had laid on the porch, and, selecting one, handed it to the colonel. The flint-head and a portion of the shaft were stained with blood.

"The Shawnee!" exclaimed Colonel Zane. Then he led Wetzel aside, and began conversing in low tones while Jonathan, with Betty holding his arm, ascended the steps and went within the dwelling.

Helen ran home, and, once in her room, gave vent to her emotions. She cried because of fright, nervousness, relief, and joy. Then she bathed her face, tried to rub some color into her pale cheeks, and set about getting dinner as one in a trance. She could not forget that broad shoulder with its frightful wound. What a man Jonathan must be to receive a blow like that and live! Exhausted, almost spent, had been his strength when he reached home, yet how calm and cool he was! What would she not have given for the faint smile that shone in his eyes for Betty?

The afternoon was long for Helen. When at last supper was over she changed her gown, and, asking Will to accompany her, went down the lane toward Colonel Zane's cabin. At this hour the colonel almost invariably could be found sitting on his doorstep puffing a long Indian pipe, and gazing with dreamy eyes over the valley.

"Well, well, how sweet you look!" he said to Helen; then with a wink of his eyelid, "Hello, Willie, you'll find Elizabeth inside with Jack."

"How is he?" asked Helen eagerly, as Will with a laugh and a retort mounted the steps.

"Jack's doing splendidly. He slept all day. I don't think his injury amounts to much, at least not for such as him or Wetzel. It would have finished ordinary men. Bess says if complications don't set in, blood-poison or something to start a fever, he'll be up shortly. Wetzel believes the two of 'em will be on the trail inside of a week."

"Did they find Brandt?" asked Helen in a low voice.

"Yes, they ran him to his hole, and, as might have been expected, it was Bing Legget's camp. The Indians took Jonathan there."

"Then Jack was captured?"

Colonel Zane related the events, as told briefly by Wetzel, that had taken place during the preceding three days.

"The Indian I saw at the spring carried that bow Jonathan brought back. He must have shot the arrow. He was a magnificent savage."

"He was indeed a great, and a bad Indian, one of the craftiest spies who ever stepped in moccasins; but he lies quiet now on the moss and the leaves. Bing Legget will never find another runner like that Shawnee. Let us go indoors."

He led Helen into the large sitting-room where Jonathan lay on a couch, with Betty and Will sitting beside him. The colonel's wife and children, Silas Zane, and several neighbors, were present.

"Here, Jack, is a lady inquiring after your health. Betts, this reminds me of the time Isaac came home wounded, after his escape from the Hurons. Strikes me he and his Indian bride should be about due here on a visit."

Helen forgot every one except the wounded man lying so quiet and pale upon the couch. She looked down upon him with eyes strangely dilated, and darkly bright.

"How are you?" she asked softly.

"I'm all right, thank you, lass," answered Jonathan.

Colonel Zane contrived, with inimitable skill, to get Betty, Will, Silas, Bessie and the others interested in some remarkable news he had just heard, or made up, and this left Jonathan and Helen comparatively alone for the moment.

The wise old colonel thought perhaps this might be the right time. He saw Helen's face as she leaned over Jonathan, and that was enough for him. He would have taxed his ingenuity to the utmost to keep the others away from the young couple.

"I was so frightened," murmured Helen.

"Why?" asked Jonathan.

"Oh! You looked so deathly—the blood, and that awful wound!"

"It's nothin', lass."

Helen smiled down upon him. Whether or not the hurt amounted to anything in the borderman's opinion, she knew from his weakness, and his white, drawn face, that the strain of the march home had been fearful. His dark eyes held now nothing of the coldness and glitter so natural to them. They were weary, almost sad. She did not feel afraid of him now. He lay there so helpless, his long, powerful frame as quiet as a sleeping child's! Hitherto an almost indefinable antagonism in him had made itself felt; now there was only gentleness, as of a man too weary to fight longer. Helen's heart swelled with pity, and tenderness, and love. His weakness affected her as had never his strength. With an involuntary gesture of sympathy she placed her hand softly on his.

Jonathan looked up at her with eyes no longer blind. Pain had softened him. For the moment he felt carried out of himself, as it were, and saw things differently. The melting tenderness of her gaze, the glowing softness of her face, the beauty, bewitched him; and beyond that, a sweet, impelling gladness stirred within him and would not be denied. He thrilled as her fingers lightly, timidly touched his, and opened his broad hand to press hers closely and warmly.

"Lass," he whispered, with a huskiness and unsteadiness unnatural to his deep voice.

Helen bent her head closer to him; she saw his lips tremble, and his nostrils dilate; but an unutterable sadness shaded the brightness in his eyes.

"I love you."

The low whisper reached Helen's ears. She seemed to float dreamily away to some beautiful world, with the music of those words ringing in her ears. She looked at him again. Had she been dreaming? No; his dark eyes met hers with a love that he could no longer deny. An exquisite emotion, keen, strangely sweet and strong, yet terrible with sharp pain, pulsated through her being. The revelation had been too abrupt. It was so wonderfully different from what she had ever dared hope. She lowered her head, trembling.

The next moment she felt Colonel Zane's hand on her chair, and heard him say in a cheery voice:

"Well, well, see here, lass, you mustn't make Jack talk too much. See how white and tired he looks."

CHAPTER 15

IN FORTY-EIGHT HOURS JONATHAN ZANE WAS UP AND ABOUT THE CABIN as though he had never been wounded; the third day he walked to the spring; in a week he was waiting for Wetzel, ready to go on the trail.

On the eighth day of his enforced idleness, as he sat with Betty and the colonel in the yard, Wetzel appeared on a ridge east of the fort. Soon he rounded the stockade fence, and came straight toward them. To Colonel Zane and Betty, Wetzel's expression was terrible. The stern kindliness, the calm, though cold, gravity of his countenance, as they usually saw it, had disappeared. Yet it showed no trace of his unnatural passion to pursue and slay. No doubt that terrible instinct, or lust, was at white heat; but it wore a mask of impenetrable stone-gray gloom.

Wetzel spoke briefly. After telling Jonathan to meet him at sunset on the following day at a point five miles up the river, he reported to the colonel that Legget with his band had left their retreat, moving southward, apparently on a marauding expedition. Then he shook hands with Colonel Zane and turned to Betty.

"Good-bye, Betty," he said, in his deep, sonorous voice.

"Good-bye, Lew," answered Betty slowly, as if surprised. "God save you," she added.

He shouldered his rifle, and hurried down the lane, halting before entering the thicket that bounded the clearing, to look back at the settlement. In another moment his dark figure had disappeared among the bushes.

"Betts, I've seen Wetzel go like that hundreds of times, though he never shook hands before; but I feel sort of queer about it now. Wasn't he strange?"

Betty did not answer until Jonathan, who had started to go within, was out of hearing.

"Lew looked and acted the same the morning he struck Miller's trail," Betty replied in a low voice. "I believe, despite his indifference to danger, he realizes that the chances are greatly against him, as they were when he began the trailing of Miller, certain it would lead him into Girty's camp. Then I know Lew has an affection for us, though it is never shown in ordinary ways. I pray he and Jack will come home safe."

"This is a bad trail they're taking up; the worst, perhaps, in border warfare," said Colonel Zane gloomily. "Did you notice how Jack's face darkened when his comrade came? Much of this borderman-life of his is due to Wetzel's influence."

"Eb, I'll tell you one thing," returned Betty, with a flash of her old spirit. "This is Jack's last trail."

"Why do you think so?"

"If he doesn't return he'll be gone the way of all bordermen; but if he comes back once more he'll never get away from Helen."

"Ugh!" exclaimed Zane, venting his pleasure in characteristic Indian way.

"That night after Jack came home wounded," continued Betty, "I saw him, as he lay on the couch, gaze at Helen. Such a look! Eb, she has won."

"I hope so, but I fear, I fear," replied her brother gloomily. "If only he returns, that's the thing! Betts, be sure he sees Helen before he goes away."

"I shall try. Here he comes now," said Betty.

"Hello, Jack!" cried the colonel, as his brother came out in somewhat of a hurry. "What have you got? By George! It's that blamed arrow the Shawnee shot into you. Where are you going with it? What the deuce— Say—Betts, eh?"

Betty had given him a sharp little kick.

The borderman looked embarrassed. He hesitated and flushed. Evidently he would have liked to avoid his brother's question; but the inquiry came direct. Dissimulation with him was impossible.

"Helen wanted this, an' I reckon that's where I'm goin' with it," he said finally, and walked away.

"Eb, you're a stupid!" exclaimed Betty.

"Hang it! Who'd have thought he was going to give her that blamed, bloody arrow?"

As Helen ushered Jonathan, for the first time, into her cosy little sitting-room, her heart began to thump so hard she could hear it.

She had not seen him since the night he whispered the words which gave such happiness. She had stayed at home, thankful beyond expression to learn every day of his rapid improvement, living in the sweetness of her joy, and waiting for him. And now as he had come, so dark, so grave, so unlike a lover to woo, that she felt a chill steal over her.

"I'm so glad you've brought the arrow," she faltered, "for, of course, coming so far means that you're well once more."

"You asked me for it, an' I've fetched it over. To-morrow I'm off on a trail I may never return from," he answered simply, and his voice seemed cold.

An immeasurable distance stretched once more between them. Helen's happiness slowly died.

"I thank you," she said with a voice that was tremulous despite all her efforts.

"It's not much of a keepsake."

"I did not ask for it as a keepsake, but because—because I wanted it. I need nothing tangible to keep alive my memory. A few words whispered to me not many days ago will suffice for remembrance—or—or did I dream them?"

Bitter disappointment almost choked Helen. This was not the gentle, soft-voiced man who had said he loved her. It was the indifferent border-man. Again he was the embodiment of his strange, quiet woods. Once more he seemed the comrade of the cold, inscrutable Wetzel.

"No, lass, I reckon you didn't dream," he replied.

Helen swayed from sick bitterness and a suffocating sense of pain, back to her old, sweet, joyous, tumultuous heart-throbbing.

"Tell me, if I didn't dream," she said softly, her face flashing warm again. She came close to him and looked up with all her heart in her great dark eyes, and love trembling on her red lips.

Calmness deserted the borderman after one glance at her. He paced the floor; twisted and clasped his hands while his eyes gleamed.

"Lass, I'm only human," he cried hoarsely, facing her again.

But only for a moment did he stand before her; but it was long enough for him to see her shrink a little, the gladness in her eyes giving way to uncertainty and a fugitive hope. Suddenly he began to pace the room again, and to talk incoherently. With the flow of words he gradually grew calmer, and, with something of his natural dignity, spoke more rationally.

"I said I loved you, an' it's true, but I didn't mean to speak. I oughtn't have done it. Somethin' made it so easy, so natural like. I'd have died before letting you know, if any idea had come to me of what I was sayin'. I've fought this feelin' for months. I allowed myself to think of you at first, an' there's the wrong. I went on the trail with your big eyes pictured in my mind, an' before I'd dreamed of it you'd crept into my heart. Life has never been the same since—that kiss. Betty said as how you cared for me, an' that made me worse, only I never really believed. Today I came over here to say good-bye, expectin' to hold myself well in hand; but the first glance of your eyes unmans me. Nothin' can come of it, lass, nothin' but trouble. Even if you cared, an' I don't dare believe you do, nothin' can come of it! I've my own life to live, an' there's no sweetheart in it. Mebbe, as Lew says, there's one in Heaven. Oh! girl, this has been hard on me. I see you always on my lonely tramps; I see your glorious eyes in the sunny fields an' in the woods, at gray twilight, an' when the stars shine brightest. They haunt me. Ah! you're the sweetest lass as ever tormented a man, an' I love you, I love you!"

He turned to the window only to hear a soft, broken cry, and a flurry of skirts. A rush of wind seemed to envelop him. Then two soft, rounded arms encircled his neck, and a golden head lay on his breast.

"My borderman! My hero! My love!"

Jonathan clasped the beautiful, quivering girl to his heart.

"Lass, for God's sake don't say you love me," he implored, thrilling with contact of her warm arms.

"Ah!" she breathed, and raised her head. Her radiant eyes darkly wonderful with unutterable love, burned into his.

He had almost pressed his lips to the sweet red ones so near his, when he drew back with a start, and his frame straightened.

"Am I a man, or only a coward?" he muttered. "Lass, let me think. Don't believe I'm harsh, nor cold, nor nothin' except that I want to do what's right."

He leaned out of the window while Helen stood near him with a hand on his quivering shoulder. When at last he turned, his face was colorless, white as marble, and sad, and set, and stern.

"Lass, it mustn't be; I'll not ruin your life."

"But you will if you give me up."

"No, no, lass."

"I cannot live without you."

"You must. My life is not mine to give."

"But you love me."

"I am a borderman."

"I will not live without you."

"Hush! lass, hush!"

"I love you."

Jonathan breathed hard; once more the tremor, which seemed pitiful in such a strong man, came upon him. His face was gray.

"I love you," she repeated, her rich voice indescribably deep and full. She opened wide her arms and stood before him with heaving bosom, with great eyes dark with woman's sadness, passionate with woman's promise, perfect in her beauty, glorious in her abandonment.

The borderman bowed and bent like a broken reed.

"Listen," she whispered, coming closer to him, "go if you must leave me; but let this be your last trail. Come back to me, Jack, come back to me! You have had enough of this terrible life; you have won a name that will never be forgotten; you have done your duty to the border. The Indians and outlaws will be gone soon. Take the farm your brother wants you to have, and live for me. We will be happy. I shall learn to keep your home. Oh! my dear, I will recompense you for the loss of all this wild hunting and fighting. Let me persuade you, as much for your sake as for mine, for you are my heart, and soul, and life. Go out upon your last trail, Jack, and come back to me."

"An' let Wetzel go always alone?"

"He is different; he lives only for revenge. What are those poor savages to you? You have a better, nobler life opening."

"Lass, I can't give him up."

"You need not; but give up this useless seeking of adventure. That, you know, is half a borderman's life. Give it up, Jack, it not for your own, then for my sake."

"No-no-never-I can't-I won't be a coward! After all these years I won't desert him. No-no——"

"Do not say more," she pleaded, stealing closer to him until she was against his breast. She slipped her arms around his neck. For love and more than life she was fighting now. "Good-bye, my love." She kissed him, a long, lingering pressure of her soft full lips on his. "Dearest, do not shame me further. Dearest Jack, come back to me, for I love you."

She released him, and ran sobbing from the room.

Unsteady as a blind man, he groped for the door, found it, and went out.

CHAPTER 16

THE LONGEST DAY IN JONATHAN ZANE'S LIFE, THE ODDEST, THE MOST terrible and complex with unintelligible emotions, was that one in which he learned that the wilderness no longer sufficed for him.

He wandered through the forest like a man lost, searching for, he knew not what. Rambling along the shady trails he looked for that contentment which had always been his, but found it not. He plunged into the depths of deep, gloomy ravines; into the fastnesses of heavy-timbered hollows where the trees hid the light of day; he sought the open, grassy hillsides, and roamed far over meadow and plain. Yet something always eluded him. The invisible and beautiful life of all inanimate things sang no more in his heart. The springy moss, the quivering leaf, the tell-tale bark of the trees, the limpid, misty, eddying pools under green banks, the myriads of natural objects from which he had learned so much, and the manifold joyous life around him, no longer spoke with soul-satisfying faithfulness. The environment of his boyish days, of his youth, and manhood, rendered not a sweetness as of old.

His intelligence, sharpened by the pain of new experience, told him he had been vain to imagine that he, because he was a borderman, could escape the universal destiny of human life. Dimly he could feel the broadening, the awakening into a fuller existence, but he did not welcome this new light. He realized that men had always turned, at some time in their lives, to women even as the cypress leans toward the sun. This weakening of the sterner stuff in him; this softening of his heart, and especially the inquietude, and lack of joy and harmony in his old pursuits of the forest trails bewildered him, and troubled him some. Thousands of times his borderman's trail had been crossed, yet never to his sorrow until now when it had been crossed by a woman.

Sick at heart, hurt in his pride, darkly savage, sad, remorseful, and thrilling with awakened passion, all in turn, he roamed the woodland unconsciously visiting the scenes where he had formerly found contentment.

He paused by many a shady glen, and beautiful quiet glade; by gray cliffs and mossy banks, searching with moody eyes for the spirit which evaded him.

Here in the green and golden woods rose before him a rugged, giant rock, moss-stained, and gleaming with trickling water. Tangled ferns dressed in autumn's russet hue lay at the base of the green-gray cliff, and circled a dark, deep pool dotted with yellow leaves. Half-way up, the perpendicular ascent was broken by a protruding ledge upon which waved broad-leaved plants and rusty ferns. Above, the cliff sheered out with many cracks and seams in its weather-beaten front.

The forest grew to the verge of the precipice. A full foliaged oak and a luxuriant maple, the former still fresh with its dark green leaves, the latter making a vivid contrast with its pale yellow, purple-red, and orange hues, leaned far out over the bluff. A mighty chestnut grasped with gnarled roots deep into the broken cliff. Dainty plumes of goldenrod swayed on the brink; red berries, amber moss, and green trailing vines peeped over the edge, and every little niche and cranny sported fragile ferns and pale-faced asters. A second cliff, higher than the first, and more heavily wooded, loomed above, and over it sprayed a transparent film of water, thin as smoke, and iridescent in the sunshine. Far above where the glancing rill caressed the mossy cliff and shone like gleaming gold against the dark branches with their green and red and purple leaves, lay the faint blue of the sky.

Jonathan pulled on down the stream with humbler heart. His favorite waterfall had denied him. The gold that had gleamed there was his sweetheart's hair; the red was of her lips; the dark pool with its lights and shades, its unfathomable mystery, was like her eyes.

He came at length to another scene of milder aspect. An open glade where the dancing, dimpling brook raced under dark hemlocks, and where blood-red sumach leaves, and beech leaves like flashes of sunshine, lay against the green. Under a leaning birch he found a patch of purple asters, and a little apart from them, by a mossy stone, a lonely fringed gentian. Its deep color brought to him the dark blue eyes that haunted him, and once again, like one possessed of an evil spirit, he wandered along the merry water-course.

But finally pain and unrest left him. When he surrendered to his love, peace returned. Though he said in his heart that Helen was not for him, he felt he did not need to torture himself by fighting against resistless power. He could love her without being a coward. He would take up his life where it had been changed, and live it, carrying this bitter-sweet burden always.

Memory, now that he admitted himself conquered, made a toy of him, bringing the sweetness of fragrant hair, and eloquent eyes, and clinging arms, and dewy lips. A thousand-fold harder to fight than pain was the seductive thought that he had but to go back to Helen to feel again the charm of her presence, to see the grace of her person, to hear the music of her voice, to have again her lips on his.

Jonathan knew then that his trial had but begun; that the pain and suffering of a borderman's broken pride and conquered spirit was nothing; that to steel his heart against the joy, the sweetness, the longing of love was everything.

So a tumult raged within his heart. No bitterness, nor wretchedness stabbed him as before, but a passionate yearning, born of memory, and unquenchable as the fires of the sun, burned there.

Helen's reply to his pale excuses, to his duty, to his life, was that she loved him. The wonder of it made him weak. Was not her answer enough? "I love you!" Three words only; but they changed the world. A beautiful girl loved him, she had kissed him, and his life could never again be the same. She had held out her arms to him—and he, cold, churlish, unfeeling brute, had let her shame herself, fighting for her happiness, for the joy that is a woman's divine right. He had been blind; he had not understood the significance of her gracious action; he had never realized until too late, what it must have cost her, what heartburning shame and scorn his refusal brought upon her. If she ever looked tenderly at him again with her great eyes; or leaned toward him with her beautiful arms outstretched, he would fall at her feet and throw his duty to the winds, swearing his love was hers always and his life forever.

So love stormed in the borderman's heart.

Slowly the melancholy Indian-summer day waned as Jonathan strode out of the woods into a plain beyond, where he was to meet Wetzel at sunset. A smoky haze like a purple cloud lay upon the gently waving grass. He could not see across the stretch of prairie-land, though at this point he knew it was hardly a mile wide. With the trilling of the grasshoppers alone disturbing the serene quiet of this autumn afternoon, all nature seemed in harmony with the declining season. He stood a while, his thoughts becoming the calmer for the silence and loneliness of this breathing meadow.

When the shadows of the trees began to lengthen, and to steal far out over the yellow grass, he knew the time had come, and glided out upon the plain. He crossed it, and sat down upon a huge stone which lay with one shelving end overhanging the river.

Far in the west the gold-red sun, too fiery for his direct gaze, lost the brilliance of its under circle behind the fringe of the wooded hill. Slowly the red ball sank. When the last bright gleam had vanished in the dark horizon Jonathan turned to search wood and plain. Wetzel was to meet him at sunset. Even as his first glance swept around a light step sounded behind him. He did not move, for that step was familiar. In another moment the tall form of Wetzel stood beside him.

"I'm about as much behind as you was ahead of time," said Wetzel. "We'll stay here fer the night, an' be off early in the mornin'."

Under the shelving side of the rock, and in the shade of the thicket, the bordermen built a little fire and roasted strips of deer-meat. Then, puffing at their long pipes they sat for a long time in silence, while twilight let fall a dark, gray cloak over river and plain.

"Legget's move up the river was a blind, as I suspected," said Wetzel, presently. "He's not far back in the woods from here, an' seems to be waitin' fer somethin' or somebody. Brandt an' seven redskins are with him. We'd hev a good chance at them in the mornin'; now we've got 'em a long ways from their camp, so we'll wait, an' see what deviltry they're up to."

"Mebbe he's waitin' for some Injun band," suggested Jonathan.

"Thar's redskins in the valley an' close to him; but I reckon he's barkin' up another tree."

"Suppose we run into some of these Injuns?"

"We'll hev to take what comes," replied Wetzel, lying down on a bed of leaves.

When darkness enveloped the spot Wetzel lay wrapped in deep slumber, while Jonathan sat against the rock, watching the last flickerings of the camp-fire.

CHAPTER 17

WILL AND HELEN HURRIED BACK ALONG THE RIVER ROAD. BEGUILED BY the soft beauty of the autumn morning they ventured farther from the fort than ever before, and had been suddenly brought to a realization of the fact by a crackling in the underbrush. Instantly their minds reverted to bears and panthers, such as they had heard invested the thickets round the settlement.

"Oh! Will! I saw a dark form stealing along in the woods from tree to tree!" exclaimed Helen in a startled whisper.

"So did I. It was an Indian, or I never saw one. Walk faster. Once round the bend in the road we'll be within sight of the fort; then we'll run," replied Will. He had turned pale, but maintained his composure.

They increased their speed, and had almost come up to the curve in the road, marked by dense undergrowth on both sides, when the branches in the thicket swayed violently, a sturdy little man armed with a musket appeared from among them.

"Avast! Heave to!" he commanded in a low, fierce voice, leveling his weapon. "One breeze from ye, an' I let sail this broadside."

"What do you want? We have no valuables," said Will, speaking low.

Helen stared at the little man. She was speechless with terror. It flashed into her mind as soon as she recognized the red, evil face of the sailor, that he was the accomplice upon whom Brandt had told Metzar he could rely.

"Shut up! It's not ye I want, nor valuables, but this wench," growled Case. He pushed Will around with the muzzle of the musket, which action caused the young man to turn a sickly white and shrink involuntarily with fear. The hammer of the musket was raised, and might fall at the slightest jar.

"For God's sake! Will, do as he says," cried Helen, who saw murder in Case's eyes. Capture or anything was better than sacrifice of life.

"March!" ordered Case, with the musket against Will's back.

Will hurriedly started forward, jostling Helen, who had preceded him. He was forced to hurry, because every few moments Case pressed the gun to his back or side.

Without another word the sailor marched them swiftly along the road, which now narrowed down to a trail. His intention, no doubt, was to put as much distance between him and the fort as was possible. No more than a mile had been thus traversed when two Indians stepped into view.

"My God! My God!" cried Will as the savages proceeded first to bind Helen's arms behind her, and then his in the same manner. After this the journey was continued in silence, the Indians walking beside the prisoners, and Case in the rear.

Helen was so terrified that for a long time she could not think coherently. It seemed as if she had walked miles, yet did not feel tired. Always in front wound the narrow, leaf-girt trail, and to the left the broad river gleamed at intervals through open spaces in the thickets. Flocks of birds rose in the line of march. They seemed tame, and uttered plaintive notes as if in sympathy.

About noon the trail led to the river bank. One of the savages disappeared in a copse of willows, and presently reappeared carrying a birch-bark canoe. Case ordered Helen and Will into the boat, got in himself, and the savages, taking stations at bow and stern, paddled out into the stream. They shot over under the lee of an island, around a rocky point, and across a strait to another island. Beyond this they gained the Ohio shore, and beached the canoe.

"Ahoy! there, cap'n," cried Case, pushing Helen up the bank before him, and she, gazing upward, was more than amazed to see Mordaunt leaning against a tree.

"Mordaunt, had you anything to do with this?" cried Helen breathlessly.

"I had all to do with it," answered the Englishman.

"What do you mean?"

He did not meet her gaze, nor make reply; but turned to address a few words in a low tone to a white man sitting on a log.

Helen knew she had seen this person before, and doubted not he was one of Metzar's men. She saw a rude, bark lean-to, the remains of a camp-fire, and a pack tied in blankets. Evidently Mordaunt and his men had tarried here awaiting such developments as had come to pass.

"You white-faced hound!" hissed Will, beside himself with rage when he realized the situation. Bound though he was, he leaped up and tried to get at Mordaunt. Case knocked him on the head with the handle of his knife. Will fell with blood streaming from a cut over the temple.

The dastardly act aroused all Helen's fiery courage. She turned to the Englishman with eyes ablaze.

"So you've at last found your level. Border-outlaw! Kill me at once. I'd rather be dead than breathe the same air with such a coward!"

"I swore I'd have you, if not by fair means then by foul," he answered, with dark and haggard face.

"What do you intend to do with me now that I am tied?" she demanded scornfully.

"Keep you a prisoner in the woods till you consent to marry me."

Helen laughed in scorn. Desperate as was the plight, her natural courage had arisen at the cruel blow dealt her cousin, and she faced the Englishman with flashing eyes and undaunted mien. She saw he was again unsteady, and had the cough and catching breath habitual to certain men under the influence of liquor. She turned her attention to Will. He lay as he had fallen, with blood streaming over his pale face and fair hair. While she gazed at him Case whipped out his long knife, and looked up at Mordaunt.

"Cap'n, I'd better loosen a hatch fer him," he said brutally. "He's dead cargo fer us, an' in the way."

He lowered the gleaming point upon Will's chest.

"Oh-h-h!" breathed Helen in horror. She tried to close her eyes but was so fascinated she could not.

"Get up. I'll have no murder," ordered Mordaunt. "Leave him here."

"He's not got a bad cut," said the man sitting on the log. "He'll come to arter a spell, go back to ther fort, an' give an alarm."

"What's that to me?" asked Mordaunt sharply. "We shall be safe. I won't have him with us because some Indian or another will kill him. It's not my purpose to murder any one."

"Ugh!" grunted one of the savages, and pointed eastward with his hand.

"Hurry-long-way-go," he said in English. With the Indians in the lead the party turned from the river into the forest.

Helen looked back into the sandy glade and saw Will lying as they had left him, unconscious, with his hands still bound tightly behind him, and blood running over his face. Painful as was the thought of leaving him thus, it afforded her relief. She assured herself he had not been badly hurt, would recover consciousness before long, and, even bound as he was, could make his way back to the settlement.

Her own situation, now that she knew Mordaunt had instigated the abduction, did not seem hopeless. Although dreading Brandt with unspeakable horror, she did not in the least fear the Englishman. He was mad to carry her off like this into the wilderness, but would force her to do nothing. He could not keep her a prisoner long while Jonathan Zane and Wetzel were free to take his trail. What were his intentions? Where was he taking her? Such questions as these, however, troubled Helen more than a little. They brought her thoughts back to the Indians leading the way with lithe and stealthy step. How had Mordaunt associated himself with these savages? Then, suddenly, it dawned upon her that Brandt also might be in this scheme to carry her off. She scouted the idea; but it returned. Perhaps Mordaunt was only a tool; perhaps he himself was being deceived. Helen turned pale at the very thought. She had never forgotten the strange, unreadable, yet threatening, expression which Brandt had worn the day she had refused to walk with him.

Meanwhile the party made rapid progress through the forest. Not a word was spoken, nor did any noise of rustling leaves or crackling twigs follow their footsteps. The savage in the lead chose the open and less difficult ground; he took advantage of glades, mossy places, and rocky ridges. This careful choosing was, evidently, to avoid noise, and make the trail as difficult to follow as possible. Once he stopped suddenly, and listened.

Helen had a good look at the savage while he was in this position. His lean, athletic figure resembled, in its half-clothed condition, a bronzed statue; his powerful visage was set, changeless like iron. His dark eyes seemed to take in all points of the forest before him.

Whatever had caused the halt was an enigma to all save his red-skinned companion.

The silence of the wood was the silence of the desert. No bird chirped; no breath of wind sighed in the tree-tops; even the aspens remained unagitated. Pale yellow leaves sailed slowly, reluctantly down from above.

But some faint sound, something unusual had jarred upon the exquisitely sensitive ears of the leader, for with a meaning shake of the head to his followers, he resumed the march in a direction at right angles with the original course.

This caution, and evident distrust of the forest ahead, made Helen think again of Jonathan and Wetzel. Those great bordermen might already be on the trail of her captors. The thought thrilled her. Presently she realized, from another long, silent march through forest thickets, glades, aisles, and groves, over rock-strewn ridges, and down mossy-stoned ravines, that her strength was beginning to fail.

"I can go no further with my arms tied in this way," she declared, stopping suddenly.

"Ugh!" uttered the savage before her, turning sharply. He brandished a tomahawk before her eyes.

Mordaunt hurriedly set free her wrists. His pale face flushed a dark, flaming red when she shrank from his touch as if he were a viper.

After they had traveled what seemed to Helen many miles, the vigilance of the leaders relaxed.

On the banks of the willow-skirted stream the Indian guide halted them, and proceeded on alone to disappear in a green thicket. Presently he reappeared, and motioned for them to come on. He led the way over smooth, sandy paths between clumps of willows, into a heavy growth of alder bushes and prickly thorns, at length to emerge upon a beautiful grassy plot enclosed by green and yellow shrubbery. Above the stream, which cut the edge of the glade, rose a sloping, wooded ridge, with huge rocks projecting here and there out of the brown forest.

Several birch-bark huts could be seen; then two rough bearded men lolling upon the grass, and beyond them a group of painted Indians.

A whoop so shrill, so savage, so exultant, that it seemingly froze her blood, rent the silence. A man, unseen before, came crashing through the willows on the side of the ridge. He leaped the stream with the spring of a wild horse. He was big and broad, with disheveled hair, keen, hard face, and wild, gray eyes.

Helen's sight almost failed her; her head whirled dizzily; it was as if her heart had stopped beating and was become a cold, dead weight. She recognized in this man the one whom she feared most of all—Brandt.

He cast one glance full at her, the same threatening, cool, and evil-meaning look she remembered so well, and then engaged the Indian guide in low conversation.

Helen sank at the foot of a tree, leaning against it. Despite her weariness she had retained some spirit until this direful revelation broke her courage. What worse could have happened? Mordaunt had led her, for some reason that she could not divine, into the clutches of Brandt, into the power of Legget and his outlaws.

But Helen was not one to remain long dispirited or hopeless. As this plot thickened, as every added misfortune weighed upon her, when just ready to give up to despair she remembered the bordermen. Then Colonel Zane's tales of their fearless, implacable pursuit when bent on rescue or revenge, recurred to her, and fortitude returned. While she had life she would hope.

The advent of the party with their prisoner enlivened Legget's gang. A great giant of a man, blond-bearded, and handsome in a wild, rugged, uncouth way, a man Helen instinctively knew to be Legget, slapped Brandt on the shoulder.

"Damme, Roge, if she ain't a regular little daisy! Never seed such a purty lass in my life."

Brandt spoke hurriedly, and Legget laughed.

All this time Case had been sitting on the grass, saying nothing, but with his little eyes watchful. Mordaunt stood near him, his head bowed, his face gloomy.

"Say, cap'n, I don't like this mess," whispered Case to his master. "They ain't no crew fer us. I know men, fer I've sailed the seas, an' you're goin' to get what Metz calls the double-cross."

Mordaunt seemed to arouse from his gloomy reverie. He looked at Brandt and Legget who were now in earnest council. Then his eyes wandered toward Helen. She beckoned him to come to her.

"Why did you bring me here?" she asked.

"Brandt understood my case. He planned this thing, and seemed to be a good friend of mine. He said if I once got you out of the settlement, he would give me protection until I crossed the border into Canada. There we could be married," replied Mordaunt unsteadily.

"Then you meant marriage by me, if I could be made to consent?"

"Of course. I'm not utterly vile," he replied, with face lowered in shame.

"Have you any idea what you've done?"

"Done? I don't understand."

"You have ruined yourself, lost your manhood, become an outlaw, a fugitive, made yourself the worst thing on the border—a girl-thief, and all for nothing."

"No, I have you. You are more to me than all."

"But can't you see? You've brought me out here for Brandt!"

"My God!" exclaimed Mordaunt. He rose slowly to his feet and gazed around like a man suddenly wakened from a dream. "I see it all now! Miserable, drunken wretch that I am!"

Helen saw his face change and lighten as if a cloud of darkness had passed away from it. She understood that love of liquor had made him a party to this plot. Brandt had cunningly worked upon his weakness, proposed a daring scheme; and filled his befogged mind with hopes that, in a moment of clear-sightedness, he would have seen to be vain and impossible. And Helen understood also that the sudden shock of surprise, pain, possible fury, had sobered Mordaunt, probably for the first time in weeks.

The Englishman's face became exceedingly pale. Seating himself on a stone near Case, he bowed his head, remaining silent and motionless.

The conference between Legget and Brandt lasted for some time. When it ended the latter strode toward the motionless figure on the rock.

"Mordaunt, you and Case will do well to follow this Indian at once to the river, where you can strike the Fort Pitt trail," said Brandt.

He spoke arrogantly and authoritatively. His keen, hard face, his steely eyes, bespoke the iron will and purpose of the man.

Mordaunt rose with cold dignity. If he had been a dupe, he was one no longer, as could be plainly read on his calm, pale face. The old listlessness, the unsteadiness had vanished. He wore a manner of extreme quietude; but his eyes were like balls of blazing blue steel.

"Mr. Brandt, I seem to have done you a service, and am no longer required," he said in a courteous tone.

Brandt eyed his man; but judged him wrongly. An English gentleman was new to the border-outlaw.

"I swore the girl should be mine," he hissed.

"Doomed men cannot be choosers!" cried Helen, who had heard him. Her dark eyes burned with scorn and hatred.

All the party heard her passionate outburst. Case arose as if unconcernedly, and stood by the side of his master. Legget and the other two outlaws came up. The Indians turned their swarthy faces.

"Hah! ain't she sassy?" cried Legget.

Brandt looked at Helen, understood the meaning of her words, and laughed. But his face paled, and involuntarily his shifty glance sought the rocks and trees upon the ridge.

"You played me from the first?" asked Mordaunt quietly.

"I did," replied Brandt.

"You meant nothing of your promise to help me across the border?"

"No."

"You intended to let me shift for myself out here in this wilderness?"

"Yes, after this Indian guides you to the river-trail," said Brandt, indicating with his finger the nearest savage.

"I get what you frontier men call the double-cross'?"

"That's it," replied Brandt with a hard laugh, in which Legget joined. A short pause ensued.

"What will you do with the girl?"

"That's my affair."

"Marry her?" Mordaunt's voice was low and quiet.

"No!" cried Brandt. "She flaunted my love in my face, scorned me! She saw that borderman strike me, and by God! I'll get even. I'll keep her here in the woods until I'm tired of her, and when her beauty fades I'll turn her over to Legget."

Scarcely had the words dropped from his vile lips when Mordaunt moved with tigerish agility. He seized a knife from the belt of one of the Indians.

"Die!" he screamed.

Brandt grasped his tomahawk. At the same instant the man who had acted as Mordaunt's guide grasped the Englishman from behind.

Brandt struck ineffectually at the struggling man.

"Fair play!" roared Case, leaping at Mordaunt's second assailant. His long knife sheathed its glittering length in the man's breast. Without even a groan he dropped. "Clear the decks!" Case yelled, sweeping round in a circle. All fell back before that whirling knife.

Several of the Indians started as if to raise their rifles; but Legget's stern command caused them to desist.

The Englishman and the outlaw now engaged in a fearful encounter. The practiced, rugged, frontier desperado apparently had found his match in this pale-faced, slender man. His border skill with the hatchet seemed offset by Mordaunt's terrible rage. Brandt whirled and swung the weapon as he leaped around his antagonist. With his left arm the Englishman sought only to protect his head, while with his right he brandished the knife. Whirling here and there they struggled across the cleared space, plunging out of sight among the willows. During a moment there was a sound as of breaking branches; then a dull blow, horrible to hear, followed by a low moan, and then deep silence.

CHAPTER 18

A BLACK WEIGHT WAS SEEMINGLY LIFTED FROM HELEN'S WEARY EYELIDS.
The sun shone; the golden forest surrounded her; the brook babbled
merrily; but where were the struggling, panting men? She noticed presently, when her vision had grown more clear, that the scene differed
entirely from the willow-glade where she had closed her eyes upon the
fight. Then came the knowledge that she had fainted, and, during the time
of unconsciousness, been moved.

She lay upon a mossy mound a few feet higher than a swiftly running
brook. A magnificent chestnut tree spread its leafy branches above her.
Directly opposite, about an hundred feet away, loomed a gray, ragged,
moss-stained cliff. She noted this particularly because the dense forest
encroaching to its very edge excited her admiration. Such wonderful
coloring seemed unreal. Dead gold and bright red foliage flamed
everywhere.

Two Indians stood near by silent, immovable. No other of Legget's
band was visible. Helen watched the red men.

Sinewy, muscular warriors they were, with bodies partially painted, and
long, straight hair, black as burnt wood, interwoven with bits of white
bone, and plaited around waving eagle plumes. At first glance their dark
faces and dark eyes were expressive of craft, cunning, cruelty, courage, all
attributes of the savage.

Yet wild as these savages appeared, Helen did not fear them as she did the outlaws. Brandt's eyes, and Legget's, too, when turned on her, emitted a flame that seemed to scorch and shrivel her soul. When the savages met her gaze, which was but seldom, she imagined she saw intelligence, even pity, in their dusky eyes. Certain it was she did not shrink from them as from Brandt.

Suddenly, with a sensation of relief and joy, she remembered Mordaunt's terrible onslaught upon Brandt. Although she could not recollect the termination of that furious struggle, she did recall Brandt's scream of mortal agony, and the death of the other at Case's hands. This meant, whether Brandt was dead or not, that the fighting strength of her captors had been diminished. Surely as the sun had risen that morning, Helen believed Jonathan and Wetzel lurked on the trail of these renegades. She prayed that her courage, hope, strength, might be continued.

"Ugh!" exclaimed one of the savages, pointing across the open space. A slight swaying of the bushes told that some living thing was moving among them, and an instant later the huge frame of the leader came into view. The other outlaw, and Case, followed closely. Farther down the margin of the thicket the Indians appeared; but without the slightest noise or disturbance of the shrubbery.

It required but a glance to show Helen that Case was in high spirits. His repulsive face glowed with satisfaction. He carried a bundle, which Helen saw, with a sickening sense of horror, was made up of Mordaunt's clothing. Brandt had killed the Englishman. Legget also had a package under his arm, which he threw down when he reached the chestnut tree, to draw from his pocket a long, leather belt, such as travelers use for the carrying of valuables. It was evidently heavy, and the musical clink which accompanied his motion proclaimed the contents to be gold.

Brandt appeared next; he was white and held his hand to his breast. There were dark stains on his hunting coat, which he removed to expose a shirt blotched with red.

"You ain't much hurt, I reckon?" inquired Legget solicitously.

"No; but I'm bleeding bad," replied Brandt coolly. He then called an Indian and went among the willows skirting the stream.

"So I'm to be in this border crew?" asked Case, looking up at Legget.

"Sure," replied the big outlaw. "You're a handy fellar, Case, an' after I break you into border ways you will fit in here tip-top. Now you'd better stick by me. When Eb Zane, his brother Jack, an' Wetzel find out this here day's work, hell will be a cool place compared with their whereabouts.

You'll be safe with me, an' this is the only place on the border, I reckon, where you can say your life is your own."

"I'm yer mate, cap'n. I've sailed with soldiers, pirates, sailors, an' I guess I can navigate this borderland. Do we mess here? You didn't come far."

"Wal, I ain't pertikuler, but I don't like eatin' with buzzards," said Legget, with a grin. "Thet's why we moved a bit."

"What's buzzards?"

"Ho! ho! Mebbe you'll hev 'em closer'n you'd like, some day, if you'd only know it. Buzzards are fine birds, most particular birds, as won't eat nothin' but flesh, an' white man or Injun is pie fer 'em."

"Cap'n, I've seed birds as wouldn't wait till a man was dead," said Case.

"Haw! haw! you can't come no sailor yarns on this fellar. Wal, now, we've got ther Englishman's gold. One or t'other of us might jest as well hev it all."

"Right yer are, cap'n. Dice, cards, anyways, so long as I knows the game."

"Here, Jenks, hand over yer clickers, an' bring us a flat stone," said Legget, sitting on the moss and emptying the belt in front of him. Case took a small bag from the dark blue jacket that had so lately covered Mordaunt's shoulders, and poured out its bright contents.

"This coat ain't worth keepin'," he said, holding it up. The garment was rent and slashed, and under the left sleeve was a small, blood-stained hole where one of Brandt's blows had fallen. "Hullo, what's this?" muttered the sailor, feeling in the pocket of the jacket. "Blast my timbers, hooray!"

He held up a small, silver-mounted whiskey flask, unscrewed the lid, and lifted the vessel to his mouth.

"I'm kinder thirsty myself," suggested Legget.

"Cap'n, a nip an' no more," Case replied, holding the flask to Legget's lips.

The outlaw called Jenks now returned with a flat stone which he placed between the two men. The Indians gathered around. With greedy eyes they bent their heads over the gamblers, and watched every movement with breathless interest. At each click of the dice, or clink of gold, they uttered deep exclamations.

"Luck's again' ye, cap'n," said Case, skilfully shaking the ivory cubes.

"Hain't I got eyes?" growled the outlaw.

Steadily his pile of gold diminished, and darker grew his face.

"Cap'n, I'm a bad wind to draw," Case rejoined, drinking again from the flask. His naturally red face had become livid, his skin moist, and his eyes wild with excitement.

"Hullo! If them dice wasn't Jenks's, an' I hadn't played afore with him, I'd swear they's loaded."

"You ain't insinuatin' nothin', cap'n?" inquired Case softly, hesitating with the dice in his hands, his evil eyes glinting at Legget.

"No, you're fair enough," growled the leader. "It's my tough luck."

The game progressed with infrequent runs of fortune for the outlaw, and presently every piece of gold lay in a shining heap before the sailor.

"Clean busted!" exclaimed Legget in disgust.

"Can't you find nothin' more?" asked Case.

The outlaw's bold eyes wandered here and there until they rested upon the prisoner.

"I'll play ther lass against yer pile of gold," he growled. "Best two throws out 'en three. See here, she's as much mine as Brandt's."

"Make it half my pile an' I'll go you."

"Nary time. Bet, or give me back what yer win," replied Legget gruffly.

"She's a trim little craft, no mistake," said Case, critically surveying Helen. "All right, cap'n, I've sportin' blood, an' I'll bet. Yer throw first."

Legget won the first cast, and Case the second. With deliberation the outlaw shook the dice in his huge fist, and rattled them out upon the stone. "Hah!" he cried in delight. He had come within one of the highest score possible. Case nonchalantly flipped the little white blocks. The Indians crowded forward, their dusky eyes shining.

Legget swore in a terrible voice which re-echoed from the stony cliff. The sailor was victorious. The outlaw got up, kicked the stone and dice in the brook, and walked away from the group. He strode to and fro under one of the trees. Gruffly he gave an order to the Indians. Several of them began at once to kindle a fire. Presently he called Jenks, who was fishing the dice out of the brook, and began to converse earnestly with him, making fierce gestures and casting lowering glances at the sailor.

Case was too drunk now to see that he had incurred the enmity of the outlaw leader. He drank the last of the rum, and tossed the silver flask to an Indian, who received the present with every show of delight.

Case then, with the slow, uncertain movements of a man whose mind is befogged, began to count his gold; but only to gather up a few pieces when they slipped out of his trembling hands to roll on the moss. Laboriously, seriously, he kept at it with the doggedness of a drunken man. Apparently he had forgotten the others. Failing to learn the value of the coins by taking up each in turn, he arranged them in several piles, and began to estimate his wealth in sections.

In the meanwhile Helen, who had not failed to take in the slightest detail of what was going on, saw that a plot was hatching which boded ill to the sailor. Moreover, she heard Legget and Jenks whispering.

"I kin take him from right here 'atwixt his eyes," said Jenks softly, and tapped his rifle significantly.

"Wal, go ahead, only I ruther hev it done quieter," answered Legget. "We're yet a long ways, near thirty miles, from my camp, an' there's no tellin' who's in ther woods. But we've got ter git rid of ther fresh sailor, an' there's no surer way."

Cautiously cocking his rifle, Jenks deliberately raised it to his shoulder. One of the Indian sentinels who stood near at hand, sprang forward and struck up the weapon. He spoke a single word to Legget, pointed to the woods above the cliff, and then resumed his statue-like attitude.

"I told yer, Jenks, that it wouldn't do. The redskin scents somethin' in the woods, an' ther's an Injun I never seed fooled. We mustn't make a noise. Take yer knife an' tomahawk, crawl down below the edge o' the bank an' slip up on him. I'll give half ther gold fer ther job."

Jenks buckled his belt more tightly, gave one threatening glance at the sailor, and slipped over the bank. The bed of the brook lay about six feet below the level of the ground. This afforded an opportunity for the outlaw to get behind Case without being observed. A moment passed. Jenks disappeared round a bend of the stream. Presently his grizzled head appeared above the bank. He was immediately behind the sailor; but still some thirty feet away. This ground must be covered quickly and noiselessly. The outlaw began to crawl. In his right hand he grasped a tomahawk, and between his teeth was a long knife. He looked like a huge, yellow bear.

The savages, with the exception of the sentinel who seemed absorbed in the dense thicket on the cliff, sat with their knees between their hands, watching the impending tragedy.

Nothing but the merest chance, or some extraordinary intervention, could avert Case's doom. He was gloating over his gold. The creeping outlaw made no more noise than a snake. Nearer and nearer he came; his sweaty face shining in the sun; his eyes tigerish; his long body slipping silently over the grass. At length he was within five feet of the sailor. His knotty hands were dug into the sward as he gathered energy for a sudden spring.

At that very moment Case, with his hand on his knife, rose quickly and turned round.

The outlaw, discovered in the act of leaping, had no alternative, and spring he did, like a panther.

The little sailor stepped out of line with remarkable quickness, and as the yellow body whirled past him, his knife flashed blue-bright in the sunshine.

Jenks fell forward, his knife buried in the grass beneath him, and his outstretched hand still holding the tomahawk.

"Tryin' ter double-cross me fer my gold," muttered the sailor, sheathing his weapon. He never looked to see whether or no his blow had been fatal. "These border fellars might think a man as sails the seas can't handle a knife." He calmly began gathering up his gold, evidently indifferent to further attack.

Helen saw Legget raise his own rifle, but only to have it struck aside as had Jenks's. This time the savage whispered earnestly to Legget, who called the other Indians around him. The sentinel's low throaty tones mingled with the soft babbling of the stream. No sooner had he ceased speaking than the effect of his words showed how serious had been the information, warning or advice. The Indians cast furtive glances toward the woods. Two of them melted like shadows into the red and gold thicket. Another stealthily slipped from tree to tree until he reached the open ground, then dropped into the grass, and was seen no more until his dark body rose under the cliff. He stole along the green-stained wall, climbed a rugged corner, and vanished amid the dense foliage.

Helen felt that she was almost past discernment or thought. The events of the day succeeding one another so swiftly, and fraught with panic, had, despite her hope and fortitude, reduced her to a helpless condition of piteous fear. She understood that the savages scented danger, or had, in their mysterious way, received intelligence such as rendered them wary and watchful.

"Come on, now, an' make no noise," said Legget to Case. "Bring the girl, an' see that she steps light."

"Ay, ay, cap'n," replied the sailor. "Where's Brandt?"

"He'll be comin' soon's his cut stops bleedin'. I reckon he's weak yet."

Case gathered up his goods, and, tucking it under his arm, grasped Helen's arm. She was leaning against the tree, and when he pulled her, she wrenched herself free, rising with difficulty. His disgusting touch and revolting face had revived her sensibilities.

"Yer kin begin duty by carryin' thet," said Case, thrusting the package into Helen's arms. She let it drop without moving a hand.

"I'm runnin' this ship. Yer belong to me," hissed Case, and then he struck her on the head. Helen uttered a low cry of distress, and half staggered against the tree. The sailor picked up the package. This time she took it, trembling with horror.

"Thet's right. Now, give ther cap'n a kiss," he leered, and jostled against her.

Helen pushed him violently. With agonized eyes she appealed to the Indians. They were engaged tying up their packs. Legget looked on with a lazy grin.

"Oh! oh!" breathed Helen as Case seized her again. She tried to scream, but could not make a sound. The evil eyes, the beastly face, transfixed her with terror.

Case struck her twice, then roughly pulled her toward him.

Half-fainting, unable to move, Helen gazed at the heated, bloated face approaching hers.

When his coarse lips were within a few inches of her lips something hot hissed across her brow. Following so closely as to be an accompaniment, rang out with singular clearness the sharp crack of a rifle.

Case's face changed. The hot, surging flush faded; the expression became shaded, dulled into vacant emptiness; his eyes rolled wildly, then remained fixed, with a look of dark surprise. He stood upright an instant, swayed with the regular poise of a falling oak, and then plunged backward to the ground. His face, ghastly and livid, took on the awful calm of death.

A very small hole, reddish-blue round the edges, dotted the center of his temple.

Legget stared aghast at the dead sailor; then he possessed himself of the bag of gold.

"Saved me ther trouble," he muttered, giving Case a kick.

The Indians glanced at the little figure, then out into the flaming thickets. Each savage sprang behind a tree with incredible quickness. Legget saw this, and grasping Helen, he quickly led her within cover of the chestnut.

Brandt appeared with his Indian companion, and both leaped to shelter behind a clump of birches near where Legget stood. Brandt's hawk eyes flashed upon the dead Jenks and Case. Without asking a question he seemed to take in the situation. He stepped over and grasped Helen by the arm.

"Who killed Case?" he asked in a whisper, staring at the little blue hole in the sailor's temple.

No one answered.

The two Indians who had gone into the woods to the right of the stream, now returned. Hardly were they under the trees with their party, when the savage who had gone off alone arose out of the grass in the left of the brook, took it with a flying leap, and darted into their midst. He was the sentinel who had knocked up the weapons, thereby saving Case's life twice. He was lithe and supple, but not young. His grave, shadowy-lined, iron visage showed the traces of time and experience. All gazed at him as at one whose wisdom was greater than theirs.

"Old Horse," said Brandt in English. "Haven't I seen bullet holes like this?"

The Chippewa bent over Case, and then slowly straightened his tall form.

"*Deathwind!*" he replied, answering in the white man's language.

His Indian companions uttered low, plaintive murmurs, not signifying fear so much as respect.

Brandt turned as pale as the clean birch-bark on the tree near him. The gray flare of his eyes gave out a terrible light of certainty and terror.

"Legget, you needn't try to hide your trail," he hissed, and it seemed as if there was a bitter, reckless pleasure in these words.

Then the Chippewa glided into the low bushes bordering the creek. Legget followed him, with Brandt leading Helen, and the other Indians brought up the rear, each one sending wild, savage glances into the dark, surrounding forest.

CHAPTER 19

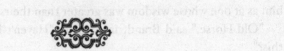

A DENSE WHITE FOG ROSE FROM THE RIVER, OBSCURING ALL OBJECTS, when the bordermen rolled out of their snug bed of leaves. The air was cool and bracing, faintly fragrant with dying foliage and the damp, dewy luxuriance of the ripened season. Wetzel pulled from under the protecting ledge a bundle of bark and sticks he had put there to keep dry, and built a fire, while Jonathan fashioned a cup from a green fruit resembling a gourd, filling it at a spring near by.

"Lew, there's a frosty nip in the water this mornin'," said Jonathan.

"I reckon. It's gettin' along into fall now. Any clear, still night'll fetch all the leaves, an' strip the trees bare as burned timber," answered Wetzel, brushing the ashes off the strip of meat he had roasted. "Get a stick, an' help me cook the rest of this chunk of bison. The sun'll be an hour breakin' up thet mist, an' we can't clear out till then. Mebbe we won't have no chance to light another fire soon."

With these bordermen everything pertaining to their lonely lives, from the lighting of a fire to the trailing of a redskin, was singularly serious. No gladsome song ever came from their lips; there was no jollity around their camp-fire. Hunters had their moments of rapturous delight; bordermen knew the peace, the content of the wilderness, but their pursuits racked nerve and heart. Wetzel had his moments of frenzied joy, but they passed with the echo of his vengeful yell. Jonathan's happiness, such as it was, had been to roam the forests. That, before a woman's eyes had dispelled it, had been enough, and compensated him for the gloomy, bloody phantoms which haunted him.

The bordermen, having partaken of the frugal breakfast, stowed in their spacious pockets all the meat that was left, and were ready for the day's march. They sat silent for a time waiting for the mist to lift. It broke in places, rolled in huge billows, sailed aloft like great white clouds, and again hung tenaciously to the river and the plain. Away in the west blue patches of sky shone through the rifts, and eastward banks of misty vapor reddened beneath the rising sun. Suddenly from beneath the silver edge of the rising pall the sun burst gleaming gold, disclosing the winding valley with its steaming river.

"We'll make up stream fer Two Islands, an' cross there if so be we've reason," Wetzel had said.

Through the dewy dells, avoiding the wet grass and bushes, along the dark, damp glades with their yellow carpets, under the thinning arches of the trees, down the gentle slopes of the ridges, rich with green moss, the bordermen glided like gray shadows. The forest was yet asleep. A squirrel frisked up an oak and barked quarrelsomely at these strange, noiseless visitors. A crow cawed from somewhere overhead. These were the only sounds disturbing the quiet early hour.

As the bordermen advanced the woods lightened and awoke to life and joy. Birds sang, trilled, warbled, or whistled their plaintive songs, peculiar to the dying season, and in harmony with the glory of the earth. Birds that in earlier seasons would have screeched and fought, now sang and fluttered side by side, in fraternal parade on their slow pilgrimage to the far south.

"Bad time fer us, when the birds are so tame, an' chipper. We can't put faith in them these days," said Wetzel. "Seems like they never was wild. I can tell, 'cept at this season, by the way they whistle an' act in the woods, if there's been any Injuns along the trails."

The greater part of the morning passed thus with the bordermen steadily traversing the forest; here, through a spare and gloomy wood, blasted by fire, worn by age, with many a dethroned monarch of bygone times rotting to punk and duff under the ferns, with many a dark, seamed and ragged king still standing, but gray and bald of head and almost ready to take his place in the forest of the past; there, through a maze of young saplings where each ash, maple, hickory and oak added some new and beautiful hue to the riot of color.

"I just had a glimpse of the lower island, as we passed an opening in the thicket," said Jonathan.

"We ain't far away," replied Wetzel.

The bordermen walked less rapidly in order to proceed with more watchfulness. Every rod or two they stopped to listen.

"You think Legget's across the river?" asked Jonathan.

"He was two days back, an' had his gang with him. He's up to some bad work, but I can't make out what. One thing, I never seen his trail so near Fort Henry."

They emerged at length into a more open forest which skirted the river. At a point still some distance ahead, but plainly in sight, two small islands rose out of the water.

"Hist! What's that?" whispered Wetzel, slipping his hand in Jonathan's arm.

A hundred yards beyond lay a long, dark figure stretched at full length under one of the trees close to the bank.

"Looks like a man," said Jonathan.

"You've hit the mark. Take a good peep roun' now, Jack, fer we're comin' somewhere near the trail we want."

Minutes passed while the patient bordermen searched the forest with their eyes, seeking out every tree within rifle range, or surveyed the level glades, scrutinized the hollows, and bent piercing eyes upon the patches of ferns.

"If there's a redskin around he ain't big enough to hold a gun," said Wetzel, moving forward again, yet still with that same stealthy step and keen caution.

Finally they were gazing down upon the object which had attracted Wetzel's attention.

"Will Sheppard!" cried Jonathan. "Is he dead? What's this mean?"

Wetzel leaned over the prostrate lad, and then quickly turned to his companion.

"Get some water. Take his cap. No, he ain't even hurt bad, unless he's got some wound as don't show."

Jonathan returned with the water, and Wetzel bathed the bloody face. When the gash on Will's forehead was clean, it told the bordermen much.

"Not an hour old, that blow," muttered Wetzel.

"He's comin' to," said Jonathan as Will stirred uneasily and moaned. Presently the lad opened his eyes and sat bolt upright. He looked bewildered for a moment, and felt of his head while gazing vaguely at the bordermen. Suddenly he cried:

"I remember! We were captured, brought here, and I was struck down by that villain Case."

"We? Who was with you?" asked Jonathan slowly.

"Helen. We came after flowers and leaves. While in full sight of the fort I saw an Indian. We hurried back," he cried, and proceeded with broken, panting voice to tell his story.

Jonathan Zane leaped to his feet with face deathly white and eyes blue-black, like burning stars.

"Jack, study the trail while I get the lad acrost the river, an' steered fer home," said Wetzel, and then he asked Will if he could swim.

"Yes; but you will find a canoe there in those willows."

"Come, lad, we've no time to spare," added Wetzel, sliding down the bank and entering the willows. He came out almost immediately with the canoe which he launched.

Will turned that he might make a parting appeal to Jonathan to save Helen; but could not speak. The expression on the borderman's face frightened him.

Motionless and erect Jonathan stood, his arms folded and his white, stern face distorted with the agony of remorse, fear, and anguish, which, even as Will gazed, froze into an awful, deadly look of fateful purpose.

Wetzel pushed the canoe off, and paddled with powerful strokes; he left Will on the opposite bank, and returned as swiftly as he could propel the light craft.

The bordermen met each other's glance, and had little need of words. Wetzel's great shoulders began to sag slightly, and his head lowered as his eyes sought the grass; a dark and gloomy shade overcast his features. Thus he passed from borderman to Deathwind. The sough of the wind overhead among the almost naked branches might well have warned Indians and renegades that Deathwind was on the trail!

"Brandt's had a hand in this, an' the Englishman's a fool!" said Wetzel.

"An hour ahead; can we come up with them before they join Brandt an' Legget?"

"We can try, but like as not we'll fail. Legget's gang is thirteen strong by now. I said it! Somethin' told me—a hard trail, a long trail, an' our last trail."

"It's over thirty miles to Legget's camp. We know the woods, an' every stream, an' every cover," hissed Jonathan Zane.

With no further words Wetzel took the trail on the run, and so plain was it to his keen eyes that he did not relax his steady lope except to stop and listen at regular intervals. Jonathan followed with easy swing. Through forest and meadow, over hill and valley, they ran, fleet and tireless. Once, with unerring instinct, they abruptly left the broad trail and cut far across a wide and rugged ridge to come again upon the tracks of the marching band. Then, in open country they reduced their speed to a walk. Ahead, in a narrow valley, rose a thicket of willows, yellow in the sunlight, and impenetrable to human vision. Like huge snakes the bordermen crept into this copse, over the sand, under the low branches, hard on the trail. Finally, in a light, open space, where the sun shone through a network of yellow branches and foliage, Wetzel's hand was laid upon Jonathan's shoulder.

"Listen! Hear that!" he whispered.

Jonathan heard the flapping of wings, and a low, hissing sound, not unlike that made by a goose.

"Buzzards!" he said, with a dark, grim smile. "Mebbe Brandt has begun our work. Come."

Out into the open they crawled to put to flight a flock of huge black birds with grisly, naked necks, hooked beaks, and long, yellow claws. Upon the green grass lay three half-naked men, ghastly, bloody, in terribly limp and lifeless positions.

"Metzar's man Smith, Jenks, the outlaw, and Mordaunt!"

Jonathan Zane gazed darkly into the steely, sightless eyes of the traitor. Death's awful calm had set the expression; but the man's whole life was there, its better part sadly shining forth among the cruel shadows.

His body was mutilated in a frightful manner. Cuts, stabs, and slashes told the tale of a long encounter, brought to an end by one clean stroke.

"Come here, Lew. You've seen men chopped up; but look at this dead Englishman," called Zane.

Mordaunt lay weltering in a crimson tide. Strangely though, his face was uninjured. A black bruise showed under his fair hair. The ghost of a smile seemed to hover around his set lips, yet almost intangible though it was, it showed that at last he had died a man. His left shoulder, side and arm showed where the brunt of Brandt's attack had fallen.

"How'd he ever fight so?" mused Jonathan.

"You never can tell," replied Wetzel. "Mebbe he killed this other fellar, too; but I reckon not. Come, we must go slow now, fer Legget is near at hand."

Jonathan brought huge, flat stones from the brook, and laid them over Mordaunt; then, cautiously he left the glade on Wetzel's trail.

Five hundred yards farther on Wetzel had ceased following the outlaw's tracks to cross the creek and climb a ridge. He was beginning his favorite trick of making a wide detour. Jonathan hurried forward, feeling he was safe from observation. Soon he distinguished the tall, brown figure of his comrade gliding ahead from tree to tree, from bush to bush.

"See them maples an' chestnuts down thar," said Wetzel when Jonathan had come up, pointing through an opening in the foliage. "They've stopped fer some reason."

On through the forest the bordermen glided. They kept near the summit of the ridge, under the best cover they could find, and passed swiftly over this half-circle. When beginning once more to draw toward the open grove in the valley, they saw a long, irregular cliff, densely wooded. They swerved a little, and made for this excellent covert.

They crawled the last hundred yards and never shook a fern, moved a leaf, or broke a twig. Having reached the brink of the low precipice, they saw the grassy meadow below, the straggling trees, the brook, the group of Indians crowding round the white men.

"See that point of rock thar? It's better cover," whispered Wetzel.

Patiently, with no hurry or excitement, they slowly made their difficult way among the rocks and ferns to the vantage point desired. Taking a position like this was one the bordermen strongly favored. They could see everywhere in front, and had the thick woods at their backs.

"What are they up to?" whispered Jonathan, as he and Wetzel lay close together under a mass of grapevine still tenacious of its broad leaves.

"Dicin'," answered Wetzel. "I can see 'em throw; anyways, nothin' but bettin' ever makes redskins act like that."

"Who's playin'? Where's Brandt?"

"I can make out Legget; see his shaggy head. The other must be Case. Brandt ain't in sight. Nursin' a hurt perhaps. Ah! See thar! Over under the big tree as stands dark-like agin the thicket. Thet's an Injun, an' he looks too quiet an' keen to suit me. We'll have a care of him."

"Must be playin' fer Mordaunt's gold."

"Like as not, for where'd them ruffians get any 'cept they stole it."

"Aha! They're gettin' up! See Legget walk away shakin' his big head. He's mad. Mebbe he'll be madder presently," growled Jonathan.

"Case's left alone. He's countin' his winnin's. Jack, look out fer more work took off our hands."

"By gum! See that Injun knock up a leveled rifle."

"I told you, an' thet redskin has his suspicions. He's seen us down along ther ridge. There's Helen, sittin' behind the biggest tree. Thet Injun guard, 'afore he moved, kept us from seein' her."

Jonathan made no answer to this; but his breath literally hissed through his clenched teeth.

"Thar goes the other outlaw," whispered Wetzel, as if his comrade could not see. "It's all up with Case. See the sneak bendin' down the bank. Now, thet's a poor way. It'd better be done from the front, walkin' up natural-like, instead of tryin' to cover thet wide stretch. Case'll see him or hear him sure. Thar, he's up now, an' crawlin'. He's too slow, too slow. Aha! I knew it—Case turns. Look at the outlaw spring! Well, did you see thet little cuss whip his knife? One more less fer us to quiet. Thet makes four, Jack, an' mebbe, soon, it'll be five."

"They're holdin' a council," said Jonathan.

"I see two Injuns sneakin' off into the woods, an' here comes thet guard. He's a keen redskin, Jack, fer we did come light through the brush. Mebbe it'd be well to stop his scoutin'."

"Lew, that villain Case is bullyin' Helen!" cried Jonathan.

"Sh-sh-h," whispered Wetzel.

"See! He's pulled her to her feet. Oh! He struck her! Oh!"

Jonathan leveled his rifle and would have fired, but for the iron grasp on his wrist.

"Hev you lost yer senses? It's full two hundred paces, an' too far fer your piece," said Wetzel in a whisper. "An' it ain't sense to try from here."

"Lend me your gun! Lend me your gun!"

Silently Wetzel handed him the long, black rifle.

Jonathan raised it, but trembled so violently that the barrel wavered like a leaf in the breeze.

"Take it, I can't cover him," groaned Jonathan. "This is new to me. I ain't myself. God! Lew, he struck her again! *Again!* He's tryin' to kiss her! Wetzel, if you're my friend, kill him!"

"Jack, it'd be better to wait, an'——"

"I love her," breathed Jonathan.

The long, black barrel swept up to a level and stopped. White smoke belched from among the green leaves; the report rang throughout the forest.

"Ah! I saw him stop an' pause," hissed Jonathan. "He stands, he sways, he falls! Death for yours, you sailor-beast!"

CHAPTER 20

THE BORDERMEN WATCHED LEGGET AND HIS BAND DISAPPEAR INTO THE thicket adjoining the grove. When the last dark, lithe form glided out of sight among the yellowing copse, Jonathan leaped from the low cliff, and had hardly reached the ground before Wetzel dashed down to the grassy turf.

Again they followed the outlaw's trail darker-faced, fiercer-visaged than ever, with cocked, tightly-gripped rifles thrust well before them, and light feet that scarcely brushed the leaves.

Wetzel halted after a long tramp up and down the ridges, and surveyed with keen intent the lay of the land ahead.

"Sooner or later we'll hear from that redskin as discovered us a ways back," whispered he. "I wish we might get a crack at him afore he hinders us bad. I ain't seen many keener Injuns. It's lucky we fixed ther arrow-shootin' Shawnee. We'd never hev beat thet combination. An' fer all of thet I'm worrin' some about the goin' ahead."

"Ambush?" Jonathan asked.

"Like as not. Legget'll send thet Injun back, an' mebbe more'n him. Jack, see them little footprints? They're Helen's. Look how she's draggin' along. Almost tuckered out. Legget can't travel many more miles to-day. He'll make a stand somewheres, an' lose all his redskins afore he gives up the lass."

645

"I'll never live through to-night with her in that gang. She'll be saved, or dead, before the stars pale in the light of the moon."

"I reckon we're nigh the end for some of us. It'll be moonlight an hour arter dusk, an' now it's only the middle of the arternoon; we've time enough fer anythin'. Now, Jack, let's not tackle the trail straight. We'll split, an' go round to head 'em off. See thet dead white oak standin' high over thar?"

Jonathan looked out between the spreading branches of a beech, and saw, far over a low meadow, luxuriant with grasses and rushes and bright with sparkling ponds and streams, a dense wood out of which towered a bare, bleached tree-top.

"You slip around along the right side of this meader, an' I'll take the left side. Go slow, an' hev yer eyes open. We'll meet under thet big dead tree. I allow we can see it from anywhere around. We'll leave the trail here, an' take it up farther on. Legget's goin' straight for his camp; he ain't losin' an inch. He wants to get in that rocky hole of his'n."

Wetzel stepped off the trail, glided into the woods, and vanished.

Jonathan turned to the right, traversed the summit of the ridge, softly traveled down its slope, and, after crossing a slow, eddying, quiet stream, gained the edge of the forest on that side of the swamp. A fringe of briars and prickly thorns bordered this wood affording an excellent cover. On the right the land rose rather abruptly. He saw that by walking up a few paces he could command a view of the entire swamp, as well as the ridge beyond, which contained Wetzel, and, probably, the outlaw and his band.

Remembering his comrade's admonition, Jonathan curbed his unusual impatience and moved slowly. The wind swayed the tree-tops, and rustled the fallen leaves. Birds sang as if thinking the warm, soft weather was summer come again. Squirrels dropped heavy nuts that cracked on the limbs, or fell with a thud to the ground, and they scampered over the dry earth, scratching up the leaves as they barked and scolded. Crows cawed clamorously after a hawk that had darted under the tree-tops to escape them; deer loped swiftly up the hill, and a lordly elk rose from a wallow in the grassy swamp, crashing into the thicket.

When two-thirds around this oval plain, which was a mile long and perhaps one-fourth as wide, Jonathan ascended the hill to make a survey. The grass waved bright brown and golden in the sunshine, swished in the wind, and swept like a choppy sea to the opposite ridge. The hill was not densely wooded. In many places the red-brown foliage opened upon irregular patches, some black, as if having been burned over, others showing the yellow and purple colors of the low thickets and the gray, barren stones.

Suddenly Jonathan saw something darken one of these sunlit plots. It might have been a deer. He studied the rolling, rounded tree-tops, the narrow strips between the black trunks, and the open places that were clear in the sunshine. He had nearly come to believe he had seen a small animal or bird flit across the white of the sky far in the background, when he distinctly saw dark figures stealing along past a green-gray rock, only to disappear under colored banks of foliage. Presently, lower down, they reappeared and crossed an open patch of yellow fern. Jonathan counted them. Two were rather yellow in color, the hue of buckskin; another, slight of stature as compared with the first, and light gray by contrast. Then six black, slender, gliding forms crossed the space. Jonathan then lost sight of them, and did not get another glimpse. He knew them to be Legget and his band. The slight figure was Helen.

Jonathan broke into a run, completed the circle around the swamp, and slowed into a walk when approaching the big dead tree where he was to wait for Wetzel.

Several rods beyond the lowland he came to a wood of white oaks, all giants rugged and old, with scarcely a sapling intermingled with them. Although he could not see the objective point, he knew from his accurate sense of distance that he was near it. As he entered the wood he swept its whole length and width with his eyes, he darted forward twenty paces to halt suddenly behind a tree. He knew full well that a sharply moving object was more difficult to see in the woods, than one stationary. Again he ran, fleet and light, a few paces ahead to take up a position as before behind a tree. Thus he traversed the forest. On the other side he found the dead oak of which Wetzel had spoken.

Its trunk was hollow. Jonathan squeezed himself into the blackened space, with his head in a favorable position behind a projecting knot, where he could see what might occur near at hand.

He waited for what seemed to him a long while, during which he neither saw nor heard anything, and then, suddenly, the report of a rifle rang out. A single, piercing scream followed. Hardly had the echo ceased when three hollow reports, distinctly different in tone from the first, could be heard from the same direction. In quick succession short, fierce yells attended rather than succeeded, the reports.

Jonathan stepped out of the hiding-place, cocked his rifle, and fixed a sharp eye on the ridge before him whence those startling cries had come.

The first rifle-shot, unlike any other in its short, spiteful, stinging quality, was unmistakably Wetzel's. Zane had heard it, followed many times, as now, by the wild death-cry of a savage. The other reports were of Indian guns, and the yells were the clamoring, exultant cries of Indians in pursuit.

Far down where the open forest met the gloom of the thickets, a brown figure flashed across the yellow ground. Darting among the trees, across the glades, it moved so swiftly that Jonathan knew it was Wetzel. In another instant a chorus of yelps resounded from the foliage, and three savages burst through the thicket almost at right angles with the fleeing borderman, running to intercept him. The borderman did not swerve from his course; but came on straight toward the dead tree, with the wonderful fleetness that so often had served him well.

Even in that moment Jonathan thought of what desperate chances his comrade had taken. The trick was plain. Wetzel had, most likely, shot the dangerous scout, and, taking to his heels, raced past the others, trusting to his speed and their poor marksmanship to escape with a whole skin.

When within a hundred yards of the oak Wetzel's strength apparently gave out. His speed deserted him; he ran awkwardly, and limped. The savages burst out into full cry like a pack of hungry wolves. They had already emptied their rifles at him, and now, supposing one of the shots had taken effect, redoubled their efforts, making the forest ring with their short, savage yells. One gaunt, dark-bodied Indian with a long, powerful, springy stride easily distanced his companions, and, evidently sure of gaining the coveted scalp of the borderman, rapidly closed the gap between them as he swung aloft his tomahawk, yelling the war-cry.

The sight on Jonathan's rifle had several times covered this savage's dark face; but when he was about to press the trigger Wetzel's fleeting form, also in line with the savage, made it extremely hazardous to take a shot.

Jonathan stepped from his place of concealment, and let out a yell that pealed high over the cries of the savages.

Wetzel suddenly dropped flat on the ground.

With a whipping crack of Jonathan's rifle, the big Indian plunged forward on his face.

The other Indians, not fifty yards away, stopped aghast at the fate of their comrade, and were about to seek the shelter of trees when, with his terrible yell, Wetzel sprang up and charged upon them. He had left his rifle where he fell; but his tomahawk glittered as he ran. The lameness had been a trick, for now he covered ground with a swiftness which caused his former progress to seem slow.

The Indians, matured and seasoned warriors though they were, gave but one glance at this huge, brown figure bearing down upon them like a fiend, and, uttering the Indian name of *Deathwind*, wavered, broke and ran.

One, not so fleet as his companion, Wetzel overtook and cut down with a single stroke. The other gained an hundred-yard start in the slight interval of Wetzel's attack, and, spurred on by a pealing, awful cry in the rear, sped swiftly in and out among the trees until he was lost to view.

Wetzel scalped the two dead savages, and, after returning to regain his rifle, joined Jonathan at the dead oak.

"Jack, you can never tell how things is comin' out. Thet redskin I allowed might worry us a bit, fooled me as slick as you ever saw, an' I hed to shoot him. Knowin' it was a case of runnin', I just cut fer this oak, drew the redskins' fire, an' hed 'em arter me quicker 'n you'd say Jack Robinson. I was hopin' you'd be here; but wasn't sure till I'd seen your rifle. Then I kinder got a kink in my leg jest to coax the brutes on."

"Three more quiet," said Jonathan Zane. "What now?"

"We've headed Legget, an' we'll keep nosin' him off his course. Already he's lookin' fer a safe campin' place for the night."

"There is none in these woods, fer him."

"We didn't plan this gettin' between him an' his camp; but couldn't be better fixed. A mile farther along the ridge, is a campin' place, with a spring in a little dell close under a big stone, an' well wooded. Legget's headin' straight fer it. With a couple of Injuns guardin' thet spot, he'll think he's safe. But I know the place, an' can crawl to thet rock the darkest night thet ever was an' never crack a stick."

IN THE GRAY OF THE DEEPENING TWILIGHT JONATHAN ZANE SAT ALONE. An owl hooted dismally in the dark woods beyond the thicket where the borderman crouched waiting for Wetzel. His listening ear detected a soft, rustling sound like the play of a mole under the leaves. A branch trembled and swung back; a soft footstep followed and Wetzel came into the retreat.

"Well?" asked Jonathan impatiently, as Wetzel deliberately sat down and laid his rifle across his knees.

"Easy, Jack, easy. We've an hour to wait."

"The time I've already waited has been long for me."

"They're thar," said Wetzel grimly.

"How far from here?"

"A half-hour's slow crawl."

"Close by?" hissed Jonathan.

"Too near fer you to get excited."

"Let us go; it's as light now as in the gray of mornin'."

"Mornin' would be best. Injuns get sleepy along towards day. I've ever found thet time the best. But we'll be lucky if we ketch these redskins asleep."

"Lew, I can't wait here all night. I won't leave her longer with that renegade. I've got to free or kill her."

"Most likely it'll be the last," said Wetzel simply.

"Well, so be it then," and the borderman hung his head.

"You needn't worry none, 'bout Helen. I jest had a good look at her, not half an hour back. She's fagged out; but full of spunk yet. I seen thet when Brandt went near her. Legget's got his hands full jest now with the redskins. He's hevin' trouble keepin' them on this slow trail. I ain't sayin' they're skeered; but they're mighty restless."

"Will you take the chance now?"

"I reckon you needn't hev asked thet."

"Tell me the lay of the land."

"Wal, if we get to this rock I spoke 'bout, we'll be right over 'em. It's ten feet high, an' we can jump straight amongst 'em. Most likely two or three'll be guardin' the openin' which is a little ways to the right. Ther's a big tree, the only one, low down by the spring. Helen's under it, half-sittin', half-leanin' against the roots. When I first looked, her hands were free; but I saw Brandt bind her feet. An' he had to get an Injun to help him, fer she kicked like a spirited little filly. There's moss under the tree an' there's where the redskins'll lay down to rest."

"I've got that; now out with your plan."

"Wal, I calkilate it's this. The moon'll be up in about an hour. We'll crawl as we've never crawled afore, because Helen's life depends as much on our not makin' a noise, as it does on fightin' when the time comes. If they hear us afore we're ready to shoot, the lass'll be tomahawked quicker'n lightnin'. If they don't suspicion us, when the right moment comes you shoot Brandt, yell louder'n you ever did afore, leap amongst 'em, an' cut down the first Injun thet's near you on your way to Helen. Swing her over your arm, an' dig into the woods."

"Well?" asked Jonathan when Wetzel finished.

"That's all," the borderman replied grimly.

"An' leave you all alone to fight Legget an' the rest of 'em?"

"I reckon."

"Not to be thought of."

"Ther's no other way."

"There must be! Let me think; I can't, I'm not myself."

"No other way," repeated Wetzel curtly.

Jonathan's broad hand fastened on Wetzel's shoulder and wheeled him around.

"Have I ever left you alone?"

"This's different," and Wetzel turned away again. His voice was cold and hard.

"How is it different? We've had the same thing to do, almost, more than once."

"We've never had as bad a bunch to handle as Legget's. They're lookin' fer us, an' will be hard to beat."

"That's no reason."

"We never had to save a girl one of us loved."

Jonathan was silent.

"I said this'd be my last trail," continued Wetzel. "I felt it, an' I know it'll be yours."

"Why?"

"If you get away with the girl she'll keep you at home, an' it'll be well. If you don't succeed, you'll die tryin', so it's sure your last trail."

Wetzel's deep, cold voice rang with truth.

"Lew, I can't run away an' leave you to fight those devils alone, after all these years we've been together, I can't."

"No other chance to save the lass."

Jonathan quivered with the force of his emotion. His black eyes glittered; his hands grasped at nothing. Once more he was between love and duty. Again he fought over the old battle, but this time it left him weak.

"You love the big-eyed lass, don't you?" asked Wetzel, turning with softened face and voice.

"I have gone mad!" cried Jonathan, tortured by the simple question of his friend. Those big, dear, wonderful eyes he loved so well, looked at him now from the gloom of the thicket. The old, beautiful, soft glow, the tender light, was there, and more, a beseeching prayer to save her.

Jonathan bowed his head, ashamed to let his friend see the tears that dimmed his eyes.

"Jack, we've follered the trail fer years together. Always you've been true an' staunch. This is our last, but whatever bides we'll break up Legget's band to-night, an' the border'll be cleared, mebbe, for always. At least his race is run. Let thet content you. Our time'd have to come, sooner or later, so why not now? I know how it is, that you want to stick by me; but the lass draws you to her. I understand, an' want you to save her. Mebbe you never dreamed it; but I can tell jest how you feel. All the tremblin', an' softness, an' sweetness, an' delight you've got for thet girl, is no mystery to Lew Wetzel."

"You loved a lass?"

Wetzel bowed his head, as perhaps he had never before in all his life.

"Betty—always," he answered softly.

"My sister!" exclaimed Jonathan, and then his hand closed hard on his comrade's, his mind going back to many things, strange in the past, but now explained. Wetzel had revealed his secret.

"An' it's been all my life, since she wasn't higher 'n my knee. There was a time when I might hev been closer to you than I am now. But I was a mad an' bloody Injun hater, so I never let her know till I seen it was too late. Wal, wal, no more of me. I only told it fer you."

Jonathan was silent.

"An' now to come back where we left off," continued Wetzel. "Let's take a more hopeful look at this comin' fight. Sure I said it was my last trail, but mebbe it's not. You can never tell. Feelin' as we do, I imagine they've no odds on us. Never in my life did I say to you, least of all to any one else, what I was goin' to do; but I'll tell it now. If I land uninjured amongst thet bunch, I'll kill them all."

The giant borderman's low voice hissed, and stung. His eyes glittered with unearthly fire. His face was cold and gray. He spread out his brawny arms and clenched his huge fists, making the muscles of his broad shoulders roll and bulge.

"I hate the thought, Lew, I hate the thought. Ain't there no other way?"

"No other way."

"I'll do it, Lew, because I'd do the same for you; because I have to, because I love her; but God! it hurts."

"Thet's right," answered Wetzel, his deep voice softening until it was singularly low and rich. "I'm glad you've come to it. An' sure it hurts. I want you to feel so at leavin' me to go it alone. If we both get out alive, I'll come many times to see you an' Helen. If you live an' I don't, think of me sometimes, think of the trails we've crossed together. When the fall comes with its soft, cool air, an' smoky mornin's an' starry nights, when the wind's sad among the bare branches, an' the leaves drop down, remember they're fallin' on my grave."

Twilight darkened into gloom; the red tinge in the west changed to opal light; through the trees over a dark ridge a rim of silver glinted and moved.

The moon had risen; the hour was come.

The bordermen tightened their belts, replaced their leggings, tied their hunting coats, loosened their hatchets, looked to the priming of their rifles, and were ready.

Wetzel walked twenty paces and turned. His face was white in the moonlight; his dark eyes softened into a look of love as he gripped his comrade's outstretched hand.

Then he dropped flat on the ground, carefully saw to the position of his rifle, and began to creep. Jonathan kept close at his heels.

Slowly but steadily they crawled, minute after minute. The hazel-nut bushes above them had not yet shed their leaves; the ground was clean and hard, and the course fatefully perfect for their deadly purpose.

A slight rustling of their buckskin garments sounded like the rustling of leaves in a faint breeze.

The moon came out above the trees and still Wetzel advanced softly, steadily, surely.

The owl, lonely sentinel of that wood, hooted dismally. Even his night eyes, which made the darkness seem clear as day, missed those gliding figures. Even he, sure guardian of the wilderness, failed the savages.

Jonathan felt soft moss beneath him; he was now in the woods under the trees. The thicket had been passed.

Wetzel's moccasin pressed softly against Jonathan's head. The first signal!

Jonathan crawled forward, and slightly raised himself.

He was on a rock. The trees were thick and gloomy. Below, the little hollow was almost in the wan moonbeams. Dark figures lay close together. Two savages paced noiselessly to and fro. A slight form rolled in a blanket lay against a tree.

Jonathan felt his arm gently squeezed.

The second signal!

Slowly he thrust forward his rifle, and raised it in unison with Wetzel's. Slowly he rose to his feet as if the same muscles guided them both.

Over his head a twig snapped. In the darkness he had not seen a low branch.

The Indian guards stopped suddenly, and became motionless as stone.

They had heard; but too late.

With the blended roar of the rifles both dropped, lifeless.

Almost under the spouting flame and white cloud of smoke, Jonathan leaped behind Wetzel, over the bank. His yells were mingled with Wetzel's vengeful cry. Like leaping shadows the bordermen were upon their foes.

An Indian sprang up, raised a weapon, and fell beneath Jonathan's savage blow, to rise no more. Over his prostrate body the borderman bounded. A dark, nimble form darted upon the captive. He swung high a blade that shone like silver in the moonlight. His shrill war-cry of death rang out with Helen's scream of despair. Even as he swung back her head with one hand in her long hair, his arm descended; but it fell upon the borderman's body. Jonathan and the Indian rolled upon the moss. There was a terrific struggle, a whirling blade, a dull blow which silenced the yell, and the borderman rose alone.

He lifted Helen as if she were a child, leaped the brook, and plunged into the thicket.

The noise of the fearful conflict he left behind, swelled high and hideously on the night air. Above the shrill cries of the Indians, and the furious yells of Legget, rose the mad, booming roar of Wetzel. No rifle cracked; but sodden blows, the clash of steel, the threshing of struggling men, told of the dreadful strife.

Jonathan gained the woods, sped through the moonlit glades, and far on under light and shadow.

The shrill cries ceased; only the hoarse yells and the mad roar could be heard. Gradually these also died away, and the forest was still.

CHAPTER 21

NEXT MORNING, WHEN THE MIST WAS BREAKING AND ROLLING AWAY under the warm rays of the Indian-summer sun, Jonathan Zane beached his canoe on the steep bank before Fort Henry. A pioneer, attracted by the borderman's halloo, ran to the bluff and sounded the alarm with shrill whoops. Among the hurrying, brown-clad figures that answered this summons, was Colonel Zane.

"It's Jack, kurnel, an' he's got her!" cried one.

The doughty colonel gained the bluff to see his brother climbing the bank with a white-faced girl in his arms.

"Well?" he asked, looking darkly at Jonathan. Nothing kindly or genial was visible in his manner now; rather grim and forbidding he seemed, thus showing he had the same blood in his veins as the borderman.

"Lend a hand," said Jonathan. "As far as I know she's not hurt."

They carried Helen toward Colonel Zane's cabin. Many women of the settlement saw them as they passed, and looked gravely at one another, but none spoke. This return of an abducted girl was by no means a strange event.

"Somebody run for Sheppard," ordered Colonel Zane, as they entered his cabin.

Betty, who was in the sitting-room, sprang up and cried: "Oh! Eb! Eb! Don't say she's——"

"No, no, Betts, she's all right. Where's my wife? Ah! Bess, here, get to work."

The colonel left Helen in the tender, skilful hands of his wife and sister, and followed Jonathan into the kitchen.

"I was just ready for breakfast when I heard some one yell," said he. "Come, Jack, eat something."

They ate in silence. From the sitting-room came excited whispers, a joyous cry from Betty, and a faint voice. Then heavy, hurrying footsteps, followed by Sheppard's words of thanks-giving.

"Where's Wetzel?" began Colonel Zane.

The borderman shook his head gloomily.

"Where did you leave him?"

"We jumped Legget's bunch last night, when the moon was about an hour high. I reckon about fifteen miles northeast. I got away with the lass."

"Ah! Left Lew fighting?"

The borderman answered the question with bowed head.

"You got off well. Not a hurt that I can see, and more than lucky to save Helen. Well, Jack, what do you think about Lew?"

"I'm goin' back," replied Jonathan.

"No! no!"

The door opened to admit Mrs. Zane. She looked bright and cheerful, "Hello, Jack; glad you're home. Helen's all right, only faint from hunger and over-exertion. I want something for her to eat—well! you men didn't leave much."

Colonel Zane went into the sitting-room. Sheppard sat beside the couch where Helen lay, white and wan. Betty and Nell were looking on with their hearts in their eyes. Silas Zane was there, and his wife, with several women neighbors.

"Betty, go fetch Jack in here," whispered the colonel in his sister's ear. "Drag him, if you have to," he added fiercely.

The young woman left the room, to reappear directly with her brother. He came in reluctantly.

As the stern-faced borderman crossed the threshold a smile, beautiful to see, dawned in Helen's eyes.

"I'm glad to see you're comin' round," said Jonathan, but he spoke dully as if his mind was on other things.

"She's a little flighty; but a night's sleep will cure that," cried Mrs. Zane from the kitchen.

"What do you think?" interrupted the colonel. "Jack's not satisfied to get back with Helen unharmed, and a whole skin himself; but he's going on the trail again."

"No, Jack, no, no!" cried Betty.

"What's that I hear?" asked Mrs. Zane as she came in. "Jack's going out again? Well, all I want to say is that he's as mad as a March hare."

"Jonathan, look here," said Silas seriously. "Can't you stay home now?"

"Jack, listen," whispered Betty, going close to him. "Not one of us ever expected to see either you or Helen again, and oh! we are so happy. Do not go away again. You are a man; you do not know, you cannot understand all a woman feels. She must sit and wait, and hope, and pray for the safe return of husband or brother or sweetheart. The long days! Oh, the long sleepless nights, with the wail of the wind in the pines, and the rain on the roof! It is maddening. Do not leave us! Do not leave me! Do not leave Helen! Say you will not, Jack."

To these entreaties the borderman remained silent. He stood leaning on his rifle, a tall, dark, strangely sad and stern man.

"Helen, beg him to stay!" implored Betty.

Colonel Zane took Helen's hand, and stroked it. "Yes," he said, "you ask him, lass. I'm sure you can persuade him to stay."

Helen raised her head. "Is Brandt dead?" she whispered faintly.

Still the borderman failed to speak, but his silence was not an affirmative.

"You said you loved me," she cried wildly. "You said you loved me, yet you didn't kill that monster!"

The borderman, moving quickly like a startled Indian, went out of the door.

ONCE MORE JONATHAN ZANE ENTERED THE GLOOMY, QUIET AISLES OF the forest with his soft, tireless tread hardly stirring the leaves.

It was late in the afternoon when he had long left Two Islands behind, and arrived at the scene of Mordaunt's death. Satisfied with the distance he had traversed, he crawled into a thicket to rest.

Daybreak found him again on the trail. He made a short cut over the ridges and by the time the mist had lifted from the valley he was within stalking distance of the glade. He approached this in the familiar, slow, cautious manner, and halted behind the big rock from which he and

Wetzel had leaped. The wood was solemnly quiet. No twittering of birds could be heard. The only sign of life was a gaunt timber-wolf slinking away amid the foliage. Under the big tree the savage who had been killed as he would have murdered Helen, lay a crumpled mass where he had fallen. Two dead Indians were in the center of the glade, and on the other side were three more bloody, lifeless forms. Wetzel was not there, nor Legget, nor Brandt.

"I reckoned so," muttered Jonathan as he studied the scene. The grass had been trampled, the trees barked, the bushes crushed aside.

Jonathan went out of the glade a short distance, and, circling it, began to look for Wetzel's trail. He found it, and near the light footprints of his comrade were the great, broad moccasin tracks of the outlaw. Further searching disclosed the fact that Brandt must have traveled in line with the others.

With the certainty that Wetzel had killed three of the Indians, and, in some wonderful manner characteristic of him, routed the outlaws of whom he was now in pursuit, Jonathan's smoldering emotion burst forth into full flame. Love for his old comrade, deadly hatred of the outlaws, and passionate thirst for their blood, rioted in his heart.

Like a lynx scenting its quarry, the borderman started on the trail, tireless and unswervable. The traces left by the fleeing outlaws and their pursuer were plain to Jonathan. It was not necessary for him to stop. Legget and Brandt, seeking to escape the implacable Nemesis, were traveling with all possible speed, regardless of the broad trail such hurried movements left behind. They knew full well it would be difficult to throw this wolf off the scent; understood that if any attempt was made to ambush the trail, they must cope with woodcraft keener than an Indian's. Flying in desperation, they hoped to reach the rocky retreat, where, like foxes in their burrows, they believed themselves safe.

When the sun sloped low toward the western horizon, lengthening Jonathan's shadow, he slackened pace. He was entering the rocky, rugged country which marked the approach to the distant Alleghenies. From the top of a ridge he took his bearings, deciding that he was within a few miles of Legget's hiding-place.

At the foot of this ridge, where a murmuring brook sped softly over its bed, he halted. Here a number of horses had forded the brook. They were iron-shod, which indicated almost to a certainty, that they were stolen horses, and in the hands of Indians.

Jonathan saw where the trail of the steeds was merged into that of the outlaws. He suspected that the Indians and Legget had held a short council. As he advanced the borderman found only the faintest impression of Wetzel's trail. Legget and Brandt no longer left any token of their course. They were riding the horses.

All the borderman cared to know was if Wetzel still pursued. He passed on swiftly up a hill, through a wood of birches where the trail showed on a line of broken ferns, then out upon a low ridge where patches of grass grew sparsely. Here he saw in this last ground no indication of his comrade's trail; nothing was to be seen save the imprints of the horses' hoofs. Jonathan halted behind the nearest underbrush. This sudden move on the part of Wetzel was token that, suspecting an ambush, he had made a detour somewhere, probably in the grove of birches.

All the while his eyes searched the long, barren reach ahead. No thicket, fallen tree, or splintered rocks, such as Indians utilized for an ambush, could be seen. Indians always sought the densely matted underbrush, a windfall, or rocky retreat and there awaited a pursuer. It was one of the borderman's tricks of woodcraft that he could recognize such places.

Far beyond the sandy ridge Jonathan came to a sloping, wooded hillside, upon which were scattered big rocks, some mossy and lichencovered, and one, a giant boulder, with a crown of ferns and laurel gracing its flat surface. It was such a place as the savages would select for ambush. He knew, however, that if an Indian had hidden himself there Wetzel would have discovered him. When opposite the rock Jonathan saw a broken fern hanging over the edge. The heavy trail of the horses ran close beside it.

Then with that thoroughness of search which made the borderman what he was, Jonathan leaped upon the rock. There, lying in the midst of the ferns, lay an Indian with sullen, somber face set in the repose of death. In his side was a small bullet hole.

Jonathan examined the savage's rifle. It had been discharged. The rock, the broken fern, the dead Indian, the discharged rifle, told the story of that woodland tragedy.

Wetzel had discovered the ambush. Leaving the trail, he had tricked the redskin into firing, then getting a glimpse of the Indian's red body through the sights of his fatal weapon, the deed was done.

With greater caution Jonathan advanced once more. Not far beyond the rock he found Wetzel's trail. The afternoon was drawing to a close. He could not travel much farther, yet he kept on, hoping to overtake his comrade before darkness set in. From time to time he whistled; but got no answering signal.

When the tracks of the horses were nearly hidden by the gathering dusk, Jonathan decided to halt for the night. He whistled one more note, louder and clearer, and awaited the result with strained ears. The deep silence of the wilderness prevailed, suddenly to be broken by a faint, far-away, melancholy call of the hermit-thrush. It was the answering signal the borderman had hoped to hear.

Not many moments elapsed before he heard another call, low, and near at hand, to which he replied. The bushes parted noiselessly on his left, and the tall form of Wetzel appeared silently out of the gloom.

The two gripped hands in silence.

"Hev you any meat?" Wetzel asked, and as Jonathan handed him his knapsack, he continued, "I was kinder lookin' fer you. Did you get out all right with the lass?"

"Nary a scratch."

The giant borderman grunted his satisfaction.

"How'd Legget and Brandt get away?" asked Jonathan.

"Cut an' run like scared bucks. Never got a hand on either of 'em."

"How many redskins did they meet back here a spell?"

"They was seven; but now there are only six, an' all snug in Legget's place by this time."

"I reckon we're near his den."

"We're not far off."

Night soon closing down upon the bordermen found them wrapped in slumber, as if no deadly foes were near at hand. The soft night wind sighed dismally among the bare trees. A few bright stars twinkled overhead. In the darkness of the forest the bordermen were at home.

CHAPTER 22

In Legget's rude log cabin a fire burned low, lightening the forms of the two border outlaws, and showing in the background the dark forms of Indians sitting motionless on the floor. Their dusky eyes emitted a baleful glint, seemingly a reflection of their savage souls caught by the firelight. Legget wore a look of ferocity and sullen fear strangely blended. Brandt's face was hard and haggard, his lips set, his gray eyes smoldering.

"Safe?" he hissed. "Safe you say? You'll see that it's the same now as on the other night, when those border-tigers jumped us and we ran like cowards. I'd have fought it out here, but for you."

"Thet man Wetzel is ravin' mad, I tell you," growled Legget. "I reckon I've stood my ground enough to know I ain't no coward. But this fellar's crazy. He hed the Injuns slashin' each other like a pack of wolves round a buck."

"He's no more mad than you or I," declared Brandt. "I know all about him. His moaning in the woods, and wild yells are only tricks. He knows the Indian nature, and he makes their very superstition and religion aid him in his fighting. I told you what he'd do. Didn't I beg you to kill Zane when we had a chance? Wetzel would never have taken our trail alone. Now they've beat me out of the girl, and as sure as death will round us up here."

"You don't believe they'll rush us here?" asked Legget.

"They're too keen to take foolish chances, but something will be done

661

we don't expect. Zane was a prisoner here; he had a good look at this place, and you can gamble he'll remember."

"Zane must hev gone back to Fort Henry with the girl."

"Mark what I say, he'll come back!"

"Wal, we kin hold this place against all the men Eb Zane may put out."

"He won't send a man," snapped Brandt passionately. "Remember this, Legget, we're not to fight against soldiers, settlers, or hunters; but bordermen—understand—bordermen! Such as have been developed right here on this bloody frontier, and nowhere else on earth. They haven't fear in them. Both are fleet as deer in the woods. They can't be seen or trailed. They can snuff a candle with a rifle ball in the dark. I've seen Zane do it three times at a hundred yards. And Wetzel! He wouldn't waste powder on practicing. They can't be ambushed, or shaken off a track; they take the scent like buzzards, and have eyes like eagles."

"We kin slip out of here under cover of night," suggested Legget.

"Well, what then? That's all they want. They'd be on us again by sunset. No! we've got to stand our ground and fight. We'll stay as long as we can; but they'll rout us out somehow, be sure of that. And if one of us pokes his nose out to the daylight, it will be shot off."

"You're sore, an' you've lost your nerve," said Legget harshly. "Sore at me 'cause I got sweet on the girl. Ho! ho!"

Brandt shot a glance at Legget which boded no good. His strong hands clenched in an action betraying the reckless rage in his heart. Then he carefully removed his hunting coat, and examined his wound. He retied the bandage, muttering gloomily, "I'm so weak as to be light-headed. If this cut opens again, it's all day for me."

After that the inmates of the hut were quiet. The huge outlaw bowed his shaggy head for a while, and then threw himself on a pile of hemlock boughs. Brandt was not long in seeking rest. Soon both were fast asleep. Two of the savages passed out with cat-like step, leaving the door open. The fire had burned low, leaving a bed of dead coals. Outside in the dark a waterfall splashed softly.

The darkest hour came, and passed, and paled slowly to gray. Birds began to twitter. Through the door of the cabin the light of day streamed in. The two Indian sentinels were building a fire on the stone hearth. One by one the other savages got up, stretched and yawned, and began the business of the day by cooking their breakfast. It was, apparently, every one for himself.

Legget arose, shook himself like a shaggy dog, and was starting for the door when one of the sentinels stopped him. Brandt, who was now awake, saw the action, and smiled.

In a few moments Indians and outlaws were eating for breakfast roasted strips of venison, with corn meal baked brown, which served as bread. It was a somber, silent group.

Presently the shrill neigh of a horse startled them. Following it, the whip-like crack of a rifle stung and split the morning air. Hard on this came an Indian's long, wailing death-cry.

"Hah!" exclaimed Brandt.

Legget remained immovable. One of the savages peered out through a little port-hole at the rear of the hut. The others continued their meal.

"Whistler'll come in presently to tell us who's doin' thet shootin'," said Legget. "He's a keen Injun."

"He's not very keen now," replied Brandt, with bitter certainty. "He's what the settlers call a good Indian, which is to say, dead!"

Legget scowled at his lieutenant.

"I'll go an' see," he replied and seized his rifle.

He opened the door, when another rifle-shot rang out. A bullet whistled in the air, grazing the outlaw's shoulder, and imbedded itself in the heavy door-frame.

Legget leaped back with a curse.

"Close shave!" said Brandt coolly. "That bullet came, probably, straight down from the top of the cliff. Jack Zane's there. Wetzel is lower down watching the outlet. We're trapped."

"Trapped," shouted Legget with an angry leer. "We kin live here longer'n the bordermen kin. We've meat on hand, an' a good spring in the back of the hut. How'er we trapped?"

"We won't live twenty-four hours," declared Brandt.

"Why?"

"Because we'll be routed out. They'll find some way to do it, and we'll never have another chance to fight in the open, as we had the other night when they came after the girl. From now on there'll be no sleep, no time to eat, the nameless fear of an unseen foe who can't be shaken off, marching by night, hiding and starving by day, until——! I'd rather be back in Fort Henry at Colonel Zane's mercy."

Legget turned a ghastly face toward Brandt. "Look a here. You're takin' a lot of glee in sayin' these things. I believe you've lost your nerve, or the lettin' out of a little blood hes made you wobbly. We've Injuns here, an' ought to be a match fer two men."

Brandt gazed at him with a derisive smile.

"We kin go out an' fight these fellars," continued Legget. "We might try their own game, hidin' an' crawlin' through the woods."

"We two would have to go it alone. If you still had your trusty, trained band of experienced Indians, I'd say that would be just the thing. But Ashbow and the Chippewa are dead; so are the others. This bunch of redskins here may do to steal a few horses; but they don't amount to much against Zane and Wetzel. Besides, they'll cut and run presently, for they're scared and suspicious. Look at the chief; ask him."

The savage Brandt indicated was a big Indian just coming into manhood. His swarthy face still retained some of the frankness and simplicity of youth.

"Chief," said Legget in the Indian tongue. "The great paleface hunter, Deathwind, lies hid in the woods."

"Last night the Shawnee heard the wind of death mourn through the trees," replied the chief gloomily.

"See! What did I say?" cried Brandt. "The superstitious fool! He would begin his death-chant almost without a fight. We can't count on the redskins. What's to be done?"

The outlaw threw himself upon the bed of boughs, and Legget sat down with his rifle across his knees. The Indians maintained the same stoical composure. The moments dragged by into hours.

"Ugh!" suddenly exclaimed the Indian at the end of the hut.

Legget ran to him, and acting upon a motion of the Indian's hand, looked out through the little port-hole.

The sun was high. He saw four of the horses grazing by the brook; then gazed scrutinizingly from the steep waterfall, along the green-stained cliff to the dark narrow cleft in the rocks. Here was the only outlet from the inclosure. He failed to discover anything unusual.

The Indian grunted again, and pointed upward.

"Smoke! There's smoke risin' above the trees," cried Legget. "Brandt, come here. What's thet mean?"

Brandt hurried, looked out. His face paled, his lower jaw protruded, quivered, and then was shut hard. He walked away, put his foot on a bench and began to lace his leggings.

"Wal?" demanded Legget.

"The game's up! Get ready to run and be shot at," cried Brandt with a hiss of passion.

Almost as he spoke the roof of the hut shook under a heavy blow.

"What's thet?" No one replied. Legget glanced from Brandt's cold, determined face to the uneasy savages. They were restless, and handling their weapons. The chief strode across the floor with stealthy steps.

"Thud!"

A repetition of the first blow caused the Indians to jump, and drew a fierce imprecation from their outlaw leader.

Brandt eyed him narrowly. "It's coming to you, Legget. They are shooting arrows of fire into the roof from the cliff. Zane is doin' that. He can make a bow and draw one, too. We're to be burned out. Now, damn you! take your medicine! I wanted you to kill him when you had the chance. If you had done so we'd never have come to this. Burned out, do you get that? Burned out!"

"Fire!" exclaimed Legget. He sat down as if the strength had left his legs.

The Indians circled around the room like caged tigers.

"Ugh!" The chief suddenly reached up and touched the birch-bark roof of the hut.

His action brought the attention of all to a faint crackling of burning wood.

"It's caught all right," cried Brandt in a voice which cut the air like a blow from a knife.

"I'll not be smoked like a ham, fer all these tricky bordermen," roared Legget. Drawing his knife he hacked at the heavy buckskin hinges of the rude door. When it dropped free he measured it against the open space. Sheathing the blade, he grasped his rifle in his right hand and swung the door on his left arm. Heavy though it was he carried it easily. The roughly hewn planks afforded a capital shield for all except the lower portion of his legs and feet. He went out of the hut with the screen of wood between himself and the cliff, calling for the Indians to follow. They gathered behind him, breathing hard, clutching their weapons, and seemingly almost crazed by excitement.

Brandt, with no thought of joining this foolhardy attempt to escape from the inclosure, ran to the little port-hole that he might see the outcome. Legget and his five redskins were running toward the narrow outlet in the gorge. The awkward and futile efforts of the Indians to remain behind the shield were almost pitiful. They crowded each other for favorable positions, but, struggle as they might, one or two were always exposed to the cliff. Suddenly one, pushed to the rear, stopped simultaneously with the crack of a rifle, threw up his arms and fell. Another report, differing from the first, rang out. A savage staggered from behind the speeding group with his hand at his side. Then he dropped into the brook.

Evidently Legget grasped this as a golden opportunity, for he threw aside the heavy shield and sprang forward, closely followed by his red-skinned allies. Immediately they came near the cliff, where the trail ran into the gorge, a violent shaking of the dry ferns overhead made manifest the activity of some heavy body. Next instant a huge yellow figure, not unlike a leaping catamount, plunged down with a roar so terrible as to sound inhuman. Legget, Indians, and newcomer rolled along the declivity toward the brook in an indistinguishable mass.

Two of the savages shook themselves free, and bounded to their feet nimbly as cats, but Legget and the other redskin became engaged in a terrific combat. It was a wrestling whirl, so fierce and rapid as to render blows ineffectual. The leaves scattered as if in a whirlwind. Legget's fury must have been awful, to judge from his hoarse screams; the Indians' fear maddening, as could be told by their shrieks. The two savages ran wildly about the combatants, one trying to level a rifle, the other to get in a blow with a tomahawk. But the movements of the trio, locked in deadly embrace, were too swift.

Above all the noise of the contest rose that strange, thrilling roar.

"Wetzel!" muttered Brandt, with a chill, creeping shudder as he gazed upon the strife with fascinated eyes.

"Bang!" Again from the cliff came that heavy bellow.

The savage with the rifle shrunk back as if stung, and without a cry fell limply in a heap. His companion, uttering a frightened cry, fled from the glen.

The struggle seemed too deadly, too terrible, to last long. The Indian and the outlaw were at a disadvantage. They could not strike freely. The whirling conflict grew more fearful. During one second the huge, brown, bearish figure of Legget appeared on top; then the dark-bodied, half-naked savage, spotted like a hyena, and finally the lithe, powerful, tiger-shape of the borderman.

Finally Legget wrenched himself free at the same instant that the bloody-stained Indian rolled, writhing in convulsions, away from Wetzel. The outlaw dashed with desperate speed up the trail, and disappeared in the gorge. The borderman sped toward the cliff, leaped on a projecting ledge, grasped an overhanging branch, and pulled himself up. He was out of sight almost as quickly as Legget.

"After his rifle," Brandt muttered, and then realized that he had watched the encounter without any idea of aiding his comrade. He consoled himself with the knowledge that such an attempt would have been useless. From the moment the borderman sprang upon Legget, until he scaled the cliff, his movements had been incredibly swift. It would have been hardly possible to cover him with a rifle, and the outlaw grimly understood that he needed to be careful of that charge in his weapon.

"By Heavens, Wetzel's a wonder!" cried Brandt in unwilling admiration. "Now he'll go after Legget and the redskin, while Zane stays here to get me. Well, he'll succeed, most likely, but I'll never quit. What's this?"

He felt something slippery and warm on his hand. It was blood running from the inside of his sleeve. A slight pain made itself felt in his side. Upon examination he found, to his dismay, that his wound had reopened. With a desperate curse he pulled a linsey jacket off a peg, tore it into strips, and bound up the injury as tightly as possible.

Then he grasped his rifle, and watched the cliff and the gorge with flaring eyes. Suddenly he found it difficult to breathe; his throat was parched, his eyes smarted. Then the odor of wood-smoke brought him to a realization that the cabin was burning. It was only now he understood that the room was full of blue clouds. He sank into the corner, a wolf at bay.

Not many moments passed before the outlaw understood that he could not withstand the increasing heat and stifling vapor of the room. Pieces of burning birch dropped from the roof. The crackling above grew into a steady roar.

"I've got to run for it," he gasped. Death awaited him outside the door, but that was more acceptable than death by fire. Yet to face the final moment when he desired with all his soul to live, required almost superhuman courage. Sweating, panting, he glared around. "God! Is there no other way?" he cried in agony. At this moment he saw an ax on the floor.

Seizing it he attacked the wall of the cabin. Beyond this partition was a hut which had been used for a stable. Half a dozen strokes of the ax opened a hole large enough for him to pass through. With his rifle, and a piece of venison which hung near, he literally fell through the hole, where he lay choking, almost fainting. After a time he crawled across the floor to a door. Outside was a dense laurel thicket, into which he crawled.

The crackling and roaring of the fire grew louder. He could see the column of yellow and black smoke. Once fairly under way, the flames rapidly consumed the pitch-pine logs. In an hour Legget's cabins were a heap of ashes.

The afternoon waned. Brandt lay watchful, slowly recovering his strength. He felt secure under this cover, and only prayed for night to come. As the shadows began to creep down the sides of the cliffs, he indulged in hope. If he could slip out in the dark he had a good chance to elude the borderman. In the passionate desire to escape, he had forgotten his fatalistic words to Legget. He reasoned that he could not be trailed until daylight; that a long night's march would put him far in the lead, and there was just a possibility of Zane's having gone away with Wetzel.

When darkness had set in he slipped out of the covert and began his journey for life. Within a few yards he reached the brook. He had only to follow its course in order to find the outlet to the glen. Moreover, its rush and gurgle over the stones would drown any slight noise he might make.

Slowly, patiently he crawled, stopping every moment to listen. What a long time he was in coming to the mossy stones over which the brook dashed through the gorge! But he reached them at last. Here if anywhere Zane would wait for him.

With teeth clenched desperately, and an inward tightening of his chest, for at any moment he expected to see the red flame of a rifle, he slipped cautiously over the mossy stones. Finally his hands touched the dewy grass, and a breath of cool wind fanned his hot cheek. He had succeeded in reaching the open. Crawling some rods farther on, he lay still a while and listened. The solemn wilderness calm was unbroken. Rising, he peered about. Behind loomed the black hill with its narrow cleft just discernible. Facing the north star, he went silently out into the darkness.

CHAPTER 23

AT DAYLIGHT JONATHAN ZANE ROLLED FROM HIS SNUG BED OF LEAVES under the side of a log, and with the flint, steel and punk he always carried, began building a fire. His actions were far from being hurried. They were deliberate, and seemed strange on the part of a man whose stern face suggested some dark business to be done. When his little fire had been made, he warmed some slices of venison which had already been cooked, and thus satisfied his hunger. Carefully extinguishing the fire and looking to the priming of his rifle, he was ready for the trail.

He stood near the edge of the cliff from which he could command a view of the glen. The black, smoldering ruins of the burned cabins defaced a picturesque scene.

"Brandt must have lit out last night, for I could have seen even a rabbit hidin' in that laurel patch. He's gone, an' it's what I wanted," thought the borderman.

He made his way slowly around the edge of the inclosure and clambered down on the splintered cliff at the end of the gorge. A wide, well-trodden trail extended into the forest below. Jonathan gave scarcely a glance to the beaten path before him; but bent keen eyes to the north, and carefully scrutinized the mossy stones along the brook. Upon a little sand bar running out from the bank he found the light imprint of a hand.

"It was a black night. He'd have to travel by the stars, an' north's the only safe direction for him," muttered the borderman.

On the bank above he found oblong indentations in the grass, barely perceptible, but owing to the peculiar position of the blades of grass, easy for him to follow.

"He'd better have learned to walk light as an Injun before he took to outlawin'," said the borderman in disdain. Then he returned to the gorge and entered the inclosure. At the foot of the little rise of ground where Wetzel had leaped upon his quarry, was one of the dead Indians. Another lay partly submerged in the brown water.

Jonathan carried the weapons of the savages to a dry place under a projecting ledge in the cliff. Passing on down the glen, he stopped a moment where the cabins had stood. Not a log remained. The horses, with the exception of two, were tethered in the copse of laurel. He recognized Colonel Zane's thoroughbred, and Betty's pony. He cut them loose, positive they would not stray from the glen, and might easily be secured at another time.

He set out upon the trail of Brandt with a long, swinging stride. To him the outcome of that pursuit was but a question of time. The consciousness of superior endurance, speed, and craft, spoke in his every movement. The consciousness of being in right, a factor so powerfully potent for victory, spoke in the intrepid front with which he faced the north.

It was a gloomy November day. Gray, steely clouds drifted overhead. The wind wailed through the bare trees, sending dead leaves scurrying and rustling over the brown earth.

The borderman advanced with a step that covered glade and glen, forest and field, with astonishing swiftness. Long since he had seen that Brandt was holding to the lowland. This did not strike him as singular until for the third time he found the trail lead a short distance up the side of a ridge, then descend, seeking a level. With this discovery came the certainty that Brandt's pace was lessening. He had set out with a hunter's stride, but it had begun to shorten. The outlaw had shirked the hills, and shifted from his northern course. Why? The man was weakening; he could not climb; he was favoring a wound.

What seemed more serious for the outlaw, was the fact that he had left a good trail, and entered the low, wild land north of the Ohio. Even the Indians seldom penetrated this tangled belt of laurel and thorn. Owing to the dry season the swamps were shallow, which was another factor against Brandt. No doubt he had hoped to hide his trail by wading, and here it showed up like the track of a bison.

Jonathan kept steadily on, knowing the farther Brandt penetrated into this wilderness the worse off he would be. The outlaw dared not take to the river until below Fort Henry, which was distant many a weary mile. The trail grew more ragged as the afternoon wore away. When twilight rendered further tracking impossible, the borderman built a fire in a sheltered place, ate his supper, and went to sleep.

In the dim, gray morning light he awoke, fancying he had been startled by a distant rifle shot. He roasted his strips of venison carefully, and ate with a hungry hunter's appreciation, yet sparingly, as befitted a borderman who knew how to keep up his strength upon a long trail.

Hardly had he traveled a mile when Brandt's footprints covered another's. Nothing surprised the borderman; but he had expected this least of all. A hasty examination convinced him that Legget and his Indian ally had fled this way with Wetzel in pursuit.

The morning passed slowly. The borderman kept to the trail like a hound. The afternoon wore on. Over sandy reaches thick with willows, and through long, matted, dried-out cranberry marshes and copses of prickly thorn, the borderman hung to his purpose. His legs seemed never to lose their spring, but his chest began to heave, his head bent, and his face shone with sweat.

At dusk he tired. Crawling into a dry thicket, he ate his scanty meal and fell asleep. When he awoke it was gray daylight. He was wet and chilled. Again he kindled a fire, and sat over it while cooking breakfast.

Suddenly he was brought to his feet by the sound of a rifle shot; then two others followed in rapid succession. Though they were faint, and far away to the west, Jonathan recognized the first, which could have come only from Wetzel's weapon, and he felt reasonably certain of the third, which was Brandt's. There might have been, he reflected grimly, a good reason for Legget's not shooting. However, he knew that Wetzel had rounded up the fugitives, and again he set out.

It was another dismal day, such a one as would be fitting for a dark deed of border justice. A cold, drizzly rain blew from the northwest. Jonathan wrapped a piece of oil-skin around his rifle-breech, and faced the downfall. Soon he was wet to the skin. He kept on, but his free stride had shortened. Even upon his iron muscles this soggy, sticky ground had begun to tell.

The morning passed but the storm did not; the air grew colder and darker. The short afternoon would afford him little time, especially as the rain and running rills of water were obliterating the trail.

In the midst of a dense forest of great cottonwoods and sycamores he came upon a little pond, hidden among the bushes, and shrouded in a windy, wet gloom. Jonathan recognized the place. He had been there in winter hunting bears when all the swampland was locked by ice.

The borderman searched along the banks for a time, then went back to the trail, patiently following it. Around the pond it led to the side of a great, shelving rock. He saw an Indian leaning against this, and was about to throw forward his rifle when the strange, fixed, position of the savage told of the tragedy. A wound extended from his shoulder to his waist. Near by on the ground lay Legget. He, too, was dead. His gigantic frame weltered in blood. His big feet were wide apart; his arms spread, and from the middle of his chest protruded the haft of a knife.

The level space surrounding the bodies showed evidence of a desperate struggle. A bush had been rolled upon and crushed by heavy bodies. On the ground was blood as on the stones and leaves. The blade Legget still clutched was red, and the wrist of the hand which held it showed a dark, discolored band, where it had felt the relentless grasp of Wetzel's steel grip. The dead man's buckskin coat was cut into ribbons. On his broad face a demoniacal expression had set in eternal rigidity; the animal terror of death was frozen in his wide staring eyes. The outlaw chief had died as he had lived, desperately.

Jonathan found Wetzel's trail leading directly toward the river, and soon understood that the borderman was on the track of Brandt. The borderman had surprised the worn, starved, sleepy fugitives in the gray, misty dawn. The Indian, doubtless, was the sentinel, and had fallen asleep at his post never to awaken. Legget and Brandt must have discharged their weapons ineffectually. Zane could not understand why his comrade had missed Brandt at a few rods' distance. Perhaps he had wounded the younger outlaw; but certainly he had escaped while Wetzel had closed in on Legget to meet the hardest battle of his career.

While going over his version of the attack, Jonathan followed Brandt's trail, as had Wetzel, to where it ended in the river. The old borderman had continued on down stream along the sandy shore. The outlaw remained in the water to hide his trail.

At one point Wetzel turned north. This move puzzled Jonathan, as did also the peculiar tracks. It was more perplexing because not far below Zane discovered where the fugitive had left the water to get around a ledge of rock.

The trail was approaching Fort Henry. Jonathan kept on down the river until arriving at the head of the island which lay opposite the settlement. Still no traces of Wetzel! Here Zane lost Brandt's trail completely. He waded the first channel, which was shallow and narrow, and hurried across the island. Walking out upon a sand-bar he signaled with his well-known Indian cry. Almost immediately came an answering shout.

While waiting he glanced at the sand, and there, pointing straight toward the fort, he found Brandt's straggling trail!

CHAPTER 24

COLONEL ZANE PACED TO AND FRO ON THE PORCH. HIS GENIAL SMILE had not returned; he was grave and somber. Information had just reached him that Jonathan had hailed from the island, and that one of the settlers had started across the river in a boat.

Betty came out accompanied by Mrs. Zane.

"What's this I hear?" asked Betty, flashing an anxious glance toward the river. "Has Jack really come in?"

"Yes," replied the colonel, pointing to a throng of men on the river bank.

"Now there'll be trouble," said Mrs. Zane nervously. "I wish with all my heart Brandt had not thrown himself, as he called it, on your mercy."

"So do I," declared Colonel Zane.

"What will be done?" she asked. "There! that's Jack! Silas has hold of his arm."

"He's lame. He has been hurt," replied her husband.

A little procession of men and boys followed the borderman from the river, and from the cabins appeared the settlers and their wives. But there was no excitement except among the children. The crowd filed into the colonel's yard behind Jonathan and Silas.

Colonel Zane silently greeted his brother with an iron grip of the hand which was more expressive than words. No unusual sight was it to see the borderman wet, ragged, bloody, worn with long marches, hollow-eyed and gloomy; yet he had never before presented such an appearance at Fort Henry. Betty ran forward, and, though she clasped his arm, shrank back. There was that in the borderman's presence to cause fear.

"Wetzel?" Jonathan cried sharply.

The colonel raised both hands, palms open, and returned his brother's keen glance. Then he spoke. "Lew hasn't come in. He chased Brandt across the river. That's all I know."

"Brandt's here, then?" hissed the borderman.

The colonel nodded gloomily.

"Where?"

"In the long room over the fort. I locked him in there."

"Why did he come here?"

Colonel Zane shrugged his shoulders. "It's beyond me. He said he'd rather place himself in my hands than be run down by Wetzel or you. He didn't crawl; I'll say that for him. He just said, 'I'm your prisoner.' He's in pretty bad shape; barked over the temple, lame in one foot, cut under the arm, starved and worn out."

"Take me to him," said the borderman, and he threw his rifle on a bench.

"Very well. Come along," replied the colonel. He frowned at those following them. "Here, you women, clear out!" But they did not obey him.

It was a sober-faced group that marched in through the big stockade gate, under the huge, bulging front of the fort, and up the rough stairway. Colonel Zane removed a heavy bar from before a door, and thrust it open with his foot. The long guardroom brilliantly lighted by sunshine coming through the portholes, was empty save for a ragged man lying on a bench.

The noise aroused him; he sat up, and then slowly labored to his feet. It was the same flaring, wild-eyed Brandt, only fiercer and more haggard. He wore a bloody bandage round his head. When he saw the borderman he backed, with involuntary, instinctive action, against the wall, yet showed no fear.

In the dark glance Jonathan shot at Brandt shone a pitiless implacability; no scorn, nor hate, nor passion, but something which, had it not been so terrible, might have been justice.

"I think Wetzel was hurt in the fight with Legget," said Jonathan deliberately, "an' ask if you know?"

"I believe he was," replied Brandt readily. "I was asleep when he jumped us, and was awakened by the Indian's yell. Wetzel must have taken a snap shot at me as I was getting up, which accounts, probably, for my being alive. I fell, but did not lose consciousness. I heard Wetzel and Legget fighting, and at last struggled to my feet. Although dizzy and bewildered, I could see to shoot; but missed. For a long time, it seemed to me, I watched that terrible fight, and then ran, finally reaching the river, where I recovered somewhat."

"Did you see Wetzel again?"

"Once, about a quarter of a mile behind me. He was staggering along on my trail."

At this juncture there was a commotion among the settlers crowding behind Colonel Zane and Jonathan, and Helen Sheppard appeared, white, with her big eyes strangely dilated.

"Oh!" she cried breathlessly, clasping both hands around Jonathan's arm. "I'm not too late? You're not going to——"

"Helen, this is no place for you," said Colonel Zane sternly. "This is business for men. You must not interfere."

Helen gazed at him, at Brandt, and then up at the borderman. She did not loose his arm.

"Outside some one told me you intended to shoot him. Is it true?"

Colonel Zane evaded the searching gaze of those strained, brilliant eyes. Nor did he answer.

As Helen stepped slowly back a hush fell upon the crowd. The whispering, the nervous coughing, and shuffling of feet, ceased.

In those around her Helen saw the spirit of the border. Colonel Zane and Silas wore the same look, cold, hard, almost brutal. The women were strangely grave. Nellie Douns' sweet face seemed changed; there was pity, even suffering on it, but no relenting. Even Betty's face, always so warm, piquant, and wholesome, had taken on a shade of doubt, of gloom, of something almost sullen, which blighted its dark beauty. What hurt Helen most cruelly was the borderman's glittering eyes.

She fought against a shuddering weakness which threatened to overcome her.

"Whose prisoner is Brandt?" she asked of Colonel Zane.

"He gave himself up to me, naturally, as I am in authority here," replied the colonel. "But that signifies little. I can do no less than abide by Jonathan's decree, which, after all, is the decree of the border."

"And that is?"

"Death to outlaws and renegades."

"But cannot you spare him?" implored Helen. "I know he is a bad man; but he might become a better one. It seems like murder to me. To kill him in cold blood, wounded, suffering as he is, when he claimed your mercy. Oh! it is dreadful!"

The usually kind-hearted colonel, soft as wax in the hands of a girl, was now colder and harder than flint.

"It is useless," he replied curtly. "I am sorry for you. We all understand your feelings, that yours are not the principles of the border. If you had lived long here you could appreciate what these outlaws and renegades have done to us. This man is a hardened criminal; he is a thief, a murderer."

"He did not kill Mordaunt," replied Helen quickly. "I saw him draw first and attack Brandt."

"No matter. Come, Helen, cease. No more of this," Colonel Zane cried with impatience.

"But I will not!" exclaimed Helen, with ringing voice and flashing eye. She turned to her girl friends and besought them to intercede for the outlaw. But Nell only looked sorrowfully on, while Betty met her appealing glance with a fire in her eyes that was no dim reflection of her brother's.

"Then I must make my appeal to you," said Helen, facing the border-man. There could be no mistaking how she regarded him. Respect, honor and love breathed from every line of her beautiful face.

"Why do you want him to go free?" demanded Jonathan. "You told me to kill him."

"Oh, I know. But I was not in my right mind. Listen to me, please. He must have been very different once; perhaps had sisters. For their sake give him another chance. I know he has a better nature. I feared him, hated him, scorned him, as if he were a snake, yet he saved me from that monster Legget!"

"For himself!"

"Well, yes, I can't deny that. But he could have ruined me, wrecked me, yet he did not. At least, he meant marriage by me. He said if I would marry him he would flee over the border and be an honest man."

"Have you no other reason?"

"Yes." Helen's bosom swelled and a glory shone in her splendid eyes. "The other reason is, my own happiness!"

Plain to all, if not through her words, from the light in her eyes, that she could not love a man who was a party to what she considered injustice.

The borderman's white face became flaming red.

It was difficult to refuse this glorious girl any sacrifice she demanded for the sake of the love so openly avowed.

Sweetly and pityingly she turned to Brandt: "Will not you help me?"

"Lass, if it were for me you were asking my life I'd swear it yours for always, and I'd be a man," he replied with bitterness; "but not to save my soul would I ask anything of him."

The giant passions, hate and jealousy, flamed in his gray eyes.

"If I persuade them to release you, will you go away, leave this country, and never come back?"

"I'll promise that, lass, and honestly," he replied.

She wheeled toward Jonathan, and now the rosy color chased the pallor from her cheeks.

"Jack, do you remember when we parted at my home; when you left on this terrible trail, now ended, thank God! Do you remember what an ordeal that was for me? Must I go through it again?"

Bewitchingly sweet she was then, with the girlish charm of coquetry almost lost in the deeper, stranger power of the woman.

The borderman drew his breath sharply; then he wrapped his long arms closely round her. She, understanding that victory was hers, sank weeping upon his breast. For a moment he bowed his face over her, and when he lifted it the dark and terrible gloom had gone.

"Eb, let him go, an' at once," ordered Jonathan. "Give him a rifle, some meat, an' a canoe, for he can't travel, an' turn him loose. Only be quick about it, because if Wetzel comes in, God himself couldn't save the outlaw."

It was an indescribable glance that Brandt cast upon the tearful face of the girl who had saved his life. But without a word he followed Colonel Zane from the room.

The crowd slowly filed down the steps. Betty and Nell lingered behind, their eyes beaming through happy tears. Jonathan, long so cold, showed evidence of becoming as quick and passionate a lover as he had been a borderman. At least, Helen had to release herself from his embrace, and it was a blushing, tear-stained face she turned to her friends.

When they reached the stockade gate Colonel Zane was hurrying toward the river with a bag in one hand, and a rifle and a paddle in the other. Brandt limped along after him, the two disappearing over the river bank.

Betty, Nell, and the lovers went to the edge of the bluff.

They saw Colonel Zane choose a canoe from among a number on the beach. He launched it, deposited the bag in the bottom, handed the rifle and paddle to Brandt, and wheeled about.

The outlaw stepped aboard, and, pushing off slowly, drifted down and out toward mid-stream. When about fifty yards from shore he gave a quick glance around, and ceased paddling. His face gleamed white, and his eyes glinted like bits of steel in the sun.

Suddenly he grasped the rifle, and, leveling it with the swiftness of thought, fired at Jonathan.

The borderman saw the act, even from the beginning, and must have read the outlaw's motive, for as the weapon flashed he dropped flat on the bank. The bullet sang harmlessly over him, imbedding itself in the stockade fence with a distinct thud.

The girls were so numb with horror that they could not even scream.

Colonel Zane swore lustily. "Where's my gun? Get me a gun. Oh! What did I tell you?"

"Look!" cried Jonathan as he rose to his feet.

Upon the sand-bar opposite stood a tall, dark, familiar figure.

"By all that's holy, Wetzel!" exclaimed Colonel Zane.

They saw the giant borderman raise a long, black rifle, which wavered and fell, and rose again. A little puff of white smoke leaped out, accompanied by a clear, stinging report.

Brandt dropped the paddle he had hurriedly begun plying after his traitor's act. His white face was turned toward the shore as it sank forward to rest at last upon the gunwale of the canoe. Then his body slowly settled, as if seeking repose. His hand trailed outside in the water, drooping inert and lifeless. The little craft drifted down stream.

"You see, Helen, it had to be," said Colonel Zane gently. "What a dastard! A long shot, Jack! Fate itself must have glanced down the sights of Wetzel's rifle."

CHAPTER 25

A YEAR ROLLED ROUND; ONCE AGAIN INDIAN SUMMER VEILED THE golden fields and forests in a soft, smoky haze. Once more from the opal-blue sky of autumn nights, shone the great white stars, and nature seemed wrapped in a melancholy hush.

November the third was the anniversary of a memorable event on the frontier—the marriage of the younger borderman.

Colonel Zane gave it the name of "Independence Day," and arranged a holiday, a feast and dance where all the settlement might meet in joyful thankfulness for the first year of freedom on the border.

With the wiping out of Legget's fierce band, the yoke of the renegades and outlaws was thrown off forever. Simon Girty migrated to Canada and lived with a few Indians who remained true to him. His confederates slowly sank into oblivion. The Shawnee tribe sullenly retreated westward, far into the interior of Ohio; the Delawares buried the war hatchet, and smoked the pipe of peace they had ever before refused. For them the dark, mysterious, fatal wind had ceased to moan along the trails, or sigh through tree-tops over lonely Indian camp-fires.

The beautiful Ohio valley had been wrested from the savages and from those parasites who for years had hung around the necks of the red men.

This day was the happiest of Colonel Zane's life. The task he had set himself, and which he had hardly ever hoped to see completed, was ended.

The West had been won. What Boone achieved in Kentucky he had accomplished in Ohio and West Virginia.

The feast was spread on the colonel's lawn. Every man, woman and child in the settlement was there. Isaac Zane, with his Indian wife and child, had come from the far-off Huron town. Pioneers from Yellow Creek and eastward to Fort Pitt attended. The spirit of the occasion manifested itself in such joyousness as had never before been experienced in Fort Henry. The great feast was equal to the event. Choice cuts of beef and venison, savory viands, wonderful loaves of bread and great plump pies, sweet cider and old wine, delighted the merry party.

"Friends, neighbors, dear ones," said Colonel Zane, "my heart is almost too full for speech. This occasion, commemorating the day of our freedom on the border, is the beginning of the reward for stern labor, hardship, silenced hearths of long, relentless years. I did not think I'd live to see it. The seed we have sown has taken root; in years to come, perhaps, a great people will grow up on these farms we call our homes. And as we hope those coming afterward will remember us, we should stop a moment to think of the heroes who have gone before. Many there are whose names will never be written on the roll of fame, whose graves will be unmarked in history. But we who worked, fought, bled beside them, who saw them die for those they left behind, will render them all justice, honor and love. To them we give the victory. They were true; then let us, who begin to enjoy the freedom, happiness and prosperity they won with their lives, likewise be true in memory of them, in deed to ourselves, and in grace to God."

By no means the least of the pleasant features of this pleasant day was the fact that three couples blushingly presented themselves before the colonel, and confided to him their sudden conclusions in regard to the felicitousness of the moment. The happy colonel raced around until he discovered Jim Douns, the minister, and there amid the merry throng he gave the brides away, being the first to kiss them.

It was late in the afternoon when the villagers dispersed to their homes and left the colonel to his own circle. With his strong, dark face beaming, he mounted the old porch step.

"Where are my Zane babies?" he asked. "Ah! here you are! Did anybody ever see anything to beat that? Four wonderful babies! Mother, here's your Daniel—if you'd only named him Eb! Silas, come for Silas junior, bad boy that he is. Isaac, take your Indian princess; ah! little Myeerah with the dusky face. Woe be to him who looks into those eyes when you come to age. Jack, here's little Jonathan, the last of the bordermen; he, too, has beautiful eyes, big like his mother's. Ah! well, I don't believe I have left a wish, unless——"

"Unless?" suggested Betty with her sweet smile.

"It might be——" he said and looked at her.

Betty's warm cheek was close to his as she whispered: "Dear Eb!" The rest only the colonel heard.

"Well! By all that's glorious!" he exclaimed, and attempted to seize her; but with burning face Betty fled.

～

"JACK, DEAR, HOW THE LEAVES ARE FALLING!" EXCLAIMED HELEN. "SEE them floating and whirling. It reminds me of the day I lay a prisoner in the forest glade praying, waiting for you."

The borderman was silent.

They passed down the sandy lane under the colored maple trees, to a new cottage on the hillside.

"I am perfectly happy to-day," continued Helen. "Everybody seems to be content, except you. For the first time in weeks I see that shade on your face, that look in your eyes. Jack, you do not regret the new life?"

"My love, no, a thousand times no," he answered, smiling down into her eyes. They were changing, shadowing with thought; bright as in other days, and with an added beauty. The wilful spirit had been softened by love.

"Ah, I know, you miss the old friend."

The yellow thicket on the slope opened to let out a tall, dark man who came down with lithe and springy stride.

"Jack, it's Wetzel!" said Helen softly.

No words were spoken as the comrades gripped hands.

"Let me see the boy?" asked Wetzel, turning to Helen.

Little Jonathan blinked up at the grave borderman with great round eyes, and pulled with friendly, chubby fingers at the fringed buckskin coat.

"When you're a man the forest trails will be corn fields," muttered Wetzel.

The bordermen strolled together up the brown hillside, and wandered along the river bluff. The air was cool; in the west the ruddy light darkened behind bold hills; a blue mist streaming in the valley shaded into gray as twilight fell.

CPSIA information can be obtained
at www.ICGtesting.com
Printed in the USA
LVHW090208050623
748880LV00021B/425